The Bayou Moon

A Duet Novel

Jerome Mark Antil

ISBN-13: <u>978-1-7332091-0-6</u>
(Paperback Edition)

Library of Congress Control Number: 2020902938

ISBN-13: <u>978-1-7332091-6-8</u>
(Kindle Edition)

ISBN-13: <u>978-1-7332091-7-5</u>
(Hard Cover Edition)

LITTLE YORK
BOOKS
New York · NY · Dallas · TX

To Leah Chase
January 6 – 1923 – June 1, 2019

Part One

One More Last Dance

A Southern Louisiana Bayou

CHAPTER 1

On February 25, 1964, fifty-one passengers and seven crew members boarded Eastern Airlines Flight 304 at the rainy New Orleans Airport for their flight to New York City. Takeoff was at 2:01 p.m. At 2:05 p.m. the jet disappeared from radar over Lake Ponchartrain.

Searchers eventually recovered the remains of thirty-two of the fifty-eight passengers and crew. "The last thing picked up was a child's red coat," reported the Times Picayune. "Floating Doll Is Grim Sight," was a headline.

This story begins forty years after the pregnant woman standing in the rainstorm saw the plane explode and sink to the bottom of the lake and she watched the doll floating on the dark water.

HE WAS BAREFOOT AND—BEST GUESS—EIGHT YEARS OLD when he first came to Carencro, having run ninety-one miles from what he thought were demons in the swamps of Bayou Chene. He rested to tend a bloody leg and hid in an empty trash bin at the slaughterhouse. Before dawn a creaking of hinges awakened him. The lid lifted under an alley lamp and a foreman with a pair of torn white rubber boots in his fist growled, "Scat, boy!" and "On your way, Peckerwood!"— before tossing the boots into the bin. Looking older than his age, the boy convinced the foreman to give him a few chores in trade for the torn boots and something to eat. Impressed with his work, the man handed the boy two sandwiches and a Saran-wrapped dill, along with the boots and tape for mending the rip.

"Check back, son. If we're ever short a man, I'll give you day work."

Feeling freedom on his face for the first time, and knowing he had run to a new life he walked about exploring the town and wound up on Bab Road in his patched rubber boots when the sharp, slithering sounds of saw blades ripping through dried lumber caused the boy to pause and look about. Nibbling on his dill like it was a dessert from Antoine's he couldn't help noticing through an opened doorway large circular saw blades hanging like Christmas ornaments in the wooden shed a man holding a clipboard stepped out of. There was a wood and canvas sleeping cot standing on its end, leaning against the inside wall behind the blades. The shed was the blade shed for the mill of the boat builder, and the boy handed the man his hunting knife.

"It's my Dundee, Mister."

"Nice knife, but I'm not in the market for a knife," the man said.

"Touch the blade, Mister, jes touch it," the boy said.

"I'm impressed son, but I'm still not—"

"Oh, it ain't for sale, Mister. I keep it sharp is all."

The boy tried to barter his blade-sharpening skills for the use of the cot in the wooden shed and asked about the broken lawn mower on its porch.

"That old mower?" the man asked.

"*Oui.*" ("Yes.")

"It's junk, only worth the metal, I reckon."

"It don' go summore?" the boy asked.

"Not in years."

"If I can spear-a-ment and fix it, will you let me use it, Mister?"

"You know motors too, do ya?"

"I t'ink I can did dat one. Dass for true."

"What's your name, son?"

The boy knew his given name— Boudreaux Clemont Finch, but as a runaway he was guarded about making it known to strangers.

"Peck, sir, most I knowed call me Peck."

"How do you keep your blade so sharp, son?"

"Egg shell, dass for true, I rub it with eggshell."

"Broken eggshell?"

"Whole egg, 'afore it's boiled, sir."

"I thought only my *grand-mère* knew that one," the man said. "That's how she would sharpen her scissors, it surely was."

The man extended his hand for a shake.

"The name's LeFleur, Peck. Marcel LeFleur."

Mr. LeFleur shook Peck's hand, said yes to his sleeping in the shed in barter for knife and axe blade sharpening. He gave him the broken-down mower and threw in the pair of pliers, two sparkplugs, and a hotplate he had in his pickup.

"That lightbulb in there stays on twenty-four hours a day, son."

"Yes sir, Mr. LeFleur."

"Unplug the hotplate when you're not using it. Wood dust sets off easy enough without help. Let's not help it with sparks."

"I'll make sure I did that, Mr. LeFleur. Ever' time I use it."

"Look in the cabinet. There should be a coffee pot, some utensils; maybe a skillet."

Peck's been grown for some time now but never certain how old he was and when the boat builder one day said he looked to be in his twenties, he was good with that. Unable to read, he'd create multiple-syllable words and convert their meanings. He knew some French. When telling stories of his past he'd reference age as—"I could swim," meaning he was eight or nine or "I couldn't swim," meaning he might have been as young as three or four—or as he would say in a Cajun patois, "I was *quatre* maybe *trois*." ("I was four maybe three.") When not mowing the lawns at the hospice, he'd be seen at shores casting a trotline or at market trading his catches—snapping turtles, mashwarohn, and frogs to fish-and-egg buyers for a few dollars on good days—for a few brown eggs if his catch was poor. He'd trade with a grocer his washing the store windows for a twelve-ounce can of French Market chicory and a small shaker of ground cinnamon from India. On the hot plate burner in the mill's blade-sharpening shed where he slept, he'd boil three eggs in his morning pot of chicory coffee. Thursday was his one day to mow. Every Thursday he would walk in the morning darkness to this hospice overlooking the calm of Bayou Carencro—it was once the stately Hildebrandt mansion. From the day he first took the job nearly ten years ago, he never missed a Thursday. At first sparkle of sun on the horizon he'd cast his baited trotline for an end of day retrieval before fueling and starting the mower.

But this was a Wednesday, and a private detective just handcuffed him to a bench on the hospice's rear lawn, warned him not to try to escape, wished him good luck and walked away. Alone he sat and waited an unknown fate, and he watched a snapper slowly climb the root of a bald cypress for the morning sun beginning to break through a layer of fog and a crawfish snake caught his eye while swimming across the shallow to where smaller frogs and crawfish were plentiful. A keen sense of observation wasn't a game to Peck, it was how he survived.

"Gators sleepin'," he muttered. "*Vous gagnez cette fois, serpent.*" ("You win this time, snake.")

He looked through smoky fog at the morning moon resting just above the horizon as if it was waiting to evaporate. A silhouette of the cypress branch appeared as if tattooed on the moon's surface, and hanging moss filtered his view like cheesecloth, but he watched just the same as if the moon was a lost mamma he didn't remember and could only imagine her looking back at him, with a sense he needed her now, more than ever before.

A lady stepped from the parking area onto the lawn, pulling white driving gloves as she approached. Peck studied her walk. Her black skirt had a designer slit baring a milky thigh. She wore a matching, finely tailored, waist-pinched, double-breasted jacket with an oversized silver and diamond-clustered brooch awkwardly pinned to its lapel; white Nike walking shoes. The shoulder bag and black leather valise she was carrying were from Torino in New Orleans. She walked directly to his bench, removing Chanel sunglasses, grasping them in her hand with the gloves, and sat down without asking. She extended a hand as though they had never met, in the likelihood of prying eyes.

"I'm Lily Cup."

Peck gave an indifferent nod as if he knew her, for he did know her from a week or so before, if only for a few hours that night in a jazz bar in the alley off Frenchman Street in New Orleans. He slouched as if body language might best express his anger, and he watched the turtle on the cypress root smiling up at the sun and he studied its carapace as if estimating its weight for soup.

"Sasha called me," Lily Cup said.

"When?" Peck asked.

"As soon as she knew which airport your flight was landing. I drove up earlier this morning."

"What they chargin' me on?" Peck asked.

Lily Cup didn't speak. She folded each glove, placed them and her sunglasses in the bag, and set it between them on the bench.

"Dey was talking murder in New Jersey, cher."

"Who was?"

"The detective, axin' me stuff."

"They haven't charged you with anything."

"So, why'd they arrest me first place?"

"They want you for questioning," Lily Cup said.

"Makes no sense, cher."

"I'm here to protect your rights—see you don't get trapped saying the wrong things."

"Just to get grilled I got to be handcuffed to a bench?"

Peck's head darted around; he cupped his free hand and pushed his arm as quickly as an attacking eel, snatching a brown beetle bug flying near him. He sat back and held it delicately between his finger and thumb, as if he were considering it as fish bait.

"Did'ja talk to Miss Lavender?" Peck asked.

"We met at Starbucks on my drive in."

"Crab say anythin'?"

"She's thinking with you being twenty-four and maybe can learn from all this, she'll likely go ahead and drop the charges and give you your lawn-mowing job back if Lafayette Parish get the answers they need and drop theirs," Lily Cup said.

"*Vingt-quatre?*" ("Twenty four?")

"Yes, you're twenty four."

"Is that what I am, cher?"

"Sasha had me search state records to find your birth certificate, so we could get you on a plane. Turns out Miss lavender found it first and gave it to that detective."

"You find it, for true?"

"You were twenty-four one month and three days ago."

"Well, I'll be—"

"Handcuffs were the detective's idea. He convinced Miss Lavender."

"But for why?"

"So you don't run— she doesn't want to be embarrassed, you gone all over again and having to explain it to her board."

"She knows I ain't no murderer, dass for true."

"Oh she knows now it's got nothing to do with anything like that."

"What, then?"

"Last week she told the sheriff about a patient being gone and he went and put a warrant out for you on suspicion of kidnapping him."

"A patient?"

"I know, it sounds ridiculous."

"It ain't like the patient don't have no name, cher. His name is Gabe, call him Gabe."

"You know very well I know what his name is Peck—I know Gabe. I'm not disrespecting him. But to the sheriff he's just a missing patient."

"Oh. Sorry."

"You're being detained for questioning. Well, it's that and the other thing the sheriff added—suspicion of taking someone across state lines against their will," Lily Cup said. "Whatever he could pile on so they could arrest you and get you here, he stacked it."

Peck thrust the beetle high so it would have time to spread its wings and take flight.

"*S'envoler gratuitement, bebette,*" Peck said. ("Fly free, bug.")

He looked for another bug.

"Any suspicion when they coming, cher?" Peck asked sarcastically.

"Soon."

Lily Cup looked at the clock on her cellphone. She lifted a mirror from her purse and checked her lipstick and eye shadow.

"Any minute, actually."

She put the mirror in the purse, opened her hand flat and studied the veins on the back of it and her polished nails in the morning sun.

"Parish sheriff's driving over from Lafayette. My guess is he'll pick up the district attorney on his way through town. I suppose they'll come together," Lily Cup said.

"Seems funny," Peck said.

"I don't see facing life in prison as funny, Peck. Kidnaping is federal and it carries—"

"Nah nah, not dat."

"What could possibly seem funny about this mess you're in?"

"Bein' handcuffed to the same bench behind this hospice where I met Gabe firs' place."

"You met him here?"

"*Oui.*" ("Yes.")

"Not in N'Orleans?"

"Here, cher. This bench."

"On this same bench?"

"*Oui.*" ("Yes.")

"That is ironic," Lily Cup said.

"Ironic. You know, dass exactly the right word, cher."

He raised his head and let it roll articulately from his tongue.

"Ironic. Sasha teached me dat one—she used it a lot."

"She does, doesn't she?" Lily Cup asked.

"I'm going to New Orl-ee-anhs to learn to read, if I can get out of this mess. I didn't kidnap nobody."

"I know it—Sasha knows it, Peck. You just have to convince a grand jury tomorrow."

"When Gabe and me first met I couldn't figure what would make a old army captain like him want to run from a place like dis, anyhow."

Peck pointed at the three-story antebellum sitting on the crest of a large lawn behind them.

"Back there was a roof over his head I gaurontee, *trois* squares a day and a view from this here bench along Bayou Carencro," Peck said. "I know it ain't much to look at for a dying man, dass for true, snakes and all; it's purdy much dead already. Look at it, cher, all lined with quiet. Cypress trees dripping with moss flowing in breezes looking like they floatin' out there in lily pad flat still water; gators minding they own business; ducks; acres of sweet green lawn smelling a fresh cut most times; fat ole magnolia trees, willows sopping up swamp and over there yonder a way, dat shiny red and yeller sign looking for a breeze so it can flop and reflect morning sun, warning about gators."

Peck stretched his free arm and yawned.

Lily Cup turned her eyes from the bayou, watched him raise an arm and flex, his muscles rippling, T-shirt hiked over ripped abs and bare stomach. Her mind seemed to wander behind a glazed stare, but she came to with a slight shake of her head.

"Did you know Sasha is Cajun French?" Lily Cup asked.

"Yes'm, I surely did."

"She likes to speak French whenever we go to Charlie's Blue Note for dancing," Lily Cup said.

"I'm Cajun French, cher. I know some French purdy good—she say I know a lot more than I let on, but she was trying to teach me a new somethin' ever' day."

Lily Cup cast an appraising glance at his thighs.

"I can only imagine," she mumbled.

"Gabe liked her a lot," Peck said. "Think she was his boo, cher? Least for a time?"

"Oh, she loved Gabe, all right—but I don't think like that. She thought he was magical," Lily Cup said. "I never saw her have such deep feelings for a man so fast...and him so old, and her with a boyfriend in Baton Rouge."

"It was the dancin', cher."

"She told me it was that and the way he would say things to her."

"I t'ink it was the dancin'—only dat."

"They sure could dance."

"Ah, Peck could watch 'em dance all night, dass for true. Even did."

Lily Cup smiled, nodding her head.

"I remember sitting on the rooftop when she got back the first time," Lily Cup said.

"Here in Carencro, you don' say?" Peck asked.

"In the Quarter, we were having a drink, looking at a full moon," Lily Cup said. "That's when she told me how it felt when he held her on the dance floor, how he smelled; how they could move as one."

"Creole man, they dance so good, dass for true."

"She was melancholy because it was after he told her he was dying, and that's when she learned how you two met."

"Ah, *oui.*"

"Did you know he ran away from the VA hospital in Pineville?"

"No ma'am, I didn't."

"He refused more treatments for his stomach cancer."

"Is dat what he's got, for true?"

"You didn't know?"

"I knowed he was sick bad off, but I didn't know it was the cancer, cher."

"He told Sasha somewhere along the way."

"I suspected he told her, but I didn't know all dat about the cancer and the treatments he run from," Peck said.

"She never knew any of it until after you were on the road."

"Memphis must be when he tole her, I guess," Peck said. "That's about when she got all weepy-eyed."

"Sasha wants me to help you if I can—for Gabe."

"T'anks, cher."

The fog lifted and Lily Cup studied the morning moon between the Cypress trees—the living monuments of Acadiana.

"Look at the moon, Peck. It's beautiful."

"*Oui.*"

"I remember a full moon one night in the Quarter, there was a smell of oyster shells in humid, still air when Sasha told me she had a feeling there was something *gris gris*—dark and cursed—about a hospice being over here in Carencro," Lily Cup said.

"Dass for true."

"Sasha is observant like that—she has been ever since grade school. She told me there was no irony in it."

"There's that word again, cher."

"She said it was mystical, Gabe being dropped here by a stranger."

"I don' know dat."

"A man found him fallen on a road outside of Opelousas, picked him up, didn't know where to take him and didn't want to take him to the law. He thought Gabe was dead but then could tell he was breathing. He brought him here to a doctor he knew. Turned out Gabe was out of his pain medicine, cramped and passed out. The doctor saw his plastic wristband ID and called the VA hospital. The VA told him Gabe qualified for hospice; he had months to live and was refusing treatment. The doctor told him he could get his pain medicine and stay if he wanted. Sasha thinks his fall on the road scared him. He agreed to stay."

"He ran from here too," Peck said.

"That's just it," Lily Cup said.

"Hanh?"

"Why from here?"

"For music, he say, but—"

"Heaven only knows," Lily Cup said.

"To him, sitting was dying, cher. He warn't ready—"

"Maybe it was this place."

"What'cha mean?"

"Listen to it, Peck."

"I hear it."

"Maybe screeching birds from the bayou spooked him."

"Maybe smelling death," Peck said.

"You could be right."

"Dass what this place is, cher."

"I believe people know when they start to die," Lily Cup said.

"Yes'm, I know dat for true," Peck said.

"And the alligators," Lily Cup said.

"People's jus' like animals—a critter's blank eyes says he knows when he's dying—being kilt or natural, it don't matter, he knows."

"This is a place where terminally ill wait to die," Lily Cup said.

"Dass for true."

"Sasha believes Gabe was dropped off here just so he could meet you, Peck."

"For true?"

"It was destiny so you could bring him to her, and they could dance."

"Sasha was good for Gabe—she woke his blank eyes," Peck said.

"She told me he refused to wait to die," Lily Cup said.

"Ain't dat for sure true? I seen him slamming a Dewar's on the bar and it didn't break so he throw'd the glass against a brick wall, smashing it and declaring under no circumstance was they a waiting room at his death's door."

Peck and Lily Cup watched a rippling in the swamp water. A large heron flew overhead.

"Sasha told me Carencro is a Cajun French word," Lily Cup said.

"Ah, *oui*."

"It means carrion crow."

"*Oui*."

"Flesh eaters—"

"*Oui*."

"—more to the point, dead flesh eaters. Vultures," Lily Cup said.

"I know buzzards—give me willies."

"Roost high in cypresses, feast on fish die-offs," Lily Cup said.

"Ever' time," Peck said.

"It's rite of passage in nature, and I wouldn't say this too loud, but they're haunting the bayou, waiting on death for supper and terminally ill patients sitting on benches watching."

"Buzzards prolly watching them back," Peck said. "*Ils ont une façon de sentir la mort.*" ("They have a way of smelling death.")

"Where in N'Orleans did you two bump into each other that night?" Lily Cup asked.

"Nah, nah," Peck said.

"It wasn't N'Orleans?"

"Nah, nah, cher."

"So how'd you both wind up on Frenchman Street?" Lily Cup asked.

"Gabe, aw he'd been here *quatre*, maybe *trois* weeks. He told me he knew it was always T'ursday he could hear my lawn mower when I walked here to mow and rake. He liked coming and watching me 'cause I near spent a full hour at sunup looking at the morning moon and throwing my trotline into the bayou and tying it off down there on dat willow root what sticks out at the water edge. He'd set and watch my floater corks to see if a mashwarohn or snapper took it under and see what else my rig might catch while I was tending lawn chores."

Peck's story seemed to place a calm on Lily Cup. She took a breath, sat back and gazed through the moss of the swampy bayou.

"Look at the moon, Peck."

"Ah *oui*."

"I love morning moons," Lily Cup said.

"I watch it most times."

"You too?"

"*Oui*."

"What do you see when you watch the morning moon, Peck?"

"Crepe."

"You see a crepe?"

"*Oui*, sometimes."

"What would you know about crepes, Peck?"

"I know'd crepes."

"To you the moon is a crepe?"

"Morning moon like dat one is, cher. *Oui.* Look at it."

"Interesting. Yes, I can see that."

"A big crepe."

"There's a red and orange sky," Lily Cup said. "Like marmalade."

"I see it."

"Red sky in morning, sailor take warning," Lily Cup said, saluting the horizon.

"Ah *oui.*"

"What does a red morning sky mean to you, Peck?"

"I only watch the moon, cher."

Lily Cup smiled at Peck's simplicity. She lightly rapped her knuckles on his arm.

"To me a morning moon is a reminder," Lily Cup said.

"Reminder?"

"It reminds me I'm alive. It reminds me to remember that my heart beats and that I breathe."

Peck rested back in the bench.

"I see mamma," Peck said.

"You see your momma in the moon?"

"*Oui.*"

"That's so sweet."

Peck lowered his head.

"Is it sad, Peck, seeing your momma?"

"Nah, nah, I'm good," Peck said.

"What's that word you said, Peck—mashwarohn?"

"Catfish."

"Just like a little boy."

"Me?"

"Gabe—coming out here to watch every time you came to mow."

"We never talked for longest time," Peck said. "We'd catch an eye or two back and forth—you know how strangers did?"

"I know what you mean."

"I knew Gabe wasn't up to his own self, spirit-wise."

"You could tell?"

"A man can tell dat sort of t'ing looking into a man's eyes no matter what color a man is. A black man's eyes, like Gabe's, are best at showing hopeless in daylight."

"And you could tell?"

"He'd set here looking unhappy all day—*mal pris.* I'd watch his eyes out of corner of my eye mostly, my arm blocking my face. One day it come to me. Why it give me chills being over there untangling my trotlines knowing a man as healthy looking as me is stuck in this godforsaken place jus' setting on a bench with nothing to did but watch me throw my trotline while he was seeing his death tunnel coming his way any day. It was 'nuff to depress any fool."

"Well, I'll be, Peck."

"Hanh?"

"You, my friend, are a poet."

"A grow'd ole man with no family like Gabe don' have nothing but himself to remember knowing."

"Aging can be so sad."

"Most he knowed is dead or long gone or out of his head. He already outlived what they told him he had in time, dass for true. Looking at his pill bottle they gived him months when they took him in—ain't no two ways about dat."

"How old do you think he was? Nobody can find his papers showing his age," Lily Cup said.

"Is he dead, cher?"

"I don't know."

"He never said," Peck said. "I never ax."

"Weren't you curious?"

"He was dying, cher. I don' 'spect a body give age much thought when he's dying. He kept to himself purdy much, didn't bother nobody."

"He wasn't one to wait," Lily Cup said.

"He told me he thought about wadin' the bayou and let gators take care of business."

"He said that?"

"He say gators would like black meat and thought he'd be good gator bait."

"How lonely it must be to grow old and not have anybody."

"*Beaucoup de viande sur les os,*" Peck added. ("Plenty of meat on the bones.")

Peck and Lily Cup sat watching the stillness of the reeds sticking out from the water. A turtle plopped from the cypress root into the bayou.

"Who spoke first?" Lily Cup asked.

"You mean me and Gabe?"

"Yes."

"It was July *quatre* week, cher."

"July fourth week?"

"*Oui*, I know, I had to mow *deux* times—once Sunday before visitors come and T'ursday regular time. It was T'ursday when I was fixing to throw my trotline dat morning. I was puttin' cut bait on fishhooks of dis here snood and I stuck hooks deep between my thumb and my palm and thought, looking over here at Gabe, hurtin' as it was, maybe it was a sign."

"You saw a sign?"

"I snipped the snood line both sides of the hooks with my weed clipper, grabbed my wire snips, turned and walked over to this here bench to get the hook out and get something off my chest same time, and I just plain come right out and ax Gabe if he wanted to get out of here."

"Is that true?" Lily Cup asked.

"*Oui.*"

"As simple as that?"

"What you mean, cher?"

"You stuck your hand with fishhooks, thought it was a sign, walked over here and asked him that?"

"True as I'm born, cher, simple as me."

"What'd Gabe say?"

"Oh, he say, 'Oh hell yes.'"

"Just like that? Sitting here he just came out and said, 'Oh hell yes'?"

"Didn't blink an eye," Peck said.

"What'd you say?"

"I say why don't ya just leave. You're free to go and where would ya go anyway, if you did get out of here, and my name's Peck, what's yours?"

"I'll be damned," Lily Cup said.

"He shook my good hand and say, 'Pleased to meet you, Peck, my brother.'"

"That's how it all began?"

"He started calling me his brother first off—he say, 'name's Gabriel—you can call me Gabe, son.' He told me if he left they would maybe take his pill bottle away and dat would kill him sure."

"He wanted to live," Lily Cup said.

"When I got the hooks out I ax him again where he'd go and he ax me if I liked jazz and I told him I liked music good and dass when he say it."

"What'd he say?" Lily Cup asked.

"I gived him my wire clipper to snip barbs off the hooks in my hand after I pushed them through." Peck held his hand up. "You can still see scars. I bled a lot."

"What did he say?"

"He ax me could I see he gits to Newport so's he and me could drink scotch and listen to jazz at some fair or festival or carnival is what I thought he say first off, ya see."

"The Newport Jazz Festival."

"I know it was a jazz festival now, cher, but I didn't knowed what he was talking about back then. It's an important one, dat jazz festival."

"You both left together from here?"

"Oui."

"His pills were an opioid. How did you get him out of here with his pills through the nurses and security?"

"I first looked him dead in the eye to see if he was worth trouble and decided quick, like Sasha did, I liked the kindly ole black man who ain't never harmed a flea. He looked like dat ole boxer man, friendly like."

"Who—you mean Muhammad Ali?"

"Yeah, dass him. Muhammad Ali, shore 'nuff."

"He did look like him, didn't he?" Lily Cup asked.

"I wanted it to be on a good foot starting out, so I flat out fessed up to him I weren't all dat bright, but I had a knack for cunning on my side, as my foster nanna used to tell me, and I might could get him out of here with his pills if he'd go put some work clothes on, drop his duffel out his bedroom window and pretend he worked for me and jus' walk out with me around worker's fence gate. Tole him I can't took him downtown, but we'd walk to a saloon down by the slaughterhouse and maybe I could fetch us a ride from there."

"Did he have to think about it?"

"Gabe just looked out over this bayou here, kind of in a stare, and told me flat out his hospice room weren't nothing but a casket wit air-conditioning and a flat-screen TV," Peck said.

"Sad," Lily Cup said.

"Being black and in army so long is what made him talk straight out 'n direct like dat—least dass what he'd say."

"He's one in a million," Lily Cup said.

"Sides, they weren't time to think. He say you'd did dat for me? I told him I weren't about to keep throwing my trotline here day after day while watching a old man die where he don't want to."

"What did he say to that?"

"We didn't have no time to talk, but a tear come down from his eye. He shook his pill bottle, making sure it was full up. I told him it'd be best if we kept looking natural, so if we didn't want to get caught and ax a lot of questions and maybe lose his pills, we had to up and did it right then and there—no t'inking about it. Told him I'd run in for a bandage, let them in there see some of my blood so they wouldn't suspect not hearing me mow for a while and I'd look to see if my pay envelope was in my slot. I'd go around and pick up his duffel and meet him by the mower on side by the fence."

"Was your money there?"

"No, but I seed a atlas map sticking out from a shopping bag, grabbed it and put it under my T-shirt. His duffel bag sure enough was outside his window."

"It was the blood," Lily Peck said.

"Hanh?"

"The blood on your hand and then you both disappear like that. I bet that's it. I bet that's why they put out a warrant. Him gone without telling anyone and you with bloody hands and gone too."

Peck lifted his hand and looked at the scar.

"And you both just walked out, no one asking why or stopping you?"

"God's my judge."

"I'll be goddamned," Lily Cup said.

"This here's Lewisana, cher."

"What's that got to do with anything?"

"A lawn boy with a bandaged up hand walking out toting a army duffel next to a overweight black man in work clothes ain't going to draw no attention in Carencro."

"You have a point."

"Walking down Guilbeaux I showed him a atlas map I stole and ax him if he showed me where this here Newport was and where we was on it, I'd figure how we'd get there. We kept walking, stopped at 7-Eleven to buy water bottles with my last five-dollar bill and to a saloon where we sure enough catched us a ride, and the driver bought us some coffee to go."

"Why did you walk?" Lily Cup asked. "Wasn't that taking a chance on being seen?"

"No money, no bus," Peck said. "I had me five dollar but figured we'd need ever' penny for water if we were running off right quick."

Lily Cup looked about for cars driving in. There were none.

"It won't be long," Lily Cup said. "Sometime tomorrow after the bigwigs have their coffee and cinnamon buns in the judge's chamber there'll be a hearing before a grand jury. The judge isn't allowed in a grand jury room. He's around in case there's an indictment, and he needs to set bail. It'll be pretty much routine, if I haven't missed something."

"I'm in trouble, dass for true."

"That depends," Lily Cup said.

"Hanh?"

"If Gabe's alive I most likely can get you off unless the DA starts getting some television coverage on it and a bug up his butt and decides to make it a reality show, with him running for office again. If Gabe is alive, everything about this whole mess is circumstantial, and he knows it."

"Do you know if he's alive?" Peck asked.

"I already told you I don't—but I'll find out from Sasha."

Lily Cup turned to catch Peck's eye. She touched his shoulder with her finger to get his attention.

"Just remember one thing, Peck."

"Hanh?"

"Sasha says you don't mean to be, but sometimes you're your own worst enemy, so try to keep your mouth shut and let me do the talking when they come."

Lily Cup turned forward, crossing her legs, widening the slit in the skirt on her thigh. Peck gave it pause. He looked at her white Nikes with no socks, the slit in her skirt and the large diamond brooch that had come undone just as she caught it and fumbled to refasten it. She pinned it, patted it with her fingers as if saying hello to her gramma who gave it to her. They sat there in the still of the morning.

"Lily Cup, how's a ravishing, voluptuous woman—ya know, dat stuff Gabe say about Sasha—like your own self come to be a lawyer?"

"What do you mean?"

"Ain' it a man's world, lawyering?"

"Excuse me?"

"Daddy close with people at the capital, is he?"

She turned and thrust her face within inches of Peck's nose. He had hit a nerve. "Peck, now I'm warning you, dammit, and you'd better listen, mister. Today's not a day to start getting ideas like pretending you're close and familiar with me out here where people can see us. It's not the least bit funny."

"Cher, I wasn't—"

"What you and I did at Charlie's Blue Note is staying in the past, and it gives you no cause. And I was drinking."

"But I wasn't—"

"This is serious business. You bring suspicions of those sorts of things, even in a joking way you do with your patois, and they may open an ethics thing and throw me off the case."

"But I—"

"Can you understand any of this, Peck?"

"Nah, nah, but I swear, Lily Cup, I won' say a word to none of them."

"And that goes for Sasha too."

"Hanh?"

"She'll be in the courthouse tomorrow."

"Why?"

"In case the grand jury wants to put her on the stand. They're calling in all witnesses. I'm warning you. If you want to get out of this mess and ever see New Orleans again, don't so much as look at her."

"Kin I call her phone to ax if Gabe's alive?"

"Not one word."

"Why, cher?"

"Not until this thing is over. That is, if you don't want me thrown off the case and the FBI taking it over. Kidnapping is a federal offense, Peck—it could carry life."

"For true? But I didn't—"

"Don't go messing it up now. Keep your business in your pants and your mouth shut."

"I won't even look at her."

"You'd better give me your phone," Lily Cup said. "I don't want you tempted."

"I won't, cher, I promise."

"Hand it over—c'mon."

"I can't call her—I don't know how to work it."

"Give it," Lily Cup said.

Peck grimaced, reached in his pocket, pulled out and handed Lily Cup his phone, still in its new packaging.

"So, women can't be lawyers, Peck?"

Peck didn't respond.

"Where'd you get such a notion? Is it how you really think?" Lily Cup asked.

Peck looked at her shoes and brooch...her thigh through the slit.

"No...but you...well, you're beautiful clear enough, and plenty smart, dass for true, but it's just sometimes how you dress in clothes looking like you're a—"

Lily Cup interrupted.

"Oh, I see, Mr. Peckerwood Finch, who doesn't own a pair of pants with a crease in them. If you're too embarrassed to let me represent you in the morning, like I cared, trying to keep your virgin boy behind out of the penitentiary rooming with rapists and murderers, you'd best put a dishcloth in that fresh mouth."

"Sorry, cher."

"I thought traveling with Gabe would have taught you manners and how to hold your tongue."

"Name ain't Peckerwood, you know," Peck said.

"I know your name. Don't try to change the subject."

"But peckerwood—"

"Don't worry, your real name is in all the papers."

"Where'd you get a name like Lily Cup, anyways?" Peck asked.

"It's my name, Lily Cup."

"For true, cher?"

"Born and raised in New Orleans and before you make some wise-ass comment, it's my real name. Lily Cup Lorelai Tarleton and I graduated law, at Harvard, and I practice criminal law in and around New Orleans, trying to keep fools like you out of prison, or from ending up in Angola, getting the needle."

"But Lily Cup?" Peck asked.

"Conceived on a picnic blanket in Chalmette, if you must know—1981, it was. As the story went, while Daddy was introducing me into my momma, so to speak, right next to a wooden bowl of potato-salad, Momma rolled in passion, her butt cheeks crushing a tube of Lily Tulip paper cups they brought for their mint juleps, and a julep wasn't a drink you can drink from a bottle. Nine months to the day Momma wouldn't let Daddy name me Tulip because of the crushed Lily Tulip cups—and made him promise her no *Tulip*. He gave her his word and then wrote Lily Cup on my birthing papers out in the hall without her knowing."

"I'll be," Peck said.

"You asked," Lily Cup said.

"T'ink of it, cher...me getting Peckerwood for being a smart ass and there you go earning Lily Cup cause your momma was getting—ya know—plowed at a picnic."

"I never have liked potato salad," Lily Cup said to herself.

"Now dass a story, I guarontee."

"Whole world hears it every Thanksgiving," Lily Cup said.

"Your daddy is something else."

"He's gone now, but he surely was."

"He didn't mean no harm wit naming you dat, cher."

"Harvard accepted me, so it couldn't have been all bad."

Lily Cup sat up at hearing a distant car's sound, turned and looked over at the entrance driveway.

"They're here, Peck."

"Where?"

"That's them parking. I'm going over to meet them."

She grabbed Peck's free hand and gave it a squeeze.

"Let's hope he's alive," Lily Cup said.

"Ain't dat for true," Peck said.

"Remember, please shut up and when they take you in, do what they tell you. They'll know to only question you outside of a grand jury room with me present. Let me do the talking."

"Yes'm," Peck said.

"Sit up straight, Peck."

"Hanh?"

"Look like you amount to something."

Peck sat up and watched a turtle crawl to the end of the cypress root and drop into the water. He rested back with a blank stare, looking at the morning moon.

CHAPTER 2

THE DAY IT ALL STARTED was the day Peck hitched a ride for them both on a cattle hauler rig to where he thought would be I-90. His plan was to follow that interstate to Newport. Turns out, this was the same day old Gabe got a taste of how unreliable Peck might be in communicating his strategic thinking too far away from a bayou. The old man wasn't taking an inch of his gratitude for the boy's big heart and heroic cunning in getting him out of hospice with his pills. He was genuinely grateful. While planning the cross-country road trip walking down Guilbeaux Street they shook on it that the goal was a simple one, to get to Newport, Rhode Island for the August jazz festival so the old man could get in a zone one last time listening to live jazz. Gabe learned in the army to lead or follow or get the hell out of the way, so on the subject of getting to Newport he stepped back and had confidence in Peck's initiative. Gabe decided early on that he'd back Peck along the way (without giving his decisions a second thought). Peck suggested early on they should make their way over to I-95 and then follow it straight north. Gabe was impressed when Peck made a point of showing him that the blue I-95 line hugged the coast pretty much all the way up to Newport. Gabe was happy and it made him no never mind which way they went as all he was thinking was stretching out on a lawn with a Dewar's, some salami or a brick of cheese, and listening to jazz and watching life and sunsets mill around for a week.

"Gentlemen," the truck driver said. "That was some good coffee and morning conversation. I've enjoyed your company."

"T'anks for the coffee, frien'."

"I'll be letting you out about a mile or so up."

"Hanh?" Peck asked, as though he'd just awakened.

"We're coming into Kenner. It's just up ahead," the driver said.

"Kenner?" Peck asked. "What do you mean let us out?"

"That's where I make my turnaround, Peck. I drop this load and pick up a load of lumber so I don't deadhead back to Carencro, don't ya see?"

"But you say you was going to I-95," Peck said.

"Naw, it was you telling me you were going to I-95, Peck."

"We ain't even took out of Lewisana."

"We did a long haul from Carencro. You're closer than you were this morning."

"But you say you were going—"

"Naw, I didn't, Peck," the driver said.

"You say—"

"You're mixin' my words."

"I'd swear to it," Peck said.

"Peck, ain' no need to be swearing. I asked you where you were headin' off to—I was watching you buy bottles of water at 7-Eleven."

"You did dat, now dass for true," Peck said. "I remember xactly. But then I remember you saying back we could hitch wit you far as you go."

"Well, 'er you go, Peck."

"I remember him saying that, Peck," Gabe said.

"Hanh?"

"This here is as far as I go."

Peck looked at Gabe.

"Seems I might'a ax him where 'far as I go' was."

As they both appeared to think back from the fix they were in—of where they started in Carencro a few hours before, they would have been better off if they had headed straight on up to Memphis and kept going north from there. It was too late for all that, and the cattle hauler-driver pulled into a truck stop in Kenner and braked the rig short of a pothole full of muddy rainwater. Peck had known the driver from drinking beers and shooting quarter-a-piece, eight-ball pool with him at a saloon down the road from the slaughterhouse where Peck worked one summer, killing calves. He liked him.

"This is it for me, boys," the driver said. "I got to drop off these feeder calves and pick up a load of lumber and head on back. Good luck to ya both."

Peck and the driver gave each other a blank stare. Peck reached out with his good hand and they shook hands.

"Peck, you might have you a better shot to 95 by starting on the interstate up at I-12," the driver said. "I'll haul you up to it. I hop on it on my way back, so if you want a ride."

Gabe and Peck looked at each other, considered the proposition and shrugged their shoulders. Gabe pulled a large, canvas, army duffel over the back of the seat and handed it to Peck, who threw it out the open door to the ground.

"Wait up a sec, Peck," the driver said.

The driver leaned and reached for a first aid kit from behind the seat. He took a tube of Neosporin disinfectant and a box of bandages.

"Here, take these, Peck," he said, holding his hand out. "Keep that hand you hooked clean and bandaged tight until it heals. Don't let it get infected."

"T'anks frien'," Peck said.

Peck crawled from the truck cab first then helped Gabe climb down. They stepped out of the way and turned as the truck's airbrakes farted their tweets, lurching the rig forward, right front tire splashing in a pothole and bouncing the diesel's stack, belching black billows. The driver tugged the leather airhorn strap, sending two friendly goodbye blasts.

When the truck was out of sight, Peck turned with a sheepish look. There was something on his mind.

"Gabe, I know what you must be t'inking about now, but I swear as I'm standing here—I sure enough thought that there rig was our ride to I-95, all the way. Now here we is put out in middle of someplace I ain't hardly heard of in one of them cities they build up and I already got us lost before we get out of Lewisana."

"Don't be tough on yourself, friend," Gabe said. "It could have..."

Peck interrupted. "Might could be I'm jus' not your guy."

"Peck, listen to you," Gabe said.

"Hanh?"

"Here we are on an adventure of a lifetime—well my lifetime, that's for damn sure—and so what if we took a wrong fork in the road? That's what life is, son. I'm telling you—so what? The fork in that road we took sure enough is all the proof we'll need to be certain we're going to have some fun. That's what an adventure is all about, Peck—having fun along the way."

"I don't see no fun, Gabe."

"Here we are in Kenner, son. Rejoice, my brother, cause because of this here fork in a road, we're just a short way from New Orleans and the Quarters and some fun."

"The Quarters, Gabe? You mean the French Quarter?" Peck asked.

"Not exactly, my brother. Frenchmen Street—it's near the French Quarter," Gabe said. "It's all a difference for those of us in the know, knowing where to go if we're on a budget and those traveling men or ladies in town overnight on expense accounts looking for beignets and seafood, or maybe a night of some out-of-town boy-toy or poonani."

"Now there you go, Gabe. You're thinking fool's gold rich, and me I'm just a lawn man. I can't afford no Quarter or no Frenchmen Street ain't no way. Oysters there are near on a buck apiece and they ain't no better dan ones from Lafayette. Ain't no better t'all. Plenty shrimpers tole me and dass a fact."

"This adventure is on me, son. You just be keeping your word by looking after your old friend here, and I'll see to it you get treated with proper adventures and maybe we'll have some fun along the way." He reached his hand to Peck. "Do we have an understanding, son?"

"We have us a deal, Captain," Peck said, shaking Gabe's hand.

Gabe smirked a satisfying grin, swiping the air with a right cross.

"Now that's what I'm talking about," he announced.

"I'll go in de truck stop yonder and ax around," Peck said.

"What for?"

"I'll see who might be goin' into de Quarter and can give us a lift," Peck said.

"It's early, my brother, and the sun's warm," Gabe said.

Peck turned slowly toward Gabe again, head down, looking at the ground in a don't-distract-me sort of way, like he was about to kick a pebble.

"Gabe, I been meaning to ax you something."

"Anything, my brother."

"Now don't go taking it to any offense or unkindliness, but I t'ink you has to stop calling me your son or your brother. It just don't seem natural coming off the tongue like dat and it ain't right your making people have to t'ink more than they ought—like they tend to without help—with you a black man and me being a boney white Cajun and all."

"Boney, you're not, my brother. I've watched the nurses stare out the windows at you with your shirt off. Ain't nothing boney about those shoulders. Why those ladies were maybe laying odds on who'd get to your Johnson first."

"Boney is my way of saying it is all, Gabe. I meant bein' white, not about my build or nothing like dat. They did? Which ones?"

"Son and my brother are figures of speech for me too," Gabe said. "I'll cut them out if it's how you feel."

"Oh it ain't me, Gabe. I'm proud to have your acquaintance and friendship, but it's other more ignorant folks, you know. It'd be hokay if it weren't for ignorant folks. They's a lot of us around, dass for true."

Gabe pointed east.

"That there's the way into New Orleans," Gabe said.

"So we can catch us a ride to I-95 all the way," Peck said.

"Let's start walking. Frenchmen Street won't be far behind."

"Hanh? Walk?"

"We'll walk steady and be there by dark or right after sure enough. I saw a mileage sign back a way. Eleven miles."

Peck balked. "Just hold on. I plumb forgot what I wanted to say. Here I go sneaking you out of hospice and there's no telling what kind of trouble I'm going to get into for dat, and Gabe, you can lie to your own self all you want but you can't lie to me—you know you ain't well or you wouldn't had been in there in de first place. Now what did you t'ink they're going to say when I let a sick old man walk from Kenner clear into New Or–lee–anhs?"

"I'll never tell," Gabe grinned.

"What will they say when you drop dead, Mr. Captain Jordan, army veteran? Why they'd get me for murder, sure as I'm standing here."

"I'm dying, Peck. I'm not sick," Gabe said. "Let's go."

Peck dropped the canvas bag and stomped a foot for emphasis.

"You just hold on another dang minute, Captain. I may be ignorant, but I ain't all dat *coo-yon. (stupid)* If you was in hospice, you is sick, right?"

"My heart and legs are fine," Gabe said. "I'm rusting out from the innards is all. It's like I got termites in my stomach. I can walk—it keeps the pain away. Now I'd appreciate you not reminding me of it every two minutes, and I would enjoy it if you'd have a mind to join me and for once stopped bellyaching."

Peck relented, and the two started a healthy pace east out of Kenner, canvas duffel over Peck's shoulder.

"Gabe, now t'ink this one good," Peck said.

"What's on your mind, son?"

"Was she blonde with nice *tétines* who was a looking at me with my shirt off? T'ink more better, old man."

"It was her and that day nurse, the sister with a green Afro," Gabe said.

"Both of em? For true?"

"Playing you with their eyes like you were a porterhouse."

"Ain' t the blonde one married or going with a dude in a Ram truck dass been dropping her off?" Peck asked.

CHAPTER 3

IT WAS JUST AFTER A RED SUNSET when the old man and his young friend first stepped onto St. Charles and paused under a streetlamp to catch their breath and watch a streetcar pass them by.

"Smell that air, Peck," Gabe said. "Take it all in, son. Inhale it big. This is what living is all about. We can surely smell for a reason, my brother. Breathing is God's doing—is what it is."

"Hanh?"

"Smells and smelling, my brother. Powder sugar, beignets, shucked oyster shells, charcoal smoke, chicory, a lady's perfume. My, my...if this ain't what heaven smells like, nothing is. I can smell termites gnawing on the roots of the dogwoods."

"Where we going to did it, Gabe? We restin' here or goin' in more?"

"Let me have a look," Gabe said.

Gabe felt for the proper pocket and took out a worn, sun-cracked, tan leather wallet. In it was his driver's license, twenty-eight dollars in bills, and two receipts from Dunkin' Donuts he kept because one had the name of the drink he liked and the other had the name of a breakfast sandwich he liked. In currency, there were two tens, a five, and three ones.

"By the looks of it, we can afford a drink or two each, a beer, not Dewar's, maybe some crawfish gumbo with rice," Gabe said. "Listening to music is free most places. At least here in New Orleans it is. Let's walk over to Frenchmen Street for some smooth jazz. It's down this track a few blocks."

"Lemme see the money," Peck said."

Gabe held up the bills.

"Dat's only *vingt-huit* dollars, Gabe."

"Twenty-eight, that's right," Gabe said.

Peck took a stand.

"You mean to tell me we going to dat Newfalls place—"

"It's Newport," Gabe interrupted.

"Hanh?"

"Newport, Rhode Island, my brother."

"Hokay, Newport. You tellin' me we heading clear across U-S-of-A and we only got us, how you say, twenty-eight dollars in our kitty?"

"In fairness, son," Gabe said, "you might at least remember the name of the place we're going off to—it's Newport. Newport, Rhode Island. We've already come three hours southeast when we might have been heading north. Let's remember the city where we're going."

"I'm trying to be serious here, Gabe. What we going to did with twenty-eight dollars?"

"That'll be enough for—" Gabe started.

"I can't took you downtown with no twenty-eight dollars."

"I got my driver's license too," Gabe said.

"It ain't funny," Peck said.

"I thought we needed a little levity."

"I like blues like anybody," Gabe, but you ain't t'inking right."

"Blues?" Gabe asked.

"You heard me, Gabe. Blues."

"Did you say blues?"

"You know I did."

"I wouldn't be saying that in too loud of voice, Peck—not here in N'Orleans."

"Hanh?" Peck asked.

"N'Orleans is jazz, my brother. It's merchants, sailors, whiskey, and whorehouses—that's what made jazz. Blues is Beale Street. Cotton-picking slaves and a back's whip-strapping gave birth to the blues. Blues is Memphis. Cotton. Get it together, son."

"Why now I don' for sure know what's more stupider," Peck said. "Me hitchin' a ride I didn't know would end us in Kenner or smuggling you out of hospice. Me quitting my job, leaving a good trotline laying on the bank of the bayou, and heading off to this here Newport, wherever, with a whole whoop-de-do twenty-eight dollars to our name. Don't dat beat all for stupid?"

"Peck, how much cash have you got on you?"

"Pocket change is all, and you know dat. Now don' you go…"

Peck paused and inhaled.

"You know we didn't wait for my pay when we run off."

"Stay calm, my friend," Gabe said, "it'll all work out. You'll see."

"With twenty-eight dollars?"

"You need to be listening to some easy jazz to calm your nerves. Jazz was born from wanderers like us with no place to go and from sweaty bodies dancing and lying together with a window open for night air and street sounds. Listening to jazz won't cost us one thin dime, and it'll heal our souls, and that's a promise. Jazz is crazy gentle on purpose. Jazz is my people talking loud at night before being quiet at church in the morning. It's freedom to fit in, fly away without goin' no place, but not talked about in the daylight. It'll show us a way, baby. Be cool, my friend. Be easy."

"It may be easy for you, ole man, you're dying. Me, they'll catch me sure enough and hang me."

Blocks from the Quarter, in a side alley off Frenchmen Street, from an old shotgun house's living room, a saxophone solo wailed out into the street.

Vaaaa vaaaa da veeeeeeee…Vaaaa ve voooo vaa vaa vava ve vooooooon, the sax jammed as though it was saying, "Come in, brothers, supper's on and you don't live here but come in anyway. Rest your feet and feed your soul away from the night."

It wailed from the house between colorful bookends of a sleazy one-room stripper saloon with a second-floor balcony rail inside above for gawking. Its door open, and a barker in front handing out leaflets promising young men walking by every imaginable personal pleasure inside. Two worn, red lacquer-painted chain-links with an empty wooden swing seat hung motionless over an emptier bar. The bookend on the other side was a room for rent walkup with a sign on the ground floor door, that read No Vacancies, and another in a second-floor window read Astrology & Massage with an email address.

The music was coming from the whitewashed New Orleans shotgun house in the middle. Soft velvet sounds of a sax rode a warm breeze into the night as if to get some air and to look for souls needing a lift. In the doorway, you could hear brushes on a snare drum's stretched skin, and a sensual slapping of a palm on strings of a base fiddle that were steady rhythm, like voodoo incantations—magnets for an old army captain's ear.

Not taking his eyes off a red neon beer sign glowing on the inside back wall, Gabe grabbed Peck's arm for balance and stepped up the two steps into the room. A four-piece quartet was playing. Bright, big white eyes of a blue-black-faced brother blowing on sax, opened wide, looked over at Gabe and closed again with a low wail, welcoming him in. The band was in the left corner on a foot-high stage. Small tables with an unlit candle each surrounded a center dance area. By the clock it was too early in the day for a crowd or to light the candles. A wooden floor that might have survived two world wars, maybe the Civil War, and more floods than termites, was shaker waxed for dancing or for sitting around and drinking if there was a show put on.

Along the right wall was a bar with eight chrome bar stools in front. A row of whiskeys, bitters and blends lined a bookshelf attached to a long mirror behind the barkeep. Looking over at the bar, their eyes were drawn to the milky white back of a lady in a red satin dress with bare shoulders, and a more than agreeable figure. Her right elbow rested gently on the bar, and her hand, with bright red nail polish, held a martini glass with lipstick marks on its rim. Next to this lovely was another, slightly shorter girl, in black shiny tights, her hair tied back. If the reflection in the mirror was true, she was as comely and curvy as the one in red. The one in shiny black tights was leaning toward a man to her right; she was holding a cigar about the size of a big thumb for him to light.

Peck elbowed Gabe in the ribs at sight of her cigar.

"Did'ya ever, Gabe?" he asked.

"I saw that a lot in Nam," Gabe said.

"I'll be waggled."

"She probably drinks cognac," Gabe said. "A good cigar is best with cognac."

The man wore a white linen suit, had a blue sapphire pinky ring on his little finger, frayed white French cuffs, and tarnished, gold-plated cuff links. His straw dress hat was on the bar between them. Three other men were seated at the bar. One in overalls, with a cap with a stevedore button on it, looked like a dock worker. He was reading a racing form. One was sipping coffee. The jigger next to his coffee cup Gabe guessed was kalua. The one on the end, a black man, was writing on a small spiral pad with a pencil in his right hand. A glass of sloe gin was in his left hand.

Gabe pointed toward the band.

"Let's sit over there."

"Hokay," Peck said.

"I'm going to go splash my face, freshen up. Grab us a table by the band, Peck. I'll be out in two shakes."

CHAPTER 4

BACK WHEN GABE WAS A YOUNG TURK, in the days of the Vietnam war and the violent war protests, sit ins and race riots, flag and bra burning, he would sport young women about like arm candy, boasting his army medals and always knowing where the keys were hidden to any American inner city's night life. A young black man back then had to go on his wits pretty much, go his own way, but with an agility, proper finesse and some street smarts, he could have a good time making do.

Young men today of any color out and about in New Orleans pretty much all look the same in the eyes—the same blank stares. They live at home with their parents and plan their future by the hour, between texts. If one had money in his jeans or a working debit card, he'd get through the next hour or two and spend it. If he didn't have means, his imagination would lock up and he'd conclude he couldn't do much. If he was straight, he'd likely try to hook up with a lady of most any age with sympathy in her eyes or one his age or younger with a similar depth of vision. He'd sweet-talk and convince his catch into letting him lie with her, at least tonight, usually underperforming her imagination's desire in between his nature's calls to a fridge for a beer in the raw and basic hope she would have the womanly instincts of his mother to see he was properly fed in the morning. A morning after meal is Millennium man's best climax. Bacon is his definition of the joy of sex.

But Gabe was not a young man of today. He was an old man from the fifties. A very old man. He was about to bring nigh on eight decades of wisdom about what celebrating freedom had been for him—a black man—back in the time when he was poorer than an alley cat.

The two settled at a table, taking it all in. They didn't talk while their eyes glanced at the band and then shifted over to the bar. The red satin rounded buttocks were firm and an hourglass waist was not unnoticed by either of them. Especially not by Gabe.

"I've always had a fondness for a fine ass," Gabe said.

"Ahh *oui,*" Peck mumbled.

"Now that's some fine ass."

"You ever bedded with a genuine prostitute, Gabe?" Peck asked.

Gabe looked at him.

"I don't mean no floozy whore what'll take a couple dollars for a quick something. Nah, nah, I'm meaning how you call classy, full-fledged beautiful high-end call girl prostitute."

"Takes me back," Gabe said.

"Have you ever did, Gabe?"

"There was a time back in my Fort Campbell training days we'd catch a bus from the base to Newport."

"Where we're going off to, Gabe—Newport?"

"No, not that Newport, son. We're going to Newport, Rhode Island. This Newport we'd catch a Greyhound to is in Kentucky, on the river."

"The Mississippi?"

"On the Ohio River."

"Hokay."

"It was back in the late fifties, son. My kind couldn't sit and eat with white folks at Woolworth's counters in Cincinnati—"

"Why not, Gabe?"

"Jim Crow, racial tensions. It was still dark times in America, son."

"I heard some of it, Gabe. Sorry, my frien'."

"But across the river in Kentucky, Peck—if it was after dark and we came alone, we could flash them twelve dollars at the door for a roll on a clean sheet."

"White women?"

"White and lovely, each and every one of them, son."

"You old houn' dog," Peck said.

"I remember I'd always carry twelve singles in each of my pants pockets so the girl could take care of whoever she needed to, to sneak me in. With two pockets of cash I could go back for another go at it."

"A black man. I heard stories about back then, Gabe."

"It wasn't any secret the ladies in those second-story whorehouses had jungle fever after wasting days with virgins only working them up—the quick-draw college white boys from across the river. They'd check me out, give me a smile at the door, look about and let me in. They could climb a black man for the full ride—they just couldn't talk about it to the wrong people."

"You horny old man. Tell me true Gabe, when you was a captain, was it different?"

"Different?"

"When you paid for it—was it different when you was a captain?"

"Only difference maybe was I could ask for my favorite girl, maybe stay a few hours if it were near closing for them," Gabe said.

"That must have been something ol' man."

"Oh, it was."

"But, you know, Peck says you deserved it, Gabe, all you had to go through. I mean being black and all, back then. I heard stories, let's don't forgot dat."

"I can tell you stories, son."

"Gabe, when you was a captain, being a real somebody and all, was it like heaven waking up with somet'ing soft laying beside you?"

"That would depend."

"Depend?"

"It would depend if I went to bed sober or drunk," Gabe said.

"Hanh?" Peck asked.

"Bedding down sober, I was most always where I wanted to be—with a woman I culled and sugar-talked for hours. That was always a pleasant morning waking up all funky-like. It was different bedding down drunk."

"Why's dat?"

"At closing time with the last woman at the bar—if she'd have me we'd bed blind drunk and waking with my nose in an armpit, afraid to open my eyes."

Drum brushes snapped to attention, scratched and snapped a solo on snare. Gabe paused, flattened his hands on the table, fingers spread to feel the vibes of the bass and closed his eyes, rolling his head gently throughout the shuffle. When the bass came back in with slaps on wire, he opened his eyes again and smiled.

"Peck, my brother, our journey is going to be a long one. I'm an old man, and it is that distinction alone from which I will teach you things you will be able to use your entire life. And my grave, when I'm in it, will bloom a golden flower if you'll give me a smile and a thought from time to time remembering it came from me."

"Gabe, we have us twenty-eight dollars in your cheap ass wallet and a thousand miles to go. I don't get no wisdom in that arithmetic, way I see it, but please go on, professor."

"See here, my friend, if there ain't music inside a place, and you're looking for music and low on capital, one doesn't bother going into the place. There's nothing to benefit."

"Sounds more like low on 'crapital,'" Peck barked with a goofy, snorting guffaw.

"In an establishment like this one, however—okay a joint—music of soul at its heart and a table of our own and our being low on ready cash, all we have to do is sit here and enjoy the music for as long as we can at absolutely no cost until someone decides it's time for us to buy a drink or libation. If they do, we have the option of ordering something or leaving. Now that's economy."

"Dat what they teached in the army, Captain?"

"It's called getting by within the rules, my brother. Survival."

"It's more like chummin' with no bait," Peck said.

Gabe looked at Peck as if he was wondering if it would be worth his time to talk more.

"My brother, I could, over a Dewar's or two, explain my life as it was in uniform in a career in the army. But there isn't enough time in this lifetime or in the next, not enough gin at the bar—nor would you be interested if there were—to describe what it's like being a black man all your life in America. End of lesson."

Gabe grabbed his chair seat with both hands and shuffled it around until it faced toward the band.

Peck's eyes furrowed. He had a look on his face like he wasn't certain if he had offended his new friend, but decided silence was best for the moment. It was then that the lady in red looked over her shoulder, turned on her barstool and began stepping down. Her high heel led a long, captivating leg, bare over a red garter strap that dripped down a warm, white thigh and snapped to black, sheer French designer stockings. With her eyes not leaving Gabe as he watched the band, she stood, straightened her dress, and walked over to their table. Her dress looked designer expensive, as did her shoes, and she had a cleavage some men could lose their sanity for. Slutty wasn't the right word for the look in her beautiful eyes, but she did have a sensuality to go along with what appeared to be perfectly shaped breasts. Her smile was genuine and that of a woman who liked jazz and the blues.

"*Bienvenue messieurs,*" she said.

Gabe turned and looked up.

"I'm afraid my French—" he started.

"The bar is self-service," she said.

"We were just getting settled, I hadn't noticed," Gabe said.

"I've been telling Charlie he needs to put up a sign or something."

"That'd help. Thank you for telling us."

"As long as I'm here, what can I get you gentlemen?"

Gabe extended his hand.

"My name is Gabe."

"Hello, Gabe, my name is Sasha, nice to meet you."

"Momma named me Gabriel, hoping I'd be an angel."

"Why, aren't you a sweet one, you little angel?" Sasha asked.

"My momma was Creole—"

"Creole? You don't say? Imagine that, I'm Cajun French."

"— from Cameron Parish she was. I was born there. Momma always said I was her angel."

"Well that certainly makes you Creole, angel Gabriel."

"Actually, my momma was quadroon—"

"You're bronzy gold, Gabriel, like Louis Armstrong's horn—such a beautiful hue—"

"More like rust. I have some years on me."

"Was it your grandma or your grandpa, you know—a slave?"

"My papaw was the slave. Mamaw was Acadian from France down through Canada. Bought and freed him and asked him to marry her."

"Way to go, Grandma—I'd have loved to have met that woman."

"Momma said Mamaw was something else."

"Most us Louisianans are a mix breed, honey," Sasha said.

"My daddy was a hard-working piano maker, mover and tuner from Joliet. Black as the sharps and flats on the keyboard," Gabe said.

"Joliet?"

"Illinois—Chicago."

"So, you're a mix—with music in your soul."

"More like a mutt."

"Your momma was right—you are an angel."

She extended her hand. "Pleased to meet you, Gabriel. My friend sitting over there is Lily Cup. She would have come with me, but she's tied up at the moment."

"Honey, we can't afford no fun with ladies tonight, sorry," Peck said.

"Excuse me?" Sasha asked.

"The lad didn't mean anyth—" Gabe started.

"Lady, we come in for a beer maybe and some jazz, dass for true, not ladies, if you catch my drift," Peck said.

Sasha smirked and looked down at Gabe.

"Is your friend for real?" she asked.

"Please excuse—" Gabe started.

"What can I get you to drink, darlin'?"

"If we haven't offended you, beautiful Sasha, I'd like a Dewar's on the rocks and a long neck for my friend."

"Dewar's and a beer, coming up," Sasha said.

"Do they have a gumbo?"

"No gumbo, honey, but the best beans and rice on Frenchman Street, for four dollars a bowl. It's a big bowl and especially good. Charlie's mother makes it in the back room."

"Then forget the Dewar's and make it two beers and two bowls of red beans. Thank you kindly, Miss Sasha."

Sasha smiled and turned away.

"They have a hot sauce?" Gabe asked.

"Tabasco for sure, and I think maybe Louisiana. I'll check."

"Louisiana, if they have it, sweetheart. I love it on chicken. Tabasco if they don't. Thank you."

By then the band members were walking past Sasha toward the bar, beginning their break. She stopped as though she had forgotten something, turned on her heel and strutted back in a march to the table, leaned down on it with one hand and looked Peck in the eye.

"I just got it," she said.

"Hanh?" Peck grunted.

"You implying we're hookers?" Sasha asked.

Peck sat up straight, speechless.

"I'm right aren't I, cowboy? You think we're goddamned hookers."

Peck looked at Gabe for an assist. No help was proffered.

"Don't be looking at him. What's your name?" Sasha asked.

"Peck."

"Nobody's name is Peck," Sasha declared.

"Hanh?"

"What's your name?"

"Boudreaux Clemont Finch, ma'am," Peck said.

"I knew it."

"Hanh?"

"Nobody is named Peck unless they've earned that distinction being an asshole. Who was inspired to name you Peck, Mr. Boudreaux Clemont Finch? Don't fuck with me, or I'll have Charlie throw you out. Who was it?"

"Mrs. Feller, at school. It was her what did it," Peck said.

Peck's hands were restless, fidgety, but he found a calm staring into Sasha's cleavage, fighting for air between two breasts as she leaned.

"Mrs. Feller didn't name you Peck, did she?"

"Mrs. Feller sure—"

"Don't lie to me."

"Well..."

"She called you a peckerwood for shooting off your mouth with no thought whatsoever, am I right?"

"Something like dat," Peck said.

"And you quit school and stopped learning manners, I'll bet."

By this time, Peck's confidence was building as he figured she wasn't about to slap or hit him with a heel of her shoe. The more he could egg her on, the more he could watch that cavern to heaven that was her chest. For maybe the first time in his life he kept his mouth shut and nodded his head in agreement, with pleasure.

"Peckerwood, listen good. Last year I put over ninety thousand in my 401K, I drive a Bentley convertible, own a caddy SUV, my three homes are paid for and I have nine full-time real estate ladies on my payroll."

Sasha paused.

She caught Peck's eyes staring down her bosom. She smiled and watched him a bit more, finding pleasure in his dancing eyes. She returned the impropriety, looked at his chest, his thighs in tight jeans and his shapely flexed arms, and raised her eyebrows with approval.

She stood up.

"Boudreaux, would you like your beer in a bottle or a glass?"

"Bottle would be good, ma'am."

Sasha extended her hand. "We going to get along easy, are we?"

"Like eatin' lettuce—easy," Peck said, shaking her hand.

She turned toward Gabe and winked.

"Angel Gabriel, maybe you can train peckerwood here what an apology is by the time I come back with y'all's drinks and beans—"

"I'll certainly give it a try," Gabe said.

"—and save a dance for me," Sasha said.

She turned, looked over her shoulder at Peck with a smile in her eyes and walked away, certain this time to do a proper sashay of hips for four eyes she was certain were glued to them.

CHAPTER 5

THE BAND WAS BACK and playing Louis Armstrong sounds when Sasha returned with a tray of beers and two bowls of red beans and rice.

"Oh my, doesn't this smell good?" Gabe asked.

"The best on Frenchman Street," Sasha said.

"Sasha, won't you join us?"

"Well, that depends," Sasha said.

"Come sit and talk?"

"I don't sit with just any man who comes in."

"Depends on what, pretty lady?"

"Are you a dancer?" Sasha asked.

"New Orleans jazz and a beautiful woman—it doesn't get any better than that. This Creole mutt is a dancer, honey. I surely am."

She smiled, gave a wink, went back to the bar, retrieved her martini and purse and returned, swaying her hips to the rhythm of music as she walked. Gabe stood and pulled a chair out.

"Why thank you, Gabe. Such a gentleman."

She leaned and kissed him on the cheek.

"Are martinis your drink of choice?" Gabe asked.

"I find them most efficient," Sasha said. "And I like the way they look in my hand."

"I went through that," Gabe said. "There was a period when I thought I looked best with a tumbler of Dewar's on rocks locked in my fist."

"Did you want a Dewar's, Gabe?"

"Not tonight, darlin'—just enjoying the music and my red beans."

"You'd still look good with a tumbler in your hand."

"When I'm dressed, holding a tumbler shows off my French cuffs and links."

"Isn't it funny what people do?" Sasha asked.

"Excuse me, darlin' but these beans and rice are about best I've ever had," Gabe said. "I wonder what her secret is, do you know?"

"She won't say, but I think she melts her butter in chicken broth, maybe dusts it first with flour and boils rice in that," Sasha said.

"Definitely the Holy Trinity," Gabe said.

"Hanh?" Peck asked.

"Nothing is cooked in New Orleans without onions, bell peppers, and celery, Boudreaux—Gabe here knows his stuff," Sasha said. "That's the Holy Trinity."

Gabe held a spoon of rice to his nose and sniffed.

"I think you're absolutely spot on about the flour," Gabe said. "Maybe a roux with flour and chicken skin fat strained into her butter melted in chicken broth secret. This is a master blend of flavors—good eating."

"How about you, Peck?" Sasha asked. "Are you enjoying the rice and beans?"

"Yes'm."

"You're in real estate?" Gabe asked.

"I am."

"I'll bet Katrina turned your whole world upside down here in New Orleans."

"You betcha it did, and BP's oil spill didn't help, either," Sasha said. "Then Harvey, Nate, they just keep coming, we just keep surviving."

"I'm delighted to know you seem to be thriving," Gabe said.

"Why thank you."

"Nothing more satisfying than a woman on top of her game."

"Gabriel, are we going to talk all night or we going to dance? I want to dance." She glanced at Peck.

"Don't look at me," Peck declared.

"I wasn't," Sasha said. "I was thinking you ought to go sit with Lily Cup at the bar or maybe get her to come over here with us."

Peck looked at Gabe with anxiety, knowing he didn't have a nickel in his pocket. He was waiting for some sign from Gabe.

"You'll like her, Peck. A bowl of beans and rice are good at room temperature. It'll hold," Sasha said. "It'll outlast the night."

"We're finding ourselves a little short tonight," Gabe said.

"How's that?" Sasha asked.

"We stepped in for a drink and maybe a bowl of gumbo and to listen to jazz. The place looked befitting our budget."

"There's nothing short about you, Gabriel," Sasha said.

"What a pleasant surprise to meet someone who dances, as lovely and as attentive as you."

"Gabriel, you bring a style into this place tonight that it hasn't seen in a long time."

"Be still, my heart," Gabe said, tapping his fingers on his chest.

"You're on my tab tonight, sweetie," Sasha said. "Both of you."

"You're too kind," Gabe said.

"I'm thinking you'd rather have a Dewar's, wouldn't you?"

Gabe smiled.

"I'll go get one, now taste your red beans and let's dance."

Sasha looked at Peck. "Kindly inform Lily Cup that her presence is required."

"Hanh?"

"Grab a chair for her when you do."

"You mean ax her to come over here?" Peck asked.

Sasha winced.

"Peck, say asked."

"Hanh?" Peck asked.

"Say the word *ask*."

"Ax."

"My lord," Sasha said. "Yes—get up and go ax her to get her ass over here."

"R'at now?"

"Right now."

"What I'm gonna did?"

"Help her walk. She's well along to being shit-faced."

Peck stood, thinking of approaches.

"And make her leave her filthy cigars at the bar," Sasha said.

Gabe pushed his bowl away, placed his napkin over the top, stood and extended his hand to Sasha.

"They're playing Joe Williams, my darling. Shall we have a go?" Gabe asked.

Sounds were deep and slow, a vibrating mellow with notes flowing out like they were paying their own rent just for coming into the room. To Gabe the sax was Joe Williams in song. Early on the two modestly held each other, as strangers politely do when they first dance. It was a second set for a sax solo when Gabe's arms reached around her waist, pulling her tightly to his body. Sasha's face gently nuzzled into Gabe's neck. She could smell sweat on his collar and the dispenser soap on his neck. She put one hand on the old man's shoulder, rested the other on the back of his neck.

"You smell good," she whispered to herself.

Gabe closed his eyes and respected the musical notes with short, deliberate steps and body sways. They became one in a room beginning to fill with local patrons. The room was also coming alive with smells of butter in red beans and rice, and respectful laughter politely subdued for an easier listening to sounds of bass and drums. It was five slow dances in a row before the two of them opened their eyes.

"What am I going to do with you?" Sasha asked.

"It's like we belong on the dancefloor," Gabe said.

"Oh my," she sighed.

They turned and walked to the table.

"Ish about time you two," Lily Cup slurred. "Sit down and join the party."

"Gabriel, meet my friend, Lily Cup," Sasha said. "Lily Cup, meet Gabe."

Lily Cup raised an unsteady hand—it swirled in small circles.

"Hello Gabe," Lily Cup said. "You'll have to pardon my—well, I may be a little..." Lily Cup hiccupped, "Oh fuck it, I'm drunk."

Gabe shook her hand, lifted his Dewar's in toast. "It is distinctly my pleasure, Miss Lily Cup. Good to meet you."

Lily Cup jerked her head, blinking her eyes like wiper blades, giving Gabe a belchy grin for his courtly gesture. She weaved her index finger around her bodice and pointed it at Peck with her eyes still on Gabe.

"Have you met Peck, Mr. Gabriel?" Lily Cup asked, pushing her finger into Peck's ribs. "This is Peck. Hee'sh vera nice."

"Do call me Gabe, Lily Cup, and yes, I have. In fact I had the pleasure of coming in with Peck earlier. We've met."

"Huh?" Lily Cup asked. She hiccupped.

"Ready for another beer, Peck?" Gabe asked.

"I can did that," Peck said. "One of doze be good."

Lily Cup broke her stare of confusion as her lips blew a bubbled, lip-snorting laugh.

"Don't you just love the way he—ya know— talks?" she asked.

"Peck's part coonass, Lily Cup. A bona fide, genuine French Cajun," Gabe said. "He gets his thoughts across in his own artful way. It takes a good ear at times, but we get along quite well, don't we my brother?"

Peck wrinkled a grin.

"You speak Cajun French?" Sasha asked. "*Vous parlez le français, Cadien?*"

"I know some," Peck replied. "*Je sais que certains.*"

"Interesting," Sasha said.

"Want to know what?" Lily Cup asked, spilling some of her drink on the table.

"What?" Gabe asked.

"At first I thought he said his name was Pecker," Lily Cup said. She snorted into her fist. "Pecker—get it? Pecker?"

"Peck, what say you go ask Charlie for some strong black coffee for Lily Cup here—lots of sugar?" Sasha asked.

Peck pushed away, stood and started toward the bar.

"Wait," Lily Cup slurred. "Lemme go with you. Charlie's my friend."

She stood, tipping the back of her chair over. Peck caught it, put his arm around her waist, propped her tightly to his side and they ambled away.

"Wanna dance, honey?" Lily Cup slurred.

"Peck!" Sasha said.

Peck turned.

"Hahn?"

"No more rye—"

"Hokay."

"Black coffee—sugar," Sasha whispered.

Peck and Lily Cup made it to the barstools.

"I have a sense that young lady has something weighing on her mind," Gabe said.

"She's in the middle of a murder case," Sasha said. "Trial starts tomorrow."

"Oh my," Gabe said.

"She believes he's innocent and the responsibility has her frightened she may lose."

"Is she the lead attorney?" Gabe asked.

"Yes, and she's damned good," Sasha said.

"That's why then," Gabe said. "No wonder she's feeling her liquor."

"This always happens when her trials start. She pretends rye clears her brain cells."

"That's one way of putting it, I suppose," Gabe chided.

"She needs a Peck tonight," Sasha said. "Let's hope he can sober her and can get her to forget her court case for a while."

"Sounds like a plan, but I wouldn't go telling Peck about her case or what she does," Gabe said.

"If you say so. You may have a reason, but may I ask why?"

"Let me put it this way...you can *ax* me...how'd that be?"

"Oh, I get you."

"This is the same peckerwood that all but called you a hooker before you were introduced."

"Gotcha," Sasha said. "You're a smart man."

"I've got some years on me, princess, and you and the music have awakened my inner spirit," Gabe said.

"Well let's dance before it goes to sleep again," Sasha said.

They stood, assumed positions like they had danced together for years. Gabe held his arms out for her.

"Jazz is mostly swing—some blue notes here and there," Gabe said. "This is free jazz—straight old school from as far back as in the fifties. These guys are good."

Sasha leaned in and kissed his neck.

"Shut up and hold me, Count Basie," she whispered. "Hold me tight."

Gabe slid his right hand down over her buttocks, giving a friendly pat, and moved it back to her waist.

"I want to take you home," Sasha mumbled. "But my boyfriend might be there."

"That does paint this scene in a new light, doesn't it?" Gabe asked.

"Oh, nothing like that, Gabe. I just want to keep you around—for dancing."

He lifted his head and kissed her ear as they turned with a dip.

"What brings beautiful women like you and your friend here to an alley off old city Frenchmen Street, when you could be somewhere fancy in the French Quarter?"

"Because you're here," Sasha said.

"You're here tonight because you knew we were coming?"

"It was a metaphor, sweetie."

"I knew that."

"It's alive in here. The booze is straight, the people are sweaty from honest day jobs, and there's the live music, the reason they come in."

"Touché," Gabe said. "I wasn't thinking."

"You smell good," Sasha said.

Gabe turned them through a sax riff back with a trombone slide.

"Better than your boyfriend?"

"Just dance."

"Can we be expecting him and there bein' a scene?"

"James is not like that."

"All men are like that, darlin'."

"James is a wimp—probably over at Commander's Palace right now, impressing his friends. He's a surgeon in Baton Rouge."

"The man lives in Baton Rouge and he dines in New Orleans?" Gabe asked.

"He's here three days a week," Sasha said.

"Interesting."

"We both have busy careers."

"I'm an old man, darlin'."

"You don't dance old."

"I know about love."

"I'll bet you do, my Creole friend."

"Doesn't sound like love to me—not that it's my business."

"Just dance."

"Do you love him?"

"I love how you smell," Sasha said.

"If smells gave us a road, beautiful lady, we'd be on the moon now," Gabe said. "You waft of powders and scented oils, of a lazy morning with sheer curtains flowing from the open window, a horse carriage clip-clopping by below, and yellow rose petals resting on gentle curves of your smooth, firm stomach."

Sasha gripped Gabe closer, as in climax.

"Damn," she whimpered. "You are good."

"I'm an old black man raised on the South Side of Chicago," Gabe said. "Momma made me read every day, play nice and to always tell girls how pretty they were. When they drafted me into the army, she told me to stay put there and learn a trade."

"What a nice momma," Sasha said.

Sasha kissed Gabe on the neck.

"You do your momma proud," she said.

"Momma would love to hear you saying that."

"What am I going to do with you? I want you to hold me like this forever."

"I'm flattered, young lady, but after the dance I'll still be an old man, and you'll still be beautiful and your surgeon man is having his dessert at Commander's Palace, waiting to bed you tonight."

"Gabe, do you know who Satchel Paige was?"

"Famous pitcher, a brother. Of course, I know Satchel Paige."

"Do you know what he said when they asked how old he was?"

"They think he was near a hundred when they asked him. Yes, I know," Gabe said. "He said— 'How old would you be if'n you didn't know'd how old you were?'"

"Where do you and Peck live? I'll give you a ride home," Sasha said.

"We don't live in New Orleans."

"Oh? Where are you staying?"

"We aren't."

"What do you mean, you aren't?"

"We have to hit the road," Gabe said.

Sasha lifted her head. "What?"

"We're going to Rhode Island."

"When's your flight?"

"We're not flying."

"You're going to Rhode Island?"

"Yes."

"Tonight?"

"We'll catch a ride somewhere."

Sasha stopped dancing and pulled away.

"Gabe, you have no money."

Gabe didn't speak but pulled her to him and into a turn.

"I know Peck has no money," she added.

Gabe turned her again with the music.

"What's in Rhode Island?"

"Newport. It's a long story. Let's not get into it now," Gabe said.

She stopped dancing and pulled away.

"You're damned straight we're getting into it now, Gabe."

Gabe looked away.

"I don't just dance with a man all night and not get attached—I'm attached. Now why Newport? Why tonight?"

Gabe pursed his lips.

"That does it," Sasha barked.

"I don't care why you're going. I'm driving you as far as Memphis, you stubborn old man."

"We'll be fine," Gabe said. "Thank you for the offer, but—"

Sasha reached for her purse.

"You're not a serial killer or anything like that are you?"

Gabe looked her in the eye with exasperated lowered lids.

"Where's Peck?" Sasha asked. "Their barstools are empty."

Peck and Lily Cup were nowhere in sight.

"I wonder where they ran off to," Gabe said.

Sasha pulled her dress down, adjusted her bodice and walked toward the bar, first looking for their drinks at the empty stools and then going into a back room where the toilets were. In a few minutes, she came out, walking towards Gabe muffling a smile.

"They'll be out in a minute."

"Uh oh," Gabe said.

"I think she's sober now," Sasha said.

"If my imagination serves me—the look on your face, woman, I'd say your attorney friend has treed a young Cajun raccoon."

"Put it this way," Sasha said. "She's not thinking of her murder trial at the moment. I'm certain of it."

Gabe pulled his Dewar's and his rice and bean bowl toward him.

"I'm going to go get my car," Sasha said.

Gabe looked at his watch and pushed his Dewar's away.

"Meet you both in front—fifteen, twenty minutes, tops," Sasha said.

"Honey," Gabe said. "This is wrong. You don't have to..."

"I had to go there sometime anyway. There's a building developer in Memphis looking to buy a hotel in the Quarter or Garden District to take condo. I'll call on him when we get there," Sasha said.

"This has been a beautiful evening..." Gabe started.

"Not another word," Sasha said. "I'm driving you to Memphis and by the time we reach Jackson, I want to know the story, understand, sir? *Comprenez-vous, Monsieur?*"

Gabe looked up from his beans and rice.

"I do, my dear. Hurry back."

Sasha took his cheeks in her hands, leaned and kissed his nose.

"Tell Peck not to go anywhere and tell Lily Cup I'll call her later, not to worry," Sasha said. "Finish your beans. I'll see you out front. We have a six-hour drive."

Gabe and Peck walked a smiling and sober Lily Cup outside and put her in a taxi. Gabe didn't ask Peck questions. He let the lad alone in whatever afterthoughts he had from his backroom encounter. When their ride drove into the alley, it was a light blue Bentley convertible with the top up.

"My goodness," Gabe said, admiring the lines of the elegant car. He swept a gentle hand across its hood. "It's blue and magnificent."

"Light blue," Peck said, "*Bleu clair.*"

Sasha stepped out, walked around behind it and clicked the trunk open with her electronic key.

"Is Lily Cup still here?" she asked.

"We cabbed her home," Gabe said.

"Damn. She has my house keys."

"Should we go get them?" Gabe asked.

"No."

"I don't mind," Gabe said.

"I can make do."

"You're not driving us to Memphis in a satin dress, Sasha."

"Put your bag in the trunk, Peck honey, it'll fit—you sit in the back," she said.

"At least let me have the honor of driving this beautiful machine, darlin'?" Gabe asked. "Part of the way. I want to see what it feels like. I have a valid license and I only nursed one Dewar's all evening."

"Good idea," Sasha said. "Let my vodka wear off."

Gabe's face grinned like a schoolboy as he stepped around to the driver's side and got in. Still in high heels and satin, Sasha pulled the passenger door open for Peck.

"Watch the upholstery, Peck," Gabe said. "Be careful. It's a classic."

Sasha leaned from the sidewalk and through the opened door.

"Do you know where we're going, Gabe?"

"To Memphis?" Gabe asked.

"You take a right at St. Charles, left at Calliope, and head to 90. We're looking for I-10 then I-55 north."

She pulled the passenger seatback forward.

"I'll find it. I know the city," Gabe said. "Do you want to look in my duffel to see if there's something in it you can put on, darlin'?"

Peck crawled into the back seat.

Sasha leaned down again.

"Peck, is there a gym bag behind the seat?" Sasha asked.

Peck lifted and held it by the door. Bending in she took it and set it on the front seat and unzipped it.

"No peeking, guys," Sasha said, lifting garments from the bag.

"You can go to Charlie's ladies' room," Gabe said.

"In my modeling days, I had to change outfits in the middle of streets and crowds of onlookers. This'll be quick."

Standing in her red Chanel satin sleeveless dress, she took black tights and a sweatshirt from the bag, flinging each over a bare shoulder. Her hand rested on the opened car door to help her keep balance as she stepped out of Dior spiked heels. In stocking feet, she reached down between her legs, grabbed and pulled the bottom of her dress up, exposing black thigh-high French stockings on beautiful, slender legs and linen white thighs; then further up to a pantyless crotch draped with a delicate saddle—a black, satin laced garter belt clinging to her hips like a café curtain above a sensual firm stomach. She caught the eyes in the car focusing on her bare lower belly.

"Heavens boys, don't sit there gaping," Sasha said. "Can't a girl get a little privacy?" she asked with a grin.

"Sorry," Gabe chuckled.

"Certainly, you've seen a girl's clamando. *L'entrejambe d'une fille?*"

There were sheepish grins but no response.

With an unsnap the garter belt fell loose from her thighs and now hung from two buttoned hooks on the top of each stocking. Draping her hips with the dress she pushed her stockings down and off a leg at a time, tossing hose and garter belt into a shopping bag. Taking black tights from her shoulder, she slipped each foot into a leg of them and swayed in jerks, her thighs and hips from one side to the other, maneuvering them up and under her dress, to her waist. She asked for an unzip. A girl on the sidewalk obliged her and the entire red satin dress dropped to her ankles, leaving her standing in tights and a black, strapless bra. She stepped one foot out of the dress, carefully lifting it with the other foot and placing it on the car seat. Still facing the car's opened door, she took the sweatshirt from her shoulder and handed it to the girl behind her to hold. She stood there in black tights and her black strapless bra showcasing a cleavage of milky white breasts. She reached behind her back, unhooked the bra, letting her supple breasts push the bra off. Both Gabe and Peck, three bystanders at the corner, and a couple waiting to walk around the opened car door that was blocking the alley's sidewalk, gave their full attention with mouths open, staring as the bra fell from her breasts. Sasha ignored the couple waiting to get by, leaned her head down, looked at Peck and grinned. She looked over at Gabe and winked.

"This is near the French Quarter, *mes amis.*"

The girl handed Sasha the sweatshirt. She pulled it over her head and down, covering her breasts before kissing the girl on both cheeks a "thank you."

"There's nothing with our natural bodies that can't be seen about in or around the Quarter, especially during Carnival—Mardi Gras and beads, am I right?" Sasha asked.

"Nothing," the girl said.

"Apparently during summer too," Gabe quipped, feeling the steering wheel with both hands. "I'm not complaining, mind you."

"It's how we do it here, honey," the girl smiled.

"Pick your chins from the floor, both of you," Sasha said. "Pull your eyes back in and let's get going. We've got a six-hour drive to Memphis."

Sasha rolled her dress, shoes, and bra into a very expensive ball and stuffed them in the shopping bag and handed it to Peck.

"Thank you honey," she said to the girl standing by her.

She then turned to the onlookers.

"Mardi Gras is over, folks." There was light applause as she climbed into the car.

"Peck, put the bag in the cubbyhole behind you, sweetie."

Eventually Gabe learned a Bentley started itself with a touch of a button, and they rolled, slowly down the alley onto Frenchman Street. Two men having a night they wouldn't soon forget and their woman accomplice along for the ride on an impulse, determined to learn the mysteries of her new friend and of the Newport she's only heard of and read about—and of the man who danced warmer than anyone had ever danced with her.

CHAPTER 6

NO ONE SPOKE. They let Gabe embrace his moment inspecting the finer details of a dazzling, state-of-the-art dashboard glowing in the night like a pilot's instrument panel. The car seemed to float from street sign to street sign as thoughtfully as the old man's feet moved on a dance floor. Gabe's smile was as though he were young again, back in his army days, on leave.

It wasn't until Ponchatoula when Sasha lifted her head from a nod off. She looked behind her to see Peck, his head back, sound asleep. She looked at the side of the old man's face, his eye, wide awake and gleaming with a pride of driving a dream car, concentrating on the road. She reached over the console and lightly scratched Gabe's inner thigh with her nails.

"You okay?" she asked.

"I'm so enjoying this piece of machinery," Gabe said, not taking his eyes off the road.

"Wanna talk?" Sasha asked.

"Talk to me, baby," Gabe said.

"Wanna tell me about Newport?"

"Did you say Newport?"

"Newport, yes."

"Nothing to tell."

"Nothing?"

"Newport. Rhode Island."

"Gabe, I thought we had something back there."

"On Frenchman Street?"

"On the dance floor," Sasha said.

"Oh, that we did," Gabe said.

"If we did, don't do me like this."

"We're headed to Newport is all," Gabe said. "What more can I say?"

"If I was wrong, then okay—I was wrong."

Gabe didn't respond.

"Vieil homme têtu!" she whispered. "Stubborn old man."

"We're going to the Newport Jazz Festival," Gabe said.

"Okay. All right, I can see that, jazz man, especially after dancing with you for five hours," Sasha said. "Now that wasn't hard, was it?"

"We're going there."

They watched the road in silence for a mile, maybe two.

"But what's with the secrets, baby?" Sasha asked.

"What secrets?"

"Why no money, why the hitching? Make it all make sense."

Gabe kept his mind on the road.

"If you don't know you can talk to me by now—"

"I have money," Gabe said.

"It seems to be eluding you tonight, darling," Sasha said.

"I have money."

"I'm not after your money, honey—I love how you dance."

"My money is what you might say tied up at the moment," Gabe said.

"Are you married?"

"It's nothing like that," Gabe said.

"Then what?"

"It's a temporary glitch, a momentary setback, and Peck and I enjoy walking, so we didn't give it much thought and started hitching rides."

"You we're doing a bad job of it, sweetie."

"Bad job of what?"

"Of hitching rides."

"How so?"

"You might consider another approach," Sasha said.

"Your point being?"

"I don't understand the part of your story about hitching rides," Sasha said. "You started with beans and rice on Frenchman Street and didn't want to accept your first hitch—my offer of a ride to Memphis. Care to explain if there's something I'm missing?"

"We started this morning."

"From New Orleans?"

"From Carencro," Gabe said.

"From Carencro?"

"Carencro."

"Carencro, like in Louisiana? Our Carencro?" Sasha asked.

"One and the same," Gabe said.

"You two might avail yourselves of a compass—"

"I know how it looks," Gabe said.

"—or a good road map."

"It's our first day on the road."

"No offense, Gabe. Carencro is west of Frenchman Street maybe two, three hours, and Newport is north, least it was last I looked," Sasha said.

"My compass is sleeping in the back," Gabe said.

"Him?"

"Him."

"Peck is your compass?"

"We've since had a shakeup of management responsibilities."

"Let me get this straight. You counted on boy wonder back there to find the way—thousands of miles?" Sasha asked.

"I'll admit if he headed a space program, young Peckerwood Finch might have landed the Apollo moon mission near Raleigh, be my guess."

Sasha looked at a console light glowing on Peck's faded, blue-jeaned thigh.

"He does have a nice bod," Sasha said.

"Lily Cup didn't want to let go of his leg when we put her in a cab tonight, seems she agrees," Gabe said.

"She needed that," Sasha said.

"So'd the boy, truth be told. It's first time since I've known him when he's stopped blabbing his mouth with blurts the way only he can."

"How long have you known him?"

"I've known him for some weeks now—met him this morning."

Sasha rested back, watching the road ahead.

"If you get tired, I'll drive."

"I'm good," Gabe said. "If I wasn't driving this fine car, I'd be sitting up all night watching out a window."

Another mile went by in silence.

"What's the story, Gabe—you and Peck?"

"Ask me no questions, honey—I'll tell you no lies."

"Talk like that frightens me," Sasha said.

She turned and lifted herself, her elbow on the console. She leaned and kissed Gabe on a cheek.

"You smell so good." Sasha whispered. "Tu sens si bon."

She kissed him on the neck.

"You're in good hands, beautiful lady. No worries."

"I take my friendships seriously," Sasha said. "I'm Cajun French, sue me."

"Baby, you make this old Creole feel like I'm in high school. You are truly blessed with a spirit all your own, like a fine wine," Gabe said.

"Then be my friend, Gabe. Don't make me a fool begging you to open up."

"Honey, I—" Gabe started.

"That's not what friends do," Sasha said.

Gabe's face tightened. He wanted the dance to go on forever, but he knew the band always had to go home eventually. A Conway truck passed their light blue Bentley. He gathered his thoughts, looking at the speedometer.

"They have everything. My social security card, my Visa card, my discharge papers, my birth certificate— everything I own is in their safe in Carencro," Gabe said. "Under doctor's orders they stripped me down like a recalcitrant child, took it all away when they checked me in."

"Why?"

"They said it was for safe-keeping."

"I don't understand, who—the police did this?"

"They even tried to take my fucking watch, but I wouldn't let them. They said I could keep an empty wallet and my driver's license in case I wandered off and someone found me."

Sasha sat back. She felt it best to let him ramble.

Still in the dark it was another mile of silence when Sasha prodded again.

"So, who is Peck to you?"

"Peck is the yardman and caretaker—"

"Caretaker?"

"And yardman."

"He mows lawns?"

"If they don't fire his ass for this—he mows at the hospice in Carencro where I was dropped off and left to die while they tested me."

Gabe gripped the wheel, disappointed the truth came out before he wanted it to. He tightened his lips.

Sasha's body fell limp in her seat.

"*L'Hospice*," she whispered.

"Hospice," Gabe mumbled.

She turned her head and looked forward into the night. She turned back, sat quietly watching Gabe's eyes. Quiet miles helped her think.

"You and Peck are running to Newport to listen to the music, aren't you?" Sasha asked.

"Jazz," Gabe said.

"One more last time," Sasha whispered to herself.

Gabe overheard her.

"Just one more last dance," he said.

She reached, gently squeezing his forearm. Neither talking for the longest time.

"It is beautiful," Sasha whispered. "*C'est beau.*"

"I'll say one thing," Gabe said.

"You don't have to, Gabe. I didn't mean—"

"That boy back there may not be a rocket scientist, but he had the heart to see an old man not wanting to die on the banks of a Louisiana bayou—he walked away from every possession he owned—his trotline rig, his mower and rakes, his job—he made a decision, kept his dignity and snuck an old man the hell out of there. The boy volunteered on his own to grant a wish and help an old man go die where he wanted to die."

"Peck did all that?" Sasha asked.

"That young man gave up everything for me. I do love him for it, so I'm tolerant of his ways."

A tear rolled from Sasha's eye as she stared at the fleeting stripes in the road rolling under the car, truck taillights ahead. She placed her palm on Gabe's thigh, scratched an x and o "kiss and hug" with her nails, patted his leg and left her hand there.

"Promise you'll wake me if you need me to drive?"

Gabe nodded. His lips pursed. "I promise, baby. Get some rest."

It was twenty miles south of the Hazlehurst exit when hail started to come down. At first a crackling of it on the hood and trunk sounded like a snare drum in a march. The cloth roof rumbled from the pelting ice storm. It then came in blistering sheets—as though the ice pellets were thrown at the car from snow shovels.

"What in the hell?" Gabe blurted.

"Wha...what's happenin'?" Peck shouted from the back seat.

Sasha's head jerked, she sat up, taking it in.

"Damn," she said.

"Storm," Peck said.

"A hailstorm—and at this time of night. The worst kind," Sasha said.

"I'm slowed to less than fifteen miles-per-hour," Gabe said. "I can't see a damn thing—afraid to stop—afraid to pull over and park—we could get hit either way or we could go off into a swamp and all drown."

A fifty-foot trailer truck crept by on the driver's side.

Sasha pointed at it. "Those taillights," she said.

"What about them?" Gabe asked.

"That truck. Follow its taillights."

"Will do."

"Keep your eyes on them."

"Makes sense, but first overpass we're pulling over," Gabe said.

"Don't take your eyes off those taillights," Sasha said. "And try to keep up with the truck."

Sasha leaned forward and adjusted the GPS on the dashboard.

The rocks of hail got larger and bolder as they pounded on the car, drowning out interior sounds.

"Hazlehurst," she shouted.

"What about it?" Gabe shouted.

"It's up ahead. There'll be an overpass or a bridge or something there that we can park under."

"Hazlehurst—got it," Gabe shouted. "Will that GPS thing tell us when we're close to it?"

"Yes. I'll watch the GPS, you watch the taillights."

Three claps of lightning turned the sky white, showing at least two inches of hail gathering on the road.

"I thought hailstorms were a spring thing," Gabe said.

"Hail knows no season in the south," Sasha said. "Auto insurance in Louisiana is half if you park in a garage away from the hail and sun."

"It looks like hell's freezing over tonight," Gabe shouted. "Lord, don't let me die in an ice storm."

"Gabe," Sasha shouted, sitting up. "Get ready to slow down and pull over."

"Tell me when, baby."

"The GPS will tell when we're about to go under the overpass. You have to be ready to pull over and stop."

"Hazlehurst," Gabe repeated.

"Hazlehurst," Sasha confirmed.

"I'll be ready," Gabe said. "Say the word."

A truck passed on the left, slush splashing on the side of the car. It brazenly drove on, passing the truck Gabe was following.

"Get ready, it's coming up," Sasha said.

Gabe leaned into the steering wheel, alert and ready.

"Almost," Sasha said.

She repeated, "Not yet…not yet…not yet…get ready, Gabe…slow down…now!"

The ravaging rattling sounds of hail hitting the car stopped.

The overpass was held up by enormous concrete trusses, easily eight feet in width each, reaching twenty or more feet to the overpass they supported above. Gabe brought the car to a crawl with his eyes peeled for a space to park.

Three cars, an RV camper, a pickup hauling a boat trailer, and a motorcycle were already under the overpass, parked on its roadside. Gabe pulled to the right of one of the cars and maneuvered up the concrete embankment that sloped under the bridge.

Sasha turned in her seat, getting on her knees. She leaned over the console and took Gabe's head in her hands and kissed his face and neck. She kissed him soundly once on the lips, leaned back and said, "Thank you, my darling. You are our hero tonight."

They sat quietly to settle their nerves from a harrowing twenty-mile drive through sheets of rock-hard hail stones. Occasionally a car would drive out from under the overpass and go on its way, and another would pull in. Gabe lowered his window and took a fistful of hail and held it for Sasha and Peck to look at.

"Let's pray this fine car isn't damaged," he said.

"To hell with the car," Sasha said. "We're safe is all that matters."

Gabe opened his door and put his foot out on the ground.

"Where're you going?" Sasha asked.

"I have some business to attend to," Gabe said.

Sasha smiled.

"I'll be behind one of those concrete pylons, if you need me."

"Leave it running, for the heat, sweetie," she said.

Gabe crawled out and closed the door behind him.

Sasha turned and got on her knees to look at Peck in the back seat. She pulled the driver's seatback forward.

"Peck?"

"*Oui?*"

"Gabe told me what you did."

"Hanh?"

"You are a good friend," she said. "Quitting your job an all."

"What's he been say'n'?" Peck asked.

"That you're about the best friend a man could ever have."

"Gabe say dat, for true?"

"He said you gave up everything you had so you could help make his dying wish come true."

"If'n your talking about me getting him the hell out of there, dass all I did, cher. I don't know about any wish, lest you're talking going to hear jazz up at Newport," Peck said.

"All that jazz," Sasha said. "Just like the song."

"You'd a did the same t'ing seeing his eyes, him sitting on dat park bench," Peck said.

"You're a good man, Peck, God will reward you."

"Is dat for true?"

"You helped a dying man," she added. "*Vous avez aidé un ami mourant.*"

"I help a frien' is all," Peck said.

"What goes around, comes around," Sasha said. "You'll be rewarded someday, somehow."

"You plenty rewarded me in the Quarter, you surely did," Peck said.

"You mean introducing you to Lily Cup?"

"Well, dat too." Peck guffawed. "I was meaning beans and rice and maybe I was t'inking your dressing on the sidewalk like dat. Whew, boy, I tell ya."

"I am so embarrassed," Sasha quipped, feigning to put her hand over her eyes. "*Oh, mon dieu, je suis tellement gêné.*"

She raised her eyebrows inquisitively and pointed each index finger at her breasts.

Peck grinned, rolling his eyes as though she were conjuring his memory of her changing outfits.

"What is it about boobies', Peck?"

"Hanh?"

"Can you tell me?" Sasha toyed. "They're just breasts."

"I see'd more than dat, cher, but if you're axin', all I can say is guys pay money to gets a look close-up, like at clubs around," Peck said. "Lots of money."

"A close look? You mean a close look at breasts?"

Peck didn't answer.

"You go to those clubs, Peck?"

"Nah, nah, I never," Peck said.

"Why not?"

"Ain' been to no club like dat."

"Don't you like to see girls naked?"

"Ain' dat—no money to go," Peck said.

"You got to see Lily Cup's titties. Did you like them?"

"Naw, I didn't."

"You didn't like seeing her—"

"We didn't got her shirt off."

"Can you see me in this light?" Sasha asked.

"Not like a giggin' lantern, cher."

Sasha flipped the map light above her head on and turned her torso enough, so the GPS and console spotlighted her front.

"Now I can," Peck said.

She pulled her sweatshirt up over her breasts.

"Me to you, Peck. Here's your Valentine."

"Ma dang," Peck yelped.

"This is thanking you, big guy, for helping Gabriel," Sasha said. "These are my girls?"

"Me oh my, they shore is purdy."

Peck took them in with a memorizing stare. To help, Sasha leaned forward with a smile, watching Peck's eyes to maybe a count of ten, sat up, and pulled the sweatshirt down again and turned around.

About then the driver door opened, and Gabe leaned in.

"Peckerwood, can I see you for a minute?" Gabe asked.

"Hanh?" Peck asked.

"Need to see you out here, son," Gabe said.

Peck's first thought was that Gabe saw the two of them—was upset and wanted words.

"Ya t'ink he seen us?" Peck whispered to Sasha.

"Peck, I have to talk to you," Gabe said.

"I think he needs help," Sasha said. "Better go see."

As Peck climbed out, Gabe took him by the arm, closed the door and forcibly walked him around back of the car. He stood Peck between him and the trunk.

"Don't be looking now, but behind me, the skinny one on the black motorcycle—he's wearing black leather, over my shoulder—"

"I see him," Peck said.

"He's the one on the bike sitting behind the boat trailer back there."

"I see him. What about him?"

"He's the motherfucker that stole my pills."

"Your pill bottle, Gabe? Whole t'ing?"

"My Contin, my pain medicine," Gabe said.

"He taked your pill or the whole bottle, Gabe?"

"The bottle. It's morphine, son. Without it I'll be doubled over wanting to die with the pain it'll give me by this time tomorrow."

"He just come up and—?" Peck started.

"I was back there peeing and then taking my pill—right behind that pylon, that one over there. The bastard slapped me on the back of the head with a fist and grabbed the bottle out of my hand and ran."

"Did you take you a pill?"

"I took my pill, swallowed it without water but I no more got the cap on, and the sonofabitch whacked the back of my head and grabbed the bottle. I fell to my knees, so I don't think he knows I got a look at him. I could see him run to his motorbike."

"Git in the car," Peck growled.

"What?" Gabe asked, confused. "Help me—"

Peck grabbed Gabe's arm firmly. "Go git bag in the car, close the door and pop the trunk."

"What are you thinking?"

Peck grabbed the front of Gabe's shirt and pulled him close.

"Now, goddammit, Gabe, 'afore he takes off. Git in the car, old man. Git in now."

Gabe stepped around the side, pulled the door and started to climb in.

"Pop the trunk," Peck yelled.

CHAPTER 7

THE BENTLEY ROCKED with the trunk being slammed shut. Peck yanked the passenger door open, saw the seat empty, Sasha behind the wheel and Gabe in the back seat. He got in and pulled the door closed.

"Take off," he barked.

Sensing the tension of the moment, Sasha nodded, brought her window down enough to look out to her left.

"Let's go," Peck grunted.

There was an opening between a small car and a large RV camper, and she edged her way through the gap. Watching for approaching headlights, she pulled onto the interstate and nervously picked up speed. The more confidence she felt behind a tractor-trailer she was following the faster she would drive to keep up. When they passed a mile north of Crystal Springs, they saw no signs of any hail or rain. The road was completely dry. It was as if they had left one room and entered another.

In the new quiet Peck reached his arm back between seatbacks, his knuckles touching Gabe's thigh. Gabe's fingers grasped Peck's hand, realizing his pill bottle was in it. He took the bottle, and with both hands he squeezed Peck's hand a *thank you, my brother...thank you.* Gabe smiled, and could finally lean his head back and wait for sleep to come.

Sasha got the speed up to seventy and set the cruise control.

She knew not to ask, but she saw in the reflection from the dash that Peck had retrieved Gabe's medicine. She was moved, watching him hand the pills to Gabe. She looked at Peck and smiled. He was a simple man. And his passion was a simple one, letting his trotline feed him at night, and earning enough mowing and sharpening blades to pay room rent somewhere; and he cared about people, risking giving up what he owned to help an old man he didn't know.

"Why if you keep this up...your helping my dancing man—Captain Jordan back there—way you do, why bless me I'm going to owe you a whole basketful of thank-you roses, Mr. Boudreaux Clemont Finch," Sasha said. "Whatever's a girl to do?"

Sasha looked into the rearview mirror and caught Gabe's smile, with eyes closed, appreciating her caring, encouraging her fun. This simple young man acted to help his friend immediately—without thinking—and in his world an immediate response was appropriate.

Peck grinned at the compliment, raised his right hand, letting his fingers welcome a sense of importance as he brushed his sun-bleached front hair to the side. Impulsively Sasha reached and took his right hand and guided it to her side of the console—Peck having to turn his body.

"Whatever am I going to do with you, Boudreaux?"

She raised his hand and kissed it. She kissed it again.

"It was a brave thing you did back there," Sasha said. "You're our hero."

She kissed his hand once more and held it to her breast.

"What's your cell number, Peck?"

"Hanh?"

"Your cellphone number, text me so I have it?"

"I don't have a phone, cher."

"When I get home," Sasha said. "I'm going to get you a phone. You ever had a cellphone before, Peck?"

"No ma'am."

"Why not?"

"I ain't had money, sides I wouldn't know who to call."

"You'd have to take care of it," Sasha said.

"I taked good care of my t'ings," Peck said.

"Peck, don't answer this if you don't want," Sasha said.

"Hanh?"

"Can you read and write?"

"No, ma'am. I didn't stay with it—school," Peck said.

"Come to New Orleans when you're ready. and I'm going to see to it you learn to read and write."

"Dass for true, cher?"

"Would you like to learn?"

"Startin' grade was about all I could take and it was firs' week," Peck said. "I run away from dat and my foster nanna. I only need my trotline to get by."

"Will you let me try?" Sasha asked.

"Nah, nah."

"I know a good tutor."

"If' I could read with nobody laughing at me?" Peck asked.

"Nobody there but you."

"I surely would."

"You'll have your own private tutor," Sasha said. "You'll pick it up fast."

"Wouldn't dat be something now? If I could read, you know contracts and t'ings, I'd might could get me a pirogue and run crab traps and sell them to fancy restaurants."

"Big money in soft-shelled crabs," Gabe said.

"I can did *cinquante* traps without a license," Peck said.

"Fifty traps without a license?" Sasha asked.

"If I could read and get me a license I could have *trois*, maybe *deux cent* traps."

"For two hundred traps you'll need a bigger boat than a pirogue, Peck," Sasha said. "Maybe we could be partners."

Sasha lifted his hand from her chest, extended hers for a shake.

"We got a deal?" she asked. "*Nous avons une affaire?*"

"We got a deal," Peck said, shaking her hand.

He leaned back, rested his head with eyes closed and a smile on his face. Gabe too. They were both asleep by the time three Mississippi state trooper cars approached from ahead and whooshed by, one as fast as the next, with white and blue lights flashing like a summer electrical storm, racing south at breathtaking speeds. Sasha watched them pass by and kept an eye on their flashing lights in the side and rearview mirror until they were out of sight. The sleeping Peck and Gabe were none the wiser.

Now Sasha had her ways about her, this was certain. She was first a fifth generation N'Orleans woman—and celebrated every moment of her femininity—but she was also an equal, diligent, confident, running her own successful real estate firm. She was chamber president two years running; she enjoyed the company of a younger surgeon from Baton Rouge, who hadn't quite made his mind up if he was ready to grow up enough to be married; and she enjoyed the independence of her occasional masquerade for men and boys, so long as they were good dancers. She enjoyed playing dress-up with Lily Cup and prancing around in low-cut, expensive Chanel and Givenchy satins and their Prada's, gathering stares and listening to jazz and dancing to slow dances at Charlie's Blue Note a few nights a month, where they were safe and celebrated as graceful New Orleans belles. Charlie always walked them home. Sasha was also a good citizen who obeyed the law—and now, after seeing those trooper cars, a concern came over her face.

She watched the road ahead, preoccupied about what to do for a spell, but went ahead and patted and squeezed Peck's leg.

"Peck?"

"Hanh?"

"Wake up, honey," she said.

Peck bolted, sat up and wrinkled his eyes, rubbing his knuckles on them.

"Yeah?" Peck asked.

"Wake up, I have to ask you something," Sasha said.

"I'm awake," Peck said. "Ax me."

In the back seat, Gabe sat up, rubbing his eyes.

"Peck, back there in the hailstorm…"

"Hokay?"

"Under the bridge, did you do anything we might be in trouble for?" Sasha asked.

Peck sat in silence.

"We need to know, Peck."

Peck sat in silence, looking ahead.

"Did you do anything that would have the police looking for us?" Sasha asked.

"Better tell her, son," Gabe said.

Peck was silent, as though he were thinking what to say.

"She knows what you did for me, my brother. We love what you did, but answer her, son."

"He told me first off to go fuck myself," Peck said.

"Talk to us," Gabe said, leaning his head over the seatback.

"So I told him if he needed an old man's medicine so bad maybe he didn't need his motorcycle key. I took the keys from his bike so he couldn't start it and run off," Peck said.

Sasha and Gabe waited.

"Dass when he pulled a knife."

"Oh, God," Sasha said.

"Two guys driving the pickup haulin' the boat come around from pissing back of the post and ax what was happening and I tole them and they offered to help me. I grabbed the robber's knife-hand quick and he wrestled me down, but I got him on the ground and edged his hand and the knife to his bike tire and pushed the blade into his tire and cut it too big to fix."

"What then?" Gabe asked.

"Then I took my elbow and whomped it back on him, whomp, whomp, but I didn't kill him."

"Talk to us, my brother," Gabe said.

"I just elbow whomped him."

"With your elbow? His neck or face?" Gabe asked.

"I know difference between a killing hit and a whomp, Gabe. Dass when one of the other guys found your medicine in knife man's coat pocket and gived it to me. They tole me t'anks and said he'd prolly gone through their truck and the RV camper too. Tole me to go on and git and they'd see to the biker."

"Is this true?" Sasha asked.

"Yes'm," Peck said.

"Every word?" Gabe asked.

"Well, nah, nah," Peck said. "Not ever' word."

"Talk to me, my brother," Gabe said.

"I wanted to kill him, Gabe—"

"Oh my God," Sasha said.

"—just like he did you by taking your pills. He could of killed ya, boss. I wanted to shore enough kill him, but I swear I didn't."

Gabe sat back. Both fear and tears grew in Sasha's eyes.

"But I didn't, Gabe. I swear it."

"I believe you Peck," Gabe said.

"I know how to kill plenty good. A whomp is just a setback, not a kill. It ain't a bonk. Sides, he was setting there holding his bloody nose and ear was bleeding when I gived his bike key to the fellers."

"I believe every word," Gabe said.

"Me too, but if those troopers were going to that bridge, something happened since we left."

"Might be an accident in the hail back there," Gabe said.

"We can't take chances. They may look for this car," Sasha said.

"A Bentley in Mississippi," Gabe said. "Spot us in a heartbeat."

"I only whomped him," Peck said.

"We believe you, Peck. Go back to sleep," Sasha said.

"He was settin' there when I walked away with Gabe's pills, I swear."

"I'm getting off the interstate in Jackson. We'll go to Vicksburg and then north to Memphis," Sasha said. "It'll keep us out of sight but add an hour or so. We'll be in Memphis by morning."

Sasha made it to Vicksburg, headed north and turned the radio on low to a blues sound. Each town she drove through seemed to pass by with a welcome and a smile and an ease of a slow dance—Yazoo City, Cleveland, Clarksdale, Helena. It was just at dawn when she turned into the Peabody Hotel and came to a stop at the outside concierge station. She lowered her window for a man approaching.

"Welcome to Peabody. May I be of service?" a bell captain asked.

"Can you give me two, three minutes, honey?" she asked.

"Of course, Ma'am, take your time."

"I'll wave you over."

The bell captain tipped his cap and backed away. She raised the window and put her cellphone to her ear.

"Welcome to the Peabody, how may I direct your call?"

"Yes, hi—room reservations, please," Sasha said.

"Certainly. One moment please."

"This is Peabody reservations, for what date of arrival?"

"Yes, hello, I need two connecting rooms. With an early morning check-in. One night only. Do you have rooms today?"

"Let me check to see if we have two connecting rooms."

"Thank you."

"Certainly, ma'am. Yes we do. When will you be arriving?"

"We're here now," Sasha said. "We just arrived."

"Name, please?"

"Michelle Lissette," Sasha said.

"Can you spell Lissette?"

"Two s's and two t's," Sasha said.

Sasha read off her credit card number, said a "thank you," and with the phone still to her ear, she motioned the concierge over.

"I have you registered, Ms. Lissette. Two connecting rooms for an immediate check in."

"Thank you."

"My pleasure, and welcome to Peabody."

"Could you send room keys out here to the concierge valet stand while we gather things from the car?"

"I'll send them right out with a bellman."

"I'll come in and sign in a few," Sasha said, hanging up.

Gabe and Peck sat in wonder. Sasha looked in Gabe's direction.

"Best there's little or no talking," Sasha said. "Don't offer anything. We're tired. We've been driving all night from a conference in Chicago."

"Michelle?" Gabe asked. "Michelle Lissette?"

She handed Gabe a twenty. "Give this to the bellman when you get to the rooms."

"Michelle Lissette?" Gabe asked.

"I'm Sasha, Gabriel," Sasha said.

Peck and Gabe climbed out of the car and stood as though they were waiting for further instructions.

"Car's no worse for wear," Gabe said. "I don't see a scratch on it."

As the bellman came out of the hotel with room keys, Sasha popped the trunk and asked Peck to lift the duffel out. She closed the trunk. The bellman followed them with a cart carrying the army duffel, and they walked down the inner ramp leading into one of the more celebrated hotel lobbies in Memphis.

Gabe had been in the hotel before. It still impressed him.

"Peck, you may not know about Elvis Presley," Gabe said.

"I knowed Elvis," Peck said.

"He signed his RCA contract in this lobby."

"Who don' know Elvis?"

Peck stopped in his tracks with eyes wide open. The lobby was a world of its own, as large as a city block. A bouquet of hundreds of red flowers sprayed over a dripping water fountain in the middle, and a lone Steinway grand piano sat beneath a crystal chandelier high above the tables and leather chairs arranged on fine oriental carpets. Shops' entrances and a bar at one end of the lobby were of matching dark mahogany. The ceiling was seventy feet high, decorated with hand-carved beams, painted murals, gold trim, and framed by a wrought-iron, second-floor balcony.

"They built this place after the Civil War," Gabe said. "It's historic, Peck. Take it all in, son."

"Bye, guys," Sasha said. "I'll call your room later."

She pointed her hand to the left at a large bank of elevators as their destination, and with a bellman following the two men, she turned right and toward the front desk to sign paperwork and check in.

It was a few minutes after noon before anyone was awake enough to think of making contact.

CHAPTER 8

SASHA RAPPED HER KNUCKLES ON THE DOOR between their rooms.

"Gabe?" she asked. "You in there?"

"One minute," Gabe said.

A bolt lock clicked, and the door pulled open.

"Come in, come in," Gabe said. "Have a seat. We woke a few minutes ago. I was just heading down to get some coffee."

"You going to go watch the ducks?" Sasha asked.

Sasha wrapped her arms around Gabe and gave him a hug and a kiss on the neck.

"By golly, that's right," Gabe said. "I forgot about the famous duck march, Peabody at noon."

He looked at the clock on the desk.

"It's too late, but I'll run down and get us some coffee."

"Gabe?" Sasha asked.

"What, darlin'," Gabe said.

"Sweetie, knowing what you told me, I just can't up and leave you right now," Sasha said.

"Sasha darlin', if I thought it could change anything, I wouldn't have told you."

Sasha watched his eyes now knowing about his hospice stay.

"Peck and ole Gabe here will be just fine. Don't you worry."

"I called my office and was able to switch appointments and open houses around. It'll give us some time to figure this whole thing out."

"Where were you, when I was half my age?" Gabe asked.

"At least one day," Sasha said. "I'll call on that hotel buyer prospect while I'm here."

She kissed him on the neck.

"You can call room service for coffee," Sasha said.

"I just want to go down and look around, walk. I want to take it all in and jog memories of when I was here in the service. I'll get a pot of coffee on a tray, maybe some Danish. I need the walk."

"Charge it to the room," Sasha said.

"I have enough money to at least treat us to a pot of coffee. I want to stroll that grand lobby again. It's been years since I've stayed in this lovely old lady," Gabe said.

"What do you know, a dancer and a romantic," Sasha said.

"You wait here," Gabe said. "Make yourself comfortable, there's a newspaper on that side table. I won't be long."

"Where's Peck?" Sasha asked.

She stepped over to the easy chair and sat down.

"In the tub," Gabe said.

"Sounds pretty quiet in there," Sasha said.

"He said," Gabe started, "—and this is a direct quote: he told me he 'didn't want no shower what needed a secret combination just to get it to run hot or cold.' Ha! He's in there soaking in a tub and looking at his map like Magellan."

"That's Peck, all right," Sasha said.

"I'll be right back," Gabe said.

"I'll be here. Enjoy your stroll. Ask when the ducks march again."

Sasha pulled a desk drawer beside her. She lifted out the WHERE visitor's guide and one from the Memphis chamber. She looked at her phone for messages. She slipped her shoes off and began paging through the magazines. It was fifteen minutes when the bathroom door opened and out walked Peck as bare-ass naked as a newborn baby with both hands gripping a towel over his head rubbing his hair dry like he was in a day spa. It was Sasha's turn to sit with her jaw open, savoring its waggle—a moment for a future memory. The lad's arms and legs were a sun-burned red, his midsection and buttocks were as white as a cotton sheet.

"Lily Cup, you lucky girl," Sasha mumbled to herself.

Peck pulled the towel from the top of his head and started rubbing his ears when he first saw Sasha sitting there, staring. He jumped back like he had stepped on a rattlesnake and lowered the towel to cover his groin.

"Commando too," Sasha said.

"How long you been here?" Peck asked.

"Long enough," Sasha smirked.

"A body needs to be tole they's a lady in the place."

"Now, who went and told you I was a lady, Peck?" Sasha asked.

"You know what I mean," Peck said.

"Remember what I told you when I showed you my girls?"

"Better tell me again," Peck said.

"What goes around comes around," Sasha said. "You got a good look at my girls and kitty, it's only fair I get a good look at—tell me, Peck, have you named your friend?"

"Funny," Peck said. "No, I ain't named it."

"How about Willy?" Sasha asked.

There was a gentle repeating kick on the door. It was Gabe, wanting to be let in.

Peck stood behind the door, with the towel over his groin and Sasha not missing the opportunity to memorize his flexing bare buttocks. Gabe walked in with a tray, balancing a pot of coffee on it, three cups, a silver milk pitcher, sugars, and an assortment of breakfast rolls.

Peck edged back into the bathroom.

"Gabe, get me my pants off the bed," Peck said.

Gabe smirked at Sasha, knowing she's had sport eyeballing a young man's personals. He set the tray on the desk and tossed Peck his jeans.

"And it ain't no Willy," Peck barked.

"I think you're right, moon pie," Sasha said.

"Hanh?" Peck queried.

"Willy is a little boy's name."

"How do you take your coffee?" Gabe asked.

"Have you seen it, Gabe?"

"Darlin' I know the boy and I are friends, but hell no I haven't—"

"Hmmm. I'd say he's such a big boy, maybe a Willard, or perhaps a William."

The bathroom door closed behind Peck with a slam.

"Two sugars and spot of cream."

"You're going to give him a nervous breakdown," Gabe said, pouring the coffee.

"Him a breakdown?" Sasha asked.

"The lad's not even housebroke," Gabe mused.

"How about me? He walked out here towel drying his hair with it swinging about, loose and looking happy. My blood pressure went up just sitting here."

"Did you say cream?" Gabe asked.

"Just a drop."

Gabe handed her a saucer and cup of coffee, took his and sat on the edge of the bed.

"Gabe, we need to talk."

"So, let's talk."

"If you still want to get to Newport."

"And I do."

"Think about it a minute," Sasha said.

"I've been thinking about it for months," Gabe said.

"You wanted to go there when you didn't think there was anything else for you, right?"

"I'll admit that was a factor, yes."

"Now there is—"

"Is what?"

"You have friends now. You've got Peck...You've got me. We'll stick by you, sweetie, through it all. No matter what."

Gabe smiled. "Where were you all those years ago?"

"You're going to need money."

"I'm becoming aware of that. Everything being so final, the thought of needing money never came to me."

 Tell me again, Gabe. How is yours tied up, exactly?"

"They kept whatever valuables I had in Carencro," Gabe said. "They pay any expenses with my insurance or my credit card. It's like I have no control over the card or what they charge to it."

"Who's your bank?"

"Bank of America."

"For us to do anything, a bank will need two forms of ID."

"I only have one."

"What do you have?"

"They kept my Social Security card, so I wouldn't have two forms. I only have my driver's license."

"I think you're being paranoid, Gabe. They really do care about you."

"If I'm so paranoid why wouldn't they allow me to leave with my medicine?"

"Your medicine is a narcotic, Gabe—they were only protecting you from getting hurt."

"Or robbed," Gabe added. "Like I was."

"Yeppers...or robbed," Sasha added.

"Hard to think straight at a place like that."

Sasha checked her phone for an address of a Social Security office close by.

"There's a Social Security place on Monroe Avenue," Sasha said.

"What about it?"

"We'll walk there, get a temporary card and then we'll go to a bank and get you another bank card."

"Can't Carencro folks trace a debit card?" Gabe asked.

"What do you mean?"

"I saw somewhere where all the ATMs take video pictures now of any transactions."

"Good thinking," Sasha said.

"Those cameras see everything," Gabe said.

"So, here's what we'll do," Sasha said. "Today we get your temporary Social Security card. We go to a bank and get a debit card. They can print one out while we wait. Then we'll go to Walgreens where you buy some prepaid credit cards with it all in one transaction and put four or five hundred dollars on each. They'll only be able to trace the one Walgreen's transaction on your card here in Memphis, but not for a few days with this going into a weekend."

"And if I buy the cards at Walgreens there won't be an ATM camera."

"I'll put you both on a plane to Rhode Island, and your trail will go cold here in Memphis."

"Smart woman," Gabe said.

"We go to Beale Street and party tonight—my treat," Sasha said.

"Let's find us some blues," Gabe said.

"We have the rooms all night," Sasha said.

"Woman, if I were younger my front hooves would be pawing like a young bull about now," Gabe said.

"Old bulls are better Gabe, don't you know that?"

"They are? Well you could have fooled me," Gabe said.

"Slow and easy—better," Sasha said.

"You are some woman."

"I bet you tell that to all the ladies, ya big ox," Sasha said, sipping her coffee.

Peck stepped out of the bathroom in jeans and no shirt.

"Well, hello Peck. Would you and William like some coffee?" Sasha asked.

Peck ignored her and sat next to Gabe on the bed.

"Look at you. You're red as Tabasco," Sasha said.

"Walkin' from Kenner to the Quarter," Peck said.

"I can't believe you two walked from Kenner to Charlie's Blue Note."

"The *trois heures* sun is the hottest," Peck said. (three o'clock)

"When we go out, I'll get aloe vera and rub your back and arms," Sasha said.

She proceeded to peruse the room service menu, reading aloud the options for lunch fare. Peck made his several selections of favorites with a flashing of his eyes.

"Where ya going?" Peck asked.

"Gabe and I have some errands," Sasha said. "They could take a couple of hours."

"Hokay."

"Will you be okay staying here and watching television until we get back?"

"Yes'm," Peck said.

"I'll order food up."

"I'm hungry...most we et since we run off was beans last night."

"I'll sign for it downstairs," Sasha said. "Just listen for them to knock and let them in."

"Yes'm," Peck said.

"I'll put a twenty on a bedside table," Sasha said. "Give it to whoever delivers the food."

"Yes'm," Peck said. "But a whole twenty dollars? *Vingt*?"

"Peck, there're two kinds of people—those who won't work without a wage—and those who work on trust," Sasha said. "Wait people work on a trust that we'll say thanks with a tip if we like the service. Give the whole twenty."

Peck appeared to understand.

Several hours later, Gabe's room door opened, and they walked in carrying an envelope from a bank. Peck jumped up to welcome them.

"Peck, honey," Sasha said, "you go over to my room— turn on the television. "Gabe needs a nap before we go to Beale Street later."

As Peck started to step in the doorway Gabe stopped him.

"Before you go, Peck. Hang on a minute, my brother," Gabe said.

He took five prepaid debit cards from the Walgreen's bag, tore the packaging off each and held them out in his hand.

"Here, you take care of the money," Gabe said.

"Hanh?" Peck asked.

"I'm an old man, my brother. Somebody will roll me and take everything we've got—like my medicine."

"Mais pourquoi moi?" Peck asked. ("But me? Why me?")

"You're my best friend, Peck," Gabe said. "See nobody gets it."

Peck felt his back pocket, then his front.

"Gabe," Peck said. "Could I borrow your wallet?"

Gabe handed his wallet to Peck. "You mean this cheap-assed old thing?"

Peck carefully placed five pre-paid credit cards into Gabe's wallet, folded it, and put it in his front right pocket for safekeeping. He looked at Gabe as a son might, indicating with his eyes he wouldn't let him down. He backed into Sasha's room and pulled the door to a near close. Gabe sat down and then stretched out on his bed. Sasha unlaced his shoes and pulled them off. She lay down beside the old man, putting her arm over his chest, her nails dancing on his shirt, lightly scratching his upper chest.

"That was a sweet thing you did," Sasha said.

"What?" Gabe asked.

"Think your friend is up to all that responsibility?"

Gabe turned his head, looking into her eyes.

"I'm sorry, I didn't mean—" she started.

"Honey, if I could figure out the words—if I could even figure how to write what it's like being a black man—being born black in America doesn't come with any set of instructions, you know. If I could, then I'd be able to express what it's like being an old black man so people like you could understand."

"You can say it, Gabe. White people, like me."

"One thing I do know after all these years is people. A black man, if he's smart, learns early on who to trust and who to just walk away from. The young man in that room over there walked up to me on his own steam yesterday morning and without thinking twice about what color I was, he said, 'Old man, you want to get out of here, don' ya? I can see it in your eyes.'"

"Peck said that?" Sasha whispered.

"You know something, pretty lady? If Peck left the hotel right now, and disappeared for good, he's already given me more honor and respect this old black soul of mine has seen from one man in this lifetime—and that's a long time."

Sasha smiled, leaned over and pecked a sweet kiss on Gabe's lips, gently touching one cheek in her hand.

"I'm sorry," Sasha said.

"You're fine," Gabe said.

There was a moment of silence.

"Gabe?"

"What, darlin'?"

"Do you want to talk about it?"

"Can you talk about Michelle Lissette?" Gabe asked.

"Michelle Lissette has a boyfriend, James. She loves him, and he says he loves her," Sasha said.

"Michelle Lissette should be with her man, darlin'."

"But he doesn't dance."

"Not a step?" Gabe asked.

"Only if I make him and never like you, Gabe. Sasha loves to dance, and she and Lily Cup dress up and go out and play a few times a month, to dance. I become Sasha."

"Girl's night out," Gabe said. "So, who is Lily Cup in real life?"

"Lily Cup is Lily Cup, the one and only."

"So it's only you incognito at Charlie's Blue Note?"

"Uh-huh."

"And you dress to the nines to attract the dancers."

"A girl can tell a lot about a man on a dance floor."

"Does Michelle Lissette love her man?" Gabe asked.

"Michelle Lissette loves James, but he doesn't, like, turn Sasha on like—well, you know."

"I don't know," Gabe said.

"Let's leave it at she's comfortable with him. Yeah, Michelle loves him...and the sex is good."

"But—" Gabe started.

"But I'm not certain Michelle would go out of her way to drive him to Memphis all hours of the night."

"The surgeon seems respectable enough by sound of it," Gabe said.

"He is."

"That goes a long way in picking a man for life."

"I know."

"I hope Michelle Lissette isn't risking a future with this young man by being up here in Memphis with us two vagabonds. Ain't much future with me, you know."

"I'm not here because I've fallen in love with you," Sasha said.

"Our bond goes beyond all that," Gabe said.

"I'm here because I've fallen in love with the person you happen to be, and what you've taught me in a matter of hours."

"I'm just an old man, not wanting to wait around to die," Gabe said.

"You're more than that, old man," Sasha said.

Gabe gave a curious nod.

"You're the most sensitive man—and the best dancer that ever held me on a dance floor," Sasha said.

"That's thoughtful, darling, but not quite..." Gabe started.

"You're a teacher of life—you stubborn old man. I thought I knew music and you go and teach me the difference between jazz and blues last night—"

"I did tell you Memphis was the home of blues, didn't I?" Gabe asked.

"—and I refuse to go back home until we've danced the blues."

"Now I remember."

"*Certains hommes peuvent être si épais!*"

"And just what in the hell does that mean?"

"Men can be so thick!" Sasha said.

"Well now you have a bedtime story for your grandchildren," Gabe said. "Your midnight ride to Memphis with two complete strangers."

"For now, it's my story. It'll be a beautiful chapter in my book," Sasha said.

Gabe turned his head and looked at the ceiling.

"Stomach cancer," he whispered.

Sasha heard the words, kept her eyes occupied watching her nails moving on his chest.

"Three months back they only gave me two months to live—said if cancer didn't kill me peritonitis would...and that's just about all I want to say about it."

Sasha had heard the hospice reference on the drive to Memphis but was stunned at the frankness of the moment. She let a quiet moment or two pass by, and she tried humor.

"Would having sex be a bad thing for you?" Sasha asked.

"My having sex would be a Goddamned miracle," Gabe mused.

"You smell good, you sweet man," Sasha said.

"My darlin', your hugs, kisses, that smile, and your scratches are better than any sex I've ever had, let me tell you."

"You are such a lovely man."

They lay quietly looking for diversions like wall art and the ceiling molding in a silence that lingered.

"Of course," Gabe said, interrupting the silence, "you do have some handsome tatas—now that's a fact."

Sasha bellowed in laughter, bolted up on her knees, straddled Gabe while yanking her sweatshirt up over her head, flipping it to his face. She grabbed a breast in each hand.

"Tatas?" she barked.

"Oh, my lord," Gabe said.

"Tatas?"

"Hee hee," Gabe wheezed.

"Why Mr. Gabriel Jordan, sir," she proclaimed, caressing her breasts. "I don't think you've been properly introduced. I want you to formally meet my girls. I'm changing their names in honor of you, darling."

"Well I never," Gabe said. "Ain't this something?"

"Gabe, this girl here is now named Gabriella—after you. Gabriella is my bold one."

"She's the Democrat," Gabe said.

"She can be naughty," Sasha said. "Say hello to Gabriella."

Sasha leaned in, letting her nipple touch Gabe's face. He smiled and kissed it gently, respectfully. She straightened, displaying her right breast.

"And from now on and forever forward," Sasha said, "this girl here is Jordan. She's kind of shy. Talk to her softly."

Sasha leaned in for Jordan's kiss. She paused, lowered her head in thought and sat up, her smile turning into tears, then silent sobs.

"I don't want you to die, Gabe."

She covered her eyes with her hands.

"This is no time for tears," Gabe said.

"I feel like crying," Sasha whimpered. "*J'ai gros couer.*"

"I'm a happy man. All I ask is that I get to live until I die. A man can't ask for anymore. Let's us live every minute we're together—and not waste a second on tears. It's been a long time since I've been happier in this old life than I am right this minute. I thank the girls, Gabriella and Jordan, but especially I thank you, my darlin'. I'm telling you your Baton Rouge surgeon is one lucky man."

"He is, isn't he?"

"Now wipe the tears."

"Is there anything in this world I can do, Gabe? Anything? Tell me."

"Now you mention it, there is one thing," Gabe said.

"Anything, Gabe."

"You can let me get some rest while you go down and get yourself something to wear on Beale Street tonight. We're dancing the blues and all you have is an expensive red satin dress rolled up in a ball in the trunk of the car—"

"That's right, I almost forgot."

"—and we'll be enjoying the best blues and ribs in the country, and that's a promise."

Sasha stood from the bed, walked towards the door when she gasped a guttural guffaw, stooping and laughing in gasps of breath.

'You okay, darlin?" Gabe asked.

"I just got it..." she stammered.

She turned and pointed to her left breast.

"Gabriella—she's the Democrat..."

CHAPTER 9

SASHA REDISCOVERED THE SHOPS in downtown Memphis before finding her way back to their rooms. She juggled shopping bags while managing to get into her handbag. She fumbled for her room key card, trying it first on Gabe's door, and then successfully on her door. Inside, she set packages on the floor. Peck in his jeans and no shirt was sprawled on his back. He was sleeping soundly with a pillow pulled over his face and the television tuned on the hotel guide channel, rolling to music. She pushed on the connecting room door and peeked in. Curtains were drawn, and in darkness she could see Gabe asleep. He breathed heavily in his sleep. Sasha went to his bed, lifted a comforter from under his legs, and covered him. His hand pawed, clutching the comforter, tucking it under his chin with a sleepy smile of appreciation. Sasha watched the old man for a moment and then stepped back into her room. She pulled the door to lessen any glare of light going into Gabe's room. She picked up a Walgreen's bag and sat down on the bed next to Peck. She lifted a jar of aloe vera, read the label, unscrewed its lid, and scooped some in her fingers.

"This might be cold," Sasha whispered to the now half sleeping Peck. She swabbed his white abdomen, that had no burn, with a flat palm of her hand. He sat straight up with a bolt.

"What...?"

"It's aloe, for your burn, honey. Relax."

Peck looked about, rested back, stuffed a pillow behind his head and neck, his eyes following her hand, and feeling it slide from one side of his waist, over his stomach to the other side and return. He made no mention that it wasn't his stomach that was burned. Sasha watched the motion of his skin rippling below her hand, of his muscles as her hand met his flesh. She scooped more aloe vera in her hand and started at his navel pushing the gel like a sensuous snowplow up the middle of his chest as far as his neck. Her hand would push the gel up and then by cupping her hand she would pull it back down the middle of his chest to his navel, gently heaving from pleasure and cold, and then slowly with her fingertips to just below the inside top of his jeans. She picked the jar up, filled a palm with gel and with the base of her palms lowered the jar to the floor.

"You going to run out," Peck said softly.

Sasha looked at his eyes dreamily, without distraction, stretching and reaching both hands, targeting his chest and nipples, flattening her hands on each, holding still enough to perhaps gather her thoughts.

"I have more," Sasha said, smiling coyly, her eyes rolling at the feel of his muscles, of pouted nipples on her palms and outstretched fingers. Her hand movement walked a thin line between the application of aloe vera on sunburn and an erotic massage. Peck was good with either distinction. His eyes studied her hands. It was as though he could feel the sensations she felt from her end.

"I'm getting a towel," Sasha said.

"Hokay."

"Unzip your fly."

"Hanh?" Peck asked, sitting up and resting back on his elbows as Sasha stood up.

"We need a towel for when you turn over, you goose," Sasha teased. "We don't want to get this messy stuff on their bed linen, do we?"

"But..." Peck started.

"Unzip and turn over," Sasha said.

Hearing "turn over" lessened his vulnerability of cheating on his new best friend, Gabe, so Peck obliged.

They had all met less than twenty-four hours ago, and he hadn't had time to learn that both Sasha and Lily Cup were, in their own right, fisherwomen of sorts, especially listening to jazz at Charlie's Blue Note in the alley just off Frenchman Street. They understood lures and the simple patience and math of when and where to cast their trotlines. They could speak it and even dressed the part, wearing their lures— designer fashions if the occasion called...and jazz dancing always called.

Peck sat up and let Sasha spread a bath towel on the bed cover. He unbuttoned his jeans, unzipped two inches down and rolled over onto his chest.

Sasha smiled, an unopened jar in her hand. She climbed on Peck and straddled him at his knees.

"Lift your butt," she said.

"Hanh?" Peck asked.

"Lift your ass a second," Sasha said.

He did, and she grabbed each side of his waistline and gave his jeans a yank, lowering his front zipper to its base.

"Oh," Peck said.

Sasha pulled the back of his jeans down to his crack and straddled the buttocks she had admired earlier that afternoon getting out of a tub. With the same care as his front, Sasha covered Peck's back and upper butt, emptying her jars of gel.

"Feel better?" Sasha asked.

"Yep," Peck muffled into a pillow.

Sasha crawled off, drying her hands with the towel.

"Want to see what I bought for tonight?" she asked.

"Hokay," Peck said. He reached under himself and zipped up his fly. He pulled a pillow to his crotch and rolled on his side to see what more Sasha might have in store.

"I got three outfits," Sasha said. "I can't decide which to wear."

"Hokay," Peck said.

"A lady at this shop said we should go to BB King's place for the best blues and dancing. You like ribs, Peck?"

"Oh *oui*," Peck said.

Standing over the shopping bags, Sasha lifted her sweatshirt over her head and off. She pulled her tights down a leg at a time, standing completely nude, looking at Peck as if she was looking through him in a thoughtful moment, thinking what to try on first. She stood as though there wasn't a soul in the room with her. As a young man who lived most of his life in a blade-sharpening shed, Peck was mesmerized by this whole experience. As a fisherman, he was curious.

"Where'd you get raised up?" Peck asked.

"Excuse me?"

"Where'd you growed up, cher?"

"What's wrong? Why are you asking that?"

"Where?"

"Where was I born or where did I grow up?"

"Growed."

"Down near Pecan Island."

"Ah *oui*."

"But I went to school in N'Orleans with Lily Cup since we were six."

"Hokay."

"Why'd you ask that?" Sasha asked.

"I knowed it be someplace like dat, you growed."

"Someplace like what?"

"An island, near the water, cher," Peck said.

"You did? How?"

"You sure get nekked a lot."

Sasha smirked, placed hands on her hips, twisting her torso.

"Are you complaining?"

"Nah, nah, oh no, ma'am."

"The salesgirl suggested we get there early to get a table on the dance floor," Sasha said. She slipped a black jumper over her head and pulled it down over her naked body.

"I always leave tags on, until I'm sure I like them, in case I want to return them," Sasha said.

The jumper had long sleeves, did not require a bra and her cleavage and upper chest were delightfully packaged and presented in a frame of fabric. The dress went down to midthigh. She turned about once, and then again, leaning back, looking over her shoulder and down. "What do you think, Peck? Do you like this one?"

"I like it a lot."

"I wish it didn't have sleeves—it's so warm out," Sasha said.

"I like it," Peck said.

"Good," Sasha said. "But it's too short for clamando, so I got some panties, just in case. Check these out, Peck."

Sasha lifted three pairs of panties, shuffled them and dropped two to the edge of the bed, stepped into a chosen black pair and pulled them over her thighs and hips, then her skirt down. She raised her eyebrows toward Peck, seeking approval.

"You look nice. Mighty nice."

"Good—you're dancing tonight, so you look nice too," Sasha said with a wry smile.

All Peck had was what he had on. He was sitting on the bed as if he were gathering his thoughts about what had just happened in front of him. Today was another world for him.

"I took a pic of you earlier and showed it to a man in a store and he guessed you had a thirty-two waist."

"Hanh?"

"Here're new jeans, a sexy belt I picked out and a T-shirt you can wear tonight. If the jeans don't fit we can take them back."

"You taked a picture of me?" Peck asked. "When?"

Sasha took off her dress and hung it in the closet. She pulled her panties down and set them on the bureau. She walked over to the bed, picked another new pair, red, stepped into them, pulled them up and stepped to the door between the rooms. Peck was distracted.

"I took it earlier," Sasha said, picking up her sweatshirt. "I'm going in to talk with Gabe. We'll let you know when we're going to walk to Beale Street so you can get ready."

Sasha may have thought it best for the safety of her phone camera that she not show Peck a picture of him toweling his head dry, swinging free in his altogether, or to tell him she had texted it to Lily Cup and got a text in return of a smiley emoticon with a tongue hanging out and a *"Where are you?"*

While Gabe slept, Sasha went through his army duffel and pulled out dress slacks and a shirt. She unfolded a hotel's ironing board and pressed both with the hotel iron and hung them in his closet. She then pulled the drapes, lifted her phone and took pictures of the setting sun.

"Time to get up, sleepyhead," she said.

She sat on his bed, leaned in, and ran her nails gently around his back and over his shoulders. Gabe rolled on his side, awake.

"Is there anything you can't eat, sweetie?"

"Pretty much everything is okay so long as I take my medicine."

"Ribs tonight?" Sasha asked.

"I love the ribs in this town, honey, but I might have to tone it down. I'll do shrimp and rice," Gabe said.

A concierge met the three at the lobby elevators and escorted them outside to a horse-drawn carriage Sasha had asked for. The night was warm and still, the sunset a blazing red and with the last few honks of afternoon traffic the carriage clip-clopped its way to historic Beale Street.

As the three walked arm-in-arm into BB King's the band was playing Beale Street Blues. Sasha wasted no time gesturing to a hostess about a table near the dance floor. A trombone was doing a riff with a tuba backing it up—banjo and drum as rhythm. Sasha motioned to Peck to follow the hostess and save a table, took Gabe's hand and led him to the dance floor, circling him around as if he was her prize for the evening. Well rested, he was up to the task, extending his hand, embracing her waist, and pulling her close to him. With feet not moving, but bodies swaying they'd begin and pause, begin and pause, rocking forms like football or basketball players, with head-motions and fakes back and forth. They'd hang on and jerk and sway to blues, with a dash of Dixie—and they'd pause and rock to and fro once, twice, three times, then still again, syncopated jerking and swaying some more back and forth to the piano, the trumpet, and the clarinet.

It was as though a curtain had opened and they were at center stage of a new play, rocking back and forth with sensuous thrusts and pulls. The night was about a trombone, clarinet, banjo, tuba, and drums—it wasn't about hailstorms, highway medicine bandits, and bad times. Gabe was feeling good and wanted to live in the moment, and he was moving well tonight. The band would end a jam, applause would fill the room and music would begin again, Gabe's thighs leading Sasha's hips as though they were both on top of a wind-up music box. Sasha's dress crawling up enough to warm the evening's curious, but still ladylike tight on her beautiful thighs, letting eyes concentrate on her motion but their souls on the rhythms of the band.

It was five sets before the band stopped for a break, and they ended with a deep dip. Sasha wrapped her arms over Gabe's shoulders and kissed him on his neck, first on the left then on the right. It was as though she were marking her territory for a crowd that had gathered to watch them dance. They joined Peck at the table.

"Whew," Sasha said.

"I'm telling you, honey," Gabe said, "there ain't nothing like the blues...it's sad and it's happy. All at once—that's the thing about it. It's being in a cotton field all day from sunup telling yourself, oo yi yi! I'm so sad now, oh, my day is so sad but there'll be music later. Lord, just get me through these rows of cotton, just get me through this one day—there'll be music tonight."

"Food," Sasha said. "Peck, have you looked at a menu?"

"Ribs and beer," Peck said, pointing at a picture of it.

"Shrimp and rice, maybe a Dewar's for me, darlin'," Gabe said.

"I nibbled some today while I was shopping," Sasha said. "I'll have a martini and just pick off your plates, if you boys don't mind."

Gabe flattened a folded handkerchief to his forehead, dabbing it, his cheeks and neck.

"Will you be okay driving back to New Orleans after you drop us at the airport tomorrow?" Gabe asked.

"You sure you want to talk about that now?" Sasha asked.

"We're waiting for food, let's talk," Gabe said.

"Can it wait?" Sasha asked.

"While we eat baby, before we dance again," Gabe said.

Sasha pointed at Peck. "And you're dancing," she said.

Sasha leaned back and checked out Peck's outfit.

"Doesn't Peck look nice in his new jeans and T-shirt, Gabe?"

"He's a new man," Gabe said. "My brother."

"You owe me a dance," Sasha said to Peck.

After picking on food, enjoying the moment and Memphis sounds, Gabe and Sasha went to the floor and embraced through five more songs, moving as one. She would end a dance with a kiss on Gabe's neck.

"You smell good," she'd whisper.

"Hotel bar soap," he'd say.

At the table, sipping her martini and picking at food, Sasha told Peck he'd better be ready, because the next slow dance was his.

"Gabe, something I need to tell you, so you don't get mad if I hadn't told you," Sasha said.

"Say what?" Gabe asked.

"I only learned today."

"What's wrong, baby?"

"You can't fly to Rhode Island tomorrow," Sasha said.

"What? Why not?"

"At least with Peck, you can't."

Gabe leaned in over the table to listen.

"I didn't want to talk about it here," Sasha said, "but I don't want you angry for me not telling you."

"Talk to me, baby. What's up?" Gabe asked.

"Peck doesn't have any ID," Sasha said.

"What's your point, darlin'?"

"No ID nowadays, and you can't buy an airline ticket. I asked a travel agent. The hotel buyer had a travel agent and gave me their number."

"Peck, is this true?" Gabe asked.

"Hanh?"

"Don't you have an ID, son?"

"Nah, nah," Peck said.

"No driver's license?"

"Nah, nah," Peck said.

"You don't drive?"

"Can't have no license in Lewisana lest you can read and write. Can't have no ID lest you have a birth certificate."

"You been walking all these years, son?"

"Walkin' or bus," Peck said.

"How about you both come back to New Orleans?" Sasha asked. "We'll have fun dancing at Charlie's. I'll look after you guys—I'll get Peck a job."

"Honey," Gabe said, "I know you mean well and you have a heart as big as the sun, but ole Gabe here is going from this place to the Newport Jazz Festival, where, God willing, I'll get to sip some Dewar's before I die."

He turned about in his chair facing the wall. The reality of the moment came over each of them. It wasn't an adventure they were on; it wasn't a joy ride; it was the final passage of a man who shared his dying wish with his new friend, a friend who came forth and wanted more than anything to help him make it come true. Sasha stood, leaned and kissed pouting Gabe on top of his head.

"We'll work it out, honey," she whispered. "No worries. I'll figure a way to get you both to Newport."

She extended her hand to Peck. He looked up when she snapped her thumb and finger and pointed her finger at him.

"C'mon, muffins," she said. "We're dancing."

She motioned to a waitress to bring Gabe a glass of port.

The band was playing a soft, slow, and painful "I believe to my soul."

Before they embraced, Sasha looked at Peck with different eyes. She was jarred by Gabe's wakeup, calling them back into the reality of the moment. She yanked Peck to her, pressing on his back with her hand so her breasts warmed his heart.

"Follow my lead," she said.

It was several minutes of dancing close before Peck got the hang of it, and Sasha worked up the nerve to try to make sense of the truth of the moment.

"He's dying, Peck."

"I know, cher."

"What do you want to do?" Sasha asked.

She leaned her head back to watch his telling eyes.

"I want to go with the old man," Peck said. "I promised."

Sasha smiled, leaned in and kissed his neck, a thank-you kiss.

"I promised the old man," Peck murmured. *"J'ai promis le vieil homme."*

Sasha squeezed Peck.

"You holding out, Peck?"

"Hanh?"

"You speak French?"

"Very little," Peck said "*Très peu*." My foster nanna teached me some, gator man teached me mostly cussin'."

They circled the floor.

"You're a good man," Sasha said. "Gabe is lucky to have you."

They turned in a sway, moving slowly to an electric guitar, wailing in tears.

"You have no driver's license, so you can't drive, or I'd rent ya'all a car," Sasha said.

"Gabe can drive, cher."

"It's too far for Gabe to drive it alone."

Peck leaned back enough to see Sasha's front pressed against his chest then he'd pulled her close again.

"You could take a train or a bus," Sasha said.

Peck lifted his head. "Can you come, cher? We all go in your car?"

"I have to work," Sasha said. "I have open houses all week."

"Oh," Peck said, pulling her into him.

Their hips locked in turns, his thigh nudging between her legs.

"Peck, honey?" Sasha asked.

"Uh huh?"

"Is that William?"

Peck didn't answer. He kept dancing.

"Why I do believe it is," Sasha said. "Oh my."

"I ain't doing that on purpose, cher."

"I'm not complaining, sweetie."

"Nah, nah."

"He certainly is proud, isn't he?"

"You can't tell Gabe."

"Our secret," Sasha said.

"Hokay, t'anks."

"Just tell me you'll help get Gabe up to Newport like you promised."

"I will, cher."

"You'll take care of him and protect him."

"I keep my promises."

Sasha paused and flexed her thighs against Peck's friend.

"I ain't trying to did dat, cher, I swear."

"William has a mind of his own."

"Won't tell?" Peck asked.

"Nothing to tell."

She kissed Peck's ear. "Does your sunburn feel better after my aloe rub?"

"Mighty good, dass for true," Peck said. "I ain't peeling."

"I should do it once more, to be safe," she whispered. "Later."

Peck gave her a look, not certain it was a threat or a medical opportunity.

The music ended. Sasha stopped motion and held Peck.

"Thanks for the dance," she said. She lowered a hand and gave his buttocks a squeeze.

"Walk close behind me, honey, no one will notice your friend."

They sat with Gabe, toasted the evening, finished the food and talked of jazz trumpeters, blues guitarists, and which ones influenced Elvis most.

"Elvis was influenced by the poor black street musicians around Beale Street during Jim Crow and the gospel singers in churches around Memphis," Gabe mused. "Roy Orbison inspired his vocal range."

"Gabe, you know more about music than anyone I know, and I grew up in New Orleans," Sasha said.

"Study people, you'll know their music," Gabe said.

"You're a Chicago boy and you've had a busy career, Captain Jordan. When did you have time to study people?"

"My army training was mostly in the south, darlin'. Rode in the back of a lot of buses down here—a person gets to study people sitting in the back of the bus."

Gabe enjoyed a gentle balance of a glass of Port and a bowl of shrimp and rice, and he was still good as late as midnight on the dance floor. At their table between dances he would demonstrate how big band leaders, Count Basie and Glenn Miller, would use a strumming guitar beat for rhythm.

Peck got the last dance while Gabe stepped out for fresh Memphis night air, and to watch the festival called Beale Street, and wait for their horse-and-carriage ride back to Peabody just after midnight.

They agreed the spirits had the better of them, and they would crash tonight and plan over coffee and breakfast in the morning. Sasha brought a glass of water to the bedside and handed it and his pill to Gabe, who was stretched out and looking up at her with a smile.

"Why do I have this feeling?"

"What feeling?" Sasha asked.

"The feeling you're not quite ready to sleep?" Gabe mused.

"You can tell that looking at me?"

"You have a look in your eye."

"How many martinis did I have, Gabe?"

"I didn't count, honey, but too many to lie down without first getting your bearings," Gabe offered.

"I'm not tired," she said.

"Maybe Peck'll volunteer to stay up and give some points of view on the merits of vodka and vermouth."

"Ya think?"

"Well, you did teach the boy how to dance," Gabe said. "It's the least he could do."

Gabe smiled and rested his head on a pillow.

Sasha tucked him in and told him she was thinking of maybe whiling away a bit of time attending to Peck's sunburn again.

Gabe chuckled. "I want to feel your arms around me one last time."

"I'll be back."

"Honey, that would make my day. You both do your whiling and attending, just let this old man wake up with you in the morning."

Sasha knelt on the floor, staring into Gabe's tired eyes. She didn't want to spoil his evening by tearing up. She pulled the blanket under his chin, leaned in and kissed him.

"Sleep well, you beautiful old man," she said. "*Bien dormir, tu beau vieil homme.*"
She rose up.

"I'll be back, darlin'," she said. "I promise."

Gabe reached for her hand and gave it a squeeze.

"Just don't give our boy a heart attack. He and I've got a road ahead."

CHAPTER 10

BOTH DRAPES WERE DRAWN in Gabe's room, blocking a Mississippi River sunrise, muffling the still of a Memphis morning on this late-night blues capital's streets. Sasha's feminine curves nestled under the blanket, motionless. Gabe, in his reading glasses, in a lounge chair with desk lamp pulled close, quietly turned pages of a newspaper. He had already made his first trek to the lobby for a walk around and to retrieve a pot of coffee with cinnamon, a cream pitcher and three cups and saucers. The captain's first cup gave him time to scour the music and arts pages, combing for the big-name talents he had known throughout his heyday. He especially liked finding pictures of them and remembering the times they conjured up. It was his second cup when he turned and folded the paper to the local news pages.

"Uh-oh," he murmured to himself. He lifted and rested his reading glasses on his forehead as he folded the page down again into a more manageable size. He held it closer to his face, letting his glasses drop from his forehead to over his eyes.

"I'll be," he said quietly.

He read on.

"Why that sonofabitch," Gabe said.

Sasha awakened, lifted her head, pulled a sheet and comforter from her face, eyes squinting in the reflection of the lamp's light.

"What?" Sasha asked.

"Good morning, darlin'," Gabe said.

"What's going on?" she asked.

"Would you like a cup of coffee and cinnamon?"

"You said, 'That SOB,' Gabe. Who are you talking about?"

Gabe poured a cup, added a bit of cream and walked it over to her. She sat up and lodged pillows behind her, taking the saucer from Gabe. He sat back down and picked up the folded newspaper.

"What time is it?" Sasha asked.

"Have a listen," he said. "It's got a whole column."

"'Two men were attacked and robbed of their pickup in Hazelton, Mississippi late Thursday evening. Brock Singleton and Winton Makaylah had parked under the Hazelton overpass during a hailstorm that blanketed one-inch hailstones over an eight-mile area that evening. The two had stepped from their vehicle, leaving it unattended, to ask a trailer-truck driver about road conditions ahead when they reportedly saw the suspect rummaging through the cab of their pickup. A scuffle ensued. The suspect allegedly pulled a knife and stabbed Singleton twice, once in the chest and once in the face. While they were distracted with the wounds and trying to stop the bleeding the thief drove off in their pickup, leaving his own motorcycle behind.

The motorcycle's tag had been removed, making it more difficult to trace. Mississippi State Police are asking witnesses to come forward. Singleton has since been moved to an emergency eye clinic in a hospital in Knoxville, where his parents live. Tennessee authorities are cooperating with the Mississippi State Police, permitting access to Singleton for informal questioning in hopes of uncovering clues. The family is offering a reward for information leading to the conviction of this highway bandit fugitive, who is considered armed and dangerous.'"

"Those were the state trooper cars that passed us," Sasha said.

"Rightly so," Gabe said. "The SOB knocked me on my head and then stabbed this fellow twice."

"Gabe, do you think they're the same two who saved Peck from being hurt?"

"There's something funny about this report," Gabe said.

"Like what?"

"They're leaving a lot of the story out."

"What are they leaving out? It sounds right to me."

"Must be a reason," Gabe said.

"You've lost me, Gabe. Like what am I missing?"

"Like what about the knife hole in his motorcycle's tire? It wasn't mentioned," Gabe said. "Like what about the scuffle with the bandit after Peck whomped him with his elbows. That wasn't mentioned."

"That's right," Sasha said. "Didn't Peck say they told him they would take care of the guy and for him to go on."

"That all would have come out in questioning," Gabe said.

"So, what are you thinking?"

"Six years in army internal affairs. I'm trained to know when facts are left out."

"On purpose?"

"There's a reason."

"Like what – give me a clue?"

"They're fishing for something."

"Hope it's not my Bentley."

"I wouldn't think so," Gabe said.

"Wait. Are they looking for Peck?"

"Probably some unfinished drug or motorcycle gang thing."

"What about what the newspaper says has you thinking?"

"Two men who tell Peck they'd take care of the bum wouldn't be calling 911 in the first place," Gabe said. "And a man who wasn't on the run already—"

"You mean the motorcycle guy?"

"Exactly, if he wasn't on the run, he would stay and fix his tire and not have to steal a truck and take off. I don't care how much he got beat up, he'd lick his wounds, but stay and fix his tire."

"So, you think he was on the run all along?"

"I think so, and I think the law knows it and is fishing for clues," Gabe said.

"What time is it?"

"Eight oh two."

"I have to get up," Sasha said.

"Finish your coffee," Gabe said.

"Our plane is at one. I'll jump in a shower and you order breakfast up."

"Hold on there."

"What?"

"Just a moment, pretty one. Aren't you going to share?"

"Share what?"

"Just when did you crawl in with me last night?"

"Not long after you were fast asleep."

"I'll be," Gabe said. "Last I remember you were on a prowl."

"I was not."

"You were howling at the moon, darlin'."

"You can't ever let me have more than two, well, three martinis," Sasha said.

"You weren't eating anything. Vodka has a way of not wanting to say good night on an empty stomach."

"Oh my God, what a head," Sasha said, standing up.

"What plane? I thought you said Peck can't fly."

"He can't," Sasha said.

"So, what's with the plane?"

"You and I are flying to Providence at one."

"Would you mind filling me in?"

"I'll find you a place to stay. I have a return flight with a nine o'clock landing. Tomorrow I'll put Peck on a Greyhound, with instructions on how and where to find you, and I'll get back to work. He'll be with you in two days, tops. I've got it all worked out."

"What's Providence have to do with it?"

"That's where we're flying to, Providence."

"But I'm heading to Newport," Gabe said.

"Newport is full up, hotel-room wise," Sasha said.

"I never thought of that," Gabe said.

"I'm getting you into a nice place in Providence. You'll have to cab it down to Newport. The long-term stay may even have a shuttle to the festival. It all starts tomorrow. You were in no mood to talk about any of this last night."

"We did do some fine rhythm and blues moves, didn't we?" Gabe asked.

"Best ever for me. You're one incredible dancer."

"So how did our boy take it—your walking in on him last night?"

"Peck?"

"Did he think he'd died and gone to heaven?"

"He enjoyed my stripping down to my panties to put my sweatshirt on, he loved my rubbing aloe on his back, but I think his watching me hold my head over a toilet bowl for an hour, puking—I don't believe it was his idea of a conquest. I splashed my face, brushed my teeth, gargled, came over and crawled in with you," Sasha said.

"So close, yet so far," Gabe mused. "Poor kid."

"I wouldn't have done him."

"You have your surgeon waiting on you back home."

"Least I don't think I would," Sasha said. "I don't know—never say never."

"It's funny how the older we get the more we stop to think about consequences," Gabe said.

"I suppose we have too many miles on us together in these—can you believe—thirty-six hours?" Sasha asked.

"It's been a wonderful journey. This one surely has," Gabe said. "I feel like I've known you both for years."

"Call room service," Sasha said. "I'm going to my room and shower. I'll send Peck over here where he belongs for appearances sake. I'll be fast. Pull the door closed between our rooms."

Gabe picked up the receiver and pointed it at Sasha. "Anything special?"

"Very large V8, Tabasco, but don't add it—send up a bottle, I'll add it—two light scrambled with chopped onion, and side of burned-to-a-crisp bacon," Sasha said. "Toasted English muffin, dry."

Gabe was on the phone with room service when Peck walked into the room, pulling its door to Sasha's room closed behind him.

"Three scrambled, sausage, biscuits, and grits?" Gabe asked.

Peck smiled his approval.

Gabe watched Peck fold his new jeans and T-shirts, setting them on the bureau. He placed the food order, gave his room number and set the phone down. Noticing the newspaper containing the article he had just read to Sasha, he picked it up.

"Peck, there's something I want to show you."

"Yep," Peck said.

"No," Gabe said. "On second thought, I better wait for Sasha. We'll talk over breakfast."

"You hokay, Gabe?"

"I'm fine, my brother. It can wait," Gabe said.

Peck poured a cup of coffee and sat on the bed.

"You were doing some mighty nice turns on that dance floor, young man. I'm here to tell you."

"For true?" Peck asked.

"Why, you were keeping up with the best of them, you truly were. You picked it up fast, son. Isn't it heaven holding on to that woman while they play the blues?"

Peck didn't answer. He nodded and seemed to stare at his memory.

"How's your sunburn doing, son?" Gabe asked with a grin.

Peck's eyes looked at Gabe's and darted away.

"No peeling. Dat stuff works," he said.

Gabe was a gentleman, a respected retired army officer, and a loyal friend. He wouldn't belabor the tease. A knock on the door signaled breakfast had arrived. Gabe opened it and held it for the bellman to roll in and set up the fold-out table.

"I'm setting this for three?" the bellman asked.

"Yes, that's right," Gabe said. "We have a guest coming."

"How far have you traveled to be here?" the bellman asked.

"New Orleans," Gabe said. We came early yesterday."

"Two cities of great music," the bellman said. "Where do you go from here?"

"Heading to Newport for the jazz festival. It's in Rhode Island," Gabe said.

The bellman finished, handed a check folder to Gabe and a pen. Gabe signed it and put a twenty-dollar tip on it.

"Thank you, good sir," the bellman said. "Safe journeys. I hope you've enjoyed your stay at the Peabody. Call us if we can be of service." He nodded his head, first to Peck and then to Gabe, and left.

"Gabe, I thought we ain't supposed to tell nothing," Peck said. "Like weren't we from Chicago or something?"

Gabe put his hand to his mouth thinking, looking over at Peck.

"Fuck it," he grunted. "I'm an old man, I can't be expected to remember everything. We'll be fine."

"I ain't trying to…" Peck started.

"Peck, if they put you on a stage under a spotlight and a hundred people were standing three feet away to guess where you were from, believe me, my brother, it wouldn't be Chicago."

Sasha rapped on the door and Gabe pulled it open.

She was dressed like a million bucks in a conservative gray pantsuit, creased pant legs with a white, heavily starched blouse, and crossed ribbon tie. She wore low black heels, and her hair was tied back in a businesslike bun.

"Well, I'll be…" Gabe started.

"Morning gentlemen," she said. "Whatcha' looking at?"

"Why…" Gabe started.

"Us Quarter girls clean up good, now, don't we, hon?"

"I'll say," Gabe said.

"It's an outfit I got yesterday, knowing we had to travel today. I wanted to look nice," Sasha said.

"You outdid yourself on looking nice, darlin'," Gabe said.

"I have some things for you," Sasha said. She reached in a shopping bag and handed him a pair of aviator sunglasses.

"Put these on."

She pulled out a Bermuda islander straw hat and handed it to Gabe. Following that she pulled out a classic golf shirt with the famous Peabody duck embroidered on the front.

"Now you're ready for a jazz festival, honey," Sasha said.

Gabe celebrated his dashing new image in front of a mirror. He set the hat, sunglasses, and shirt on his bed, pulled up a chair for Sasha to sit and gestured to another for Peck.

As they ate, businesswoman Michelle Lissette picked up her alter ego Sasha's cellphone and brought herself up to date, checking her appointment schedules and flight tickets. A moment or two later, she was reading an incoming text. She looked up at Peck.

"Peck, where were you born?"

"I don't know," Peck said.

"We have to find a birth certificate for you."

"Hanh?"

"We need one so we can get you an ID."

"Before we got to Kenner in that rig you were talking with the driver about a foster nanny, my brother. Do you remember a name or town?" Gabe asked.

"Prudhomme," Peck said. "Alayna Prudhomme, 'tween Bayou Sorrel and Choctaw."

"Lily Cup is going to help," Sasha said.

"Hanh?" Peck asked.

"You remember Lily Cup, don't you, Peck?"

Peck grinned.

"She's an attorney."

Sasha winked at him and texted the information to Lily Cup.

"Boudreaux Clemont Finch, right?" Sasha asked.

"*Oui*," Peck said.

"And she's already met William."

Peck put his head down sheepishly with a grin.

"I'll pay any cost," Gabe said.

"It's handled," Sasha said. "Helping a friend. *Aider un ami.*"

"Cho! Co!" Peck said.

He leaned and thank-you kissed Sasha on a cheek.

Sasha held his head to hers and took a selfie, texting it to Lily Cup. She waited for a response, set her phone down and picked up her fork.

"Peck, you're going to have another boring day at the hotel," Sasha said. "I'm taking Gabe to Rhode Island, but I'll be back tonight, and tomorrow I'm putting you on a bus."

"Why can't I go today?"

"Because you won't know how to find him until I find a place for him to stay and come back and tell you," Sasha said. "Tomorrow we put you on a bus and you'll be there overnight, in two days, tops."

Peck looked at Gabe.

"You be good with dat, Grandpa?"

"I'm good with it, my brother," Gabe said, smiling at Peck. He raised his fist, and Peck raised his, and they fist bumped.

"Peck, give Gabe his wallet. He'll need his license and charge cards. I'll see you have pocket money today and tomorrow on your trip."

"You're a sainted woman," Gabe said. "God will bless you for this."

"He already has," Sasha said. "He put me here to get you two to Newport. Peck, there's something you need to know."

"What I need to know, cher?"

"The man you fought with in Mississippi stabbed another man and stole his pickup truck."

"Dass for true, cher?"

"He's on the loose."

"I only whomped him."

"Point is we know he was heading north," Sasha said.

"Hokay?"

"So he could be coming through here. And they may be looking for witnesses," Gabe said.

"Did he kill a man?" Peck asked.

"Stabbed him in the chest and face," Gabe said. "The man's in the hospital."

"Witness like me?" Peck asked.

"We just have to be careful," Sasha said.

"Not so much the law," Gabe said. "The biker. If he sees you he may remember you can be a witness. He's already stabbed one man."

"So I stay?" Peck asked.

"Until I get back tonight," Sasha said. "Maybe we'll dance before you get on a bus tomorrow."

"Now, remember you two," grunted Gabe with a sly grin.

"What?" Peck asked sheepishly.

"No more than three martinis," Gabe said.

"Ain't dat a true?" Peck asked.

"No worries there," Sasha said.

"How so?" Gabe asked.

"I have to get back to work tomorrow. I'm dropping Peck on an early bus, and I have a six-hour drive to Vieux Carre."

"Be careful, darling," Gabe said. "You're precious cargo."

"What if the stabber sees her Bentley?" Peck asked.

"He's pointed north. Sasha is heading south," Gabe said.

After breakfast Peck moved his clothes into Sasha's room. Sasha tried unsuccessfully to buy Gabe a proper suitcase. He preferred his army duffel with *Cpt. Jordan* stenciled on it. Sasha checked out of the room Gabe was in and extended her room for one more night. Peck settled in for a day of watching television and eating in the hotel.

CHAPTER 11

FASTEN YOUR SEATBELT, HANDSOME," Sasha said.

"It's going to be a bumpy night," Gabe chuckled.

"Buckle your seatbelt," Sasha said.

"I took my butterfly to that movie."

"What movie?"

"All About Eve, 1950. Maybe it was '51. I was at Fort Benning. You're too young for that one."

"I like classics," Sasha said. "I'm here with you, aren't I? Buckle up."

"I got it," Gabe said.

"Want me to put your hat in an overhead?"

"Oh no, ma'am," Gabe said. "I'm enjoying my new sporty look. It's been a while. And first class too—can you just imagine?"

"Gabe, were you ever married?"

"I've been a widower for thirty-six years come September. Woman was the love of my life."

"Was she that butterfly you took to the movie?"

"She was."

"That's so sweet," Sasha said.

"We had a son, Harold. Strapping image of me. He made us proud."

"Had? Is he gone?"

Gabe squeezed her hand. "He's still in my heart. Lost him in Iraq. He was career army, like me. Would have made captain too."

Gabe turned his head, staring out the window. Sasha motioned to a flight attendant for two coffees.

"His platoon was at chow in a big tent, nowhere near any action."

Sasha held his hand.

"They say a mortar hit an ammo truck parked outside. Took them all out."

"I'm so sorry," Sasha said.

"They think it was friendly fire."

An attendant interrupted, handing each a coffee.

"Was your wife a dancer?"

"My, but how she could move," Gabe said.

He rested his head back and stared up at the ceiling of the plane.

"There wasn't a dance we wouldn't try, and believe me, we tried them all. That woman taught this Chicago know-it-all some moves."

"If she was a dancer, I know she had your heart."

"That woman was my everything, from the first day I saw her eyes. She was putting a nickel in the Coca Cola machine."

"A nickel?"

"That's what a Coke cost in those days. We met while I was on a transfer leave back to the states from Korea. First thing we did when we looked in each other's eyes was put a quarter in a jukebox at the non comm Officers Club and dance."

"Non comm? You were a Captain, weren't you?"

"Not then I wasn't. My, but how my butterfly could dance."

He turned his head and looked at Sasha.

"Without saying a word to each other, we danced."

"You can say her name, Gabe."

"Fort Dix, it was."

"You said Fort Benning."

"I did?"

"It doesn't matter, Gabe. Try to rest."

"I'm losing it. The more time that passes, the more I lose," Gabe whispered to himself.

"She'll always be with you if you say her name, Gabe."

"It was Fort Dix. We danced and caught a train into Harlem."

Gabe's eyes glazed in thought.

"I mean it," Sasha said. "It's good luck to mention a loved one's name, Gabe. She'll always be with you, and she'll be with you when...well, you know."

"Beverly," Gabe said.

"Beverly, a sweet name."

"I called her Butterfly."

He turned his head and looked out the window.

"Beverly sounds perfect for you," Sasha said, handing Gabe a napkin.

Gabe looked back at Sasha.

"How about you, Michelle Lissette? Any past you want to share?"

"I've never been married. Been engaged twice, but something in me won't let a man rule my roost. I like making my own money and feeling independent. I always seem to run them off somehow."

"You and Lily Cup go to Charlie's a lot, do ya?"

"I wouldn't say a lot. Maybe when the moon is full, or we just get in a mood to be held. We'll doll up as sexy as we can and check them out as they walk in the door. Sometimes we get lucky."

"Does your surgeon man condone this extracurricular—sometimes lucky?"

"Well, there's partying, and there's cheating. By lucky I meant that we find a good jazz dancer. I don't cheat."

"The red gown you wore when we met was striking. It left little to the imagination but certainly stirred my libido."

"Wearing Chanel and Givenchy is half the fun. A sensual dance in them to the best jazz on Frenchman Street is the other half. Our fun may get risqué on a dance floor, but mostly we go home alone. Charlie walks us home."

"So, you two had an eye on us when we walked in?" Gabe asked.

"Oh yes," Sasha said. "Sized you up the second you came in."

"And me an old man, pray tell how?"

"As soon as you stepped in, I knew it just watching you through the mirror behind the bar."

"How'd you know I was a dancer?" Gabe asked.

"When you sat by the band. That's how. I saw you point at a table and tell Peck to go save it while you went to the bathroom."

"How about Peck? Any first impressions of him?"

"Lily Cup poked me with an elbow when Peck walked in with you. She was speculating if Peck was, well, as, shall we say, 'packaged' as he was sunburned and good looking, like boys his age."

An attendant retrieved their coffee cups, and the plane landed in Charlotte, giving them time to walk the terminal to a gate for the connecting flight to Providence. This time Gabe let Sasha put his hat in an overhead and leaned back in his seat and snoozed. Sasha read magazines. In Providence, Sasha found the Courtyard Hotel and computed their long stay rate per week. Gabe left his card number to guarantee it and put his duffel in his room before taking an elevator down to the lobby, where Sasha was gathering information leaflets about the city and the festival.

"You hungry?" she asked.

"I am."

"Let's get something to eat," Sasha said. "We can talk while we eat."

Sasha held Gabe's arm as he led her from the hotel two blocks to the Woonasquatucket River. The river was narrow and had iron baskets resting on concrete pilings lined maybe thirty yards apart down the center of the river.

"Have you ever been here?" Gabe asked.

"I haven't."

"At night, they'll stack those iron baskets with firewood and light them. They call them *WaterFire*. It's quite a sight," Gabe said.

"I bet it's beautiful," Sasha said. "Romantic."

"Let's go to Canal Walk." He pointed. "It's just over there. We'll get a hot dog or something from one of the vendors."

They walked to the Canal Walk crossing.

"Which way are we headed?" Sasha asked.

"Let's see," Gabe said. "If that's Point Street Bridge—it should be over there. Yes, there it is, this way. It's not far."

The two walked, taking in the sights of a city's downtown. They bought food from two carts and carried it to the Point Street River overpass before sitting down on a bench.

"He's still here, I can tell," Gabe said.

"Who's still here?"

"See across the river, up there under the bridge?"

"Yes, but I don't see anyone."

"You can tell where he stands and leans on the wall to play," Gabe said. "The wall's worn smooth where he leans back on it."

"Who?" Sasha asked.

She squeezed a mustard packet onto her hotdog.

"He wails the prettiest alto sax—prettiest I've heard north of Memphis," Gabe said.

"Point Street Bridge," Sasha said. "Learn something new every day."

"Great sax," Gabe said.

"How can one man make a smooth mark on the wall?"

"His leather jacket," Gabe said. "He leans back in his leather jacket, I don't know. Over the years— he's still here, I can tell."

"I believe you."

"It'll be after dark."

"Be careful walking alone after dark," Sasha said.

"I promise, darlin'," Gabe said.

"Maybe leave your valuables in your room and put on the *Do Not Disturb*," Sasha said. "Always keep your driver's license with you. Maybe a color copy of it and leave the original in your room."

"Seems as the time floats by, the more vulnerable an ole man gets," Gabe said.

Sasha finished her food and scanned her phone while Gabe ate some fries.

"Okay, Gabe, according to this, preliminary entertainment and some sideshows for the Jazz Festival start tomorrow. I'll get you a pass that'll cover everything."

Gabe fumbled in his pocket and pulled out a charge card. "Use this." He handed it to Sasha.

"Weather's good," Gabe said. "Lucky—let's hope it holds the week."

Sasha concluded a ticket purchase transaction in her phone.

"Okay, you're set. We have festival passes for you and Peck," Sasha said. "We'll print them out at the hotel. Newport is thirty miles away."

"There'll be buses, I'm sure," Gabe said.

"Gabe, instead of the hassle of trying to find shuttles, take Uber. We'll open an account on one of your cards. You call a special number and order a car and tell them where you're going. They pick you up and it's all paid when you arrive. You don't have to sign. It'll have fare and tip already included, and you don't have to carry cards or a lot of cash."

"You've thought of everything, baby," Gabe said. "I can't thank you enough."

Sasha looked deeply into Gabe's eyes.

"That's just it," she said. "I'm trying *not* to think of everything."

"Live every day until we die," Gabe said. "It's the best we can hope for, darlin'."

As they walked to the hotel listening to city sounds, Sasha held back tears and fumbled through her purse. She lifted out a fifty, folded it and pressed it into Gabe's palm.

"Give this to your friend," Sasha said.

"My friend?"

"Your alto sax friend under the bridge," Sasha said. "Have him play 'When Sunny Gets Blue' for me."

Gabe clutched her hand and the fifty, wrapped an arm around her shoulders. They stopped in front of his hotel. She kissed his neck, first on one side, then the other. She flagged a waiting cab. She held Gabe, head resting on his chest, neither saying a word. She took his hand and goodbye kissed it twice.

"I've got to go," she said. "I'll call your room tomorrow and tell you when Peck's coming in on the bus. If you don't answer the phone, I'll leave a message or keep calling until you do. Maybe you could meet him at the bus station. Don't forget to call Uber."

Sasha handed Gabe business cards with her contact information.

"Best I meet him," Gabe said. "The city could overwhelm the boy."

"I'll get him a couple of shirts at the airport or in Memphis when I land," Sasha said. "See he looks nice when you take him to the festival. Don't let him wear a T-shirt."

Gabe smiled. "You're such a momma hen."

"Have you got enough medicine?"

Gabe looked at her eyes. He kissed her hand and let it go.

"Until we meet again, my love," Sasha said. "*Jusqu'au revoir, mon amour.*"

"I'll wait while the music plays," Gabe said.

Sasha landed in Memphis at 8:45. A ride to the Peabody gave her time to answer emails, buy Peck's bus ticket to Providence, and text Lily Cup she would be on her way to New Orleans early in the morning as Peck's bus departed at 4:30 a.m. She thanked the driver, stepped out and tipped a bellman for pulling a hotel door for her, welcoming her back.

"What did you do all day?" Sasha asked.

"I walked and learned some of Memphis purdy good," Peck said.

"I thought you were going to stay in and not risk being seen by that motorcycle creep."

"Nah, nah."

"You promised."

"Sides, I had to get me a bag to hold stuff."

Peck held up a new canvas sport duffel.

"That's a nice bag for your things."

Peck picked up a large spool of black fishing line.

"Got me this too," Peck said.

"What on earth for?"

"*Deux-cent*, how you say?"

"Two-hundred."

"*Oui*, two-hundred-pound line, dass what for."

"Why did you buy that?"

"Man gave it to me free for buying a duffel bag."

Having slept on her flight Sasha was alert, but muscle weary from sitting. She handed Peck a shopping bag with two new shirts, set her purse on a bed table and stretched her arms, suppressing a yawn.

"Put these in your bag, Peck."

"Is Gabe hokay?" Peck asked.

"He's fine. He's in a nice hotel, he knows how to get to the festival, and he has a ticket for you."

"A ticket?"

"A pass to the jazz festival and the side shows. You need one to get in."

"I miss ole captain already," Peck said.

"Your bus is at 4:30 in the morning."

"Ah...hokay."

"You feel like dancing tonight?"

Peck looked at her eyes, remembering last night.

"Ribs," he said, rolling his eyes from her into the bag with shirts.

Sasha removed her jacket, her blouse, her shoes and slacks, and laid them on the bed. She unsnapped her flesh-colored bra and tossed it on the pile. She walked toward the bathroom. Peck looked up from the bag she had handed him. She caught his eye and turned.

"I'm jumping in the shower."

"I'll sit here, cher."

"We'll go in half an hour or so. Look nice," she said.

Peck held up one of his new shirts.

"Perfect, sweetie. Be a dear and hang up my suit and blouse?"

Peck picked up garments as the bathroom door closed behind her.

In time, Sasha came out in the black jumper she had worn the night before. She stepped into her shoes next to the bed.

"Toss me the panties on the bureau, baby," she said. "The red ones."

Peck obliged and watched her bend to step into the panties and pull them up to her waist.

BB King's was crowded with a blend of locals and tourists. Blues wailed slow from an inviting electric guitar solo. Sasha handed the maître'd a twenty to find seats. Two opened, if they didn't mind sharing a table on the dance floor. Sasha took Peck by the hand and led him to their table, pulling out a chair for him. The couple sharing were young, early twenty-something newlyweds, enjoying ribs. Holding a neck of a beer bottle in one hand and a rib in another, the groom was in cargo shorts and a golf shirt and a hand-molded straw hat he bought from a street vendor on his way in; she was holding his arm with her arm wrapped through his and holding a rib in her hands like an ear of corn. She was wearing jean cutoffs and a T-shirt.

Sasha said "hey" to both and then leaned toward Peck.

"I'm not drinking tonight. I have a long drive tomorrow."

"Me too, then," Peck said.

"How about a Virgin Mary?"

"What's dat?"

"V8 with Tabasco and a stalk of celery," Sasha said. "It's hot."

"Hokay," Peck said.

Sasha ordered the drinks and a rack of ribs to share. As the waitress walked away, she leaned, gave Peck a kiss on the ear.

"Let's dance."

She held Peck tight, her arms over his shoulders, face resting on his neck; his arms around her waist, hands spread and holding her close. Peck could feel her tears on his neck and back as they moved slowly from one blues guitar solo to the next. Her breasts heaved, her stomach contracted as she sobbed quietly to herself, thinking no doubt of Gabriel, a friend she was about to lose forever. They danced four sets and returned to their table. The groom's stare at Sasha from across the table was met with a deadly stare from his bride and a knuckle into his ribs. He picked up his long neck, put it to his lips and gave Sasha a come-on smile.

Peck picked a rib and gnawed. Sasha looked away, lifted her drink with her left hand and sipped. With her right hand, she took a cloth napkin and reached under the table to rest it on Peck's lap. She slid her palm over Peck's thigh, unintentionally nudging a waking William. Peck's neck bolted. Sasha smiled and leaned into his ear.

"Thanks for being Gabe's friend," she said.

"Ol' Gabe is my frien' now, cher," Peck said. "Proud to even knowed the man."

Sasha gave his thigh a quick nail scratch and pulled her hand away. She picked up a rib and waited for another set to start.

"Honey, if you can't read, how do you remember things you have to remember?"

"I just remember is all."

"So, if I told you Gabe was at a Courtyard hotel downtown, you could remember?"

"Can you write it for me?" Peck asked.

"I thought you couldn't read."

"I can't, but if you write it I show it to folks and find it dat-a-way."

Sasha leaned in, keeping her eyes on the groom still copping looks at her chest. She kissed Peck on the ear as though she was appreciative of his simple, innate thought process.

"Let's dance," she said.

They moved to sad wails of the guitar. Peck held her close. Her sobbing stopped but her grip around his neck and head gave him a feeling she sensed a desperation of emptiness that comes over caring people at times.

"I have a phone for you in the hotel."

"Hanh?"

"It's prepaid. I put three hundred dollars on it. You'll have to get somebody to show you how it works."

"Yes'm, but why, cher?" Peck asked.

"I want you to be able to call me if anything happens."

"Ah, *oui.*"

"Understand?"

"Yes'm," Peck said.

"You be sure to call me right away, if anything at all happens," Sasha said.

Her face buried on Peck's neck and the contractions of her stomach against his body signaled quiet sobs. It was after midnight when Sasha's awareness of Peck's William on her inner thigh distracted her as the electric guitar begged a high libretto, as if it were a tear falling into a wailing climax.

The set ended with them motionless in embrace. Thinking only of herself, this emotionally drained Sasha placed her hands around Peck's waist, lowered them to his butt cheeks, firmly pulling him to her flexed thighs. Her eyes opened as she woke from loneliness. She clung blindly to Peck's arm as he led them back to the table. The groom had gone to the men's room, and the bride was stirring her daiquiri with a straw. Sasha flagged a waitress for a check and leaned in over the table.

"Honey," she said, "all guys are lookers."

"He's always doing it," the bride said.

"When were you married?"

"Yesterday. We got married in Little Rock."

"He's a lucky man," Sasha said.

"It's so embarrassing. I know he loves me."

"How long have you known him?" Sasha asked.

"Since fourth grade," the bride said.

"Do you love him?"

"More than anything, I love that man."

"Then don't let it bother you, honey—"

"I know he loves me."

"Next time you catch him looking, just point at a dude in the room and whisper in hubby's ear you wonder how big the guy's dick is."

The bride snickered.

"Point at a real looker… and ask your guy how to tell a dick size."

The bride's eyes squinting as she lifted her hand and held delicate fingers over her mouth.

"He'd kill me."

"He won't kill you, honey. Tell him now he knows how it feels when he gawks. He'll learn to behave."

She paid the check, winked at the bride, now with a grin on her face, took Peck by the hand outside and flagged a carriage to Peabody.

Under the lamp glow Sasha set the alarm on her phone for 3:30 a.m. and set it on the bedside table. She stripped from her jump suit, pulled her panties down, leaving them on the floor next to the bed, and crawled under a comforter and top sheet as Peck came out of the bathroom in briefs and edged around the bed.

"What time did I got to be on my bus?"

"I'll get you there by four," Sasha said.

"T'anks, cher."

"I'll come back here and sleep before I check out and drive to New Orleans."

"Hokay, good."

On the other side of her bed he started to pull a blanket.

"Where do you think you're going?"

"Oh?" Peck asked. "Maybe on the floor then, maybe?"

Sasha smiled, reached and pulled the sheet up, inviting him in.

"If I'm naked, you have to be naked," Sasha said. "*Si je suis nu, tu dois être aussi.*"

Peck snorted a nervous guffaw and started to crawl in.

"*Mais non, mais non,*" Sasha said. Still with a raised sheet in her hand, she pointed at his underwear.

Peck crawled in, kneed the sheet up and bounced as he pulled his underwear down and threw it over to the bureau.

Sasha turned the light off. The room became still and quiet for the longest time. There was no motion on the bed, as neither had turned about, or so much as pulled on the sheets or comforter for positioning.

"Peck?"

"*Oui?*"

"You're a good dancer."

"*Merci*, cher."

"You'd look dashing in white tie and tails—in a tuxedo."

Peck didn't respond.

"There's a Mid-Winter Cotillion in N'Orleans."

There was no response.

"Peck, would you be Lily Cup's date to the Mid-Winter Cotillion?"

"Hanh?"

"It's a grand ball in N'Orleans. I'm a chaperone. I'll be in Givenchy. Lily Cup is in my court and she'll be dripping in diamonds and with you on her arm in a tuxedo and white tie, you'll dazzle them."

"Maybe, cher."

There was a long silence. Moments of a quiet uncertainty filled the darkness—like times when you feel like you're the only one awake.

"Peck?"

"*Oui?*"

"You have a girlfriend?"

Peck's head turning toward Sasha made sounds of rustled starched pillow linen.

"Nah, nah."

"No girlfriend?"

"Nobody special," Peck whispered.

"Have you ever had one?" Sasha asked.

"Hanh?"

"You know, a real love, have you ever—?"

"You sad for Gabe, cher?"

"I'll never get to dance with him again," Sasha said.

"You dance good with him, cher."

"I'm so sad."

"Dreams can be good," Peck said.

"You mean memories?"

"*Oui.*"

"Memories are good."

"I bet he dreams of you."

"You do?"

"He dreams of you dancin' with him, cher."

"Do you dream of a girl?" Sasha asked.

"I know a girl, cher."

"You do? Where is she?"

"Down in Anse La Butte," Peck said.

"Does she love you?"

"She no boo, cher."

"Do you love her?"

There was a silent pause.

"Do you do it?" Sasha asked.

Peck leaned his head back and grinned into his pillow, like he had been caught with his hand in a cookie jar.

"Do you?"

"She ain't no boo, but we do it good, I'll say."

"Is she pretty?"

"Yes'm, surely, she is."

"Who's sexier? Me, Lily Cup, or your lady boo? Be honest."

Peck's warm hand gently touched Sasha's firm breast in the dark. It searched about slowly, found a nipple and gently played with it.

Sasha delicately placed her fingers on the back of Peck's hand and lightly followed it as it explored the curves of her breast, nipple, and soon the other breast and nipple.

"You like my girls, Peck?"

In the dark, his tongue found her breast, and his warm lips rested on her aroused nipple and suckled. Sasha placed the back of a hand over her mouth and closed her eyes. She was patient with his tenderness.

"We'd better not, Peck," Sasha whispered.

Peck licked her breast around her nipple.

"We're both sad and vulnerable," she said.

Pecked sucked.

"I wonder if Gabe is asleep."

Peck lifted his head slightly but kept his hand gently fondling and kneading her breast in a silence of not knowing what to say.

"Do you love her?"

"Her man is on a rig," Peck said.

"She's married?"

"Not married, but she have a man on a rig, though, *trois* weeks out, *deux* weeks back," Peck said.

"So, William is there to lend a hand, is he?"

"Can I touch you down there, cher?" Peck asked.

"Why, Peck," Sasha said.

"Can I?"

"What are you up to?"

Peck's hand made its way down a warm, smooth stomach, cupping Sasha's own.

"You have gentle hands," Sasha said.

Peck didn't speak. As he found her pearl, he favored it gently with soft touches of his finger until her thighs lifted slightly to his hand, her head pressing her pillow. He slowly, patiently circled her pearl with his finger, rolling it between two as he would a small, wine-soaked raisin.

"We'd better stop, Peck," Sasha whimpered.

"*Faut-il aider vous oubliez, jolie dame*?" Peck asked. ("Does it help you forget, pretty lady?")

"It helps," Sasha said. "*Il aide.*"

Peck's fingers patiently circled her pearl in the silence, waiting for the sounds he would recognize. It was when Sasha's thighs lifted firmly, her buttocks flexing again and again in twerks, rising off the mattress into Peck's hand, her fingers gripping and pulling sides of the pillow around her face. She made no sound. She didn't have to. Her buttocks and thighs quivered a peak, then released, and sank deep and motionless into the warm mattress. Peck moved his hand and rolled on his back and looked off into the darkness.

It was quiet again.

"What's her name?"

"Elizabeth."

"She speaks French, doesn't she?"

"*Oui.*"

"I could tell."

"How, cher?"

"Your French is good."

"I knowed her a long time."

A quiet filled the room again. Perhaps anxiety, contemplating what next.

"Let's get some sleep," Sasha said.

"Yes'm," Peck said.

Sasha rolled toward Peck, lifting her leg over his thigh, pushing past William and saddling his hip, resting her leg on his stomach. She could feel a throbbing on the base of her thigh.

"Elizabeth is lucky to have you and William on lonely nights," Sasha whispered.

Peck didn't speak.

"Night," she said.

"Good night, cher."

Sasha leaned and softly kissed Peck's ear, resting her head on his pillow.

"Thank you," she whispered.

Peck didn't respond. When Sasha was asleep, he turned his head toward her face. He could feel cold teardrops on the pillow. He knew he owed it to her friendship and to Gabe's to just sleep.

CHAPTER 12

LIKE A ROBOT, THE BENTLEY'S GPS POINTED THE WAY on an early morning navigation from the Peabody to the Greyhound terminal. Between Sasha and Peck, no mention was made of the dalliance. Tears on a pillow told her story. Sasha parked, and they went inside a brightly lit bus terminal.

"You want a breakfast sandwich?" Sasha asked. "We have time before they board your bus."

"You don' have to wait," Peck said. "You be tired. Go get some sleep."

"Let's sit over there and have a coffee while we wait," Sasha said.

Sasha went to a counter and retrieved two coffees, a sausage and egg bagel for Peck, and a toasted everything bagel for herself.

"Your bus ride is thirty-six hours. It's a day and a half."

Peck looked up from his sandwich.

"You should be pulling into Providence sometime in the afternoon day after tomorrow."

"Hokay," Peck said.

Sasha lifted an envelope and package from her handbag.

"I bought you a Discovery pass for the bus."

"Cher, you don't have to be buying—"

"I didn't buy it, Gabe bought it with his card."

"Ah."

"It's good for thirty days, so hang on to it. And here are some twenties in this envelope—don't open it here. Put it in your pocket. It's enough to buy food along the way and pay cab fare or emergency money if you need it when you get there," Sasha said. "Gabe will meet your bus in Providence, but just in case."

"T'anks cher. What's a discovery pass?"

"It's a ticket that will get you on any Greyhound and take you anywhere for thirty days from today. You can use it to come back to New Orleans. It's a pass to get on any bus."

"Ga-lee," Peck said.

"Peck, this is your new phone. This is from me. It's prepaid. Have Gabe or someone teach you how to use it."

"Gabe don have no cellphone, cher."

"Then ask someone else. They'll show you. Or I'll show you back in New Orleans. Put it in your bag."

"T'anks, cher."

"I wrote down Gabe's hotel, phone number, and address in case you need it. And here's my business card. Put it in your pocket and don't lose it. If you ever need to find me no matter what, ask someone to help you use your phone to call or text me. Use a charger cord and plug it in on the bus so it keeps charged."

"Peck's gonna miss you," Peck said.

"Remember the motorcycle creep?" Sasha asked.

"*Oui*," Peck said.

"I'm worried he's still on the loose," Sasha said.

"I know."

"You be careful, Peck."

"I will."

Public-address announcements echoed as they called the bus gate for boarding. Sasha walked Peck to the bus. She gave him a long last hug and a kiss on his cheek.

"Think Peck can maybe read sometime?"

"Soon," Sasha said. "Bye, baby. Give Gabe a hug for me. Take good care of him. I'll set up a tutor when I get back to the Quarter."

Peck boarded, stepping up and in cautiously, studying faces on both sides of the aisle—some asleep, some reading, some looking on their iPad screens, some looking back at him. He took an empty seat toward the rear by a window behind two sleeping girls wearing torn jean cutoffs and the same T-shirts (Princeton University). He looked out and saw Sasha waving. She couldn't see through the dark-tinted windows, but she waved lovingly at her new friend. As the bus's engine roared to a start, it backed into the night and drove away with a sweeping curve onto an empty city street. Sasha turned and walked to her car.

Peck had no sense of how long he had slept when he woke to motions of the bus comfortably making its way down the interstate. The sun was up and well off the ground. He raised his head and sat tall, looking over the rows of heads in front of him. He watched the road ahead with a Walmart truck far off in the distance.

"Good morning," a fellow sitting next to him said. He was a hefty, broad-shouldered young black man. He had a gentle smile and a conservative haircut. He sat tall, with earphones in both ears. His collar was starched and pressed, and a cellphone rested on his thigh.

Peck rubbed his eyes. "Where we are?" he asked.

"We'll be in Nashville soon," the young man said. "Where're you headed?"

"I'm going to Providence," Peck said. "A long way up a bayou. How 'bout you?"

"I'm headed to Parris Island," the young man said.

"Paris?"

"It's in South Carolina," the young man said.

"Ahh."

"I've joined up with the marines. Boot camp is in Parris Island."

"Coo-Wee, you're a marine?" Peck asked. "How long you in for?"

"I was supposed to go to San Diego, but I'm going to Parris Island."

"Hanh?"

"Parris Island is boot camp if you live east of the Mississippi," the marine said.

"Hokay."

"I live in West Memphis, and I was supposed to go to San Diego."

Peck looked at the young man, a bit confused.

"The recruiter in Memphis said they won't look close at the paperwork and think it being West Memphis I lived in— they'll think it's in Tennessee like Memphis is, so I'm going to Parris Island."

"West Memphis? I don't get—"

"West Memphis is in Arkansas."

"Hokay?"

"That's west of the Mississippi. If you live west of the Mississippi marines are supposed to be going to San Diego for basic, but I'm going to Parris Island."

He stopped trying to justify his traveling to Parris Island and picked up a portfolio from the floor filled with orders and printed materials regarding his marine training. He pulled a glossy picture of a marine in full formal dress uniform, holding a sword. He admired it and held it out for Peck to see.

"They don't give me this. They call them dress blues. I have to pay for my dress blues," the marine said.

"Nice uniform," Peck said.

"My daddy signed me in, and they're giving the checks to him to keep for me. They're paying for all my college if I keep staying in."

"When did you get on?" Peck asked.

"The bus?"

"Yeah."

"I got on the same time you did, in Memphis. I sat in front, but I had to go to the bathroom and came back and sat here. S'okay with you, I sit here?"

"Nah, nah. It's all good," Peck said.

"Girl next to me up front keeps reading a Bible. I don't have nothing against Bible reading, but it's a distraction with me trying to be online reading about Parris Island."

Peck pointed to the marine's phone.

"I got me one of them," Peck said.

"An iPhone?"

"A new one. My frien' going to teached me how to use it."

"How many megapixels does your camera have?" the marine asked.

Peck sat there stymied, as if he was wondering what the marine was asking and then he looked out the window, then back at the marine's iPhone resting on his knee.

"She goes to Baylor," the marine said.

"Bible girl?" Peck asked.

"She told me her father is a Baptist minister."

"Ah, poor *peeshwank*," Peck said.

"Her school let out two months ago. None of my business why she's only coming home now."

"Long time?" Peck asked.

The marine held up both hands, fingers outstretched.

"Ten weeks, that's a long time not to be coming home."

"Ah, *oui*. Dass for true," Peck said.

"I didn't ask," the marine said. "None of my business."

"Maybe dat be why she's reading a Bible," Peck snorted. "She's going home to papa."

They both watched the pine trees and a cliff through windows for a mile or so around a hillside curve.

"A marine life is a good life," the young man said. "Free room and board, cash bonuses, world travel."

"What's room and board, frien'?"

"Bed and food is free."

"Good on you, man," Peck said.

"They pay for my uniforms too, but not the dress blues."

"Your family, they'd be proud in Memphis for you."

"West Memphis. It's in Arkansas."

"They'd be proud," Peck said.

"I wrestled in high school."

"You wrestle? Dass for true?"

"Won county," the marine said. "Hope I can wrestle in the marines. You ever wrestle?"

"Nah, nah, never did dat," Peck said. "I seed a man wrestle a gator one time—Bayou Cane, but jus' for show. He won him fifty dollar."

"You ever wrestled an alligator?"

"Nah, nah, I stay clear," Peck said. "I dive a turtle, jump a snake, but stay clear of gator shore t'ing."

"Where're you from?" the marine asked. "Mind me asking?"

"Raised up near Petit Anse Bayou," Peck said.

"I don't know that."

"I have a bed near Carencro."

"Is that near Memphis, where you got on?"

"Lewisana."

"You really eat snake?" the marine asked.

"Bait, I catch 'em for bait—snakes," Peck said. "Trotline, I hook half a snake on my snood lines."

"Snakes make good bait for fish, do they?"

"They too small for gators to waste they time on—just right for turtles. Mostly want bluegill sunfish or bass. They fry best."

"My grandmother makes turtle soup," the marine said. "She lives in Forrest City."

"Ah, *soupe à la tortue*," Peck said.

"How old are you?" the marine asked.

"Twenty-five, I t'ink," Peck said.

"Nineteen," the young man said.

"You a big'un," Peck said.

"You like to fish?" the marine asked.

"I did it purdy good," Peck said. "I guess I like it."

"Some friends and I tried the Mississippi a few times. We didn't have any luck, so we gave up."

"Mississippi too fast," Peck said. "Bayou best—lake's good, if you have to eat."

The two stared over heads through the front window of the bus, the marine looking for road signs, Peck looking for the angle and pitch of the sun, so he could tell the time. They sat for nineteen miles without saying a word.

"Here's my stop."

"Hanh?"

"See the sign? Westel Road, eleven miles ahead."

"Dass where you going, marine?" Peck asked.

"No, it's where I board a marine bus with other recruits. It'll take us in."

"Ah," Peck said.

"I have some time before we stop, I can show you how to use your phone if you want. I'm good at teaching."

"T'ank ya, no, man," Peck said. "T'anks though."

The bus slowed down to exit on Westel Road. There were three chartered buses filled with marine recruits waiting. The marine stood and retrieved his suitcase and a paper sack from the overhead. He reached his hand out.

"I'm Eddie," he said.

Peck shook his hand.

"Peck," Peck said. "Good to meet ya, Eddie."

The marine handed Peck his paper sack.

"There're two sandwiches in this and a pear," he said. "Take it in case you get hungry. My mom made them. She's a good cook."

"T'anks frien'," Peck said, accepting the sack.

"I don't know what they are, but they'll be good. She's a good cook. She loads them up."

Peck smiled a thank you.

"Good luck on your trip, Peck," the marine said. "I hope you catch a lot of fish."

Peck smiled.

"I'll write your name down when I do my diary tonight," the marine said.

My name is Boudreaux Clemont Finch," Peck said.

The marine lifted his phone, spelled out Peck's formal name with his lips and texted it to himself.

"So, when I write my book, I'll remember your names—Peck—as the first person I met on the first day of my life's journey. I'll get the name right."

"How 'bout Bible lady?" Peck asked.

"Oh yeah, her," the marine said. "I don't know her name, so she doesn't count."

He offered a military salute to Peck, turned and made his way down to the front and off the bus. Peck watched his new friend walking over and being welcomed by a marine drill sergeant in uniform. The sergeant checked his name off on a clipboard list and motioned which bus he was to board. Peck's bus door closed, and its engine revved, moving back onto the pavement, rolling onto an entry to the interstate and back up to speed.

Peck looked in the sack, smelled it approvingly, rolled its top closed and set it on the seat next to him. He pulled his cellphone from his pocket to have a look when a young girl with shoulder-length cinnamon hair and freckles made her way from the front of the bus. She looked about for the bathroom door and stepped up to the last row of seats, grabbed a seatback for balance. The girl wore no makeup, conservative Bermuda shorts and Nike running shoes. She was pretty. There was an innocence about the sparkle in her eyes. She pointed at the empty seats across the aisle from him. Peck couldn't read her T-shirt. It said "Baylor Bears Sic 'Em."

She held her fingers over her mouth to mask her teeth braces.

"Sir, would you watch my bags if I put them over there?" she asked. "I have to use the bathroom."

"I'll watch 'em, cher—dey be good."

"Thank you."

"You pass a good time," Peck said.

Bemused by his Cajun patois, she raised her brows in wonder. "You don't mind?" she asked.

"*Pouponer*," Peck said, motioning her to the bathroom. ("Powder your nose.")

She offered Peck a grinning smile, her teeth lined with thin braces and wires. She studied his eyes, his arms, and the paper sack on the seat next to him as she moved toward the bathroom. She paused, stepped back and leaned her head over the seatback, pointing bashfully at the seat with his paper sack.

"Could you save me this seat, maybe?" she asked.

"The seat is yours," Peck said. "*Le siège est à vous.*"

The girl beamed. "I'll only be a sec," she said. "Thank you so much."

Peck was holding his lunch sack and contemplating opening it when the girl came back. She had taken time to apply makeup, lip rouge and powder. Her cinnamon hair brushed. She had delightful, twinkly eyes. Peck stood and moved to the window seat, offering her the aisle seat across from her bags. She smiled and sat next to Peck.

"Oh," Peck said, looking over at her. "Who is dis lovely woman they send out of the *pot d'chambre*? What they did with my frien' I saving dis seat for?"

"You silly," the girl said. "I just wanted to look nice."

"Oh, you look more than nice, cher. Ooo la la."

The girl extended her hand.

"My name is Millie," she said.

Peck wasn't certain what to do so he took her hand and shook it.

"This is where you tell me your name," Millie said.

"Ah, *oui*. People call me Peck." He shook her hand.

"Is Peck your real name or a nickname?" Millie asked.

"Name's Boudreaux Clemont Finch," Peck said. "They call me Peck for talking so much. You call me Peck, cher."

"I don't know. Boudreaux is such a forceful sounding name," Millie said. "But I like Peck. I'm good with Peck...So—hi, Peck."

Peck held up his paper sack.

"You hungry?" Peck asked.

Millie looked at Peck's eyes, decided she liked him and could be his guest for a snack.

"I'm starved," Millie said. "I slept through the break stops in Dallas and Memphis. I haven't eaten since Waco, and that was last night."

Peck pulled a sandwich in a Ziploc bag and held it for Millie to take.

"Hold on," Millie said. "I have water."

She stood and reached across the aisle for a cloth shopping bag next to her suitcase on the seat. She retrieved it and sat down with the shopping bag in her lap.

"I know, I know—I must look like a bag lady," Millie said. "But I have water in here somewhere, I promise."

She lifted another, smaller cloth bag from the outer bag, handing the straps to Peck.

"Can you put this on the floor between us, please?" Millie asked.

"Yes'm," Peck said, taking the bag and placing it on the floor.

"Be gentle, it's my Charlie," Millie said.

"Charlie?" Peck asked.

She lifted a black Bible from a bag and handed it to Peck.

"Hold this. It's in here somewhere," Millie said.

Peck held the Bible.

"Here we are," Millie said, uncovering her packet of water bottles. "Told'ja I had water."

She took the Bible back and handed two bottles for Peck to hold while she put the shopping bag back on the seat across the aisle.

"*Qui est* Charlie?" Peck asked.

"Oh, you'll only laugh," Millie said.

"Hanh?"

"My boyfriend always picked on me about Charlie. He isn't my boyfriend anymore. Anyway you'll only laugh and think I'm silly."

Millie pulled half of the tuna fish and tomato sandwich from the sandwich bag and bit into it, holding a hand up covering her mouth as she chewed.

"Peck won't laugh," Peck said.

Millie looked into Peck's eyes with a twinkle.

"I promise, cher. You can tell Peck."

"I get off at Kingston," Millie said. "Help me watch for signs. I can't get off with makeup on. Daddy would freak, so I need to watch for signs so I have time to take it off."

Peck spared her the fact that he couldn't read road signs.

"He strict, your papa?" Peck asked.

"He's a Baptist minister in Kingston," Millie said.

"Ah, *oui*. Is that—?"

"He would kill me. He thinks I'm still a virgin. Watch for the Kingston signs."

"Charlie?" Peck asked.

"Oh," Millie said.

"Charlie," Peck said.

"But only if you promise not to laugh or make fun of me."

"Oh, cher," Peck said. "Never would I—"

Millie turned toward Peck. She stared into his eyes for confirmation. She held her little finger out, hooked around.

"Pinky swear," she said. "Pinky swear on your life you won't laugh."

Peck locked little fingers with her.

"Charlie," he said.

Millie reached between their legs and pulled a doll from the bag on the floor. It was a doll of a baby boy, life size and weight and dressed in pajamas. Millie handed her sandwich to Peck to hold, and she cradled the baby in her arms.

"This is my Charlie," Millie said. "I've had him since I was three. He goes everywhere with me."

"Charlie's a fine looking boy," Peck said.

"I know you're just saying that," Millie said. "But it's all right."

"Nah, nah—he's a handsome boy, Charlie is," Peck said.

Millie smiled up at Peck, raised her eyebrows, lifting her doll in his direction, gesturing she would like him to hold her baby Charlie. Peck put sandwiches in the paper sack, rested it on his lap and held her baby. Two people making bathroom trips would see the doll in Peck's arms and give him a look.

"How old is Charlie?" Peck asked.

"Seventeen," Millie said.

"*Qu'est-ce qu* seventeen?" Peck asked. ("What is seventeen?")

Millie bit into her sandwich, pretending she understood.

"Charlie's heavy," Peck said.

"Doesn't he feel real?"

"I like Charlie."

"You don't think I'm silly?"

"Nah, nah," Peck said. "I still have Dundee."

"Dundee?"

"My hunting knife. Dundee, *mon enfance, couteau de chasse.*"

"What does that mean?" Millie asked.

"My hunting knife all my life," Peck said. "I name it Dundee, all my life I have it. Under my pillow."

"That's so sweet," Millie said. "So, you understand."

"Ah, *oui.*"

While handing baby Charlie back to Millie she noticed fresh scars on his hand from the fishhooks. She took his hand in hers, balancing Charlie in her other arm.

"What happened?" Millie asked.

"Fishhooks," Peck said. "Wasn't paying attention."

Millie leaned down and gave his scars a kiss. She set Charlie in his cloth bag on the floor and covered him with a baby blanket.

"I can tell, Charlie is pleased to make your acquaintance," Millie said.

She picked up her iPhone and scrolled several messages with her thumb, shrugged, and put it back in her shoulder bag. Peck handed her the other half of her sandwich and they sat in silence, eating and drinking water.

"Why does a man tell a girl he loves her and then cheat on her with another woman?" Millie asked.

"He's a liar?" Peck queried.

"He probably had lots of girls," Millie said.

"And he lies to them all," Peck said.

"I know I'm not beautiful," Millie said. "But when a man tells you he loves you, it makes you feel beautiful. Shouldn't he try to mean it?"

Peck grasped her hand.

"You beautiful, cher. Dass for true."

"With all these freckles, my braces?"

He gave her hand a slight squeeze.

"You a bouquet of spring flowers."

Millie looked at his hand on hers, turned her head sideways, and with a blush looked up at his face. She grinned shyly and turned her head back down.

"How old are you?" Millie asked.

"*Vingt-cinq,*" Peck said.

"Is that old?" Millie asked.

Peck shrugged his shoulders.

"Not old, cher."

"Where do you live?"

"Carencro, down bayou," Peck said.

"Is that in Texas?"

"Lewisana."

"Oh."

"Saving for a pirogue and running crab traps and selling them to fancy restaurants."

"What's a pirogue?"

"A boat."

"Oh."

"A small boat."

"When grownups ask me what I'm going to be," Millie said, "I always tell them I want to become a doctor, so they'll leave me alone—"

"Ah."

"But I really want to be a teacher and have lots of babies and maybe live on a small farm and raise chickens."

"*Une bonne vie*," Peck said. ("A good life.")

Millie leaned her head over and touched it to Peck's shoulder.

"I love it when you do that," she said.

"What?" Peck asked.

"You know," Millie said, "talk French."

"Ma English not so good, but I hokay with the other, I say."

Suddenly Millie's head perked. She sat tall, pulling herself up by the back of a seat in front of her.

"Oh, no—oh my God!" she shouted.

"Hanh?"

"That was my sign."

"Where?"

"Kingston. We just passed the sign for Kingston."

She jumped up and bolted back to the bathroom, slamming its door and locking it behind her. Peck leaned toward a window to see if he could see towns or villages approaching. The driver pushed a button on his overhead microphone and announced a special stop in Kingston and for everyone to stay on board.

Peck could feel the bus slowing down—Millie still in the bathroom. As they came to a stop, the bus door opened. The driver stood and looked back for Millie, as he knew she would be getting off. The bathroom door burst open. She reached and grabbed her suitcase and her cloth shopping bag.

"Do I look all right," Millie asked, seeking approval.

"Ah *oui*," Peck said.

Millie reached, grabbed Peck's hand and squeezed.

"Goodbye, Peck," she said. "It was nice meeting you and thank you for the sandwich."

Her words followed her scampering down the aisle apologizing to everyone along the way for delaying the bus, and finally to a waiting driver. She jumped off, the door closed soon after, and the bus engine roared again.

As the bus rolled off the concrete curb shoulder and back onto the pavement Peck looked down and saw the bag on the floor with Charlie in it. He grabbed it and hurried to the front.

"Wait! Stop the bus, mister. She forgot a bag," he shouted.

"Can't stop," the driver snapped.

"You have to stop."

"It'll go into lost and found."

"Stop the bus. I'm getting off too, then," Peck blurted.

"We have a schedule, pal. I stop, you get off, you don't get back on."

"Stop the bus," Peck yelled. He dashed to the back to get his duffel. The bus pulled over and its door opened. Peck jumped off, gripping his duffel and the cloth bag holding Charlie. He turned and watched the driver giving him an annoyed look while pulling the door closed. The bus rolled away.

Peck started to trot back to the place where he saw Millie get off the bus to meet her ride home. Soon in the distance he could see Millie standing by an open door of a Suburban, speaking with a woman with a small dog on a leash.

He broke into a run. "Millie," he shouted.

No response.

"Millie," he shouted again.

This time both Millie and the woman looked his way.

Peck held the cloth bag high above his head.

"Charlie!" Peck shouted.

"Oh, my God, I forgot Charlie," Millie exclaimed.

Millie's mouth dropped open, her eyes burst wide, and she grinned with grateful delight, both hands nervously covering her braces. She sobbed in awe of learning she had forgotten her baby, and in a miracle of all miracles it had been found. Her eyes fastened on Peck's eyes and beamed with thankful tears.

"Charlie," she mouthed. "You saved my Charlie."

CHAPTER 13

MILLIE LIFTED BABY CHARLIE FROM THE BAG, bounced up and down, giving him a proper hug. Nestling the baby's head to her cheek, she put her hand on Peck's arm.

"Momma, this is Peck," Millie said. "His real name is Boudreaux but call him Peck."

"How do you do, young man?" the mother asked.

"We met on the bus, Momma, and he's going to..." She paused in midsentence and turned. "Exactly where is it you are going anyway?" Millie asked.

"Providence," Peck said. "Dat be in Rhode Island."

Millie gave pause with the patois and stared at his eyes.

"And you got off the bus just to bring me my Charlie?" Millie asked.

"*Oui.*"

"You mean you weren't getting off in Kingston?"

"*Vous avez oublié votre Charlie,*" Peck said. ("You have forgotten your Charlie.)

"Don't you love his French, Momma?" Millie asked.

"It's charming," Millie's momma said.

"So what is it you just said, Peck—just now."

"I say you forgot your Charlie, cher."

"Can we take him to a bus station, Momma?"

"What kind of ticket do you have, Peck?" the mother asked.

Peck pulled a Discover Pass from his pocket and held it up.

"Oh good," the mother said. "You can get on another bus with that."

"Are we going to take him to Knoxville, Momma?" Millie asked. "To the station?"

"Millie, let's take Peck home and feed him. I'm sure you both can eat something," the mother said.

"Momma, we had a sandwich on the—"

"We'll call from home and find when another bus goes through. We'll see to it he gets to the station in plenty of time."

"Take him home, Momma?" wide-eyed Millie asked, holding fingers over her mouth.

"I have stuffed bell peppers."

"*Delicieux,*" Peck said.

"What about Daddy?" Millie asked.

The mother turned and raised her hand in prayer. "'Or what woman, if she has ten silver coins and loses one coin, does not light a lamp and sweep the house and search carefully until she finds it?'" her mother asked.

"Luke," Millie said. "It's from Luke."

Millie covered her mouth with an edge of her hand and leaned toward Peck. "It's from the Bible," she whispered.

The mother smiled at Peck, took Charlie from Millie's arms and cradling the baby doll, continued another verse.

"'When she has found it, she calls together her friends and neighbors, saying, 'Rejoice with me, for I have found the coin that I had lost!'"

Millie tweaked her shoulders up and down, grinning with squinty eyes. She took Charlie from her mother, placed him in his cloth bag, and stepped up and into the back seat of their Suburban, motioning for Peck to climb in.

"Does what you said—you know, the *delicieux* thing—does it mean you like stuffed peppers?"

"*Oui*," Peck said.

The Suburban soon pulled onto a driveway and rolled down a grade toward a large colonial house. Peck could see a lake in back at the base of a hill behind the house.

"*Grande bass, j'ai parié*," he said. ("Big bass, I bet.")

Millie giggled.

As an explorer would, Peck looked for flood lines and other tell signs of the lake's culture. As a fisherman, he was trying to get a feel for what could be caught in a lake like that.

On a desktop computer in a room just off the kitchen, Millie sat and went online to see when the next bus to Providence would come for Peck. She saw it wasn't until 1:00 p.m. the next day, and he had to catch it in Knoxville. She asked Peck his last name and went ahead making reservations for him.

"One o'clock tomorrow, Momma," Millie said.

"Knoxville is about forty minutes," the mother said. "You'll have to leave by eleven to be safe, Millie."

"Does it mean he can stay here tonight?" Millie asked.

"Your father would insist. Any young man who has sensitivity and caring to go out of his way to bring a friend happiness and joy is a man of God."

"Do you need to tell somebody you'll be late getting where you're going, Peck?" Millie asked.

Peck lifted Sasha's card from his pocket.

"Would you call Sasha at dis number, cher?" Peck asked. "Tell her when Peck gets to Providence?"

"You can use my phone," Millie said.

"Nah, nah, you talk better," Peck said. "Tell Sasha."

"This card says Michelle Lissette," Millie said. "Is this the wrong card?"

"Nah, nah. Ax for Sasha. She knows," Peck said.

Millie took the card, stepped out on a back patio and spoke with Sasha. She smiled several times throughout the conversation and grinned once.

"Sasha's so nice," Millie said, returning to the kitchen. "She's going to call the man you're meeting in Providence and tell him when you'll get in."

"Was she worried?" Peck asked.

"She wasn't worried at all," Millie said. "She told me to make sure you don't sunburn."

The two of them sat on barstools on either side of the kitchen's granite island and went through stuffed peppers and an assortment of leftovers from sausages to cheese. Millie watched Peck's eyes as he glanced with interest around the room at different wall coverings, bric-a-brac, family pictures, and art. If he turned his head out of her line of vision she would look at his arms and chest. She handed him a clean paper napkin and dabbed her lips with hers.

"It's early. What do you want to do?" Millie asked.

Peck looked out a window at the lake.

"You got tackle?" he asked.

"Tackle?" Millie mused.

"*Oui.*"

"You mean wrestle?"

She placed a hand over her braces and gave him a teasing grin as if she was amused, while a bit confused.

"Nah, nah," Peck said. "Fish poles, rods, fishin' tackle."

Millie blushed at her devilish misunderstanding. Peck smirked, apparently guessing what she had thought. She liked his smirk.

"In the garage," Millie said.

She stepped to the bedroom hallway. "Momma? Peck and I are off fishing, okay?"

"In the boat?" the mother asked.

"No, Momma. We'll be on the dock."

While Peck organized two sets of gear, Millie told him she knew nothing about fishing and would count on his patience to put bait on and to take fish off, if she was lucky enough to catch one. Peck listened to her patiently with nods of his head every so often, so she would feel connected. Before long they were sitting five feet apart on a long wooden dock her father had built.

"Is Sasha your girlfriend?" Millie asked.

"Nah, nah," Peck said. "A frien'."

"She told me to tell you she got back in New Orleans at four the same day she took you to the bus station," Millie said.

"Ah, good," Peck said.

"Peck, can I ask you something?"

"Sure," Peck said. "Ax."

Millie got up and walked over and sat next to Peck, hanging her legs off the side of the dock. "I didn't want to say anything in the house," she said.

"Ax," Peck said.

"Who's the bad man Sasha told me to tell you to look out for? Should you be worried?"

Peck cast several times out and reeled in while he was thinking how best to answer the girl's question. He handed his pole to Millie and asked her to hold it for him. He reached in his pocket and pulled the folded-up newspaper article Gabe gave him in Memphis. He handed it to Millie.

"Read dis," Peck said.

Millie read it carefully.

"My goodness. Is this about you?"

"Nah, nah," Peck said. "He's a bad guy, knife man."

"Is he after you?" Millie asked.

"Big hailstorm in Mississippi and we pull under a bridge," Peck said.

"Who pulled under a bridge?" Millie asked.

"Gabe, my frien', Sasha, my other frien', and Peck here, we stopped under a bridge in a hailstorm. The knife man stole my frien's medicine while he was peein'. He hit him on his head, knocked him down. My frien' could have died, cher, without his medicine. I got it back."

"This man in the newspaper hit him?" Millie asked. "The same man who stabbed the man?"

"Same man," Peck said. "Man he stabbed and his frien' helped me get Gabe's medicine back. We left outta there and knife man did dat—all dat in dat paper there, after we gone."

"And he's still on the loose?" Millie asked.

"*Oui.*"

"No wonder Sasha is worried."

"I feel bad," Peck said. "Bad for the man he stabbed. He helped Peck."

"This says he's in Knoxville," Millie said.

"Who?"

"The man who got your friend's medicine back. He's in a hospital in Knoxville."

"Where we are to Knoxville?" Peck asked.

"We have to go there tomorrow, to Knoxville, for your bus," Millie said.

"Dat for true, cher?"

"You want to go see him at his hospital?"

"Oh, cher, dat be so good," Peck said.

"We can't tell Momma or Daddy about any of this, Peck," Millie said.

"Hanh?"

"They would freak and not let me drive you in—maybe not let you stay here."

"You hokay with me?" Peck asked.

Millie leaned her head on Peck's shoulder.

"I'm so okay with you," she said.

Peck folded his paper and pushed it deep into his jean pocket.

Millie placed both hands around Peck's arm, feeling his muscle.

"Did you really fight that man?"

"My frien's medicine keeps him alive. I had to," Peck said.

"You're so brave," Millie said.

"*Tu me faire sentir bien, cher,*" Peck said. ("You make me feel good, cher.")

Millie pulled close to his arm, resting her head.

"Is that good? What you just said?"

"*Oui,*" Peck said. "It is good. *C'est ci bon.*"

"Why Providence?" Millie asked.

"My frien' go there," Peck said. "Newport Jazz Festival. He need Peck to look after him."

"Look after him?"

"He's old," Peck said. "Very old. Not too long now."

"Not long?"

"You know hospice, Millie?"

"Yes," Millie said. "Sad place."

"Gabe from hospice I work at. He wanted to see jazz. I see he hokay and take care of him."

"You're going to be with him, your dying friend?" Millie asked.

"He be dyin' soon, maybe," Peck said. "Last wish for the ole man, to go see Jazz Festival."

Millie looked up and watched Peck's eyes staring off over the lake.

"You're such a nice man," Millie whispered, a tear filling her eye.

Peck knew the setting for a good fishing time wouldn't work with more talking than patience going on. He did enjoy an outing and watching a new body of water, but he packed it in, and they walked with the tackle back up to the house and into the garage.

Reverend queried Peck at dinner. Peck told of the hospice where he worked and threw his trotline and how he was taking care of an old dying man from there—how he was going to meet him in Providence. Reverend opened dinner by calling Peck a good shepherd, leading by example, the way he was so thoughtful, sacrificing his own time to get off his bus and bring a doll back to his baby girl. Before they broke bread, he said a special prayer blessing Peck on his travels ahead and asked for God's guidance and safety.

Peck learned during dinner that the more he kept his mouth shut, the more recognition and seconds he received. On into the evening the mother told Peck he'd be sleeping on a sofa in their den, so televisions in the bedrooms wouldn't keep him awake. She made a point of telling him he was welcome to raid the refrigerator. With every message of acceptance of her new friend, Millie would crunch her shoulders up in personal victory and down in tingly salute, and grin.

Reverend raised his glass of iced tea in toast.

"Tonight," the reverend said, "we celebrate our new friend, Peck. Tomorrow we'll celebrate the return of our college girl."

"Momma, I'm driving Peck to Knoxville early in the morning," Millie said. "I can show him downtown, and we don't have to rush."

"How thoughtful," the reverend said.

"Now Peck," the mother said, "if you come again, call or text Millie, and we'll be happy to pick you up at our Kingston stop, ya hear?"

"Yes'm," Peck said.

"I'll pick up and do the dishes tonight, Momma," Millie said.

The parents stood, walked down the hall calling their dog and went to bed, leaving Peck and Millie at the table.

"Momma put a sheet and pillow on the sofa," Millie said. "Will you be okay?"

"I be fine," Peck said.

"You get comfortable, Peck. I'll just put the dishes in the washer and give you some privacy."

Peck stood, stretched, and yawned. Millie glanced his way as she stacked the dishes. He went into the darkened den to make up his bed as she wiped the counters and gave the kitchen a final look. As if with a thought in mind, Millie stepped into the den.

"Peck, I want to go online..." she started, then bolted to a stop. In the distance by the sofa Peck was standing shirtless in tight white briefs with his jeans on the floor around his ankles. She lowered her head, put her hand over her braces and raised her eyes, staring at his briefs as if he couldn't see her look.

"Online?" Peck asked, paying no mind to her presence.

Millie composed herself, perhaps imagining being in a school dorm. She lowered her voice.

"Give me that newspaper you have," Millie said. "I'll go online in my room and see what I can find out—and if they caught him yet."

Peck stepped out of his jeans and bent to the floor to retrieve them, giving Millie ample ogle time, with the added benefit of Peck finding his folded newspaper clipping and walking over and handing it to her.

"Can I get you anything?" Millie asked.

"No, cher. I'm good," Peck said.

Millie nodded and mouthed "good night," turned the kitchen lights off and went to her bedroom. First thing she did was scan the newspaper article, saving it on her desktop. Then she folded it and put it deep in her purse. She left no chance her parents could find it laying around and maybe causing a scene. She put her pajamas on and brushed her teeth, staring into the bathroom mirror as though she were thinking of the boyfriend who had betrayed her, and was it her braces or her Charlie or some other flaw? And maybe it was kismet, her meeting Peck. The only thing she knew about him was his kindness and gentle nature, and that he was good-looking, muscular, and spoke French. Her mirror stare didn't seem to overlook her memory of his chest as he walked across the den in tight white briefs, to be certain. She spit into the sink bowl and returned to her computer desk.

It was two and a half hours after midnight when Millie found herself in her unbuttoned pajama top kneeling in the dark next to the sofa Peck was sleeping on, watching him sleep. An aquarium in a corner dimly lit the room. She leaned on the sofa's edge and kissed his bare shoulder. Peck startled, but settled, and waited without a word spoken. He turned his head toward hers, and she leaned even more forward and kissed his mouth, softly and gently with moist lips. She lifted her head to see his eyes.

"I wanted to do that all night," Millie said.

"*Très bien*, cher."

"Have you ever heard the scripture Song of Songs 7:6?" Millie whispered.

"Nah, nah," Peck whispered.

"How beautiful you are and how pleasing, my love, with your delights!" Millie whispered the verse.

Her warm left hand rested on his chest and traveled slowly down over his stomach and under his briefs, gently grasping the base of his erect William, now in full throb.

"Your stature is like that of the palm, and your breasts like clusters of fruit," Millie whispered.

Peck reached and with his thumbs pushed his briefs down over his thighs. Millie kissed his left nipple again and again, licked it once and crawled up and straddled Peck's stomach, her face kissing his chest.

Her scripture continued. "I will climb the palm tree; I will take hold of its fruit."

Millie reached down in between her legs, held Peck's William and directed it in between her wet lips, leaning back on it until it was deep inside, rubbing her G. Her pelvis rolled in steady motion, her buttocks lifting, squeezing and lowering, devouring every friction, savoring every throb from his William. As her buttocks rocked and heaved, she lifted his hands to her breasts, reciting more verse.

"May your breasts be like clusters of grapes on the vine, the fragrance of your breath like apples," she whimpered.

It was not an endless moment but it seemed every answer to a prayer and when it came, it was a long, silent, writhing mutual climax, his head lifting from his pillow, their bodies flexing with messages of ecstasy, filling one another as if their nerve ends embraced.

Millie squatted on Peck for the longest time, tasting his chest, savoring its memory, feeling secure. She lifted her head and slowly leaned forward toward Peck's face, causing William to come out from the warmth of her love and fall limp. She kissed his lips a soft, warm kiss.

"We have to leave early," she whispered. "We'll get breakfast in the city and then go to his hospital."

She kissed him again and crawled off.

"Night, cher," Peck said.

Millie didn't answer. She grinned, smelling her fingers, and hurried down a hall to her bedroom, quietly pulling the door.

CHAPTER 14

THEIR SUBURBAN PULLED OUT of the drive at dawn with Peck's duffel on the floor in front of him. Both had coffee thermoses in their hands as she drove east into a Tennessee sunrise.

"I went online. I found a lot of things about what happened under that bridge and about this man who got hurt," Millie said.

"You did?"

"First off, his name is Brock, but I can't tell if he and his friend are lovers or traveling companions, but they're close, I can tell."

"Maybe brothers?" Peck asked.

"No, I don't think so. One is Brock Singleton, and his friend is Winton Makaylah," Millie said.

"Ah...you so smart, cher," Peck said.

"I'm going to miss you, Peck," Millie said. "Do you think you'll miss me?"

"*Peck va manquer ta bonheur*," he said. ("Peck will miss your happiness.")

"Is that good?" Millie asked. "What you said?"

"Ah, *oui*, Peck will so miss beautiful Millie," Peck said.

"I'll write you and maybe when I get back to school, you can come see me, or I'll come over to Louisiana and see you," Millie said.

"Where you go to school?" Peck asked.

"Really?" Millie asked.

"*Oui*. If Peck knows I maybe come there."

Millie slowed her speed, pulled off onto a shoulder and brought the Suburban to a stop. She placed it in Park and turned to Peck.

"You can't read, can you?" Millie asked.

Peck looked at her as though she was disappointed.

"The newspaper article you have, you can't read it, can you?"

Peck turned his head and looked at the road ahead.

"You can tell me," Millie said. "It doesn't matter to me. You're perfect just the same."

"*Oui*," Peck admitted. "Sasha is teaching me when I get back to New Or–lee–anhs. You sad...with Peck?"

"Never, ever. Don't ever say that," Millie said. "You're my favorite friend so far."

"How you know, cher, I can't read?"

Millie pointed to her T-shirt.

"This," Millie said. "This says Baylor University. It's where I go to school."

"Ah," Peck said.

"I'm still writing to you," Millie said.

"*Je vais apprendre à lire un jour*," Peck said. ("I'll learn to read someday.")

"Show me your friend Sasha's card," Millie said. "The lady I called last night."

Peck reached in his pocket, retrieved it and held it up. Millie steadied his hand and took a picture of Sasha's card with her cell phone.

"I'll write you at this address," Millie said. "You'll figure it out."

Millie set her phone down, leaned over the console, took Peck's head in her hands, looked deep into his eyes and kissed him a long, warm, passionate kiss—a kiss they had matured into on the sofa earlier that morning. She sat back, buckled her seatbelt and drove off.

"Someday," Millie said, "you'll maybe even write me back."

"You honey sweet," Peck said. "You're a special frien'."

Neither spoke for several miles.

"When we get to hospital, I'll go in with you—as your girlfriend or your sister—or something," Millie said. "They may give you a form to fill out, or you may have to read signs. Who knows?"

"*Je te remercie*," Peck said.

"That's good, right?" Millie asked. "Is that good?"

He reached his hand over and gently squeezed her thigh.

"Very good," Peck said. "*Très bon.*"

Millie turned in on Henley Street, crossed the Tennessee River and went to Main Street.

"You ever been to Knoxville Old City area?" Millie asked.

"Nah, nah," Peck said.

"It's historic," Millie said. "It's close to the university campus so they have neat food and places."

Carefully slowing the Suburban while passing the US Courthouse, Millie let Peck take it all in. She turned left on Gay Street and pointed out a history center, the Tennessee Theatre. She found a parking spot on Union Avenue. They got out and walked into Market Square.

"I don't think anything is open yet," Millie said. "I just wanted you to see."

"It's a nice city," Peck said. "Old like New Or–lee–anhs."

They walked the Market Square, making their way back to where the Suburban was parked.

"When you can write, are you going to write me?" Millie asked.

"I don't know computers," Peck said.

"No computer," Millie said. "A real letter I can read and put under my pillow."

"Ah *oui*," Peck said. "*Je vais tu écrire ma toute première lettre.*"

"Is that good?" Millie asked. "What you said?"

Peck took Millie by the hand, held it to his lips and smiled.

"My first letter is for you, cher," Peck said.

Millie beamed a blush, holding fingers over her braces. He lightly kissed her hand, and they turned and climbed the steps to find the Suburban.

"Let's go to the hospital, and we'll see if there's a place to eat," Millie said. "There's got to be something open."

The hospital towered in the background over Knoxville, a block from a McDonald's. They pulled in and parked, settling for coffee and breakfast sandwiches. They had worked up an appetite. Millie brought a complimentary copy of a Knoxville newspaper to the booth, while Peck picked up creamers and sugar packets from the condiment table. As Peck unwrapped the first of his two sausage, egg, and cheese biscuits, Millie found the hospital on her cellphone.

"Give me that newspaper article," she said.

"I don't have it," Peck said. "I gived it to you last night."

"Oh!" Millie said. "In my bag. Sorry."

She reached deep into her bag and retrieved his newspaper article, unfolded it and set it on the table. She picked up two French fries, bit them in half, and with an available finger, touch-dialed her phone and put it to her ear. The hospital answered.

"Hello?" Millie asked. "What are your visiting hours?"

"Maternity?" the operator asked.

"Oh no. Just a patient."

"Eleven to nine. No children under fourteen," the operator said.

"Thank you," Millie said. "Can you tell me if Brock Singleton is there?"

"One moment, please."

"Thank you."

"Mr. Singleton is here."

"Thank you."

"Are you family?"

"Why?" Millie asked.

Millie stuffed the rest of two fries into her mouth listening.

"He can only see family members."

"Really?" Millie asked.

"Are you family?"

"Can you tell me why, please?"

"I'm not at liberty, only family members permitted. Are you a family member?"

"No ma'am. Thank you."

Millie clicked her phone off. She opened her burrito and took a bite.

"Family only," Millie said.

"*Que?*" Peck asked.

"She said he can only be seen by family members," Millie said.

"Ah," Peck said. "You tried, cher. *Merci.*"

Millie looked into Peck's eyes without saying a word. There was no telling what she was thinking. She sipped her coffee, lifted the breakfast burrito to her mouth and bit a third of it off and chewed.

"What's a pirogue look like?" she asked with a full mouth.

"Ah," Peck beamed. "A pirogue."

"What does it look like, is it like a motorboat?"

"It's a flat boat carved from a tree, to find gators or lift crab traps."

"Alligators?"

"*Oui.*"

"How many traps does it take to catch your crabs?"

"Maybe *cent*, maybe *deaux cent*." (hundred, maybe two hundred)

"Is that a lot?"

"Ah, *oui*," Peck said.

"A lot of traps," Millie said. "It must be a big tree for that pirogue."

"Nah, nah," Peck said. "Only some crabs in trap. Peck lift it from bottom, take 'em out, put shicken bone in and drop it to bottom again. No traps in boat. Jus' basket with crabs I catched."

"Interesting," Millie said, not taking her eyes from Peck's eyes.

"Crabs to all restaurants," Peck said. "Softshell to best restaurants. They pay good money."

"And you figured that all out yourself?" Millie asked.

"*Oui*," Peck said.

"And you won't ever give up until you get it to work?" Millie asked.

"*Mais oui*," Peck said.

Millie bit into her burrito.

"My boyfriend gave up on me," Millie said.

"He not for you, cher."

"So, he's loser?"

"*Oui*."

She chewed in thought, staring through Peck.

"Peck?"

"Hanh?"

"We aren't giving up today, either. We're going to go see Mr. Brock Singleton."

"How?" Peck asked.

"I have an idea."

"Family only, cher, remember?"

"My Europe to 1600 history teacher—"

Peck placed his hand on Millie's hand to calm her.

"—Professor Thayer told us how a bad man got his grandmother to send him five thousand dollars," Millie said. "He was a crook, and he just called her, and she sent him money, and she didn't even know him."

"She didn't knowed the man she sended money to?"

"No, she didn't know him. He pretended she did and she believed him."

"*Bâtard*," Peck said. ("Bastard.")

"Does that rhyme with what I think it means?" Millie asked.

"*Oui*, rhyme," Peck said.

"He called her and said, 'Gramma?'" Millie said.

"And *bâtard* didn't even know her?" Peck asked.

"No, that's just it," Millie said. "The second he said, 'Gramma,' my teacher's grandmother said, 'Baby Tim?' like she knew him. The crook then told her yes, he was Baby Tim, and he was in trouble and needed five thousand dollars and didn't want anyone to know. It was all too embarrassing."

"*Mille*, cher, how you say, thousand?"

"Five thousand."

"Aye yi yi! And?" Peck asked.

"And she wired him the money, five thousand dollars, every cent," Millie said.

"*Bâtard*," Peck said.

"A total *bâtard*," Millie said.

Millie methodically picked up fry after fry, lifted them to her mouth and chewed, as her mind churned in thought. Her eyes would twinkle on occasion. She'd sip coffee. Then she paused, sat up straight, and pointed a finger up, as if she had a thought.

"Hold on," she said.

Millie picked up her phone and redialed the hospital.

"Wish me luck," she said.

"Hanh?"

"Let's see if they'll ring him."

Peck lifted her free hand, kissed it, and released it.

Millie squinted shyly and grinned. When the hospital answered, she straightened up again.

"Yes, patient Brock Singleton, please," Millie said. "That's Singleton."

Millie's eyes bulged, telegraphing they were about to ring his room.

"Hello?" the voice asked

"Brock?" Millie said into the phone.

"Yes, who—?"

"Brock, is that you?"

"This is Brock. Who's this?"

"Guess," Millie said.

"Tell me."

"You have to guess. One hint. I'm your favorite cousin."

Millie nervously put her fingers over her mouth, hoping, waiting.

"Kristen, is that you?"

"Yes!" Millie said.

"Are you really here in Knoxville?"

"Yes!" Millie said. "This is Kristen and I'm really here."

"Are you sure you want to see me? I look a mess."

"Can we come see you? We're only here for a while."

"Of course, of course," Brock said. I'll tell the nurse you're coming."

"With a friend," Millie said.

"I'll tell the nurse. I can't wait to see you, Kristen. Visiting hours aren't until eleven, though."

"That's okay," Millie said. "We'll come after eleven. Bye-bye."

Millie set her phone on the table, picked up one of Peck's breakfast sandwiches, took a huge bite, and then broke into a nervous giggle.

Peck could only stare at her, thinking what a good fisherman she would be—patient, cunning, knowing the right bait. Millie lifted her hand for Peck to shake.

"Hello," she said. "I'm Kristen, and how are you?"

They shared a laugh, refilled their coffee, and enjoyed each other, Millie's eyes going from wondrous, curious, thoughtful, to indifferent.

"He's such an asshole," Millie said, staring into Peck's chest.

"Who?"

"My boyfriend."

"He's not your boyfrien'," Peck said. "He betrayed Millie."

"Oh, right," Millie said. "*Bâtard.*"

"Ah, *oui, cher*," Peck said.

"He'll regret losing me," Millie said. "Someday he'll regret it."

"Nah, nah," Peck said. "He won regret anything."

Millie looked up at Peck, her mouth in a pout. "He won't?"

"*L'homme est trop stupide pour savoir ce qu'il est perdu,*" Peck said. ("He's too stupid to know what he loses.")

Millie tweaked her eyebrows at the thought of what Peck said, his using the word *stupide*. She smiled and sat back, enjoying the moment.

At the hospital, Millie walked to the nurse's station and asked someone to announce her—Brock's cousin, Kristen. They did and on the fourth floor Millie and Peck stepped by a uniformed policeman across a hall, walked into Brock's room, and let the door close behind them. Brock was sitting, resting his back on a pillow. Bandages covered half his face, including one eye and his jaw.

"Brock," Millie hurried, "I'm not Kristen. I had to say that or they wouldn't let us come see you."

Brock sat up in fear. "Who are you?" he stammered.

Millie pointed at Peck. "Remember him?" she asked. "You saved him under a bridge when he was fighting a knife man and you got his friend's pills back. Remember?"

"Hailstorm," Peck said.

Brock squinted an eye and looked keenly at his features.

"I remember," Brock said. "Now I remember. He knocked your friend down and stole his medicine."

"*Oui,*" Peck said. "*Oui.*"

Millie leaned in and looked at the damage to Brock's face.

"My name's Millie. Are you going to be all right, Brock?"

"They saved my eye," Brock said. "I need dental surgery on my upper jaw."

"It's so lucky they saved your eye."

"How did you find me?"

"The newspaper said you were here," Millie said. "Peck wanted to see if you were okay."

"He stabbed me twice in my face."

"Do they know who he is or have they caught him?" Millie asked.

"No," Brock said. "He got away. They're still looking for our truck, but they said he'd have changed my plates on it and there are a million white pickups."

"Do you live in Knoxville?" Millie asked.

"I teach in St. Louis," Brock said.

"All the way over in St. Louis?"

"We went to New Orleans for vacation and were driving back when this happened. My parents live in Knoxville. They brought me here."

"Is Winton, the man in this paper, here with you?" Millie asked.

"He had to get back to St. Louis—summer school," Brock said.

"I'm going to pray for you every day," Millie said.

"Thank you," Brock said.

"And my daddy is a minister," Millie said. "I'm going to ask him to say a special prayer for you."

"You're sweet," Brock said. "That's nice. Where do you know Kristen from?"

"What?" Millie asked.

"You used cousin Kristen's name to get in, where do you know her from?" Brock asked.

"Oh, I don't know her, I guessed—long story," Millie said. "We had to get in here to see you."

"I appreciate you coming," Brock said. "I'm glad you got away okay, Peck."

"T'anks to you, *mon ami*," Peck said.

"How's your friend—the one with the medicine?" Brock asked.

"He's good. You saved his life," Peck said.

"God bless you, Brock," Millie said. "You're going to do fine—I just know it."

"Thank you," Brock said.

"Let me get a picture of you two—a keepsake for you," Millie said.

She picked Brock's phone from the bedside table and stepped back.

"Peck, get close to Brock for a picture," Millie said, finding a camera button and holding the phone up in anticipation. She clicked.

"One more," she said.

Peck leaned in, shaking Brock's hand and smiling.

"Perfect," Millie said.

She opened the photo file of the phone to look at the results. Behind the two pictures she had just taken were four more—two of a black motorcycle, one with a white pickup in front of it, and another side view of a black motorcycle with Peck on the ground, fighting the knife man.

"You're in this one Peck, fighting the man."

"I am?"

"Oh, these are good of the motorcycle," Millie said. "Did the police see these pictures?"

"Yes. I signed a release and they downloaded them, but they said he already removed the license plate from his motorcycle, so they can't trace him by using the pictures."

"What a rat that creep is," Millie said.

"I wonder if they looked at my video," Brock said.

"What video?"

"See if there isn't a video of him or his motorcycle on my phone."

"Hold on," Millie said. "There is."

She stood motionless for a second, her face without expression.

"Mind if I text this video to myself?"

"Be my guest," Brock said.

Millie texted to her phone the two pictures of Peck and Brock and the video taken under the bridge in the hailstorm. She deleted the outgoing texts from Brock's phone, turned his phone off and rested it on the bedside table. She held Brock's hand and smiled.

"We're all praying for you," Millie said. "And I can't thank you enough for saving this big lug here. Thank you and your friend."

"Thanks for coming in," Brock said. "And don't worry, I won't break your cover—Kristen."

He winked his one eye as they left his room. They didn't speak a word in the hall, walked past the policeman, stepped on an elevator, walked out through the lobby and climbed into her Suburban. That was when Millie burst.

"Wait 'til you see this," she said.

"See what?" Peck asked.

"Wait," Millie said.

Millie opened her cellphone and found her recent text to herself. She opened the video and leaned over the console.

"Look," she said.

She started the video. "Watch what happens."

The video showed knife man jumping into the pickup, but after he pulled the door closed, he threw a small license plate on the dashboard.

"What did he throw, cher. Was that his motorcycle plate?"

"I'm certain it was."

"Can you read it?" Peck asked.

Millie played it again and froze it with the plate in clear view.

"08N391," Millie said. "Underneath the number it says Motorcycle."

"Aye, yi, yi," Peck said.

Peck's fist clenched—his lips tightened as the memory returned to him. He didn't even wonder how Millie got the video. He only stared at an evening that was a nightmare. Millie lowered her hand holding her phone and turned toward Peck.

"If we could catch him, would you want to?" Millie asked.

"When you t'inking, cher?"

"Now."

"Oh, *oui*," Peck said.

"I'll have to come up with a lie to tell my parents, and you'll have to miss your bus and catch the next one."

"Hokay."

"You okay with all that?" Millie asked.

"To catch this man, *oui*," Peck said. "Gabe would say yes too."

"Do you know where he is, so you can call him?"

"Who, cher?"

"Your friend, Gabe."

Peck pulled out the papers Sasha had written the information on. In no time, Millie had the hotel in Providence on her cell and handed it to Peck.

"Hold this to your ear," Millie said.

"Courtyard, how may I direct your call?"

"Hello?" Peck asked. "Mr. Gabe Jordan."

"Hello?" Gabe asked.

"Gabe? How you are, my frien'?"

Millie stepped down from the Suburban, giving Peck privacy.

"Gabe, your liking the jazz?" Peck asked.

"The jazz is phenomenal, my brother. The big show starts this weekend, but I've heard the best jazz since New Orleans."

Peck listened to Gabe as Gabe was dropping names from the world of jazz and of the sounds he'd been listening to.

"Gabe, I seed the man what helped us get your medicine under dat bridge," Peck said. "He purdy tore up, but he's hokay."

"How on earth did you find him? I hope you told him thank you for me."

"Ya, ya—the newspaper say his hospital, so I got off the bus. Gabe hokay with dat?"

"Totally okay with that. Take your time getting here, son."

"You sure Gabe?" Peck asked. "More time, Peck be there?"

"See the sights, take it all in, make it an adventure my brother—it's a beautiful country."

"Bye Gabe," Peck said. "I see you soon."

"Goodbye, my brother. I love you."

Millie watched him take her phone from his ear, and she climbed into the Suburban.

"Gabe is fine," Peck said. "He say lots more days of jazz, so I be good another day."

"Perfect," Millie said. "I'll figure something to tell Daddy why I won't be home tonight. I know lots of girls in Knoxville. That will help."

"How we going to find knife man," Peck asked. "You dreamin' it?"

"Let me show you the video again, Peck. Take a good look at it."

Millie opened her albums and scrolled to the video of the black motorcycle and pickup truck.

"See?" Millie asked.

"His motorbike?" Peck asked. "*Oui.*"

"No," Millie said. "Look closer."

"*Que?*" Peck asked.

"His license number," Millie said. "We can find who he is from his license plate number."

"*Sainte merde,*" Peck said.

"That's good, right?" Millie asked. "What you said?"

Peck raised his left hand behind Millie's head, gently touched her cheek and directing her face to his.

"*Tu es si* special," he said.

"Mmm...I know that's good, right?" Millie asked. "What you said?"

Peck kissed her on one cheek, on her forehead, her nose and then the other cheek.

Millie turned forward in her seat, grinned, and buckled her seat belt, savoring the moment. She started the Suburban.

"We've got to find a computer," Millie said. "We have lots to do. Then we'll find this *bâtard.* He can't hide now."

"Gabe," Peck said, sitting back in his seat. "He sound happy. Much jazz for him there—dass good."

The Suburban backed out and rolled forward into a late morning.

CHAPTER 15

WHERE WE GOING, CHER?"

"We'll go to a public library and see if my Baylor card will get us in to it," Millie said. "If it does, we'll go online and check what buses you can get on later today or tomorrow. Then I'll call Momma with some excuse why I won't be home and we'll look up the knife man in the DMV."

"DMV?" Peck asked.

"The Department of Motor Vehicles know who owns the license plate numbers," Millie said.

The librarian was cordial. A woman at the desk knew of Millie's father and invited them in to use the facilities. Peck looked in awe at the number of books on shelves. He followed Millie to a computer desk where she sat down.

"Go ahead and walk around," Millie said. "Check it out. I'll be right here."

Peck made his way down one aisle and then the next. He would stop and touch a book cover. He would look between books on a shelf, watch someone sitting at a library table reading. He circled around approaching Millie, her face illuminated by a computer screen.

"Okay," Millie whispered. "There's a bus you can catch at midnight if we get lucky and find him. If not, another one tomorrow, same time as today, one o'clock."

"Hokay," Peck said.

"I cancelled your reservations for today. We'll make new ones when we know what we're doing."

Peck pulled a chair and sat beside Millie. Millie took the newspaper clipping from her bag, flattened it in front of her, reread it, whispering passages.

Two men were attacked and robbed of their pickup in Hazelton, Mississippi late Thursday evening.

"Okay, it happened in Mississippi, not Tennessee—"

"Ah, *oui*," Peck said.

"—so we need to check a DMV in Mississippi first," Millie said.

She continued whispering as she read.

Brock Singleton and Winton Makaylah had parked under the Hazelton overpass during a hailstorm that blanketed one-inch hailstones over an eight-mile area that evening. The two had stepped from their vehicle, leaving it unattended, to ask a trailer-truck driver about road conditions ahead when they reportedly saw the suspect rummaging the cab of their pickup. A scuffle ensued, the suspect allegedly pulling a knife and stabbing Singleton twice, once in the chest and once in the face.

"That's wrong, Peck."

"Hanh?"

"Remember Brock telling us he was stabbed in the face two times?"

"*Oui*," Peck said.

"That poor man. Wasn't it awful how his face was wrapped?"

"Yes'm," Peck whispered.

Millie continued reading.

While they were distracted with wounds and trying to stop bleeding the thief drove off in their pickup, leaving his own motorcycle behind. The motorcycle's tag had been removed, making it more difficult to trace. Mississippi State Police are asking witnesses to come forward. Singleton has since been moved to an emergency eye clinic in a hospital in Knoxville where his parents live. Tennessee authorities are cooperating with Mississippi State Police, permitting access to Singleton for informal questioning in hopes of uncovering clues. The family is offering a reward for information leading to the conviction of this highway bandit fugitive who is considered armed and dangerous.

"Okay, here it mentions Tennessee," Millie said. "So, if we don't find him in Mississippi, then we have to try Tennessee."

"Why?" Peck asked. "Why Mississippi and how come Tennessee, cher?"

"Because we don't know which state to check first," Millie said.

"But, cher—"

"Peck, I know what I'm doing—I've been researching papers for three years now, sweetie."

"Don't a license plate tell you where a motorcycle from, cher?" Peck asked.

"Yes, but..."

Millie paused in midsentence. It dawned on her what Peck was leading up to—the video she had of the pickup truck and the motorcycle license plate on her cellphone. She looked at Peck, covered her braces with her hand, grinned, and shrugged her shoulders. She had completely forgotten the video.

"And you're the one who can't read," Millie mused. "You're smarter than me, that's for sure."

She lifted her cellphone and opened to the video of the pickup truck with the license plate on the dashboard. She froze the screen and the license plate state was legible: Kentucky 08N391.

"What do you know about that?" Millie quipped rhetorically. "As easy as that. Our *bâtard* lives in Kentucky."

She reached her left hand over and patted Peck's leg.

"Good job, Sherlock," she whispered. "Just like fishing, eh?"

"*Tu es la magie, cher*," Peck said.

Millie's fingers danced about the keyboard, her eyes focused on the screen and the occasional pop-up.

"I'm thinking that's good," Millie said. "What you said."

"*Oui*," Peck said.

Millie combed the web, searching for a Kentucky DMV site.

"Every state does public information differently," Millie whispered. "I learned this doing research for characters in a book. My business law professor wanted us to voir dire an author's facts presented about characters in his book to see if he did good research, or if he was trying to pull the wool over our eyes."

"Pull wool?" Peck asked.

"It means to bullshit us," Millie said.

"Ahh."

"I had to find stuff in Minnesota and in Michigan, and that's when I figured out that every state does it differently."

Peck sat patiently, not having the faintest idea what she was talking about.

"Here we go," Millie said. "Plate numbers by county. Kentucky."

She entered Kentucky's website and typed in DMV County. She then keyed in 08N391, pressed *enter* and waited.

"Laurel County," Millie said. "He lives in Laurel County. Now let's see if there's an address for him in Laurel County. Peck, reach in my bag and find my pen, will you please?"

The screen led her from one website to another until she found a complete DMV listing for London, Kentucky. There it was: his name, his address, and a registration and plate number for a black 2014 Harley Davidson.

"Mr. Eric Tandino, you are about to go to jail for a long, long time," Millie said.

Millie took the pen from Peck's hand and jotted down the street address. Not taking her eyes off the screen she handed it back to Peck to hold.

"Let's see how far London, Kentucky is from here," Millie whispered.

"Why?" Peck asked.

"Drive time," Millie said.

"Can't we just tell somebod—"

Millie turned sharply, leaning to Peck with a determined look.

"I'm really good at this," she said softly. "Let me do my thing."

Peck nodded and sat back.

"*Oui.*"

"How far is London, Kentucky from Knoxville, Tennessee," she whispered to herself tapping the keyboard. She watched the screen.

"Hmmm," Millie said to herself. "One hour and twenty-nine-minutes driving with no traffic. There's no heavy traffic during the day. So, we don't have to worry."

Millie took the pen from Peck's hand and scribbled a note on the driving time and interstate routes.

"I'll set the GPS with this address."

She handed the pen to Peck and looked at her screen, striking keys as she spoke.

"Let's see if Greyhound goes to Providence from London, Kentucky, or if we'll have to come back here?" Millie asked herself.

Peck smiled at her confidence, her taking charge. A good fisher she was—she thought of every detail.

"Oh, good," Millie said. "Peck, there's a bus to Providence from Knoxville that goes to London, Kentucky, and then up that way to New England. So, the bus that leaves here at midnight, gets into London at one fifty-six in the morning and leaves London at two thirty. It's a break stop, or they're picking up mail or something."

"What are you saying, cher?" Peck asked.

"I made you reservations from London for two thirty tomorrow morning, so what I'm saying is we're going after this *bâtard*."

"Cher, don't we jest tell the cops?" Peck asked.

Millie folded Peck's newspaper article, put it in her shorts' pocket, stuffed written notes in her bag, and closed computer windows she had opened. She stood and motioned Peck out of the library, where they could talk. There was a new confidence in her stride—one Peck hadn't seen before. Outside she stepped down four steps to the first landing and waited for three people to pass by. She turned to Peck and looked up.

"This *bâtard*, this Tandino guy could have killed your friend, Peck."

"Dass for true," Peck said.

"Your friend could have died without his medicine."

Millie turned a full circle, thinking. "Look what he's done to poor Brock," she said. "Scarred his face for life."

"Ah, *oui*," Peck said.

"We've got to go to Kentucky and watch while they take him away to prison."

Peck saw in Millie's eyes a determination to make her life important, after a boyfriend had deflated her self-worth.

"Millie, will you call Sasha and tell her after my bus leaves so she can tell Gabe when I get there?" Peck asked.

"So, you'll do it?" Millie beamed. "You'll go with me?"

"Let's go," Peck said. "*Allons-y.*"

"Are you hungry?" Millie asked.

"*Oui*," Peck said.

"We'll stop along the way," Millie said.

"Hokay."

"Wait a second first. I have to call Momma."

Millie pointed to her Suburban and motioned Peck to go get in while she handled some personal business. She'd walk and pause—then she turned and walk the entire width of the library's step she was on. She smiled, clicked her phone off and hopped down the five steps to her Suburban and climbed in.

"I'm going straight to hell," Millie said.

"Hanh?" Peck asked.

"Straight to hell."

"Why, cher?"

"I just told Momma the biggest lie, and I'm going straight to hell for it," Millie said, starting the Suburban.

"What lie?" Peck asked.

"I told her I ran into a girl who goes to Baylor, and she was crying at McDonald's and told me she was pregnant, and her mother wouldn't let her get an abortion, and her boyfriend didn't want to marry her, and she may have to quit school," Millie rambled. "I told Momma I had to stay with her in Knoxville tonight and cheer her up and help her talk to her momma."

"*Whoo!* aye yi!" Peck blurted.

"Ya think?" Millie asked.

"Whoo! Whoo! Whoo!" Peck said.

"Straight to hell, right?" Millie asked.

"Hmm," Peck said sitting up in his seat. "Maybe not hell, cher."

"Hell and damnation," Millie said. "My daddy would skin me."

"Let me ax."

"Go ahead," Millie said.

"You know girls at dat"—Peck pointed to her T-shirt— "Baylor, what are pregnant?"

"Do I ever," Millie said.

"You know girls whose boyfrien's don't wanna marry 'em?"

Millie looked over at Peck, lowered her eyelids in a dull stare.

"Duh?" she grunted.

"Oh, *oui*, sorry," Peck said.

"What's your point?" Millie asked.

"So everything Millie say to your mamma is true, just backwards out of order," Peck said.

"And I won't go to hell?" Millie asked.

"Oh, you can go to hell, cher, but for something good, I'm t'inkin'. Not for a bad lie."

Millie dabbed a happy tear from a corner of her eye, grinned and drove off. She smiled at herself in her rearview mirror.

"Better read your Bible, cher," Peck said, leaning back. "Just in case."

As Millie found Interstate 75 to London, she soon saw an exit sign touting a Subway sandwich shop. She exited, found it, pulled in and parked. They ordered. Millie filled cups with iced tea, found a corner booth and sat down, waiting for Peck to bring sandwiches. He joined her, sliding her sandwich over the table. His was a meatball—a foot long and hers was a traditional salami, lettuce, tomatoes, and cheese with olives and jalapeño slices.

"I always carry a toothbrush in my bag," Millie said.

"What for?" Peck asked.

"Seeds," Millie said. "Tomato and jalapeño seeds stick in my braces." She opened wide and took a decisive bite from the end of her Subway sandwich.

"Ah," Peck said. "Good t'inkin'."

Millie looked over at Peck, mouth chewing and an afterthought twinkle in her eyes. Through a muffled mouthful she asked, "When you learn to read, Peck. What kind of books do you think you'll like?"

Peck paused reflectively, holding his sandwich like a saxophone right outside his waiting mouth.

"Panography," Peck said.

He bit into his sandwich.

Millie sat tall with a 'huh?' in her eyes.

"Yeah, dass for true, cher—panography," Peck muffled.

Millie's lips puffed a guffaw like a deep-sea blowfish, spitting parts of a tomato slice, a bite of chopped onion, and half a slice of jalapeño pepper onto the table. She gasped for air, red faced giggling near to tears. She lowered her face to the tabletop.

"Are you dying, cher?" Peck asked.

Face down, Millie nodded yes. In a few seconds, she lifted her head, hand over her mouth, her giggle calmed, and inhaled. Neither of the star struck lovers had to say another word. The dashing young man who couldn't read or write entertained a well-educated, sophisticated princess just as in a Disney fairy tale. To Millie, Peck was as charming as any prince. To Peck, Millie was a delight to listen to and to watch.

By late afternoon they were driving into London, Kentucky. Millie pulled into a gas station, handed Peck a credit card so he could pump gas while she located the address on her phone GPS.

"Regular," Millie said. "It's the button on the left."

They drove slowly through the streets, listening to the instructions voiced from her phone. It took them into several twists and turns.

"Maybe this wasn't such a hot idea, Peck," Millie said.

"Just keep moving, cher," Peck said.

"This is not a good area," Millie said. "Look at these places."

The small homes were not only poor, they seemed disheveled— cluttered. This was not just a poor neighborhood—it was a dangerous neighborhood. GPS brought them to the side of a two-story home that looked like an old farm home the city grew around. It appeared vacant, with weeds crawling high on its exterior walls.

"Back up," Peck said.

"What?" Millie asked.

"Go back a way."

"We're getting out of here, right?"

"Nah, nah, just back up a way and stop."

Millie put the car in reverse and backed up slowly.

"Stop," Peck said.

Like a hunter he leaned his head around and looked. He pointed to a mobile home fifty yards behind the vacant house.

"Look," Peck said.

"Where?"

Peck pointed.

"A motorcycle," Peck whispered.

"It's blue, not a black motorcycle," Millie said.

"Is this the address that thing say, cher?"

"My GPS? Yes. That's the address.

"That's him then, I can tell," Peck said.

"Wait, let's see if it's the same plate number as the black one under the bridge," Millie said.

She opened an album on her phone and scrolled two pictures with a motorcycle in them.

"It's not the same motorcycle," she said.

"Prolly he stole this one," Peck said.

"Same number," Millie said.

"Same number?" Peck mumbled, almost as though seeing it made him relive an evening's hailstorm and a bridge in Mississippi.

"What do we do, Peck."

Peck didn't respond. He was preoccupied with looking around at all the houses, looking for clues.

"So, do we call the police?" Millie asked.

"Nah, nah," Peck said. "Not this neighborhood, nah."

"Why not?"

"They not come—or they on the take from drug here in dis place."

"Now I'm frightened," Millie said.

"Let me t'ink," Peck said.

"Let's just get out of here."

"Nah, nah. Let's wait," Peck said. "Let me t'ink."

Inch by inch, as though he were studying the telling ripples on a water's surface at a marshland bayou, estimating where best to throw his trotline, Peck studied with his eyes, inch by inch, every foot, every yard, every porch, every discarded, rusted-out junk, fallen bicycle, and appliance.

"Wait here," Peck said, reaching for the door handle.

"I'm going with you," Millie said.

"You should wait," Peck said.

"I'm scared, Peck."

"We don' know..."

"I'm going with you," Millie insisted. "He's hurt people. He could have killed your friend stealing his pills. He stabbed Brock, could have killed him. I'm going with you and that's settled."

Millie knotted her eyebrows into a serious expression, insisting Peck relent.

"Hokay, then," Peck said. He pointed to a house across the street. "But you wait here while I get something and I'll come get you before we go to his place."

"You promise?"

"I promise, cher."

"Okay," Millie said.

"Lock the doors," Peck said as he stepped out.

He walked at a quick, attentive pace, crossed the street and picked up an aluminum bat resting on a fifty-gallon barrel. He pulled a baseball glove from the bat and set it on a barrel lid. He hid the bat next to his side as he hurried back to the Suburban, where he asked Millie to unlock the door.

"You sure?" Peck asked.

He lifted the bat for her to get a sense of danger in what they were about to do.

"I'm going with you," Millie said.

"Get my duffel bag," Peck said.

"Besides, I'd be too scared alone here."

"Leave your bag inside and carry my duffel."

"I'll get it."

"Don't drop it."

Millie reached over the console, lifted Peck's duffel from the floor, and stepped out of the Suburban. She touched a button and locked the doors.

"Put the keys in your pocket," Millie said.

"Hokay."

"We can't afford to lose them."

"Stay with me no matter what, cher," Peck said as he moved around the front of the Suburban and picked up speed.

"I will," Millie said, determined to allay her fears and be brave.

Peck walked straight towards the blue motorcycle, first in a stroll, then in a hurried sprint, and when they were within thirty feet of the mobile home, the screen door was pushed open by the knife man, and as it slammed to an exterior wall of the mobile home a hundred plus-pound, teeth-baring, growling Rottweiler ran through the doorway at full speed and sprung from the porch, lunging at Peck and Millie. Peck swung the bat a full, deep sweeping circle from the ground, bringing it up over his head and with two hands down full-strength square on the charging dog's head with a hollow but decided *clonk*. The dog yelped once and instantly fell dead at their feet.

"Now you're a dead man, you motherfucker," the knife man screamed. "You killed my dog. You fucking killed my dog." He let go of the screen door and backed into his mobile home to grab a two-foot-long machete. He pushed the screen door open again. Peck lurched toward him, slamming knife man's wrist with his bat, jarring the machete loose. He kicked it away, dropped the bat to the ground and pushed him back inside the mobile home, and they struggled. Millie stood outside shaking with nervous tears, physically shuddering as she stared at the dead dog. Inside a window shattered from a fist smashing through it. A chair was turned over; another was tossed as a weapon.

"My duffel," Peck shouted.

"Peck?" Millie stammered.

"Bring my duffel."

"Me?" Millie shouted.

"Bring my duffel, cher," Peck said.

"Inside?"

"It's safe now. Come in."

Millie stared at the dead dog as she stepped around it and up on the stoop pulling the screen door open to see Peck straddling the knife man whose wrists were bound with Peck's belt. Peck had stuffed a dishrag into his mouth to shut him up. Peck had blood dripping from his forehead, and his knuckles were scraped and a bloody raw. It moved her.

"My fish line," Peck said. "In my bag."

Millie shook as she looked at the knife man's eyes staring up at her. Not taking her eyes off him she unzipped the duffel and pushed her hand in and around and retrieved a large spool of black, two-hundred-pound tested fish line.

"This?" Millie asked.

"Oui," Peck said. "Open it up. Take the wrap off."

His determined voice commands stirred her. Millie's fears evolved to a feeling of confidence in Peck as her protector. Going about his business while bleeding, protecting her. She watched him use the fishing line to painstakingly tie the knife man's arms, hands, legs, and ankles, totally immobilizing him, her freckled cheeks turned a deep red flush with an excitement she hadn't known before. She looked around at the carnage, the broken window with blood on it, thrown chairs and the bleeding scars on Peck.

"Can he move?"

"He'll never move from here."

"Won't he die if we leave him?"

"We'll call the police, cher. He won't die here."

As Peck knelt back to see his handiwork in binding the knife man immobile— even tied to a refrigerator leg—to hold him until the law came, Millie grabbed his hair in her fist, pulled his head back snarled her mouth with unbridled passion kissing him upside down, causing him to turn toward her. Peck moved and sat on the floor, clutching her breasts and squeezing through her T-shirt, Millie straddling his lap, kissing him. Millie lifted to a squat, unbuttoned and pulled her shorts below her buttocks and sat down on his lap again. She kissed as she reached between her legs and managed to unzip his fly enough to grasp his fully erect, pulsating William. Her lips and tongue licking his sweat and kissing his face.

She lifted her pelvis and with her fingers guided William's head to the moist lips of her warmth in welcome and plunged slowly down its throbbing length, feeling the entire shaft stretch every centimeter of the walls of her lust. Fully engulfed, she lifted and lowered her squeezing, flexing, buttocks on his firmness, holding the back of his neck with her hands for balance and sucking his lips and kissing his closed eyes. In time Millie's eyes rolled back, and she began to writhe, her body shaking with Peck's as if they were in dance, his falling back onto his elbows.

Their climax was the perfect ending of an experience they would share in future memories.

Millie sat, engulfed with William, and pointed at a clean towel on the counter. Peck reached, grabbed it, and handed it to her. Millie watched Peck's eyes as she lifted from his lap and stood over him, unconsciously letting the knife man stare at her. Catching his looks, she stared back with a sneer, wishing him a special spot in an eternal hell. He looked at her crotch. She smirked, wiping her inner thighs with the towel before pulling up her shorts. She tossed the towel on the counter and lifted the newspaper clipping she had stuffed into her back pocket. She placed it on the floor in front of the knife man for the police to see, but out of his reach.

Outside, Peck rubbed the bat free of fingerprints and dropped it on the ground next to the dog.

"I want to tip his bike over," Millie said.

"Nah, nah, cher, keep moving."

They hurried unseen and drove to downtown London before Millie, still shaking, pulled into a gas station and parked. They both gasped for breath, looking at each other, not a word spoken between them on the drive in, as if they were feeling a bond and realized they would have this moment all their lives, regardless of where life took either of them.

"That dog could have killed us," Millie said.

"Oui," Peck said.

"Would it have killed us, Peck?"

"I wouldn't let it," Peck said.

Millie looked at the blood dripping down Peck's forehead. It jarred her. It stirred her. She handed him a tissue.

"You were brave, cher," Peck said.

Millie smiled, took her phone and dialed 911.

"Laurel County Sheriff," the voice answered.

"Hello," Millie said.

"How can we help?"

"I want to report seeing a wanted murderer."

"You saw a murder? What's your name?"

"No, we saw a murderer. We know he's wanted, and we know he's at his home now."

"Do you have his name and address, ma'am?"

Millie gave the address. "His name is Eric Tandino, and he's wanted in Mississippi for stabbing a man in Hazleton."

"This murder happened in Mississippi?"

"Yes sir. He stabbed Brock Singleton, who's in the general hospital in Knoxville."

"And this Brock Singleton, he passed, did he?"

"I have to go."

"Your name, ma'am?"

"Can I be anonymous?"

"You can, but there may be a reward."

"I want to be anonymous."

"Thank you for the tip."

"You can give the reward to Brock Singleton's family. They may need it for medical bills."

"If that's allowed, we'll see that Brock Singleton's family get any reward, if this is the guilty party."

"Oh, he is, and if you need proof he's the man, look on Brock's cell phone. He has a video of the crime happening—his motorcycle and everything. It even shows him stealing the pickup."

"I'm sure we'll have that."

"No. The police took pictures off his phone but didn't look at his video."

"We'll check it out. Thank you."

"Okay then, goodbye."

Millie clicked her phone off.

"Murder?" Peck asked.

"I had to," Millie said.

"But murder?"

"You said it yourself, Peck. Cops won't come to a bad neighborhood jus' for a gang fight."

"*Oui*," Peck said.

"I learned the trick in my psych class," Millie said.

"Trick?"

"A master magician taught our class sleight of hand. He said all magic is a matter of tricks, it was about getting an audience to look away at one of your hands—being distracted—while in the other hand you're preparing the trick, unnoticed. State troopers certainly will come in for a murderer. They even said so."

"*Ah, très intelligent*," Peck said.

"I need the bathroom," Millie said.

"Inside, cher."

"To freshen up," Millie said, "and I got your blood on my T-shirt. Want anything?"

"Nah, nah. I'm good," Peck said.

Millie returned to the car, smiling, cinnamon hair brushed and with makeup.

"Let's find a place for coffee, where we can talk and then I'll drop you at the bus depot, and go back," Millie said.

"Where will you go?" Peck asked.

"I wish I could go with you," Millie said.

"Ah *oui*," Peck said. "Ma frien' waits on Peck. He needs me."

"I know. I'm going home and tell Momma the truth," Millie said.

"The truth?"

"It's time she and I had our mother—daughter talk."

"Ever' t'ing?" Peck asked.

"Well, maybe not everything, like about all of this up here," Millie said. "She'd be hysterical."

"Dass for true."

"Just that I've been grown up a long time now, and I like to wear makeup, and I like frozen daiquiris, and so what if I do? She'll have to get used to it."

"How 'bout Reverend?" Peck asked. "Your poppa?"

Millie reached in her bag and pulled out a wheel of birth control pills and held it up.

"Him too," Millie said. "I love my daddy more than anything, but it's time he knows his baby girl Millie could vote more than two years ago."

Peck reached and gently squeeze Millie's thigh. Millie grabbed his hand and held it.

"Peck, I'm scared."

"Why share? Don't be scared," Peck said.

Millie turned and put her arms around his neck and held him tight. Peck embraced her and assured her he would always protect her.

"I know I'll probably wake up in the night a lot, screaming about all this, Peck."

"Ah *oui.*"

"Especially that dog, or that man's machete— everything," Millie said.

"*Oui.*"

Millie let go, smiled and turned in her seat.

"But right now, I feel so good. Let's go get some coffee."

CHAPTER 16

GABE, DID I WAKE YOU?" Sasha asked.

"Sasha?"

"Hi honey."

"My baby," Gabe's voice smiled through the phone. "I've been up, already on my second cup. How grand it is to hear your voice."

"I have you on speaker, sweetie," Sasha said. "Do you mind?"

"I'll take you anyway I can get you, my darling," Gabe said.

"I'm opening mail while we talk," Sasha said. "I have an easy foot tall pile I'm behind on."

"A big pile for the Big Easy," Gabe said.

"Spare me. It's too early. Haven't had my coffee, yet."

"His name is Donald," Gabe said. "He goes by Don."

"What on earth are you talking about?"

"Point Street Bridge," Gabe said. "Mister sax."

Sasha looked up from her letter opener and smiled.

"I gave him your fifty and he rolled into "When Sunny Gets Blue" so beautifully people gathered to listen," Gabe said.

"Oh my."

"When Sunny gets blue..." Gabe sang a verse into the phone. *"...her eyes get gray and cloudy..."*

"And then the rain begins to fall," Sasha sang.

"Did he wail, sweetie...when he played it?

"Pitter patter, pitter patter," Gabe sang.

"Could you feel us dancing to it?"

"He watched me the whole riff," Gabe said. "He knew it was special to me... important for you."

"Sweet man."

"I miss you, baby."

"So how is...you know...everything?" Sasha asked.

She pulled a tissue from the box behind her.

"Be honest."

"Early mornings are my worst time—early like around four or five."

"Do you still have your pills?"

"It used to go away with a pill. Now I break one in half and take one and a half. It helps."

"Are you worse than when you were here?" Sasha asked.

"We don't want to be talkin' about me, darlin'," Gabe said. "Let's talk about you, let's talk about jazz, about when we'll dance again."

Sasha put her letter opener down and lifted another tissue from a box. She patted her eyes, no doubt thinking of Gabe dying alone in a hotel room in Providence.

"Peck will be there tomorrow at two a.m.," Sasha said. "I'm supposed to tell you not to pick him up. He'll catch a cab to you."

"I wrote it down, honey. I'm usually awake. I'll go get my friend. I miss him."

"Gabe, do you have your pot of coffee there with you?"

"You know I do."

"Fill a cup, honey, I have a surprise for you."

"Hee hee, my baby," Gabe mused. "Hold on."

Sasha waited.

"Okay, full cup," Gabe said.

"You know that bastard who hit you and stole your pills?"

"Hailstorm, he stabbed a man, how could I forget?"

"That's him."

"How could I forget?"

"Well—"

"Don't tell me, they found him?"

"Better than that."

"They caught him?" Gabe asked.

"Take a sip," Sasha said, "and swallow."

"Hee hee. My baby."

"Peck caught him."

"What?"

"Our Peck caught the guy who stole your pills," Sasha said.

"How on earth?"

"It's true."

"Where? How?"

"Troopers are picking him up and hauling him into jail, holding him for extradition to Mississippi."

"Picking who up?"

"The pill thief."

"Wait, wait," Gabe said. "I want to hear the whole story, but nature's calling, can you hold?"

"Go, go," Sasha said. "Someone's at the door with a delivery. I'll be right back too."

Sasha went to the office door and signed for a courier envelope. She looked at its receipt. It was from Lily Cup's law offices. She walked back into her office, pulled her door closed and sat down as Gabe came on again.

"I'm here," Gabe said.

"Me too," Sasha said.

"So, tell me everything. Don't leave anything out," Gabe said.

Sasha placed the courier envelope on top of her pile.

"A girl helped him. You know about her already," Sasha said.

"Just a minute."

"What?"

"What girl?"

"Didn't Peck tell you about the girl?"

"All I know is Peck called me yesterday and told me he'd be another day. He didn't mention any girl."

"Oh?" Sasha asked.

"Better start at the beginning," Gabe said. "My Uber ride doesn't come for an hour."

"Seems our boy met a girl somewhere on the bus he was riding. Her name is Millie. In fact, they met on a Greyhound while going through Tennessee."

"Good for him, but what's this—?"

"She got off the bus—"

"This Millie got off?"

"—and she forgot something, a bag or something on the bus. Seems our Peck made the driver stop to let him off so he could give the girl her bag."

"My brother."

"Seems the driver was pissed at him for making him stop."

"This was in Tennessee?"

"Tennessee, but the bus wouldn't wait and left him."

"Is that boy something or what? What a guy."

"He found the girl, gave her whatever it was she forgot, and she and her mother took him home for dinner."

"Well I'll be," Gabe said.

"Can you believe it, Gabe?"

"But what's this got to do..."

"So, he stays over, and she's a senior at Baylor University. "

"That's in Texas—Waco. I was stationed in Killeen, Texas not far from there.

"Texas, yes. So, I'm guessing red hair, freckles, maybe twenty, but she somehow sees a newspaper clipping about the stabbing under the bridge and looks things up on her iPhone, and one thing leads to another, and so he sleeps on their sofa."

Gabe mumbled a snicker into the phone. "How does your 'one thing leads to another' wind him up on a sofa?"

"I don't know, Gabe, the girl wasn't talking."

"Kids keep some secrets," Gabe said.

"I don't even know how they could, you know, do anything with her parents at home and her father a Baptist minister."

"So, what did he say?" Gabe asked.

"Who, the father?"

"No, Peck. What did he say?"

"Oh, I didn't talk to Peck. She called me. The girl Millie called."

"My man," Gabe said. "What a guy."

"Like I said, it seems one thing led to another, and then she drove him into a Knoxville hospital where they met the man who got stabbed. Apparently, his family lives in Knoxville, so that's where they put him in the hospital. The one who got your pills back for you. On his cellphone he had a video of a license plate from that motorcycle under the bridge, and that's how they traced this guy and the troopers arrested him."

"Arrested him in Mississippi or Tennessee?" Gabe asked. "I'm lost."

"That's just it," Sasha said. The motorcycle guy lived in London, Kentucky. That's where they found him and that's where Peck caught his bus last night after midnight—London, Kentucky."

"There has to be more to this," Gabe said. "Why would he be leaving out of London, Kentucky, and not from Knoxville? How did he even get to London?"

"I just told you. Maybe he'll tell it better," Sasha said. "The girl, Millie, was pretty tightlipped about it all. That's all I know."

"My brother, my Peck," Gabe said. "He has a way with the ladies, he surely does."

"He's a sensitive guy, if he filters his thoughts," Sasha said. "Girls like a sensitive guy."

"I hope the knife man goes away for a good ten years or more," Gabe said. "He needs to be off the streets."

"Are you enjoying your jazz festival, honey?" Sasha asked.

"It's heaven. Right here on earth, and it doesn't start for two days."

"So, what do you do all day?"

"The prelim shows are grand."

Sasha picked up another tissue, held it and listened to Gabe.

"Kamasi Washington played a rehearsal yesterday—saxophone. Oh, my God, how good was that? Sasha, when that man played I'm telling you, you could hear a pin drop. People swaying and in tears, in chills—every emotion. We all loved it."

"Good for dancing?" Sasha asked.

"If you were here baby, such good dancing. At the opening of the festival I'll get to see Chick Corea and Gregory Porter. They're what it's all about. Going to be fifty or more playing at different places around Newport, different venues."

"So much fun," Sasha said.

Gabe went on about the food in the area—how he preferred southern catfish to the flakier cod in New England; while corn on the cob in this neck of the woods was a delicacy it was so good with butter. He rambled as Sasha opened the courier envelope.

She interrupted.

"Gabe—Lily Cup just sent over Peck's birth certificate and his Social Security card."

"She found it?"

"She found it."

"Good for her," Gabe said. "Now he can be a somebody."

Sasha read the papers aloud.

"Boudreaux Clemont Finch—born 1996—"

"That makes him twenty-four, not twenty-five, like he thought."

"His parents are the state of Louisiana—it has him as a ward of the state somehow—and his race is unknown."

There was a moment of silence.

"What does that mean, Gabe—race unknown?"

"Southern slave states let parents mark the birth certificates with whatever race they wanted. It was because of the sex between slaves and slave owner family members. The color of the baby at birth would determine which plantation house, or slave cabin the baby would grow up in. That's what it sounds like."

"With it saying 'unknown' does that mean they don't know who the father was?"

"We're all the boy's got," Gabe said.

"Seems so."

There was another moment of silence.

"Gabe, if I overnight these papers, can you check around and find out where you can get him a legal ID? Tell them it's an emergency so he can get an airline ticket."

"I'll call the VA office here in Providence. They'll tell me."

"Okay."

"But I wouldn't send it until he gets here."

"Oh?"

"He's missed two buses," Gabe said. "And me...well, let's wait until he's here, baby."

"Okay," Sasha said. "Maybe you're right."

While Gabe and Sasha, Providence and New Orleans, were chatting through her stack of unopened mail, the Greyhound driver made an announcement on Peck's bus that they were stopping in Charleston, West Virginia, for a thirty-minute break. Peck looked over at the portly black lady sitting next to him.

"Where'd he say?

"Charleston," the lady said.

"Wonder how food is in Charleston?" Peck asked.

"Should be good."

She began organizing her bags.

"Po folks eats good," she said.

"Charleston poor, is it?" Peck asked.

"Where they's a Greyhound station, it will be," the lady said. "Food should be good."

"You getting off?" Peck asked.

"My niece is havin' a baby," the lady said. "Here to hep."

"Dass nice," Peck said.

"How far you goin', hon?"

"Providence. Dass in Rhode Island...got me a way still."

Peck looked out through the window, watching people passing by on the streets of downtown.

"Can I ax you something, maybe?" Peck asked.

"What'cha need honey?"

"What makes po folk food better?"

"Fat. Cheaper food has fat. We leave the fat in."

He looked in store and restaurant windows going by. He watched a delivery boy riding a bike on a sidewalk. Their bus slowed and pulled into a station and eased itself into a slot at an angle. The bus driver said everyone could get out, eat, stretch their legs, walk about, but be certain to be back in half an hour or the bus would leave without them. Inside Peck couldn't read a menu board, so he watched food preparers hand plates to customers until he saw a plate he wanted.

"What's dat?" Peck asked a man with a tray in his hand.

"Huh?" the man asked.

"Dat?" Peck asked, pointing to his bowl.

"Cheeseburger and bowl of chili," the man said, still walking. "Ask for a number two."

"T'anks, frien."

Peck turned, stood fourth in line and ordered a number two—a cheeseburger, a bowl of chili, with a Dr. Pepper.

After eating, he strolled by the rack of magazine cover pictures to take a walk outside smelling of diesel fuel. In time Peck saw people gathering at his bus, so he boarded. He stepped to the back and got a seat by a window. As usual he kept his duffel underfoot, where he could see it. At two different break stops, Wheeling and Harrisburg, two different people sat with Peck. The first was an older man with a cane resting between his legs who kept his eyes on a *Wall Street Journal*. The second, a high school history teacher, who spent time reading on his laptop and searching the web for vacation, camping, and canoeing spots in Maine. When the teacher pulled his cellphone from his pocket it was the first time Peck spoke a word since Wheeling.

"I got me dat same phone," Peck said.

He reached down into his duffel bag and retrieved it, still in its wrapper.

"It's a nice phone. You'll like it," the teacher said. "It's not so loaded it needs a lot of battery. It'll do a good job for you."

"*Bon*," Peck said.

"It looks new, is it connected?" the teacher asked.

"I don' know," Peck said. "My frien' just gived it to me."

"Are you French?" the teacher asked.

"Cajun French," Peck said.

"Interesting," the teacher said. He folded his laptop down. "I can set it up for you, if you'd like."

"Really?" Peck asked. "You know how?"

Peck handed his phone to the teacher, who removed its wrapping and protective adhesives from the sides and the screen.

"Do you have its charging cord?" the teacher asked.

Peck reached into his duffel again, pulled out a cord. The teacher plugged it into Peck's phone and then into an outlet on the bus. A yellow light began flashing in the center of his screen, indicating a charge.

"Let's give it ten or fifteen minutes," the teacher said. He rested Peck's phone on the lid of his laptop.

"What's your email account?" the teacher asked.

"*Non, je prends des leçons de lecture*," Peck said. ("No, I'm taking reading lessons.")

"*Oh, si vous lisez le français, pas l'anglais?*" the teacher asked. ("Oh, so you read French, not English?")

"*Je n'ai pas lu, désolé. Si pas de mail, juste parler par téléphone*," Peck said. ("I don't read, sorry. So no mail. Just talk for phone.")

The teacher picked up Peck's phone and looked at its charge. He turned the phone on and waited for it to come awake. In a few seconds there was a *tink* sound on the phone. Then another *tink* and a third.

"What's that?" Peck asked.

"Those are texts," the teacher said. "You have three text messages already."

"Quel est three?" Peck asked.

"Trois," the teacher said.

Peck looked at the teacher, not certain what a text was in the first place, and not certain if he had to do anything because of the messages.

"Can you read 'em?" the teacher asked.

"*Non*," Peck said.

The teacher looked at Peck, waiting for instruction. Peck motioned that perhaps the teacher could look at the messages and relay them to him.

The teacher nodded and scrolled down to the first text received.

"It says it's from a Michelle Lissette, and it says, 'Hello Peck, I hope you like your new phone. Call me.'"

"She gived me the phone," Peck said. "Dass Sasha."

The teacher waited for Peck to signal to open the next text. Peck nodded.

"This one is from Michelle Lissette too. It says, 'Your Millie sounds sweet, happy they caught that bastard and locked him up. Call me.'"

The teacher furrowed his eyes as though he was uncomfortable, as if he didn't know from the sounds of the last text how distant Peck was from his own culture. He appeared nervous after reading the second message. He was prepared to abandon the notion of setting up Peck's phone.

Peck could see one more line on his phone that read *Michelle Lissette*, He couldn't read it, but he was aware there was one more message. He motioned to the teacher to kindly open and read it. The teacher reluctantly obliged. He opened the text and read it to himself. He shut the text and held Peck's phone out for Peck to take.

"It was nothing," the teacher lied. "Just a repeat of the other one."

"Repeat?" Peck asked.

"It happens a lot," the teacher said.

Peck looked at his phone, still unaware how to use it. He pulled his power cord from the outlet, wrapped it around his phone and put it back in his duffel.

The teacher opened his laptop again and got busy working, sending messages and going online. Peck reclined his chair back and took a nap.

In Trenton, New Jersey their bus curiously pulled to a curb and stopped a block away from a Greyhound depot sign on the side of the terminal building. The door opened and three police officers boarded quickly and charged back up the aisle with their guns out and arms cocked, pointing them at the ceiling. They edged in quick shuffling steps to the last seat. The teacher immediately pointed at Peck and edged himself out of the seat and back by the bathroom.

"Hands where I can see them and don't move a muscle, buddy," barked one officer, pointing his gun at Peck's head. "Not one muscle."

Peck sat there, stunned. He furrowed his eyes and tried to look around at the teacher, but an officer touched the side of his head with his pistol and barked again.

"Do not move. Keep your hands where I can see them. I'll blow your head off."

All the passengers, except the teacher, were asked to leave the bus.

As the bus emptied an officer grabbed Peck's wrists and snapped cuffs on.

"Get him off and then we'll cuff him behind his back," the first officer said.

"Shackles?" the second officer asked.

"Oh, hell yes. This one's a runner."

They pulled Peck up by his cuffs, got him in the aisle, a gun still to his head.

"Hand me that, will you pal?" the officer asked the teacher. He was pointing at Peck's duffel bag.

Peck didn't move a muscle. He watched, taking everything in and waiting, as if he were a gator surveying a still bayou. Peck wasn't one to overthink too much, but he suspected this was about the knife man he fought with in Kentucky, and maybe the knife man didn't make it. Maybe he pulled the refrigerator over on himself—or maybe a wild dog got him. Peck froze his emotions and followed instruction. Turning to be led down the aisle of the bus he caught the eye of the schoolteacher.

"Sorry, man," the teacher said. "I'm sorry."

Outside onlookers stood and stared as Peck's handcuffs were switched from his front to behind his back. Two officers knelt on either side of Peck and placed shackles on both ankles and fastened them. It was then they thoroughly frisked him. They grabbed under his crotch; they went through his bag, dumping its contents out on the ground and then picking everything up and putting it back.

"Well lookee here," an officer said. "Now what on earth would a man traveling a thousand miles on a bus be doing with a half-used spool of fishing line? What do you suppose?"

Two officers walked Peck to a squad car.

First officer looked Peck in his eye. "You have the right to remain silent and refuse to answer questions. Anything you say may be used against you in a court of law. You have the right to consult an attorney before speaking to the police, and to have an attorney present during questioning, now or in the future. If you cannot afford an attorney, one will be appointed for you before any questioning if you wish. If you decide to answer questions now without an attorney present, you will still have the right to stop answering at any time until you talk to an attorney. Knowing and understanding your rights as I have explained them to you, are you willing to answer my questions without an attorney present?"

Peck stared back with cold, gray eyes. It was a dark, distant stare. There was no telling what was going on in his mind. He was a gentle young man by nature, orphaned since birth, not knowing a mother or a father. He had nightmares of having been toughened by an abusive foster nanna who made him sleep in a drawer, then on a kitchen floor while keeping the state's bed and board money and slaving him out as soon as he was old enough to carry bait buckets for her drunkard of a boyfriend. He remembered being in grade school when he ran away, running trotlines and mowing lawns to survive. Peck understood about being alone and about the darkness in his life. He knew no one had friends in the bayou. You were a hunter or you were food.

The first officer brought his nose within inches of Peck's nose. "Can ya hear me, punk? Do you understand your rights, sir?"

Pecks eyes were a gray, cold stare, like a gator.

"*Vous n'a pas d'importance pour moi—va te faire foutre,*" Peck said, turning his head away. ("You don't matter to me—fuck you.")

"Lock him up, fellas," the first officer said. I'll see to him in the morning."

"What do we book him on?" the second officer asked.

"Warrant says kidnapping, unlawful interstate trafficking," the first officer replied.

They pulled open a back door of a squad car, placed a hand on the top of Peck's head, shoved him into the seat, lifted his legs in, and slammed the door.

"IHOP or the diner?" the second officer asked.

"Doesn't kidnapping mean we leave the jewelry on," the first officer asked.

"Shackles and cuffs? You bet," the second officer said.

"Let's do the diner," the first officer said. "Roast beef and mashed potatoes night, all you can eat."

"The diner doesn't have mashed potatoes, they have whipped," the second officer said.

"What's the difference?" the first officer asked.

"Lumps, they're mashed. No lumps, they're whipped," the second officer said.

"Then they're whipped. Let's go."

"First we dump nature boy in the backseat off, lock him in the holding tank, and then we'll go eat," the second officer said.

CHAPTER 17

THE OFFICERS DIDN'T REMOVE his leg shackles. They dragged his feet from the car and pulled him out to a stand. They held his arms, helping him keep his balance as he climbed the stairs into a Mercer county lockup. A Trenton officer photographed Peck's front and side profile and fingerprinted him. Two officers followed him, as he shuffled down to the end of a long, dark, windowless corridor, where they slid a cell door open and motioned him in. Peck slid his feet through the cell's doorway, going in halfway, then he stopped and stood frozen, looking at a brick wall filled with graffiti and no window.

"I don't know if they're going to..." the second officer started.

He stopped abruptly, wanting Peck's attention.

"Hey," the second officer barked.

Peck didn't move.

"Hey," the officer shouted.

"Hey!" he repeated. "Fella, I'm talking to you."

Peck shuffled further to the back wall, turned around looking down at the floor, and sat on a thin mattress-lined steel shelf.

The officer stepped in and walked up to Peck.

"You goin' to teach him, Sarge?" queried one of the inmates in a next cell.

"Stand up," the officer said.

"Pretty boy needs to learn respect, don't he, Sarge," another voice asked from an adjoining cell.

"Stand up, nature boy," the officer barked.

Peck stood, gaining balance.

The officer looked over at the adjacent cell. "Turn around, fellas," he said.

Two of four in the cell complied. One was sleeping.

With his elbow cocked back, the officer slammed Peck in the gut with his closed fist, doubling him over. Peck gasped for air. The officer pulled Peck's head up by his hair and slugged him in his stomach again. Then he pushed him back on the cot. Peck fell over on his side, gasping and wheezing for breath.

"When an officer is talking to you, best you don't be rude, nature boy," the second officer said. "Is that understood?"

The officer backed away, stepped out of the cell and locked the door.

"Like I was saying, they might feed you tonight, or they might feed you in the morning, but I suggest you be polite when they do."

He turned and walked the dark corridor and slammed its door shut.

"What ya in for?" came a voice.

Peck lifted his shackled legs up on his cot and laid down on his side, his hands still cuffed behind his back.

"Ain't for shoplifting," came a voice. "Looks of him."

"The man don't hit a face, d'ja see that, Harry?" another voice asked. "The man always goes for the gut but not the face."

"What you mean?" another voice asked.

"If the man marks your face, judge don't like that," the voice said. "Slamming your guts out can't be seen. No evidence. The man don't hit the face."

"Fuck," a voice said.

"Too much paperwork, if a judge sees a busted lip or somethin', and he gets mad," a voice said.

"Damn," a voice said.

Peck's world was now little more than a dark five-by-seven holding tank. Being the only prisoner on the floor in cuffs and shackles didn't bode well for his situation. His eyes stared a gray stare. He had no idea why he was there. Was it the teacher who had turned him in? If it was, what did the teacher know? What did he suspect? Peck closed his eyes long before he fell asleep.

Beams of a morning sun cut bright lines slanting down through shadows of adjoining cells. Dust particles floated like stars illuminated by the beams and disappeared again into the shadows. Peck had urinated in his jeans as he couldn't maneuver with his hands cuffed behind his back, even though a stainless-steel toilet bowl with no lid was a foot from his head next to his cot. Peck heard a bolt key in the cell door, and it slid open. He turned and sat up.

"Aww shit," the first officer said.

"What Sarge? The second officer asked.

"Didn't anyone ask him if he had to piss?" the first officer asked.

There was no answer.

"Goddammit," the first officer said. "You got pants in the bag, nature boy?"

Peck nodded his head.

The first officer looked at the two officers standing behind him.

"Get his pants. Get those off him and roll them up in a paper towel and put them in a plastic bag or something—but get him cleaned up and take him down to Interrogation Room A," the first officer said.

He stepped back and behind the second and third officers.

"See he eats before you bring him down," he said. "Have him there by ten, no later."

"Yes, Sarge," the second officer said.

"And look," the first officer whined, pointing to the toilet. "There's no shit paper. Get the man some paper. Where's the fucking toilet paper? Who prepped this cell, anyway?"

"Sorry, Sarge," the second officer said.

"This is county, guys. Let's show some class." The first officer stepped out and walked the dark corridor, looking at his watch.

Two officers unshackled Peck, removed his cuffs, and went to find his duffel bag in the property room. One returned and tossed in clean jeans and underwear, a half roll of paper towels and stepped back and checked the locked door. Peck distanced his eyes and his awareness, as though he were alone in a bayou. He took care of his personal needs and flushed the toilet. He splashed himself at the sink and used paper towels to dry his face and body before he pulled fresh underwear and his new jeans on. The two watching him and the cellmate's eyes down the hall were nothing more than eyes in a swamp, bog or tidal flow. They meant nothing to Peck. A cart was pushed down the corridor and to his cell. Another uniformed officer lifted a pie tin and a spoon from it and handed it to the second officer.

"When you're done, leave it on the floor over here," the food cart pusher told Peck. He pointed at a spot near a door to his cell.

The second officer handed Peck a tin of macaroni and meat sauce, a spoon and a plastic bottle of water, stepped out of the cell, and slid the door closed.

"It's nine thirty-seven," the first officer said. "We'll be back in twenty minutes to get you."

Peck watched them walk the corridor and out the door, letting it slam behind them. He looked at his wrists. It was the first time he could see them since last night. He turned his hand and looked at the scars from the fishhooks. He held the pie tin with one hand and twisted his other wrist. He shifted the pie tin to the other hand and twisted the other wrist about. It was as if he were appreciating what little freedom he had, even though he was caged like an animal. He picked up his spoon, looked at it in his hand, and shoveled food into his mouth until the pie tin was empty. He set the tin and spoon on the floor where the food cart man had said and stepped back and sat on a portion of his cot not dampened by his urinating in the night.

He waited. Steeped in thought, he turned and studied the scratching of letters and sketches of faces on the brick wall behind him. He stood, walked over and picked up the spoon, walked back and touched the wall with the spoon handle, seeing that the girth of the spoon handle fit most of the wall carvings. He stepped back and dropped the spoon into the pie tin, walked to the bunk and sat down.

When they came, there was no talking. They cuffed him in front this time, left the shackles on the bunk and walked him the length of the corridor into an eye-squinting, brightly lit county police station area and to a door out of a Philip Marlow detective movie with a frosted glass pane on the top half and the letter A painted in black on its center. They pushed the door open, walked Peck to a table where a middle-aged detective in a suit and a detective woman in her thirties in a black pantsuit sat and waited with indifferent looks on their faces. The officers sat Peck across from the two and pushed his chair in.

"Thank you, officers," the lady detective said. "We won't need the cuffs. You can take them off."

The second officer obliged, removing Peck's cuffs and carrying them out with him.

"We could use some coffee," the male detective said.

He looked first at the lady detective who nodded yes and then over at Peck. "How do you like your coffee?"

Peck pursed his lips as though he would trust them one time. "Black," he mumbled. "Sugar."

There was no talking while they waited. Three Styrofoam cups were brought in and set on the table. The male detective handed Peck his cup, black with sugar.

"Do you know why we're here, Mr. Finch?" the female detective asked, breaking the quiet.

"We're not thinking about what happened to the money yet," the male detective interrupted.

The female detective rested back and sipped her coffee.

"Tell us what you did with the body," the male detective said.

Peck's head bolted up.

"You know the bayous and the swamps," the female detective said.

Peck watched her eyes.

"Where'd you hide the body?" she asked.

Peck sat with a cold blank stare at the tabletop.

"I bet it's easy getting rid of a body when you know the swamps," the female detective said.

"Okay, let's start with the money," the male detective said.

Peck looked up.

"Three grand's a lot of money," the male detective said.

"Where did you spend it?" the lady detective asked.

"You only have a few hundred on you now," the male detective said.

Peck stared at the tabletop.

"A casino, right?" the lady detective asked. "You lost it at tables or was it in the slots?"

"My money says it was the tit bars," the male detective said.

"Now, be nice, Lieutenant," the female detective said.

"Did you drop three thousand dollars on lap dances? Easy to do," the male detective said.

There was a knock on the door and the first officer stepped in.

"Detectives? the first officer asked.

"We're busy," the male detective said.

"There's a call," the first officer said.

"No interruptions," the lady detective said.

"Tell them we'll call back," the male officer said.

"The prisoner has a phone call on line three, sir."

"Officer, we're in an interrogation, here," the male detective said.

"But it's his call, Detective," the lead officer said.

"What are you saying?" the male detective asked.

"He's allowed a call. It's his call," the first officer said.

"Are you telling us he hasn't had his call?" the lady detective asked.

"No, Detective," first officer said. "I mean, yes that's what I'm telling you. Not yet. This will be it."

"God damn it," the male detective barked. "He's been here all night. Why hasn't he been permitted to make his call?"

The first officer had a look on his face that any answer he gave would be a wrong answer. He stood there.

"Did anyone even read him his Miranda rights?" the lady detective asked.

"Oh, yes, Detective. We recorded that," the first officer said.

The two detectives looked at each other and shook their heads.

"Line three," the first officer said.

The male detective slid a phone over the table to Peck. He and the lady detective stood and left the room.

"We'll be outside," the lady detective said. "Finish your call."

When the door closed behind them Peck looked at the flashing light on the phone. He picked up the handset and put it to his ear.

"Hello?" he asked. There was no sound at the other end. Peck saw a light still blinking, and he chanced pressing on its button.

"Hello?" he asked.

"Peck, is that you?"

"This is Peck, who dat?"

"Sasha," she said. "This is Sasha, Peck. How are you?"

"Oh cher, what I did?" Peck pleaded. "They talkin' crazy talk about dead body and gamble money. What I did, cher?"

"Did you get my text, Peck?" Sasha asked.

"Not the last one. The teacher never read it to me. What'd I did?"

"Peck, I don't know anything more than they put a warrant out on you so I can't tell you anything," Sasha said. "Hold on, and I'll put Lily Cup on the phone. She's a lawyer. She'll help you."

"What I did?" Peck asked.

"Hello Peck?"

"Yeah," Peck said. "What'd I did, cher? They lock me up."

"Peck, listen," Lily Cup said. "Until you're back here in Louisiana it's maybe safer if we don't talk, so please don't ask me anything, but trust me, I'll help you get out of this mess."

"Tell Peck something anyhow," Peck said.

"A private detective is coming to get you out of jail. He's going to fly you to Baton Rouge or New Orleans, and he'll drive you to Carencro. I'll meet you there."

"Carencro?" Peck asked. "What body they talkin' about? They talking a dead body, cher."

"Peck...Peck...did you understand me?" Lily Cup said. "A detective is coming and he'll fly you to Baton Rouge or New Orleans and then he'll drive you to Carencro. Do you understand?"

"What dead body?" Peck asked.

"Tell me you understand," Lily Cup said. "Do you understand?"

"*Oui*," Peck said. "*Je comprends.*"

"Good," Lily Cup said. "Now promise me you won't say a word to anybody unless I'm with you."

"Yes'm," Peck said.

"Say you promise," Lily Cup said.

"What about the body?"

"They're just fishing, Peck. Don't think about a body."

"But—"

"Peck, this is important. Tell me you understand and you promise."

"I promise, shore t'ing," Peck said.

"Good, they're fishing, get what they say about a body out of your head."

"Hokay, cher."

"Good, here's Sasha to say goodbye," Lily Cup said.

"Peck, are you okay?" Sasha asked.

"I'm scared like Bayou Chene," Peck said.

"You mean that girl—the girl you go see?" Sasha asked.

"Nah, nah, like gator man, I—"

"Don't be frightened, honey. Do what Lily Cup tells you. She knows what she's doing."

"I growed in Bayou Chene with my foster nanna who slaved me to gator man when I was *quatre* or *trois* maybe, I t'ink."

"Peck, we don't have long to talk and they could be listening. Tell me when you get here."

"I feel like dat all over again now."

There was a silence on the phone as Sasha thought of his loneliness and despair, clasped her mouth with a palm and quiet sobs. She handed the phone to Lily Cup.

"We've got to get off the phone, Peck," Lily Cup said. "Remember, everything is going to be all right, and no talking. Promise?"

"Promise," Peck said.

The call ended.

Peck watched shadows of people through the frosted glass—detectives milling about outside the interrogation room. It was twenty minutes of Peck sitting there looking at the phone when the door opened and the third officer came in and without talking, he cuffed him and walked him through the main station and down the dark corridor to his cell. This time he picked up the shackles, removed the handcuffs and left Peck alone in the cell.

The lunch cart came with a tin pie plate of food and a spoon. This time it was a knackwurst sausage, beans and a plastic bottle of water. Three hours later a guard came to the cell and had Peck stick his hands between the bars; he cuffed him before opening the door and he led Peck to the main station lobby. A heavy-set man with a balding head and twigs of hair stubble in his ears, a gravy stain on his shirt, and a tattered briefcase with worn straps, walked up to the guard. He looked Peck over and then in the eye. The officer removed Peck's handcuffs and the man with the briefcase pulled a new set from his belt.

"Here's the plan, Finch," the private detective said. "Name's Conway. You don't try anything funny, and we'll get along just fine."

He cuffed his left wrist to Peck's right wrist.

"You come along easy and we'll be best friends, Finch," the private detective said.

He turned around with his back to the station crowd, lifted brass knuckles from his pocket and held them up to Peck's nose and growled a whisper.

"Fuck with me or try to run, I'll bust your face open, rip your arm off and stick it up your ass. We pretty much understand each other?"

Peck nodded.

"Well good," the private detective said. "We're off to a good start."

The private detective put the brass knuckles back in his pocket and looked at the guard. "Where do I sign for him, and how can I get a ride to the airport?"

"Over here," the guard said, walking them to a desk. "You want Trenton-Mercer?"

"What in the hell is a Trenton-Mercer?" Conway asked.

"It's a local airport," the guard said.

"Hell no," the private detective said. "I want Newark. I don't want no Mickey Mouse scramble through some bush-hop airport with a prisoner in tow."

"I'll call you a van," the guard said.

Peck caught the private detective's eye.

"Mr. Conway?" Peck asked quietly.

"What?" the private detective grunted.

"I can't fly," Peck said. "I got no ID for true."

The private detective gave a wily smile. "You do now, Finch. I've got your social security card in my bag and the warrant."

"Oh," Peck said.

"You ever even been on a plane, Finch?"

"Nah, nah," Peck said.

"Be a good fella and just enjoy the ride," Conway said. "It's free, and we'll have us a good lunch at the airport before we board."

Peck somehow felt more secure now. As secure as one could feel being handcuffed to a private detective. It was something about the private detective's candor he felt he could trust. He watched New Jersey go by as the van crossed through farm country, past horse stables, and pastures, and skimmed over historical industrial cities. The interstate in New Jersey was an overpass through manufacturing and warehouse buildings dating back to the Civil War, not like the great bayous it would pass over in Louisiana.

The like of the Newark airport was a new experience to Peck. It was hard for a down bayou boy to imagine anything so large being so well organized. He accepted the humiliation of being handcuffed and stayed within tow, climbed steps in unison, clearing security doing what he was told to do, and then they sat in a booth at Chili's restaurant. Conway placed his jacket over their arms, which remained cuffed together.

"With only one arm, kid, we're better off ordering something we can eat with one hand," he said. "Things I don't have to cut for you—and things that don't take two hands to hold."

Peck nodded as if he was open to suggestions.

"How about a bowl of chili, some potato salad, a couple of hot dogs and a Coke? Fries too."

Peck nodded his approval.

A plane was something Peck had only seen leaving a vapor trail high over the wetlands. He could not imagine what it would be like to sit in one, much less fly in one. The takeoff had Peck spellbound. His eyes gleamed at the experience, the feel of it, being pushed deep back into his seat. He looked out at a wing and at clouds rolling by, trying to imagine the mystery of how this all happened to him, almost like wondering how a snake or gator can just float on top of the water. The exhilaration of this flying experience seemed to let him forgive slugs in his stomach and wetting his pants in front of others. He'd keep them forever in his memory, though. Nature's way had no option for forgetting, but it appeared he had gotten it behind him for the moment.

"Can I ax you, something, sir?" Peck asked.

"Ask," the private detective said.

"Back there, in jail they was a smell," Peck said.

"It's a county lock up. They call it a holding tank. Folks usually don't shower before getting locked up," Conway said.

"Nah, nah, not inside but from outside," Peck said.

"Outside? Outside of the lockup?"

"*Oui.*"

"Did you say the smells?"

"*Oui.*"

"From outside?"

"*Oui.* What dat smell, you know?"

"Are you meaning like the fishy smell, outside?"

"Dass it. What dat smell, sir?" Peck asked.

"Oh, that, and call me Conway."

"What it is, Conway?"

"Shad," Conway said.

"Shad?"

"Shad."

"You don't say. Shad like row and river catch?" Peck asked.

"Same shad," Conway said.

"They net 'em?" Peck asked.

"They use a dart," Conway said.

"Dart?" Peck asked.

"A dart is a small tiny little thing—looks like a hook but there's no barb on it. Why it ain't no bigger than your little finger's nail. It's called a dart. Shad go upstream by the millions to spawn, just like salmon, but when they're on a spawning run, they don't feed along the way, you see, so they won't bite a hook."

Peck looked at the private detective intently, listening to his story.

"When they swim upstream and they see one of these darts they'll snub it with their snout—push it out of the way. Shad won't feed when they're going upstream to spawn. They snub it away with their snouts and it hooks into them—and that's how they're caught. The dart sticks into their gill or their side, and you reel them in. Oh, they'll put up a fight—jump two, maybe three times."

Peck smiled as he so enjoyed the story of shad.

"I've seen them—big ones over 23 inches—jumping two, three feet out of the water, and they're full of row, you know, the fish eggs."

"T'anks," Peck said.

"Mr. Finch," proclaimed the private detective as if it were a historic moment, "in County, you were on the shores of the great Delaware River. You've heard about the famous Delaware River, haven't you?"

"No sir," Peck said.

"George Washington crossed the Delaware River right there where you were in Trenton."

"For true?" Peck asked.

"Right about where you were in the tank," Conway said.

"Ah," Peck said.

"They're having their annual shad festival now," Conway said. "All up and down the Delaware, from the jetty dam there in Trenton—why they're skinning them in yards, pulling row and cleaning them all around the courthouse where they're being judged."

"T'anks," Peck said. "Good story."

"The fish smell comes from the fryers," Conway said. "They stack 'em high for the taking. It's all for charity or something."

Peck leaned his head back, looked out at the clouds floating by and fell asleep. There was no moon.

CHAPTER 18

TWO UNIFORMED POLICE OFFICERS stood guard in the historic, echoing, marbled entry hall of the Carencro City courthouse. On a distant bench on the north side of the hall sat Sasha (Michelle Lissette). Sasha was wearing a tailored gray pantsuit and jacket, a black satin blouse buttoned to her neck, and conservative heels. Purposely ignoring Peck and Lily Cup directly across the lobby corridor, she thumbed an iPhone, reading and answering emails. There was a Starbucks cup on the bench next to her bag. Sitting a few feet over from Sasha on the same bench was Miss Lavender, director of the hospice in Carencro. Miss Lavender was reading a book. Several feet from Miss Lavender, private detective Conway was sitting with a wrinkled, empty sandwich wrap in one hand, pinching two donuts and a large Styrofoam coffee cup in the other. Several napkins lay on the bench seat beside him. Every time someone would enter or leave the courthouse, the tall brass doors would sound a deep clunk together, like shrimp trawlers bumping a dock coming into port. The whispering of people in the hall echoed like they would inside a basilica.

"You look nice, Peck," Lily Cup said. "Is that a new shirt?"

"Sasha, up bayou in Memphis give it," Peck said.

"Peck, the detectives or the district attorney may try to hassle you and call you Boudreaux Clemont Finch. Just don't let them fluster you," she said.

"Dass my name, cher," Peck said. "I good with it."

"And what's going on here isn't a trial. They're asking a lot of people a lot of questions, trying to find out what happened to Gabe."

"Did Gabe die, did he? You can tell me, cher."

Lily Cup either didn't hear Peck or ignored the question.

"Attorneys aren't allowed in the grand jury room but that's not the point," Lily Cup said. "Remember, they want to learn what you know, not what you don't know. Don't be offering things for them to think about. It could only dig a hole deeper. Don't tell them things they don't ask for."

"I know bait good and trotlines," Peck said. "I be hokay."

What Peck wasn't sharing with Lily Cup was how his treatment in that New Jersey lockup jarred him, and how it reopened memories of times when he was four, five and six, forced to carry bait buckets for the drunkard gator man until his hands bled or his back burned from the sun a tar red so raw he would try to sleep at night sitting up leaning on his shoulder. He has nightmares of a rope tied around him under his armpits being dragged behind a flat boat as bait on alligator hunts—rifle shots over his head—praying someone would pull him in the boat in time. He wasn't sharing how he learned patience by waiting hours on end hiding from gator man in cypress trees watching alligators float like logs without moving a muscle until the time was right. He wasn't sharing how gators must know everything, being they were a million years old and man was fish bait at maybe seventy, eighty.

The grand jury room door opened. A man stepping out let it close behind him. He walked in a gracious pace the length of the hall toward the judge's chambers at the east end.

"Morning, Miss Tarleton," the man said, tipping two fingers on his forehead as a friendly salute, greeting counsel as he passed.

"Good morning, your honor," Lily Cup said.

"Welcome to Carencro," he said.

She watched him walk the hall and into his chambers. "He's the local judge," Lily Cup said. "He was in there telling them he'd be around in case they make a decision on indicting you, if he's needed to set bail."

"Decision?" Peck asked.

"This is a grand jury, Peck. It's not like a jury trial. Behind those doors they can't say you're guilty or innocent. All they can do is say they don't think you should be charged with a crime or they could say they think you should be charged," Lily Cup said.

Peck clenched his fists, as though in fear.

"Just be yourself and tell the truth," Lily Cup said.

"They was asking about murder in New Jersey, cher. Will you be in there with me?" Peck asked.

"I can't go in with you, but I'll be with you all the way," she said.

One of the uniformed officers answered his cellphone. As he talked he walked over to private detective Conway and paused, waiting to finish the call. He leaned and spoke with Conway. Conway stood, and they both walked over to Lily Cup and Peck.

"Counselor Tarleton?" the uniformed officer asked.

"Yes, officer?" Lily Cup asked.

"The grand jury has begun, and I'm to stay here with you and your client while they call everyone in one at a time. Your client will be the last one called."

"That'll be fine. I'll go get some coffee. My treat, would you like a cup officer?" Lily Cup asked.

She stood and picked up her valise and shoulder bag.

"That'd be nice, counselor," the uniformed officer said. "An iced black is fine. Thank you, ma'am."

"Peck," Lily Cup said. "I'll be right back. Like the officer said, if they call you, it will be after everyone else."

"Do they call you?" Peck asked.

"Honey, listen to me," Lily Cup said. "Attorneys aren't allowed in a grand jury room. There's no need to be frightened, just tell the truth."

"Peck, I know it's all pretty secret stuff. I think they try to make it scary. They can't even take notes or minutes in there," Private Detective Conway offered.

"I'll have to cuff him to a bench, counselor," the uniformed officer said. "Regulations, ma'am, in case I get called away."

"That'd be fine," Lily Cup said.

Lily Cup gave a look at Peck as if to try to explain the handcuffs. He simply raised his wrist, offering it for cuffing.

"Private Detective Conway," the uniformed officer said. "You may go in now."

Lily Cup gave Peck a deserving smile of thanks for helping with the handcuffs, turned and headed out the front door to a Starbucks.

Private Detective Conway was the first witness called into the room. The bailiff held a Bible before him and asked him to place his hand on it and swear to truthful testimony.

"Private Detective Conway," the district attorney said. "Do you know why we're here today before a grand jury of Lafayette Parish?"

"No sir," Conway said. "I was fulfilling a portage assignment and asked to appear, but other than what I read on the warrant, I don't know details."

"Private Detective Conway, what if I were to tell you suspicions before this grand jury are those of kidnapping, grand theft, and possibly murder?" the district attorney asked. "Might you see where the observations and opinions of a professionally trained and experienced eye like yourself might be of help in determining a person of interest's likelihood for committing the crimes we've outlined?"

"Yes, sir," Conway said. "I can see that."

"Private Detective Conway, how many years have you been a private detective or in a similar capacity?"

"I tried twice but I did not pass the law boards after I graduated LSU in 1994, so I apprenticed with a bounty hunter and got my license as a private detective in Shreveport. I found the work rewarding and I bought him out last year in May, when he retired."

"Are you active as a bounty hunter?" the district attorney asked.

"I mainly do out-of-state portages—" Conway started.

"They seem to run from Louisiana, don't they, Private Detective Conway?" the district attorney mused.

"—transferring in prisoners, like young Peck, who's sitting out there, thanks to me."

"Young Peck?"

"My portage," Conway said.

"You're of course referring to a Mr. Boudreaux Clemont Finch, is that correct Detective Conway?"

"Yes. His name is Finch, but he preferred I call him Peck."

"Do you always do what a prisoner prefers?" the district attorney asked.

"I try to get along with them, best I'm able," Conway said. "We'll get along if he knows the rules, and if I know his requests are within my power—and it's an easy portage. Two thousand or more miles is quite a spell being handcuffed to a man—bathrooms, restaurants, things like that. Best we get along."

"Private Detective Conway, in your experienced observation could Mr. Finch, or Peck, as you call him, murder a man?" the district attorney asked.

Detective Conway started, thinking.

"In your opinion, of course, detective Conway."

"I don't think so," Conway said.

"You're saying you don't think this man could murder someone."

"Doesn't seem the sort."

"Private detective Conway, could this Peck you brought here from a jail cell in Trenton, New Jersey—could he kidnap someone—anyone, in your opinion?"

"If you mean kidnap, like for ransom or for money?" Conway said.

"Is there any other kind, Detective Conway?"

"Well there are many cases of parents abducting children during divorce proceedings," Conway said.

"I was referring to the more nefarious kidnapping, private detective Conway."

"I don't think he would do a thing like that. No sir, I don't."

"Private detective Conway, if I were to tell you there is a matter of a missing four thousand dollars belonging to the victim that was in this party of interest's care, would that maybe cause you to rethink your position?"

"You mean about Peck?" Conway asked.

"Your position about Peck, yes," the district attorney said.

Private detective Conway scratched his jaw. He reached up onto his bald forehead and scratched. He lowered his eyelids and grimaced with determination.

"No sir, I don't," he said. "I don't think any of that would change my opinion of him one whit."

"Most curious," the district attorney said.

"Well, you asked," Conway said.

"Oh, I'm not questioning your veracity, private detective Conway, not in any manner...but would you please share with this grand jury just what insights you might have that enable you to think of our party of interest as not capable or as unlikely of such crimes? A man you met and were with less than a day?"

"The shad," Conway said.

"Excuse me?" the district attorney asked sarcastically.

Conway sat and waited.

"Did you say, the shad?"

"It was the shad," Conway repeated.

The district attorney swept his arm around as though he was presenting the private detective on a center stage.

"Kindly illuminate the men and women of this grand jury, private detective Conway," the district attorney said.

Sensing a trap but showing in his eyes he was sincere and certainly wanting justice served for the boy in the hall, Conway sat up in his seat.

"It was on the plane when the young man out there—"

"The man you call Peck, Detective Conway?"

"Yes sir, the man I call Peck asked me about the fish smells around the courthouse in Trenton."

"Let me get this straight. Did you say fish smells?"

"Trenton and other places were having their annual shad festival going all around the Delaware River," Conway said. "It's a very popular festival along the historic Delaware, I've heard. The length of it, actually. We were buckled in on the plane waiting for takeoff when he asked me. This Peck. He turned in his seat and looked me right in the eye, and he asked me—I remember he asked— 'back there, Mr. Conway, he said, what was that smell?'—that's sure enough what he asked me."

"Private detective Conway, a prisoner asks about a shad festival—"

"Oh, he didn't know about the festival."

"—a prisoner asks about the smell of fish and you can assume he's incapable of committing a crime?"

"He didn't ask about fish, he asked about the smell."

"On the plane, this Peck out of the blue asked you about a smell."

"He could smell it from his cell," Conway said.

"Ladies and gentlemen," the district attorney said. "This is beginning to sound a bit fishy to me."

"It's the way he did it," Conway said.

"Oh, enlighten us, please continue, private detective Conway," the district attorney said. "We're all ears."

"He did more than ask," Conway said.

The district attorney didn't bother talking; he waited.

"I know he couldn't have done those things because of the way he listened to me," Conway said.

"Things, Detective Conway?"

"Kidnap and murder," Conway said.

"Because of the way he listened to you?"

"I've been doing this for close to thirty years. I've seen it all pretty much. In my line of work, I see up close the kidnappers, murderers, and thieves, see—and one thing I know is they don't want to learn."

"You're saying that murderers and thieves don't—"

"They know it all. Least that's my look on things, anyway. I remember sitting on that plane near half an hour—could a been forty minutes—describing to this Peck fellow what it was like catching a shad—how they had to hit your dart just right; how they'd jump two, maybe three times when they did. I'm telling you as God is my witness, this boy didn't once take his eyes off me while hearing my story, not for one second. I don't think he's your man."

With his back to the detective, the district attorney watched the eyes of the jurors.

"Could money be a motive?" the district attorney asked.

"He had money on him," Conway said.

"Four thousand dollars is unaccounted for, detective Conway."

"He didn't have much, but he had enough to get by. He had a Greyhound travel pass on him."

"I assume travel passes are pricey, detective Conway."

"I don't know, but I would imagine they are."

"A travel pass would take money, Detective Conway."

"A thief doesn't carry a Greyhound travel pass on him."

"And just what does a thief carry?" the district attorney sniped.

"He sure doesn't carry a bus pass," Conway said.

"And your theory is, Detective Conway?"

"He'd steal a car. A thief would steal a car."

"Thank you, private detective Conway. You may step down. Thank you for your insightful testimony."

"Can I say one more thing?" Conway asked.

"You're still under oath," the district attorney said, waving his hand and inviting Conway to speak.

"The boy was as feared and as frozen as a jack rabbit," Conway said.

"What's your point detective Conway?"

"If he was a thief or a killer, he'd have nerves of steel, have tattoos, gold watches, something fancy—a ring, maybe. But he wouldn't listen to a story about catching shad like he was a schoolboy. He has a duffel bag with one pair of jeans, two shirts, a spool of fishing line and some underwear in it. On his person he had pocket money, a bus pass, some handwritten notes and papers."

"Noted, private detective Conway," the district attorney said. "You may step down."

Conway stepped down and walked out through the large door. He held it as Sasha walked in. The district attorney gestured for her to take the stand and she obliged.

The bailiff held the Bible and swore her in.

"Miss Lissette," the district attorney said. "Can you state your name and where you live?"

"My name is Michelle Lissette. I've lived in New Orleans all my life. I attended Tulane. I have a real estate business and primarily deal with Garden District residential sales, rentals or historical restoration."

"Thank you, Miss Lissette," the district attorney said. "Do you know the nature of a grand jury, ma'am?"

"Not really. I think you indict people?"

"A grand jury listens," the district attorney said. "They listen to all known witnesses or parties of interest, and then they decide the viability of a case against someone moving forward. As the district attorney, it would be my decision, after hearing their feedback, as to whether to move a case forward or any other disposition."

"Now I understand," Sasha said. "Thank you."

"Miss Lissette, our interest is anything you might know that would be relevant to the party of interest we have before us in the name of one Boudreaux Clemont Finch and his relationship with one Gabriel Jordan," the district attorney said. "Miss Lissette, are either of these names at all familiar to you?"

"I know them both, Peck and Gabe," Sasha said.

"Please enlighten the grand jury as to your relationship with these men, Miss Lissette."

"Peck is Boudreaux Clemont Finch and Gabe is Captain Gabriel Jordan, retired."

"Continue."

"I met them at Charlie's Blue Note. It's a small neighborhood jazz bar off Frenchman Street near the Quarter. My girlfriend and I sometimes go there to dance. It's safe because Charlie always walks us home. Peck and Gabe came in one night. They had red beans and rice, and a couple of drinks. Gabe drank Dewar's—that's a scotch and Peck drank beer."

"Was there anything suspicious about their behavior?" the district attorney asked.

"No," Sasha said.

"Were you able to observe them throughout their time at Charlie's?"

"I danced with Gabe. He's a very good dancer."

"Would you say you were able to learn his demeanor by dancing with him?"

"In fact, I think we danced until almost midnight."

"Miss Lissette," the district attorney said, "the grand jury is here to listen to evidence given by parties who have had contact with the party of interest. It is in their purview to determine whether in their opinion after listening to your testimony there may or may not be a case going forward against that party."

"A criminal case?"

"That's in their purview, Miss Lissette."

"With those two?"

"That's why we're here, Miss Lissette."

"A case like what?" Sasha asked. "I can't imagine one."

"Miss Lissette," the district attorney said. "It'd serve our interest if you would let me ask the questions."

"Fine with me," Sasha said. "But I think I know those two pretty well, and I can't imagine either of them as bad guys."

"Miss Lissette," the district attorney said, "one of the charges pending on the outcome of this grand jury is that of transporting a person against their will across a state line. Are you aware of any conversations you overheard that would lead you to believe Mr. Jordan was being forced to leave Louisiana against his will, particularly by Mr. Finch?"

"I can do better than that," Sasha said.

"By all means, Miss Lissette. Please illuminate us."

"Peck wasn't even with us when Gabe told me he was going to the Newport Jazz festival in Newport, Rhode Island," Sasha said. "He and Peck were headed there because Gabe wanted to go, not because Peck wanted to go."

"Miss Lissette," the district attorney said, "all well in good, but did you personally witness Mr. Jordan leaving this Charlie's with Mr. Finch?"

"No," Sasha said.

"So, all of this conjecture is supposition on your part, might that be fair to say, Miss Lissette?"

"No," Sasha said.

"So you did see them leaving together, Miss Lissette?"

"Not exactly, if you want me to be exact."

"Miss Lissette, you're trying the grand jury's patience," the district attorney said. "Would you care to explain?"

"I said I didn't see them leaving Charlie's," Sasha said. "But I did see them come out of Charlie's."

"Games with us can be costly and punishable with a contempt of court, Miss Lissette," the district attorney said. "Kindly be warned."

"When Gabe told me he was heading to the Newport Jazz festival, he said they were hitchhiking. I offered to drive them as far as Memphis is all," Sasha said. "I went home and got my car and came back. That's when I saw them coming out of Charlie's."

"So, it was you who drove Gabriel Jordan and Mr. Finch out of state, Miss Lissette?" the district attorney asked.

"Well not that, either," Sasha said. "Gabe liked my Bentley and asked if he could drive. He had a valid license, so I let him. So, you see, Gabe drove himself out of the state of Louisiana in my Bentley—and with Peck asleep in the back seat. If Peck was taking someone across a state line against their will he was not doing a good job of it. He was sound asleep most of the way."

The district attorney dropped his papers on the table on top of his briefcase. He turned in a circle, thinking. He turned again.

"Ladies and gentlemen of the grand jury," he began. "Let's say we're able to corroborate the veracity of this witness. After all, she would appear to have a substantial equity in her local community interest and not be inclined to play with risks. If what she says is the case, and we are to believe her, and also the testimony prior to Miss Lissette, what we might have is a local kidnapping."

"Peck didn't kidnap anyone," Sasha said.

"Young lady, if Peck so much as walked that dying old man out through the gates of the hospice," the district attorney said. "A case for kidnapping might bear listening to."

"I don't know any of that," Sasha said. "All I know is Gabe wanted to go to Newport. He would have tried even without Peck."

The district attorney raised his index finger in the air as if with a thought. "And if this man, one Gabriel Jordan, has deceased," the district attorney said. "This could be involuntary manslaughter. Removing a man from a facility who needs close and constant medical attention. This could be the case, if the man struggled from dementia and has passed."

"Gabe did not have dementia," Sasha said.

"Are you a doctor, Miss Lissette, an expert on dementia?"

Sasha was too upset and angry to cry at the thought of Gabe dying.

"It's not like that," Sasha said wringing her hands.

"Miss Lissette, to your knowledge, is Gabriel Jordan alive or dead?" the district attorney asked.

"I spoke to him two nights ago," Sasha said. "He was alive."

"I ask again, Miss Lissette, is Gabriel Jordan, a man allegedly taken from the protection and safety of hospice care alive or dead?" the district attorney asked.

This time Sasha lifted a tissue from her bag and dabbed her eyes.

"I don't know," she said.

"How long would it take you to determine if Mr. Gabriel Jordan is alive or dead with absolute provable verification from credible witness testimony?"

"Maybe an hour or so," Sasha said.

"Grand jury members," the district attorney said. "I propose we walk to an enjoyable lunch. The county is treating today. We'll give Miss Lissette her hour or so and reconvene back here at one thirty. In the meantime, Miss Lissette, you are under a full gag order not to divulge anything about this line of questioning with any other awaiting witnesses. We'll see you back here at one thirty."

Sasha stepped down from the witness stand and dashed out.

CHAPTER 19

SASHA MADE HER WAY into the hall, letting the grand jury room door close freely behind her. Miss Lavender was still seated on the far wall bench with an open book in hand; Lily Cup, Peck, and one uniformed officer on the bench closest to the grand jury room door. Sasha dashed across the hall, heels spiking cold marble over to the far bench, where she sat down and proceeded to text Lily Cup without looking across the lobby at her.

"Not allowed to talk with anyone about the grand jury," she texted.

"You can if they've released you."

"They haven't."

"Explain."

"In deep shit. I have to prove Gabe is alive."

"So? Call his hotel and see if he answers," Lily Cup texted. "If he does, he's alive. Duh!"

"Not that easy," Sasha texted.

"He's in a hotel, right?"

"Yes."

"Well, if he doesn't answer, ask the front desk if they have seen him this morning," Lily Cup texted.

"I have to have a credible witness," Sasha texted.

"I'll be your witness," Lily Cup texted.

"Can't."

"Why not?"

"Gag order, I can't talk to any witnesses or their attorneys," Sasha texted.

"You have a f#!?ing gag order like that and you don't bother to tell the lead defense attorney about it in your first text?!!!!" Lily Cup texted.

"PULEEZE no drama. Save it for a trial if I fuck this up," Sasha texted. "You know your way around courts. Who can I get on short notice as a credible witness?"

"Now? Today?"

"I have an hour and a half to put it together or else the kid could be in big trouble maybe."

Lily Cup set her phone on the bench, opened her valise and shuffled papers. Then, almost as if it were a stroke of brilliance, she snapped her finger, picked up her phone and started texting again.

"Judge Thibodaux," she texted.

"What's a Judge Thibodaux?" Sasha texted.

"See the door marked 'Chambers'?"

"Where?"

"Down at the end of the hall?"

Sasha looked down the length of the marble hall.

"Not that end, the other end of the hall," Lily Cup texted.

Sasha saw the door.

"That's Judge Thibodaux's office," Lily Cup texted. "He's in there. I saw him."

Sasha smiled, nodding her head.

"Word is he's an old fart— likes tits," Lily Cup texted.

Sasha's smile turned into a cartoon smile.

Sasha stood, straightened her suit coat, saw to it her pants creases were aligned and blouse tucked. She was reaching and tightening the velvet ribbon knot tying her hair back as her phone signaled. She picked it up.

"Watch y'self," Lily Cup texted.

Sasha stood erect, at first as if she was rising to accept the challenge, then let her shoulders droop in thought, knowing what was at stake. Fueled with resolve, she began walking in quick, short steps while unbuttoning a blouse button, then the next button down, then the next, her heels echoing through the grand marble foyer. With her back to Lily Cup and Peck she looked down quickly, assessing whatever cleavage she was able to liberate on short notice, and raised an arm, giving a thumbs-up signal as she pushed the door with the gold leaf lettering marked *Chamber*. The reception area was pecan wood paneled, empty and deep, and rolling films of cigar smoke billowed from an office two doors back. Holding her phone in one hand, her carryall in the other, she made her way down the short hallway and peered in the doorway where the smoke emanated.

"Excuse me?" Sasha queried.

Behind the desk a silver-haired man in a leather wingback crushed his newspaper down with both hands and bug eyes, nearly dropping the cigar from his mouth.

"Excuse me?" Sasha repeated.

"Ma'am?"

"I'm looking for Judge Thibodaux. Are you Judge Thibodaux, by any chance?"

The man took the cigar from his mouth. "Why, yes, I am...I'm Judge Thibodaux, but the lady out front will be more than obliging, I'm certain..."

Sasha took charge and stepped in the office, making her way to the front of the judge's desk. She strategically leaned over and down from a standing position, setting her carryall bag on the floor.

"How may I be of service, young lady?" the judge asked, taking his cigar from one hand and placing it in the ashtray. "Please, take a seat. I'm at your service."

Sasha sat down, leaning forward in the chair.

"Judge Thibodaux, there's no one out front and I know this is short notice—a man as important and as busy as you—but I need a credible witness because if I don't have a credible witness and proof that a certain man is alive by one thirty today there's going to be all kinds of trouble."

"Young lady, does this by chance have to do with any case before me now?" Judge Thibodaux asked anxiously.

Sasha looked at her phone and began thumbing through local restaurant menu pages, answering the judge remotely.

"On? Case? Before you? Oh, no sir, how could it?" Sasha asked.

Sasha stood again and leaned in, offering her hand to the judge. The judge accepted the offer, lingered as he gently shook her hand.

"My name is Michelle Lissette, and I'm in real estate. I've come from New Orleans to get papers in order for a project and to the best of my knowledge you wouldn't be trying any cases down in New Orleans, since it's a different parish and district. Did you know there were 64 parishes in Louisiana, Judge? I just have to prove a man's alive and I could do it myself, but you know how they are. They want me to have a credible third-party witness give a statement, so I need a credible witness to help me, and do you like calamari, Judge?"

Sasha sat down with a bounce.

The judge's head limped forward in anticipation. Then he caught it and paused as his mind caught up.

Oh, I do love calamari—I'm partial to a Béchamel red sauce with just a touch of butter." he said.

As the judge folded his newspaper and spoke on about how much cream should be in the sauce, Sasha touched her phone keys and held it to her ear.

"Drago's Seafood."

"Hello? I'd like two orders of calamari, please."

"Is this a pick up?"

"Can you add a Béchamel sauce with butter and...hold on, please," Sasha said, looking over at Judge Thibodaux.

"How many oysters, Judge?" Sasha asked.

The judge fanned both of his hands open as if he were surrendering in the battle of New Orleans.

"We don't have Béchamel, ma'am, we have a private recipe red sauce for the calamari."

"Send that sauce and send two dozen fresh oysters on shaved ice, horseradish, cocktail sauce—but do not mix them. We'll do it here," Sasha said.

"Two calamari, red sauce on the side, two dozen oysters, anything else?"

"Can you send it over to Judge Thibodaux's chambers, please?"

There was a pause.

"Yes ma'am, we'll bring it right over."

Sasha raised her brow.

"You know where that is?" she asked.

"We know."

"Good, see you soon. Oh, and there's no one out front, so just bring it back here, okay?"

"We'll bring it soon."

Sasha ended the call and held her finger up as if to hold the moment and dialed one more restaurant.

"Antoni's, how may I help you?"

"Hello. You have Italian, right?" Sasha asked.

"Only the best."

"Good, do you have a Béchamel sauce?"

"Of course, we have Béchamel—the best."

"Is it red?"

"It's pink, ma'am. A light pink."

"Can you send a pint of your Béchamel sauce right away?"

"What entree?"

"No entree, just a pint of Béchamel."

"Of course."

"You can? Send it to Judge Thibodaux's office."

"Twenty minutes."

"You know where?"

"We know the judge."

"Just walk on back. There's no one up front."

Sasha set her phone on the table next to her chair.

"You are one popular guy, Judge."

"Are all realtors from New Orleans as scrappy?" the judge asked.

"We have to move quick down there, Judge. We could all be under water at any minute."

"How may I help you?"

"Judge, does your phone do conference?"

"It does."

Sasha stood, leaned over his desk and picked up his phone receiver.

"Nine?" Sasha asked.

"Yes, ma'am. Dial nine for an outside line."

Sasha dialed the Courtyard Marriott in Providence and as it started ringing, she set the receiver down and pushed the conference speaker button.

"Courtyard by Marriott, how may we direct your call," the operator queried.

"Hello. I'm trying to reach a Mr. Gabriel Jordan," Sasha said. "He's a guest there."

"One moment, I'll ring Mr. Jordan's room," the operator said.

Eight rings with no answer and the phone went into voicemail. Sasha hung up, picked up the receiver and dialed again.

"Hold on, Judge," she said.

"Nothing on my docket today, take your time."

"Courtyard by Marriott, how may we direct your call," the operator queried.

"Hello, I just called for a Mr. Gabriel Jordan, and he didn't answer in his room," Sasha said.

"Would you like me to try again?" the operator asked.

"No, no. Could you ask people at the desk if they'd seen him around this morning—maybe getting coffee or catching an Uber? Please? It's important."

Sasha tapped two fingernails impatiently on the desktop, leaning down on one arm, waiting for answers from the conference speaker.

"No one remembers seeing Mr. Jordan this morning," the operator said. "But we have busy mornings with checkout and our continental breakfast. Very busy indeed."

"Thank you," Sasha said. She pushed the button to hang up and sat down.

"Might I ask where you were calling?" Judge Thibodaux asked.

The judge's question was interrupted by the first deliveryman from a restaurant. Sasha handed him her credit card to swipe and pointed at a side conference table for the man to place the bags. She invited the judge over with a welcoming smile. She signed the tab and thanked the deliveryman. As he exited, he was interrupted by the delivery of the Béchamel sauce. Sasha lifted a twenty from her bag and held it up.

"Will this take care of it?" she asked.

"Oh yes, ma'am," he answered. "Hi, Judge," he threw in, snapping the twenty from her hand and leaving.

With calamari and a Béchamel dip and fresh raw oysters on shaved ice, any gathering becomes family in kind. In southern Louisiana, it's almost a religious experience—as sacred as morning beignets with chicory coffee and cinnamon.

"Were you reared in the Big Easy, child?" Judge Thibodaux asked.

"Judge, I was born in a ladies' toilet in Vieux Carré," Sasha said. "Momma lived in Faubourg Lafayette, and she found making it home an inconvenience when her water broke while she was standing in line to get a praline at the oyster bar."

"Oh my," Judge Thibodaux said. "You certainly were christened Mardi Gras early. It's no wonder you have fire in your blood. I can tell you're a woman who controls her own destiny."

"*Jeanne d'Arc était stupide*," Sasha said.

"Young lady, I do understand enough of the French to know without ample reason, my momma, a devoted follower of the church might have suggested you've blasphemed against a holy saint who was publicly burned at the stake, with such sentiment," Judge Thibodaux said.

Sasha swallowed an oyster, smiled, shaking her head a definite no.

"So, tell me, for the record, and in your humble opinion, of course, why was Joan of Arc stupid?" the judge asked.

"She should have peed on the matches," Sasha said.

While it sank in, the judge choked and snorted cocktail sauce into his nose, causing him to stand coughing, laughing, guffawing, gulping water, trying to get in control. Sasha's giggle turned into a nervous tremble as she watched his contortions, hoping he didn't have a heart attack. By the time he got in full control and sat down again all they both could do at first was inhale and then give a loud exhale.

Composure gained with a vocal sigh, the judge picked up a ring of calamari, and asked again, "Just where are you trying to call?"

"Providence, Rhode Island, Judge. My friend is up there going to the Newport Jazz Festival every day all week."

"Those are great fun," Judge Thibodaux said.

"You've been there?"

"The Newport Jazz Festival?" the judge asked."

"Yes."

"Oh, my yes. More than once."

"More than once?" Sasha asked.

"We stayed in Newport the times we went," Judge Thibodaux said.

"We couldn't get him reservations in Newport, Judge. That's why he's in Providence."

"We'd sail the Intercoastal Waterway all the way up. We actually moored in the center of Newport, and we'd jitney to shore daily during the festival. We saw Mel Torme and George Shearing together one night, and so many others. It was a marvelous time. Your friend is fortunate."

"Did you dance?" Sasha asked.

"Oh, my yes, we danced," he said, gazing at a ring of calamari in a memory trance. "My Barbara hated the smell of cigar on my dinner jacket, but how she loved to dance."

"He's there now, Judge, at the festival...the man I have to prove is alive...he probably left the hotel early this morning in Uber," Sasha said. "Oh well—we just missed him."

"He couldn't have," Judge Thibodaux said, looking at his tall floor clock, which was about to chime on the half hour.

"Excuse me?"

"He couldn't have left yet."

"What do you mean, Judge? Did you say he couldn't have?"

The judge held up two oysters, one in either hand, offering one to Sasha, holding his up like a glass of fine wine.

"Let's toast," he said. "A toast to the Newport Jazz Festival and to the music that binds this ruptured nation together and sees that it'll always remember Southern Louisiana."

"Here's to Louisiana," Sasha said.

"Here's to Louis Armstrong," Judge Thibodaux said.

They tipped back, swallowing their horseradish-cocktail oysters whole. Sasha set the shell down and licked her fingers.

"What'd you mean, Judge—you said he couldn't have—like he couldn't have left yet is how you put it? What did you mean?"

"This is a weekday, darlin'."

"So?"

"So, any performances before the festival on three weekdays are in concert halls and private venues, but mostly at night. These are what you might say added attractions, but not the actual Newport Jazz Festival itself—which is presented after regional fans get off from work for the weekend. The weekend is festival time for the all-daytime and late nighttime sitting out under a summer sky or in the tent. The festival is three days away."

"So, there's nothing going on up there this morning, Judge?"

"I wouldn't think so."

"Judge, you are amazing, you blessed, blessed man." Sasha hopped up, stepped around the table, bent down before him and kissed the middle of his forehead, leaving a Lancôme red lipstick mark ablaze.

"Oh my," Judge Thibodaux said.

Sasha stepped behind the judge's desk, lifted the receiver and called the Providence information operator.

"Providence?" Sasha asked. "Connect me with the main downtown police station for Providence, please."

There was a pause.

The judge looked over, a bit puzzled, but his docket was clear. He went back to work on the calamari.

"Hello, I'm calling from the district courthouse in Carencro, Louisiana," Sasha said.

"Yes," Sasha said. "Yes, Louisiana. I need one of your officers to go to the Point Street Bridge. We have reason to believe an elderly gentleman is lost. Can you please send someone there to look for him? He may even be under the bridge."

The answering officer took down Sasha's name (Michelle Lissette), the name of the target, one Gabriel Jordan, and finally the private, unpublished phone number for Judge Thibodaux's desk line that Sasha read off the phone itself. Sasha shared in whispers to the judge that Officer Brandon Kelsey was being assigned to go over to the bridge, and Officer Kelsey would indeed be calling back with a full report. With that Sasha stepped around the desk.

"Officer Brandon Kelsey," Sasha said. "Thank you so much. We'll be here waiting."

Sasha set the phone receiver down.

"I need a drink, Judge Thibodaux, can I buy you a drink?"

Judge Thibodaux stood, dabbing his fingers with a napkin. "I have some sherry or a fine port, or perhaps a smooth Angel's Envy Bourbon," he said.

"Whatever you're having I'll have," Sasha said. "And go ahead and get a fresh cigar, Judge. I like your cigar smoke."

Judge Thibodaux held the bottle of Angel's Envy Bourbon and two tumblers for Sasha to take.

"You pour, I'll get a cigar," he said.

Sasha turned toward him while snipping the end from one she had already pulled from his cigar humidor. She handed it to the judge."

"Such a delight you are," Judge Thibodaux said.

Sasha looked at the clock on her phone and tapped it with her fingernails. She had thirty-five minutes before her time ran out.

As they waited, they mused and talked about family history and the state of the economy, and if they'd ever get the lumber barons to stop supplying big box store chains with Cypress chips for mulch. How tens of thousands of acres of Louisiana cypress trees were being cut and ground into mulch each year while southern Louisiana was sliding into the gulf, causing the annual flooding in New Orleans.

The phone rang. Sasha jumped up and grabbed it on the second ring.

"Judge Thibodaux's office," Sasha said. "Oh, yes, hold on."

Sasha hit the conference button.

"Officer Brandon Kelsey?" Sasha asked. "Is that you?"

"It is me, Miss Lissette," Officer Brandon Kelsey said. "We have found and identified—picture ID and Social Security card—your man, one Gabriel Jordan, alive and well."

Sasha reached for a tissue.

"Was he under the bridge?" Sasha asked.

"Under the bridge, Miss Lissette, just as you suggested he would be," Officer Brandon Kelsey said.

The judge leaned toward the desk.

"Officer, this is Judge Thibodaux, Carencro, Louisiana District Court. Officer Kelsey, what is your station's ID and may we ask your badge number, for our records?"

"Providence Central, Judge," Officer Brandon Kelsey said. "My badge number is 4S014, and I'm a sergeant, Your Honor."

"Thank you, Officer Kelsey," Judge Thibodaux said. "And for the record again, did you make a positive ID on this person?"

"Yes, Your Honor," Officer Brandon Kelsey said. "Physical, picture ID and Social Security."

"And do you find him in visibly good health?" Judge Thibodaux asked.

"I do, Judge," Officer Brandon Kelsey said. "He was sitting under the bridge with others, listening to one of the locals play his saxophone."

"Thank you, Officer Kelsey. Will you kindly fax me a report of this when you get back to your station?"

"I will, your honor."

The judge gave him the fax number.

"Your honor, Mr. Jordan would like to use my phone to speak," the officer said. "Would that be permissible, sir?"

"Of course," Judge Thibodaux said. "Put him on."

"Sasha?" Gabe shouted.

"He calls me that sometimes," Sasha whispered with a grin.

"Hi honey," Sasha said. "How's the festival?"

"When's he coming?" Gabe asked.

"Gabe, I thought he only played the sax after dark?" Sasha asked.

"All day and almost all-night during festival week. This city is packed. He's here now," Gabe said. "When is Peck coming?"

"Soon," Sasha said. "Maybe tomorrow."

"Sasha, I've been thinking a lot, and I want you to do something for me," Gabe said. "You're going to need a witness. Can you get a witness, darlin'? You can call me at the hotel later, when you have one."

The judge winked at Sasha.

"I've got one here and now. What's up?"

"You have a witness there with you on the phone?" Gabe asked.

"Sitting here with me," Sasha said. "A good one."

"This is as good a time as any, let me get something out of my pocket I wrote down," Gabe said. "Okay, here goes."

Gabe cleared his throat on the speaker and began to read.

"I, Gabriel Jordan, being of sound mind do bequeath all my worldly possessions, holdings, pensions, and financial accounts to Boudreaux Clemont Finch, currently residing in Carencro, Louisiana..."

Sasha broke into tears.

"And I want it all in a trust for him effective immediately and I name one Michelle Lissette as the sole trustee to see he has a real home and he gets his GED, into college and a degree, at which time there should be more than enough to get him started with a shrimp boat or a small farm. I am Captain Gabriel Jordan, retired, and Officer Brandon Kelsey here is my witness on this end."

There was silence.

"Well?" Gabe asked.

"I don't have the words," Sasha said.

"Well, is it legal?" Gabe asked.

"I'll have it typed up, he'll have to sign it and it'll be good to go," Judge Thibodaux said.

The judge then gave her a thumbs-up.

"It'll be legal," Sasha said. "I'll fax it to your hotel, you sign it."

Gabe may have pumped a victory fist in the air, knowing it was legal, as the saxophone wailed in the background "When Sunny Gets Blue" in celebration. It flowed from the conference speaker, and tears rolled down Sasha's cheeks.

"Sasha?" Gabe asked.

"I'm still here."

"Go find that peckerwood and tell him to sign me out of that coffin and come up and listen to some jazz and drink some wine."

"I promise," Sasha sobbed into the phone. "I love you, Gabe."

"Baby, you should have heard the harmonica trio last night," Gabe said. "They played Scott Joplin for two hours. Oh, my god—do you remember the old Harmonicats, or are you too young?"

"I'll call you tonight," Sasha said. "It'll be late. Love you."

She hung up.

Sasha walked over to the judge, in tears. She motioned him with a repeated swirling turn of her hand to stand up. He stood and she gave him a look and a long, warm hug. She took her tissue and rubbed the lipstick from his forehead and cheek and kissed him on the neck.

"You are the best, Judge Thibodaux. You are a wonderful man."

"Thank you for a delightful morning," Judge Thibodaux said. "My recorder picked up everything and once that officer's fax comes through, I will have all the papers drawn up, the will and everything. I'll see you get it in New Orleans. You see it gets signed before a Notary."

"I don't know how to thank you," Sasha said.

"You might save a dance for me when I come down for my monthly Brennan's breakfast sabbatical."

"I promise that dance. There's a place off Frenchman Street."

"I look forward to it and will wait with bated breath."

"Judge, I need one last little favor. I have to get something signed by you saying you know Gabe is alive."

The judged looked over at Sasha, contemplated and smiled.

"I'll do better than that, little lady," Judge Thibodaux said. "Walk with me over to that grand jury, and I'll tell them personally." Judge Thibodaux took his robe from a coat hanger, swirled it around behind him and put it on.

"You knew about the...you know...me and the grand jury?"

"Not at first, young lady, but when certain names were bantered about over calamari and oysters, it all started to become more familiar," the judge said.

"Why the robe, Judge?" Sasha said. "It's not a court, is it?"

"Batman to the rescue," he said.

Sasha closed her eyes and rested her head down on the judge's shoulder. She gave him a squeeze.

"I thought judges and attorneys weren't allowed in a grand jury room, Judge."

"We aren't—as spectators—no law against interruption. Now we'd best start walking that long hall, Michelle," Judge Thibodaux pointing to his clock. You barely have seven minutes left."

CHAPTER 20

"HELLO?" Gabe asked.

"Did I wake you, sweetie?" Sasha asked.

"What time is it?"

"Eleven thirty here, so it's after midnight for you."

"I was reading a book," Gabe said. "A northern white boy in 1953 sees a young black girl in trouble in Little Rock, and he works up the nerve to ask Ernest Hemingway to help him help her."

"I'm reading mail," Sasha said. "Street's lousy with drunks."

"Did you tell him?" Gabe asked.

"I think you should be the one to tell him," Sasha said. "He'll be there with you tomorrow."

"Is that when his bus gets in?"

Sasha sat straight up, hand over her gaping mouth.

"Oh, my God, you don't know," Sasha said.

"Know what, baby?" Gabe asked.

"The hospice put a warrant out for Peck."

"What? When?"

"Last week. They only found him two days ago on a bus."

"What on earth?" Gabe shouted.

"After you left the hospice, they saw the blood on his hands and when he disappeared they thought he kidnapped and killed you, and the district attorney had him arrested and pulled off his bus up in Maryland or New Jersey or somewhere. It was awful, Gabe."

"This all happened today?"

"Yesterday and today, Gabe. I swear it's been a nightmare."

"Are you pulling one on me, darlin'?"

"As God is my judge, Gabe. That's what yesterday was all about. I had to prove to a grand jury you were still alive. They were trying to pin kidnapping and murder charges on him. It's why the judge was in the room with me as a witness when I got you on the phone."

"What?" Gabe asked.

"I'm so sorry I completely forgot to tell you. I wasn't allowed to talk to anyone about it or I would be held in contempt of court."

"This is like a bad dream," Gabe said.

"Tell me about it," Sasha said. "More like a nightmare from hell."

"All this happened yesterday?"

"Today, here, we're an hour behind you," Sasha said. "They were talking involuntary homicide for Peck if I couldn't prove you were alive. It's been a nightmare for the past two days. Lily Cup represented him. She was good."

"So, how's Peck?" Gabe asked. "Is everything cleared now?"

"Thanks to you, you sweet, sweet man," Sasha said. "And to a judge I owe a dance to."

"My baby," Gabe said. "What would we ever do without you?"

Sasha pulled tissues from the box and dabbed her eyes. "I miss you, Gabe."

"You never told me—is he back on a bus?" Gabe asked.

"No. We have an ID for him now, so I'm putting him on a plane in Lafayette early. He'll be there tomorrow."

"Is he with you?" Gabe asked.

"Lily Cup drove him to the hospice in Carencro after the grand jury today," Sasha said. "He wanted to mow their lawn and pick up the place. I'll get him from his saw blade shanty in the morning and take him to the airport."

"Sombitch wanted his trotline," Gabe mused.

"That too, I'm sure."

"You must be exhausted."

"I could use a martini."

"How about a dance, my darlin'?" Gabe asked.

There was a long, quiet pause. Sasha's knuckles were rolled on her lips. She thought of her dying friend, alone in the night and so far away as tears streamed down her cheeks and chin.

"You need to bond with Peck," Sasha said. "This will be a good time for you two to talk."

"You're one amazing, unselfish woman," Gabe said. "I'm blessed you're in my life now, and God knows I love my butterfly—but you fill my soul, my friend."

Her mind lost in a moment—Sasha wept into the phone.

Gabe placed a marker in his book and set it down. With the receiver to his ear he leaned over and poured a cold cup of coffee. He was stalling for time as he thought. What would Captain Jordan do?

"Okay, okay," Gabe said, as though he just called a meeting to order.

"What?" Sasha asked.

"Here's the plan."

Sasha perked, eyes widened as if she had been awakened.

"Yes?"

"The festival is in three days. The big finale is under the tent."

Sasha wrenched her eyes with Gabe's use of the word *finale*.

"And?"

"Easy. I want you up here for the big finale," Gabe said.

"Gabe, I don't think I..."

"And I don't want any arguments."

"You're up to something, I can tell," Sasha said.

"I need you here to watch after Peck while I see a doc."

"Are you worse?" Sasha asked.

"No," Gabe said. "I've met two doctor partners who want to put me through the ropes at their clinic. I don't put much hope in it but thought maybe I'd check it out."

"Where did you meet them?" Sasha asked.

"One plays a good sax, and we met sitting next to each other at an exhibition concert. His partner had surgery during the concert, so I met him at another time, during the Scott Joplin celebration."

"Who are they again?"

"They're specialists," Gabe said. "I was telling them how I was on borrowed time and they told me no one was ever on borrowed time, and they'd like to have a look."

"You always run away from doctors Gabe."

"I think I could trust these two, darlin'."

"Oh, my God," Sasha said.

"Woman, get on a plane and come dance with old Gabe."

"Only if you promise to go see them."

There was a long pause.

"I promise."

"Okay, I'll come."

"My baby."

"Make me room reservations. I'll see you in two days. Meantime I have to go talk to some people, change a few things around."

"Go, darlin', I'll wait here for Peck all day tomorrow if I have to."

They hung up.

Sasha made it over to Charlie's Blue Note just after midnight. Lily Cup was sitting at the bar with a cigar and a glass of port.

"No rye tonight?"

"No court tomorrow, I'm on vacation."

"Would you put that stinky thing out?" Sasha asked, climbing on to a barstool.

"It's not lit," Lily Cup said.

"Charlie, a martini please, darling?" Sasha said.

"Where've you been?" Lily Cup said. "Why're you looking so...like that?"

"I've been at the office. I wanted to tell you you've been great. I'm so proud of you and Gabe says thanks for helping Peck. It's pro bono and everything, right?"

"Oh, you'll pay for it," Lily Cup said.

"I'm sure I will."

"I need to borrow a Caddy SUV to go to an Ole Miss game."

"This summer?" Sasha asked.

"No, this fall when they start up playing. Bunch of friends have been talking about going."

"The keys are in my desk anytime you need it."

"What'd you do in there today?"

"Where?"

"With Judge Thibodaux. How'd you pull it off—get him to virtually cause a shutdown of a grand jury?"

"Oh, that. I don't know."

"That's bullshit."

"He listened to reason, I guess, and came to our rescue."

"You mean he wasn't a dirty old man?"

"He was a perfect gentleman."

"Old tit man, a gentleman? Give me a break."

"Oh, the judge enjoyed a casual glance at my girls, but other than that, not a lewd word or unwelcomed gesture."

"Imagine that—the word on the street is—"

"He was a perfect gentleman."

Lily Cup lighted her cigar.

"We enjoyed a lovely brunch and some smooth bourbon, a sipping whiskey."

"He didn't even come on?" Lily Cup asked.

"We talked about saving the cypress trees. We talked about the best seasonings for a good Béchamel. We even talked about how he and his wife loved to dance before she died."

"You just can't listen to some people," Lily Cup said. "They just talk. They like gossip. Here I thought he was an old rake."

"Everybody sees things differently," Sasha said. "I learned it in real estate."

"How's that?"

"A husband will want a house because it's close to his work and the trees are mature; the wife will want it because of the schools, and she smelled a chocolate cake in the oven; a kid will want it because it has a lock on his bedroom door."

"It's all pretty simple," Lily Cup said. "People talk gets involved and fucks everything up."

"Pretty much," Sasha said.

The two sat at the bar sipping drinks for another half hour. They didn't speak a word. They would offer gestures. They would watch people dancing in the reflection of the mirror on the wall. They'd known each other since—Sasha says since six; Lily Cup says she exaggerates and that they were five. They'd been through school together; they'd been through boyfriends and breakups together, heartaches and lost relatives. They knew what they had done for Peck and for Gabe. They knew they had done it because it was who they were.

"What's next for Peck, ya think?" Lily Cup asked.

"Gabe's leaving him everything," Sasha said.

"What's that mean?"

"He made out a will."

"Everything?"

"I didn't see you to tell you."

"Does he even have anything?"

"He's been collecting Social Security and Army pension for a lot of years. He's a saver."

"That makes good karma," Lily Cup said.

"It was in the stars," Sasha said.

"They really love each other."

"Yep," Sasha said.

"You could see it," Lily Cup said.

"Peck worships the man. Gabe's like the father he never had."

"Is Gabe just going to, like, turn it all over? Just give it to him?"

"I'm the executor," Sasha said. "It'll be in a trust. We'll get him in school and maybe college or trade school."

"Think Peck will want to do all that?"

"He says he does."

"That's good, then, right?"

"Yep."

Sasha took a sip of her martini.

"Maybe we can use Peck. What say we pay him to clean our offices. We'll cancel the service we have now," Sasha said.

"He'll be able to afford an apartment," Lily Cup said.

"You know what it means, don't ya?"

"No, what does it mean?"

"Just means now he's family, you can't fuck him."

"What?"

"He's family now. You can't fuck him."

"Why, I never—!"

"Now, now, now, girlfriend," Sasha said. "Don't be bullshitting a bull-shitter."

"You don't know what you're talking about," Lily Cup growled.

"You seem to forget, girlfriend, I saw him nailing your ass right back there in that bathroom—you were three sheets to the wind, screaming for Jesus."

"You did? I was? I didn't think anybody…"

"You might have pulled it off in the men's room, but to walk into the ladies' room and see his pants down around his knees and that fine ass of his pumping between your turkey legs—"

"Shut up. No way."

"—his head bumping the Tampon dispenser…"

"Okay, okay—enough!" Lily Cup said.

They each took a sip of their potable while staring at each other, a reflection in the mirror behind the bar.

"If I can't fuck him again, you surely can't, that's for damn sure."

"I've never—" Sasha started.

"Yeah, right— I still have the pic you texted me from Memphis of his schlong."

"Oh, that," Sasha said.

"I'm not saying you did or didn't, but you can't fuck him now."

"That's right," Sasha said, in a proper, responsible tone of voice. "We can't fuck Peck—I suggest you write it on your wrist so when you drink your rye you won't forget."

"I can be a lady," Lily Cup said.

Sasha furrowed her brow looking at the cigar in Lily Cup's hand. Lily Cup huffed a scowl in return.

"I'll have you remember, Michelle Lissette, that I got a certificate of achievement at Mrs. Winston's finishing school that summer and you didn't."

"That was well over thirty years ago."

"It's framed and on my bedroom wall if you ever want to see it."

"Are you going to keep bringing that up forever?"

"What? Me bring up Mrs. Winston walking in on you holding your panty band out, showing yourself to Hank and Kenneth Buchanan?" Lily Cup asked.

"I lost a bet."

"You lost a bet? Oh, that's rich."

"I bet that Hank couldn't get Mariah Randall to kiss him," Sasha said.

"Some bad bet, they married each other after college," Lily Cup said.

"At least I pay my bets."

"At least I have the good sense to know propriety and social mores," Lily Cup said. "I shan't think of fucking Peck ever, ever again. It hasn't so much as entered my mind."

"That's what you said about Kenneth Buchanan," Sasha said.

The two looked into the mirror through several sips, savoring their memories, listening to the music, perhaps letting the events of the day unwind in their minds while Charlie emptied a bottle in Lily Cup's glass.

"So, would a blowjob be out of the question?" Lily Cup asked.

Sasha spit her olive, snorted four short gravelly snorts, pounding one fist on the bar, the other hand shaking her full martini glass loose from her fingertips up, over and behind the bar, shattering it on the back wall below the mirror. Her forehead now on the bar, her nostrils writhing in snorts and gasps of laughter.

Lily Cup reached into Sasha's handbag and "borrowed" her credit card, holding it in the air.

"Charlie?" Lily Cup asked. "Check please?"

CHAPTER 21

GABE WAS LIGHTLY SNOOZING when there was rapping on the door.

"Just a minute," he said.

The old man got to his feet, stepped over to the door in his socks, and pulled it open. Young Peck stood in the hall with a grin. The fish out of water was learning the trotlines and snoods of a completely new world barely a week old to him. A world outside the bayous he always called home. He was learning of a world filled with fears and surprises. At this moment, however, he was taking delight in that he had taken his first ever flight alone and managed to get to the hotel from the airport in a strange city.

He was delighted to see his friend once again.

"How y'all are, Gabe?"

Gabe grabbed his arm and pulled him for a hug.

"My brother," Gabe said. "My brother."

"What I'm gonna did is take care of you now," Peck said.

They stepped into the room and Peck dropped his duffel.

Gabe was an old soldier. He wanted to hear how Peck caught the pill robber and knife stabber, but he knew army debriefings, and he knew the story would come in its own time. Right now, he just wanted to greet his friend.

"Gabe, I flied a whole *dix* states. Nothing to it, kind of. Lewisana is how you call the Pelican state all the way to this here Providencial, Rhode Island," Peck said.

"That's right," Gabe said. "That's right. Ten states."

"Whoo!" Peck said.

"Peck, where'd you pick up all those fanciful names? And it's Providence, not Providencial."

"Providence, Rhode Island," Peck said. "I knowed that."

"Did you figure it out yourself?"

"Nah, nah. A lady told me, dass for true," Peck said. "I told her lots of land down there under the plane, and she say *dix* states we fly over and she say I'm going to told you about them."

"A lady taught you all that in that short amount of time?" Gabe asked.

Peck grinned.

"And you remembered it just like that?" Gabe asked.

"Dass for true, Gabe. I like to did dat, learning like dat."

Gabe stepped to the coffee urn and poured two cups. He handed one to Peck.

"*La dame parlait français,*" Peck said

"The lady spoke French?" Gabe asked.

"*Oui,*" Peck said.

"Was she traveling alone?"

175

"*Trois*, ah— how you say, t'ree of dem I'm t'inking."

"Three?"

"*Oui*, t'ree. Dass it."

"Peck, I couldn't love you more if you were my own son, I hope you know."

"Makes Peck proud, dass for true," Peck said.

"I'm going to ask you something, son, but it'll have to be in English, I'm not up on my French as I should be."

"Ax," Peck said.

"Now it doesn't matter one way or another, but can you count...you know...do you know numbers, son?" Gabe asked.

Peck's eyes looked as if he knew it was a test he was willing to take because he respected Gabe too much to mislead him. He demonstrated his number skill limitations in his own way. He handed Gabe his coffee cup to hold and reached in a pocket, pulled out an assortment of bills, selected four and stuffed the balance back in his pocket. He held them up one at a time.

"One dollar," Peck said. "Five dollar, ten dollar, twenny dollar."

"That's good," Gabe said. "That's real good, my brother."

Peck grinned.

Gabe held up three fingers. "How many is this, Peck?"

"*Trois*," Peck said.

Gabe held up seven fingers. "Do you know how many this is?"

"*Sept*," Peck said.

"No problem, no problem," Gabe said. "Let's try it another way. Hold your hands up in the air," Gabe said.

"Hanh?"

"Go on, hold your hands up," Gabe said. "You've got the bills down pat, now I'm going to show you how easy counting in English is."

Peck raised both hands in the air.

"Spread your fingers," Gabe said.

Peck spread the fingers of both hands.

"Hold them steady."

Gabe touched each finger and thumb in turn and counted.

"One, two, three, four, five, six, seven, eight, nine, ten," Gabe said. "Now you do it. You count them."

Wiggling each finger in turn, Peck recited.

"*Un, deaux, trois, quatre, cinq, six, sept, huit, neuf, dix.*"

Peck grinned, kept his hands up, encouraging Gabe to do it again.

"One, two, three, four, five, six, seven, eight, nine, ten," Gabe said.

Peck shook his fingers in the air as though he could feel knowledge entering his brain.

"*Encore*," Peck said.

"One," Gabe said.

"One," Peck repeated.

"Two," Gabe said.

"Two," Peck repeated.

"Three," Gabe said.

"Three," Peck repeated.

"Four," Gabe said.

"Four," Peck repeated.

Two grown men stood in the middle of the hotel room and counted together from one to ten eleven different times. By the eleventh time Peck could recite the numbers one to ten in English on his own and in order. He was beside himself. He was like a boy with an ice cream treat. The look on his face was almost as if it was his first flight in a plane alone, challenging him not ever to be afraid again, to demand more from his mind, to explore the worlds that had been shut out for him in the past from ignorance. He kept repeating one through ten in English, and the more he repeated them, the faster he could say the numbers.

"Wait, Gabe, look what I'm going to did."

Peck pulled bills from his pocket and sorted out a small pile of singles. One at a time he dropped them on the bed as he counted.

"One, two, three, four, five, six, seven," Peck said.

Gabe reached to shake Peck's hand. It was an eye-to-eye shake, like a proud poppa and son shake neither would forget.

"Okay, that's the lesson for today," Gabe said. "I'm proud."

"I like dat," Peck said. "I like to did dat."

"Put your money away," Gabe said. "I had some time on my hands yesterday, so I bought a few things. Open the shades so we can see them in the daylight."

Peck pulled the shades and moved his duffel to the footstool. Gabe pulled the top bureau drawer under the television, lifted out three plastic shopping bags and handed them to Peck.

"Here's a couple of Polo shirts, cargo shorts, a belt, and some leather boat-deck moccasins. I got twelves, Peck. What size foot do you have, son?" Gabe asked.

Peck shrugged his shoulder, leaned and pulled a sneaker off. He held it up and pointed to the numeral 12 on the inside of the shoe. Gabe saw the number, and Peck shrugged his shoulders again, as though he couldn't read the number.

"*Difficile*," Peck said. "*Douze?*"

"Oh, I get it," Gabe said. "You can't read it in English. It's twelve."

Gabe took the shoe from Peck's hand, looked at the number and contemplated how best he might teach Peck how to read it. He handed the shoe back.

"*Douze*," Gabe said. "*Douze* is twelve."

"Ah," Peck said.

"Another lesson for another day," Gabe said. "I'll be down in the lobby, getting some air. You try on anything you'd like and meet me there, and we'll go to lunch, and then we'll head over to Newport for the festival," Gabe said. "Take your time."

"I be down," Peck said.

"Peck," Gabe said, "I'm taking you to a diner two blocks from here. Only seats maybe twenty people. They have the best chicken pot pie and steamed corn on the cob with a block of butter to rub it on. Son, I'm telling you, it'll melt in your mouth."

Gabe arranged for Uber to be at the hotel at three for their ride to Newport. Before leaving they walked to the diner, Gabe pointing out Providence landmarks and downtown attractions, especially the river. As they entered the diner, the owner welcomed Gabe with a "good morning, Captain," and Gabe found his favorite booth empty and gave Peck his pick of the seats.

"I can only eat half of their chicken pot pie. I'm good for two ears of corn, but if you're getting pot pie, I'm going to ask them to put half of mine on top of yours."

Peck was open to any proposition when it came to food. He was celebrating having made it through an ordeal with the law he still didn't fully comprehend, but now he was with his friend.

Gabe placed the order for the food and coffee.

"I want to tell you something," Gabe said. "Do you know up in that hotel room you learned in ten minutes what it would take a youngn' a week to learn in school?"

"For true?" Peck asked.

"Ten minutes," Gabe said. "Now why do you suppose nobody's taken the time to teach you basics like counting in English? It boils my grits, it does—selfish bastards."

"Maybe nobody ain't had the ten minutes, Gabe, dass for true," Peck said.

"Try the corn," Gabe said. "Rub it in butter, get some pepper on it."

The two busied themselves.

"That's all going to end here and now, my friend," Gabe said.

"What you mean?" Peck asked.

"Sasha knows," Gabe said.

"Knows?" Peck asked.

"She wanted me to be the one to tell you," Gabe said. "I've gone and adopted you."

"Hanh?"

"I'm going to put you in school, help you get a driver's license. Hell, maybe you can even start a crabbing or shrimping business someday."

"Dass for true, Gabe?"

"It all starts here and now, my brother. You good with that?"

"I don't want to forgot nothing, Gabe," Peck said. "Can you told me dat again?"

"It's not a legal adoption, Peck, but you're twenty-four, and I'm an old man and I reckon a handshake between us is all we need to tell the world we're family—that is, if you're good with me being family, son."

"I'm good with dat," Peck said.

"From now on, you're going to a tutor and get your high school diploma," Gabe said. "You'll learn how to read and write and how to drive, and you're not going to stop learning until you want to, and from the looks of it what you learned flying a whole ten states up here, you've only just begun."

"T'anks, Gabe. T'anks."

"Eat your pie before it gets cold."

Peck's eyes were a wondrous gaze, staring at Gabe's that had nothing but truth in them. Peck stuffed a forkful of chicken and carrot in his mouth. Not taking his eyes off Gabe, he chewed, swallowed, and took a sip of coffee in thought.

"What about lawn mowin'?" Peck asked.

"Witch can mow her own goddam—" Gabe started. He caught himself. He had to set an example for his new student.

"They'll do fine without you," he said. "Sasha will call them and see they pay you what they owe you."

"Is school hard to did? Do you for real t'ink...?"

"Peck," Gabe said. "Slide me four sugar packets, son."

Without thinking, Peck lifted the sugar packets from the silver bowl, counted out four and slid them over the table, mouthing in turn a one, two, three, four, as he pushed each. As soon as Gabe stopped them with his palm they both looked up at each other and smiled.

"See how easy learning is, son?" Gabe asked. "We'll get your coon-ass gibberish as good as your French— why hell, you could be governor or something someday."

Peck beamed.

"Those two ears are yours, my brother," Gabe said. "Get butter."

He sipped his coffee.

The Uber ride to Newport was, for Peck, a chance to take in every detail and nuance of a world new to him. For the first time he was in a land where it snowed regularly in the winter; where they ate a northern cod caught in nets more than they did bayou southern catfish caught on poles or trotlines.

Gabe reached a folded twenty-dollar bill over the seat to the driver and asked him to take the extra time to show them around the historic city, the rambling palatial mansions, the ocean-front, the grass tennis courts, and churches dating back to the pilgrims. Peck took it all in, this time not as a hunter or predator he had to be growing up in marshland wilds and surviving in the bayou, but this time as the student awakened in him.

CHAPTER 22

GABE RESERVED A CAR AND DRIVER for the afternoon. He had been in New England during his early army days and enjoyed sharing his memories of it with Peck, the sights of Newport. Peck watched from the moving car's window, point a finger and count things—up to ten of them—as they'd drive by: stop signs, boats in a bay, people strolling on sidewalks. They heard music, had the car stop and wait as they sat on the stoop of an open door listening to a jazz piano competition in a filled studio hall. After hearing three players, Gabe looked at his watch and they headed back to Providence. It was on the way when Gabe thought he could make use of the drive time and help Peck tackle *th* sounds. He was inspired by Peck's ability to pronounce properly the word *three* when he counted out loud. As they drove into Warwick, he attempted to back into a pronunciation topic.

"Peck," Gabe asked. "Why is it you say *three*, and not *t'ree*?"

"Hanh?" Peck asked.

"You say three—like when you count, you say one, two, three," Gabe said. "Why is it you don't say one, two, t'ree? Just curious."

Peck squirmed like a child who had to go to the bathroom. "Ain' *three* right, Gabe?"

"Count to ten for me," Gabe said.

"Hanh?"

"Go ahead, count it out in English. I'll show you what I mean."

Peck looked warily from the corner of his eye, as if he were about to walk into the barbed hooks of a trotline. "One, two, three, four, five, six, seven, eight, nine, ten," Peck said. "Are you funnin' at me, Gabe?"

"Say *three*, Peck," Gabe said.

"Three," Peck said.

"Perfect. Now see, when you say *three,* you don't say *t'ree*," Gabe said. "Now say it again: *three.*"

"Three," Peck said.

"Okay, now say this: 'Look at that truck over there.'"

"What?" Peck asked.

"Go on, say it. Say, 'Look at that truck over there.'"

"Look at dat truck over dare," Peck said.

The driver stared at them in the rearview mirror.

"You mind watching the road, Robert?" Gabe asked.

Gabe turned to Peck.

"Peck, say the word, thanks."

"T'anks," Peck said.

181

"Peck, this time try saying this one. Say, 'Look at *three* trucks over *three* miles.'"

"Hanh?" Peck asked.

"Just try it. Say, 'Look at *three* trucks over *three* miles,'" Gabe said.

"Look at *three* trucks over *three* miles," Peck said.

"See, you can do it. You can do the *th* sounds. Once more: 'Look at three trucks over three miles.'"

With an accomplished grin on his face, Peck repeated, "Look at *three* trucks over *three* miles."

"So, if *three* isn't *t'ree*, then doesn't it make sense that *that* isn't *dat*, and *they* isn't *dey and thanks isn't t'anks*?" Gabe asked.

Peck looked as if he might be open to listening to the question again for clarification. Not certain he'd broken through, Gabe scratched his head, searching for another approach. Peck watched the agony Gabe seemed to be in, smiled sympathetically at his friend's good intentions and opted to put him out of his misery.

"You dance, old man," Peck said. "Let Peck do the t'inkin'."

Gabe smiled and pointed at the front window.

"Look yonder, Peck," Gabe said. "Look who's here."

Sasha was strolling in front of the hotel, her cellphone to her ear. She had no bag visible.

"No bags. Looks like she's checked in or can't stay," Gabe said.

The Uber car circled toward an unloading space.

"Pull over there, Robert," Gabe said. "We'll get out."

Sasha saw Peck stepping out of the car and smiled, holding up a finger for more time to finish her phone call. Gabe told his driver they'd be calling him tomorrow.

Sasha clicked her phone off, gave Peck a hug around his neck and then Gabe. She held Gabe tightly, motionless, without a word said between them. When they finally let go, she stepped back and became all business.

"I want the number for those doctor guys," she said, holding her hand out.

"Well hello to you too," Gabe said, with a frown.

"Give it," Sasha said. "I want their names and numbers."

Gabe dug into his pocket.

"Can I show you something we learned today?" Gabe asked.

"Sure," Sasha said. "But no stalling. Give me their numbers."

"Peck, show Sasha how you can count to ten."

Gabe handed a business card to Sasha. Sasha looked at the card then impatiently up at Peck.

"One, two, three, four, five, six, seven, eight, nine, ten," Peck said.

"And?" Sasha asked.

"Peck can count in English," Gabe said. "He counts from one to ten. Want to see it again? Watch."

"One, two, three, four, five, six, seven, eight, nine, ten," Peck said.

Sasha looked at the card in her hand again and then up at Peck.

"Does he make you 'arf' like a seal and throw you a fish every time you do it?" Sasha asked.

Peck snorted a goofy, guttural guffaw. Gabe smirked in defeat.

"You two get lost," Sasha said. "I have some calls to make."

"Are we doing dinner tonight?" Gabe asked.

"Will the sax man be under the bridge tonight?" Sasha asked.

"He'll be there," Gabe said.

"Then we're doing takeout," Sasha said. "Anything you want, but we're eating under Point Street Bridge."

"He knows you'll be in town," Gabe said.

"Good," Sasha said.

Sasha held her opened hand pointing toward the hotel doors and waited for Gabe and Peck to go through them.

"I'll be up in a minute."

She walked to a park bench pressing numbers on her phone.

"Fineman Docherty Clinic," a voice answered.

"Hello, my name is Michelle Lissette, and I'm looking for a Doctor Michael Docherty."

"Doctor Docherty is not in."

"Do you know when he'll be back?"

"Doctor Docherty is gone for the day."

"Do you know if Doctor Larry Feinman is in?"

"He is."

"He is?" Sasha asked. "May I speak with him, please?"

"This is Doctor Feinman."

"You're Dr. Feinman?" Sasha asked. "Hello Dr. Feinman, my name is Michelle Lissette, and a friend, Gabe Jordan, told me about meeting you and your partner and I'm in town and wanted to see if you were serious about wanting to check him out like he said you told him you were. Were you serious?"

"We're both quite fond of Gabe, and yes we're serious."

"Good," Sasha said. "How soon can you do it?"

"We'll look at the schedule in the morning; it might be a few weeks out."

"Weeks?" Sasha asked.

"Typically, we book up several weeks in advance. I'll look in the morning and see what's available."

"Can't you do it any sooner? I mean it was a wonderful gesture on your part, but can't it be done sooner?"

"By sooner, just what did you have in mind? Our schedules are full."

"How about tonight?" Sasha asked.

Dr. Feinman snickered into the phone.

"Could you do it tonight?" Sasha asked.

"You were serious?"

"Yes."

"Tonight?"

"What's wrong with tonight?"

"We have long days here at the clinic. Today was another long day."

"You already said your days are all booked up," Sasha said.

"And they are, but—"

"So, what's wrong with doing it at night?"

"I'm not certain—"

"Doctor Feinman," Sasha said, "if you got told you only had days to live would you actually care whether your last day on earth was during daylight or dark?"

Sasha looked at the clock on her cellphone.

"Would he have to fast before the tests?" she queried.

"Eight hours. Only water."

"Eight hours? He can do that."

"Have him here at one in the morning."

"Thank you, Doctor Feinman. We'll be at your lab at one."

"See you at one. Now I'd better go get some rest," Dr. Feinman said.

"God bless you and God bless everyone in your lab, Dr. Feinman," Sasha said. "Goodbye."

Sasha's hotel room was on a different floor. She stopped at Gabe's room. Peck let her in.

"Here's the deal, guys," she announced. "Gabe, your doctor friends are opening their lab tonight just for you, and they're going to put you through every test."

"What?" Gabe asked.

"I want no arguments."

"Tonight?"

"Well, at one a.m. in the morning, actually. We have to be there then, but you have to fast for eight hours first, so you go to bed now and only drink water. Peck and I will leave you alone and come get you when it's time."

"It'll just be another big waste of time."

"Be a good boy, Gabe. Tomorrow we'll see sax man."

"A lot of poking and prodding. I only suggested it to—"

Sasha grabbed a towel from a bureau and threw it at Gabe.

"Shut up!" she snapped.

"Well, it's true," Gabe said.

"Gabe, when's the last time anyone told you that you might be able to live? Answer me that."

"A big zero," Gabe said.

"These two guys are brilliant," Sasha said. "You said it yourself."

"Are they saying I might be able to live?"

"No."

"Well, there you go."

"But they're not saying you're going to die, either."

"And your point is?"

"They're saying they don't know. When's the last time anyone has said they don't know?"

"What time?" Gabe asked.

"Go to bed," Sasha said. "We'll wake you. You'll need your strength."

Gabe relented and moved to his bed and sat down.

"Peck, come with me. Let him sleep," Sasha said.

They pulled the drapes and left Gabe alone. Peck and Sasha went to the front of the hotel and watched the setting sunset. Sasha led Peck to a park bench overlooking the river. A small boat was floating from one iron basket to another, lighting the fire logs. They cast a warming glow.

"Peck," Sasha asked. "Has Gabe talked to you about school?"

"He teached me how to count, dass for true," Peck said.

"And that's a good thing," Sasha said. "But has he talked about your going back to school full time?"

"You mean with kids?" Peck asked.

"No kids," Sasha said. "With a tutor, but after you get your high school GED, maybe then college or a trade school. Would you like that?"

"He teached me to count *en anglaise*."

"A tutor will teach you all that—counting, reading, writing. What do you think?"

"Could I t'row my trotline and mow lawns and do dat?" Peck asked.

"We were thinking we'd get you an apartment in New Orleans. You could earn money cleaning my real-estate office and Lily Cup's law offices at night. You could go to your tutor most of the day."

"For true?" Peck asked.

"Wouldn't you like to learn all you can and start your business and have a place of your own?" Sasha asked.

"Peck know who he's going to marry, cher."

"Marry?"

"*Oui.*"

"Who?"

Peck didn't answer.

"I know, you're thinking that Elizabeth girl down in Anse La Butte, right? The one you diddle while her boyfriend is offshore?"

Peck sheepishly looked about as if he were hoping no one heard Sasha announce his indiscretions to the world.

"Millie," Peck said.

"Who?"

"I'm gonna marry Millie."

Sasha sat up. "Millie? The girl who called me?"

"I love Millie," Peck said.

"Does she love you?"

"I t'ink so, maybe," Peck said.

Sasha saw contentment in Peck's smile.

"Peck, if you could make wishes come true, and you only had one wish, what would you wish for? What would your life be like?"

"Gabe don' die," Peck said.

Sasha looked at Peck's eyes, smiled gently, pursed her lips and held back a cry while witnessing Gabe's friend—as unconditionally devoted to him as a son would be.

"You still want a pirogue?" Sasha asked. "To pull traps?"

"If I be smart, like you say," Peck said. "I'd want me a farm with one, two, maybe three acres for planting, like melons and zucchini, like dat. And then one, two, three, four, five acres' marsh bottom for burying my own crawdad traps."

"Not blue crab?" Sasha asked.

"Blue crab for sure, but mo money in crawfish," Peck said.

"That sounds nice, Peck. A nice dream. Think city girl Millie would go for the farming and crawfish beds? It's pretty hard work."

Peck didn't answer. He stood and walked Sasha to Gabe's favorite Providence diner, stepped in and waved hello to its owner. He talked Sasha through his and Gabe's favorites—corn on the cob with fresh creamery butter, sliced whole tomatoes with salt and pepper, and chicken pot pie. Sasha took her business jacket off, hung it on a hook and let Peck order the entire meal. She watched his eyes as he confidently told the lady server what they wanted. He was particularly proud to say,

"We gonna cahoot together and can we start with two ears between us, if dat be fine? Dat be two for the lady and two for me...and we gonna did shicken pot pies too. Two of them too—but only one each."

The waitress knew Peck from his visits with Gabe. She made him comfortable with a simple, "Yes sir, will that be all?"

Peck held up two fingers. "Two beers," he said.

Sasha studied Peck's eyes, recognizing what Gabe had said earlier— that Peck had counted on his fingers the three acres of planting land for farming he wanted and the five acres of low, wet marshland he wanted for crawfish traps—and his being able to count those acres was light-years from twenty-four years of a mentally muted silence, as he scratched a life in the bayous, not having to know how to count in English, just having to know how to avoid snakes and alligators and how to catch a dinner he'd eat alone and how to mow and sharpen axe blades to pay for a small cot in the back of the boat-builder's blade-sharpening shed.

"Millie would be lucky to get you," Sasha said.

CHAPTER 23

"MICHELLE, YOU TWO CAN WAIT here in the waiting room, or go to your hotel and come back," Dr. Feinman said. "If you'll give me a cell number, I can text you when we're finished."

"How long do you think?" Sasha asked.

"Several hours. Maybe four."

"We'll either stay here or find an all-night place around," Sasha said. "The diner or something else."

"Suit yourselves," Dr. Feinman said.

"Will you call me, Doctor?" Sasha asked. "At any time, please?"

"One of us will, I promise."

Sasha took Gabe's hand.

"Bye, honey," Sasha said. "Play nice."

Sasha and Peck watched Gabe and several nurses in smocks pass through double doors and walk out of sight. Sasha looked at the time and ordered an Uber with her cellphone app.

"We wait for Gabe?" Peck asked.

"I've got an idea," Sasha said. "Come with me."

Sasha asked the driver to take them to a Dunkin' Donuts and wait for them in the car. Sasha stepped over to the menu board to read it.

"Peck, tell the nice lady which donuts you want," Sasha said, pointing to a donut assortment case. "Pick out ten you like."

"You want a dozen?" the waitress asked.

"He'll pick ten," Sasha said.

"They come in dozens, lady," a manager said in the background.

"I don't think he can count a dozen," Sasha said. "Peck, go ahead and pick out ten."

The manager came to the front, ready for battle.

"Our donuts come in singles or they come in dozens, ma'am. We would have to charge you for singles if you only get ten, but we'd charge you the dozen rate if you select a dozen. It would be much cheaper if your friend got twelve."

"So, let him pick ten—give him two free ones, and charge him for a dozen," Sasha said.

"Carole," the manager growled. "Just handle it."

He left in a miff.

When he was out of earshot.

"Who starched his undies, Carole?" Sasha asked.

"He gets like that sometimes," Carole said.

"Lucky you," Sasha mumbled.

"He shouldn't work nights," Carole said.

"He shouldn't be allowed out of the house," Sasha said.

"That'd sure get my vote," Carole said.

"Peck," Sasha said. "Pick ten, then pick two more, does that work?"

"That's clever," Carole said.

"Dat be good, cher," Peck said.

"While he's thinking what can I get you, hon?"

"Is there like a big thing, maybe a large thermos you sell we can get with five or six cups of coffee in it?" Sasha asked. "I'll buy the thermos."

"We have the Box O' Joe," Carole said.

"The box of what?" Sasha asked.

"It holds ten, ten-ounce cups."

"A box would be good, ten cups would be good, but is there a thermos or something to hold coffee, keep it warm?" Sasha asked.

"It's our Box O' Joe. Let me show you one, hon."

Waitress Carole brought an empty Box O' Joe container from under the counter and handed it to Sasha.

"See this here?" she asked. "It'll hold ten cups and keeps it warm and everything."

"Imagine that, a cardboard coffee container," Sasha said.

"It's popular," Carole said.

"Well okie-dokie, then. You've sold me, Carole. We'll take a Box O' Joe."

"Where you from, hon?" Carole asked.

"N'Orleans."

"I figured you weren't from around here."

"It's a long way away," Sasha said.

"Don't have Box O' Joe down there, I don't suppose," Carole said.

"We don't get out much in the Quarter. We have Café du Monde," Sasha said. "There we get it in china cups if we sit in, with a couple of beignets typically. Tourists get disposable cups."

"Bet them Café du Monde folks don't give you a hard time like our manager, huh?" Carole asked.

"Haven't you heard, Carole? Down there we just flash our tits and they give us beads with our beignets and coffee."

Carole grinned.

Sasha winked at Carole.

"Don't believe everything you see about New Orleans on YouTube, honey—night Carole, and thanks."

Peck carried the package to the car and put it in the trunk.

"Take us to the Point Street Bridge," Sasha said.

Sasha told the driver he was welcome to join them for coffee and donuts or leave and she'd call him as soon as she heard from the doctor. The driver opted to go home and sleep. Peck carried the donuts and coffee down the slope and in under the bridge.

"He's gone," Sasha said.

"Who's gone, cher?" Peck asked.

"Donald," Sasha said. "He plays sax here."

Peck poured two coffees and handed one to Sasha. He lifted the lid of the donut box, took a glazed and sat on the lawn and watched the river flow by.

"Is it true you don't know your mom or dad, Peck?" Sasha asked.

"Dass for true, cher," Peck said.

"You don't have to talk about it if you don't want to," Sasha said.

"S'hokay."

"I'm happy you and Gabe found each other."

"I knowed Gabe was good straight off," Peck said. "He got honest eyes."

"He does, I agree," Sasha said.

They sipped their coffees. Sasha picked a powdered donut, broke it in half with her fingers and let half stay in the box.

"Was your foster nanna lady nice?" Sasha asked. "Do you ever see her?"

"*Elle me laisser utiliser l'homme gator,*" Peck said. ("She let gator man use me.")

"*Comment ça?*"

"He maked me carry bait shrimp buckets to his boat," Peck said. "If I drop one he whack me with a strap."

"How old were you?"

"Couldn't swim."

"Can you swim now?"

"Yes'm."

"How old?"

Peck looked at her as if he had told her already.

"When you say you couldn't swim, are you saying you were really young?" Sasha asked.

"*Oui.*"

"Like maybe you were young, like three, four or five? Is that what you're saying?"

"*Oui?*"

"And that man would beat you?"

Peck didn't answer.

Sasha picked up the other half of the powdered donut.

"Where was your foster nanna all this time?"

"Bayou Chene, I t'ink cher, by Choctaw."

"I don't mean where did she live. I meant why wasn't she protecting you from this man?"

"I run off after he maked me gator bait."

"Gator bait?" Sasha asked.

"*Oui.*"

"Explain that to me."

"Gator man taked me long way into bayou in boat."

"I know, a pirogue."

"Nah, nah, not a pirogue, in a boat with a motor. He make me jump in the water with a rope tied on me. He start the motor and pull me off back a long ways, looking for gators to come get me. If he seed one he'd pull me up and shoot it."

"This sounds like a bad dream, Peck," Sasha said. "Are you imagining all this or did he really do that to you?"

Peck didn't answer.

"What's his name?"

"Gator man."

"Where does he live?"

"Bayou Chene, 'tween Bayou Sorrel and Choctaw, with foster nanna, dass for true."

Sasha lifted her phone and started a text to herself.

"What's her name?"

"Prudhomme," Peck said. "Alayna Prudhomme, 'tween Bayou Sorrel and Choctaw."

"When he did that— pulled you— did you ever see alligators?"

"Nah, nah, I died," Peck said.

"You died?"

"I died."

"What do you mean, you died?"

"Gator man throwed me in off the boat and I turned my whole self dead with no eyes or no air—just dead is all."

A tear rolled down Sasha's cheek and glistened in reflection of the full moon.

"How many times did gator man make you die, Peck?"

"Don't know."

"Did he do this a lot?"

"Couldn't count den, cher."

Sasha held her coffee cup to her cheek and looked off into the river. "Did you tell your foster nanna?"

"*Oui.*"

"What'd she say?"

"*Tu devrais être reconnaissant qu'il t'enseigne.*" Peck said. ("You should be grateful he's teaching you.")

"How did you get away?"

"I climb a bald cypress and hided in the hollow up over the limb. I stay hid there." Peck held up four fingers. "This many day, cher."

Then he remembered he could count now.

"Four days," Peck said. "I hided in the cypress hollow four days then run off and didn't stop until Carencro. I lied about how old I was and got me a job killing calf at the slaughter barn."

Sasha keyed in the towns into her phone.

"That's sixty-five miles," she said.

"I run all the way, cher. No stop."

"How old were you when you ran away?"

"I cud swim."

"You say slaughter barn."

"*Oui.*"

"You mean you swept up, carried feed?"

"I bonk 'em dead."

Sasha winced.

"Got good at it. Dey drop with one bonk on head between eyes. Foreman string 'em up after dat."

Sasha looked as though she were in a bad dream. She'd heard stories like this, but hard to believe they really happened.

"Dey seen I was too young and a lady fired me."

"What did you do then?" Sasha asked. "Where did you go?"

"I heard the sawing down by the track and ax the boat builder man man if'n he need a worker. He say I could sharpen axe blades for sleeping on the cot in his saw blade shed. I told him I do it if I could earn out the lawn mower he had setting there doing nothin'. He say *oui* and gived me a trotline too."

Sasha's phone sounded. She read the name on the screen.

"Hello, Doctor Feinman?"

"It is."

"Everything okay?"

"He's resting."

"Is he okay?"

"All his signs are good."

"When will he wake up?"

"In several hours."

"Did you find anything out?" Sasha asked.

"We'll be reviewing lab results soon."

"When can you talk about it?" Sasha asked.

"We'll meet this morning, sometime. We could see you at one."

"Doctor Feinman, you have no idea what this means to us," Sasha said. "You people are kind, and God will thank you for this."

"Are you staying in the city?"

"Yes. I'm checked in at the Courtyard."

"That's where Gabe is staying, if I'm not mistaken."

"That's right," Sasha said. "So, we come get Gabe around nine, and meet you for the results at one?"

"Yes."

"He'll be starving," Sasha said. "Tell him we'll eat in the morning with him."

"I will."

"Okay, thank you, Doctor," Sasha said. "Oh, Gabe loves his morning coffee."

"I'll see he gets some."

Sasha ended the call.

"He's asleep. We'll get him in the morning."

"I heard," Peck said.

"Let's walk to the hotel. I'll set an alarm and wake you if you want to go with me. We'll get Gabe and take him to the diner," Sasha said.

"*Oui.*"

He stood, gathering the Box O' Joe and remaining donuts.

Sasha stepped over to Peck and put her hand on his cheek. She gave him a gentle kiss on the other cheek.

"I want you to listen to what I have to say, Mr. Boudreaux Clemont Finch."

Peck stood motionless.

"I mean this from the bottom of my heart."

"You died back there all those years ago. I can't begin to imagine what it was like for you—your dying like that every time that gator man did that to you."

Peck closed his eyes.

"Look at me, Peck."

Peck opened his eyes.

"I want you to know God cared because He saw to it you couldn't count all those deaths you had to go through."

Peck lowered his head. Sasha put her hand under his chin and raised his head up.

"Now you have Gabe, Peck. It's all different now. You have a daddy who loves you and wants to care for you."

A tear bubbled in Peck's eye.

"You'll never have to die again, Peck. Never, ever."

Peck leaned his head down on the top of Sasha's head, a tear dropping onto her forehead.

"Peck, Gabe is your resurrection. You'll never have to die again."

Peck and Sasha held hands climbing the knoll and walking back to the hotel.

CHAPTER 24

"GOOD MORNING, SUNSHINE," Sasha said. "Did you get a good night's sleep?"

"I could eat a horse," Gabe said.

"I'll bet you could."

"Where's Peck?"

"I let him sleep in. We'll go to the hotel, you change your clothes and we can all either go to the diner, or the Dunkin' Donuts we found."

The car was waiting. Sasha held Gabe's door while he climbed in and went around and got in beside him.

"Saxman Don wasn't there when we got to the bridge last night," Sasha said.

"Sorry you didn't get to hear him."

"It was fine, Peck and I sat there, watched the river and talked."

"I think he stays until one. My guess is the earlier crowds like to listen, and are the tippers. Later crowd the drunks and noise makers."

"Peck and I had a long talk," Sasha said.

Sasha tapped Gabe on the thigh and gave him a sign she didn't want to talk about it in front of the driver.

"So which is it?" she asked.

"Which is what?"

"The diner or Dunkin' Donuts."

"The hotel has a breakfast set up in the lobby."

"I thought you'd want some corn on the cob you keep going on about," Sasha said. "At the diner."

"I bet if I showed her how, Ruth could make corn fritters," Gabe said. "Corn fritters and scrambled eggs—oh, brother."

"So, it's Ruth, is it?" Sasha asked with a tease.

"That's her name."

"Have you been messing around Providence on me, Gabe? Getting pretty personal, aren't we? She's Ruth, eh?"

"Ruth is the morning waitress at the diner," Gabe said.

"I'll just bet she is," Sasha winked.

"They like to be called servers nowadays, but she's the niece of the owner—his name is Doug—and her brother plays backup rhythm guitar around the area if anyone needs it."

"What?"

"I've been here awhile, darlin', I know some people."

"Do you like sleep over at the diner, for Pete's sake?" Sasha asked.

"I'm an inquisitive guy, what can I say?"

"Lily Cup and I've been going to Charlie's Blue Note for ten years and you know more about this Ruth gal in three days than we know about Charlie."

"I'm a social animal, I guess," Gabe said. "There's more to life than dancing, you know."

Sasha smirked. "Yeah, sounds like it—there's corn on the cob."

"Holding those ears, watching the butter drip," Gabe said.

"I love it when you talk dirty," Sasha said.

The car pulled up to the hotel. They got out and watched it drive off.

"What time?" Gabe asked.

"We have to be there at one o'clock."

"Okay."

"If you don't want to go, I'll go alone," Sasha said.

Gabe didn't answer. Sasha put her arms around him and hugged.

"Let's get Peck," Sasha said.

"I'm starving," Gabe said.

"Go get dressed. We'll see what Ruth thinks about your corn fritter idea."

"I'm certain Ruth could talk her uncle into making them," Gabe said.

"That's not what I'm worried about," Sasha said.

"What?" Gabe asked.

"She probably will want to smear corn fritters all over your body, you dirty old man."

Gabe shook his head, rolling his eyes, choking in an early morning grin. "Are you coming up?"

"I'll wait down here," Sasha said. "I'll check my emails."

Gabe stepped away and walked to the elevator. Sasha watched the door close, then went outside to a distant park bench on the lawn in front of the hotel. She pressed dial, then speaker.

"Hello?" Lily Cup asked in a weak, crackly morning voice.

"Did I wake you?" Sasha asked.

"What time is it?" Lily Cup asked.

"Oh shit," Sasha said. "I totally forgot the time difference."

"Don't worry about it," Lily Cup said.

"I'm so sorry."

"I had to get up to answer the phone anyway."

"Very funny."

"Is Gabe all right?" Lily Cup asked.

"They gave him tests, ran him through their machines, I don't know what all, but we won't know until one this afternoon."

"So, what's the real reason you called? Whut'cha' need?"

"You are so rude," Sasha said.

"Me?"

"Why would you just come out and assume I only called you because I needed something. How rude."

"Because I know you," Lily Cup said.

"Girlfriend you only think—"

"I know when you wake me up you need something."

"You fresh thing."

"It's not just to talk."

"Why I never. I can't ever remember calling you this early— ever."

"LSU homecoming, 2011—"

"What?"

"You called me at four-seventeen in the morning to tell me some basketball dude had just given you three orgasms."

"I would so never call you to tell you that," Sasha said.

"No, you're right," Lily Cup said.

"I know I am, I would so never—"

"You called to tell me you wanted to marry him, but you were at the ice machine in the hall filling an ice bucket and you couldn't remember his name or his hotel room number."

"Honey, what do you know about swamps or marshes in the Bayou Chene area, between Bayou Sorrel and Choctaw?"

"Doesn't ring a bell," Lily Cup said.

"Damn."

"Why?"

"As a kid, Peck was abused by a pig he called gator man," Sasha said.

"Gator man?"

"Peck calls him gator man."

"Sexually abused him?"

"Not that, but have you ever heard the term 'gator bait'?"

"In the movies, yes."

"Well this gator man would drag Peck behind his boat—"

"That's deep bayou spooky talk, girlfriend— gator man."

"Like from the time he was four. You wouldn't believe what he went through."

"Oh yeah, I would. I'm up at Angola prison at least once a month. I saw a man in chains who was caught feeding wise-guy-killed bodies to feral hogs he kept half-starved in concrete pens. I've seen—"

"Enough," Sasha said.

"I'm sorry," Lily Cup said.

"Enough...too early in the morning."

"Now you know why I can't sleep half the time."

"I love you," Sasha said.

"I love you too, baby cakes. I'll light a candle for Gabe at Saint Louis Cathedral."

"Would you do that?"

"Just be with your friends—some quality time. You deserve it."

"Thank you," Sasha said.

"Michelle?"

"Yeah?"

"Get me some names, without being too obvious."

"I'll work on it."

"People and places, get me what you can."

These women had a pact since the sixth grade that they won't ever say goodbye to each other. Sasha clicked her phone off and walked back to the lobby to wait for Gabe and Peck to come down.

The wait at the diner was no more than fifteen minutes. Most of the work crowd was already at work.

"Ruth, I'd like you to meet our friend, Michelle. She's up from New Orleans," Gabe said.

Waitress Ruth poured three cups of coffee, smiling at Sasha while listening to Gabe.

"Gabe, I already had the pleasure of serving your friend when she came in with Peck. Good morning," Ruth said. "Good to meet you. What can I get everybody?"

"Ruth, I've been meaning to talk to you about your fabulous corn on the cob," Gabe said.

"We pick the best," she said. "Well we don't actually pick it. We go to the farmer's market and pick out the best, is a better way of putting it."

"You're missing a golden opportunity, Ruth," Gabe said.

"Oh? And how's that, Gabe?"

"There's so many other things you can do with corn," Gabe said. "Especially as good as the corn you serve."

"You mean things like corn chowder, corn fritters, cornbread, corn waffles, and corn pancakes?"

Gabe's mouth dropped open. Waitress Ruth turned the menu in his hand over to nearly half a page of corn items.

"Only August and September, though. Best months for fresh corn, Gabe," waitress Ruth said. "Now what can I get everybody?"

Following breakfast, it was too early for music. Sasha didn't want to stress Gabe out and purposely chose not to talk about what Peck had told her under the bridge. She opted for a nap and a meet-up in the lobby at twelve thirty for their one o'clock meeting.

The Uber driver was there on time, and both Dr. Feinman and Dr. Michael Docherty welcomed Sasha and Gabe at the door and walked them back to a conference room. Peck took a seat in the waiting area.

Gabe, Sasha, the two doctors settled in their seats as Dr. Feinman opened a file folder.

"How are you feeling, Gabe?" Dr. Feinman asked. "Were you able to get some rest?"

"I feel fine," Gabe said. "They've come a long way in the poking and prodding departments. I felt nothing. Slept like a baby."

"Good," Dr. Feinman said. "Gabe, you're a soldier. And as a soldier you know that when you plan the strategy for battle, you have to weigh the risk for every move you take."

"Like chess," Gabe said.

"Yes, like chess," Dr. Feinman said.

"The King can't really die in chess," Sasha interrupted. "You just tip him over, but he doesn't die."

"Point taken," Dr. Feinman said.

"How long I got?" Gabe asked.

"Gabe, we've confirmed you have stomach cancer," Dr. Feinman said. "Not long, unless something is done."

No one spoke.

"We've also confirmed that it hasn't metastasized."

"Meaning?" Gabe asked.

"Meaning it's just in your stomach."

"Am I missing something?" Gabe asked. "Or is there supposed to be some good news in here somewhere?"

"The good news is both Dr. Docherty and I think a total gastrectomy might be your solution. It would take all of the cancer out of your body."

"Take it all out?" Gabe asked. "How?"

"It's complex surgery," Dr. Docherty said. "We remove the entire stomach. That way we remove all the active cancer cells."

"Would it add anything to my life?"

"It could be years," Dr. Feinman said.

"Years?" Gabe asked.

Tears bubbled in Sasha's eyes. She sat watching Gabe's eyes.

"Tell me how it works," Gabe said. "If I have no stomach."

"You'll receive a general anesthesia for sleep and pain control," Dr. Feinman said. "We make an incision from below your breastbone down to your navel. We surgically remove the stomach and the nearby lymph nodes. We may also need to remove your spleen and portions of your esophagus, pancreas, and intestines. After the cancer has been removed, we attach your esophagus to your small intestine to form an alternate stomach. This will enable you to continue to swallow, eat, and digest food. Because of the limited capacity of your new stomach, you'll need to eat smaller amounts of food on a more frequent basis."

"Corn kernels are tiny, honey," Sasha said, smiling through tears.

"How long does it take, doc?" Gabe asked.

"A total gastrectomy takes two to three hours to perform. If you undergo this procedure, you should plan on staying in the hospital for at least a week. You'll need three to six months for recovery."

"Doc, after the week, can I fly?" Gabe asked.

"I'd like to have you around for regular checkups for a month," Dr. Docherty said. "After that you can fly, sure."

"You said risk," Sasha said. "What risks?"

"Gabe's not a young man," Dr. Feinman said. "It could be a shock to his heart. He could have a heart attack."

"Dr. Feinman and Dr. Docherty," Sasha said. "With all due respect—our Gabriel here walked from Kenner, Louisiana all the way to the Quarter, and then we danced until midnight. Oh, I think his heart can take it."

"You a dancer, Gabe?" Dr. Docherty asked. We knew your love for jazz, but you're a dancer. Great exercise."

"Why do you think I've followed him up here?" Sasha asked. "Do you know how hard it is to get a lug on the dance floor these days?"

"You do have a point," Dr. Feinman said.

"A girl finds a good dancer, we stalk them," Sasha said.

"And all this time I thought you've been following me around for my looks and that jungle fever experience I read about in the tabloids," Gabe mused.

"So what say you, Gabe?" Dr. Feinman asked.

"Years?" Gabe asked.

"Could be years," Dr. Feinman said.

"I'd rather lose you trying, than lose you for not taking a chance of giving you years," Sasha whispered.

"Will my veteran's insurance pay for it?" Gabe asked.

"Every cent, and if it didn't, it'd be on us, dancer man," Dr. Docherty said.

Sasha reached and pinched Gabe's ear. "Say it," she said.

"Ow," Gabe said.

"Say it!" Sasha said.

"Yes."

"Louder."

"All right, all right, yes! Let's do it. Now, woman, let go of my ear."

"Tuesday, then," Dr. Feinman said. "Gabe, fast from midnight, drink only water. I'd eat light today and tomorrow."

"Anything else?" Sasha asked.

"I'll text you the name of an agent for temporary housing in the area if you'll need a place for the month or so," Dr. Docherty said.

"I think the Courtyard will be better for him. Breakfasts already there, housekeeping," Sasha said. "The diner's close by."

"That makes sense," Dr. Docherty said.

"Well then," Dr. Feinman said. "Go enjoy your day, and we'll see you on Tuesday."

"Gabe, will you be at the finale today?" Dr. Docherty asked. "It's a piano tribute to George Shearing."

"We wouldn't miss it," Gabe said. "Did you know Shearing started playing at three—in England—and he played the accordion as well?"

Gabe's voice was energized, like that of a schoolboy. He felt an honest confidence there could be a quality future of many more dances and saxophone wails in years to come.

"I didn't know about the accordion," Dr. Docherty said.

"Oh yeah. As a boy, young Shearing would listen endlessly to all the jazz and blues greats on 78 records, and he got so he could mimic them. That's how he became so versatile. An all-time great."

"You certainly know your jazz," Dr. Docherty said.

"Tell you what, let's all go to the festival together next year," Gabe said. "My treat."

"Gabe, if you make me cry…" Sasha started.

"Okay, sorry, see you gentleman on Tuesday," Gabe said as he led Sasha to the door.

He paused and turned.

"Thank you both."

Chapter 25

"*DO WE HAVE SEATS* for the performance in Newport?" Sasha asked.

"Some of the festival is under an open tent," Gabe said. "We sit on the lawn. It's right in front of a bay where yachts are moored."

"Then we'll do a picnic lunch," Sasha said. "We can listen to Shearing and talk about what we have to do to get ready for a crazy week ahead."

"My baby," Gabe said. "You've done enough, and I love you for every minute of it. You don't have to hang around. I know you have a business to look after and your days are valuable. I'll be all right."

"*Oh, tu vieil homme têtu!*" Sasha cried. ("Oh, you stubborn old man!")

Sasha leaned forward.

"Driver? What's your name?" Sasha asked.

"Robert," the driver said.

"Please don't listen, Robert," Sasha said, turning toward Gabe.

"Why you self-centered old fool of a man," she said. "When will you stop pretending you're Sir Lancelot and start knowing who your friends are?"

"Darlin' I didn't mean..." Gabe started.

"Mean, schmean. You don't have the slightest clue how women think if you thought I would up and leave you to go through this alone."

"I don' t'ink ole Gabe meant he..." Peck started.

"You shut up, peckerwood. You're no better. Just the same as your twin, here. You don't know the first thing about women, either."

"What you mean?" Peck asked.

"Millie."

"What about Millie?"

"Didn't you tell me under the bridge you were going to marry her?" Sasha asked.

"Millie?" Peck asked.

"Yes, Einstein, I just said it—Millie," Sasha said. "Who was she to you—you said it under the bridge—the girl you're going to marry?" Sasha asked.

"I stay at her house there," Peck said.

"Did you kiss her?" Sasha asked.

"Hanh?"

"I'll know if you're lying. Did you kiss her?"

"Hokay," Peck said.

"For two days you were in Carencro at the grand jury and not until under the bridge last night did you ever talk about her."

Peck sat speechless.

"Have you kissed her?"

"Ah, *oui*."

"I knew it. Look at him, Gabe, he's a mess."

Gabe smiled.

"Is she all you can think about, son?" Gabe asked.

"Yes," Peck said.

"Day and night?"

"Purdy much."

"You're in love with her, Peck," Sasha said.

"Yes'm."

"Does she know it?"

"I dunno," Peck said.

"You talk to me about marrying her—you're up here eating donuts under a bridge, and she doesn't have a clue?" Sasha asked.

Peck stared out the window.

"Either a man tells a girl he loves her so much he can't sleep or eat or think straight, or he doesn't. Which is it?"

"I love Millie dat much."

Sasha pointed to Gabe.

"You really want to help this man get well?"

"Yes'm, I sure..." Peck started.

"Then get your head straight and start living your life like it means something," Sasha said.

"Hanh?"

"Only you can make it mean something, Peck. Nobody else can do it for you. Do it for Gabe—but especially do it for yourself. You can't make excuses for not taking chances and wasting your life."

"I understand," Peck said.

"You haven't even told her, have you?" Sasha asked.

"Dat I love her?" Peck asked.

"That's what we're talking about. Have you?" Sasha asked.

"Nah, nah," Peck said.

"Men!" Sasha barked.

"Hanh?" Peck asked.

"You're another piece of work," Sasha said.

She turned and looked out the window.

"You and Gabe belong together."

Sasha pulled herself forward by the back of the front seat.

"Robert, drop these bums at the hotel and let me out at that bench."

"Yes, ma'am," the driver said.

"We have three hours before it starts, but it'll be crowded if we want to sit close to the bandstand," Gabe said. "We should get there early."

"I have to make some calls," Sasha said. "Meet in an hour."

"What will we do about food and a blanket to sit on?" Gabe asked.

"I'll ask around, maybe find a cooler or a picnic basket somewhere," Sasha said. "A deli will have salads and sandwiches. You two wait in the hotel. I'll go see, after I make my calls."

"How about a bucket?" Gabe asked.

"A bucket?"

"Kentucky Fried Chicken—a bucket."

"Oh, my lord."

"A big bucket, potato salad, and biscuits," Gabe said.

"Peck?" Sasha asked.

"I like shicken, cher," Peck said.

"I should have known. I'm traveling with Chef Paul and James Beard," Sasha said. "I'm picking the wine. We'll get it on the way to Newport. Robert, drop me and wait here while we get organized. Then we'll go to Newport."

"No problem," the driver said.

When Sasha sat on the bench, she gave a sigh of relief. It was dawning on her there was hope for Gabe. He might be able to live out the rest of his life getting to the things he now only has a keener awareness of. She touched *Lily Cup* on her phone and looked around to be certain she was alone and touched *speaker*.

"Where are you?" Lily Cup asked.

"Exhausted and still in Providence," Sasha said.

"Everything okay?"

"I need you to tell the ladies at my office I won't be in for a week at least," Sasha said. "They have to cover my open houses and closings. If they need me, we can Facetime."

"Is Gabe getting worse?" Lily Cup asked.

"That's just it," Sasha said. "These two internal specialists met Gabe at the festival. They have a high-tech oncology lab. They tested him all through the night and now they think they can operate and remove all the cancer."

"Oh, my God," Lily Cup said. "He must be ecstatic."

"They're operating on him Tuesday."

"It's a miracle."

"Somebody should be here with him."

"Of course," Lily Cup said.

"We're sending Peck back to New Orleans," Sasha said. "Can you pop over to my office and ask Amy if she can find him a reasonable studio or efficiency apartment?"

"How close in?" Lily Cup asked.

"The tutor is in the Garden District," Sasha said. "Close enough to walk or bike between that and our offices."

"He can have my dad's old bike," Lily Cup said.

"Come up with some kind of cleaning schedule for him. Tell Nettie she doesn't have to clean our offices anymore. No cut in pay but she'll still clean our homes. Figure out what to pay Peck."

"Our office will pay our share."

"Whatever you think is fair."

"Your James came by yesterday," Lily Cup said. "He's asking where you are, and if you've dumped him."

"I can't think about James now," Sasha said. "I'll call him tonight."

"At least leave him a message or something," Lily Cup said. "Put him out of his misery."

"Peck's in love," Sasha said.

"No."

"He's a goner."

"In this short time—what's it been, a few days?"

"Blind love."

"With who—not you, please tell me?"

"A girl named Millie he met on the bus."

"I'll be."

"I mean, the boy's unwired."

"On a bus?"

"He jumped off the bus at her stop, somewhere in Tennessee."

"Maybe you and I should take more bus rides," Lily Cup said.

"I'm thinking Peck stays through the operation Tuesday," Sasha said. "I'll put him on a bus to New Orleans on Wednesday."

"He can fly now, why not on a plane?" Lily Cup asked.

"He has business in Tennessee," Sasha said. "The lady he's cottoned to lives there."

"His love?"

"He's down for the count."

"Our Peck—cheating on us already, eh? Bet she's young and, well young."

"He hasn't said, only that he loves her," Sasha said.

"Did he meet her before he got arrested and was flown in for the grand jury?"

"Yes."

"That little shit," Lily Cup said.

"Why?"

"He didn't mention her to me," Lily Cup said.

"Nothing?" Sasha asked. "You with him all day at the grand jury. He didn't say anything to you about her?"

"Not a word, but I'm sure he had prison on his mind."

"That's true."

"Speaking of Peck," Lily Cup said. "Did you get any names—you know?"

"I did. Hang on, let me look at my phone."

Sasha scrolled emails, looking for one she sent to herself. She remembered texts and looked for a text she might have sent.

"Here," she said, "his foster nanna was an Alayna Prudhomme. I have Bayou Chene...and this one says it's between Bayou Sorrell and Choctaw."

"This is good. And the guy?"

"All I have is Peck called him gator man," Sasha said.

"Got it," Lily Cup said.

"I think the guy has his own place—maybe boats."

"Got it."

"So, what can you do with all of that?"

"I can smell around."

"They're not good people."

"I've got it."

"Are you still in trial?"

"I lost," Lily Cup said.

"I'm sorry," Sasha said.

"Well, I actually lost, and won at the same time."

"Oh?"

"I got Andre off the murder charge."

"You got him off murder? That's a big win, sweetie."

"Too circumstantial, but—and this is a big but—he got two years in Angola for selling firearms without a license...and basically from the trunk of his Lincoln, actually. The circumstantial was that the murder weapon had serial numbers on it. To win the murder rap I had to rat him out and prove all the guns in his trunk had their serial numbers removed, so he couldn't have done it—the murder."

"The murder weapon could have had serial numbers on it," Sasha said.

"Shadow of doubt," Lily Cup said. "The jury liked my theory."

"And so they busted him for weapon sales," Sasha said.

"At least he doesn't get the needle for murder."

"You're a genius, girlfriend."

"Andre thinks so."

"Do you still get paid?"

"Oh yeah. He paid plenty."

"That sounded pretty smart, what you did."

"I'm driving up to Angola tomorrow—see that he behaves himself. Maybe I can get him out in six months with good behavior."

"Are you ever afraid of going to Angola alone?" Sasha asked. "I heard it's nasty."

"Honey, Angola is safer for me than the streets of New Orleans after midnight," Lily Cup said. "Andre will protect me."

"Really?" Sasha asked.

"Andre has his fingers in everything. He knows everyone he needs to know. It's like he's an octopus with arms all throughout Louisiana."

"Amazing," Sasha said. "Harvard would shit."

"Andre wouldn't let anything happen to his star attorney," Lily Cup said.

"You are a star," Sasha said. "And thank you for making sense out of that whole kidnapping thing Peck was in."

"You made it happen," Lily Cup said. "You and Judge Thibodaux, you vamp."

"Okay, sweetie. Love you," Sasha said.

"Let me know when Peck will be here," Lily Cup said.

"I will. Give Charlie and the band hugs for me."

The ride to Newport, Rhode Island was pleasant, a reflective ride. Sasha sat in the middle of the seat with her head rested back, holding each of her boy's hands, like a mother.

Peck appeared contented that the dark moment that started in New Jersey was behind him, and he was now with a man who thought of him as a son.

Gabe's smile out the window made it appear as if a great weight had been lifted from his shoulders; as he felt for the first time in months there wasn't the finality of a giant brick wall facing him, but perhaps an open tunnel to a hopeful reality.

Sasha, exhausted and weary, was content to put her emails aside for the drive through historic Rhode Island. The past twelve days had changed her life, between that of impetuously following a shooting star from a dance floor in a jazz joint just off Frenchman Street to Beale Street in Memphis and now to feeling more family warmth than she had known most of her adult life. Other than her childhood friend, Lily Cup, she had never been more attached to such sincere, interesting characters. She's become connected, as if she has known them for years.

The tent crowd was quiet and respectful; plastic cups kept the noise of tinkling ice cubes down. Two entertainers from local groups took turns playing their own Shearing impressions. They played "Lullaby of Birdland," "Misty," "How High the Moon," and "Let there be Love." They played the entire *Guys and Dolls* score as performed by the velvet fog, Mel Torme and accompanied by jazz pianist George Shearing in concert at a Newport Jazz Festival a long time ago.

"This wine is mellow, smooth, buttery," Gabe said.

"Listen to you," Sasha said.

"What is it?"

"I don't believe we have a bucket of fried chicken with two ninety-dollar bottles of Arnot-Roberts Chardonnay, Trout Gulch 2014," Sasha said.

"It reminds me," Gabe said.

"Why would that not surprise me?" Sasha asked.

"Back when I was active in the army, I remember a time when I was being self-conscious."

"You? Self-conscious?" Sasha asked.

"About being black. After we got back from 'Nam I'd go out of my way to avoid all the black clichés, like chicken and grits and greens."

"Are you talking soul food?"

"That too, but everything changed in Paris."

"Oh, do tell," Sasha said.

"Another captain and I were walking in Paris, enjoying the sights and the fountains. We started up to Sacre Coeur basilica, approaching the Montmartre steps."

"I've been there," Sasha said.

"Well now, if you've been to Paris you know this is almost a religious experience."

"It is."

"The fact that this marvel lasted through two wars that decimated most of Europe was a miracle in its own right."

"And?"

"And coming down the long steps of this holy experience were two brothers—black dudes talking with each other about what a groovy visit Paris was, each holding a bucket of Kentucky Fried chicken in one hand and a bottle of French wine in the other."

"Ha!" Sasha bellowed.

"Can you imagine? Two buckets of Kentucky Fried coming down the Montmartre steps in Paris—with French wine."

Sasha picked up a leg of chicken, held it and looked at it.

"Well, excuse *moi,* boys," Sasha said. "*Bon appetite.*"

That evening they sat in Gabe and Peck's room with coffee, cognac, and conversation.

"Tell us how, Peck. Tell us what happened," Gabe said. "You caught the under the bridge knife guy...tell us how it all went down."

Peck told the story of his meeting Millie on the bus. He told of her doll, of the braces on her teeth, of her Bible, and of the twinkle in her eyes. He told of how he remembered the image of the Kingston sign as the place they got off the bus, and that was where Millie told him to get off if he ever came back. He told of how Millie knew her way around a library as well as he knows his way around a bayou. He told of how they tracked and found the knife man, how he had to kill the dog, and how he tied him up like a gator with his two-hundred-pound test line that would only tighten if the knife man fought it or tried to get loose.

"You mean the spool of fishing line you got free for buying that bag in Memphis?" Sasha asked.

"Yes'm," Peck said.

The story gave Sasha and Gabe great pause. Peck came from another world than theirs, but in his world good was just as good and evil was just as universal. They shared their amazement at how the college girl and Peck worked together as a formidable team, looking back only after the police were notified and an arrest was made. They understood the life-threatening dangers both walked into—facing a man who had already stabbed a man in the chest and face and wouldn't be selective about his victims. The more they listened, the more Sasha and Gabe felt that Millie was the perfect foundation Peck needed—and they both needed each other. Sasha hinted that she'd have a talk with Peck about schooling and outline a plan for him to think about. She left the two to go to her room and get a night's sleep.

"Don't sit up and talk all night," Sasha said.

Back in her room, Sasha touched *Lily Cup* on her phone.

"Hi," Lily Cup said.

"Did I ever tell you about the hailstorm and the bridge and Gabe getting hit?" Sasha asked.

"You drinking?" Lily Cup asked.

"No."

"Tell me again. I like that story."

Sasha proceeded to tell Lily Cup about their road trip to Memphis and how Peck and this girl Millie he met on the bus figured out where the knife man was and how they went and caught him.

"Holy shit," Lily Cup said.

"What?" Sasha asked.

"I don't know that part. Peck and the girl Millie did all that?"

"When they arrested him in New Jersey and were asking him about bodies and money, he thought he'd killed the knife man. Until they took him to you in Louisiana, he thought he'd murdered the guy."

"If he thought he could have killed him he must have hurt him pretty badly," Lily Cup said.

"That's just it," Sasha said. "He tied the guy up with two-hundred-pound test fishing line. He bought a bag, you know like a duffle or workout bag in a sporting store in Memphis, and they gave him a spool of two-hundred-pound test fishing line. He tied the dude up with his fishing line. He said he's seen gators tied like that."

"You couldn't book this act," Lily Cup said.

"The girl called the troopers and told them he was tied up in his trailer and anchored to the refrigerator," Sasha said.

"Millie called the police?" Lily Cup asked.

"Yes, Millie," Sasha said.

"Fishing line?" Lily Cup asked.

"Two-hundred-pound fishing line."

"I lit a candle for Gabe."

"Love you," Sasha said.
"Love you," Lily Cup said.
They ended the call.

CHAPTER 26

LILY CUP CHECKED HER HANDBAG with a guard and pulled a chair around to sit down opposite Andre. She looked about, scanning the placement of the inmate's visitors, leaned forward and lowered her voice.

"Andre, do you know any good cops down in Bayou Chene, near Choctaw or maybe Bayou Sorrell?" she whispered.

"Andre knows good cops everywhere," Andre said. "Some he knows, how you say, better than others is all. Why you ask?"

"This kid I know was in a jam there."

"Talk to Andre."

"Well, he's not a kid—he's twenty-four now. This happened when he was a young kid. Someone, I can't tell you who, asked me to help him so I helped him," Lily Cup whispered. "It was nothing he really did—no crime or anything like that—it was all circumstantial and a grand jury was just asking if he was main witness to something. Anyway, I got him off, but while doing all that I learned he grew up there, you know, in that Choctaw area—like back in the swamps, bayous, and marshlands. A hard life growing up, he was made to do bad things for a man they called *gator man.*"

"Swamp people have their ways," Andre said.

"The kid can't read or write, so we're helping him, a friend and me—we're getting him into school. You know, like we're giving him a break, a second chance."

"You talking or dancing with Andre, *mon ami?*"

"I'm serious, Andre."

"You talking a hard life—a gator man—or are you talking a break and a second chance?" Andre asked. "You're dancing with Andre."

Lily Cup leaned in, her elbow on the table, her knuckles covering the sides of her mouth.

"Andre this kid was dumped when he was just a baby somewhere back in that marshland or bayou around there, in '90—maybe '91," she whispered. "Alayna Prudhomme is one of the names, somewhere between Bayou Sorrel and Choctaw, I think. Least that's what I hear."

"This Prudhomme," Andre said. "She knows this gator man?"

"They must have been fucking, that's what I'm thinking," Lily Cup said. "The bitch probably collecting state money for keeping the kid. It's been fifteen years. Who knows now? They both could be dead. All I know is this *gator man* is nasty."

"Man cannot stoop so low as to not get love from a woman or a dog," Andre said.

"When the kid could walk, she'd let this guy, *gator man*, chain him with a dog collar under a porch. Enslaved him for hard labor in daylight when he was like six, carrying bait shrimp buckets to his boat, used him as gator bait at night. The kid got his mouth taped so he couldn't scream, and he'd get pulled in dark bayous behind a boat far enough back he would attract the bigger gators. He was just a helpless kid."

"This gator man is not a nice person," Andre said.

"Ya think?"

"Not what you would call the fatherly type."

Lily Cup looked into Andre's eyes as if she knew she connected.

"He's a good boy, this boy?"

"He's a good boy, Andre. A decent kid."

Using no names Lily Cup went on to tell Andre how she and Sasha met Peck and how Peck was helping Gabe make a dream come true living out the last days of his life by going to Newport to listen to jazz. She told how Gabe was beaten and robbed of his cancer pain medicine under a bridge in Hazelton, Mississippi, and how the robber stabbed another man in the face and how Peck and a girl tracked him down three states away and caught him, and how Peck tied him with two hundred-pound fishing line and left him bound to the refrigerator leg while they called the troopers and told them where the robber was tied up.

"Three states?" Andre asked.

"Can you imagine?" Lily Cup asked.

"That's a long way from a bayou."

"The kid and this girl he likes tracked him."

"The kid's a good tracker."

"He's a good kid, Andre."

"He sounds like a good boy."

"Just needs a break."

"Two hundred-pound line, you don't say?" Andre asked.

"He saw gator man tie alligator snouts with it," Lily Cup said.

"This gator man only hunt gators?"

"Gators and I think he sells shrimp bait and I think he has a fishing boat for charter."

"How did he get away? This friend you can't talk about—how'd he get away from this gator man? His kind is hard to get away from, especially for good gator-bait boys, anyway."

"He told my friend he climbed a bald cypress and hid in its trunk hollow, standing barefoot in the dark on broken buzzard eggs and live ants for four days until he heard the gator man throwing empty whiskey bottles against a rock all pissed off that he couldn't find the kid and driving off with another bottle probably to see the Prudhomme skank. I think the kid was like eight or nine. He ran seventy miles before stopping with his feet bloody. He's been alone ever since, mowing lawns, fishing for food. He lives in a saw shed. He sharpens blades for a mill or boat builder or something in barter for a sleeping cot, hot plate and a trotline."

"What you want a good cop for?"

"I want—"

"For a bad man?"

"He's a bastard," Lily Cup said.

Andre looked into Lily Cups eyes with a cold stare.

"I want a good cop to find the bastard, Andre."

"I need good coffee," Andre said. "I need Scotch."

Lily Cup knew from experience, that in the world she worked in if someone changes a subject, best she change it too. She also knew Andre knew she couldn't get him Scotch.

"Anything I can get you?" Lily Cup asked.

Lily Cup made mental notes of requests Andre had for simple things like writing paper, magazines, and cans of peaches. They made light conversation until a guard signaled it was time for him to return to his cell and for her to leave.

"You behaving yourself, Andre? Are you being a good boy so I can get you out of here early?"

Andre leaned into Lily Cup.

"Leave it to Andre."

"I don't want him hurt, Andre."

Andre stood.

"Just find the bastard."

Andre waited for a guard to come over and walk him to his cell.

It was 11:45 a.m. in Providence when both Dr. Feinman and Dr. Docherty came to a waiting area in scrub smocks and invited Sasha and Peck into a conference room, closing the door behind them.

"Gabe has a wonderful constitution," Dr. Feinman said.

"You should see him dance," Sasha said.

"He came through with flying colors," Dr. Feinman said.

Sasha held the palms of her hand to her mouth in prayerful thanks.

"His heart rate hardly fluctuated," Dr. Docherty said. "Usually we see a change in heart rate with the stress of a major surgery like this."

"Gabe's a black man," Peck said. "He seen worse, bein' black."

There wasn't a person at the table who didn't understand what the man who grew up in the wilds of a Louisiana bayou meant. They reflected on the thought, like it was a poetic riff from a jazz instrument.

"Is he awake?" Sasha asked.

"It'll be an hour or so," Dr. Feinman said.

"Can we see him then?"

"He'll be groggy at first, but it'll be good for him to see you."

"We'll grab lunch and come back," Sasha said. "Is there anything special we need to know? Any rules?"

"We'd like to see a couple hundred feet before we let him out of here," Dr. Docherty said.

"You want centipedes, Doc?" Sasha quipped nervously.

"We need him to get out of bed and walk as soon as he can. Each day he needs to walk a little further. The goal is to get him up to two hundred or more feet in one stretch. Let's say a week—seven days in a row he does two hundred feet. Then he can move to the hotel."

"Perfect," Sasha said. "When the man isn't dancing, he's walking."

"It may take several days, could take a week. Let him pace himself. Just encourage him," Dr. Docherty said.

"He's got an incredible constitution," Dr. Feinman said.

"He's a regular Forrest Gump," Sasha said.

"He's a lucky man."

"We'll see you after lunch, gentlemen. Thank you for everything."

Before they walked to the diner, Sasha sat with Peck on the park bench and gave him a tutorial on how to use his new cellphone.

"You can count to ten in English, Peck, so this should be easy for you," Sasha said.

Just as Gabe repeated the one to ten count eleven times, Sasha pointed at each number in order and counted them aloud again and again. Eventually Peck took the cell from her hand and pointed to each number and said its name.

"One, two, three, four, five, six, seven, eight, nine," Peck said. "And dis one here is zero."

Sasha showed him how to dial, how to make a call, and how to hang up. She taught him how to answer a call.

"Who's the most important person in your life, Peck?" Sasha asked.

"Hanh?"

"The most important person in your life."

"Gabe."

"That won't work. Gabe doesn't have a phone."

"They's one in his room at the hotel," Peck said.

Sasha grinned at Peck's simple awareness, seeing all things.

"So there is," Sasha said. "Okay, so Gabe is the most important, so he'll be number one. I'll put a one before his name, and if you want to call him you just touch the name here that has a one in front of it. When the hotel answers, you ask for him. Got it?"

"I t'ink so," Peck said.

"I have Millie's number in my cell from the time she called," Sasha said.

One at a time Sasha filled his phone contact directory with the important names with a leading number in front, so he could identify who he'd be calling. 1 was Gabe; 2 was Millie; 3 was Sasha. A good start.

"Let's go eat," Sasha said.

On the way to the diner Peck asked what the text slots were and she explained they didn't matter as he couldn't read them until after he learned to read.

"This here one is Millie," Peck said, pointing to the number 2 on his directory."

"That's Millie all right," Sasha said. "Don't press it yet. We have to see bus schedules and all that first. Do you still have your Discover America pass?"

"Yes'm," Peck said.

Sasha and Peck celebrated lunch discussing the miracle that Gabe had made it through an operation that could add years to his life.

"Isn't it good to know Gabe might be around to see you get your schooling, Peck?" Sasha asked.

"You t'ink I can did dat?"

"Only if you try. If you like it, will you go all the way?"

"Hanh?"

"Like to college?" Sasha asked.

"Yes'm," Peck said.

"Want to talk about Millie?"

"Hokay."

"You really love her?"

"Oh, *oui,* cher."

"So, if you love her, and let's say she loves you, you should give her time to finish her school, and she should help you finish yours," Sasha said.

"So we get married?" Peck asked.

"After she finishes school," Sasha said.

"Ahh, *oui*."

"We'll give you the biggest wedding the Quarter has seen—well Frenchman Street anyway, in Charlie's Blue Note."

"*Hoot!*" Peck said.

"After you finish school you can buy that farm, or crawfish bog or be president or anything you want."

"And Gabe live with us, hanh?"

"He would love it."

Sasha scrolled her phone, found Greyhound bus lines and booked an evening seat for Peck on a bus that went through Knoxville.

"You're set, Peck," Sasha said. "Now you can call Millie and see if she wants to see you, and if she can pick you up tomorrow at eleven forty-five at the Kingston stop."

Peck took a gulp of his coffee.

"What time is that, cher?"

"*Onze quarante-cinq*, Peck. That's eleven forty-five."

"He picked up his phone and touched the name with the number two in front of it and held it to his ear. Soon a big grin came over his face.

"Hello?"

"Hello, cher, this is Peck."

"Peck? I dreamed about you last night."

"How you are, cher?"

"I miss you so bad."

"Can you pick me up in Kingston at eleven forty-five?"

"You're here? I'll be right over."

"Tomorrow, cher."

"Yes! Yes! I'll be there waiting—eleven forty-five."

"You wanna see me, cher?"

"More than anything in the world."

"I wanna see you too, dass for true."

"I love you, Mr. Boudreaux Clemont Finch. Eleven forty-five. I'll be there."

"Bye, cher," Peck said.

Peck ended his first call with a grin that plastered his face.

"Feels good, doesn't it?" Sasha asked. "Love."

"Oh, *oui*," Peck said. "So good."

Gabe was awake. There were tubes down his nostrils and wires on his chest and wrists. He was weak in voice, but his eyes twinkled at the sight of Sasha and Peck walking into the room.

"Not too long," the nurse said. "Tomorrow will be better. He's been through a lot."

"Hi honey," Sasha said, sitting on a chair next to the bed and holding Gabe's hand.

Gabe squeezed her hand.

Peck held his hand up as a waved hello for Gabe. Gabe smiled at Peck and raised his thumb.

"Honey, Peck is going to catch a bus to New Orleans. Lily Cup will set him up in a small apartment, and he starts schooling with a tutor on Monday, in the Garden District."

Gabe nodded agreement.

"He's going to see his Millie on his way down," Sasha said. "And it's okay because he agrees if they do anything they're going to wait until she's out of school."

Gabe nodded and smiled.

"And when Peck buys his crawfish farm, he's going to need you for swimming around distracting the alligators so he can pick up his traps," Sasha said.

Gabe started to laugh, then grimaced, and motioned to Sasha that it was pulling at his sutures.

"Oops. Sorry," Sasha said.

Gabe squeezed her hand, telling her thank you for another chance. A tear formed in her eye as she stood to leave. He held her hand and pulled her close to him and whispered in her ear.

"Go see Don," Gabe whispered. "Have him play 'When Sunny Gets Blue.'"

His hand loosened, and he fell asleep.

CHAPTER 27

LATE THAT EVENING, sitting in the Greyhound depot waiting area, Sasha pulled a debit card from her bag and handed it to Peck.

"Can you remember this combination: four, three, two, one?"

"Yes'm," Peck said. "Four, three, two, one."

"Good. Remember those four numbers in that order and keep them secret. This card will get you anything you'll need on your trip. It'll get you school supplies when you get to New Orleans. Hand it to the clerk at checkout, and if they ask you to enter your pin number, remember that code—four, three, two, one—and touch those numbers in that order."

Peck pointed to the name on the card.

"What this say, cher?"

"That's you, Peck. It says Boudreaux C. Finch. They couldn't fit Clemont on it. But that's you, Mr. Finch."

Peck smiled and held the card for a closer look. The embossed name matched the name on his new ID card. He turned it over and there was a signature on the back.

"I signed your name on it," Sasha said. "That's how you will sign your name when you can write. I just did it for you."

"T'anks."

Sasha held out a sealed envelope.

"This has some cash for the road. Use the card when you see things you need, though," Sasha said. "Don't lose it."

At the depot exit they found his bus. Sasha held Peck for a long goodbye. He was family now. Knowing Gabe was going to have a chance at more time was a game-changer for everyone somehow. It made this moment real, more permanent. She almost felt maternal.

"You go slow with Millie," Sasha said.

Peck listened, nodding his head.

"Don't overwhelm her. Give her plenty of time to know if she really loves you enough to be with you forever—"

"I will, I promise."

"—and that you're not just a rebound love for her."

"Rebound?" Peck asked.

Sasha stepped back looking Peck in the eyes.

"Peck," Sasha said. "You ever have a big fish on one hook and a smaller fish on another hook at the same time—?"

"*Oui.*"

"—and you can't pull the big one in through the briar barbs under water, only the small one?"

"*Oui,*"

"You take the small one home and eat it, right?"

"*Oui,*"

"But wouldn't you have rather had the big one?"

"Oh, *oui,*" Peck said, understanding the metaphor.

"Get it?" Sasha asked.

"*Oui,*" Peck said. "Be sure Peck is big fish, not little fish, cher."

Sasha walked him to the bus, handed him a sack with bottled water and sandwiches, and kissed him on the cheek.

"What do I tell her momma and daddy?" Peck asked.

Sasha reflected but didn't answer.

"I'll see you in New Orleans, honey," Sasha said. "Maybe you and I can fly up here on weekends to see Gabe and take him to the diner until he can come home."

"Corn," Peck said.

"You know?" Sasha asked. "I think corn would be perfect for him. You're right."

"Bye, cher," Peck said. "I love you for what you are, dass for true."

"Parents like the truth, Peck," Sasha said. "Just be yourself."

Sasha watched the bus pulling around the back of the station, bouncing a tilt from the driveway to the street and then on down to the highway, its roof washed with the gold of the streetlights as it passed under them on its eventual journey south.

Knowing her life had changed since an evening of dancing at Charlie's Blue Note, Michelle Lissette walked alone the many blocks through downtown Providence to the river and then to Point Street Bridge. As she neared it, she could hear the wail of the sax.

In the still of a cloud covered and seemingly moonless night she became Sasha again, making her way down the grassy slope and under the bridge, waving a gentle hand toward Don. He riffed from his slow blues wail into "When Sunny Gets Blue" without pause.

Sasha sat in tears. The torment of what Peck had been through and of almost losing Gabe stirred on her face like the shadows of a lonely get well card. The moment of change closing in, and it may have been dawning on her how lucky she was to have these two new friends, and how rewarding it was to be able to be there for them.

She sat and listened to gentle saxophone sounds until the others and lovers dwindled and moved on with a threat of rain, and Don began folding his tent from another early morning of jazz and mellow blues. He raised a plastic bottle of water and swallowed it all without stopping for breath. He stepped around the ledge, picking up cups and pieces of paper his listeners had left behind. He removed the mouthpiece and packed his instrument in the royal blue velvet lining, closed and locked the leather case.

He held his hand outstretched and offered Sasha a hand up the grassy knoll to the sidewalk. The two walked together, slowly, without talking for three blocks. Sasha folded a hundred-dollar bill, held it up for him to see and slipped it in his pocket.

"Gabe thanks you for being here for him," Sasha said.

Don smiled, and they split with a fist pump, Don going straight for three more blocks to his apartment to smoke cigarettes and drink vodka alone in the dark with his memories, and Sasha going left a block to the hotel to be alone maybe with her thoughts of her boys and of getting some rest.

Peck learned how easy it was to sleep through the night on an all-nighter bus. It wasn't until after the bus departed the bedlam of that New York City stop and the bustle of the Newark New Jersey terminal. He couldn't help noticing how much activity there was at city stations, alive with people moving about, while only one or two boarded buses. It was as if big city terminals were clubs of warmth and welcomed noises for the homeless or for people who couldn't sleep alone. Soon the bus made its way up into the Pennsylvania mountains under a rich, full moon. Could it be, Peck wondered to himself, that Gabe or Sasha were looking at the same moon and thinking of him? He remembered watching the moon as a child with a dog collar padlocked around his neck, chained under gator man's side porch. He'd grasp the wooden lattice with his little fingers and look up at the full moon as if to wonder if his real mother and real father ever looked at the moon while he did, and if they ever thought about him. He would pray to the moon to tell them he was certain they would like him now, because he wasn't a crying baby anymore, and now he could carry buckets of bait shrimp and not spill them and he could earn his keep. He would ask the moon to tell them if he saw them.

Under the glow of the moon and gentle swaying motion of the bus Peck dozed off about the same time Gabe opened his eyes.

"Lord," Gabe said under his breath. "Lord, I've been meaning to thank you. Actually, before the operation I thought I'd be thanking you in person, but since I made it through I've wanted the right moment and the right words and it's going to take me some time to get through this, and I don't have so much breath, so just bear with me as I'll need some time, and my catheter friend is taken care of my business, so there won't be any interruptions. Lord, I'm not good with words, you already know that, but you've bestowed on me so many other blessings, and I feel like I'm almost reborn today, just waking up after this operation, and I've been brought up to show appreciation, to always say thank you, and I'm going to do it properly if it takes all night.

"When I lost my boy in Iraq, and then I lost my butterfly, Lord, I thought you were truly telling me it was quitting time. I apologize for my doubt and questioning you. Please forgive the words I might have used those days. And when I found the cancer I figured it was your plan all along that we three go together and be done with it, but then you go and put that turn in my road, in Carencro, Louisiana it was, and I would never besmirch the Almighty with a presumption that this tattered old soul was the least bit worthy of a miracle, but Lord you put me on that dance floor off that Frenchman Street alley and one night of red beans and rice and Joe Williams, and it was a rebirth in me that could only be heaven-sent.

"I don't know what you have in store for me now—whether I'll live out a good life or get hit and run over by a truck when I walk out of here, but I want to thank you from the bottom of my heart—which is just about all that's left in there. Thank you for the time I had with my butterfly, and thank you for my son, and thank you for my new family—Michelle and Boudreaux. Oh, my Lord and God, you couldn't have aligned the stars any better than how you blessed us all the ways you have. Boudreaux is a good boy, you already knew that. He's the reason I'm here praying tonight and not days closer to pushing up dandelions. I feel like you put him here for me to look after, and you made me whole again to do it. And our Sasha friend doesn't have a bad bone in her body, and she'll watch after the boy long after I'm gone. So, thank you, Lord, I'll get some rest now. Thank you for listening. Amen."

Gabe closed his eyes and slept.

Peck's bus pulled into the Knoxville station for a thirty-minute food break. The next unscheduled stop would be Kingston Pike, where Millie would be waiting for him. Peck grabbed his duffel and stepped off the bus to stretch his legs. He figured there would be vittles when he arrived in Kingston, so he chose to just walk around, exploring outside the terminal. Across the street was a used bookstore. Peck couldn't read the sign, but his eyes brightened when he saw the posters of books in the window. He crossed the street and cautiously stepped in. After a small conversation, the clerk seemed to know to be patient with Peck, and he was helpful.

"I'm going to learn to read and write," Peck said. "You have a book with all the words maybe?"

The clerk went to the second row and picked three new books from a shelf and brought them forward.

"Here is a dictionary. It's one of the best there is," the clerk said. "These two come in a pair—a dictionary and a thesaurus."

Peck pointed at the one book. "All the words?"

"Yep," the clerk said.

"How much?" Peck asked.

"Twenty-four ninety-five, plus tax."

Peck knew his range went only to ten on the counting in English scale, so he opted to reach in his pocket and pull out his debit card. Within seconds he counted to himself, four, three, two, one—and within minutes he was crossing the street to the bus station with the safely wrapped dictionary he was looking forward to learning from. Carrying it gave him an emboldened sense of confidence. As he crossed the street, in the distance he could see his bus driver consoling a woman, her head down, who seemed as if she was crying.

"Lady," the bus driver said. "I'm really sorry, I just don't think your friend was on my run. He could be on the one that comes through at two thirty. If he's not on the bus, and you didn't see him in the terminal, I sure can't help you, lady. Anybody you can call?"

Peck stepped around, his bag with his new dictionary in one hand, his duffel in the other. He saw that the girl covering her eyes with a tissue and sobbing was his Millie.

He paused, stood there in awe, shifted both bags to one hand with a grin on his face and tapped her on the shoulder. Millie looked up as if he was annoying her, but after seeing him her brows shot up, her eyes burst open, and then came a toothy grin as she leaped with one hop up on him. He caught her, her arms over his shoulders, hanging on, as he held her waist. She kissed him again and again.

"Lady, it appears you have found your man," the bus driver said.

Millie's arm reached out and waved.

"We're loading, buddy," the bus driver said. "If you're going."

"I'm with her," Peck said. As she continued to kiss his chin and cheeks and nose, he freed his one arm and pointed a finger to the back of her head.

"I'm going with this one," Peck said.

The driver smiled coyly, crawled into his seat, and closed the door, giving Peck a thumbs up.

They loosened their clinch and grabbed a booth in the café where Millie spoke a mile a minute, explaining that when she knew the bus number she could find out all the stops and she decided she wanted to come to Knoxville and get him here, so they could talk before she took him home, and when he wasn't on the bus and not in the terminal her heart sank, and she couldn't stop crying. She ordered two orders of French fries and two BLT sandwiches and water and threw a glance at Peck to see if he was okay with a BLT.

"That poor man," Millie said of the bus driver.

"Oh, I bet he's seed some t'ings," Peck said.

"Daddy and Momma are so happy you're coming. Daddy's cooking brisket just for you, and he wants to take you out on his boat. Momma is making you bread pudding."

Peck smiled.

"There's just one little thing, Peck," Millie said.

"Hanh?"

"Nothing we can't get around, mind you."

"Like what?"

"I thought I should tell you before we get there, and you find out that way."

"Tell me, cher," Peck said.

"I love it when you call me cher."

Millie reached over the table and placed her hand over Peck's and was completely distracted.

"Oh, did you hear about our stab-in-the-face friend?" Millie asked.

"Nah, nah," Peck said. "The Brock guy or the bad guy?"

"The bad guy, of course, silly," Millie said.

"Tell me, cher," Peck said.

"So the state troopers went to his trailer and found him just as we left him. He couldn't move a muscle the way you tied him. It was in the newspaper. They even had to shoo a raccoon that had wandered in and was in the creep's garbage can—and they found a bag filled with all sorts of stolen pharmaceutical pills and capsules. A garbage bag full. The paper said it was a legal discovery as they had probable cause to search his place. The reporter even said the dog was probably killed in self-defense."

"This all good?" Peck asked.

"There's more," Millie said.

"*Bon*," Peck said. ("Good.")

"*Le bâtard* pleaded guilty to stabbing Brock if they didn't press charges on the pills," Millie said. "Daddy says he'll get ten years as he's done this before—robbed people on the highway, usually at truck stops. They have him on videos, but he would always leave the state where he robbed people."

Peck held Millie's hand and remembered Sasha's advice to go slow.

"Is that what you were tellin' me cher?"

"Okay," Millie said. "So the deal is the vermin showed up, and he's going to be having dinner with us, and I don't blame you if you get mad, but he just dropped in, and nobody invited him, and he's been apologizing and all that stuff, and are you mad at me?"

"Vermin?" Peck asked.

"The snake," Millie said.

"Snake?"

"The old boyfriend," Millie sang melodically. "Stephen."

"Ah," Peck said. "Stephen, the snake."

"He's more like an ingrown toenail."

"He knows 'bout Peck, this Stephen Toenail?"

"He will in forty minutes," Millie sang again.

"Won't your momma alretty did tole 'em?" Peck asked.

"Oh, no way," Millie said. "Daddy said why spoil the fun by telling him and miss out on all the fireworks."

"Do your daddy and momma know, like dat we...?" Peck started.

"No," Millie said, lifting her nose. "Nobody's business and nothing to tell anyway."

"So, what he mean 'bout fireworks, cher?"

"Oh, that," Millie said. "Stephen is so jealous he can't stand boys around me ever. He still thinks he owns me."

Peck looked at the smile of satisfaction in her eyes.

"You like the farm, for true, cher?" Peck asked.

"Chickens and tomatoes?" Millie asked, leaning forward.

"*Oui.*"

"More than anything."

"So, what you do when you seed a snake, hanh?" Peck asked.

"Simple," Millie said. "If it's little, I'd shoo it away. If it's big, I run get you to catch it for bait."

Peck's mouth dropped. Millie put her hand over her braces, grinned and raised her brows.

"Did I say that right?"

Pecked took his phone from his pocket, opened it and touched the number two button in front of Millie's name. Her cell rang within seconds, and she looked at it curiously and put it to her ear.

"Hello?" she asked.

Phone to his ear, Peck leaned forward, looking into her eyes while talking into his phone.

"I need to brought myself with a beau'tinous lady to some brisket and puddin', cher, can you did dat for me, farm girl?" Peck asked. He watched her eyes sparkle and tear up. He closed his phone and held her hand.

"If we sit here all day, they'll be no brisket or bread pudding left," Millie said.

"Snakes don't eat much," Peck said.

For the entire trip from Knoxville to the Kingston exit the two held hands when it was safe, and the only thing said between them was Peck asking Millie how much longer she had in school, and Millie telling him three semesters, but she was taking French as well, and not to ever mention to her folks what they did last time he was there when they caught the knife man.

"*C'est bon*," Peck said, holding up three fingers for three semesters.
"I know that's good," Millie said.
"*Oui*," Peck said.
They pulled onto the drive, and Peck lifted his package and duffel from the floor.

Late the same afternoon, Sasha, with the help of two nurses, got Gabe out of bed, and he walked in slow, short steps ten feet, to the other side of the hall and ten feet back to the bed.
"Only one hundred eighty to go," Sasha said.

CHAPTER 28

AT THE HOUSE, PECK OFFERED CORDIAL HUGS to the momma and the reverend. They were warm and gracious and asked how long he could stay—the special young man who would stop a bus just to make a person happy. The momma's interest was inspired in spreading the gospel with the example he set, the daddy's was to get some fishing in. While they made their pleasantries, the Ingrown Toenail was in the bathroom skulking. Peck took the opportunity of his absence to inquire about the fishing tackle in the garage. Reverend offered it and asked if he could join him on the dock while waiting on the brisket and potatoes in the smoker.

"Peck," the reverend said, "I have a package of frozen shrimp we can try as bait. I hear they use frozen shrimp offshore in Galveston. I'd like to try it here. Would that do us?"

"Shrimp *bon* in saltwater," Peck said. "Les' try it in fresh water."

Millie's expression was pleased that her two favorite men would be down on the dock and out of harm's way from an inevitable Ingrown Toenail drama.

"You two be back in an hour," the momma said. "Millie and I will have the salad and deviled eggs done about then, and we'll be ready for the brisket and potatoes."

At the dock, the reverend gave Peck two rods and kept two for himself. He used frozen shrimp on one and a lure on the other that he stood and cast. Peck took some time and prepared frozen shrimp on both rods. He tied eight shrimp just above three pronged hooks and lowered them to the bottom, letting the bait rest on the bottom with floating bobbers to watch. He sat on the dock with his legs hanging over.

"Have you always lived in Louisiana, son?" the reverend asked.

"Oui," Peck said. "I growed some at Bayou Chene, near Petit Anse Bayou 'tween Bayou Sorrel and Choctaw, but then I go to Carencro."

"Do you have family there?" the reverend asked. "In Carencro?"

"Je ne connais pas mes parents, Révérend. Jamais fait," Peck said. ("I don't know my parents, Reverend. Never did.")

"I never..." Peck started.

"I understand what you said, son," the reverend said. "And I'll be proud to tell you you've done one outstanding job of knowing life's values and of being a good and merciful Christian."

"When I growed I'd talk to the moon and pretend my mamma was the moon telling me how to behave, Reverend," Peck said. "The moon told me good, dass for true."

"You were your own parent," Reverend said.

"I don' know what that meaned," Peck said.

"Such a heartfelt story. You're a special person, young man."

"T'anks," Peck said.

"It's none of my business, son," Reverend said. "But can you read and write?"

Peck lifted the debit card from his pocket and held it up.

"I'm going to New Or–lee–anhs and learn me to read, Reverend," Peck said. "I starting right away, then school and university."

"Can you manage that on your own? May we help?"

"Nah, nah, t'ank ya," Peck said. "Captain Gabe Jordan adopted Peck and he put me in learning all everything."

"What a nice man he must be," Reverend said. "This Captain Gabe fellow."

"*Oui*," Peck said. "God gived me Gabe to save his life from hospice, and He gived Gabe me to save mine and put me in school."

"Praise the Lord," the reverend said.

The reverend reeled in a bass, unhooked it and dropped it in the ice chest. He cast the lure out again.

"So how have you supported yourself all this time?"

"I mow and rake lawn at hospice on Bayou Carencro, and I throwed my trotline and catch things I sell— snappers, mashwarohn, like dat."

Reverend reeled in another largemouth bass, unhooked it and placed it in the ice chest.

"Mashwarohn?" the reverend asked just as he got another strike. "What's that?"

He reeled in a bass.

"Catfish," Peck said. "Mashwarohn is Cajun for catfish."

"Where do you live?" the reverend asked.

"I catch the crawfish snakes and cut them for bait for my trotline and I got a cot and hot plate in a boat builder's blade shed in back of the wood mill, barter it for sharpenin' they saw blades."

As reverend reeled in another bass he said, "I need to go turn the brisket one last time and take out the potatoes. You stay here a few more minutes, son. See if you can have some luck."

"Okay," Peck said.

"Bring the ice chest when you come up," the reverend said.

"*Oui*," Peck said.

As the reverend walked up the hill, Peck watched until he was out of sight. He got on his knees and hand over hand pulled one of his fishing lines until he surfaced what was a ten-pound mashwarohn. He smiled and snipped the line, letting it swim away. He tugged on his other line. It was empty, so he reeled it in and discarded the shrimp that was on that line, throwing it in the lake.

They each had a plate in their hand and lined up near the smoker for the reverend to slice portions of brisket and fork over a potato.

"So how do you know Millie?" Ingrown Toenail asked.

Peck learned long ago that brevity always worked to an advantage in a negotiation with an alligator, or an arm-wrestle with a drunk.

"Bus," Peck said.

"What do you mean, bus?"

"Bus."

"Don't you live around here?"

"Nah, Nah," Peck said.

"So, you just got off a bus here?"

"*Oui.*"

"Talk English."

"Yes, I got off here."

"What are you, a stalker?"

"I'm a fish'r."

"A fisherman?" Ingrown Toenail asked.

"*Oui.*"

"Oh, that's rich. As if Millie would actually be the least bit interested in a Frenchie frog fisherman."

"Nah, nah," Peck said.

"Like you would know what Millie likes."

Reverend placed portions on Peck's and then on Ingrown Toenail's plates, and they turned toward the house. Peck leaned into Ingrown Toenail.

"I know what Millie don't like, cher," Peck said.

Ingrown Toenail looked at him in disgust.

"She don't like you," Peck said.

He stepped in the doorway and walked over to get an iced tea. He waited for the momma to come in and seat everyone. She was at the head of the table. Peck was to her left and Millie was to her right.

Ingrown Toenail sat with a pout to the right of Millie. He'd throw snarly looks over at Peck, but Peck has seen worse on snapping turtles staring him down.

Reverend said the blessing and thanked the Lord for all gathered at the table. He asked for a blessing of the food and of the lives of each there. He said they were blessed for having met Peck and prayed for every success for Peck in his school days ahead.

"School?" Millie asked, interrupting the reverend. "Sorry, Daddy."

"*Oui,*" Peck said.

"When?" Millie asked.

"When I get to New Or–lee–anhs," Peck said. "Right away, I start."

"Ask me, he's going to need a lot more than school," Ingrown Toenail said. "Can't make a pig out of a sow's ear—right, Reverend?"

"Stephen, behave," the momma said. "That's not polite. Be Christian, son."

"And it's a purse," Millie said. "Can't make a purse..."

"Even if you did have school, what could you do with it?" Ingrown Toenail asked.

Millie looked at Stephen as if she were tired of his rudeness.

"Why look at me? He's too old to be good anywhere, Millie."

Peck set his fork down and waited, as if he challenged Ingrown Toenail to dare give him the floor.

Ingrown Toenail accepted the challenge with a sneer.

"How would you know what to do with an education anyway? You'd still be a redneck."

"I'd ax Millie to marry me," Peck said.

Everyone's fork hit their plates. Millie's mouth dropped open—her eyes teared up. She sat frozen with her hand over a grinning mouth.

Reverend looked down at the momma and then he looked at Peck with a curious squint in his eye.

"Just what are your intentions, young man?" he asked.

Peck stood and stepped over to the computer table near the back door and picked up his shopping bag. He walked back, sat down and lifted out the package and unwrapped the dictionary and held it up.

"Reverend, sir?" Peck asked, then looking over at Millie's momma. "Momma?"

Once he had their undivided attention he began.

"I know I ain't intelligent, and I know'd they is smarter, but there won't ever be nobody who will love Millie more'n me ever, and dass for true. Now Millie has herself three (he held up three fingers) semesters more in university and I got all dat time and more after dat to get it did right, but I promise with all my heart, cher, if your daddy, the reverend say yes and your mommy say yes and you say yes, in three semesters I will know ever' word in this here book, and I spend every day of our life telling you one or two and what they mean."

"This is such a crock," Ingrown Toenail said.

"Hush, "Millie said. "The man is talking."

"Reverend, sir?" Peck asked. "If'n Millie will have me after we both get our school, can I marry her?"

The reverend didn't think twice. He simply looked over at Millie.

"Millie?" the reverend asked.

"Oh please, Daddy," Millie said.

The reverend looked down at a smiling momma.

"Young man needs his education, Momma," the reverend said. "He can't fish."

"Is that a yes, Daddy?" Millie asked.

"And you'll wait until after school for both of you?" the reverend asked.

"Yessir," Peck said. "My word."

"Then the yes would have to come from our dumplin', it would seem. Millie?"

Millie looked at Peck, her eyes streaming in tears. "Yes, yes, I will marry you."

"This is such a crock..." Ingrown Toenail said.

Millie pushed her seat back, stood and ran to her room. On her return she carried her baby doll, Charlie. She walked over and handed it to Peck to cradle it in his arm. He did so and picked up his fork with his other hand and stabbed a piece of brisket. Millie stepped around to her side of the table.

"Stephen," Millie said. "Either stay and be a gentleman or leave."

It was nine o'clock in Providence while Sasha was walking with Gabe through the hospital hall.

"You did a hundred feet two times today, honey," Sasha said.

"I'm ready for the Boston Marathon," Gabe said.

"If you keep this up, you'll be in your hotel by next week and able to travel in September."

"When can we dance?"

"Whenever you ask, pookie."

Sasha pushed the door to his room, and he made his way in. Just before he got to the bed Sasha took him by the arm to steer him around by the window.

"Come over here," Sasha said. "I have a surprise for you."

"What the...?" Gabe started.

Sasha opened the window and stuck her head out.

"Over here," Sasha shouted. "He's here in this one."

She pulled her head back in and smiled at Gabe just as a saxophone on the lawn below began playing "When Sunny Gets Blue."

"My baby," Gabe said.

VaaaaaVeeVeeVaaVoooooOVaaaVaaaVaVaVaVeeeeeVa...

"You are something else."

The velvet wails of a saxophone echoed off hospital walls, and people gathered on the lawn.

"Wanna dance?" Sasha asked.

Gabe moved his walker aside and embraced her. He swayed once, twice. Sasha kissed him on the neck just as she looked down and saw flashing police lights on a patrol car below.

"Uh oh, there's trouble," Sasha said.

Gabe looked out. "Will they arrest him or just ticket him?"

"I'll go down," Sasha said. "Watch my bag."

Most of the staff enjoyed the antics of the sax. The head nurse was the one who had called the police. No one had to tell Sasha that. She could tell by the scowl on her face.

"Officer, officer," Sasha shouted as she ran toward the scene. "It's all my fault, officer. I'm to blame."

"Don was disturbing the peace, lady," the officer said. "We leave him alone if he stays under the bridge, but the hospital called and reported the nuisance."

"Nurse Cratchet up there is a bitch, officer," Sasha said. "Everybody else loved it. He was playing for an old man up there just out of an operation."

"If you want to defend him, ma'am, you'll have to go tell it to the judge," the officer said.

"Say that again, officer," Sasha said.

"Excuse me?" the officer asked.

"Say what you just said," Sasha said. "About the judge."

"I said you'll have to tell that to the judge, lady."

"You're Officer Kelsey, aren't you?" Sasha asked.

"Lady, do we know each other?"

"Officer Brandon Kelsey," Sasha said.

"I am."

"I knew it. I'm good with names and voices. I'm in real estate."

"But—"

"I was the one with Judge Thibodaux in his chamber in the Carencro Louisiana courthouse when you found and were witness to a man being alive and then witnessing his living will."

"Now I remember. That's right," the officer said. "I did do that. So, you're the—"

"I'm her," Sasha said, extending her hand for a shake.

"Well, I'll be," the officer said. "Don, you got lucky tonight. I'm letting you go without a ticket."

"You remember the man?" Sasha asked. "The man you witnessed for?"

"I do," the officer said.

Sasha pointed up to Gabe, looking out the window three flights up.

"That's him," Sasha said. "That's the one and only Gabriel Jordan."

The officer looked up at Gabe and waved.

"He was operated on and is going to live."

The officer stepped around and looked at Don. "So, what are you waiting for, Don?"

"I'm going, I'm going," Don said. "I'm out of here."

"The hell you are," the officer said.

"What?"

"What were you playing for our friend up there?"

"'When Sunny Gets Blue,' officer," Don said.

The officer looked at Sasha.

"Nobody but Nurse Cratchet complained?"

"Not a soul," Sasha said.

"Finish it," the officer said.

"What?" Don asked.

"Finish it," the officer said. "Or I'll run you in."

Don started a new riff of "When Sunny Gets Blue." The officer told everyone to disperse, and he told Don to go back to the bridge after he was finished. Sasha kissed the officer on the cheek, thanked him, and went back inside.

Sasha stepped off the elevator with Nurse Cratchet standing there, as if stalking her, arms folded, and scowl matching her personality. She wasn't about to give Sasha the benefit of acknowledging how Sasha managed the softer side of the law, allowing the lovely music to entertain patients.

"Visiting hours are over."

Sasha walked toward Gabe's room.

"You'll have to go," Nurse Cratchet said.

"In a little bit," Sasha said, brushing by her.

"Now," Nurse Cratchet said. "Or I'll call security."

Sasha turned on a dime. "Look, here, wicked witch of the north. I don't know what got your panties in a wad, but if that man doesn't do his walks he won't get out of here, and I'm his official walker, so you call security, and I call my lawyer, and this time next week you'll work for me, as I'll own the hospital."

Nurse Cratchet harrumphed and walked away.

In the room, Gabe was in bed with a broad smile.

"My baby," Gabe said. "That was something. Please tell Don thanks for me. Tell him that was special."

"You know who that cop was?" Sasha asked.

"I do," Gabe said. "From under the bridge."

"Isn't it a small world?"

"Your phone has been making all kinds of sounds," Gabe said.

Sasha picked it from her purse.

"A text," Sasha said. "Listen to this. *'Hi Michelle, this is Millie. Peck asked my folks if he could marry me after we're out of school, and they said yes and I said yes and I love him so much, and he wanted me to tell you and his dad, Gabe, and he is going to stay here again tomorrow, and then he will be on the bus to New Orleans and start school. XOXOXO Millie.'*"

"We picked a winner in that boy," Gabe said.

"You picked him," Sasha said. "I was a hooker, remember?"

"Oh my," Gabe giggled. "That's right."

"But he is a winner," Sasha said. "She sounds like a winner too."

"She does," Gabe said.

"So where are you going to live when you get out of here?" Sasha asked.

"How much do I have put away?"

"Enough to be comfortable."

"I'm a dad again," Gabe said. "You're a realtor. Do I have enough to get a small three-bedroom in the Garden District?"

"So, we don't get Peck an apartment?"

"He'll live at home," Gabe said. "Least until he's out of school."

"One floor," Sasha said. "So you can save your knees for dancing. I'll look at some shotgun houses. There're some deals."

"See you tomorrow, baby?" Gabe asked.

"Yeppers," Sasha said. "Hundred fifty feet tomorrow."

Sasha kissed Gabe on the neck and went back to the hotel.

In her room she soaked in a hot tub bath, lifted her phone and answered Millie's text. *"Thanksgiving or Christmas, pick one. But you and your family come to New Orleans, and we celebrate you and Peck. XOXO Michelle."*

CHAPTER 29

BY MID OCTOBER GABE AND PECK WERE SETTLED in a modest three-bedroom shotgun cottage in the Garden District. Peck could count change, had mastered the alphabet and was reading at a fourth-grade level. He was taking French, as the thinking was learning conjugations and sentence structure in English might be easier for him if he learned it in a language that he already knew quite well. The tutor found his animal science aptitude to be particularly strong and was pushing him into working on projects and visiting museums around the city.

Peck was becoming an avid reader. He'd look up a word he wasn't certain of in his dictionary. He memorized the pronunciation of vowels and consonants, and he would master one child's book, reading it aloud several times by memory, and go on to the next. Daily he would dictate to his tutor messages that he wanted texted to his Millie, and she would help him read Millie's responses.

On Thanksgiving Millie's family joined her and visited New Orleans for the holiday weekend. The reverend and the momma stayed at Sasha's, and Millie stayed in the third bedroom with Gabe and Peck. They took to Gabe right off, admiring his kindness and generosity toward others. They were most impressed when Peck greeted them at the airport with a "Welcome to New Orleans and Happy Thanksgiving," without a hint of patois. Oh, he could turn it on when he wanted to, but with his new knowledge of diction he so enjoyed feeling a part of society. He and Millie held hands and were inseparable, walking through the Garden District and on daylight tours in the Quarter. They would talk of children and of gardens and crawfish beds and catfish farms, and Peck would read a book to Millie, and Millie would sit there in tears and know that every word he read was him saying *I love you* to her. She would ask him what would grow best in the soil they would have, and he said tomatoes and onions, maybe zucchini and melons.

"Lots of shickens," he would say. "But you have to put them in at night to keep them safe from the critters."

Gabe cooked turkey and stuffing; the momma made her bread pudding, and Sasha brought a green bean casserole and rolls and salad. Millie made the sweet potatoes with marshmallows; and with his reading and counting skills and with some help, Peck was able to master the recipe and oven temperatures for pecan pie with Karo syrup, and he made three. He also used his debit card to buy a pot of turtle soup for those curious enough to try.

Each morning Peck and Millie would catch a streetcar and then walk the distance to the Café du Monde for coffee and beignets and look into each other's eyes as Gabe would say coffee and chicory and a beignet in New Orleans was not a luxury but a morning prayer.

The reverend and the momma joined Sasha and Gabe at Charlie's Blue Note one evening, and although they drank iced tea, they did enjoy the red beans and rice and slow dancing to authentic New Orleans jazz. While they were away, Millie and Peck made haste, expressing their passion for each other being alone at home.

"We could cut quite a rug, in college," the reverend would say.

It was at the Blue Note when they decided, and Sasha as well, that everyone should come for Christmas in Tennessee. They could get to see Knoxville decorated and have a grand time, and it was certain Santa would come to the house on the Kingston Road exit. Weather permitting, they could also get some fishing in.

To get them off on their Christmas trip, Lily Cup drove Gabe, Sasha, and Peck to the airport and pulled up to the curbside attendant, leaving the car running. Peck and Gabe wished Lily Cup a Merry Christmas and got out to grab the bags.

"What are you doing for Christmas, sweetie?" Sasha asked.

"Mom needs the company," Lily Cup said. "With Dad gone she's happiest if we just go out somewhere. We'll think of something."

"We'll be back on Sunday," Sasha said.

"Let me know," Lily Cup said. "I'll pick you up."

"You look nice," Sasha said. "You going to a party?"

"Christmas party at Angola," Lily Cup said. "Going to see some of my clients, take them a little something."

"Are you allowed to give them gifts?" Sasha asked.

"They open them up and rewrap them, but yes," Lily Cup said. "And the inmates can give visitors gifts. Things they have or made while in there. It helps them feel part of the human race. At Christmas, they even let the prisoners who are in for nonviolent crimes visit their guests in lounge chairs in the main sitting area. So I'll see Andre out there today. He was a good boy—only busted for gun-running."

"Love you," Sasha said.

"Love you back," Lily Cup said, and they air-kissed goodbye.

Lily Cup drove into Angola, parked and took a shopping bag filled with gifts out of her trunk. Most were simple trinkets or souvenir keepsakes she had wrapped, just so a prisoner would be able to unwrap a gift. Andre's gift was a jigsaw puzzle.

"You look lovely," Andre said. "So festive."

"Why thank you, Andre," Lily Cup said. "You look nice. You've shaved, a nice shirt and everything. Are you being a good boy?"

"I deliver mail on my cell block. Know most everybody. Being good so you can get me out," Andre said.

"Well, you can be good to be good too," Lily Cup said.

"So I heard a story, Lily Cup," Andre said.

"Is it a Christmas story, Andre?"

"It's kind of like a Christmas present, this story."

"Open your present first, Andre."

Lily Cup pulled the package from the shopping bag. Andre opened it to find a jigsaw puzzle.

"A paddlewheel," Andre said.

"It's the Mississippi Queen," Lily Cup said. "500 pieces."

"A Mississippi River steamboat," Andre said.

Andre studied the box as a child would on Christmas morning. The colors, the steamboat, the pelicans along the Mississippi River shore.

"Look at the pelicans watching it go by, it's coming into N'Orleans—headed to Bourbon Street," Andre said.

"Some people frame their puzzles after they put them together, Andre. They can look nice all framed pretty in like a TV room or den or someplace."

"Thank you, my friend," Andre said.

Andre reached to the floor and picked up a small box wrapped with paper and ribbon. He didn't hand it to Lily Cup but set it on the table before him.

"You want to hear a Christmas story?" he asked.

"I love Christmas stories, Andre," Lily Cup said.

"Now I don't know where I heard this one, Lily Cup. Important you know that," Andre said. "Could have been on television or something like that."

Lily Cup looked as if she sensed Andre was sending a message with the buildup.

"Okay," Lily Cup said, with a bit of hesitation.

"This rich guy, see, could have been from England or France or somewhere like that—yeah, England," Andre said. "He wants to get him an alligator. Oh, he wants a big one, that's for sure—like to have it stuffed and put over a bar or in his den somewhere, maybe his club."

Lily Cup listened.

"So, somebody—I don't know who, maybe a park ranger. You know, those guys with the hats," Andre said. "Well maybe this park ranger tells this English guy he needs to go to Choctaw and ask for gator man, you know, like the one with old lady Prudhomme somewhere down there, like she's his old lady, he tells the guy. So, they find the gator man and the English guy tells him he wants a big gator, maybe over seventeen feet and he'll pay five thousand to shoot one. Well that gator man says for five thousand he would take him out personally, but it had to be at sunset, when gators and crocs wake up, and they'd have to be in two boats. Gator man always goes alone in his pirogue because he has to stand all the way, and stand and pole row, and he don't want more people who might tip it so he falls in. And the other boat had to stay thirty feet away, and there was a fancy video camera with the infrared lenses that would shoot in the night on that boat to make sure it didn't get too close and maybe bump the other boat."

Lily Cup listened.

"So, Lily Cup, they go out in two boats, just like the gator man says, and they're back in the bayou just where the swamp begins. The pirogue got on the deep side of some big old bald cypress, and this near twenty-foot gator comes up from behind like a fast log and gator man signals back to English in the other boat to get ready to shoot, and wouldn't you know, his pirogue went and jerked, and gator man lost his balance, dropped his pole, and he fell out?"

"Did he get back in his boat?" Lily Cup asked.

"Oh no," Andre said.

"What happened?"

"A young gator he don't waste no time and took his head clean off with one snap and a quick twist, and the big ole one, the near twenty-footer? Why that gator took him under to bury until he rots and seasons good to eat later. That gator man didn't feel a thing, or so the English guy who was telling the story told somebody."

"Did he call the police?"

"I'm glad you asked that, *mon ami*. You see, the Englishman he come to shore. He sees these two what you call vagrant trappers. They not doing so good with their traps, don't you know, cause one of them asks English for money to buy cigarettes, see, so he tells the trappers what happened and what should he do? They looked at his anchor rope and saw that it was dry, so he couldn't have used the anchor rope to pull and jerk gator man's pirogue, and then they watched the video recorder and saw that the boats weren't close to each other, but sure enough they saw gator man's boat jerk good and him falling in the bayou."

"And?"

"One of them said he must have hit a root. They couldn't see nothing jerking the boat, one said," Andre said. "The other wondered should they call the sheriff."

"Did they call?" Lily Cup asked.

"The storyteller, he never finished the story. I don't know," Andre said.

"If those two took the time to check the anchor rope and watch the video, seems they would have called the sheriff," Lily Cup said.

"As the story goes, *mon ami*, English gave them—the vagrants who asked him for cigarette money—why he gave them two thousand dollars each and told them to be sure to go look up the Prudhomme lady and give it all to her. He counted it out in their hands, two thousand dollars each. Then he left. I guess for England or France or somewhere those rich guys travel. Nobody ever said what happened after that."

Lily Cup sat back. She didn't say a word. She knew better than to talk or ask questions. She knew everything Andre had told her he presented to her as third-party hearsay. It was worthless as evidence anywhere.

Andre handed the small box to Lily Cup.

"Merry Christmas, my friend," Andre said. "Open this later."

"Thank you, Andre. Merry Christmas."

"Maybe you can, how they say, re-gift it to someone."

Lily Cup stood, holding the package, looking Andre in the eye.

"Andre don't mind, *mon ami*."

When Lily Cup got to her car, she unwrapped the box and opened it. It was a large spool of black, two-hundred-pound test fishing line. The spool was empty.

She texted Sasha.

"Hey," she texted.

"Hey," Sasha texted.

"You in Knoxville?"

"Nearby, yes."

"He's gone."

"Who's gone?"

"Gator man."

"Where?"

"You don't want to know."

"You're right. I don't want to know."

"You never will."

"Love you," Sasha texted.

"Love you," Lily Cup texted.

Part Two
Mamma's Moon
(Nine months later)

CHAPTER 30

GABE BOUGHT A THREE-BEDROOM SHOTGUN HOUSE in the Garden District that he and Peck shared. Peck now drove to his work cleaning offices and to a private tutor. One morning Gabe decided to take a walk, for a stretch of the legs and to go to Walmart to get some housekeys made. It had been nearly sixty years since the retired veteran had been in a Penny Arcade and played with the pinball machines long before there were video games. Penny Arcades near army bases were nostalgic for the homesick soldiers when he was young and when his Army friends had day passes from Korean battlefields and only had time to kill in the 1950s.

Needing extra sets of keys, Gabe remembered hearing of the credit- card-operated vending machine that could make duplicate keys while you watched and waited and he heard of other vending machines lining the front hall of Walmart that could virtually do anything else.

Gabe's buddy, a retired sergeant at the VA hospital in Pineville was first to stir his imagination by telling him about the machine.

"Just put a card in and a key you want copied and hit a few buttons and tell it how many you want and if you want it plain or with a favorite NFL team logo on the bow for fifty cents more," his friend would say.

Gabe's imagination did the rest.

He set his mind on the Saturday morning errand to witness this gadget he'd been promised and to get extra house keys made.

The store's front hall lined with machines was everything his veteran friend had told him, and the key machine was as promised. So fascinating was the machine Gabe bought a pair of reading glasses for $9.95, just to catch all the action behind the window.

"Hey, mister," the young man at the next machine said.

Gabe glanced over at the boy. Twenty, twenty-two was his guess. Clean cut, clothes neat, a book bag on his back. Gabe didn't answer, busy reading the directions on the key-making machine.

"Mister, can you let me use your card for just a second, please? I'll give it right back," the young man said.

"No," Gabe said without looking up.

The young man turned and asked a passerby and was turned down. He turned to Gabe again.

"Mister, this machine won't charge anything to your card, but it'll give me ten dollars and I'll give you two dollars just for letting me use your card. It'll only take ten seconds, and I'll give it back."

"No," Gabe said.

"Not even for two dollars, you won't let me use your card?"

"I can't son, sorry," Gabe said.

"You can't? You can't? A grown man telling me you can't? You lying old motherfucker, mister, telling me you can't."

Gabe looked over at the boy.

"Old man you're a dead man the second you walk out of this store—you're a dead motherfucker. You hear me, old man?"

With cold, gray eyes, the boy stared at Gabe and backed down the hall, pointing a finger at him and cursing his threat.

Visibly shaken, Gabe turned to his left and went looking for the store manager.

CHAPTER 31

GABE'S FRONT DOOR PUSHED OPEN. Lily Cup stepped in. "I just spoke with the coroner, the kid's dead," Lily Cup said.

The aging army captain, veteran of Korea and Vietnam, lowered his newspaper just enough to see over the entertainment page.

"Was it murder, Gabe?" Lily Cup asked.

"Close the door, honey, AC's on," Gabe said.

In a black skirt with a tailored matching waistcoat and white Nike walking shoes, she leaned and propped a black leather briefcase against the wall by the door. She stood like an exasperated tomboy, adjusting and refastening her grandmother's diamond brooch on her lapel.

"I heard you've been walking with a cane, dancing man. What's that all about?"

"So?"

"You don't carry a cane."

"I've owned canes for years."

"You jazz dance for hours on end a couple of nights a week and all of a sudden, out of the blue, Sasha tells me you started carrying one everywhere? I know you don't need a cane."

"I just prefer wearing a cane now."

"Wearing a cane?"

"A gentleman wears a cane—a color befitting his ensemble."

"Well excuse me."

"A gentleman carries an umbrella or walking stick."

"Wearing or carrying, it smells premeditated to me, Gabe. What's up with the cane thing?"

"Does Sasha know about this morning?"

"I've been putting out fires all over the CBD. I haven't had time to tell her anything. She'd have a canary."

Gabe lifted the paper again to read.

"I need to know if it was premeditated," Lily Cup said.

"I don't want to talk about it," Gabe said.

He closed the paper, folded it in half, and in half again. Dropping it on the arm of the chair, he stood and left the room.

"Define premeditated murder," he said from the kitchen.

She tossed a handbag and white driving gloves onto the other chair, lifted Chanel sunglasses to the top of her head.

"Gee, I'll have to think on this one. Hmmm...Oh, I know. How about the police have a cane with blood on it and there's a dead man who had no weapon?"

"It's a walking stick. My cane is over by the door."

"Well now it's a goddamned murder weapon, Gabe. They checked for prints, and yours are the only prints on it, and their guess is the lab will say the blood has his DNA."

Gabe came out with a coffee urn in one hand and his finger and thumb through two empty cup handles. He held the cups out for her to take one.

"No more," Gabe said.

"You're rather nonchalant for the spot you're in. Why'd you clam up on me like that at the precinct? It didn't set well with any of them. The DA entered a charge of second-degree murder. With pressure from New Orleans tourism folks the police chief put out a warrant for you from his lunch at Brennan's."

He held the empty cups closer to her.

"Just made it. Chicory and cinnamon."

"If you had a damn television here, you'd have seen it— 'Daylight killing on St. Charles Avenue.' It's all over the news, freaking out the DA and the Visitors Bureau. No telling how many videos from streetcars going by will wind up on You Tube."

"That's enough," Gabe said.

"People can live with violence after dark. That's expected in any city, but when it's in broad daylight, forget about it. The DA pushed for an early docket and it's Tulane and Broad for you at nine a.m. tomorrow."

"What's Tulane and Broad?"

"Why don't you have a television?"

"What's Tulane and Broad?"

"Magistrate Court."

Gabe was silent.

"You're being arraigned in the morning."

Gabe glanced at the coffee mugs in his hand.

"Congratulations, Gabe, you made the big time. You have to appear before a magistrate to hear the second-degree murder charge against you."

"What then?" Gabe asked.

"We enter a plea. Guilty, not guilty, or nolo contendere."

She took an empty cup in one hand, pinched his arm with the other.

"Gabe, look me in the eye and swear it wasn't premeditated."

"Is this some technique they teach at Harvard Law, Miss Tarleton?"

Gabe poured her coffee.

"Now is not the time to fuck with me, Gabe. You're a big boy—you know the difference— premeditated and self-defense."

Gabe returned the coffee pot to the kitchen, came back out and sat down.

With his silence she rolled her eyes and turned to the other chair.

"The only reason they haven't busted down your door and you're not behind bars is they trust me, Gabe. I know the system and how to get around in it."

"If they come, they come."

"You're a decorated veteran, and I'm your attorney, and I promised you'll show up in the morning."

"Tell me where and when, I'll be there."

"Sasha warned me about you."

"Oh, I'm sure she has."

"You're an ornery, stubborn old coot when you have a mind to."

She sat down.

"I'm never ornery," Gabe said. "But that's enough."

"I should have listened to Sasha."

"You're a damned good attorney, Lily Cup."

"Yeah?—well if I'm that good why are half my clients in Angola."

"I know you're good."

"Gabe—now that we're on it, there's something I need to tell you."

"I appreciate you."

"You may want to get somebody else."

"You were third in your class at Harvard—"

"Gabe, I was bottom of my class at Harvard—I had to take my bar exam three times."

Gabe sipped his coffee, looking into her eyes.

"Sasha tells everybody I was third in my class—"

"Drink your coffee while it's hot."

"—but I'm smart."

"I know you are, little sister—that I do know."

"I wasn't good with books, even in high school. I'm what they call an observational learner—a hands-on learner. I learned more after I got out of school than I ever did in. It was painful just going to class—but I never missed a class and that alone got me through."

"You're dogged," Gabe said. "That makes you good."

"You still want me after tomorrow, Gabe?"

"It's you and me, little sister—it's you and me all the way."

Lily Cup clenched her coffee mug with both hands and a grin like a school girl with a cup of hot chocolate.

"We're lucky we have Judge Fontenot."

"Why is that?"

"I heard her dad was killed in Vietnam."

"I wonder if I knew him."

"She's always been fair to me in the past. A new school gal, tough on the letter of the law, but she'll listen to reason if it solves a case. She hates red tape with a passion, and seldom lets the DA or the defense use the system for delays. If things can get resolved out of court she doesn't get hung up on tradition."

"Have you heard?" Gabe asked.

"Heard what?"

"Our Sasha asked me to give her away."

"Gabe, like she's been my best friend since kindergarten, she tells me everything," Lily Cup said.

"How about them apples?"

"It's sweet."

"I'm thinking Peck and I throw her a party," Gabe said. "Something she'll remember."

"Costumes, she'll remember costumes."

"We'll commemorate their engagement Mardi Gras style. Lots of pictures; close friends."

"Will you print invitations, like a formal do?" Lily Cup asked.

"But of course," Gabe said.

"It's party time! She would flip over a costume party, all our friends would," Lily Cup said.

"We have to come up with some music," Gabe said.

"You and Peck celebrating her engagement will mean a lot to her."

"Should we do it here or over at Charlie's Blue Note with live jazz?"

"Gabe, you've got one picture on your mantle, two chairs, and a cardboard box in the living room."

"More space for people," Gabe said.

"This isn't exactly what I'd call a Commander's Palace party room, Gabe."

"I was thinking a streetcar *day pass* in the invite if we do it here."

"That's a great idea—parking sucks on this street."

"I have to make a list," Gabe said.

"When are you going to buy some furniture?"

"I'm too old to impose furniture on Peck."

"You need furniture for you."

"Peck would only feel obligated to keep it after I'm gone. I'll let him and Millie pick out the furniture doodads, curtains, and the dishes when they play house. There's time."

"How's your stomach?"

"What stomach? They removed it."

"I don't mean since the operation. Were you hurt today?" Lily Cup asked.

"He missed me with his knife."

"The DA is having a problem with that, Gabe."

"What problem?"

"They found no knife anywhere at the scene."

Gabe watched the bubble floating on his coffee and took a sip.

"I'm a hospice survivor with some time left in me, hopefully. At least enough time to plan a party."

"You might be partying in Angola if the DA decides to push this to a grand jury," Lily Cup said.

Gabe stood, got the coffee urn from the kitchen and brought it into the living room.

"Let me warm your coffee?"

"Do you two at least have beds?"

"Of course we have beds, little sister. Peck thinks he's a prince—a mattress and sheets after sleeping on a canvas cot most of his life with a saddle blanket that wouldn't cover his legs."

"This all must be a new world for him," Lily Cup said.

"For fifteen years he slept in a shed with no heat at a boat maker's wood mill," Gabe said.

"No heat?"

"He had a hotplate for his coffee pot. Saw blades hanging over him like Macy's parade balloons. It took him weeks getting used to sleeping on a bed."

Lily Cup stared in wonder.

"I'll find him curled on the floor, no blanket, with his window wide open," Gabe said.

"Peck and Millie," Lily Cup said.

"Peck and Millie," Gabe repeated.

"They do seem like a good fit, don't they?" Lily Cup said. "At least they did when I saw them together. That seems forever ago—last Thanksgiving."

"She's loved that boy with a passion from the day he made the Greyhound pull over so he could jump off just to give her the doll she left on the bus," Gabe said.

"That's right—now I remember—her baby doll—Charlie, wasn't it? Sasha told me about the doll."

"Her Charlie."

"Hell, I had my Teddy bear all through Harvard. I still have it," Lily Cup said.

"Millie does love her Charlie," Gabe said.

"Does she like the house?"

"The girl loves New Orleans."

"What's not to love about New Orleans?" Lily Cup said sarcastically. "Killings in the streets before brunch."

"It's a different world for her from the strict Southern Baptist home life in Tennessee and Baylor University," Gabe said.

"Millie is Baptist?"

"She is."

"Oh, my Lord."

"A Southern Baptist."

"Gabe, I had an old maid great aunt one time who used to lecture me. She'd sit next to me at the dinner table and say, "Honey, a person can't help being black, but they sure can help being Baptist."

"I would have loved your great auntie," Gabe said.

"Does Millie know about the ambiance, the dancing, drinking, and debauchery that goes on at Charlie's Blue Note?"

"Little sister, that girl would love Milwaukee if Peck were there."

"Good fit then, I guess."

"Her folks love Peck like a son, and he's a Baptist preacher and she's a missionary."

"As for her liking Charlie's Blue Note," Gabe added, "I'm not certain Millie's even had a good look at this house the few times she's come on her school breaks at Baylor. I know she hasn't been to Charlie's."

"They don't waste any time dancing, I'm guessing."

"She hits that door, pauses just long enough to hug ole Gabe here a genuine hello and kiss on the cheek, then she'll grab Peck's arm like it's an empty egg basket, pull his bedroom door behind them and climb his bones."

"Damn—" Lily Cup said.

"That pretty much sums up her visits here."

"Sounds like an Erskine Caldwell?"

"What's an Erskine Caldwell?"

"*God's Little Acre*. Caldwell wrote *God's Little Acre*."

"I thought you didn't like books?"

"I like the dirty parts. This one's a hottie about religion and sex."

"I don't know about any praying going on in that bedroom, but our Peck will come out looking peaked, step on the porch for air and go back in for another round."

"Whoa," Lily Cup said.

"The lad has the stamina of a young bull."

"Now that takes me back," Lily Cup said.

"I can only imagine."

"I remember those younger days of wild, reckless abandon," Lily Cup said.

She sipped her coffee, smiling.

"Innocent times," Gabe said.

"They weren't so innocent," Lily Cup said.

"Oh?"

"I remember after school sometimes—Sasha and I'd be feeling randy and we'd corner us a couple of momma's boys we thought showed promise. We'd sneak into one of those backyard storage rooms on Magazine Street and wear them out."

"Lord help 'em," Gabe said.

"The Lord stays off Magazine Street, Gabe. Sinners only."

"Impetuous youth."

"We had perfect lures."

"A pint of rye?"

"Nope."

"A joint?"

"Oh, nothing that prosaic."

"I'm afraid to ask."

"Sasha was the first in our grade to wear a D cup bra," Lily Cup said.

"Her girls," Gabe said.

"They were magnets for high school bad boys dying for a peek," Lily Cup said. "The bigger her girls, the 'badder' the boys."

"Youth," Gabe said.

"We developed our fancies. Hers was arousing a dude with his stares and putting his condom on him. She'd ride it like a sailor on a rowboat—the boy gawking up at and feeling her girls in her Victoria's Secret bra she saved her allowance for. She wouldn't take it off. She'd say a boy appreciates a cleavage—why spoil the fantasy?"

"And you?"

"Let's just say I developed a liking for the feel of a firm cigar."

"Ha!" Gabe guffawed. "Is that why you smoke the short Panatelas?"

"Over the years I've learned to keep my expectations low."

"Youth is uncouth," Gabe said. "At least you're sophisticated and couth now, little sister."

"Too couth. I like to get mussed up on occasion."

"You're an attractive woman. It'll happen."

"She's talking about the wedding reception maybe being at Charlie's Blue Note," Lily Cup said.

"If that's true, I'm surprised James hasn't put up a scuff," Gabe said.

"Why?"

"A jazz joint in an alley off Frenchmen Street isn't what I'd call his cup of tea."

"I think the house would be best for the engagement party, fixed up a little. I'll help," Lily Cup said.

"It would be more personal here," Gabe said.

"I think so," Lily Cup said. "This is like home to her."

"This little shotgun? Our Sasha lives in a Garden District mansion."

"But you two are family."

"I'll have Peck paint the porch ceiling," Gabe said.

Lily Cup stood, coffee cup in hand. She walked to the door looking out at the porch ceiling.

"Why?" she asked.

"I'm changing the sky-blue to another color, maybe a white."

"It looks freshly painted."

"It's a tradition thing," Gabe said.

"What tradition?"

"A lady at the library told me a sky-blue ceiling on a front porch signals an available woman-of-age living in the house."

"That's phooey," Lily Cup said.

"You've never heard that?" Gabe asked.

"I heard that one and three others like it. Like sky-blue wards off spiders and attracts bees away from people sitting on porch swings. I wouldn't bother painting it."

"I'm a Chicago boy—what would I know from superstitions?"

"It's an old wives' tale," Lily Cup said.

"I thought maybe it was voodoo superstition," Gabe said.

"Blacks weren't allowed to practice voodoo back then, Gabe. It was considered savage, and the French made voodoo illegal for blacks. The practitioners were criminalized and arrested."

"That doesn't make sense—during Korea and our docking in the port of New Orleans, I saw plenty of it. Black voodoo— how'd they get away with it without getting caught then?"

"They added a statue of the virgin Mary and some rosary beads and passed it off as a Catholic ceremony. That kept the law away."

"The things I'm learning, little sister—and me an old man."

"Sasha and I still sit on a roof in the Quarter under a full moon if it's not lightning—bad *Gris-Gris* if there're thunderstorms under a full moon. We light candles and talk through the night about the mystical, mumbo jumbo, and voodoo. It's fun. It's how we play when we're not dancing."

"And I thought most girls play with dolls," Gabe said.

"Only voodoo thing I've heard about front porches in Acadiana is some still clean them with red brick dust to ward off bad spirits," Lily Cup said.

"Can these séances tell my future?" Gabe asked.

"I saw no alligator under the house when I got here. It's life, not death in this house today. I can't speak for Lee Circle, where you did the kid in this morning."

"I still can't quite wrap myself around it," Gabe said.

"Around killing him?" Lily Cup asked.

"A tired old black man like me owning a house here in the Garden District."

"And why not?"

"Fifty years ago, all I could have done here would be scrub floors or wash dishes for *massah*."

"We're sinful and excessive, Gabe, but the survivors grow character, usually in our twenties."

"Talk to me."

"New Orleans is an anomaly of prejudiced behavior," Lily Cup said.

"I see it every day. It's not like any other city," Gabe said.

"We're a melting pot of French, Spanish, African and English—Native American. My daddy made me study it—family cultures—before I took my Louisiana bar exam the third time. Family law was always stumping me. My daddy told me if I didn't study people and cultures along with the law books on family and I failed again it would be my own fault, and I might ought to think of working in a hardware store."

"Your daddy sounds like a smart man," Gabe said.

"Throughout and after the Civil War, the French-speaking Creoles of color had racial alignment that was like no other place in the south. That's a big reason we love to cook and eat well, and we live, work, and play together. We respect each other. It was the Jim Crow laws at the start of the twentieth century that fucked it up. Even the streetcars were segregated in 1902. We've had our problems since, but after the Martin Luther King times, prejudice hasn't been that much of an issue here. Oh, don't get me wrong, Gabe. When a black man offs a white kid on St. Charles in broad daylight, all bets are off."

"So how is it we've gone full circle?" Gabe asked.

"Did Sasha think twice about dancing with you that first night you came into Charlie's Blue Note?"

"She asked me to dance," Gabe said.

Lily Cup pulled a cord, lifting a venetian blind and pointed across the street.

"The Garden District you live in Gabe, is just a Monopoly box with play money, houses, and hotels in it."

She pointed.

"Huge houses like that one that nobody lives in, but the maid and gardener still come to once a week. Mansions in the heart of a pauper–poor, diversity–rich city. The wealthy from the corners of the earth buy here just to show off owning a piece of New Orleans—a city like no other place. They don't need reservations to party with locals during Mardi Gras week. You're special, Gabe. You own and live here. Streetcars here work for you just as they have for Anne Rice and for Tennessee Williams and Truman Capote."

"It's still something," Gabe said. "Fifty—sixty years ago, Louis Armstrong couldn't have lived in the Garden District."

"If he had the cash and could afford it, I wouldn't bet he couldn't."

She lowered the blind and turned toward him.

"I don't want you scrubbing floors for 'massah' in Angola. I know you, Gabe, and I know Angola."

Gabe looked at his coffee mug.

"My guess is you had a reason for killing him, but that's not good enough. I have to hear from your lips that it wasn't premeditated. I'll defend you in any case, but I have to hear it. There's a lot of fucking prep work to do."

"It's not much to look at—Lily Cup—missing furniture, draperies and the trappings—but it's more than a house. This is our loving, blessed home. As long as we're here, it is Peck's and my private sanctuary away from those parts of our lives that have haunted their full share of pain and suffering. This is our safe haven—our resting place. It's always welcome to good friends like you and Sasha—"

"Gabe, I can't help you if you won't—"

"Our home is not the place for these words and for conversation of this nature. I'm asking you as a friend to kindly respect our space."

"I'll pick you up in the morning. We'll talk then," Lily Cup said.

"I'll have Peck drive me in the morning. He likes sporting me about in his new pickup."

"Peck drives?" Lily Cup asked.

"He does."

"In this short a time? What's it been—a couple of months since he's been here?"

"Nine months—" Gabe started.

"Has it been nine months already?"

"And he can read every word in the driving manual."

"He reads?"

"He only missed two questions on the written test. He didn't know what 'yield' meant. I forget the other. Now he's trying to read a John Steinbeck novel, can you imagine?"

"Which one? Like it matters."

"*Cannery Row.* He got it with his library card."

"He's like one of those big fat cans, you know, the restaurant ones, I think they call them number–ten cans. They fill them with beans, but he's filled with brains waiting for someone to come along with a can opener," Lily Cup said.

"That's Peck," Gabe said.

"He's amazing."

"Listen to this one," Gabe said. "He's reading out loud, one word at a time, after telling me it was harder for him to read out loud than it was reading to himself."

"Huh?" Lily Cup asked.

"I know, it makes no sense, right? So I ask him why he doesn't just read to himself with no talking it out."

"What'd he say?"

"He said, 'Gabe if'n I don't say 'ever' word out loud so I can hear 'em good, how am I supposed to know what they sound like so I can say 'em good when time comes to use 'em proper?' Can you imagine?"

"Know what's scary?"

"What?"

"He has a point," Lily Cup said.

"How can you not love the boy?" Gabe asked.

"When will he get his GED?"

"This month. Illiterate to a high school diploma in months."

"Jesus."

"Sasha's tutor friend is a miracle worker," Gabe said.

"Polly Lou, she was the smartest one in our school."

"She actually taught him conjugations in a French he understood—and had him translate them into English. He was reading in weeks."

"She's damn good."

"When Millie comes in for the ceremony, we'll celebrate at Dooky Chase's—you too."

"Does Peck know about today?"

"No, he was gone when I got home from the police station."

"Where's he now?"

"Probably on his way."

"Should I not be here so you can tell him?"

"Stay. He went over to Tulane, talking with a guidance counselor. After that he may be talking with Xavier. Depends on how it goes at Tulane."

"You must be proud of him."

"We knew he had it in him," Gabe said.

"We did," Lily Cup said.

"Do you think James is right?" Gabe asked.

"What?"

"James."

"You mean right for Sasha?"

"Yes. Think he's right?"

"Where in the hell did that come from?"

"You're her best friend."

"What does that have to do with it?"

"Think James is the man?"

"Why are you asking now?"

"No reason."

"What's on your mind, Gabe?"

"I mean she's full of life, she's giving—she's successful, intelligent—a great dancer," Gabe said.

"But?" Lily Cup asked. "I know there's a *but* coming..."

"But—and girlfriend, this goes no further than these walls..."

"I swear," Lily Cup said.

"The woman has much more to offer the world and James is a...well, James is a..."

"Yeah, I know," Lily Cup said.

"James is a self–indulgent dilettante, full of himself," Gabe said.

"He's all that all right."

"I mean is he just a bad habit or does the woman love him?"

"She says she does."

"Sombitch doesn't even like to dance," Gabe said.

"James is an asshole," Lily Cup said.

"You took the words right out of my mouth."

"Maybe he's hung like a polo pony and knows how to use it," Lily Cup said. "Ever think of that?"

"You mean like our Peckerwood, little sister?"

Lily Cup swung her head around, eyes in a wide–open glare.

"Hush," she declared, grinning through clenched teeth as if someone could hear. "That was one night—and I was drinking rye. Murder case on my mind."

"Oh, I've heard, little sister. Sasha shares."

"No one is to know about that night. You're my friend so keep it between us that Peck and I ever...you know."

"I saw the smile on your face, I put you in a cab," Gabe said. "I think they call that particular smile an afterglow."

"It's not fair that I can't remember it that well."

"I think you remember, lawyer lady, and you weren't drunk when the two of you had coffee and disappeared. You skipped from the bar to the lady's room to knock one off. You remember."

"I always get drunk before a murder trial."

"Your only regret is people gossip."

"Drunk and horny—I can't help it—before every murder case, ever since I finally passed the bar."

"Murder makes you horny?"

"Drunk makes me horny—murder makes me drink. Rye."

"You choose to mask that tryst the night you met Peck behind rye? Your secret is safe with me."

"Thank you."

"Does Sasha smile like that after James stays over?"

"Like what?"

"Like you did that night?" Gabe asked.

"Not even," Lily Cup said.

"I've wondered."

"She says it's good sex, but I never catch her looking into space."

"What do you mean?"

"Women know these things."

"Do tell."

"We play good nights over in our minds. There're girl signs only girls know how to read about a morning after. Her and James? Not even close."

"Sex isn't all there is, I suppose," Gabe said.

"It isn't?" Lily Cup asked.

"There's more to life than a roll in the sheets."

"Damn."

Lily Cup's eyes brightened in a mischievous smile while interrupted by the front door opening and Peck walking in.

"Hey, cher, how you are?" Peck asked.

He gave her a hug and a kiss on each cheek. He picked up her cup from the cardboard box, slurped a mouthful and set it back down.

"Hey, Captain," Peck said.

"How'd Tulane go?" Gabe asked.

"I'm goin' to night school—I start in June," Peck said.

"My man!" Gabe snorted.

"I can work the days and school and study the nights. I liked him a lot. Nice man."

"Didn't laugh at you, did he?" Gabe asked.

"Nah, nah," Peck said. "Not ever."

"No one worth a salt will ever laugh at a person trying to get ahead, trying to improve themselves," Gabe said. "I told you."

Peck turned to Lily Cup.

"Lily Cup, can I clean the law offices daytime instead of night when I start night school?"

"Sure—but it'll have to be on Sundays or early mornings and be out of there before nine."

"I can did that. Sorry, cher— I mean I can do that."

"I knew what you meant," Lily Cup said.

"I'll clean before you open up," Peck said.

"Congratulations, Peck—"

"Hanh?"

"—on getting into Tulane," Lily Cup said.

"T'anks, cher."

She paused a reach for her coffee, copping a reminiscent glance at his package, then up at his eyes.

"How come I don't ever see you come and go?"

"I always come after dark."

"When are you coming this week?"

"Midnight tonight."

Peck's cellphone beeped. He opened the text and with a wrinkled brow studied the words. Gabe flicked his finger at Lily Cup so she could watch Peck reading.

"It's Millie," Peck said.

He reread the text.

"Gabe, it say here she'll be in New Or–lee–anh in May, she coming for all summer," Peck said.

"Your lady is always welcome in this house, Peck," Gabe said.

Peck read another text.

"Millie say here can she meet my mamma," Peck said.

Peck lifted his head and looked over at Gabe.

Gabe looked at him, turned his head catching Lily Cup's eye, winked as he leaned on the chair arm to bolster getting up and standing.

"Peck, my brother—we've been blessed with Sasha's and James's engagement and now with you— a bonafide Tulane man, and we're blessed with our Millie. I'm going for a walk and when I come back I'll take my nap. What say you and I grab shrimp and grits and a couple of drinks at the Columns tonight? The streetcar will give us some quality time to talk and catch up."

"Hokay."

"We have a deal, son?"

"We got a deal, Captain," Peck said.

They shook hands.

Peck kissed Lily Cup on both cheeks and exited to go read in his room. Seeing the bedroom door pulled closed, Gabe leaned toward Lily Cup, lowering his voice.

"Has Sasha ever told you anything about Peck's childhood—about his foster mother or nanna or whatever and her old man—gator man?" Gabe asked.

Lily Cup stood, paced nervously as if she was hoping to avoid any subject only Sasha knew she was far too familiar with. Lily Cup knew gator man had "disappeared" and how. She believed if it got out it could get her disbarred, or worse. She walked to the coffee maker, filled her cup and returned. Seated again, she placed her cup on the cardboard box and played with her driving gloves as a distraction. She looked up at Gabe.

"Not much. Oh, I heard some things, but not much."

"Apparently they're a couple of mean bastards—vicious drunks," Gabe said. "I'm surprised Sasha hasn't told you."

"Does Peck ever talk about it?" Lily Cup asked.

"Not to me."

"He's blocking it. Nothing wrong with that," Lily Cup said.

"Oh, he called himself a boney white French Cajun boy one time but not much else."

"I'm surprised he hasn't told you more, Gabe, as close as you are."

"I don't think he likes to talk about it. I know he told Sasha some things that time we were all up in Providence," Gabe said.

"Do you think Millie knows anything?" Lily Cup asked.

"Anything?" Gabe asked.

"He ran away from home when he was ten or something, didn't he?"

"Eight or nine," Gabe said.

"Jesus."

"I hear you, little sister. And since an age of eight or nine, whichever it was, the boy hasn't taken a handout or one penny of welfare."

"Do you know where he got the name *Peck*?" Lily Cup asked.

"I can guess," Gabe replied.

"Where?"

"Around these parts they'll call a poor white man, usually a no- account from the swamps and bayous a *Peckerwood*."

"Meaning white trash?"

"Yeah. Like calling me nigger. Same thing."

"Lucky he wound up in Carencro," Lily Cup said, "and not here."

"How so?"

"Beggary and the handout are a way of life in New Orleans."

"A city's poverty wouldn't have changed him, I don't think," Gabe said.

"You don't think it would have swallowed him up?"

"The boy has character in his blood."

"I can see that, look at the year," Lily Cup said. "And now Tulane."

"I think he would have assimilated with blacks, the French, and the Spanish— but still he would have mowed lawns and sharpened knives to get by, just as he did in Carencro. I could see him throwing his trotline somewhere each morning and selling his catches to restaurants or trading at the market for his eggs and chicory."

"His character had to come from someone," Lily Cup said.

"My thought exactly," Gabe said.

"It'd be interesting to know from whom."

"Knowing would be the Holy Grail," Gabe said. "Maybe one day we'll know the story and can give him a past he can be proud of."

"I heard some of it..." Lily Cup started as she prepared to leave.

Gabe lifted his walking stick from the corner it leaned against and stepped out of the house alongside her as she headed to her car. He pulled the door closed and adjusted his honey–cream, linen newsboy cap.

"Charges for second degree murder are no easy thing," Lily Cup said. "We have to declare a plea to murder—guilty or not guilty—no in–between—there's no getting out of it."

Gabe nodded his head, with an understanding of the situation.

"It's not smart to be cavalier, Gabe. They know you killed the kid. I need to know if it was premeditated."

Gabe stood there motionless.

"The DA can really hurt you. Why won't you tell me? I can help. I'm good—I know my way around."

He paused on the step above the sidewalk.

"If I knew myself, darlin', I'd tell you in a heartbeat, and that's the truth," Gabe said. "I'm not holding anything back. I'm not being cavalier."

"Then why won't—?" Lily Cup started.

"I'm just not sure, yet. I need time to think it through."

"We have no time, Gabe."

"It's the way I am. Sorry."

"Whatever you do, don't talk tomorrow. Don't say a word unless I tell you it's okay to speak. Putting your foot in your mouth can wind you up in prison."

"Fair enough."

"And if I say you can speak and you don't know something tell them you don't know. Don't be caught in a lie."

"Let me work it out in my mind, "Gabe said. "I'm an old man. I need to make it right in my head and with God."

"It'll take more than the Almighty in the morning, Gabe."

"There's a young man lying naked on a cold, stainless–steel table in the city morgue because of me," Gabe said.

"I think I need a drink," Lily Cup said.

"God gave me a longer life to live. He didn't give me a longer life just so I could take another life. I have to work it out in my head."

"What are you going to tell Peck?"

"About what?"

"You know about what, Gabe."

"Millie meeting his mother?"

"Well that too, dancing man," Lily Cup said, "and about the trouble you're in?"

Gabe didn't answer.

She stepped down to the sidewalk and started walking toward her car. She turned and looked at him standing on the step as a gentleman would, waiting for her to reach her car.

"Sasha isn't sure that lady is his mother, right? You knew that much, didn't you?" she asked.

"I knew."

"I'm going over and light a vigil candle at St. Patrick's for you, Gabe, and the Almighty."

"You mean that, little sister?"

"I'll see you at the courthouse in the morning. Don't be late."

"Light two," Gabe said stepping down to the sidewalk and turning away for his walk. "Better light two."

Lily Cup turned again.

"Gabe?"

Gabe paused and looked around.

"Yes?"

"In there you said I was smart—did you mean that?"

"I meant every word, my little sister. Every damn word."

"I'm not all that book smart, Gabe, in case you want to get somebody else."

"You're street smart, Lily Cup."

"I am that."

"Plenty street smart, little sister."

"I know my way around pretty good."

"Lily Cup, you're Peck in a skirt."

"Peck is plenty smart. You really think I'm—?"

"Street smart is better than book smart any day," Gabe said.

"I'm lighting three candles," Lily Cup said.

CHAPTER 32

THEY STEPPED FROM THE SEVEN-FIFTY STREETCAR, and it rolled on behind them, whining off into the night. Soon they were at the front gate of the Columns Hotel, brightly aglow with floodlights washing historic columns and walls of a porcelain white majesty.

"Stand a minute, my brother—let's take it in."

"Take what in, Gabe?"

"This place—the Columns—one of the few things that still belongs to New Orleans and isn't for rent like some cheap, painted-up whore that sells her soul once a year so the rich world can come for pre-Lenten entertainment, throw money for plastic beads and gloat at their lot in life. They have an arrogance about them. It's like they can leave when they want and leave us to pick up. This one is ours, Peck. Isn't it magnificent?"

"*Tres grand,*" Peck said.

"It looks big—I'm not sure how many rooms they have for hotel guests. Not many, I suppose—but I don't know. It was a private home in its day."

They climbed the steps, paused on a landing surrounded by various size tables with linen cloths, couples silhouetted by a moonless night, drinks in hand, chatting and listening to their partners, as in a Toulouse Lautrec print.

"Look around, Peck. Locals enjoying the night away from toils of a long day, the streetcar sounds, the smells of New Orleans."

Peck understood Gabe's sense of living every single moment of what life he had left in him.

"My brother, would you prefer sitting here on the patio in the night air or inside?"

Peck didn't answer.

"We might talk better inside," Gabe said. "Night folks congregate in the bar or out here. Let's take our chances in the front room."

A server carrying a tray of drinks told them to find a table—she would be back to take their order. The smaller parlor room that Gabe preferred had a front window with dark-stained indoor shutters that dated back a century. Bay and framed, the window looked on St. Charles Avenue and its glass pane height rose from the floor to a twelve or fourteen–foot ceiling. Romantics like Gabe could imagine children of the 1800s who were supposed to be taking their naps sitting on the floor in the bay, watching the parade of horses, carriages, and streetcars going by. The table was for four, but he and Peck sat on both sides of a corner V with an avenue view, their backs to the next room with its round red leather settee and an ornate, wood-carved barroom behind that.

Peck reached out and rested his hand on Gabe's.

"*Quel problème avez–vous, mon ami?*" ("What trouble are you in, my frien'?")

"My brother," Gabe said, "I know as sure as I'm born when you speak with the French, you have something important on your mind. I only made out the word *problem*—and I'm here for you. What problem do you have—let it out, my brother."

"Nah, nah...not me. What trouble you in, frien'?" Peck asked.

Gabe reeled his torso, eyes wide, mouth open, caught off-guard. He pointed to the seat across from him.

"Sit over there, son, so I can look into your eyes."

Peck got up, moved, and sat again.

"Just what do you know about so–called trouble you speak of, my brother?" Gabe asked.

"Gabe, I dunno—"

"What exactly have you heard, son?"

"I heard nothing, Gabe."

"I'll be damned."

"I see plenty though."

Peck stared into Gabe's eyes.

"You in trouble, old frien'—tell Peck about it.

"I swear—" Gabe started.

"Hanh?"

"I spend a lifetime in the army learning to be aware of things around me, and in all those years—not one time—have I seen anyone even come close to having your sense of observation. My brother."

The waitress came to the table, about to interrupt. Gabe interrupted her first.

"Honey, how about bringing us two shrimp and grits and maybe bring one crawfish *etoufee* that we'll share. Bring a couple of spoons, if you will, and two small plates and start us with a Dewar's on the rocks for me and a long neck for my brother here and keep them coming."

"Yes, sir," the waitress said.

"Young lady, the streetcar will be our driver tonight."

"Thank you, sir."

Gabe waited for her to step away, turned his head and looked Peck in the eye, while leaning in over the table.

"Okay, sure," he said.

"Sure what, Gabe?" Peck asked.

"I'll tell you my story, my brother—"

"Hokay."

"But only after you tell me how you found out."

"Hanh?"

"Who told you about this morning?"

"Lily Cup," Peck said.

"Hogwash," Gabe said. "She's a total professional. She wouldn't say a word."

"Lily Cup at the house," Peck said.

"Not buying it. She's been to the house before."

Peck just looked at Gabe, lifted his beer.

"What gave you the idea there's trouble?" Gabe asked.

"Her satchel by the door," Peck said.

"Her briefcase tipped you!?"

"If no trouble, satchel would be in her car. She took it into the house. Only could mean trouble for my frien'."

Gabe sat back.

"The eyes of a fucking bald eagle," Gabe said.

He inhaled and exhaled, as if in defeat. He sat rubbing his chin and shaking his head, as if he was letting the moment sink in. Peck's keen observation had picked up the scent of trouble just as if the boy were on his pirogue in a bayou swamp tracking a gator for bounty or turtles for soup. Gabe leaned in and lowered his voice.

"I killed a lad today, I surely did."

Peck rested his beer on the table.

"He couldn't have been twenty, maybe twenty–two."

Peck was motionless.

"Killed him deader than a cold mackerel." He put the flat of his palms to his eyes and rubbed as if he wanted to wake from a bad dream.

"Old Gabe here is in big trouble with the law, my brother, and bigger trouble with the Almighty."

He looked around for prying ears, leaned in further.

"That's the mess I'm in, son."

Peck reached across the table and held his hand again.

"Tell Peck, Gabe. When?" Peck asked.

"Happened this morning, after you left for your meeting at Tulane."

"Where you was, Gabe?"

"Thought I'd stretch my legs on Andrew Higgins Boulevard."

"You walk all that way?"

"Not all the way. I thought I'd take the streetcar to Lee Circle for a look at the World War II museum; thought maybe I'd sit with a coffee on the park bench and have a chat with President Roosevelt."

"You been there before, Gabe."

"I stepped from the streetcar and was crossing St. Charles. There was no traffic, and I remember looking up at the tree branches and phone wires still draped with strings of beaded necklaces from Mardi Gras hanging from them. I remember thinking it must be they get caught in trees when they're thrown from the tall parade floats. That's about when he came up."

"Who?"

"The kid."

"From behind you?" Peck asked.

"No—from straight on in front of me."

"On the sidewalk?"

"Well, it was when I was stepping onto the sidewalk, he was there."

"He was standing there or walking?"

"I don't remember but I do remember when I caught his eye he was smiling a big, cold smile."

"He smiled, Gabe?"

"He pulled a knife from under his shirt—I'd say six, eight–inch blade. He walked toward me grinning and smiling, pointing and poking the knife at me and he kept saying, "Wallet, mister...give me your fucking wallet, old man...wallet...your fucking wallet...""

A woman at the next table turned in her chair.

"Sir, do you mind? The language."

Gabe looked at her—lifted his scotch and nodded his head.

"What'd you do?" Peck asked.

"I lifted my stick with both hands and turned sideways—took a stance. I poked the tip at his eye. I missed his eye, but I know I hurt him. Then I reeled and slammed the back of his upper calf full force with my stick, just like it was a baseball bat and took him down."

"He go down, Gabe?"

"He buckled and went down hard, but he didn't drop the knife."

"What'd you do?"

"He grabbed my shirttail with his fist and swiped up at me, cut my shirt—took a button off, and that's when I did it. God'll judge me, I could only see red. I turned the stick around and struck his head. I remember bashing it down—hearing it—feeling it hit his skull. I don't remember anything after that, but that someone grabbed me and held me until I came to."

"Bonk him dead, frien'?"

"I didn't look—but he was dead."

"People see?"

"For damn sure, at least I think."

"Did you stay there?"

"I didn't run. A cop cuffed me, put my stick in his trunk and drove me to the station. He was a vet, a brother. He called Lily Cup for me while he drove. She was at the station waiting when we got there. They booked me and let me go home because of her. I have to go before the judge in the morning."

"*Mais vous essayiez seulement de vous defender*," Peck said. ("But you were only trying to defend yourself.")

"Are you saying self-defense?"

"*Oui.*"

"Lily Cup said the DA can build a case proving the boy was defending himself from me."

"She say that, for true?"

"She did."

"Hmm."

"It's a pickle."

"And why you not in jail, Gabe?"

"Lily Cup. They trust her that I'll show up. Tomorrow I have to hear the murder charges against me and plead something."

"Oh, hokay."

"It's a big dill pickle."

The waitress served them. Both men paddled forks through the fragrances and tastes of the town. Family secret ambrosias of red sauce warming the shrimp and grits made things all right.

"All right" in the Big Easy is when the tastes of the food to the palate can make you forget all else, at least for the moment.

"Peck, can I ask you something personal?"

"Ax."

"You don't have to answer if it makes you uncomfortable."

"Ax."

"I was thinking about Millie—you know, her text to you today."

"Ah *oui*."

"Her wanting to meet your mamma."

"*Oui*."

"What can you tell me about your youth, son?"

"Hanh?"

"We never talk about it."

Peck looked up from his shrimp and grits.

"How far back do you remember, Peck?"

Peck placed his fork in the bowl and sat back.

"If it's uncomfortable, we'll drop it," Gabe said.

"I grow'd somewhere at Bayou Chene, I t'ink—there and Petit Anse Bayou, 'tween Bayou Sorrel and Choctaw. Foster nanna is most all I remember good. There was gator man. Gator man belt-strapped me if I dropped the bait shrimp buckets. I had to scoop shrimp and carry the buckets until his pirogue was full. He'd sell bait to tourists at the fishing docks."

"How old were you?"

"I couldn't swim is what I remember."

"Did he pay you?"

"Nah, nah...he'd dog collar me around my neck and chain me under porch back of his house. I worked, is all."

Gabe sat silently.

"My foster nanna would tell me gator man was lar'ning me and to see I mind him good. He'd tow me for gator bait. When the moon come out, I'd look up near all night pretending the moon was my mamma looking down, and I'd talk to her and I'd promise her I was a good boy now and no trouble, and I'd be quiet and behave if she ever come back. I talked to the moon."

"She heard you, son."

"For true, Gabe?"

"Your mother heard every word, I'm certain of it."

"I don't even knowed my mamma, Gabe— what do I tell Millie?"

Gabe lifted his scotch for a sip, waiting for Peck to speak again.

"Peck is scared, Gabe. Scared she'll run away when she knows I don't know my own mamma."

"Listen to me, my brother. Listen good. Millie may still hug her baby doll, but she's stronger than you think, son."

"Dass for true, ain't it, Gabe?"

"Spoon some *etoufee* and let me think a minute. I need to think."

The lobby of the hotel and both party rooms to its left were empty. The front desk was an ornate wooden antique table with carved legs—a man sitting behind, chin in hand, dozing off. Some guest was at the piano in the bar among laughter and an occasional cheer of a celebrated moment.

"Peck, you owe it to your Millie," Gabe said.

"Owe her?"

"Tell her the truth."

"Hanh?" Peck grunted.

"You have a problem, Peck. You don't know the truth."

"Ain't dat for true."

"This all took place a long time ago in your life. You've been gone from that world like fifteen or more years. It's impossible for you to remember the truth, my brother—the whole story."

"What you sayin', Gabe?"

"I'm saying you have to go back to that Bayou Chene—or Choctaw or wherever—and find out for yourself."

"Go back?"

"When you know the truth, that's when you can tell Millie the story."

"Tell her the truth?"

"She's strong. She'd never be afraid of the truth coming from you."

"Ya t'ink?"

"That woman loves you so much—."

"I knowed."

"—but it's now up to you to learn the truth—if not for her, then for your children."

"I love her too, frien', just as you say—so much."

"It's settled, then."

"It is?"

"You'll go search it out, my brother."

"Good idea, Gabe, after I help you."

"I love you, Peck, but old Gabe here needs to get out of my fix on my own. I got into it—I must get out of it on my own one way or another. You don't have a minute to waste. I'll handle my mess. You want to make me happy, son—go find your answers for you and Millie. Promise you will, my brother."

"I'll go, I surely will."

"You'll leave in the morning, son."

"I'll go in the morning, Gabe."

"Now remember this, Peck. You're a strong man. Look them straight in the eye. Don't let anybody frighten or intimidate you."

"I'm not scared no more, Gabe."

"Take your time. You have some weeks before night school starts," Gabe said. "Take all the time you need to get the answers you're looking for."

"Gabe, can I ax you something?"

"Anything, my brother."

"Why did that boy with a knife smile?"

"What?"

"You say he kept smiling at you? Why did he smile at you like that?"

Gabe picked up his Dewar's with an eye like the military in him was wondering where Peck might be coming from. He took a sip.

"Where you know the boy from?" Peck asked. "A body with a knife pointed for business don't smile at a stranger. He only smiles when he knows him. Where you know him from?"

Gabe set his drink down.

"Remember that day I went to have keys made for the house?" Gabe asked.

"I remember. You wanted to walk then too."

"I was in Walmart. I was at their key-making machine and it was next to another tall vending machine. The same kid was at that machine next to me, working it."

Gabe described how the kid pressured him for the use of his credit card and threatened to kill him when he refused to provide it.

"What'd you do?" Peck asked.

"I've never been so street-scared. I'm not agile or strong like I once was. I found the manager and told him. He said he'd walk me to the streetcar. Outside he asked me if I could recognize the kid and I told him yes, if I saw him again. We stopped for a light, and when I turned around, there he was—the kid was waving a knife. He was leaning on a bicycle looking me in the eye with a smile and waving his knife. 'That's him,' I told the manager. 'That's him.' The manager told me to stay put and he turned and ran toward the guy, yelling and waving his arms until the kid pedaled away in a scoot. The manager walked me to the streetcar and waited until I boarded."

"So that's when you started with a cane, Gabe?"

"Learned self-defense with one in the army."

"You're innocent," Peck said.

"Peck, I know I— "

"Tell Lily Cup the story, cher."

"What story?"

"Walmart."

"What about Walmart? It's only my word."

"Tell her to find the manager and get the video. They'll have it."

"I'll be damned," Gabe said.

"It's all the proof you need, frien'," Peck said.

"I'll be damned."

"Video—it's how we catch'd the Kentucky motorcycle knife man, remember, Gabe?"

"How can I forget that night?"

"Innocent, my frien'. Tell the story to Lily Cup."

"When are you going back to learn the truth, my brother?"

"To see my foster nanna?"

"To learn the truth," Gabe said.

"Tomorrow."

"Promise me you will, son."

"I already promised, Gabe."

"Good."

"I clean offices tonight. I'll go tomorrow."

"Let's get some pecan pie and call it an evening," Gabe said.

"You sure you be okay tomorrow, without Peck?"

"I promise you I will— I have Lily Cup."

"Lily Cup is plenty smart, dass for true."

"What a night, my brother."

"Good we talk like this, Gabe."

"A guardian angel brought you to me, my brother."

Gabe caught the waitress's eye and indicated dessert and coffee for both. He looked at the ceiling and into the heavens.

"Thank you, Butterfly—thank you, my darling."

"Butterfly?" Peck asked.

"Butterfly, my brother. Butterfly was my girlfriend, my lover, my wife, and the mother of my son...longer than I can ever remember. Now she's my guardian angel—my Butterfly."

CHAPTER 33

THE LAW OFFICES ON CARROLLTON AVENUE where Peck had cleaned every week for nine months were in a nineteenth-century, French-styled, mansard-roofed, three-story building. A florist on the ground floor looked orchid expensive and a tall, narrow, dark, forest-green wainscoted stairwell next to an elevator in the adjoining side hall rose to the second and third floors. Walking from his truck parked a block away, he could see lights in one window on the second floor. The elevator was locked after hours, so he made his usual climb and let himself in, shouting "Peck" as he pushed the door open, not wanting to alarm anyone after midnight.

As routinely as he once prepared, baited and would cast his trotline every morning in Carencro to catch turtles or mashwarohn he'd barter for eggs and coffee, he dusted the floor moldings, the conference table, and desktops. He vacuumed carpet; he sponge-mopped restrooms and kitchenettes of both upper floors. He was leaning down into the trash container inserting and fastening a new liner when a hand came up under his crotch from behind with a grab, causing a startled jump and a turn so off-guarded he fell back into the container, folding the side in.

"What?" he snarled.

"Oops," Lily Cup said.

Peck stood motionless.

"Sorry."

"You thinkin' I was someone else?"

"I knew it was you."

"Scared me—"

"Just thought I'd say hello to William."

"Hanh?"

Lily Cup offered a wry smile.

"Who?"

"William."

"Who told you about—?" Peck asked.

"About William?" Lily Cup interrupted.

"Who told you?"

"How William got his name?"

"You drunk."

"I know."

"How long you been drinking, cher."

"I always get drunk before a murder case."

"Who told you?"

"Sasha's my best friend since we were six. Who do you think?"

"What'd she told you?"

"We have no secrets...she told me she named him William seeing it through a crack in the door when you stepped out of a bathtub in Memphis."

Lily Cup moved toward Peck, drink–tumbler in one hand, gazing into his eyes in a daze as she moved closer.

"You need to close bathroom doors, Peck. But no worries. William is a secret safe with me."

She touched her flat hand on the front of his jeans, moving slowly in search of William.

"You remember that night?" Lily Cup asked.

Peck watched her hand.

"What night, cher?"

"At Charlie's Blue Note, when we met?"

"I remember."

"I had a murder case that next morning too."

"Last year. I remember. Do you remember, cher?"

Her hand found William, who was visibly not annoyed with the warmth of her touch.

"Things happened pretty fast that night," Lily Cup said.

"Gabe and me went to Memphis with Sasha," Peck said, not taking his eyes off her hand.

"Oh, a lot more than that happened that night. You remember?"

"I remember."

"I won the murder case the next morning, Mr. Boudreaux Clemont Finch. William brought me luck. Well, I sort of won it. How about some luck for my murder case tomorrow?"

Peck stood tall and motionless, thinking—weighing options as the hunter he was—while her palm and fingers took turns gripping William playfully through his jeans, as if it were a fine cigar.

"You're a plenty smart lawyer, Lily Cup."

"You think I'm smart, baby?"

"You don't need luck."

"Oh, I do."

"You letting the wine talk."

"Rye—" Lily Cup said.

"Rye," Peck repeated.

"—and I'm not all that smart."

"You smart, cher."

"I was having a cigar, sipping my rye, scared to death, thinking about my murder case tomorrow."

Peck looked through the dark front offices to Lily Cup's office in the back.

"Don't worry, my window was open to let the smoke out."

"I'll be waggled," Peck said.

"It bothers you, doesn't it?"

"Hanh?"

"Bothers you, women smoking cigars."

"Ain't seen it until you."

Her hand clenched his throb.

"I like the way one feels in my hand—"

She pinched the zipper toggle to his jeans and began to pull down.

"—the way one feels in my mouth."

He gently lifted her hand and pulled it away.

"Gabe your murder case, tomorrow, cher?"

Lily Cup bolted in a sobering stupor, stepping back.

"Huh?"

"I know, cher."

"Know?"

"I know."

"You know what?"

"I know about Gabe, cher."

"What do you know?"

"Can you help him?"

"I have no idea what you're talking about—"

Peck lifted his brow as if to ask her to admit Gabe was her case. He lightly kissed her hand.

"And even if I did, I can't talk about it. It's the law. It's called attorney-client privilege."

"*Peut–etre que vous pouvez ecouter*?" Peck asked. ("Maybe you can listen?")

"I can listen?" Lily Cup asked.

"You speak the French?" Peck asked.

"I understand sometimes when Sasha speaks it...but I won't discuss Gabe in any way."

Lily Cup turned to walk away and then turned back.

"What did you mean, I can listen?"

"Just listen, is all."

"Listen to what?"

"Listen to a story, cher."

"What kind of story?"

"A story that will make you a most happy lady."

Remembering she was buzzed, Lily Cup slurred another awkward invitation.

"Can we play after?"

Peck stood there.

"Just a little...a quickie?"

"Nah, nah."

"Millie is so lucky."

"Millie?"

"You're such a fucking prince."

Peck placed his hands on her shoulders, turned her, pointing her toward her back office.

"You won't have to do anything, Peck. I'd do it all."

"*Non, désolé.*" ("Sorry, no.")

"Can I smoke my cigar?"

"*Oui.*"

She took him by the hand and led him to her office in the back. She pointed at where he could sit and stepped to the side of her large walnut desk and pulled the window up a foot. From a neighboring saloon, sounds of a trumpet softly flowed up and into the room, as if a songbird of a New Orleans evening was flying by, making its rounds.

She plopped down into her desk chair and leaned back. The big leather wingback seemed to swallow her. She kicked her heels off one at a time, lifted and rested her feet on the desktop, crossing bare legs at the ankles, concealing the black satin panties that had just seconds before made their first curtain call under her short tight skirt during her shoe removal and leg lift. She snipped the end of a cigar as though it was in the way, held a platinum lighter, rolled the Panatela with her fingers and puffed until the end was a burning coal glow. She caught his eye and winked.

"Tell me a story, big boy," she said, taking a puff.

"Once upon a time..." Peck started with a guffaw.

She snickered as best she could—sobering up and cigar smoking at the same time took thought and coordination. She didn't change her expression. She waited.

"It was after Valentine's Day, cher—I remember sure. I watched 'em dance late that night at Charlie's. You were there that night."

Lily Cup nodded.

"Gabe had to get house keys made next day. I didn't have my license, so he said he'd streetcar and walk or maybe, how you say, Uber."

"Taxi," Lily Cup said. "Gabe doesn't have a phone."

"Can I open the window bigger?" Peck asked.

"I'll do it," Lily Cup said.

She stood and pulled the window another foot higher. The trumpet sound was the same tone—a sad blues sound. She sat down and lifted her legs, Peck looking away so he wouldn't be obvious seeing her personal nature wrapped in smooth satin.

"Go on with the story."

"Gabe was using the machine that made keys, and a kid was at the next machine. Kid ax him for a credit card to use in his machine...and Gabe say no."

"Well of course he'd tell the little snot, no," Lily Cup said.

"The kid say he was going to kill him, so the manager walks Gabe to the streetcar— "

"The kid was a creep. This kind of thing happens every day."

"But he sees the kid outside the store waving a knife."

Lily Cup sat up and folded her legs Indian style in the chair, oblivious to the view from Peck's side of the desk.

"Knife?" Lily Cup asked.

"Knife," Peck said.

"The same kid who asked Gabe for his card had a knife? Pointing it?"

"Dass for true, cher. Kid had a knife."

"Were you with him, Peck?"

"Nah, nah, Gabe was alone."

"Did Gabe tell you this when it happened?"

"Tonight, cher—at the Columns. You know the Columns."

"The kid was a bully. But what's all this got to do with Gabe now?"

"The kid is dead now, cher," Peck said.

"The same kid is dead? The bully?"

"*Oui.*"

"What's that got to do—?"

"Same kid Gabe killed today."

"How did you know?"

Peck sat there.

"Why are you telling me this, Peck?"

"Maybe there's a video?"

"What store?"

"Walmart," Peck said.

She stood, pushed her skirt down on her thighs and stepped into her shoes.

"Did Gabe tell you all this in secret, Peck?

"Nah, nah, cher. We were eating shrimp when he told me."

"Did you drive tonight, Peck?"

"*Oui.*"

"Where's your truck?"

"Around the corner."

"You okay to drive?"

"*Oui.*"

She reached in her purse, pulled two fifties and tossed them to Peck.

"Here."

"Hanh?" Peck asked while stretching to catch the bills.

"You're now my investigator, Peck. That's a retainer. If anyone asks, you were paid to do research for one of my cases."

"Coo coo," Peck said.

"You can't tell what we talk about, got it?"

"Peck keeps his word and secrets, cher."

"Drive me to Walmart. I've been drinking and don't want a cab or Uber this late."

"Let's go," Peck said.

He sat in the pickup waiting in front of the Walmart for Lily Cup to come out. He was patient, as he took pride in her confidence in him, and that he understood the seriousness of her helping Gabe in the morning.

Eventually she walked out with a paper sack. She opened the door, set the sack on the seat and reached her hand for him to pull her up and in.

"Holy shit," Lily Cup said. "It doesn't get any better than this."

"How'd it go, cher?"

"You were right on the money, Peck. They have two tapes—and they're perfect," Lily Cup said.

"Two tapes?"

"One from inside the store and the manager says he can see things so clearly he could read his lips."

"That's good, then?" Peck asked.

"There's one taken outside with him waving the knife, just like you said. They'll be perfect."

"Did the manager remember?"

"The manager from that day wasn't working tonight, but this one— Larry Albright— called him at home. He remembered it all happening, he remembered Gabe, and he will be at the court whenever I need him."

"Que Dieu vous benisse, Lily Cup." ("God bless you, Lily Cup.")

"Back at ya, Mr. Boudreaux Clemont Finch. None of this could have happened without your help, Mr. Investigator."

"That mean it's over now, cher?"

"Oh no, it's only started—but it's a hell of a start!"

"Does it mean Gabe innocent?"

"It means Gabe can maybe plead not guilty and get out on bond."

"That's good then, right?"

Peck reached in the bag to look at the DVD cases. There were none, only two pints of rye.

"Where they are, cher? The tapes?"

"Oh, they have to download them and copy them—I'll get the copies in the morning when the manager comes in."

"Ahhh."

"I have to figure a way to use this information."

"What's that mean, cher?"

"I've got to get the DA to see them without opening a legal can of worms."

"Tell Peck."

"If Gabe goes to trial before I get the right people to see the videos, having them at all will be a gamble. The court may not allow them in—it happened in the past and now the kid is dead and can't defend himself. They can trump up legal bullshit like that."

"So, the more you give the DA man that proves Gabe is innocent before court, the better your chances?"

"Something like that."

"It's like baiting three snoods, cher."

"I have no idea what a snood is, Peck."

"If Peck need to catch a *bait* snake real bad, there's a special way to do it."

"Who's the *bait* snake, Peck, the DA?"

"Nah, nah, he the snapper, cher—he the prize."

"What do snakes have to do with snappers and what's a bait snake?"

"Bait snakes are for bait. They're crawfish snakes?"

"Snakes for bait?"

"Oui. Need bait snake to catch snapping turtles."

"So what are you sayin?"

"You in control, cher. Think like you the fisher."

"You're saying I need a snake for bait?"

"Oui."

"And how do you propose—?"

"Jess catch one, cher."

"Are you saying you can catch a crawfish snake for bait anytime you want?"

"Pretty much, cher."

"Anytime you damn well please—guaranteed?"

"Oui."

"Okay, I give—tell me."

"If you want a snake right now, quick-like, use you a live frog and hide the hook good."

"You use a frog that's still alive?"

"*Oui.*"

"How?"

"You hide the hook somewhere on it."

"And a live frog will guarantee you catch a crawfish snake?"

"*Oui.*"

"I'm not getting it, Peck. I thought crawfish snakes liked crawfish."

"They like frogs better."

"Crawfish snakes like frogs better than eating crawfish?"

"Cher, I seen a crawfish snake climb on the back of a gator sleepin' on a big ole log just to catch a frog settin' in the sun. They sure do like frogs good, dass for true."

"So what's your point? What's any of this got to do with a kid who's lying dead in the morgue and the DA?"

"You say you can't talk about nothin' without Gabe being there."

"It's the law."

"Maybe you should stop t'inkin' what you can't do, cher and start t'inkin' what you can do."

"We're back to the frog, I suppose."

"*Oui.*"

"You're saying I need a frog?"

"*Oui.*"

"So, you're saying if I could figure out what my live frog is, and I hide the hook on it and then find a way to get the DA and some others to see these videos and hear what the store manager has to say—"

"That would end it, maybe?" Peck asked.

"Not sure."

"Why?"

"I haven't seen the dead body yet."

"What's that mean, cher?"

"Are you sure it's the same dude I saw on the video?"

"Same one. Gabe told me he crossed over St. Charles Street and on the sidewalk the same kid came up, pointing a knife at him and this time ax'n for his wallet and money."

"They didn't find a knife."

"He had a knife, cher."

"You know for sure the kid had a knife today and was pointing it?"

"Dass for true, cher."

"But they didn't find a weapon, Peck. That's pretty serious for Gabe."

"Gabe don't ever lie to Peck."

"If Gabe tells me it was self-defense when he saw the guy he killed today, I'll believe him. He's just not saying anything."

"He told me it was, cher."

"He hasn't told me anything, yet."

"He's sad, cher."

Out of the blue Peck bolts.

"That's it, cher!" he barks.

"What's it?" Lily Cup said.

Peck sat up tall and with inspired confidence. He clicked his thumb and finger.

"Cher?"

"What!?"

"You say dat you can't talk what Gabe say—how you say— ?"

"What?"

"Cher, in the breakroom you say there was a law you can't talk about anything what Gabe say."

"Attorney-client privilege?"

"Dass it, cher— attorney-client privilege."

"That's the law, Peck."

Peck started the truck and slowly pulled out of the parking lot.

"And you say Gabe won't talk?"

"He clammed up on me at the station—he won't talk."

"Then from now on maybe don't talk to Gabe about nothin' cher."

"What in the name of Blaze Starr are you talking about?"

"Dass your frog, cher."

"My frog?"

"To catch our bait snake."

"I need a drink, Peck. Take me home."

"Say tomorrow Gabe say it, say—self-defense—would the DA go away then, cher?"

"If not guilty is his plea tomorrow, the DA won't go away. It would go to preliminary hearing and then most likely the grand jury and then go to trial."

"Trial?"

"Not right away. The DA has to decide. He can take it to a grand jury or drop it."

"What's he t'inking, cher?"

"You mean with what he's got?"

"*Oui.*"

"A kid is dead—he knows Gabe killed him and he knows there's no weapon on the kid."

"Hokay."

"Gabe is screwed."

"What you need, cher?"

"If the defendant doesn't tell his attorney what happened—"

"You mean Gabe."

"—I can't build a defense if he won't talk. Take me home. I'll sleep a few hours."

Peck made his way through the nightlife like a gator in a murky swamp, avoiding traffic that might have been drinking and partying. He pulled in front of her house and brought the pickup to an idle.

"Can I ax you something, cher?"

"Park, I feel like talking."

"Hokay."

He pulled into her driveway.

She kicked off her heels and grabbed the paper sack. She hiked her skirt to mid-thigh while turning on the seat facing him, her back now leaning against the door. She folded her knees, her bare feet on the seat steadying her like a bookend. She pulled a pint of rye from the sack, opened it and took a swig.

"Turn it off," Lily Cup said.

He obliged.

"What did you want to ask?"

"Let me understand something, cher—"

"Okay."

"You say if Gabe tells you a whole lot of t'ings about what happened and how it happened and where and when, you know all that stuff—"

"I get it, I got it—what's your point?"

"If he tells you everything you can fight his case, right?"

"That's the way it works. At least I can try."

"But you can't tell what Gabe tell you to nobody who could help you before trial, right?"

"Right, not without Gabe's permission."

"What if Gabe don't never tell you anything?"

"Nothing?"

"Nothing, cher."

"Where're you going with this, Peck? What are you thinking?"

"Gabe don't say a word—what is it when all you know you hear the truth from what Peck here tole you—remember Gabe never tole you nothing?"

"Fuck."

"Is that how you say—?"

"Attorney-client privilege?"

"—attorney client privilege, cher?"

"You sure he didn't tell you about what happened in confidence, Peck?"

"What that mean, cher, confidence?"

"Did he tell you to keep it secret when he told you?"

"No way."

"Are you sure?"

"Like I say, he tole me while we was eating shrimp and grits. People at next table could hear. The lady even told him to watch his language."

"Then it would be hearsay."

"What's that, hearsay?"

"Somebody telling me what happened, not Gabe—that's hearsay."

"Dass your frog, cher—"

"You're saying?"

"—you can talk about what I tole you and maybe show the video too. I give'd you that too."

Lily Cup lifted the bottle for a belt, her eyes glazed over at how naturally instinctive it was for a boy who grew up in the swamps to put food on the table.

"That'd be all hearsay," Peck said.

She took another swig.

"Peck here is your frog, cher. Don't let Gabe talk—I'll tell you what I know."

"I wonder why he didn't tell me about the tapes?" Lily Cup asked.

"It's cuz I figured it out for him," Peck said.

"What do you mean?"

"He didn't remember. I t'ink old man was sad from killing the kid."

Lily Cup gazed at Peck as if she were in awe of his insight. She had listened to stories of his accomplishments from Gabe and Sasha. He went from illiterate to earning his GED in nine months.

Peck was waiting for a reaction.

"Can you talk about what I say, cher, you know, that hearsay stuff if Gabe never say nothing to you?"

"Yes, I can."

"Then you need to bait some snoods with it, cher."

"I'll read up and figure approaches that won't land me in hot water."

"Read then, cher. Promise you'll read good."

"Do you believe him, Peck?"

"Ever' word, cher, Gabe don' lie."

She had a gaze of trust as if Peck was the brightest, most perceptive mind she'd seen, even at Harvard. He reminded her of a young her, a street-smart survivor.

"Are you really reading *Cannery Row*?" Lily Cup asked.

"Yes'm."

"Why *Cannery Row*?"

"I ax the lady for a book about oceans, fish, and frogs," Peck said. "She tell me, *Cannery Row*."

"Talk to me about why you ran away from home, Peck."

She reached between her bare knees and handed the opened pint to him. He sniffed the piquant, took a swig and handed it back, swallowing with wrenched lips.

"What you mean, cher?"

"When you were a little boy. You ran away from home."

"*Oui.*"

"Sasha told me."

"Ah *oui.*"

"How old were you?"

Peck started.

"I want to know what it was like."

He didn't appear offended with the question. To him his new friends like Lily Cup were genuine, loving, and honest to the core. He just wasn't certain how to answer.

"Scared."

"I can't imagine what it must have been like."

"I didn't have no shoes."

"You ran away barefoot?"

"I remember, dass for true."

"Didn't anyone try to help you?"

"Nah, nah."

"Didn't anyone see you running?"

"I hided from cars passing me, I run to Carencro."

"How long were you running?"

"I run to Carencro."

"No, not miles—how many hours?"

"It was night two times before I got to Carencro."

"Why Carencro? Did you know someone there?"

"Nah, nah—my leg was bleeding bad. I had to stop and sleep. Slept in a container at the slaughter house."

"Did you know it was a slaughter house? You couldn't read, could you?"

"I know'd the smell. I can tell the sounds. When I waked up I see a man and ax him what they was killin'. He say veal calves. I told the man can I bonk 'em full day for some rubber boots and sandwiches."

"Jesus, how old were you?"

"I could swim."

"You mean you just learned to swim?"

"*Oui.*"

"So, you were maybe eight or nine?"

"*Oui.*"

"Were you big for your age?"

"Big maybe. I just look old, I t'ink."

"Did the man give you boots?"

"*Oui.* They had a rip on the side.

"And?"

"I bonk calves that come through the opening. One bonk after the first couple times."

"What do you mean, bonk?"

"A steel pipe." He held his hands out. "About so long, filled with lead. I'd hold it tall and bring it down like a sledge between their eyes. I'd bonk 'em dead, one bonk."

Lily Cup lifted the bottle, took a cold, glassy-eyed swig, slowly shaking her head.

"Did the man give you sandwiches?"

"*Oui.* Many days I go back and work then come a lady she ax me how old I was. I told her I didn't know, and she fired me."

Lily Cup stretched her arm, held the pint between her spread bare knees. He took it and raised it for another swig.

"Did she let you keep the boots?"

"I walked away in 'em."

She shook her head as though she was waking from a bad dream.

"It's good it was so long ago. You probably don't remember a lot, and now you have Gabe and Millie."

"I'm going in the morning to find the truth," Peck said.

Lily Cup sat up, away from the door, looking startled, confused, and tipsy.

"What?"

"In the morning, I'm going. You can pick Gabe up maybe?"

"Where are you going?"

"Gabe say I need to find the truth about where I grow'd, so I can tell Millie the truth."

Lily Cup took a swig, corked the bottle and set it on the floor.

"Can you even remember where to go after all this time?" she asked, as she repositioned herself. Hoping to change the subject, she lay on her stomach, knees bent, putting a distracting palm on his thigh, resting her chin on the back of her hand.

"S'okay if I rest here?"

"Hokay."

"It's been a long time, Peck. Can you remember names and what any of them look like?"

"Foster nanna, gator man, Elizabeth—'tween Bayou Sorrel an' Choctaw. I remember."

"Who are they to you?"

"My foster nanna; gator man her boo—least he was then...Elizabeth, a special frien' in Anse La Butte."

Hearing 'gator man' Lily Cup perked her head up, reached and lifted the bottle from the sack on the floor of the truck.

"So, this gator man— "

"*Oui?*"

"Like is he, this gator man guy your father?"

"Nah, nah."

Lily Cup took a long thankful swig, put the bottle back in the bag and leaned her chin on his thigh again.

"And the special friend? What kind of special friend was she?" Lily Cup asked, looking up.

Peck grinned.

Her eyes devilishly smiling, she moved her hand to the bulge on his inner thigh pant leg and clenched William.

"Would you say Elizabeth is this kind of a special friend?"

"A frien', cher. She ain't no boo."

"Boo? You mean girlfriend?"

"*Oui.* Lover."

"Did you fuck?"

Peck's grinned silence spoke for him.

"Wait! When you were nine?" Lily Cup started.

"Nah, nah." Peck laughed. "Elizabeth in Anse La Butte long time after Peck run away."

Without moving her right hand from his thigh, she rose to her knees and unzipped his jeans with her left. Peck sat frozen, wondering his next move. Her warm hand slithered into the unzipped cavern, retrieving a throbbing William. She grasped and held it.

"This kind of special friend?" she repeated.

He pondered. It wasn't as if they weren't sexually familiar, but Millie was now in the equation—the girl he'd promised his heart and hand to. Lily Cup fondled William, stroking it with her forefinger and thumb watching it impatiently, like she was stopped and waiting for a red light to turn green. He glanced down at her hand touching William as though he was considering surrender. He looked out his side window to see if the coast was clear. He turned his head to look out the passenger side when he first saw a possible compromise. He prolonged his watch of the reflection from the passenger window of her on her knees, her butt up as she leaned down on him, her sensual black satin crotch and the seductive curves of her butt cheeks, her linen–white bare inner thighs. He pulled her hand away, lifted and kissed it and put William back in the barn and zipped up.

"It's the rye, cher," Peck said.

Lily Cup looked up in defeat and pouted. She pushed on his thigh for leverage, rising tall on her knees. Turning completely around on her knees, she bent over in the opposite direction, this time looking again for the bag and her bottle. He reached between her thighs up under her skirt from behind, gently cupping her love island with a soft hello just as she had earlier grabbed him.

"Oh?" She churned, jerking her head up like a kitten in heat with opportunity. She braced one arm on the front dash, the other on the door, arching her buttocks as a sign of welcome. Peck maneuvered his thumb gently in and under her panty crotch elastic and in between a moist warmth of love lips. With the feel, he started, opened his eyes, finding his outstretched arm reaching his hand under her panties his curled knuckles masking her pearl.

"Yes," she whispered, this time lowering her head.

His welcomed thumb moved inside her wet warmth and in slow, steady, never-ending circles it massaged the velvet wall of her inner G nerve endings until the streetlamp spotlighted her milky white silken–thighs flex and grip on his arm, again and again, her butt cheeks lifting and squeezing in aggressive, quick thrusts as in a hope the moment would become a day. The clenching of her crotch and the short, crisp gasps were signal of climax in perfect rhythm with her heaving stomach contractions. At the end a tight quiver and she went limp and rested.

She exhaled a "whew!" as if she were perfectly satisfied, followed by a deep breath and "Hot damn!" as if it was 'back to business.' He slowly removed his hand, patting her love island tenderly.

Her head fell, she looked under herself down between her legs and then reached and adjusted her panties.

A newsboy bicycling by threw that day's edition of an *Advocate* on her porch and caught Peck's eye.

"Don't worry, he's gay," Lily Cup panted.

Climbing from the pickup, she stood with the passenger door open and pushed her skirt down her thighs. She gathered herself and finger-brushed hair strands from her face. She reached in for the pints of rye in its paper sack. All in hand and leaning on the passenger seat, she looked over into Peck's eyes and smiled.

"You okay?" she whispered.

"Make it good for my frien', cher."

"The frog idea is genius, Peck."

"Pirogues are slow, cher, but they find gators."

"Don't worry about Gabe, honey. I'll take care of him."

He nodded.

"Peck, hint to Gabe to let me do the talking tomorrow."

"He'll be asleep."

"Wake him and tell him to catch a cab in the morning and that I may be late getting to court, but don't tell him why. I have to pick up the tapes. I'll text you the address and court he has to be in. But don't say any more to him."

"Hokay."

She straightened upright and stepped back.

"You sure we're okay, Peck?"

"We good, cher."

"What time are you heading out?"

"When I get up," Peck said.

"Take a phone charger."

"Yes'm."

"This Elizabeth, does she live in the area you're going?"

"Oui. Anse La Butte—near t'ings."

"Does she know about what happened to you there?"

"*Oui.*"

"Does she speak French?"

"Cajun French, *oui.*"

"Is she a good friend?"

"*Oui.*"

"Is she smart?"

"Ah *oui.*"

"Why don't you go see her first?"

"For true?"

"She maybe can help you. Go see her first."

"Hokay," Peck said.

"Be careful, Peck. It can be dangerous in those swamps."

"I know."

"You'll need a base so you won't have to sleep in the truck. Maybe Elizabeth will let you stay with her while you're looking around."

"Ah, *oui.*"

"Be careful."

Lily Cup lipped a smooch at Peck and stepped into her house.

CHAPTER 34

IT WAS A SMALL CAJUN RESTAURANT in a strip mall, just big enough to keep secrets in a corner with its blue and white checked tablecloths and curtains. A touting of Creole chicken and home-battered fish was on a hand-painted sign over the door. To the right of the restaurant was a locksmith; to the left an empty space that once sold lawn mowers and sparkplugs, with a *for rent* sign taped to the window.

Pulling in front of the restaurant, Peck stepped on the brake, paused in an idle as if he was thinking back, before he met Millie, how he and Elizabeth once passed lonely nights away from his fishing and mowing and away from her man on some oil rig weeks at a time. They were unintentional lovers; they chose to be friends. Their bond was in the holding and the talking and the laughter. Peck had grown up learning to be there for Elizabeth since their eyes first met. He had just turned nineteen, a lawn mower and fisherman. She was twenty-four, a sous chef.

Nearly eight years before, he had walked the dozen miles from Carencro that 103-degree day in search of fishing holes and stopped to quench his thirst. Something brought them both to that store in nearby Anse La Butte at the same moment of the same day. At first sight, it was as if they were already together as he caught his own reflection in a glass door of the refrigerated water cabinet behind her. His hair was sun-bleached and trim; hers, long, brunette and brushed, framing a quiet beauty in her face and blocking her view of impressions her nipples made through the yellow T-shirt. His face and arms were a ruddy tan, while her face was ashen and her eyes an emerald green, and she seemed open for smiles over quiet delicate pastries or for sitting for an artist's canvas.

It was generally not in her nature to stare, so there must have been a reason they could not take their eyes from each other as Peck reached behind her for a bottle of water. Destiny nudged him to buy two bottles and the strangers refreshed with cold swallows on the hot summer sidewalk like pollywogs at play, and he walked backward in front of her and made things up to talk about in French, and she laughed and pulled a lock of hair away from her eyes and rolled it in her fingers and studied his eyes until they didn't seem like strangers and found themselves in front of her house. She liked him and invited him in.

"*J'ai plus d'eau dans la maison*, Peck," Elizabeth said. ("I have more water in the house, Peck.")

Only they knew the roads they'd traveled in secret moments of second lives. With or without a moon, they could sense when the loneliness of an empty bed would fill their night, and Peck would walk the eleven miles to be with her after his mowing in Carencro and Elizabeth would have a candle lit on the mantle.

They'd sit in the tub, her legs wrapped around his waist and she'd wash his back and they would talk of where he could buy a spark plug for his mower and if she should frost her hair and would he like crepes and jam?

Peck climbed from his pickup, stepped over to the restaurant and pushed the door, ringing the same bell he remembered, sat on a stool at the red Formica counter and asked the waitress if she knew Elizabeth and if she might be coming in.

The girl disappeared behind the curtain of beads into the kitchen to inquire. A man in a white T-shirt, red bandana around his neck, and sporting a Saints' cap, came out, wiping his hands with a white towel.

"Elizabeth don't cook here no more, mon," he said.

"Did she move? I went by her house. It has a rent sign on front," Peck said.

"Elizabeth, she know you, *mon ami*?" he asked.

"*Oui, ça fait un moment que je l'ai vue*," Peck said. ("Yes, it's been some time since I've seen her.")

"Let me call d' wife. She know, sure. Have you some creole chicken, *mon ami*. It's so good."

"Shicken, red beans, and coffee," Peck said.

"You like d' white or dark meat, *mon ami*?"

"I like shicken," Peck said.

"Comin' up. I call d' wife."

The man disappeared through the beads.

Peck turned and glanced out the front window at his khaki-colored pickup. His road trip to the Anse La Butte suburb of Breaux Bridge had taken the better part of three hours, but he was refreshed. He'd been to Anse La Butte many times to see Elizabeth, but he had walked before, from Carencro after his Thursday lawn-mowing duties at the hospice, and this was the first time he felt he wasn't an outsider. It was as though he belonged, having driven alone on an Interstate and parked in front of a Cajun restaurant in Breaux Bridge, just like other customers.

The girl came from the kitchen and placed a plate of chicken and a bowl of red beans in front of Peck, then a paper napkin, fork, and spoon. She set a coffee cup in front of him and filled it.

"It's fresh," she said. "Need cream?"

"Nah, nah," Peck said. "Sugar. T'ank you."

He spooned into the beans.

A firm, stocky, lady of medium height wearing cargo shorts and a white cotton shirt, a denim apron tied in the back, and a straw gardening hat, opened the door, ringing its bell. She walked over, removing gloves and stuffing them into her apron pockets.

"You the one asking about Elizabeth, hon?"

"Yes'm," Peck said.

"Can I sit with you?"

"Sure, yes ma'am."

She sat down.

"I'm Flora. What's your name, hon?"

"Peck is what they call me." He extended his hand. "I'm Boudreaux Clemont Finch."

"Carol," Flora said. "Get me a cup of green tea, will ya, sweetie?"

"She's told me about you," Flora said, shaking his hand. "Pleased to make your acquaintance."

"You know where Elizabeth is, Miss Flora?"

"Baton Rouge."

"Baton Rouge?"

"Moved over a month ago."

"Ahh."

"She didn't tell you?"

"Nah, nah," Peck said. "Peck's not seen her for a long time."

"Baton Rouge. She has a nice apartment in Baton Rouge. It's right downtown, close to her school," Flora said.

"She hokay? Elizabeth hokay?" Peck asked.

"She's fine, hon. Woman just got bored waiting on him every few weeks out here. She's a young girl. She told me she felt strangled, couldn't breathe. She wanted a city where she could meet people, go to restaurants, take some classes—you know, live a little."

"I know," Peck said. "She still his boo?"

"She's still with him, but I think it's getting a little thin, if you know my meaning—him gone a month at a time out on the rig."

"*Oui.*"

"She's getting into a cooking school, hon. Our Elizabeth will make quite a chef," Flora said.

"She like cooking, dass for true," Peck said.

"I'm thinking it was fine when you were coming by, but when you stopped coming around, things changed," Flora said.

"Changed, cher?"

"She seemed to get anxious, impatient about the little things."

"*Je comprends*," Peck said. ("I understand.")

"She told me you might be by," Flora said. "She wanted me to tell you to come see her. She misses seeing you. I have her number. You want it?"

"Yes'm, please," Peck said.

"Where'd you drive in from? Carencro?"

"Nah, nah. New Or–lee–anh," Peck said.

"Honey, you must have already come through Baton Rouge to get here," Flora said.

She sipped her tea, staring off into the limbo of a wall as though she were thinking of Elizabeth feeling vibrations of Peck driving past her earlier.

"Imagine," Flora said. "Did you come through Baton Rouge or the other way, hon?"

"Baton Rouge, *oui*," Peck said.

"Imagine that."

"I know."

"Maybe it's a sign."

"*Oui.*"

"Such a shame you didn't know."

"*Oui.*"

"Baton Rouge isn't far, though. Finish the chicken. You can make it by early afternoon."

She penned Elizabeth's phone number on a slip of paper and handed it to him.

"What'd she say about Peck?"

Flora held her teacup with the palm of both hands and looked him in the eye.

"It was all good, hon. She said nice things about you."

"She did?"

"I know she misses you."

"We were just…" Peck started.

"Ain't none of my business what you two are," Flora said. "You're grown adults; life has its twists and turns. Good friends are not that easy to come by."

"Dass for true, Miss Flora."

"Ain't nobody's business how some steer through the turns, Peck."

"I'm tracking for truth now," Peck said.

"Truth?"

"About my real mamma. I'm going to go find my foster nanna and ax," Peck said. "I'm trying to know the truth about my real mamma."

"You from around here, honey?"

"Well—"

"Acadiana?"

"Yes'm, but Elizabeth's French is better. I'm t'inking she maybe could help me good."

"Where exactly are you from?"

"Raised up in Bayou Chene," Peck said.

"Bayou Chene, you say?"

"Yes'm, and Bayou Sorrell, I think—over near Choctaw."

"Are you sure it was Bayou Chene?"

"Ah *oui*, I runned two whole nights. Bayou Chene."

Flora placed her palm on the back of his hand.

"Honey, just how long has it been since you've been back home?"

"Sixteen, fifteen years about, I reckon," Peck said.

"In all that time have you been in touch with your foster nanna?"

"Nah, nah, no ma'am," Peck said. "I runned away when—"

"That ain't none of my business why you left, hon—when you left—none of my business."

"*Pardon*," Peck said. ("Sorry.")

"And you say you haven't spoken with your foster nanna for a time?"

"Not since I runned."

"And you think she's in Bayou Chene?"

"Yes'm."

Flora looked over at waitress Carol.

"Carol, honey, get me a fresh tea."

She placed her palm on his hand again.

"Honey, there ain't no Bayou Chene."

"Hanh?"

"I hate to be the one to tell you, but Bayou Chene was flooded. Word was if it wasn't the water, it was the silt that buried people and animals alive. There ain't no Bayou Chene, hon."

"No Bayou Chene?"

"The whole town is under ten, twelve feet of silt."

He turned the spoon in his half-empty cup, staring out, as if he were trying to get his mind around what Flora had said.

"Dass for true, cher?"

"The whole town sunk, it's only a memory now—it's not even a ghost town, hon."

She nodded at Carol. "Get him some coffee, sweetie."

"Are you going to be all right, Peck?" Flora asked.

"Nah, nah, I'm hokay."

"I'm sorry to be the one that had to tell you, hon."

"T'anks for tellin' me, though."

"Your foster nanna must be up there in years."

"Been a long time since I seed her."

"How old would you say she'd be today?"

Peck held both hands out, counting on his fingers.

"I don't know, maybe sixty—maybe fifty."

"Oh no, hon," Flora said.

"Ah *oui*, I t'ink of her now as her bein' maybe thirty, maybe twenty back then."

"That couldn't be."

"I t'ink so, *oui*. I remember she didn't look old when I runned off," Peck said. "She was young."

"How old are you, Peck?"

"Twenty–four

"You're twenty-four?"

"*Oui.*"

"Then you sure didn't run from Bayou Chene," Flora said. "I don't know what I was thinking."

"Hanh?" Peck asked.

"You couldn't have, hon."

"I couldn't?"

"Bayou Chene sunk in the sixties. Your foster nanna would have to be in her eighties, maybe in her nineties, if she was ever in Bayou Chene. The Atchafalaya Spillway levees kept flooding until it busted and the whole town and every living thing in it disappeared."

He stirred his coffee.

"I'm t'inking sixty, maybe fifty maybe."

"Maybe you just don't remember things right," Flora said.

Peck watched his spoon stir.

"You've been gone a long time, hon. Maybe it was another place and maybe your foster nanna could still be alive."

Peck lifted his phone from his pocket and began keying in a number.

"What're you doing?" Flora asked.

"Text Elizabeth."

Flora placed her palm on his hand, stopping his movement.

"Wait, hon."

"Hanh?"

"Why don't you let me text her for you?" Flora asked.

"I can text her good," Peck said.

"Carol," Flora said, "Get him a slice of key lime. On me, hon."

She leaned into his ear. "Ain't none of my business, but if a certain someone out on a rig sees a number showing up on his phone bill, there could be questions. Get my meaning?"

"*Oui,*" Peck said.

"Let me text her for 'ya, hon. You use my phone to call her if she says okay."

"Good idea," Peck said. "I forgot…"

"Not to worry."

"T'anks, Miss Flora."

"Ain't none of it my business; nobody's business."

Her thumbs danced on the keys. There was an instant response. She read it first and held it up for Peck to read.

"Good," Peck said. "I'll go there."

"Finish your pie, hon. I'll run to the house and get her address. I'll send you with some fresh okra and tomatoes."

"T'anks, Miss Flora," Peck said.

"If you need to get her a message, text me, and I'll get her answer for you."

"You're a nice person, cher," Peck said.

"I try to be a good Christian like I was raised, praise Jesus," Flora said. "I'm a child of God doing His work. The paths we take are our own chosen journeys and the self–righteous can butt out. Ain't none of it anybody's business but your own."

As Flora was stepping from Breaux Bridge's only Cajun chicken and fish restaurant to go to her house behind, exactly 126 miles away, at the corners of Tulane and Broad avenues in New Orleans, the bailiff was opening the morning like a rooster crowing.

"Order in the court. All rise. Section M of the Criminal District Court is now in session. The Honorable Judge Lindsay Fontenot presiding. Silence is commanded under penalty of fine or imprisonment. God save this state and this honorable court. Please be seated. There is no talking in the audience. Good morning, Judge."

The bailiff stood in this magistrate court and spoke with loud, officious resonance.

"The State of Louisiana calls Gabriel Jordan. The defendant will rise," the bailiff said.

Gabe looked about for Lily Cup, who was not in the court room. He stood.

"Remain standing," the bailiff said as he turned and walked to a waiting chair by the court reporter, busily typing away.

The judge adjusted her microphone.

"District Attorney Holbrook?" the judge asked.

"Your Honor, the defendant is being charged with second-degree murder."

"Mr. Jordan, do you have an attorney? If you can't afford one, I will appoint a public defender for you."

"I have one, Your Honor. I'm sure she'll be along."

"Who's your attorney?" Judge Fontenot asked.

"Lily Cup Lorelei Tarleton, Your Honor."

"Be seated, Mr. Jordan, "Judge Fontenot said. "Bailiff do you have Ms. Tarleton's cell number?"

The bailiff scribbled on a piece of paper and handed it to the judge. The judge handed it to her assistant who lifted a cellphone, tapped the number and put it to her ear.

"She's not answering her phone, Your Honor," the assistant said.

"District Attorney Holbrook, as this is an arraignment, we can either move it to another day or have a public defender stand in for Ms. Tarleton during her absence."

"The state wishes to move forward, Your Honor," District Attorney Holbrook said.

"Will the defendant rise," Judge Fontenot said.

Gabe stood.

"Defendant Gabriel Jordan, at the time you were arrested were you read your Miranda Rights?"

"Yes, Your Honor, they read them to me."

"Murder is a serious crime," Judge Fontenot said. "The court has options of temporarily appointing—"

Lily Cup interrupted by pushing the court room doors open wide, announcing her attendance as she rushed down the aisle.

"I'm sorry, Your Honor—I had to pick something up and it wasn't ready—I had to wait, the traffic—the whole morning."

"We have a busy docket, counselor."

"Your Honor, I didn't know about this until one a.m. this morning. I'm sorry and ask the court's indulgence. I'm here now."

Lily Cup set her leather satchel on the table and sat next to Gabe, who was still standing.

"Counselor Tarleton is your attorney, Mr. Jordan?"

"She is, Your Honor," Gabe said. He pointed to Lily Cup seated beside him. The judge spoke to the court reporter.

"Let the record show that counsel for the defendant is Ms. Tarleton."

The judge looked at Lily Cup, then at Gabe.

"Gabriel Jordan, you are being charged with the violation of a criminal code written and enforced by the Louisiana State Legislature. The code is RS 14:30.1. I must inform you that statute 30.1 is second-degree murder—the killing of a human being. Under the definition of the charges—the offender, that would be you—had a specific intent to kill or inflict great bodily harm."

The judge lowered her head and peered over the tops of her reading glasses.

"Do you understand the charges as read by me?"

"I understand them, Your Honor," Gabe said.

"By this statute, whoever commits the crime of second-degree murder shall be punished by life imprisonment at hard labor without benefit of parole, probation, or suspension of sentence. Do you understand the penalties as I have read them?"

"I understand, Your Honor."

"How do you plead to these charges?" Judge Fontenot asked.

Lily Cup stood.

"Captain Jordan pleads not guilty, Your Honor."

Lily Cup leaned and whispered into Gabe's ear, "I have a plan." She straightens and addresses the judge.

"The court will now consider bail and—" the judge started.

"Your Honor," the district attorney said. "This was a most heinous crime. A young man in the prime of life—of college age—bludgeoned repeatedly by a hardened military officer. I pray the court refuse bond. The man is capable of doing it again, Judge Fontenot."

"District Attorney Holbrook—"

"I'm not speaking without cause, Your Honor. The man has scurrilously rearmed himself and sits here defiantly in your courtroom, a weapon at his side."

"Weapon?" Judge Fontenot asked.

"He has a cane, Your Honor."

"Counselor Tarleton, just how did the defendant get that cane past security?" the judge asked.

Lily Cup leaned toward Gabe and whispered.

"They didn't stop you?"

"I showed them my military ID, they ran my cane through the x-ray conveyor and handed it back to me. Nobody said a word."

"Your Honor, the defendant did not slip through security—security permitted him through."

"How did the defendant get through security with a cane?" Judge Fontenot asked.

"Your Honor, the District Court's security inspected the cane and let the defendant pass," Lily Cup said. "By law's definition a cane is not considered a weapon, no more than a wheelchair is. There is nothing hidden in his cane. My client walks with a cane."

Judge Fontenot penned a note and handed it to her assistant for follow-through.

"Your Honor, the defendant has served honorably in the Korean and Vietnam conflicts," Lily Cup said. "He has been decorated numerous times. He does not run from his responsibilities. He walks with a cane. There is no law prohibiting the use of a cane. They are allowed on commercial airplanes."

The judge's assistant returned to the bench and handed the judge a slip of paper.

The judge read it and looked at the court reporter.

"Let the record show the defendant's cane had been examined and approved by security."

"I would like my concern noted—" the DA started.

"So noted," Judge Fontenot said.

"—and the state will fight bond, Judge Fontenot."

"Your request is noted. Will the defendant stand?" Judge Fontenot asked.

Gabe stood, and Lily Cup stood as quickly.

"Your Honor," Lily Cup said. "May I approach the bench?"

"So soon?" the judge asked.

"Your Honor?"

"Approach."

Lily Cup stepped to the aisle and walked to the right of the bench, the DA by her side. Judge Fontenot put a hand over the microphone and leaned in.

"Your Honor, I have good reason to ask—"

"You're here Counselor Tarleton, ask."

"I'm asking the court to consider a pretrial conference."

"You mean a preliminary hearing. I plan to schedule it—after bail is determined," the judge asked.

"No, Your Honor, I mean a pretrial conference."

"Now?"

"Yes, Judge."

"Counselor Tarleton, this case hasn't even been to the Grand Jury. We're nowhere close to a trial."

"There are extenuating circumstances in this case, Judge, I think—"

"Your Honor," the DA barked in a whisper. "The facts are clear."

"Let me understand. You're asking for a pretrial conference before we even know there'll be a trial?" Judge Fontenot asked.

"You have the power to request one, Your Honor."

"Counselor, you'll have opportunities to negotiate a disposition."

"I don't wish to negotiate a disposition, Your Honor."

"You're asking me to interrupt proceedings and have it here, now?"

"Your Honor, there are times when legal issues must be resolved before a trial."

"That's what Preliminary Hearings are for, Counselor Tarleton," District Attorney Holbrook whispered.

"Counselor, we're not—" Judge Fontenot started.

"Perhaps if we discussed it in your chamber, off the record, Judge, that would be best," Lily Cup said.

"I could clear the courtroom," Judge Fontenot said.

"This is a stall, Your Honor," the DA said.

"Please, Judge Fontenot," Lily Cup said.

"Give me a good reason," Judge Fontenot said.

"Your Honor, television documentaries have named New Orleans the most violent city in the western hemisphere."

"I'm well aware, Counselor."

"Murder capital, they called us."

"Do you have a point to make, Counselor?"

"We have an audience of hungry press people sitting in this courtroom waiting to be fed so they can draw conclusions just to make news at our expense."

"A man has been murdered, Counselor."

"Clearing the courtroom so we can meet in here will only raise their ire," Judge—"

"The press is paid to be here, Counselor."

"—if, on the other hand, you call a pretrial conference, which you have the power to do, closed, off the record, and in your chamber. That won't raise suspicion."

"District Attorney Holbrook?" Judge Fontenot asked.

"I think it's a stall, Judge, but I'll oblige the court's decision."

"If we're all together—the district attorney, the assistant district attorney, you and me, Judge, it can be off the record—" Lily Cup started.

"What you're really saying is with no press," the judge said.

"No press, no court reporter, and no New Orleans Visitor Bureau."

"It's that important to you?" the judge asked.

"It's that important to New Orleans," Lily Cup said.

"Go back to your seats. Let me consider it and look at my schedule," Judge Fontenot said.

After a quiet visit with her clerk of courts Judge Fontenot looked at Gabe, still standing.

"Captain Jordan," the judge said. "The court is ordering a pretrial conference in my chamber. I'm releasing you on a twenty-five-thousand-dollar bond."

"But Your Honor," Lily Cup said.

"No bail, Your Honor, the defendant is a dangerous man," District Attorney Holbrook said.

"Twenty-five-thousand dollars for a man who is a decorated military officer, a veteran who served honorably in two wars?" Lily Cup asked.

"Twenty-five-thousand dollars."

"Your Honor, the ordeal alone has taken a toll on his health."

"Murder often does that," District Attorney Holbrook said.

"Bail is set," Judge Fontenot said.

"Your Honor, my client doesn't pose any threat of skipping out."

"I want to send a clear message of how seriously the people of Louisiana take these matters. Twenty-five-thousand-dollar bond."

The judge slammed her gavel.

"Your Honor," the DA said. "I would like it noted that counselor's request for pretrial conference is a delay tactic of the unprepared—an unnecessary delay."

"Miss Tarleton is respected in our courtroom," Judge Fontenot said. "I am trusting she won't waste the court's time. Captain Jordan, you're excused. Counselor Tarleton, please see the defendant settles with the bailiff. Captain Jordan, your attorney will be apprised of the date and time you will need to be in court."

"I'll be here. You have my word, Your Honor," Gabe said.

"This court is adjourned until further notice," Judge Fontenot said, pounding the gavel.

"Will counsel for the defense, District Attorney and the Assistant District Attorney meet in my chamber?"

Lily Cup whispered to Gabe.

"Go straight home, Gabe. Talk to no one out in the hall or in front of the courthouse. Catch a cab and go home."

"I will."

"When you get there, don't answer the door for anybody. I'll come by later."

CHAPTER 35

IT WAS A SECOND-FLOOR APARTMENT in a newer building on South Fourteenth Street in Baton Rouge—city transit commutable to the cooking academy and her restaurant job. Elizabeth pulled the door open. She was barefoot in sun–bleached jeans with threaded holes in the knees and a short-sleeve, yellow V–neck sweater and no bra. Elizabeth didn't need a bra. She leaned her head on the door and smiled a lingering "hold me" smile, but it was the city, and there were neighbors.

"Come on in," Elizabeth said.

He stepped in, closed the door behind him and turned into her arms, folding around him tightly, her cheek pressing into the side of his neck with a pout as if she was remembering her nightmares of never seeing him again.

"Hi, cher..." Peck said.

"Shhhhh," Elizabeth whispered.

The hold lingered.

"*Un sandwich aux oeufs?*" Elizabeth asked. ("An egg sandwich?")

"Bien," Peck said. ("Sure.")

"You didn't walk?" Elizabeth asked.

"*Non.*"

"I have to hear about the man who doesn't walk now, *mon ami.*"

He picked a postcard from the kitchen counter.

"See this?" he asked. He turned the card over and read it slowly, deliberately.

"Special pre–summer carpet cleaning."

She raised her hands to her face. "You read?"

"*Oui.*"

She approached with arms out and hugged him with warm, happy congratulations, a pride in having believed in him.

"*Je suis si fierè. Tellement heureuse,*" Elizabeth said. ("I am so proud. So happy.")

"What does *pre–summer* mean?" Peck asked.

"Before. Pre–summer means before summer," Elizabeth replied.

"Ahh," Peck said. "Maybe it's good help if we speak English?"

She took his face in her hands, leaned in, kissing him sensuously, her tongue darting under his upper lip, nibbling it, pulling on it with her lips.

She leaned back. "We still do some French things maybe, *non?*"

"*Oui,*" Peck said.

"*Bonne.*"

She kissed his nose and stepped back.

"Egg sandwiches," she said, turning into the kitchen. "Did you bring a bag?"

"How long before...?" Peck started.

"Before we're not alone again?"

"*Oui.*"

"He left for the rig two days ago. We have a few weeks. Can you stay a few weeks?"

"Nah, nah," Peck said. "But some time, sure. Maybe you can help me with something."

"Do you have a bag?" Elizabeth asked.

"*Oui.*"

"Make sure you're parked legally. They ticket around here. The gate code is seven, three, two, five—can you remember that?"

"Seven, three, two, five. I'll remember."

"Are you still living in Carencro?"

"Nah, nah. I'm in New Or–lee–anh."

"We are so fancy. I must hear about my big-city boy. Get your bag. You're my cousin, don't forget," Elizabeth said.

"I won't forget, cher."

As Peck pulled the door behind him on South Fourteenth Street in Baton Rouge, it was in the Orleans Parish Criminal District Court in New Orleans, that Judge Fontenot's chamber door was being closed by the judge herself.

"Sorry for the delay, folks," the judge said. "I had some reshuffling with my bailiff. Would anyone like coffee?"

Judge Fontenot sat in her chair. Seated in the room were the district attorney, the assistant district attorney, and Lily Cup.

"Judge Fontenot," the DA said, "this is—"

"I'd like some coffee," Lily Cup said.

"I would too," the judge said. She picked up her phone, buzzed her assistant.

"Pamela, can you arrange coffee and trimmings for two...?"

She looked around the room for other coffee takers. The assistant district attorney raised his finger, much to his senior's scowl. "Three cups. Thank you, Pamela."

"Your Honor..." the DA began.

"I mean what's the pleasure of having a conference in a judge's chamber if the judge can't show off and serve coffee?" Judge Fontenot asked.

The judge noticed the district attorney looking at his wristwatch impatiently. "The city has enough crime," she said. "I'm only trying to lighten the tension."

"With all due respect, Judge—"

"There's blind justice, District Attorney, and there is blind rage. I ask you to join me in respecting our colleague and let's have a listen to what she has to offer."

"—the people of Louisiana are protected under the law and only the law," the DA said.

"How was it, Bob, that you waited nearly forty minutes with a filled courtroom to express concern about a weapon? A wrong party might consider that a bit of grandstanding."

"I didn't see the cane until the defendant stood up, Judge."

The coffee came and was served about.

"Should we have a court reporter, Your Honor?" The DA asked.

"This is a pretrial conference and so long as you, the district attorney, the assistant district attorney and the defendant's council—in short, all sides are present—there can be no surprises. We can be off the record."

"Thank you, Judge," Lily Cup said. "I'm asking for a forty-eight-hour delay in scheduling a preliminary hearing."

"Your Honor, criminal pretrial conferences are for—" the district attorney started.

Lily Cup snapped. "I know what they're for, Bob—if you'll give me a chance."

"Tell us why we're here, counselor," Judge Fontenot said.

"I need some time," Lily Cup said.

"The people will need more than a 'the defense needs time' to delay a preliminary hearing," the DA said. "They're looking for answers."

"Judge, on February fifteenth, a man was inside a Walmart, at the key-making machine, making house keys for his home."

"This is not a trial, Judge," the DA said. "Why is counsel presenting evidence?"

"I'm not presenting evidence, I'm telling you a story that may be of interest to the city of New Orleans and the court," Lily Cup said.

"Counselor Tarleton, are you toying with a defendant's right to attorney-client privilege?"

"Judge, I haven't spoken with my client about the case."

"Excuse me?"

"I've asked, but he's not talking. A police sergeant called me when the defendant was arrested. I bailed him out—"

"This seems to be your problem and not the court's," the judge said.

"Judge, my client is a friend of mine, a hospice survivor. He's not a murderer. I just need a forty-eight-hour delay. Please, Your Honor."

"Forty-eight hours to try to get your client to talk to you?"

"Without a weapon, we're screwed, Judge. I need time."

"District Attorney Holbrook?" the judge asked.

"What's on your mind, Lily Cup? I have a city to answer to," District Attorney Holbrook said.

"You know me well enough, Bob. I wouldn't be asking this if I wasn't right. Give me an hour with you in your office and then give me 24 hours to sniff around."

"It's your call, District Attorney Holbrook," Judge Fontenot said.

"Thank you, Judge," Lily Cup said. "I need your help, Bob."

"My help for what?" the district attorney asked.

"You can pull strings—I've helped you before. You owe me."

"A quid pro quo on a murder?" Judge Fontenot asked.

"One day?" the district attorney asked.

Lily Cup looked at her watch. "I need forty-eight hours."

"We can't meet here," the district attorney said.

"Let's go to your office first and then to Dooky Chase for lunch, my treat," Lily Cup said.

Judge Fontenot picked up her cellphone and pressed a key.

"Commander's Palace, how may we be of service?"

"This is Judge Fontenot. Might I get a table for three at seven, please? No occasion—a night out with my daughter, just home from college."

She stood, gathering her purse and her briefcase.

"Judge Fontenot, if you'll give her the forty-eight hours, I can give her an hour in my office."

"Done," the judge said. "You have forty-eight hours, counselor."

"Thank you, Judge," Lily Cup said.

"Preliminary hearing in two days," the judge said. "Play nice, you two."

In the DA's office a clerk handed Lily Cup and District Attorney Holbrook bottles of water, waited for them to go into the office and pulled the door closed behind them.

"You have the floor," Holbrook said.

"Bob, on February fifteen," Lily Cup said, "a young man was standing at a vending machine at Walmart that was beside a machine a man was making house keys on. The young man turned several times, asking the key man for the use of one of his credit cards for the vending machine he was standing in front of. The key man turned him down each time. The young man turned again and threatened to kill the key man the minute he left the store and got outside."

"Were you there?" the DA asked.

"I wasn't," Lily Cup said.

"I'm to listen to hearsay?" the DA asked.

"I have it on this tape," Lily Cup said, holding it up. "It's the Walmart security video tape showing that incident, just as I said."

"That incident has nothing to do with this docket and security tapes do not record conversations," the DA said.

"I had a lip reader read the man's lips. I have it typed here."

"You know it won't be admissible."

"I know, but I just want you to read it."

"You read it," the DA said.

"Here goes: The young man says—'You can't? You're telling me you can't? You're a lying old motherfucker. You are dead, you motherfucker, the second you step out of this store. You are a dead man.'"

"You say this happened weeks ago? What is the relevance?" the DA asked.

Lily Cup placed the DVD into a television monitor. She pressed play and ran it through, reversed it and ran it through again and again.

"This proves nothing," the district attorney said.

"I have another DVD," Lily Cup said. "Same day, same Walmart, nine minutes later. Watch this."

She turned the player on.

"Bob, the kid is brandishing a weapon. A knife. The old man he's threatening is my client."

The DA did not respond. He sat back in his desk chair, he swirled around and looked out the window. Lily Cup sat and waited for his reaction.

"I take it this kid in the video is the corpse we have in the morgue."

"Same one."

"Any idea why the courtroom was full?" the DA asked.

"The NOLA Film Festival this weekend. They're filling hotels with Hollywood and press," Lily Cup said. "Press snooping around, is my guess."

"Without a weapon you don't have much of a case," the DA said.

"Without a weapon, I'm fucked," Lily Cup said.

The DA lifted his bottle of water and took a swig. Lowering it he paused as though he had an inspiration.

"Yes!" the DA said to himself with a snap.

His chair swiveled around.

"Larry Gaines," he said.

"Larry Gaines?" Lily Cup asked.

"Larry Gaines."

"I know the name," Lily Cup said. "Larry Gaines, where do I know it."

"Lieutenant Larry Gaines, he's a detective. He works the Quarter."

"That's where I know him. What about him?"

"He's the best there is, and I trust him," the DA said.

"I think I know—" Lily Cup started.

"Call him up. Ask my clerk for his number. Tell him the spot you're in."

"Can he just drop what he's doing and—?"

"He's on vacation. I had dinner with him Saturday. Call him."

"Thanks, Bob. I owe you."

"You're good for it."

Lily Cup stood and smiled, embracing her valise and DVDs.

"You mean that?"

"I know you, Lily Cup. This guy is too close to you somehow."

"I've known him almost a year. He's a friend. This is so not him, premeditated murder."

"You're way too close to him."

"I am, I know."

"Don't let it get so close you can't see straight."

"I'll be careful."

"Call Larry."

"Thanks, Bob."

"Good luck, but know right now, if you don't come up with something more than what you've got, your client's dead meat. I'll nail him."

Lily Cup left the office, found her car and drove to Orleans Avenue and parked around the corner of the Dooky Chase restaurant. She was still burning off a rye hangover, the stress of the arraignment and Leah's gumbo was just the ticket she needed. She made her way up the steps, looked at the picture of President Obama and the inimitable Leah Chase eating together and she stepped into the dining room and up to the hostess podium.

"No reservations, sorry," Lily Cup said.

"Not a problem, Ms. Tarleton, let me take a look," the hostess said.

"Is Ms. Leah here, hon?"

"She is, Ms. Tarleton, how are you today?"

"Hungry and hung over."

"Well you've come to the right place."

"Think I can see Ms. Leah before I leave?"

"I'll tell her you're here. I'm sure she'll want to see you. Let me seat you and I'll come let you know."

Lily Cup chose to do the buffet. Her first order of business was a bowl of New Orleans' world-famous Dooky Chase seafood gumbo. Two pieces of cornbread, of course. At the table Lily Cup spooned her gumbo in a pensive manner, as if her mind was stirring about what a dangerous position Gabe was in. It was as if she was thinking he was giving up on life and wanted to be punished for taking a life, regardless of the reason. She enjoyed a small helping of potato salad when the hostess came to her table.

"Leah would love to see you, Ms. Tarleton."

When she was finished, Lily Cup settled her tab and stepped back into the famous Dooky Chase kitchen. Chef Leah Chase wearing her iconic red chef coat was sitting behind a small table stacked with papers. It was in the heart of the kitchen's activity. Leah caught Lily Cup's eyes walking in and beamed her famous smile. They kissed cheeks with Lily Cup squatting down to talk, resting her arms on the table top.

"Gabe's in trouble, Leah."

Leah started. She rested her hand on Lily Cup's hand and patted it gently.

"Why, how can that beautiful man be in trouble?"

"He's killed somebody?"

Leah started again, sat up, her hands clasped. She lifted her hands to her face and rested fingers on her mouth. It was as if more than seventy years of Jim Crow was coming back. The civil rights movements she had lived through, Martin Luther King eating and meeting in her back rooms—memories of her Dooky Chase serving all colors regardless of the law—it was as if it was all coming back."

"Who did that beautiful man—?"

She couldn't say the word.

"He's a kid, Leah—twenty-two, we think."

"A child," Leah said.

"Pretty much," Lily Cup said.

"Does the young man have a name?"

"He was a John Doe."

Leah knew the buzz words, the slang. She listened.

"Prints came back, identified him as a Kenneth Bauer."

"Why did it take prints to identify that boy?"

"He didn't have any identification on him?"

"Was he a brother?"

"No, Leah, he wasn't."

"Gabe—and a white boy?"

"Yes."

"A local?"

"We don't know."

"An Acadian boy?"

"We don't know yet, Leah."

"There was no identification on his person?"

"No."

"So, his wallet was missing?"

"His wallet was on him, Leah—and it was filled with various things, but no identification, no photographs, no addresses of any kind."

"Officers were on the scene?"

"Immediately."

Leah looked into Lily Cup's eyes for the big answer. Lily Cup knew what she was looking for.

"The officer, was he?"

"The officer was black, Leah."

"How did—?"

"Gabe's cane. He did it with his cane—you know, his walking stick. The young man pulled a knife on him and I'm pretty sure it was self-defense, but Gabe's totally depressed about killing someone. He's not talking."

"Would you tell that beautiful man he has my prayers?"

"I'll tell him, Leah."

"The boy has my prayers, as well."

Leah reached and took Lily Cups hand and held it.

"I've seen it too many times," Leah said. "The spoils our floods and desperate hurricanes cause attract wrong intentions. They come to New Orleans like pirates. After the shop windows are repaired and the evacuated homes are again inhabited, they turn from looting to menacing our citizens and tourists, and in this case a vulnerable senior—a beautiful black man."

"My problem, Leah, is without a knife my hands are tied—the law is the law—and it goes to trial if there is an indictment, which sounds likely."

Leah took and squeezed Lily Cup's hand.

"Lily Cup, you listen to Leah now. I've seen it all. There's some good in everybody. Sometimes they have trouble finding it. New Orleans is like no other place. There are times—times in the shadows and devastation of our hurricanes and our floods—when to the world we—under sea level and where the Mississippi empties into the world—we must resemble the old untamed west."

"Leah, that's beautiful—and saying it politely."

"We must be strong and streetwise for everyone's survival and sanity and for our community's benefit.

"The judge has given me forty-eight hours."

"That's a lifetime, my friend. Anything you need from Leah, you come by. You've got my prayers."

"Thank you, Leah."

Minutes later Peck's phone beeped, waking him. It was a text from Lily Cup. He also had an unread one from Millie.

"Pray," Lily Cup's text said. "We'll know in a couple of days. I'm at Dooky Chase for chicken."

He looked at the next text, from Millie:

"I love you, hunk—baby Charlie says hello."

He closed his eyes and rolled over, returning to his nap. Elizabeth was in the kitchen, wooden spoon in hand, a fresh French loaf on the counter and her butter sauce carefully being stirred in a copper pot; a dark Bordeaux stood by, waiting to be opened and decanted.

Elizabeth was smiling.

CHAPTER 36

THE LONELY DRONE OF THE SAX floated from Charlie's Blue Note as Gabe stepped from Frenchmen Street into the alley. It was as if another night was celebrating the old man's life and welcoming him with a grace.

Vaaaa vaaaa da veeeeeeee...Vaaaa ve voooo vaa vaa vava ve voooooon.

Familiar velvet sounds were reaching out, as they had the night he and Peck first walked into the city a year before. The sax seemed to offer promise and calm for the old man, jazz aficionado, dancer, and troubled soul. He pushed the door open, stopping its return with his cane. Holding the jamb with a grip, he stepped up and in. On the small stage in the far-left corner, his favorite quartet was playing blues. The tall, broad-shouldered sax man, a blue-black faced brother with gentle eyes, caught his friend's eye and winked welcome during a rambling ride down to a long and low B flat.

Sasha's perfect form perched on her preferred stool at the end of the bar. She was in one of her dance-night ensembles—a red satin strapless Chanel designer gown so haute it was insured. Her elbow posed on the bar, a lipstick-smudged martini glass delicately balanced in her fingertips. Eyeing Gabe through a wall mirror, she begged Charlie's pardon for the interruption and for a Dewar's on the rocks for their friend. Turning on the stool, she lowered a Cyd Charisse–like long leg to the floor, baring a slender, snowy white thigh above a sheer stocking carefully puckered to a black satin garter strap button. She stood and organized the dress as if it were a first dance at the prom, lifted her martini in one hand, a tumbler of scotch in the other, and ambled with a sway to the music, elbows out, balancing the drinks, her celebrated cleavage leading the way toward his usual table by the band. Gabe rose, pulling out a chair.

"You look ravishing, darling," Gabe said. "Make an old man happy. Do sit."

"Give us a hug, baby," Sasha said. "Been worried sick all day."

She set the drinks down and they embraced, her cheek buried into his neck. She lifted her head, kissing his neck.

"Buy a damn phone so I can find you," Sasha said.

"Never," Gabe said.

"Did he hurt you?"

"Who told you?"

"Peck. He texted me some of it and said that Lily Cup would explain but she hasn't answered her phone all day."

"It's been a day. No telling where she is."

"You okay, Gabe?"

"Okay is not the word that comes to mind, darling. A boy is dead," Gabe said.

"What happened in court must have been good, you're here?" Sasha asked.

"Let's dance," Gabe said.

The band was midway into a sax rift of "Louisiana Blues." He took her by the hand, wrapped an arm around her waist and pulled her to him. He tapped his toe three times slow—a fourth time—a fifth time, then pulled her hips in syncopation, and they swayed, turned, and started it again. They moved about their corner of the room like they were instruments in the band—as if they'd spent a lifetime together on dance floors just off Frenchmen Street. In one turn Gabe caught the eye of the sax man and winked as the song's sound was fading to close. The sax man looked over at his drummer, caught his eye, then at the bass, then the trumpet man.

"Our brother wants it easy, just one more time, gentlemen," sax man said. "And one, two, three," he said, clicking his finger and thumb.

The band ripped into "Louisiana Blues" again. Gabe was now in the zone, moving in perfect sync with her, the lady who saw to it he was able to dance one more time. She had saved his life the year before. As the sounds of the second playing faded, he turned her slowly, carefully dipping her, smiling into her eyes.

"If I was only half my age, James would be out the door, my darling," Gabe said.

"Now you tell me," Sasha said.

"I would wrap you in my arms and blanket your body with roses," Gabe said.

"I love it when you talk dirty," Sasha said.

He righted them and they embraced. Arm-in-arm they made their way back to the table. Seated, she reached both hands across and held his.

"How are you?"

Gabe looked at her.

"Tell me true."

"Much better now that I've danced with my best girl," Gabe said.

"Lily Cup's phone is still turned off. All her office says is she's in meetings," Sasha said. "How'd it go in court?"

He looked at his watch. "I guess they're still at it. The judge said they'd let me know when I had to be back."

"That bastard," Sasha said.

"The judge?"

"No, the prick that tried to kill you."

Gabe lifted his hand, softly touching her lips with two fingers. "Not tonight, baby," he said.

She knew what he was saying. Ever since they met, Charlie's Blue Note was off limits for business talk. It was their escape. Dance was their escape, away from the real world. Several nights a month Sasha would leave the real estate world behind her and *slut-up*, as she and Lily Cup still called it, just to dance to jazz and blues. In priceless strapless Chanels that presented her "girls" to best advantage, the finest Prada heels, and Cartier ornaments Sasha dressed to the nines with the sole intention of coming to Charlie's Blue Note to dance.

"They're playing Joe Williams, baby," Gabe said.

He stood, his hand extended. The two intertwined like fine Christmas ribbon wrapping each other in sway and turn with the sounds, the vibrations of the sax, a skitter scattering of brushes on a snare, a heart-thumping, stringed bass.

With the twisting and turning he mumbled into song, his own Joe Williams in her ear.

"Git out my life, woman. You don't love me no more... no, no," Gabe sang.

They would jerk into a turn, then back and forth as one.

"Git out my eyes, teardrops...I got to see my way around," Gabe sang.

She pulled her left hand from his, reached up and placed fingers over his mouth.

"Dance, Joe Williams, just dance," Sasha said.

She took his hand again.

He lowered his right hand from her waist and patted her buttocks a sensual scold, and then held her waist again. She grinned and kissed his neck. The sax player quietly clapped his hands, celebrating Gabe's vocal rendition. It was five more dances before they sat and ordered red beans and rice, and more drinks.

"My darling, can old Gabe here broach a subject—something that's been preying on my mind?"

"Broach?" Sasha asked. "Sounds like bad jewelry."

"About James," Gabe said.

"Where's Peck?" Sasha asked.

"Did he mention in his texts? He got accepted into Tulane," Gabe said.

"What a guy," Sasha said. "His tutor told me he was ready."

"He starts night school in a few weeks. Isn't that something?"

"Where is he tonight? You shouldn't be out alone this late."

"Peck's gone," Gabe said. "A trip."

"What sort of trip? To see Millie?"

"He wanted to check out his past," Gabe said.

"You mean he's gone to mow the old bird's lawn at the hospice in Carencro?" Sasha asked. "That's a long drive just to mow a lawn."

"Not exactly."

"Where, exactly?"

"Millie's been asking about his momma."

"And?"

"Asking if she could meet her," Gabe said.

"We knew it was a matter of time," Sasha said.

"You think? I always thought she knew—thought maybe he'd have told her."

"I actually figured she'd know better than to bring it up. I haven't held anything from Millie or her family," Sasha said.

"I told him to go, for his own good."

"Go?"

"I told him it might be best if he finds the answers for himself, so he could know."

"Go? Go where?" Sasha asked.

"The man deserves at least that—answers."

"He went alone?"

"Why not?"

"Please tell me you're not serious, Gabe?"

"He left this morning."

"Jesus," Sasha said.

She turned in her seat and stared at the wall.

"So, I'm getting your back? Now it's all on me?"

"Do you know how dangerous it can be traveling into those swamps and bayous?" Sasha asked.

"He knows the swamps."

"You've heard the stories, the serial killers."

"I've heard the stories."

"How could you let him go?"

"Peck knows the swamps better than most. He'll be fine," Gabe said.

"He hasn't been back there since he was ten," Sasha said.

"He was eight or nine, and now he has maps," Gabe replied.

The band took a break and walked by the table.

"I can't imagine you're letting him go alone," Sasha said.

"He's a grown man."

"You, of all people."

Gabe tightened both fists, raised them and brought them down on the table with a dull thud.

"God damn it to hell. I'm just about fed up with the bullshit of being talked down to like I'm a delinquent schoolboy or a recalcitrant child that's not sitting in the room. All day I've been pulled on and prodded and poked—even threatened with a knife—and all day not one, 'are you all right?' All I hear is what I've done wrong, or where I've made a bad decision. I'm tired of it."

She sat, staring at him.

"Peck is a grown adult," Gabe said. "He's mature. He knows bayous and swamps better than any alligator—he has an affinity for people we can't even begin to imagine, and he's considerate of them, and how dare anybody tell me he's not person enough or man enough or mature enough."

"You mean me."

"What?"

"You said anybody. You meant me."

"The band's back, baby," Gabe said. "Dance with me."

They stood and held each other without speaking, waiting for any sound. The sax wailed into their favorite, the daydream-soft sounds of "When Sunny Gets Blue," and they moved with it, her cheek nestled into his neck.

"I'm sorry," Gabe whispered.

"It's not you, darlin'."

"Maybe I didn't think it through."

"I'm sorry, Gabe. This has been a day of hell for you."

"I've been too long black," Gabe said.

"Shut up," Sasha whispered.

"It's true, baby. An American black doesn't think about potholes on the road ahead. We count on them. It's been our culture for four hundred years. Trouble has a way of hovering over us like a high-noon sun. I wasn't thinking when I sent him off alone."

The song lingered. They turned, sliding feet slowly with a sadness, a melancholy in motion, Gabe humming the song.

"Do you think we're in love?" Sasha asked.

He turned her and stepped in tune.

"Do you?" Sasha asked.

"I've loved you from our first dance last year the night we met," Gabe said.

"Me too," Sasha said.

He put his arm around her with a loving squeeze, not missing a motion, a step in the dance.

"If James is right for you, it'll be good," Gabe said. "You'll have a long, happy life."

"I guess," Sasha said.

The song ended. They stood, holding each other, waiting. The next piece was upbeat jazz—not appropriate for their mood. They walked to their table and sat down, looking at each other with different eyes for the first time.

"You have me worried about the boy," Gabe said. "Maybe I should call and ask him to come home."

She was silent. She reached and held his hands.

"I mean it," Gabe said.

Sasha didn't speak.

"I know he can deal with the swamps and the bayous and the back roads. I'm not worried about that. He may even get some good fishing or crabbing in, but if this gator man has a long memory and he meets up with him, it could be a problem."

"You know about the gator man, Gabe?"

"You told me about *gator man* when we were in Providence. I haven't mentioned it or let on to the boy I knew."

"Peck'll be okay, Gabe."

"This gator man is dangerous," Gabe said.

"Gator man won't be a problem."

Gabe set his Dewar's down, jerking his head to attention. "Excuse me?"

Sasha just looked at him.

"I didn't hear you," Gabe said.

"Gator man is dead," Sasha said.

"Say again?"

"Gator man is dead."

"That for certain?" Gabe asked.

"He's dead."

"How? When?" Gabe asked. "How do you...?"

"Gabe, you remember when we drove to Memphis last year, and I begged you to tell me what was wrong with you?"

"I remember like it was tonight," Gabe said.

"Remember what you told me?"

"Remind me."

"You said, ask me no questions, and I'll tell you no lies...remember?"

"So, he's..." Gabe started.

"Gator man will never hurt Peck again," Sasha said. "That's all you need to know, and Peck sure as hell can't hear it from us. He's wakened from that whole nightmare. Let's leave it be."

Gabe placed his elbows on the table, rested his cheeks in his hands, thinking to himself.

"Gabe, do you know why every woman in love is like a black man?" Sasha asked.

He sat up.

"This ought to be good. Why, baby?"

"They both know when it's time to keep a secret, and they know how to keep one and take it to their graves," Sasha said.

He smiled, accepting the sanctity of the moment.

"You sure you don't have some color in your veins, darlin'?" Gabe asked.

Sasha sipped her martini with an inquisitive smile.

"My momma's water broke while she was standing in line waiting to get some pralines. I was born in a restroom in Treme, so who the hell knows?" Sasha asked.

"From Congo Square to Everywhere, baby," Gabe mused.

"You got that right, dancing man—so who knows?"

"You were thinking all along Peck will be okay?" Gabe asked.

"Yes."

"You were just putting on..."

"He'll be fine," Sasha said.

"Woman, order some more beans and rice. I need one more Dewar's—you need a fresh martini—and go fix your hair. I mussed it with the dip."

"Aye aye, Captain," Sasha said and saluted.

"Let's dance until Charlie throws us out."

"Don't you sound like a hottie," Sasha said, standing to go to the bar.

"It's not every day a man learns a woman's been in love with him for nine months."

"Unrequited love, you softy," Sasha said.

"I want to dance tonight, baby—and I'm a curmudgeon."

Sasha's phone chimed in her purse. She lifted it out.

"It's her," Sasha said. "Hey."

"Have you seen Gabe?" Lily Cup asked.

"He's here—at Charlie's."

"Goddammit, I told him to go home and wait for me."

"He's here."

"Tell him not to move a muscle. I'll be right over."

Sasha put her phone in her purse.

"She's on her way. You're not to move," Sasha said.

"I'm going to do my business. I shall return," Gabe said.

He walked away.

Sasha adjusted her bodice, pulled her dress down to proper and walked toward the bar, swaying her hips to the music.

They were dancing to a Duke Ellington sound when Lily Cup first came through the door. She looked around the room for them.

"Can I have a rye, Charlie?" Lily Cup asked.

"Coming up, LC," Charlie said.

"Better make it a double, straight up—no ice."

"You got it," Charlie said. "Go sit, I'll bring it over."

"Thanks, hon," Lily Cup said.

She eyed Sasha's purse on the table by the band, approached, sat and waited. It wasn't long before she had her drink and the dancers were back and seated.

"All things considered, it was a pretty good day today," Lily Cup said.

"It's over?" Sasha asked.

"Far from it," Lily Cup said. "But it was a good day."

Gabe ate his beans and rice, listening passively.

"How can it be good, if it's not over?" Sasha asked.

"Any day a DA doesn't say, 'fuck you, we're going to trial,' is a good day," Lily Cup said.

"The man nearly gets killed, your phone's off—I wish someone would tell me what's going on," Sasha barked.

"Nothing to tell, yet," Lily Cup said.

"You mean you don't want to talk about it," Sasha said.

"That too," Lily Cup said.

"I'll shut up," Sasha said.

"Gabe, I'm going to finish my drink and take you home," Lily Cup said.

"How'd it go?" Gabe asked.

"I need you to get a good night's sleep, and I'll pick you up early. We'll have a busy day."

"What's going on?" Gabe asked.

"I'll fill you in in the morning," Lily Cup said.

Gabe looked at Lily Cup as if she was dismissing him.

"I just want you to get a good night's sleep. Big day ahead," she said.

He pushed the bowl away.

"Woman, for six days I crawled on my belly under a barrage of machinegun fire on Pork Chop hill in Korea; in Nam I sat in a foxhole next to a kid from Teaneck and watched a sniper's bullet go through his eye and blow the back of his head out while he was telling me about his new seven-pound baby girl; I can tell you what napalm smells like on burning bodies in rice patties infested with venomous snakes. Woman, don't patronize."

"Let's all calm down," Sasha said. "We're friends here."

"I've been in the DA's office all afternoon," Lily Cup said. "Watching the tapes over and over. We had the store manager on conference call telling his recollection of the day you had the keys made. They had the lip-reader come in to demonstrate how she did it. When she saw them again, she read the lips of a passerby in Walmart lipping, 'asshole,' at the kid while she walked behind him while he was threatening you."

"And?" Gabe asked.

"We looked at the body," Lily Cup said.

Gabe froze.

"The FBI prints came in on him," Lily Cup said.

"Anything?" Gabe asked.

"His name is Kenneth Bauer and he tried to buy a handgun in Tucson and was turned down. He tried again at a gun show in Las Vegas and was turned down. So a hunting knife became his weapon of choice. Probably bought it at a hardware store."

"Kenneth Bauer," Gabe said.

"There's more," Lily Cup said.

Gabe looked up in anticipation.

"It happens our Mr. Kenneth Bauer is wanted in Dallas for five possible robberies where his prints were found—"

"He's a street robber," Gabe said.

"And for a stabbing murder of a man in a Dallas parking lot," Lily Cup continued. "A camera at the Greyhound depot spotted Mr. Bauer following the guy. They've since found Mr. Bauer's thumbprint on the dead man's eyeglasses."

"What does this mean for Gabe?" Sasha asked.

"It means Gabe and I have our work cut out for us," Lily Cup said.

"The man's wanted for killing a man in Dallas," Sasha said. "Doesn't that prove he's a killer?"

"First of all, he's a suspected killer," Lily Cup said. "But killing a suspected killer is still murder...and Gabe killed the man."

"I don't get it," Sasha said.

"I do," Gabe said.

"All this may give us a break by giving Gabe's story credibility, but we have a lot of work to do," Lily Cup said.

"He's a suspected killer, that should prove— "Sasha started.

"We can't prove the kid had a knife. Gabe's charged with the murder of Kenneth Bauer, and an hour ago the police commissioner told the police chief to have him followed and bring him in if he made any wrong moves."

"But it's so obvious the guy killed that man in Dallas, they have his prints and the video," Sasha said.

"Will you please listen to me, Michelle? There's no such thing as a 'vigilante' defense," Lily Cup said. "As far as the DA sees it, Gabe killed a man who had no knife, and Gabe will have to be there through preliminaries the day after tomorrow to see if they're going to indict him."

"So, maybe I'm not getting it," Sasha said. "He pleads innocent, they take all of the evidence into consideration, and they drop their case."

"He's already pled not guilty, Michelle."

"This is Charlies, I'm Sasha," Sasha said.

"What you're not getting is that this is fucking America," Lily Cup said.

"So?" Sasha asked.

"There are two courts in America."

"Amen to that, little sister," Gabe mumbled.

"We have Judge Fontenot's court, and then we have the court of public opinion."

"The media," Sasha said.

"The media," Lily Cup said. "That one is truly a circus. There's no way in hell the media will allow the DA of a world's most violent city let the killing of a young white 'tourist' by a black army officer on St. Charles Avenue in broad daylight just go away. I don't give a good goddamn how many medals Gabe has, the visitor's bureau would hang the DA out to dry if he buried it, and they represent a lot of his votes."

"Jesus," Sasha said.

"They nailed him to a cross too, remember?" Lily Cup asked.

"Little sister is right," Gabe said.

"I have a plan, though," Lily Cup said.

Gabe put his spoon down. "What do you need me to do?"

"The DA liked my Harvard story I told him," she said.

"Harvard story?"

"When I was at Harvard, a second-year law student—I remember he was the son of some governor somewhere. Anyway, the kid was stoned and he wheeled a homeless drunk and all his belongings in a red wagon to the quad after listening to the guy hallucinate on a soapbox in a park about trial law. The homeless guy had wanted to be a lawyer but flunked out, dropped some acid and dropped out and lived on the streets, pulling his red wagon around."

"Where's this going?" Gabe asked. "Sounds like a sick joke."

Lily Cup threw back her rye and set the glass down upside down for emphasis. "We lawyers are sick fucks, Gabe, or haven't you heard? In trade for a fifth of bourbon, the man revealed to us fledgling law students his *National Enquirer* defense theory."

"*National Enquirer* theory?" Gabe asked.

"This guy told us most people would listen to any goddamned thing you tell them if the first sentence is a question."

"A question," Gabe said.

"He called it the *National Enquirer* defense."

"I don't see the point," Gabe said.

"It's impossible to lie with a question," Lily Cup said.

"I get that," Gabe said. "I'm good with that little sister."

"Tomorrow we're going to find that needle in the haystack—that one shred of evidence that raises that one or two questions that could write an end to this whole mess."

"Isn't *the National Enquirer* over the top for the 'media' metaphor?" Gabe asked.

"Gabe, you're old enough to remember when they could only swear or show sex on cable television, right?" Lily Cup asked.

"I am and I do," Gabe said. "There was family television and there was cable television."

"It's all cable now," Lily Cup said. "It's streamed—it's You-Tubed. The so-called news can say anything it damn well wants, show anything it damn well wants and without libel—just as long as their first sentence is a question."

"What do you need me to do?" Gabe asked.

"Gabe, the DA pulled some strings and got the police chief to assign a Lieutenant Gaines to be your arresting officer. I know him."

"There's a warrant for me?"

"No, they're watching you."

"I'm being followed?"

"That's what a watch is, Gabe."

"So, what's next?" Gabe asked.

"Lieutenant Gaines told me he would meet us in the morning, and if you're cooperative he'll try to help you, and we would go from there. I want you to go home like a good boy, get a night's sleep. I'll get you in the morning. We'll go through the details of what happened for the millionth time, and if we can find what we need and have the DA where we need him, then maybe we can prevent an indictment."

Gabe stood, dropped three twenties on the table.

Lily Cup picked up her phone, tapped the keys, waited, and tapped the keys again.

Gabe rubbed Sasha's neck and shoulders.

"This has been a special evening. Thank you, darling," Gabe said.

Sasha stood and embraced him. "I love you, you old bear," she said. "Listen to her, she's good."

"I'll flag a cab," Gabe said.

"Uber is outside, waiting," Lily Cup said. "If it's not, wait a few. It will be. It's paid."

The ladies walked Gabe to the door. He stepped outside, climbed into the Uber and rode off.

"Let's go talk," Sasha said.

"I can't, hon," Lily Cup said. "I have a full day tomorrow. I'm going to the office."

"Peck's taken off," Sasha said.

"I know," Lily Cup said.

"You know?"

"I knew last night."

"How does everyone know things but me?"

"I gotta run," Lily Cup said.

"Will Gabe be okay?" Sasha asked.

"At his age, he's facing life in prison. Having no witnesses makes it tough. Having no knife makes it impossible. I'll do my best."

Knowing she had just told Gabe the secret of gator man disappearing, Sasha put her arms around Lily Cup's neck and whispered. "Remember when we were seven, our pact of never holding secrets from each other ever, ever?"

"No telling and no holding, and we were six, but I remember," Lily Cup said.

"I have one now," Sasha said. "Can I hold this one, please?"

"Depends what it is."

"I told Gabe about gator man."

"Fuck."

"I had to."

"Pay Charlie for my rye?"

"Of course."

Lily Cup kissed her on both cheeks.

"Love you," Lily Cup said, stepping to the door.

"Love you," Sasha said, turning to the bar.

CHAPTER 37

ELIZABETH SAT ON THE BED gently running fingers through sleeping Peck's hair, scratching his scalp with loving French manicured nails.

"*Il est temps de se lever, la tête endormie. J'ai pris le jour de congé,*" Elizabeth said. ("Time to get up, sleepy head. I took the day off.")

He rolled over, blinked open his eyes and stared as if he was trying to remember where he was.

"You slept like a little baby," Elizabeth said.

"The food was so good."

"I love cooking for you."

"Too much wine for Peck."

"You're in love, Peck."

"Hanh?"

"I can tell the way you hold me now. Who is she?"

"You would like her, cher. Millie."

"Do you love her?"

"I'm in love, dass for true.

"I'm so jealous, but we'll always be..."

"*Mais oui,*" Peck said. "Always."

"Besides, when I become a chef I may have to move to New York or Paris, and you always need water and a pirogue near you."

"*Oui.*"

"So, will you tell your Millie about your Elizabeth?"

Peck smiled. "*Oui.* Cousin."

She crawled onto the bed, straddled him over the covers and leaned down to his face.

"*Embrasser des cousins?*" ("Kissing cousins?")

"I go to university soon, cher. Elizabeth becomes an important chef and Peck learns to be smart, ha."

"You're plenty smart already," Elizabeth said. "The university will make you wise."

She kissed his lips softly and leaned back, first watching his mouth, then soulfully looking into his eyes.

"Will you forget me?"

"*Jamais.*" ("Never.")

Elizabeth's eyes didn't believe him, but they smiled.

"So, get up Mr. Peck. Take a shower and I'll make breakfast, and we'll talk."

"*Oui.*"

"Then we can go for a long walk."

"*Oui.* Go to the kitchen, cher."

"Are you pushing me out?"

Peck smiled.

"Ah, I know."

Elizabeth reached down between her legs and felt William through the blanket, morning erect and throbbing.

"You are such a naughty little boy. You are so shy and don't want Elizabeth to see our friend."

Peck rolled, moving her off.

"Crepes, cher?"

"Boudin or bacon?"

"Boudin."

"Grits?"

"*Oui,* and jam on crepes?"

Elizabeth smiled into his eyes, kissed the tip of his nose and left the room.

Just as Peck was stepping into a shower in Baton Rouge, Gabe and Lily Cup, in New Orleans, were stepping into the Silver Whistle Café for eggs and coffee. A plainclothes detective stood at his table and greeted them with handshakes.

"Gabe, this is Lieutenant Gaines. He's a detective in the city, but he's an acquaintance of mine and a friend of the district attorney. Lieutenant Gaines is going to try to help us. He's on vacation, so be good to him."

"It's good to see a brother wanting to help," Gabe said. "Thank you, Lieutenant."

"Has Ms. Tarleton explained to you that I've been assigned as your arresting officer?"

"She has."

"It's just a formality, but I'm required to read the Miranda Warning."

"I understand."

"You have the right to remain silent. Anything you say can and will be used against you in a court of law. You have the right to an attorney. If you cannot afford one, one will be provided for you. Do you understand what I've read?"

"I do, Lieutenant."

"One more detail—one you might want to talk over with your attorney," Lieutenant Gaines said.

"Which is?" Gabe asked.

"I need to know if you are giving up your attorney-client privileges in what we discuss today?"

"The Miranda Warning pretty much takes care of that, doesn't it, Lieutenant?"

"It pretty much does, but I thought I'd ask."

"I'm fine with it," Gabe said.

"We're fine," Lily Cup confirmed.

"Captain, Miss Tarleton was telling me you lost a son in Iraq."

"I did."

"I'm sorry to hear that. Which conflict, sir?"

"Desert Storm," Gabe said. "Friendly fire."

"That was an historic engagement," Lieutenant Gaines said.

"General Norman Schwarzkopf—truly heroic," Gabe said.

"Your son was a hero. I served in Iraq, but our second time in."

The three ordered breakfast and waited for coffee to be poured.

"Captain, Miss Tarleton and the district attorney brought me up to speed on the situation you're in. I've read the notes and the files. I have some ideas of what we can do this morning that can be productive and might help with the DA's deciding whether or not to take this to the grand jury," Lieutenant Gaines said.

"I'm at your service, Lieutenant. Please call me Gabe."

"If you're not *Captain*, my brother, then I'm *Larry* to you," Larry said.

Gabe stretched his arm, offering his hand.

"Good to meet you, Larry."

"Nice to meet you, Gabe."

"Maybe you two should get a room," Lily Cup mused. "There's a hotel through that door and upstairs."

"Gabe, according to the notes, you say you were attacked. Did you know the man who allegedly attacked you?" Larry asked.

"To say I knew him wouldn't be accurate. I had seen him before, on February fifteen. I knew his face."

"How can you be certain it was that date, February fifteen?"

"I remember it because it was the day after Valentine's Day, and it's also the date on my receipts for my house keys."

"Did you know this person before that time—before the day after Valentine's Day—or was that the first time you saw him?"

"That was the first time."

"Tell me how you met him."

Gabe methodically recounted the details of his morning in the store where he had his keys made.

"You're an experienced veteran—a soldier, Gabe. What was your state of mind when this happened?"

"I went through boot camp in my teens, Larry. I've been two years in Korea under gun and mortar fire. I've fought mosquitoes, rain, and sniper fire, and napalm for two years in Nam. Like the rest of them, I handled it best I could. My brother, in all that time I have never been as scared as I was that day at that Walmart, the day that snipe stood with his eyes watching my eyes in a deadly cold glare and promised to kill me the second I walked out the door. Never have I ever been so fearful."

"With all you've been through, Gabe, why this one particular time were you so frightened?" Larry asked.

"Twenty years ago, I would have grabbed him by the collar and tossed him into a wall. I think it was that all of a sudden I realized what being old is. I'm an old man now. Sometimes I need help just trying to stand up from a chair. I was scared, my brother. I've never been so scared in my life...not of what the little pissant was threatening to do...I was frightened of what I wasn't anymore."

"Your cane offered you no sense of security?" Larry asked.

"I wasn't wearing my cane."

"You left your cane at home?"

"Yes."

"You must not have relied on it as a defense piece."

"I never wore my cane or carried my walking stick before. I learned cane defense from a communications specialist years ago."

Lieutenant, you understand that *wearing* a cane thing?" Lily Cup asked.

"I have a dad, I surely do understand it, counselor. Man steps out, he wears his cane."

"My brother," Gabe said.

Gabe continued.

"He was a private in a VA hospital in Guam. I've kept two canes and one stick since, just in case I was ever in need—one black cane and one brown, to match whatever suit or shoes I might be wearing at the time. I've owned them more than thirty years, but I only started wearing one after that day I was making keys."

"Was it by the book SOP army instruction or a casual one-on-one from the private?"

"He had a manual we paged through, but I don't think it was army issue. I remember it. When threatened, grab cane firmly with both hands and never loosen the grip. Second, assume a side posture to prevent getting kicked in the nuts. Third, distract him with quick jabs to the face and eye if he's in my space. Four, hit the back of the leg, upper calf just under the knee joint, as hard as you can until he goes down."

"Interesting," Larry said. "What was number five?"

"What would you suppose it was, Lieutenant. Number five?"

"Was number five to kill him?"

"Number five was to run—unless he had a gun. If he had a gun, hit it away and then run."

"Did your experience that day at Walmart make you want to kill him when you saw him again, Gabe?"

"It made me want to go home and lie down. I had to stop my heart's pumping from busting my chest open. I went straight home."

"The second time you saw Mr. Bauer—"

"Yes."

"Did you recognize him right away?"

"Yes. It was after I came out of the store. I was waiting for a streetlight with the store manager, and we saw Bauer leaning on his bicycle, waving the knife."

"I meant to say the next time after that. Did you think of killing him when you first saw him two days ago?"

"No."

"You said he pulled a knife on you."

"He did."

"After he pulled a knife, did you think of killing him then?"

"No."

"What happened next?"

"He demanded my wallet and money."

"When he demanded your wallet, did you think of killing him?"

"No."

"What went through your mind?"

"I thought of defending myself."

"What did you do?"

"I took position, poked him near his eye twice and then slammed his upper calf and he went down."

"Was that when you thought of finishing him off?"

"I thought he'd stay on the ground and let me walk away."

"And did he?"

"He started getting on one knee, grabbed my shirttail in his fist and swiped at me with the knife. Pulling, poking, and stabbing. He cut my shirt twice—cut a button off. I felt the blade and that's when I went blind. That's when I clubbed him. You know the rest."

"I don't, Gabe. That's why we're here."

"From all you've heard and read, Lieutenant, don't you think it's a pretty cut-and-dried case of self–defense?" Lily Cup asked.

"It could be, if witnesses came forward," Larry said.

"And with no witnesses?" Gabe asked.

"And no knife?" Larry asked.

"Sounds like I'm cooked," Gabe said.

"We have to satisfy the DA that it was self–defense and not a revenge crime," Larry said. "We have to help with some clue or clues that prove your testimony is true. We have to come up with more than a no-witness, no knife, 'trust me' self–defense."

"Help me understand, Larry," Gabe said.

"Gabe, a prosecutor's job is to put murderers away for life. A district attorney prosecutor will try to do that by convincing the jury you're a heinous murderer. If the judge allows the videos in, he won't hesitate to raise doubts about you wanting revenge. The prosecutor is the first to talk to the jury. He's going to tell the jury that poor Mr. Bauer was walking along, minding his own business and you, an angry man, recognized him and attacked him in broad daylight, and your claim that young Mr. Bauer pulled a knife to protect himself was a lie—and you, an experienced, highly trained, battle-savvy army captain viciously murdered him."

"Why are we even here then, Larry? I could have saved a few dollars and eaten at home. It sounds like I'm at the gallows already," Gabe said.

"Miss Tarleton, perhaps you can step in and help Gabe understand the whole picture."

"Gabe, the DA has the local media on his back. They're looking for answers to a daylight killing on one of the most celebrated avenues in the world—St. Charles Avenue, home of the streetcar. The DA believes me. But he needs more than that to drop the case against you. He needs some corroborating evidence in your favor that can be documented. Isn't that about it, Lieutenant?"

"That's it, exactly," Larry replied. "And the knife would help."

"What now?" Gabe asked.

"Let's finish our breakfast. I hear they make a delightful blueberry muffin. I want to do one of those and one more coffee before we start our search," Larry said.

Just as the three were focusing on a Silver Whistle Café breakfast at Josephine Street and St. Charles Avenue, Peck in Baton Rouge had finished shaving and was toweling his face when his phone chimed.

"*Bonjour.*"

"I love you so much, mister. Have I told you lately?" Millie said.

"Who is this?" Peck asked with a grin.

"It's Millie."

"Hi, cher."

"Have you forgotten me already?"

"Nah, nah," Peck said. "I was having the fun."

"Did you get my text?"

"Text?"

"Last night. I texted and I waited all night and you didn't text me."

"I was asleep. Are you still coming?"

"Yes, and I've been thinking."

"T'inking?"

"I was thinking maybe Lily Cup or Sasha could suggest where I might get summer work in New Orleans."

"All summer, cher?"

"Something like research or canvassing maybe. You know, looking for things or talking to people. I don't know. Could you ask them?"

"When I get back, sure."

"Get back?"

"*Oui.*"

"Where are you? Are you in Carencro again?"

"Baton Rouge."

"What's in Baton Rouge?"

"Can I tell you something you will be happy, cher?"

"Yes."

"I start night school. Tulane in June."

"You are amazing."

"Tulane, cher."

"I love you so much. Daddy will be excited to hear that."

"Tell your daddy I'm reading *Cannery Row*. It's a whole book."

"I will. I love you."

"I love you, cher."

"What are you doing in Baton Rouge?"

"Can Peck tell you that when you come? It'd be better then."

"That's fine."

"Try to call me tonight, will you? Please? Please?"

"I will."

"Bye, I love you," Millie said.

"*Je t'aime*, cher."

Peck pulled his briefs up, his T-shirt on and stepped into the kitchen for breakfast.

"Smells so good."

"Did you find the shampoo?"

"*Oui.* I finded it."

"Who were you talking to?" Elizabeth asked.

"That was Millie."

"Sit and eat. Did you tell her where you are?"

"I told her Baton Rouge."

"So, she doesn't know about me?"

"I maybe could tell her tonight."

"You are such a naughty boy."

"I'm not naughty. We slept good last night. I was a gentleman."

"I let you sleep, is why," Elizabeth said.

Peck kissed her good morning.

"There's blueberry and there's marmalade for the crepes."

"*Merci*," Peck said.

"What was it you wanted to talk to me about?"

"Hanh?"

"Your Millie?"

"Talk?"

"Flora told me you were looking for your momma."

"Ah *oui*, cher. I need to find people I runned from way back. I need to find who I am, cher. *Tu comprend*?" ("Understand?")

"Are you thinking your foster nanna?"

"*Oui*."

"Do you even know where to begin to look to find her?"

"I thought I did, but that Flora lady say Bayou Chene is flooded and gone—gone so long it couldn't be where I growed."

"You told me of the gator man, Peck. What can you remember about him? Maybe that will help."

"He maked me carry bait shrimp buckets and would tar me if'n I dropped one before his pirogue was full."

"Bait shrimp?"

"*Oui*."

"Are you sure it was shrimp and not crawfish or mussels?"

"I remember big, white plastic buckets of bait shrimp," Peck said.

"If it was shrimp it had to be closer to Choctaw, Peck."

"Choctaw, cher, I remember that."

"Long River," Elizabeth said.

"*Quelle*?" ("What?")

"Atchafalaya Swamp, off the river, Peck. That river is the only place he could get shrimp. It must have been there, somewhere."

"Shrimp is from the gulf, *non*?"

"There's shrimp there, Peck. In fact the only fresh-water shrimp in America is from the Atchafalaya river. I learned that in cooking school."

"Dass a big swamp, must be."

"*Tu as du mal à te souvenir de tout ça, Peck?*" ("You're having a difficult time remembering, Peck?")

"*Oui*."

"Finish breakfast. I'll get dressed and we'll go for a walk so you can think."

"Hokay." Peck said.

"Butter in the fridge if you want more," Elizabeth said, stepping into the bedroom.

Peck enjoyed three crepes, two with blueberry and one with marmalade jams and melted butter. The boudin reminded him of who he was, and he ate it and his grits with contentment.

Elizabeth was in the bathroom when Peck went into the bedroom to pull his jeans and shirt on. They met in the kitchen, Elizabeth with a backpack.

"Why so much to carry, cher—for a walk?"

"I have an idea," Elizabeth said.

"Hanh?" Peck asked.

She pulled the front door open and took him by the hand.

"Come with me," she said.

CHAPTER 38

AT THE SILVER WHISTLE CAFÉ IN NEW ORLEANS, the server held a breakfast check out. Lily Cup handed her a credit card.

"Let's walk through that morning," Larry said.

"I can do that," Gabe said. "It started out..."

"I don't want to hear it, Gabe. I want to actually walk through every step you took. Like if you walked out of the house. I want to do that just as you did. If you caught a streetcar, I want to do that."

"I got it. So, the house is fourteen blocks or so. Care to walk?"

"Wait for the Uber I already ordered," Lily Cup said. "We'll ride it."

They left the café, stepping into a bright, sun-rich midmorning. Arriving at Gabe's home, the lieutenant was given a tour of the small, typically southern styled, shotgun house. Gabe offered to make coffee.

"I'd rather we be about our business at hand," Larry said.

Gabe looked at his watch. "If we're going to be accurate, I didn't leave for eighteen more minutes."

"We can wait," Larry said. "What were some of your army career assignments? After Korea and after Nam?"

"I was in Fort Hood a dozen or so years. I ran a communications group. Hood is the largest base in the country. Lots of battalion field combat drills. I had a pretty big staff."

"Were you ROTC in college?"

"No ROTC—no degree. I just liked to read, thanks to a mother not letting me leave the house to play stickball until I could tell her about the chapter I just read. She'd tell me that people who read had an advantage in life. It seemed Momma was right. The army needed troops who liked to read. Most of what we did was shuffle paper."

"Did you enlist?" Larry asked.

"I was drafted, but I would have joined anyway. I told the draft board I'd go army if they let me be a career soldier. If not, I'd go marine or air force."

"To make captain on a high school diploma, you must have been a special trooper."

"I liked to read." Gabe looked at his watch. "It's time."

He stood, picked up his cane and pulled the door open.

"My walking stick is with the police. I'll have to use my cane today— we can pretend it's my walking stick."

"That's fine," Larry said.

"Shall we?"

"After you," Larry said. "Best you can remember, retrace your steps, exactly as you went on that day. We'll try not to distract you and we'll follow behind."

"Yes sir," Gabe said.

"Just do what you did. Walk the same speed, try to duplicate your trip to Lee Circle."

"Yes sir."

He stepped from the house and to the sidewalk just as Elizabeth's and Peck's bus stopped on South Tenth Street in Baton Rouge.

"There's a small bistro near here if we get hungry," Elizabeth said. "I want to show you something first."

She held his hand and they walked several blocks to France Street.

"*Regarde, mon amour, c'est Paris,*" Elizabeth said. ("Look, my love, it's Paris.")

"Hanh?" Peck asked.

"*Eh bien, c'est comme un tout petit Paris, mais faisons semblant,*" Elizabeth said. ("Oh well, it's a little Paris, but let's pretend.")

Peck pulled on her hand until their bodies and eyes met. She kissed him softly, at first coquettish and then, wrapping her arms around his neck, she opened her warm mouth, devouring his smile, kissing first one lip and then another, sucking on his tongue—open hands now on each of his cheeks. Peck placed his hands on her hips and gently pushed her away from the kiss.

"People can see," Peck said.

"*Nous sommes trop loin de l'appartement. Pas de soucis,*" Elizabeth said. ("We're too far away from the apartment. No worries.")

"*Si'il te plait, on peut parler Anglais, cher? Ça aidera Peck beaucoup si nous parlons en Anglais,*" Peck said. ("Can we speak English, cher? It will help Peck better if we talk in English.")

"Only if you kiss me whenever I please."

"Ah, *oui.*"

Elizabeth pointed at a sign for Government Street.

"Paris is like a big wheel, Peck. The designer of Paris drew a circle and then had the streets and avenues come together. At the center I know there's the Notre Dame Cathedral and the Louvre. But, so sad, I've never been there. I've only heard stories."

"Someday you be a famous chef in Paris."

"Peut–être." ("Maybe.")

"Peck doesn't see a circle, cher. Where is the circle?"

"It's more of a big x, Peck. That's Somerulis Street, and it crosses that one, Penalver Street, and then there is Beauregard Street, which crosses that one over there, Grandpre Street, and they come together like a big x."

Peck looked confused.

"Never mind," Elizabeth said. "Let's just keep walking. I want you to meet someone."

"Who?"

"A lady. She's a diviner."

"Hanh?"

"She's a reader too."

"Reader like Peck?"

"She reads tarot cards. She tells the future. People trust her word."

"But Peck want to find the past. Is that the right word—past?"

"It's the right word. The thing is, she can maybe do that too. She's also a hypnotist."

"What's that for?"

"What you've forgotten about from so long ago. She might be able to get you to remember people and places. Maybe she can help you find your foster nanna from what your subconscious remembers."

"Thank you for showing me Paris."

"Are you being sarcastic?"

"When I get home I look *sarcastic* in my dictionary and then I'll tell you, cher."

Short blocks and narrow streets showed the Spanish and French influences on the historic city. Walking downtown was being in another state of mind a world away from the Carencro or the New Orleans Peck knew. Baton Rouge was a quiet-busy place, with government buildings, a state university, bustling restaurants, celebrated public libraries, galleries, and cooking schools. The downtown felt secure and civilized, away from the beggary, the faceless tourism of New Orleans and its transient scavengers, who fed on the coattails of floods and hurricanes. Baton Rouge might be Louisianans' hidden treasure, the true soul of a gentle people, while New Orleans was the elephant in the room, a wanton mistress where personal pleasure became its own excuse, a folly to the world. They held hands, only stopping to kiss or take a picture.

As Elizabeth and Peck walked, taking in the sights in Baton Rouge, eighty-three miles away in New Orleans, two blocks from his house, Gabe was walking east on St. Charles Avenue with Lily Cup and Larry following.

"Up here is where I caught the streetcar."

"Which stop, Gabe? The one just across the street or that one farther down?"

"The one farther down. I'm a walker."

"Do you remember where you crossed over?"

"Yes. It was up there by that fire hydrant. There was a black Mercedes parked. I remember the passenger door was open and they were talking. St. Charles right behind their car. There was space to cross between the Mercedes and the fire hydrant."

"Do the same now, Gabe."

Gabe stepped off the curb and waited for three cars to approach and pass by. He crossed in the middle of the block and onto the other side. He walked along one of the two tracks until he was at the streetcar stop. He stopped and turned.

"Gabe, was there anyone standing here when you got here?"

"No. I think it was after the commuters went to work. I usually try to avoid them. If the car's full, they make you stand the whole trip. I was alone here."

The streetcar rolled to a stop, the front door opening and the stairs edging out. Gabe stepped up and in. Lily Cup and Larry following suit.

"Three day passes, how much?" Gabe asked.

"Just buy yours, Gabe," Larry said.

Gabe inserted bills enough for a day pass, retrieved it and stepped back to the third seat.

"Want to sit up here on the bench, Gabe?" Lily Cup asked.

"This is where I sat," Gabe said.

He knew the more he could accurately demonstrate remembering, the more his story about how the killing happened would be believed.

"Is St. Josephs the best stop for the World War Two museum, conductor?" Gabe asked.

"It is, yes sir," the conductor said. "I'll shout it out for you."

"Thank you, young lady."

Gabe looked at Larry.

"Just like I did it," Gabe said, "but the conductor was a man."

Lily Cup sat with Gabe. Larry sat in the seat across the aisle.

"Any word whether James will move here after the wedding, or will he still commute in three days a week, like he does now?" Gabe asked.

"Sasha hasn't said. We don't talk that much about it. She knows what I think," Lily Cup said. "I just leave her alone."

"They live different lives," Gabe said. "It makes no sense to me. Sasha is well respected in the community."

"They wanted her to run for mayor."

"She'd be a good mayor. She's involved and generous with local charities."

"She knows everybody."

"I get a kick out of watching the woman celebrate the city's culture and romance. How you two gussy up just to dance jazz."

"She got me into that scene when we were in our twenties."

"You were just starting out."

"We love to dance. You know, the dirty dancing scene—but we were into jazz."

"Blues and jazz, it doesn't get any better than that."

"She convinced me old dudes were better jazz dancers, and we knew Charlie was opening a jazz bar in his mother's place, so we picked Charlie's Blue Note for our dancing."

"She's a pistol," Gabe said.

"She told me if we were going to do it right we had to dress the part, always strut our stuff, so we looked nice on the dance floor."

"Sounds like what she would do to present a house for sale."

"I'll be goddamned," Lily Cup said.

"What?"

"That's exactly what I told her. It was like she was prepping for an open house."

"You lost the debate, is my guess," Gabe said.

"Damn straight. She stood in front of the mirror lecturing me on her world-class tits and how they needed a proper stage and how I had a *boy* ass."

"Boy ass?"

"I don't know. She just said men liked cleavages and bubble butts, so we had to accent our positives. Men pick dance partners like peacocks pick mates—she'd say."

"Boy ass?"

"Boy ass, bubble butt, all the same," Lily Cup said.

"To a cracker, maybe. But brothers like their women with a wagon."

"Women with a wagon? A wagon? What the hell is that, some kind of urban ebonics?"

"A cushion," Gabe said.

"Cracker means white, right?" Lily Cup asked.

"Yes."

"Well, we went shopping for our uniforms. I remember I was in third year law school and Sasha was trying to sell condos in the Quarter. We charged over ten thousand bucks in four hours."

"Canal Street must have lit up," Gabe said.

"We did do a number—a big number. Nothing but the best. My sunglasses were four hundred bucks. Just imagine, in those days."

"Well you did good, little sister. The tights you wear at Charlie's does your boy ass proud. I've seen glances you get walking away."

"I'm a cigar smoking tomboy, but I do have a nice ass, don't I?"

"This James guy is only about himself," Gabe said. "It's about how well he can eat or how he can walk into a place and get a table because of who he is."

"That about sums him up," Lily Cup said.

"I don't get it," Gabe said.

"Being held in someone's arms a few nights a week goes a long way in overlooking some things. It could be worth it to her," Lily Cup said. "It's lonely being a single woman."

"She could do better. There's many good men who would jump at the chance to embrace her," Gabe said. "Peck, half her age, would be better for her than James."

"Sasha's only thirteen years older than Peck," Lily Cup said.

"I knew it was something like that, but he'd be better than James for her."

"Aren't you the feisty old matchmaker?"

"I'm not pushing anything. We're only talking. I was trying to make a point."

"Do you really think Peck would be good for Sasha?"

"I was using him as an example of an alternative, but actually, I don't. I think he would be good pajamas for her lonely nights, not so good for everyday wear...let's just say she wouldn't be into crabbing or splashing around for snapping turtles, and he wouldn't be into two martini lunches in the Quarter."

"I'm glad you cleared that up, because I got dibs."

Gabe turned in the seat with a surprised grin on his face.

"Excuse me? Dibs?"

"You heard right. Between you and me and no one else, I put dibs on Peck, at least in my dreams I have. We already know he loves my boy bubble ass and the fucker is smarter than a *Jeopardy* champ. He actually reminds me of a young me."

"I thought you didn't remember your go with the lad at Charlies?" Gabe asked.

"So, I lied. Actually, I think he and I would be a perfect set."

"I'll be damned."

"Mum's the word, Gabe. We all have our fantasies, and I'm not into busting him and Millie up. I think they're perfect together."

"I'll be cool, my sister. My lips are sealed."

"Good," Lily Cup said.

"Fascinating."

"Saint Joseph—Lee Circle—Saint Joseph, next stop," the conductor said.

Gabe turned to Lily Cup. "If I get through this mess, let's take Sasha out and have a talk."

"Good idea. We'll do it. Two on one."

While they waited, Gabe glanced at Larry. "This is it," he said.

A statue–less, tall, granite column surrounded by lawn was all that remained of the iconic New Orleans landmark at Lee Circle. City fathers had removed General Robert E. Lee in deference to offending African Americans. As the streetcar came to a full stop, Gabe stood, cane in hand, and stepped to the front and down one step to just behind the conductor's chair, thanking her for calling out the stop.

"Have a blessed day," the conductor said.

"From your lips to God's ears, my sister," Gabe said as he stepped off the streetcar. He stared up at the tall column that once supported General Lee. Larry and Lily Cup stepped off and joined him, a few feet away from other passengers boarding.

"Okay, Gabe," Larry said. "Let's get started."

"Right."

"Where were you standing when you first got off the streetcar? Was it where you're are now?"

Gabe walked ten feet to his right and stood.

"It was over here."

"What did you do then?"

Gabe pointed at the tree and the power lines across the eastbound side of St. Charles Avenue. There were beaded necklaces hanging on tree limbs and on the wires lining the street. Necklaces of all colors.

"When Sasha was showing me houses, she told me that the Mardi Gras parade came up St. Charles. It wasn't until two days ago I noticed those hanging over there."

"What did you do then?" Larry asked.

"I stood here, taking it in, trying to imagine floats going by, beautiful girls tossing the necklaces; the streets lined with parade watchers and revelers. I stood here for fourteen minutes."

"Fourteen minutes?"

"I had looked at my watch and knew the World War II museum wouldn't open for fourteen minutes, so I just stalled while enjoying looking up at the necklaces."

"Then what?"

"I crossed over to that sidewalk over there."

"Where did you cross? Did you go down to the corner, or did you cross here?"

"Here, from where I'm standing."

"Okay, let's talk it through," Larry said. "Gabe, did you walk straight across or at an angle?"

"Straight across. I saw a necklace on that fence over there I thought I would get."

"When you were standing here, did you see Mr. Bauer anywhere in sight?"

"No, sir."

"And when you crossed, was there any time while you were in the street when you could see Mr. Bauer?"

"Never. No sir."

"I'm asking you to stay here, Gabe. Miss Tarleton and I are going to walk over to the sidewalk to observe. We need you to wait until I ask you to come across."

"I'll wait."

Lily Cup and Larry stepped onto St. Charles and walked across. There was a chalk outline of a body and blood stains. Both had been washed to a faint image by a power washer. Just before they got to the curb of the sidewalk, Larry touched Lily Cup's arm, asking her not to move. On the street, Larry walked to the left until he reached the corner. He turned and slowly walked back, leaning down and looking at each inch of the sidewalk's gutter. Just beyond where Lily Cup was standing he lowered himself to a knee.

"Bingo," Larry said.

He stood, retrieved a pair of tweezers from his left pocket and a property baggie from his right. He knelt down again and carefully picked up something.

"What?" Lily Cup asked.

"A button with what appears to be blood on it," Larry replied.

He placed the button in the baggie, locked it closed and put it in his vest pocket.

"If we only had the shirt," he said.

"It's in my valise," Lily Cup said. "Want it now?"

"No. Stay there a bit. I want to walk up the sidewalk and take a look."

He looked over at Gabe.

"Gabe, which direction was he coming from?"

Gabe pointed west, away from the corner. Larry stepped up on the sidewalk and walked west slowly, leaning down, studying every inch along the sidewalk. It was a good fifteen feet when he stopped, retrieved his tweezers again and another property baggie. He knelt and carefully placed several objects in the baggie, sealed it, and put it in his vest pocket. He walked back to where Lily Cup was standing.

"Gabe, go ahead and come across, just as you did."

"Yes, sir."

"Before you come across, I want you to take a minute and think. Think about how and where you crossed over."

"I do remember I was blowing my nose," Gabe said.

"Blowing your nose?" Larry asked.

"Yes, sir. I'm a four-time sneezer, and I remember I had sneezed once, and knew I had three more to go, so I was getting my handkerchief out."

"Captain, I want you to repeat that again right now, just as it happened—and just how you came across, sneezing."

Gabe tucked and braced the cane under his folded right arm. He pulled the handkerchief from his left pocket with his left hand as he stepped onto St. Charles. As he crossed, Gabe pretended two sneezes with both elbows scrunched to his sides, his hands were occupied holding the handkerchief and wiping or blowing his nose. He sneezed again as he stepped onto the curb on the other side, glanced quickly at the bloodstains, grimaced and turned his head away.

"Exactly where were you when Mr. Bauer approached?"

"I was right here where I am now. I had just gotten on the sidewalk and didn't have time to turn the way I was going to walk when he came up."

Larry made some notes in his booklet.

"Miss Tarleton, I think I've seen enough. That's all I'll need from either of you for now. If you'll get me the shirt, I'll take it in and go write my report."

"Do you want me to run get it now, Lieutenant?" Lily Cup asked.

"You all go on. I want to stay here for a while—look around. We can meet in the DA's office at three p.m. Should give me enough time. Will that work for you?"

"I'll be there, Lieutenant. Just me?" Lily Cup asked.

"Just you."

Larry turned to Gabe, extending his hand.

"Thank you for being so patient and professional with me, Gabe. I am honored for the opportunity to try to help a brother in any way I can."

"You're not going to arrest me and take me in?" Gabe asked.

"You've got a good, caring attorney, Captain. She'll have you at the preliminary hearing. That's all I need to know."

"My brother," Gabe said.

They clutched a hug.

"I wish you all the luck, Gabe."

CHAPTER 39

JUST AS GABE WAS CROSSING ST. CHARLES to wait for a streetcar home, Elizabeth and Peck were in Baton Rouge standing at the door of the tarot reader and spiritual diviner on College Street. The door was a glossy black enamel with small brass stars surrounding a street number. A card above the doorbell read, "Ring the doorbell and be patient."

Elizabeth pushed the button.

"Don't be frightened, Peck. I think she can help you," Elizabeth said.

"I'm good," Peck said.

To pass the time, Elizabeth hugged Peck around the waist and nuzzled into his neck.

"*Je n'aime pas si longtemps ne pas te voir*," Elizabeth said. ("I don't like so long not seeing you.")

The interior curtain of a side window was pulled back and released. Finally the door opened and a woman in a satin robe smiled and welcomed both of them in. There was a freshness about her, as if she had just stepped from a tub. While they stood, the woman grouped her hair from the side to the back of her head and attached a band to it. She had an attractive face because of inquisitive, caring eyes. She looked to be in her late thirties.

She hugged Elizabeth welcome. "It's good to see you, *mon amie.*"

"I brought my friend," Elizabeth said.

"Is this the special friend we spoke of?"

"Yes. Peck."

"I am Audrey," she said. "It is my pleasure to meet you."

Peck tipped his head.

"He's everything you said he was."

"I know."

"I told you he would come back."

The diviner looked deep into Peck's eyes. She took his hand and raised it to gently touch her cheek.

"His hand is warm," she said to Elizabeth. "A fire is burning inside him."

Audrey spoke to Peck. "You are searching for answers?"

"Yes'm," Peck said.

"Come into the next room and sit with me. We'll begin there."

"Would you want me to wait here?" Elizabeth asked

"You come too. You are to be his guide through the journey ahead, yes?"

"*Tres bien*," Elizabeth said.

"I told you he would come to you one day. Please join us at my table."

Peck looked about the room. There were crosses and dolls hung on walls and resting on a mantle. Rosary beads hung on the edge of a picture frame. There were many drapes of velvet and satin in rich, dark colors, and there were scented candles. On the wall was an unpainted wooden shelf with twenty or so unopened decks of tarot cards in several short stacks. Audrey reached back and took a deck in her hand and opened it, removing the cards. She held them to Peck.

"Here, Peck. Shuffle these."

Peck looked at the deck and began to spread the cards with his fingers.

"Later, Peck—take them home with you. Feel each one of them carefully. They will listen and absorb your most inner feelings. Take them home with Elizabeth when you leave, keep them safe, and bring them back tomorrow."

"I don't understand," Peck said.

"Your touch will warm some cards, wake them up. They will serve you and tell your story. They will offer to help us find a way," Audrey said.

"*Merci*," Peck said.

Audrey put her hand on Peck's as he touched the cards. He rested them on the table, his hand covering them.

"Tell me who you are, Peck."

"Hanh?"

"Each of us are three people," Audrey said. "We are who we think we are. We are who others think we are, and we are who we actually are. Who are you, Peck?"

"Peck is a fisher, dass for true. I like larn'ing to read and I catch the turtles and mashwaron. I like boiled eggs."

"And you love friends, *non?*" Audrey asked.

"Ah, *oui*," Peck said.

"Are you in love, Peck?"

"Ah, *oui*. I love my Millie so much."

"Do you want to tell me about Millie, Peck? She must be a special person to have your love."

"Millie is so special. She make Peck feel good about myself and she wants to be with me and have children and raise shickens and okra."

"Do you love Elizabeth?"

"*Oui.*"

"Do you love Elizabeth like you love Millie?"

"Different love. Elizabeth and Peck hold each other. It makes loneliness feel better some nights. We are there for each other."

"That's beautiful," Audrey said. "You have a soulfully tender heart."

Peck reached over and rested his hand on Elizabeth's thigh.

"Elizabeth helps Peck find who I am, so I can tell my children who they are."

"A good start is starting in positive thought. Are there any nice things you can remember about your early childhood, Peck?" Audrey asked.

"I remember the moon, cher."

"Do you want to tell us what you remember about the moon?"

"When the moon was full I kneel in the dirt under the porch and pray to it. I talk to the moon and tell it things. Sometimes it tell me things."

"What would you tell the moon?"

"Sometimes, if the moon was my mamma true, I would tell her I be good if she ever come back to me. I work so hard and not make noises to keep her awake."

"Do you think your momma heard you?"

"Gabe say yes, ma'am. He say my mamma heard ever' word. I believe him."

"Did you talk with any others in the moon?"

"I wanted a sign. I wanted the moon to tell me what to do, how to get out, where to go."

"And did you get a sign?"

"Yes'm, I surely did."

"Can you tell me?"

"The big ole bald cypress in the swamp was my frien'. The moon say that to me. It say I can trust the ole cypress."

"Can you explain?"

"The moon say gator man was bringing the pirogue back empty the next day, and he would be so mad he got no gators, and Peck should hide, so he don't find me and belt strap me."

"Did you hide?"

"I climbed the dead Cypress frien' on the swamp edge, you know, where the moon say to and sat in its hollow while gator man shouted my name, looking for me, and he drank whiskey and he broke bottles on rocks."

"Did he find you?"

"I stayed there three days. He never seen me."

"Was he there for three days looking for you?"

"Nah, nah. Gator man left for foster nanna's place right off. Peck stayed in the tree two more days, thinking what to do."

"So, the moon was a good friend, and the cypress tree was a good friend. Can you remember any other good things, Peck?"

"The vultures helped Peck, I say."

"How did the vultures help you, Peck?"

"Peck ate their eggs. Four eggs in the tree hollow. I don't like vultures, but they were good to Peck that time, I'll say. I stepped on three and broke them, but four were good. Ants ate the broke ones."

"Peck, have you ever been hypnotized?" Audrey asked.

"What is that, hypnotized, cher?"

"When you get hypnotized you go into a deep sleep, and sometimes the subconscious can remember things that the conscious mind has forgotten."

"Ah," Peck said.

"Our brain is like a big filing cabinet or a tool box filled with tools. We sometime forget what files we have or what tools we have, but with hypnosis, we can see things more clearly."

"So hypnotized is good, maybe?" Peck asked.

"It can be helpful."

"I like that," Peck said.

"First you must take Elizabeth to help you find some things we'll need. Then come back when you've found them, and I will have a reading of the cards you have with you. After that we will have a private divination to hear what the spirits have to say."

"What things you need, cher?"

"I need you to go to a library and find some maps of areas you think you have been to in your life, Peck."

"I been to Rhode Island."

"Just maps of your childhood, Peck. Places you remember during early youth. Maps sometime speak to us."

Audrey stood and politely asked them to leave and do their work. She reminded Peck to shuffle the tarot cards and touch each one and to keep them safe on his person. As Elizabeth and Peck moved to the door and stepped out, the phone rang inside with Audrey waving goodbye, while answering it.

Pulling the door closed, Elizabeth wrapped her arms around Peck's neck and kissed him passionately.

"*Je peux etre ta lune a l'avenir, mon amour?*" Elizabeth asked. ("Can I be your moon from now on, my love?")

"*Pour toujours, cher.*" ("Forever, cher.")

"Wherever we are, whoever we're with, when we look at the moon we will see each other, promise?"

"*Oui.* That be good."

"Audrey wasn't scary or weird or anything like what you hear about readers, was she?" Elizabeth asked.

"Nah, nah, nice lady."

Elizabeth was moved by talk of the moon. She backed Peck against the door and kissed him again, this time leaning on him. She lifted her head back and smiled into his eyes, her hand reaching down and feeling William through his jeans.

"It still there, cher?" Peck asked.

"Oh, it's still there."

"The Bistro?" Peck asked. "Can we go eat now?"

Elizabeth playfully squeezed William.

"*Peut–être que Peck va me nourir avec ça?*" ("Maybe Peck will feed me this?")

"Bistro, cher. Take us there and we'll eat and talk."

Elizabeth laughed and held his hand as they walked. They chose a sidewalk table at the bistro.

"Would you want wine, Peck?"

"Nah, nah. Can you tell Peck what's good to eat here, my chef frien'?"

Elizabeth ordered calamari they would share and two Hawaiian chicken and pineapple barbeque wraps. Elizabeth drank Chardonnay and Peck drank water. They relaxed and spoke of the city; of the beautiful LSU university campus; of Peck's New Orleans, and of night school at Tulane. They spoke of Millie and her baby doll Charlie and of Peck's devotion to her, and how important it was to learn of his past.

"Your boo, cher. Is he still good to you when he's not on the oil rig?"

"He's still a good man, Peck. He works hard, long hours when he's out there. It takes him some time to rest up when he comes home."

"Do you have the good times?" Peck asked.

"We'll go for walks. We sit in the park and watch people. Sometimes we pack sandwiches and wine."

"Is he, how you say—romantic?"

"It's more like we're good friends and we fuck, Peck. Understand?"

"*Je comprends,*" Peck said. ("I understand.")

"He's a nice man and he'd be a good father."

"Hokay."

"I wouldn't say he's romantic."

"Dass good. That he's nice."

"With me in cooking school he knows one day I may be going to New York or Paris to try to be a chef."

"Would he go with you?"

"We've talked about it."

"What'd he say, cher?"

"He said he'll have to cross that bridge when we come to it. He said there were rigs in Europe."

"Would he be upset if he knew about us?"

"He'd be hurt. He'd probably understand, but he would be hurt."

"*Oui.*"

"Would you be hurt if Millie made love to another man?"

"Peck would be surprised a lot...and hurt, *oui*. I would come to you and ask for advice."

"I would say come to Paris," Elizabeth said.

"Peck would maybe go, but Millie loves me so, we are meant to be."

"She sounds perfect for you, Peck. I'm happy for you both."

"Is there a library we can get maps Audrey wants us to get?"

"A few blocks away. Let's get a dessert and split it."

"Good," Peck said.

They ordered key lime pie.

"Peck, are you okay with this whole thing? Of being with Audrey tomorrow?"

"*Oui.*"

"What's going through your mind about it?"

Peck lifted the tarot cards from his pocket and began to fan them out on the table, faces up.

"These are so good to look at, but so mysterious, *Gris Gris*. Are they good?"

"Each one is supposed to tell a story of where a mind and soul are the day they are turned over. We'll see how you think about them tomorrow."

"I think sometime if I'll ever know'd if my foster nanna just finded me or did somebody didn't want me and just gived me to her when I was born. I just think sometime I'll never know."

"Maybe you can find her and she'll tell you things. She must have loved you. Was she nice when you were there with her?"

"I don't remember. I know she let gator man slave me, carrying bait shrimp, and he make me gator bait is all I remember. So, I runned away to Carencro."

"Did your foster nanna know what gator man was doing to you, about how badly he was treating you?"

"Nanna would say to mind him—he was church-goin' and teaching me things to make me a man. She didn't like to talk too much. Told me to go with gator man and mind him."

"Tomorrow, then?" Elizabeth asked.

"Tomorrow?" Peck asked.

"Tomorrow maybe Audrey can help."

"*Oui.* Maybe."

"Finish the pie, Peck. We'll walk to the library, then to the grocer for tonight."

"Hokay."

"I'm doing a special chicken tonight, a light lemon butter sauce and capers."

"I like shicken, cher."

CHAPTER 40

ORDER IN THE COURT," the bailiff announced. "All rise. Section M of the Criminal District Court is now in session. The Honorable Judge Lindsay Fontenot presiding. Silence is commanded under penalty of fine or imprisonment. God save this state and this honorable court. Please be seated. There is no talking in the audience. Good morning, Judge."

The district attorney stood in this magistrate court and waited as the bailiff spoke.

"The State of Louisiana calls Captain Gabriel Jordan, US Army retired."

Gabe stood. The bailiff approached.

"Captain Jordan, raise your right hand and place your left hand on this bible. Do you swear that the evidence that you shall give shall be the truth, the whole truth and nothing but the truth, so help you God?"

"I so swear." Gabe said.

"Captain Jordan, I have read the charges. Are they clear to you?" Judge Fontenot asked.

Lily Cup nodded.

"They are clear Your Honor," Gabe said.

"The defendant has plead not guilty to the charges," the judge said. "This preliminary hearing is to determine probable cause. We're here to determine further disposition."

Judge Fontenot was adjusting her microphone while the bailiff was taking a seat. Gabe and Lily Cup at their table and across the aisle, Lieutenant Gaines (Larry) the DA and assistant DA were in the front tables. Seated behind the DA were three people unknown to Lily Cup. Gabe leaned over.

"Who are those three?" Gabe asked.

"I don't know," Lily Cup said.

"District Attorney Holbrook, Counselor Tarleton, a sidebar please?" the judge asked.

Lily Cup stood and stepped into the aisle and waited while the district attorney lowered the lid of his briefcase, stepped into the aisle and joined her. They walked to the judge's right side of her bench. The judge pushed her microphone away and leaned in with a modulated voice.

"Don't look now but three news networks, two civil rights group representatives, New Orleans' Visitor Association, a Tulane professor and an author writing a mystery novel are joining us today. The police are at the door, prepared to remove demonstrators."

"Why all the hullabaloo, Judge?" Lily Cup asked.

"The New Orleans Film Festival always draws a crowd of hungry news people," the district attorney said.

If this goes smoothly, it will be thanks to you, Counselor Tarleton," Judge Fontenot said. "And to you District Attorney Holbrook."

"Excuse me?" Lily Cup asked.

"Counselor, you asked for a pretrial conference before we began. District Attorney Holbrook agreed. Any other setting and a lock-out wouldn't stand their speculations and we couldn't have avoided the press."

"Thank you, Judge."

"District Attorney Holbrook and Counselor Tarleton, this is the million–dollar question. Have the past thirty–six hours been helpful so we can move forward?"

"We'll know soon enough, Judge," the district attorney said.

"Ms. Tarleton?" Judge Fontenot asked.

"Your Honor, I am honored to work with a court with grace and compassion and a district attorney with such integrity and caring for the benefit of the community. I'm speechless."

"It appears you have found the words, counselor. Such a pleasant way to open a day."

"I agree, Judge," the district attorney said.

"Before we run off to Tipitina's for some Zydeco dancing, I have something to share, and I'll let you two decide," Judge Fontenot said.

Lily Cup and the DA stood, waiting.

"District Attorney Holbrook and Counselor Tarleton, with the thought of containment of, shall we say, prying media eyes with jaundice on this particular case with its racial overtones, you might consider meeting the press after we've concluded."

"It would appear you've done some homework, Judge," the district attorney said.

"I'm thinking about New Orleans," Judge Fontenot said. "The last thing this town needs is unfounded *Gris Gris* becoming headlines for months to come and messing up our private walks in the park."

"I agree, Judge," Lily Cup said.

"Are you ready?"

"Your Honor, speaking for the state, I believe we can present a case in a manner that will leave no question unanswered," the DA said.

"Counselor Tarleton?" Judge Fontenot asked.

"I agree, Judge."

The district attorney and Lily Cup took their places at the tables.

Lily Cup leaned into Gabe's side.

"Stay cool, Gabe. Today we're going with the flow. It's the DA's show, just be patient and let's see how it goes."

"I'm ready for anything," Gabe said.

"District Attorney Holbrook, call your first witness," Judge Fontenot said.

"Your Honor, the State of Louisiana calls the assistant district attorney from Lafayette, Louisiana, Ms. Berkin."

The Lafayette assistant district attorney stood and walked to the stand and waited for the bailiff to swear her in.

"What's this about? Why Lafayette?" Gabe whispered.

Lily Cup looked at Gabe with a look as if be still, and to not over react to things.

"Ms. Berkin, do you know why you're at this preliminary hearing?" the district attorney asked.

"I believe so," Ms. Berkin said. "I'm here to offer witness to Captain Jordan's physical and mental state."

"And why would the defendant's physical and mental state be important at this hearing."

"I assume to find if he was disturbed in any way—to the point of being prone to violence."

"Can you share with the court when you first met the defendant, Captain Jordan?"

"I can," Ms. Berkin said.

"Would you tell us the time and circumstance?"

"It was a little more than nine months ago. Our offices received an anonymous call about a suspected homicide in Opelousas," Ms. Berkin said.

"And was it a homicide?" the DA asked.

"The call was referencing the defendant. It seemed that the defendant was not a victim of a homicide as the caller thought but he had collapsed on the side of the highway and was taken by a good Samaritan to a doctor in Carencro. In fact two persons had witnessed this and called it in as a suspected homicide."

"Was the defendant taken to an emergency room?" the district attorney asked.

"It was a hospice in Carencro, District Attorney," Ms. Berkin said.

"Can you explain why the good Samaritan chose a hospice, Ms. Berkin?"

"The good Samaritan was a friend of a doctor at the hospice, so that's where he took the defendant."

"What happened then?" the district attorney asked.

"Two things," Ms. Berkin said. "The first was that it was almost fortuitous that the good Samaritan had taken the defendant to the hospice, as it seemed three months before this incident, the defendant had been diagnosed with stomach cancer and given two months to live by the staff at the VA hospital in Pineville."

"What was the second thing?"

"Because it was reported as a suspected homicide, and we learned that the defendant had run away from the VA hospital in Pineville, I was asked to investigate his background for criminal records or mental issues that might be threatening to the general public."

"Will you share with the court what you found?"

"That's when I found that the defendant had been diagnosed with stomach cancer and had voiced a weariness of the treatments the VA was administering to him," Ms. Berkin said.

"Anything else?"

"From the accounts of witnesses at the hospice, the losses of his wife and only son weighed on his mind, and these witnesses felt the defendant was in a state of depression."

"Do you know the circumstances of how the defendant lost his wife and son, Ms. Berkin?"

"What do you mean?"

"Were their losses of natural causes or—"

"Are you asking me if they were violent deaths?"

"Are you aware of the circumstances of their deaths, Ms. Berkin?"

"The defendant's wife died of a heart attack in her midsixties. I'm not certain of the date. His son was lost in Iraq—Desert Storm."

A tear came to the corner of Gabe's eye. He lowered his head.

"Ms. Berkin, was the defendant clinically tested for depression, to determine if he needed confinement?"

"No," Ms. Berkin said.

"Excuse me? Are we to understand that the investigation of the defendant who was deemed suicidal didn't include a clinical evaluation and diagnosis?"

"Suicidal?"

"The defendant refused any more treatment, Ms. Berkin. Isn't it true he actually ran away from the VA hospital and their treatments?"

"But we couldn't," Ms. Berkin said.

"Couldn't test him? Can you explain why you couldn't test him, Ms. Berkin?"

"I never got an order for an evaluation but had I, by the time the order would have come, Captain Jordan had run away from the hospice as well."

"Run away?"

"Yes."

"Wasn't he free to leave?"

"When a patient carries opiods—"

"Narcotic?" the district attorney asked.

"Yes."

"It would seem hospice care includes a more watchful eye and security in such. How was it possible he just ran away, Ms. Berkin?"

"At first we suspected foul play."

"Please continue," the district attorney said.

"The yard maintenance man was seen with heavy amounts of blood on his hands the same day both he and the defendant disappeared from the hospice."

"What took place then?"

"We were asked to investigate, but this time for a possible kidnap and homicide."

"The defendant, Captain Jordan, is here with us today, looking alive and well, Ms. Berkin. Might we assume the matter of the disappearing duo and the bloody hands were resolved?"

"They were," Ms. Berkin said.

"And can you describe for this hearing how it was resolved?"

"Captain Jordan apparently wanted to run away to Newport, Rhode Island, and the gardener employed by the hospice offered to help him get there."

"Does the defendant, Captain Jordan, have relatives in Newport?"

"No."

"What was the attraction?"

"We were told he wanted to listen to the jazz at the Newport Jazz Festival. The gardener arranged to get him there."

The courtroom seemed to pause and take a deep breath in quiet reverence for a story of a dying man's last wish.

"Assistant District Attorney Berkin, were there any findings of a criminal nature in Captain Jordan's past?" Judge Fontenot asked.

"Your Honor, the defendant had no criminal record, no lawsuits or liens, no unpaid traffic tickets. We found he was decorated four times—twice in Korea, once in Vietnam and once again on his retirement—for exemplary service to his country."

"Thank you," Judge Fontenot said.

"Thank you, Ms. Berkin. Your witness, Counselor Tarleton," District Attorney Holbrook said.

Lily Cup stood.

"Ms. Berkin, for the benefit of this hearing—was there ever any explanation offered for the blood seen by witnesses on the gardener's hands the day he and Captain Jordan disappeared from the hospice?"

"There was."

"Can you tell the court?"

"The first thing the gardener was known to do when he came to work on his day to mow, was prepare, bait, and throw a trotline into the bayou behind the hospice. He would catch fish and turtles he would later trade for money or food. The hospice administrator had given him permission to do this. The morning they disappeared he had cut his hand trying to remove fishing hooks that had stuck into his hand. That explained the blood to our satisfaction."

"Ms. Berkin, do you know the whereabouts of this gardener today?"

"Yes."

"Where might he be?"

"The defendant has unofficially adopted the gardener and is now putting him through college," Ms. Berkin said. "I learned that from the hospice administrator and according to her the gardener lives with the defendant."

"Thank you, Ms. Berkin, no further questions," Lily Cup said. She turned to the judge. "Your Honor, for the record, Captain Jordan underwent major stomach surgery while he was in Rhode Island, and the result was the total removal of his cancer."

"A serendipitous outcome—his surgery during a Newport Jazz Festival," Judge Fontenot said. "District Attorney Holbrook, call the next witness."

"The state calls Lieutenant Larry Gaines, of the New Orleans Police."

Lieutenant Larry was sworn in and took the stand.

"Lieutenant Gaines, how long have you been with the New Orleans police department?"

"It'll be a total of fourteen years this October."

"What do you mean, a total of, Lieutenant?"

"I was on the Storyville patrol as a police officer for six years before the second Iraq war. I enlisted and served in 2011 and 2012, and I rejoined the New Orleans police department when I was sent home."

"Thank you for your service, Lieutenant—to our nation and to our city," the district attorney said.

There was no response.

"What position do you hold today, Lieutenant?"

"I'm full detective. I've been a detective for two years."

"Were you called in on this case, Lieutenant?"

"Actually, I was on vacation, still am for ten more days. Our chief called me at home and asked me to assist in any way I could. He said it was an important matter that needed to be cleared up."

"Can you share with us the process you went through and what you found and whether or not you came to any conclusions, Lieutenant?"

"That's why I'm here."

"Thank you, Lieutenant. Please continue."

"The first thing I did was watch the Walmart security videos to get a look at both parties. I knew this wasn't relevant to the day, almost three weeks later, of the killing, but I wanted to see if the videos offered any clues."

"Would you explain to the court the Walmart security videos, Lieutenant—they've not been brought up before?"

"Yes. There were security videos that captured a confrontation between the defendant and the victim—a confrontation that took place three weeks before the homicide in question."

"I can see these videos you speak of as not being admissible in a trial, Lieutenant."

"I agree."

"So why would you bring them up?"

"They show that the defendant and the victim knew each other."

"So, are we to understand the defendant knew the victim for several weeks?"

"According to the security tapes, yes."

"What did you see, and what could you conclude from watching the tapes, Lieutenant?"

"The defendant was having keys made and the victim had visibly accosted him, he badgered him, demanding the defendant give him the use of a credit card."

"Was that it—a verbal threat?"

"On the second video, taken outside the store, the victim brandished a long blade knife and was jabbing it at the air in the defendant's direction. He was jabbing it aggressively. The store manager could be seen running toward the young man and his escaping on a yellow bicycle."

"Were you able to conclude anything from this, Lieutenant?"

"Two things. It did help me narrow my focus—I concluded that the young man was violent, aggressive, appearing to be without conscience at the time this happened in Walmart."

"And number two, Lieutenant?"

"The defendant did have a possible motive. Revenge."

"Would premeditated murder be a possibility, Lieutenant?"

"It's possible."

"What the fuck?" Gabe whispered to Lily Cup.

Lily Cup elbow nudged Gabe's arm.

"He's setting the stage," Lily Cup said.

"Please continue with the investigation's findings, Lieutenant," the district attorney said.

"I was aware the defendant pled innocent to second-degree murder. I was asked by the commissioner to step in as the arresting officer and to investigate the homicide. I asked to meet the defendant and his attorney, Ms. Tarleton, to see if I could question him."

"For what purpose, Lieutenant?"

"Speaking with the accused I find helpful. It was my own coroner's inquisition, you might say," the lieutenant said.

"And were they cooperative?"

"Most cooperative, District Attorney Holbrook. We met the first time for breakfast."

"You interrogated a murder defendant over a public breakfast table with beignets and cinnamon?"

"No, sir. At breakfast I told him the seriousness of the charges and that it was in his interest to help me prove his innocence."

"And the defendant's attorney agreed to his cooperating with you?"

"She did."

"Lieutenant Gaines, did you read him his Miranda Rights?" Judge Fontenot asked.

"I did, Your Honor. His attorney was witness to it."

"And both Captain Jordan and his attorney agreed to cooperate?" Judge Fontenot asked.

"They did, Your Honor. They were aware that with no eye-witnesses coming forward the defendant's innocence was in question knowing the young man was— well, a young man—and that Captain Jordan was an experienced, battle-proven army man...and..."

"And what, Lieutenant?" the district attorney asked.

"There was no knife at the scene."

A grumbling rolled about the gallery. Judge Fontenot slammed the gavel three times.

"Order in the court," the judge said.

"In your opinion, were the store's videos a help to the defendant's case?" the district attorney asked.

"They could help him, but without a knife not so much," Lieutenant said.

"Can you elaborate?"

"As I said before, if they were admitted into evidence the security videos could help, by demonstrating that the young man was an aggressor—an armed aggressor at that."

"Go on, detective Gaines."

"The video could also suggest motive for Captain Jordan."

"And if the defendant 'sought' revenge, that would be premeditated murder."

"Yes.

"While the defendant has only been charged with second degree murder."

"Yes."

"You were at breakfast, Lieutenant. Please continue," the district attorney said.

"My instincts told me that from his many years in the service, the defendant knew and understood the army way of investigation—and that was to duplicate the details of the entire day from the minute he woke up until the moment he was handcuffed and taken into custody."

"And what would prompt these instincts, Lieutenant?"

"I was an officer in the army and...well..."

"You were an officer in the army and what? I didn't quite hear you, Lieutenant."

"And, like the defendant, I'm black," the Lieutenant said.

You could hear a pin drop. Papers were not being rustled. The whoosh of the ceiling fans seemed silent. The district attorney stepped back and looked at Lieutenant Gaines.

"The people for the state of Louisiana are colorblind, Lieutenant, I don't see a relevance—"

"If you were a man of color, Mr. District Attorney, you would see the relevance."

"Although I appreciate your candor—your insight," Judge Fontenot said. "There are few places other than in our beloved New Orleans where many cultures are more respected. It's a respect that has grown over a century of living and working together that bring us to the same family supper tables. Our blend of cultures is what make us one in mind and soul."

"I agree," the lieutenant said. "Your Honor, there is tolerance between our cultures, but it's natural that each culture understands their own with an innate sensitivity."

"Please go on, Lieutenant. This is not a trial and the court will keep our interruptions to a minimum," Judge Fontenot said.

"We went to the defendant's home and waited for the exact time that he left the house the day before."

"The day of the incident?" the district attorney asked.

"Yes. From there he walked as he had done on that day and we followed him, to St. Charles Avenue and turned left—east. In the middle of the block he crossed the avenue and walked to the streetcar stop and waited. We rode the streetcar to St. Joseph's just as he had done two days before. I questioned him about what he did next, what he saw. We repeated each step and he told me everything he could remember seeing. He was most cooperative."

"Go on."

"It was the way he described coming across the street when I felt his innocence was a definite possibility," Lieutenant said.

"You stated that you had taken the streetcar to St. Joseph's. Did you get off there, Lieutenant?"

"Yes."

"This should be interesting, Lieutenant. A man crosses the street and it indicates his possible innocence?" the district attorney asked.

"It's the way he was crossing the street."

"So, you're telling the court the defendant made an impression by simply crossing the street—I take it the street is St. Charles Avenue."

"Yes."

"Please continue."

"He was crossing the avenue while blowing his nose," the lieutenant said.

"Would you repeat that for the court, Lieutenant Gaines?"

"The defendant was blowing his nose," the lieutenant said.

"Would you favor the court with the significance of a man's blowing his nose with his not committing murder, Lieutenant?" Judge Fontenot asked.

"Your Honor, to cross the street while blowing his nose, his cane had to be tucked in under his arm, elbows close to his body, with both hands on the handkerchief or tissue. He had sneezed five times, one time standing by the track when he got off the streetcar and four times while crossing St. Charles Avenue at St. Joseph and stepping up on the curb."

"Is there a point to this?" the district attorney asked.

"There is. It seems natural that if a man were blowing his nose all the way across the avenue, he couldn't have been in an aggressive posture, especially one that would result in the death of another. He was wiping his nose, probably not looking up, and my theory is he never saw the victim until he was approached on the sidewalk at knifepoint and threatened."

"Sound detective work, Lieutenant, but there has to be more," Judge Fontenot asked.

"Your Honor, according to the defendant when the young man threatened with knife thrusts and demanded the his money and wallet, I think I can prove my theory that the defendant went into a self-defense mode, brandishing his cane as a weapon as he had been trained to do—and I think I can prove he dropped the assailant to the sidewalk with one blow to the upper side of his back calf."

"Did he strike the victim's head?" the district attorney asked.

"Other than a defensive attempt to poke him in the eye, no, not at that time. He put the young man on the ground with one blow to his upper calf, just as he was trained to do, and then I believe it was his intent to leave as quickly as he could."

"Continue," the district attorney said.

Lieutenant Gaines lifted a property bag that held the torn shirt with the missing button.

"The young man grabbed the defendant's shirttail, making it difficult for him to break away—and according to the defendant he kept stabbing up with the blade. You can see that the button was not pulled from the shirt. He cut the button thread clean from the defendant's shirt and slashed the shirt four other times. It was his own pulling of the shirt away from the defendant's torso that may have saved the defendant from being cut with the knife."

"Had Forensic examined your evidence and the scene?" the district attorney asked.

"They had. I worked Forensic a year and a half, so I returned to the scene several times and examined it as well."

"What did you find?" Judge Fontenot asked.

"On the first time I went, I found the button that was cut from the Captain's shirt. I found it under some leaves."

"Without the proper lab work how could you possibly know the button was from the defendant's shirt, Lieutenant?" the district attorney asked.

"I called in a favor from a friend at the state troopers lab in Baton Rouge who reported that the button had the victim's blood on it, and a partial print of his thumb. I drove it up and waited."

"Some favor," the Judge said. "Lab work usually takes weeks."

"It was a Super Bowl bet he owed me, Your Honor. I traded it for an early lab result."

"Please continue," the DA said.

"I believe the victim cut his own thumb when his blade cut the shirt button off. It was his blood on the button which indicated to me he did have a knife. I also found seven cigarettes stepped out in the same spot more than thirty feet away from the scene. Every cigarette had the victim's fingerprints on them."

"What would that tell you—spent cigarettes, Lieutenant?" the district attorney asked.

"It proves nothing but, gathered as they were and with his prints it suggested to me that the victim could have been loitering near a corner he knew was a popular corner for people going to the WWII Museum. I imagined his standing there smoking for a long period of time, lying in wait for a prospective score, and when he recognized the defendant stepping onto the sidewalk, remembered his face, a man who he knew had a wallet filled with credit cards, he approached the defendant to rob him."

"You've presented an intriguing case to the benefit of the defendant, Lieutenant."

"It's only my theory, Your Honor," the lieutenant said.

"Were there any discoveries leading to a self-defense?"

"My theory went a long way to pointing me toward self-defense—I went over everything a hundred times but I needed more."

"What you've presented is impressive—that it was likely not a random act by the defendant, Lieutenant. But the people still see no weapon the victim was purported to having used," Judge Fontenot said.

"Where's the knife?" the district attorney asked.

"I still didn't have a knife."

"Are you implying, since there was no knife, the people should see a probable cause?" the district attorney asked.

"Not yet. What I had was either the Captain's word, or my own investigative experiences—a gut sense if you will—of the purposes of the clues I found—like the cigarettes—the button with the victim's blood on it."

"Without a knife, Detective Gaines, I don't see a strong case for self-defense."

"I knew I needed a knife, but I needed more."

"A knife alone would go a long way, what more would you need?"

"I needed to bring theories into credibility."

"Go on."

"I needed to corroborate the defendant's account he was crossing St. Charles Avenue, while sneezing, wiping his nose and in a non-offensive posture. As a trained military man, it could be self-serving for him to tell me he was sneezing and distracted while crossing the street."

Lieutenant Gaines lifted an evidence bag.

"I'd like to present this into evidence. I found it under a bush between the building and sidewalk—on the complete other side of the sidewalk from where the captain had stepped up."

"What is it?" District Attorney asked.

"I found this handkerchief with the initials GJ sewn into it. With his initials monogrammed on it, it would appear it belonged to Captain Jordan, but it can be tested for DNA. Where I found it convinced me the defendant was sneezing as he told me and couldn't have been in an aggressive posture, or an offensive stance before he threw the handkerchief toward the building and he was threatened the moment he was in the middle of the sidewalk."

"A handkerchief tells you that, Lieutenant?"

"The positioning of the handkerchief does. As a good soldier, he knew to throw the handkerchief out of the way to do battle without distraction or impediment."

"And that's when he killed the victim?"

"I believe he put the man down and tried to walk away."

"Please tell the court what you think this means, Lieutenant," Judge Fontenot said.

"Your Honor, the defendant was trained for 'civil' self-defense, not for a military defense. It was 'man on the street' cane and walking stick self-defense training 101, Your Honor—put the aggressor down and leave quickly."

"The man is dead, Lieutenant," the district attorney said.

"The attacker wouldn't let the defendant retreat. He grabbed and held his shirt as he attacked him with swipes of his knife. As a soldier, Captain Jordan defended his life by striking his attacker twice, once in the head, once at the knife."

The lieutenant lifted Exhibit #1, Gabe's walking stick, in the air.

"This is the walking stick Captain Jordan used to strike the victim. If you examine it closely, although it isn't a new stick, it shows no wear. Captain Jordan even admitted he had only started wearing a cane or carrying a walking stick since his scare at Walmart. If you look at it, the walking stick that looks new has a quarter-inch gash in it. By first impression it's as if a knife had struck it and cut into it."

The lieutenant set the walking stick on the table.

"On a hunch, I went back to the scene just before dusk. I wanted another look."

"You have us on pins and needles, Lieutenant," Judge Fontenot said.

The lieutenant lifted a property baggie in the air.

"I'd like to enter this into evidence, Your Honor. It is the knife, and it does have the victim's prints on it."

A murmur swept the courtroom. The judge answered with three gavel knocks.

"Order."

"Your Honor, the lab confirmed the knife is tipped with a drop of the victim's own blood."

"How did the knife mysteriously reappear?" the district attorney asked.

"My combat training, District Attorney Holbrook."

"Your combat training found the knife?"

"It was my hand-to-hand combat training that reminded me of self-defense tactics with a rifle or stick. My hunch was the victim didn't cut the cane with his knife which was my first theory or impression."

"What changed your mind?"

"The gash in the stick was too deep for a swipe of a knife."

"Are you an expert on such matters as to probabilities involving physics, Lieutenant?" the district attorney asked.

"I'm not."

"But you state it was a knife cut on the stick, Lieutenant."

"My combat training tells me it was Captain Jordan, the defendant, who used his stick to hit the knife out of the victim's hand as opposed to the knife striking the stick offensively. The defendant followed his military training by knocking the knife out of the victim's hand with his walking stick. Following that hunch and looking everywhere, I found the knife on the second-floor balcony of the house behind the scene."

"The lab has determined the knife you found is the knife used in the attack?"

"Yes. Blood and prints."

"So, your testimony is the defendant struck at the knife with his walking stick like he would a bat or a golf club?" Judge Fontenot asked.

"Exactly, Your Honor, the knife landed on the second-floor balcony of the house close by."

"That is impressive detective work, Lieutenant. Any more?" the DA asked.

"The victim was not an unarmed man. This is the weapon we needed. I believe there is substantial evidence that the defendant was only protecting himself."

"Thank you, Lieutenant. He's your witness, Ms. Tarleton."

"We have no questions, Your Honor," Lily Cup said.

"I would like to call my last witness, Your Honor. I would like to call Mr. Chris O' Sullivan, coroner for the city of New Orleans and Orleans Parrish."

The coroner fumbled papers in his hands while walking to the stand. He was sworn.

"Coroner O' Sullivan, have you examined the body of the deceased in question?" the district attorney asked.

"I have, superficially," the coroner said.

"What do you mean superficially?"

"I have an autopsy scheduled for tomorrow. I only had time to examine the body for external wounds."

"What did you find?"

"A severe trauma to the head was the probable cause of death. Death by homicide. Just under the right eye there was trauma, but it was not life-threatening. There was a fresh knife cut on the left thumb of the deceased."

"Could that cut be from cutting himself when he cut off the button of Captain Jordan's shirt?"

"I wasn't told the circumstance or the bloodwork results, but if the blood matched the deceased's blood it could be the result of being cut by his own knife."

"Would you say that the blow to the head was pretty conclusive as to cause of death, Mr. O'Sullivan?" the DA asked.

"I would."

"Anything further before I turn you over to the defense?"

"We were served with a court-ordered request from the Dallas County District Criminal Court in Texas, asking for exhumation rights of the body. They need the body to settle several cases in Dallas, Texas," the coroner said. "Their legal system allows for exhumation, if a violent crime was involved."

"If a body is evidence in a murder trial here, Judge, I'm thinking we hold precedent and can hold the body?" the DA asked.

"Before I answer, District Attorney—Mr. O'Sullivan sir, do you have a copy of the order from the Dallas Criminal Court?" Judge Fontenot said.

"I do, Your Honor."

"Would you please read the 'several cases' portion of it?"

The coroner put his reading glasses on and lifted the page from his file folder.

"'Kenneth Bauer's prints were found on three empty wallets and one empty purse in downtown Dallas dumpsters and alleys. His print was found on the eyeglasses of a man who was stabbed to death and robbed while entering his car in a downtown parking lot a block from city hall. There is video of him following the man. In the video the man was carrying a briefcase. There was no briefcase at the scene.'

That's about it, Your Honor."

"Who would pay to ship the body to Dallas?" Judge Fontenot asked.

Lily Cup stood and raised her hand in the air. "If Dallas doesn't pay it, I'll pay it," she said.

Lily Cup sat down and gently knuckled the side of Gabe's thigh.

The judge reached for her gavel.

"District Attorney Holbrook, you asked if Dallas Criminal Court could do that—request a body for examination for five crimes, one being murder?"

"I did, Your Honor."

"It would seem they have," Judge Fontenot said. "District Attorney Holbrook, I find no probable cause for second-degree murder here. Now what say you?"

"Your Honor, at this time the State of Louisiana will not be moving forward for an indictment against Captain Gabriel Jordan."

"Clerk of courts, you may release the body to Dallas. If it's necessary please arrange billing the expense of sending the body to Dallas to Counselor Tarleton," Judge Fontenot said.

"Yes, your honor," the clerk of courts said.

"Captain Jordan, your case is dismissed," the judge said. "Your bond obligation is extinguished. This case is closed."

Her gavel fell a decisive knock.

Lily Cup and Gabe stood.

The press emptied the room into waiting cameras in the hall.

"You are quite a woman," Gabe said. "Best attorney I've ever seen, and I've seen a few."

"Gabe, I can't do lunch. I have a lot of paperwork and the DA and I have to meet with the press. You go home and rest. I'll pick you up later. We'll go to Charlie's Blue Note and celebrate."

"Will you tell Sasha?"

"She's busy with closings all day today. I know she's dying to know what's going on, but let's surprise her together, tonight," Lily Cup said. "Peck too, later."

Gabe gave Lily Cup a long embrace.

"Thank you, little sister."

"Go get some rest, Gabe. You must be exhausted from all of this. We'll party tonight."

CHAPTER 41

NOT LONG AFTER Gabe walked out of the criminal court room in New Orleans, Peck and Elizabeth had walked from lunch at the Bistro. Peck was reading public notices pinned on the Baton Rouge Library bulletin board while Elizabeth spoke with a librarian at the front desk about procedure.

"The lady said we can use any of the reference materials here, but we can't take anything home unless we have a library card," Elizabeth said.

"I have a library card, cher," Peck said.

"It's for New Orleans, not Baton Rouge." Elizabeth said. "It won't work here. Let's just look around and see what we can find. We can make copies to take home."

"Copies be good."

As they walked between the shelves full of books, Peck occasionally reached his hand out to touch the spine of a book with his fingers. Elizabeth wasn't quite certain where to start. She circled back around, reading off the nameplates over each door. She held Peck's arm.

"Peck, let's sit down a minute and talk."

They sat side-by-side at an empty library table. She gathered her thoughts while looking around the room.

"In cooking school, they teach us that the first time we try to do a menu item we don't experiment—we follow the recipe. After we know what we're doing we can experiment."

"*Oui,* cher—like baiting a snood. First time you watch and learn from somebody, then you know."

"Something like that, so I'm thinking if you only remember this foster nanna and then there was gator man, I'm thinking we should maybe look at maps and see what you can remember from them."

"Maps is what Miss Audrey say we was to get her, remember?"

"That's right she did, didn't she?"

"Maps, she say to get maps."

"You have a good memory Peck. I only wish you could remember more."

Peck leaned into Elizabeth with a nuzzle.

"I remember your neck, cher."

He kissed her neck.

Elizabeth scrunched her neck and shoulder in a "now don't get me started" gesture and stood, looking about for the best room where maps might be. She pulled atlas map books and Louisiana reference books from shelves and stacked them on the table.

They sat together as she turned each page.

"Look at this one, Peck. Didn't you say Gabe came from Pineville?"

"*Oui.* He stayed at a VA hospital in Pineville. He runned away from there."

"Look at this—see this dot right here? It's Opelousas. I think you said that's where they found him. Imagine that distance. He walked almost seventy miles."

"He fell down is when somebody bringed him to the hospice."

"Here's another one. Does the Mississippi River make you think of anything when you were young, Peck?"

"Nah, nah. I heard stories but never see'd it until after I runned away."

"Does the Atchafalaya River mean anything?"

"Yes," Peck said.

"What does it mean?"

"I been on that, the Atchafalaya, I think with gator man."

"*C'est un bon debut,*" Elizabeth said. ("This is a good start.")

"Bayou Chene too," Peck said.

"See this water, Peck? Does Lake Maurepas mean anything to you?"

Peck sat tall, as if he bristled.

"Maurepas Maris. *Oui.* Frenchman Settlement, Killian. *Je me souviens d'eux,*" Peck said. ("I remember them.")

"You really remember?"

"I remember floater house."

"You mean houseboat?"

"*Oui. Péniche.*" ("Yes. Houseboat.")

"Does she live on the houseboat?"

"*Oui.*"

"And did you live on it too?"

"*Oui.*"

"Did the houseboat have a motor, Peck?"

"Nah, nah. A pole, cher. A pole would push the houseboat around."

"Did you travel in it?"

"Nah, nah. It was tied to a willer tree—tied tight."

"You were a little boy. How can you remember it was a willow tree?"

"Mamma Nanna would say to Peck, she say it was a sad tree. It, how you say...?"

"Weeps?"

"*Oui,* cher—weeps."

"Willow weeps," Elizabeth said.

"*Oui.*"

"It's like the song," Elizabeth said.

"Hanh?" Peck asked.

"*Saule, pleure pour moi,*" Elizabeth sang. ("Willow, weep for me.")

"Peck, I know Audrey is going to have you do this tomorrow, but shall we peek at the tarot cards? Would we be in trouble?"

"She tolded me to touch them. I don't see no trouble."

"Take the cards out of your pocket and spread them on the table."

Peck turned the deck face down on the table.

"*Leur eventail.*" ("Fan them out.")

Peck spread the cards in a two-foot trail.

"Okay, now one at a time, when I tell you, pick one," Elizabeth said.

"Hokay."

"Go ahead, pick one and turn it over."

Peck turned a card. It had an angel in the sky blowing a golden horn and there were naked people on the ground with their arms outstretched.

"Hmmm," Elizabeth said.

"What it mean, cher?"

"*Je n'ai pas la moindre idée, mon ami*," Elizabeth said. ("I don't have the faintest idea, my friend.")

"Humph," Peck said.

"Turn another card."

Peck turned a card with a knight on a white stallion. The knight was a skeleton in full armor and there was an archbishop on the ground praying over what looked like a dead body with a little girl fainting.

"*Merde*," Elizabeth said. "Put them away, Peck, hurry. Turn them over and put them away. We'll make a copy of these two maps and then go to the grocery."

When they got to the apartment, Peck put sacks on counters, then lifted his phone, indicating he was going in the bedroom to call his Millie. Elizabeth looked at her watch and motioned approval, and that she would cook.

Peck took his shoes and jeans off and stretched out on the bed, pressing call keys on the phone.

"Hello?" Millie asked.

"How you are, my Millie?"

"Hold on, sweetie. Let me get out of the shower and grab a towel. Don't go away."

Peck smiled.

"Is this my darling, my superhero?" Millie asked.

"I'm anything my baby want, cher. Peck misses you so much."

"If I think of how much I miss you, Peck, I would not get my schoolwork done so I could come this summer. I take a lot of cold showers."

"Do it good. Schoolwork makes you smart to run our farm."

"I can't wait. Chickens and a garden."

"When you sleep, you think of Peck?"

"Always. Where are you now?"

"Baton Rouge. I spend'd time at the library. We looked up books—maps and things."

"I was at the Baylor library today. They scolded me for keeping books too long. I tried to explain to them I was madly in love, and I could not be held responsible for my tardiness with their books—as time had absolutely no meaning to me anymore."

"Ha," Peck said.

"What are you going to do tomorrow, Peck?"

"I see Audrey."

"Audrey?"

"Audrey, this lady who reads what you call tarot cards and tells Peck things."

"Tarot cards—I've seen them do that at a UT party in Austin."

"You turned the tarot cards?"

"I don't think Baptist girls are allowed to play with tarot cards. I'm not sure."

"Are Baptist girls allowed to be with Cajun French fishers?"

"This one is. Do you have anyone in mind?"

"I have something in mind, cher."

"You little diablo, you. Are you talking naughty?"

"My William make Peck do it—talk dirty."

Millie laughed. "You don't like it called William. What makes you talk about William now? Are you being a bad boy?"

"Peck is perfect gentlemen. It's William is so bad."

"William is so good," Millie said. "Don't be picking on him."

"So, Peck will call tomorrow and tell you what the Audrey lady say, hokay?"

"I love you, Peck."

"I love you, cher. Study hard."

Peck got up from the bed and in his briefs and T-shirt walked out to the kitchen where Elizabeth was talking on her phone. She raised a finger over her lips, indicating "be quiet." Her boo was on the phone.

Peck went to the refrigerator next to the counter Elizabeth was leaning on. He opened the door and looked through and behind on its shelves and lifted out a bottle of iced tea. He stood beside her, removing the cap. He held the bottle out, offering her a sip. She shook her head *no* while reaching a hand out and pulling the top of his briefs away from his stomach. She looked down in at his prize, rolled her eyes and let it snap closed, smiling.

He stepped into the living room, plopped on the sofa and picked up his *Cannery Row* novel. He opened the chapter where the brothel owner, Nell, saw Doc in the general store. Peck read each word to himself while Elizabeth finished her phone business and prepared a candlelight dinner of chicken in butter cream sauce with capers and thin asparagus Hollandaise.

As Peck turned the page he learned that brothel owner Nell was telling Doc that he worked too hard and was living alone. He needed to get out more. She had a new girl at the house, Suzy, that he might be interested in. "She don't quite fit in, she don't belong there—just needs the work, Doc. She ain't like my other girls, Doc."

Peck turned another page to see if Doc makes a decision to go meet the girl, Suzy, and add some fun to his life of collecting sea urchins and frogs for science labs in schools.

Peck read until Elizabeth called him to dinner.

CHAPTER 42

ABOUT THE TIME Elizabeth and Peck were sitting down for dinner in Baton Rouge, in the alley off Frenchmen Street, Lily Cup was pushing the door to Charlie's Blue Note open to slam with an attention-getting irreverence.

"A round of drinks for everyone, Charlie—the boys in the band get two, and where's my box of cigars?" Lily Cup asked, as Gabe stepped into the room next to her.

She lifted his arm as though it were after the fifteenth round of a heavyweight prizefight.

"Ladies and gentleman, the winner and still a champion, let's hear it for our own Captain Gabriel Jordan," Lily Cup said.

Sasha, in a gray business suit, reached over the bar and grabbed a fresh cigar and a clean ashtray. She climbed from her stool, pranced toward Lily Cup and handed them to her. She then turned to Gabe with arms open. They hugged to a round of applause from Charlie and four at the bar, the eight sitting at tables with their bowls of red beans and rice, and four on the dance floor. The band stopped a piece of jazz and counted into "When Sunny Gets Blue," knowing it was Gabe's favorite. The three joined arms and walked like musketeers over to Gabe's table by the band.

"Don't get me wrong, darling, you look fresh out of Bloomingdales, but what's with the suit?" Gabe asked. "This is Frenchmen Street."

"Forget the suit. Didn't I tell you she was one incredible attorney? Didn't I tell you?" Sasha asked.

"You did indeed, and just watching her two days ago and today and how it all came down could bring me to happy tears. I could not agree with you more," Gabe said. "What a ride it's been."

"What is with the gray suit?" Lily Cup asked.

"I just came from a closing and didn't want to miss you guys if you came here and your phone is off, thank you very much."

"Was it an agent's closing or your own closing?" Lily Cup asked.

"One was mine, a place in the Garden District on Coliseum Street. It's a redo. Four and a half million, my listing, my client, my sale," Sasha said.

"Gabe, our queen of the strapless gown here just made more coin today than everyone in this alley will make all year combined."

"You do pretty well yourself," Gabe said.

"Not if I keep handling pro bono bums like you, I won't," Lily Cup guffawed.

"I'm not pro bono. I'm paying you, little sister."

"No, you aren't. It's on me. Shut up and have some fun tonight."

"Tonight, we celebrate," Gabe said.

"I'll go get our drinks," Sasha said. "We'll do beans and rice later."

"And grab a couple more cigars for me," Lily Cup said.

"I've been meaning to ask, little sister. Isn't smoking banned in N'Orleans restaurants and bars, counselor?" Gabe asked.

"You are correct, my friend. Cigars are absolutely banned from bars and other confined spaces…"

"I thought I read that somewhere," Gabe said.

"But you didn't read the fine print, Captain. Cigar bars in New Orleans existing before the smoking law are grandfathered."

"And Charlie's Blue Note is a…?" Gabe asked.

"I personally took the matter into my own hands. I set up the corporation for Charlie ten years ago. It's Charlie's Blue Note and Cigar Bar, Inc." Lily Cup said.

"You are something else, little sister…something else," Gabe said.

"You're talking to a fucking visionary, Captain. Half my clients, half the judges—even the DA's people—smoke cigars. This is New Orleans."

"Sweetie pie, you can smoke all the cigars you want tonight," Sasha said. "You saved Gabe, you genius best friend all my life, and otherwise nice person who I'll love until I die," Sasha said.

"Lily Cup, we've never danced. Would you do me the honor?" Gabe asked.

Sasha removed her suit coat and rested it on the back of a chair.

"Behave, you two," Sasha said, smiling and walking away.

A three-piece band took stage in a break for the jazz band. The music was a boogie-woogie Sewanee River on a lap piano, snare drums, and fiddle. Gabe stood, held his hand out for Lily Cup as she reached for an ashtray.

"Keep the cigar with you, little sister. You've earned that privilege," Gabe said.

She stood, smirked and strolled to him while bending over with a jazz step and hip motion, cigar in her fingers. Gabe took her free hand, pulled her to him and held her waist. Then he faked a jerk with his hips, then one with his shoulders, then back and forth and a step forward and back. The two were in perfect sync on their row down the Sewanee River with the band. As the music faded with a violin ending and bow removed, Gabe stood motionless, put his hands tenderly on each of Lily Cups cheeks.

"Thank you, little sister," Gabe said.

"My pleasure, poppa bear," Lily Cup replied.

"Make room for the tray," Sasha said.

Lily Cup stepped away from Gabe and moved her ashtray to the corner of the table.

"The lady can dance," Gabe said.

"What do you think we've been doing here at the Blue Note for ten years? Arts and crafts?" Sasha asked.

"Now don't get me started, darlin'. I've heard about the days on Magazine Street. Woman, you can't put one over on old Gabe, here."

Sasha put her hand on her waist, braced up with a smirk.

"Whatchu talkin' 'bout, dancin' man?" Sasha asked.

"You know what I'm talkin'. I'm talkin' the Victoria's Secret brassiere you saved up for and the shows—I'm keeping it clean—the shows you put on in those back sheds on Magazine Street," Gabe said.

"Lily Cup, you are such a blabber puss," Sasha said.

"Gabe and I were making conversation over chicory coffee, girlfriend. Thought I'd tell him how your girls could quench a hot afternoon's free-time boredom on school days."

"The Brewster kid—remember him?" Sasha asked.

"That's the one. Gabe, we took his virginity, took him around the world, and I convinced him to ask Mrs. Conklin how to spell *ménage a trois*—that she would be so impressed she would give him an A."

"You two have a book to write," Gabe said.

Lily Cup threw back a swallow of rye. "Gabe, can I ask you something?"

"Anything, my heroine."

"It's personal," she said.

"I have no secrets at this table, little sister."

"It's something that's been kind of, you know, gnawing on me, inside...and I was trying to figure out how to ask."

"So, ask already," Gabe said.

"I started thinking about it in the courtroom today when Lieutenant Larry was telling the judge that because he was black he could understand your messages. He said he could communicate with you better than others, because it was a black to black, a culture thing," Lily Cup said.

"Just as a man can't talk good menstrual, a white can't talk good black," Gabe said.

"We communicate on the dance floor, baby," Sasha said.

"We do, and that ain't no lie," Gabe said.

"Gabe, when you said—I don't know—I think it was right after Larry told the judge the Walmart videos could make you look like you had a motive for murder...you leaned over and said to me, 'I'm ready for anything.' Do you remember saying that? Did you mean that?"

"I remember and I meant it," Gabe said.

"What did it mean?"

"It's a black thing. Now you two, of all people, know ole Gabe here don't dwell on being black. But what you may not be able to see is being black dwells on me and my brothers for all our lives. We don't all go through life with chips on our shoulders, but we do go through our lives with a clear understanding that the Declaration of Independence, where all men were created equal, was written by a man who owned slaves until the day he died. We know what it's like, in most cities, when we cross a street and we can sometimes hear car doors lock."

"Are you saying you expected the worst and were ready not to fight...just give up?"

"I was."

"I'll be damned."

"Sorry."

"But why? You knew it was self–defense."

"Yes. I did, and you did, and the chief of police did, and the DA did. But—and you even said it—the media upset the Visitors Bureau, and it then became second-degree murder."

"Let me ask. Did OJ expect the worst just because he was black?"

"OJ was guilty. He expected it...and maybe his murder trial was just another Tuesday night NFL game for him—who knows?"

"How about Bill Cosby?"

"I think he expected a public lynching."

"But he gave them pills."

"He admitted to giving them Quaaludes years before the trial. He was a big star. I wouldn't be surprised if he had a bowl of pills and a pile of cocaine on his dresser. You don't go to a man's bedroom to have tea."

Gabe lifted the bottle and swallowed some Dewar's.

"Cable changed the world. It's divided us. It's now the court, judge, and jury," Gabe said.

"Your case wasn't a race case," Lily Cup said.

"I know exactly what it was, little sister. It was a case of all eyes on New Orleans, and tourism had to cover its ass by whupping mine. Nothing personal. My being black only helped ratings. Pundits had five victims for stories—me being black for one, me being an old man, me being military, and don't forget the homeless white boy."

"Television changed everything," Lily Cup said. "I had to take six hours of crisis management on handling media. Nothing is local anymore. It all goes global."

"Pavarotti has left the building," Gabe said.

"You mean Elvis?" Lily Cup asked.

"Pavarotti," Gabe said.

"The opera singer?"

"Our lesson of any sense of world-class humility we had was watching an entire world at war when eighty million people died. Showing respect for others was a given; it was how we were raised. Good behavior was drummed into us in the sixties and seventies, when the world was still young and Pavarotti lived and set the example on the world stage. When Luciano Pavarotti died, little sister, with his broad smiles and long scarves; with his hand-sewn tuxedos with black ties and white ties and a passion for brilliance...When he died it just seemed feeling good about the simple, respectful dressing up to go out and the saying of *please* and *thank you* eroded from our culture. It was as if our sense of world class took a bow with him and exited, stage left," Gabe said.

"Will you two give it a rest? Dance with me, Gabe," Sasha said.

"Absolutely," Lily Cup said with a hiccup. "I have to pee. I'm going to call Peck and tell him."

As Lily Cup got up, Gabe stood and offered his hand to Sasha. The bass slap-strummed the beat, brushes on a soft snare offered the way...and the riff began. Gabe pulled Sasha in full circle. He didn't know the tune, but he knew the right moves. The clarinet took him back to Benny Goodman, and they swayed in a syncopation of celebration—not of court battles, not of life going by. It was a celebration of New Orleans. For the bad that happened in this particular bend in the Mississippi river, there were two things good that happened, and there was the music.

"Hello?" Peck asked.

"Hey Peck, I have good news," Lily Cup said.

"You sound like an echo, cher. Where you are?"

"I'm in the restroom. We're at the Blue Note."

"A restroom?"

"I had to pee. Now can I tell you my news?"

"Tell Peck."

"Gabe got off. He's free as a bird. We're celebrating at Charlie's."

"That is good news. You the best."

"It happened with you telling me about the videos, Mr. Investigator. You're the brains behind this whole thing."

"You plenty smart. T'ank you for helping my frien'."

"Hey, Peck."

"What?"

"My panties are down around my knees. Want a selfie?"

"You drinking that rye again, cher?"

"Is there any other drink?"

Peck laughed.

"I was just fooling with you. If I took a selfie like that it would probably wind up on Facebook in an hour."

"Cher, tell Gabe I'm happy? Tell him for Peck?"

"I will."

"T'ank you."

"Is that Elizabeth gal helping you?"

"Yes'm, she is big help. Tomorrow we go see Audrey. She's a tarot lady."

"Where are you?"

"I'm in Baton Rouge."

"Please be careful, Peck."

"I be careful, dass for true."

Lily Cup flushed the toilet.

"Shit, I didn't want you to hear that," Lily Cup said.

"Hear what?"

"Never mind. Keep us posted?"

"Hanh?"

"Bad connection. Just let us know how it's going."

"For sure, cher."

"Night, Peck. Good luck."

"Bye."

CHAPTER 43

THE BEDROOM WAS DARK, and the time was somewhere between bar closings and when the brushes of washers would sweep through the streets of downtown Baton Rouge. A city sound, a siren, wailed in the distance behind buildings in another neighborhood. In a deep sleep, Peck mumbled with a restless roll, and he turned over with a flop, facing the center of the bed. Now they sleep as friends, not the lovers they once were but as he rolled over, his arm followed him like a boa, the back of his hand landing on the heat of a warm blend of soft satin and silky–smooth skin. His hand turned from back to palm instinctively inquisitive, feeling the warm buttock, and it met the touch with an unconscious squeezing and Braille–like feel. This awakened Elizabeth's curiosity and she rolled on her side, her back to him. Her head on her pillow, eyes open, she looked up at a ceiling she couldn't see. Peck's free hand went from the flat of his stomach it was resting on down into his briefs, and William was pulled summarily from a restless sleep and directed between the hidden warmth of Elizabeth's crotch from behind. Her legs straightened and flexed her buttocks, holding her thighs together like a vice. William began pumping between her legs, slowly at first, teasing the awakened but hidden lips of her island while rubbing the softness of their satin gatekeeper.

"Peck."

William thrust slowly.

"Peck."

William's motion between a heaven-sent triangle of thighs and a warm, satin-covered crotch became more deliberate, upper thighs softly slapping her buttocks. A sleeping hand fumbled in front of her like a lost puppy in search of breasts.

"I'm not Millie."

William was relentless.

"Peck, wake up."

"Hanh?" Peck asked.

In the dark of night, Peck woke, and as if he saw the light of what he was doing on the backs of sleeping eyelids, he pulled his hips away, freeing William into the night air and rolled on his back. He rubbed his eyes and cheeks and raked stiff fingers through his hair in a scratch.

"Peck's got to stop drinking the wine, cher, dass for true," Peck said.

He tucked William in his briefs.

Elizabeth was silent as she smiled, still looking toward the ceiling in the darkened room.

"No more wine for me."

Elizabeth rolled toward Peck and nuzzled his neck.

"Mais le poulet et les câpres ètaient bons, non?" Elizabeth asked. ("But the chicken and capers were good, no?")

He thought for a moment, and with stomach muscles contracting, broke into a silly laughter.

"What time is it?" Peck asked.

"It's three–thirty. We should sleep."

"What time does Peck have to see Audrey?"

"Ten in the morning. I'll show you where to catch the bus and when to get off. I'll write it down."

"You go with me, cher?"

"I have to be at the cooking school at ten. I'll be back here at three. You should be done by then. Want me to cook tonight, or want to eat out?"

"Bistro?"

"Parfait!" Elizabeth said. ("Perfect.")

"We'll meet here and then go to Bistro," Peck said.

"Oui." Elizabeth said. She kissed Peck on the neck. She knelt up in the dark.

"Tu veux que je retire ma culotte?" ("Do you want me to take my panties off?")

"Peck doit être bon, cher," Peck whispered. ("Peck need to be good, cher.")

She pulled her T–shirt up over her head and off, flipping it to the bureau. She leaned in, felt around for William and kissed it a quick goodnight through his briefs and lay down, her bare back to Peck, tucking a pillow between her legs and falling asleep.

When Peck stepped out of the shower he could smell fresh-brewed coffee. He toweled his hair, wrapped a loosely knotted, dry towel around his waist and walked the hall to the kitchen for a cup. Elizabeth was barefoot in her chef school pants with no top. Bell–shaped breasts flexed as she reached into the upper cabinet for cooking utensils and then into the refrigerator for eggs. Peck watched her nipples, likely remembering the first time they met, and he saw them through her yellow T–shirt so many years ago.

"Bonjour," Peck said.

"Bonjour," Elizabeth said.

"Tu as l'air reposè. Tu as bien dormi?" Peck asked. ("You look refreshed. Did you sleep well?")

Elizabeth smiled.

"I was sleeping so well until this naughty boy with a big, long broom handle molested me," Elizabeth said.

"I was dreaming. You are so lovely in the night, I could not resist touching you in my sleep. Ha ha. Don't be upset with Peck, cher."

"You were more fun when you weren't in love," Elizabeth said. "You finished things you started back then."

Elizabeth poured a cup for Peck, dropped two teaspoons of sugar in it and stirred. She held it out.

"C'est tellement triste, cher," Peck said. ("It's so sad, then, cher.")

"Why sad?" Elizabeth asked.

Peck took the coffee from her hand.

"It's so sad because Peck won't ever finish with Elizabeth, ever. So sad."

Elizabeth reflected and smiled at the oral embrace. Her eyes felt good about it. She reached and with her thumb and finger loosened the knot and let his towel drop to the floor, exposing skillet flat abs, carved pecks and a resting, chubby, William. He smirked, not moving a muscle. He nonchalantly sipped of his coffee.

"*Oh mon dieu, on dirait que notre ami a eu une attention particulière dans la douche peut–être?*" Elizabeth asked. ("Oh my, it looks like our friend got special attention in the shower, maybe?")

Elizabeth put a pot under the faucet and turned the water on.

"Our friend has a name, cher. Don't be rude," Peck said.

"A name? What name?"

"William. He is William."

Elizabeth grinned, turned the faucet off, lifted the pot to the stove and turned the gas flame on.

"I would shake William's hand, but I'm certain he's exhausted from being in the shower with you."

They continued their repartee with smiles and grins, and it reminded them why they had been such good friends for so long a time.

"I'm going to shave. I'll be right out. Will Elizabeth have breakfast with me?"

"I'll have toast, but then I have to leave. We eat what we cook, and I'll get so fat if I eat more now. Go shave."

Peck sipped his coffee and turned down the hall. Elizabeth watched him walk away and then turned to crack the eggs into the three ceramic coddlers. Peck came out dressed and ready to start his journey.

"Do you have money, Peck? You have to pay Audrey."

Peck took a debit card from his pocket.

"This?"

"That will work. She'll take a card. Do you have bus money?"

"*Oui.*"

"Don't forget the tarot cards."

"I have the cards."

Peck twisted the lids off the coddlers and peppered the contents of the first, and with a spoon enjoyed its sunken treasures for the palate. Elizabeth liked watching the adventure in his eyes. She was happy for him with his new love and continued education. Sometimes she would wonder if Peck and her man should meet, and if they did, how it would be arranged.

"Here's a spare key. Hang on to it. I'll see you when I get home."

"T'ank you, cher."

Elizabeth went back into the bedroom and came out buttoning the top of her cooking school chef uniform. It was a heavily starched white. Her nametag was pinned to it. She walked over to where Peck was sitting and nudged her knee into his thigh so she could sit in his lap. He turned and she sat on his lap sidesaddle.

"Don't be afraid today, Peck."

"I'm not afraid."

"Audrey will tell you what she sees in the cards, but it's what she thinks she sees, so don't be afraid."

"I'm not afraid, cher."

"It's good to listen to her, though, so listen to her and remember what she tells you."

"Peck is a good listener. Have to listen for turtles."

"Turtles don't make noises. Why do you listen for turtles?"

"Frogs make noises when they jumpin' away from snappers, cher. Crawfish snakes chase after frogs."

Elizabeth put her arms around his neck and smiled into his eyes. She found great warmth, a security in knowing how closely her friend communed with nature.

"Will it be all right if I kissed you goodbye, Peck?"

Peck sat there without speaking.

"Well?" Elizabeth asked.

"I'm t'inking," Peck said.

Her right hand lifted from his neck to the top of his head and grabbed his hair and pulled his head back. Her open mouth plunged his smile with a morning kiss of passion between friends. Her hands held his ears as they kissed. She kissed his lips, his chin and sat up with a happy sigh.

"Now good, cher?" Peck asked.

"Needs more pepper," Elizabeth said. "Use the white pepper on the other coddled eggs, Peck."

With that she stood, clutched her bag of books and notepads and headed to the front door.

"*Au revoir, mon ami*," Elizabeth said.

She left for school, and Peck was not far behind. His phone showed he had an hour to be at his appointment with Audrey, so he decided to walk. He would walk to South Tenth Street and go from there.

Audrey was waiting for him. She opened the door and invited him in. She then hung a "do not disturb" sign on the door, closed and locked it behind them.

"Let's step into the next room, Peck. We'll be more comfortable there."

With the exception of a strand of blue LED lights hanging over a velvet-draped table and a burning wax candle, the room was darkened.

"Have a seat, Peck. I use these few lights and one candle so we are not distracted by things in the room."

"I understand."

"Would you prefer I use your given name, Boudreaux Clemont, or Peck. I want to use what is comfortable for you. Do you have a preference?"

"Peck is good."

"Did you bring the tarot cards?"

"Yes'm."

"Before we begin, would you shuffle them?"

Peck shuffled the deck of cards in several different manners before setting them on the table.

"Now fan them out."

Peck ran the palm of his hand tightly over the deck and dragged them into a trail of about two feet.

"Do you have a number you feel most comfortable with? It may be what some call a lucky number...or a number you think of more than other numbers?"

"Eight."

"You feel good with the number eight?"

"Eight hooks on a snood. Eight fingers, no thumbs. Eight is good."

"One at a time, Peck, slowly run your hand over all of the cards and pick eight cards you feel may be sending you a message. Take the time you need. One at a time, hand them to me."

The first time, Peck ran his hand over the cards and selected one card and handed it to Audrey. She held it face-down in her palm. The second and other times he put his left hand on the left end of the card trail, closed his eyes and ran his right hand over the cards and picked one at a time and held it out for Audrey. With each card he selected, he became more concentrated on the task at hand.

Audrey picked up the remaining portion of the deck and placed it on the wooden shelf behind her. She fanned the eight cards in her hand.

"Pick one of these cards, Peck. The card you select will tell us the road before you that destiny has willed you to travel. Let the card speak to you. Be patient."

Peck placed his palm under her hand holding the fanned cards. He held his other hand over them. He closed his eyes and moved each hand back and forth slowly. His index finger came down and touched one.

"This one," Peck said.

He pulled it from her hand and held it out for her. Audrey placed it face-down in front of Peck. She then placed the remaining seven cards face-down and side-by-side in the middle of the table.

"We first reveal a lead message, and then we will turn one message at a time and see in what direction they lead the journey," Audrey said.

She took the first card Peck had selected and turned it over.

"Your hand selected this first. It's the Death card. Death means change in your future. It could be any aspect of your life. It might be something you learn about yourself. It could be something about someone you love. Death means a complete severance from the past and future. Do you wish to hear more?"

"*Oui.*"

"The change in your life will be painful. It will be permanent. You must have death before you can move on to a new phase of your life. Something has been approaching you. It will arrive soon. You are about to lose something valuable to you."

"Foster nanna, I t'ink," Peck said. "She's coming, I t'ink."

"It could be a person, but it could also be a thought, a dream."

Audrey placed her hand on his. "Do you wish to continue?"

"*Oui.* Continue."

She turned another card.

"This is the High Priestess card. You possess good judgment and have strong intuition. You will be rewarded if you maintain discipline. Although this is a time of renewal for you, you need help from someone."

"Elizabeth," Peck said.

"Would you like me to continue, Peck?"

"*S'il tu plaît, ne me demande plus. Je n'ai pas peur d'entendre ça,*" Peck said. ("Please don't ask me again. I'm not afraid to hear this.")

"Ahh, the Justice card. A very good card if you are kind and fair, or if you've been a victim. For the unjust it is a warning, for you it is a blessing. You are going to receive an outcome you truly deserve."

Peck clenched his fists and held them to his lips in heavy thought.

"This one is the Strength card. You have chosen cards well, my friend. This shows you have the rawest of power. You have a balance of mental and physical strength. It does come with advice. You shouldn't turn down any offers that will change your future."

As if he were waiting for the nibble on his trotline that would feed him that day, Peck gazed at the remaining cards.

"Oh my. This is the Hanged Man card. With it comes two interpretations. Either the old must die to create the new, or it lets you let go from a past—a sacrifice. The Hanged Man is a metamorphosis."

"I runned away once. Do I run back now, maybe?" Peck asked.

"Time will give you the answer, Peck."

She turned another card.

"This is the Lovers card. Love comes to you in many forms. You will come to two paths. One of them will take you to a good place. You have a conflict approaching. Choose wisely."

"Between Millie and Elizabeth, you mean?" Peck asked.

"No. I think you'll have to choose between love and a career. I'm not certain."

"I pick love," Peck said.

"I believe you can pick both. I just think the card is telling you to keep a balance."

"D'at is good then," Peck said.

"Now, third from last of the cards you picked—the Fool card."

"Hanh?" Peck asked.

"Oh, but it's a most powerful card, the Fool card. It's a new beginning. It means something is going to change in your life. You ran from home when you were nine. Imagine the risks you took. It has only brought you success."

"Millie, Gabe, Peck's frien's so good," Peck said.

"There are two more cards. You must select carefully now. The card you select will anoint your journey. But the one left on the table—the last one—will seal the fate of all that is meant for you in the days ahead. Choose carefully. Take your time."

Almost without thought, his hand, like a darting eel, reached and grabbed a card and held it out for Audrey.

"Oh my, you have a strong will. Let's see what you selected."

Audrey turned the card.

"Interesting. You selected the Judgment card. It tells of the transition we speak of. It tells that it's been long in the making and it is coming to a fruition. It also says you will have to make decisions."

"*Si seulement Peck était plus intelligent, Mlle Audrey. Je pourrais mieux comprendre, je pense,*" Peck said. ("I wish Peck was more intelligent, Miss Audrey. I could understand better, I think.")

"It will come to you in time, Peck. It's important that you're pure of thought and true to those around you. Follow your heart."

"Yes'm."

"Now there is one more card. It is a window on your destiny. Are you ready?"

"*Oui.*"

"Peck, try to think of your entire life. In this lifetime, what one thought or dream have you turned to time and time again, for balance, for warmth, for hope?"

"My mamma, cher. I talk to my mamma."

"Turn the last card, Peck."

Peck turned the card, looked at it and set it on the table as a tear formed in his eye.

"The Moon card, Peck."

"I know," Peck said.

"Something in your life is not what it seems."

"My mamma, maybe?"

"The Moon card is a strong indicator that you must rely on your own intuition."

"The moon is my mamma, I know for true."

"Your understanding of the past is distorted."

"It's my mamma for true, cher."

"Peck, the moon is your imagination. Don't ever lose that."

"I'll never lose the moon, cher."

"That's the end of our reading, Peck. How do you feel?"

"So much to t'ink about. I feel like there are so many—how you say—doors to open now?"

"That's a perfect description. Yes—doors that need opening."

"Thank you, Miss Audrey."

"Peck, is it possible that you come back in the morning and bring Elizabeth with you?"

"*Pourquoi*?" Peck asked. ("Why?")

"I want her to be a part of a decision that has to be made. I'm thinking a hypnotist can help you now. I think you're ready to open some of those doors, and your subconscious has many of the keys."

"I'll ask Elizabeth and if she say yes, I bring her. What time?"

"Same time. It won't take long. After that I'll set an appointment with the hypnotist."

Peck dug in his pocket and pulled out his debit card.

"Pay me tomorrow, Peck. How do you feel about today?"

"I feel good. So many things to t'ink about."

"Good."

As Peck walked to the apartment his cell phone rang. It was Lily Cup.

"Hey, cher. How you are?"

"Peck, I'm in Baton Rouge. I have meetings in the courthouse until four. Can you have dinner with me?"

"Elizabeth in school to three o'clock. Maybe all of us for dinner?"

"Perfect," Lily Cup said.

"So, you will call me later, cher?"

"I will. See you later. Pick your favorite restaurant," Lily Cup said.

Peck put the phone in his pocket and smiled as he crossed a street. He would go to the apartment and call his Millie and tell her of the day, and then he would read more chapters of *Cannery Row* until Elizabeth came home.

A traveling cloud seemed to block the sun, but only for a moment. The air cooled as it passed over. Peck enjoyed walking through downtown Baton Rouge.

CHAPTER 44

NOT KNOWING PECK'S MOOD following his tarot reading, Elizabeth took care to unlock the apartment door quietly. The living room and kitchen were empty, and the bathroom door was ajar. Through the hall she could see his bare feet on the bed. He was sleeping on top of the bed cover on his back in his briefs and no T-shirt. His arms wrapped around a pillow pulled over his face. She took her cooking school chef uniform top off, checked it to see if it needed laundering and hung it in the bedroom closet.

She stood bare-breasted and watched Peck sleeping in his briefs, the John Steinbeck novel beside him. She quietly pulled a drawer, removing a yellow-gold T-shirt with LSU's, "Tiger Bait" imprinted on it in black. She dropped the T-shirt on the bed and began untying straps holding up her school chef pants. She lowered them enough to realize she was *sans* panties that day, pulled them up and refastened the strap. She took a hairbrush from atop the bureau and placed a knee on the T-shirt at the edge of the bed as she crawled on over it and sat beside Peck. She ran her fingers gently around his chest.

"*Ma cheri?*" Elizabeth asked.

His body didn't move as he lifted the pillow from over his face and rested it behind his head.

"Brush my hair?"

Peck opened his eyes at the sound of her voice and without moving he looked at her eyes, at the brush in her hand, and at her breasts.

"I need to brush before we go out."

"*J'aime comment tu me brosses les cheveux,*" Elizabeth added. ("I like how you brush my hair.")

"Run the tub hot, cher," Peck said.

Elizabeth grinned, her eyes awakened with a twinkling. The tub had been a special place for all the years they had been friends. A hot bath usually followed good sex, sometimes bath time led to it, but whichever way the compass pointed, a tub was their secret place, their tree house.

Elizabeth would say the tub was special because they would take the time to talk while he brushed her hair or she washed his back or clipped his toenails. Peck held his secret from Elizabeth that she had taken his virginity when he was almost nineteen and fresh out of their first tub bath, and Elizabeth held hers from him that she knew. Peck would say the water was good when it was hot like a bayou swamp but without alligators or snappers. Elizabeth would say her time with Peck in the tub bonded them together like the Holy Trinity of Cajun cooking –onion, celery, and bell pepper.

Hearing the faucets turned off, Peck got up and stepped into the bathroom and dipped a toe into a full tub. He pushed the curtain to the far left, out of the way. Elizabeth reached and pinched either side of his briefs, pulling them to the floor and he stepped out of them.

"Get in," Elizabeth said.

He did and sat down. She handed him the brush, dropped her chef uniform pants to the floor and stepped in the tub in front of him, sitting between his legs. Peck took her hair into one hand and brushed it down from her scalp and off the end into his flattened hand. He would pull brushstrokes with an endless patience, like a fisherman casting his line from a lonely reef.

"*Qu'as-tu cuisiné aujourd'hui, cher?*" Peck asked. ("What did you cook today, cher?")

Elizabeth pouted her lips. Her voice cracked.

"*Le chef Elizabeth a cuisiné de la merde aujourd'hui. J'ai brûlé le saumon, brûlé une sauce au beurre, et j'ai râpé une putain de carotte et pas julienne. Merde, merde, merde,*" Elizabeth said. ("Chef Elizabeth cooked shit today. I burned the salmon, burned a cream butter sauce, and grated a fucking carrot and not julienne. Shit, shit, shit.")

"Anyone can burn a salmon."

"Not when it's supposed to be poached, they don't."

"Oh?"

"Yeah...oh."

"Your hair is so pretty, cher."

"Don't make me ask. Tell me what Audrey said."

"She told Peck the moon was my frien', and she say there is change coming in my life. She say not to be scared, but I need somebody to go with me when I go to my past."

"Did she say who?"

"And she say that the death she saw is for changes in my life, and that something always had to die to make, how you say, room for the new thing—at least I think dass what she had to say."

"Who will die, did she say?"

"Your salmon is dead, maybe that counts, cher."

With a grin in her eyes, Elizabeth's pouting lips bristled a tight pucker.

"Do you think butter sauce dies?" Peck asked.

Elizabeth reached behind her back with her hand, threatening to grab William or his personals, but she paused and rested her arm on his knee.

"It didn't frighten you, the things she said?"

"Nah, nah."

"Did she say who should go with you?"

"No, but she ax if you could come with me to see her tomorrow, same time. She say to bring maps."

"Peck, I can't be the one to go with you. You know that, don't you?"

"So, I tell Audrey you have cooking school and can't come see her with me."

"No, I don't mean that. I can go tomorrow. I just can't be the one that goes with you wherever it is you have to go in your past."

"I know that, cher. You have your boo on the rig. I've been thinking maybe Millie should go with me."

"Your Millie? Interesting. Do you think she could handle the swamps and things you might see and hear?"

"My Millie can handle it. I just don't want to disappoint her maybe."

"How could you possibly disappoint her?"

"What if I'm a nobody bag dare where I grow'd, cher?"

"Tell me about Millie. What's she like?"

"Millie ax me if I could watch her t'ings on the bus that time. She had to go to the *salle de bain* (bathroom) and I saw her eyes good, and I knew there was something about her come over me. When she come out she sat with Peck, and we talked about her boyfrien' what cheated on her all the time and how her daddy was a reverend and strict. She has a little doll, you know, like a baby ever since she was three or two. Peck not sure how old it is now, but she keeps it with her. It's her baby Charlie."

"She had a boyfriend when you met her?"

"No. She told him goodbye when she got on the bus to go bag home in Tennessee from university. Dass when I meeted her. On the bus."

"Is she pretty?"

"Oh, *oui*."

"When did you know you were in love, Peck?"

"On the bus. When she ax me to watch her t'ings, dass for true, cher. It was magic."

"*C'est tellement beau, Peck. Je suis contente pour toi*," Elizabeth said. ("That's so beautiful, Peck. I'm happy for you.")

"Do you know why Audrey wants to see us both tomorrow?" Peck asked.

"I'm certain she wants to let me in on her thoughts while we're both in the room. I told her stories about what you went through with the gator man and with the foster nanna you ran from."

"You told her all dat, for true?"

"And more."

"What more?"

"I told her you are the most romantic men I have ever known."

"Dass for true?"

"For true," Elizabeth said.

"*Ta Millie vous rend tous les deux si chanceux. Garde-la et ne la laisse jamais partir*," Elizabeth said. ("Your Millie makes you both so lucky. Hold her and don't let go.")

"If Millie come here, would it be good or bad if she meeted you, cher?"

"I would love to meet Millie. What would you tell her about us?"

"Millie and Peck so much in love, I wouldn't have to tell her anything."

"What kind of woman would she think I am, cheating like I do?"

Peck stopped brushing and set the brush on the tub rail.

"You don't cheat."

Elizabeth paused, squeaking the tub floor with her bottom as she turned around and looked into Peck's eyes.

"I'm a cheater on my man, no?"

"You have to be in love to cheat, cher. Elizabeth not in love."

Their gaze into each other's eyes churned memories of nearly ten years of nights together. Ten years of Elizabeth watching Peck grow up and years of Peck knowing he had the privilege in lying with a masterpiece not yet painted. He knew

Elizabeth was a woman with destiny, and it comforted him in knowing they would always be the closest of friends.

"You are such a lovely, lovely man, *mon ami.*"

Elizabeth raised up and stood over Peck in the tub, soap suds melting down her thigh. They looked into each other's eyes with understanding that the change in their lives was happening, and they could feel it. Peck looked up at her perfect body, waiting to be sculpted in his dreams of her and in her own fulfillment of life's adventures.

"*Qu'est–ce qui va m'arriver, cher?*" Elizabeth asked. ("What will happen to me, cher?")

"Elizabeth will become a chef in Baton Rouge, this red stick city with an x at its heart, and then she will go to Paris where the big wheel is, where the tower glows at night and the wine is good—the Paris you told me stories about—and she will not kill the salmon or burn her butter sauces anymore."

"And what will happen to my man out on the rig?"

"He is just a man on a rig. He is not your man on the rig. He will find someone who is right."

"Will I ever again be held like you hold me, Peck?"

"*Oui.* A lucky man will see your eyes and find you and he will hold you forever."

"For true, Peck? How can you be sure?"

"Paris will hold you, cher. He will follow."

Elizabeth cupped her island with a palm almost as if someone had walked into the room.

"Cher, it do no good to hide yourself. Won't do no good."

"I don't know what you're saying. I'm not hiding anything."

"You are. It'll do no good."

"Why won't it?"

"Peck has memorized all of you to his brain—dass why."

Elizabeth laughed, stepped from the tub and wrapped herself with a towel.

"My frien' Lily Cup called Peck today. I forgot to tell you, cher, she wants to take us someplace for dinner."

"Lily Cup?"

"Dass for true. Lily Cup. She's a frien' of mine and Millie too. Her daddy named her Lily Cup when she got born. You'll like Lily Cup."

"Where do you know her from?"

"Lily Cup is a lawyer in New Or–lee–anhs. She helped me one time and I clean her offices. She comes to the capital for business, I t'ink. She's in Baton Rouge and wants to take us to dinner."

"We'll have to go someplace where nobody knows me," Elizabeth said.

"Why?"

"My man? The rig? Remember?"

"Today Audrey showed Peck the Hanged Man card. She say it meaned upheaval and change. What does upheaval mean? Can you tell me?"

"*Oui.* Upheaval means your salmon is dead and the sauce is merde and the carrot is a joke."

"Ahh. Well we go to any restaurant we want with Lily Cup, then. Audrey say upheaval is so good. We do it for me, and for Paris, for my good frien' Elizabeth."

Lily Cup was standing just outside Ruffino's when Peck and Elizabeth walked up. Peck hugged her and introduced Elizabeth while pulling the door open. The maître d' sat them at a comfortable corner table. Lily Cup handed him a twenty and asked for a bottle of his driest Bordeaux, and if he didn't have French, the driest Italian red in the cellar. She instructed him to have it decanted, to awaken it in the night air.

Elizabeth looked about for faces she knew but settled in and hung her purse strap over the back of Peck's chair.

"So, you are Elizabeth?" Lily Cup asked.

"*Oui, madame*," Elizabeth said.

"Peck, she is as beautiful as you said she was. Every bit."

"Cher," Peck said, looking at Elizabeth. "I didn't tell..."

"He certainly did. He told Sasha when they were in Memphis just how beautiful you are—and he was right. You are."

"Ha, I forgot to tell you Lily Cup and the Sasha she speaks of are best friens' since like six years old," Peck said.

"And we have absolutely no secrets," Lily Cup added.

"Tell me about Gabe," Peck said.

"The judge made us work with a detective and the district attorney's office to study what happened that day...well, you know. The detective proved Gabe was acting in self-defense, just as you said, Peck. They dropped the case. He's home free."

"Elizabeth, Lily Cup is the best lawyer in the state of Louisiana. She the best."

"That reminds me," Lily Cup said.

She opened her bag and pulled out three one- hundred-dollar bills and put them in front of Peck's bread plate.

"I owe you this. We won."

"Nah, nah, cher. You don't owe—"

"If we had lost you are paid, but we won, and you get a bonus for your research. Take it. You earned every penny."

Peck raised an arm and motioned for the maître d'.

"May I be of service, sir?"

Peck held up the three bills.

"Will this be enough for a bottle of what Miss Lily Cup just ordered? The wine?"

"More than enough, sir."

"Well, bring the bottles it will pay for, and don't open them until we say."

"Yes, sir. Right away, sir."

"Well, well, well...just look at you, Mr. Boudreaux Clemont Finch. Elizabeth, I do believe our friend here is propositioning us to party tonight."

Elizabeth nodded. "That's how it looks, for certain."

"I'd better get a hotel room. I'll be in no shape to drive back tonight," Lily Cup said.

"Stay at my apartment. I can make coffee later."

"And crepes?" Peck asked.

"It's settled. We'll have crepes with cream and jams for dessert, of course," Elizabeth said.

"So Elizabeth is who taught you about crepes, Peck."

"Ah, *oui*, cher."

"Now it's all making sense."

They celebrated and talked about life, and of friendship and of Acadian charms and of hoodoo and full moons. Lily Cup told the many bad things she learned while practicing criminal law and how Peck must take care and not be followed, and to be cautious of who he talks to and what he says when he travels back into the swamps and bayous.

Peck told Lily Cup how proud he was to be her friend, and maybe they would dance when they next go to Charlie's Blue Note, and Elizabeth talked of Paris and how one day she would like to perhaps have a breakfast spot or a bakeshop of her own. Lily Cup talked of Peck and how genuine he was, and she asked Elizabeth if he had introduced her to William, and Elizabeth told her that she and William were once close friends, but lately he's been standoffish and like "un poisson froid," ("a cold fish") as she put it.

They laughed and they sipped wine and shared the tastes on each of their many plates, and the candle burned out to a stream of smoke and a new one was lit.

"Why did you pick Baton Rouge?" Lily Cup asked.

"Cooking school, why?" Elizabeth said.

"I don't know, it's something about Baton Rouge."

"What about Baton Rouge?" Elizabeth asked.

"New Orleans is where food is celebrated worldwide, honey."

"Why don't you like Baton Rouge?" Elizabeth asked.

"I think it's the way the Mississippi River just turns and cuts through the middle of it. It's like Baton Rouge is the vulva of the whole country."

Elizabeth lifted her glass with a devilish grin.

"To the vulva," she said. "To Baton Rouge."

"Peck, don't let me forget," Lily Cup said. "I brought papers that might help you. I have your birth certificate and other things in my briefcase. I'll give them to you later."

"T'anks, cher."

Peck hiccupped and leaned over to Lily Cup. "Lily Cup, can I ax you something?"

"Don't you just want to squeeze him? He is so cute the way he talks sometimes," Lily Cup said. "What do you want to ask, sweetie?"

"Millie is maybe wanting to do research, like she say—maybe work for you during summer, or for a judge—I don't know."

"First, let me ask you something, Peck—and no bullshit," Lily Cup said. "Was it true, you know, what I heard about how you caught the guy who stole Gabe's pills a year ago, under that bridge?"

"For true, cher."

"Like did Millie really follow you and carry your bag when you killed the dog with the baseball bat?"

"Dog was Rottweiler, attacking us, dass for true. I bonk him dead."

"And she saw the whole thing and didn't scream or run away?"

"She saw more, cher. She saw Peck fight the knife man who had a machete and Peck tie him up in his trailer."

"And she wasn't afraid?"

"She was plenty afraid, but always by my side, and we did it good, with the pill stealer tied up."

"Did it? You mean—what do you mean?"

Peck grinned.

"Oh, that! Like, you did it? Right there?"

Peck lifted his glass of wine and smiled.

"Whoo hoo!" Lily Cup said.

Elizabeth gasped. "The, how you say, bad man was watching while you made love?"

Peck clicked his glass on her glass, then on Lily Cup's.

"That settles it. I'm hiring the bitch. Give me her number. I'm going to have her meet you here and help you do research—help you drive while you're looking around."

Peck looked at Elizabeth for an opinion.

"Invite her to stay, Peck. Millie is welcome to stay with us."

"Won't that be a little awkward with your man?" Lily Cup asked.

"You know about...?" Elizabeth asked.

"Peck, Sasha, Memphis, remember?" Lily Cup asked. "I think she got him drunk. He told her everything."

"Perhaps I can explain two people, like a couple, quite easily. Explaining only one would be hard," Elizabeth said.

"She's smart, Peck. Hang on to her friendship."

"Peck always will."

"What are you both doing tomorrow?" Lily Cup asked.

"I go see the tarot lady again," Peck said.

"So, what's next with tarot lady?" Lily Cup wanted to know.

"We're both going in the morning to see her," Peck said.

"You have an empty sofa, Elizabeth?" Lily Cup asked.

"I do."

"I'm going with you both in the morning. I want to meet your tarot reader, Peck. Maybe I can help."

Lily Cup picked Peck's cellphone up from the table and scrolled through it. She pushed a button and put it to her ear.

"Hi sweetie," Millie said.

"I'm not your Peck, Millie. This is Lily Cup."

"Hi, I was thinking of you, and..."

"Peck told me you want a summer job."

"Yes, oh that would be so good."

"You're hired. I'll wire travel money. Where are you, anyway?"

"I'm in Waco, Texas."

"Do they have an airport in Waco?"

"I catch a bus to New Or-lee-anhs."

"I want you to catch a bus to Baton Rouge. I'll call you tomorrow to explain."

Lily Cup gave Millie her cell number.

"Text me your full name so I'll have your number and can send money, and I'll be in touch."

"Thank you, thank you," Millie said.

"We're out at dinner. We'll be late. Peck'll call you tomorrow after we have a meeting we have to go to, and I'll call you when I get back to New Orleans tomorrow afternoon."

"Tell Peck I love him."

"I'll tell him—and he loves you too, sweetie. Night, night."

Lily Cup smiled at Peck and set the phone down in front of him.

"Now, then," Lily Cup said. "That's out of the way, and we have a bottle and a half left, and we have the promise of crepes with cream and jam – what say you both we head to the apartment for our treats?"

"*Ça m'a l'air bien*," Elizabeth said. ("Sounds good.")

"*Oui*," Peck said.

The dinner's finale of pear salad with Roquefort was put before each of them, and they celebrated future great adventures with a toast and a salute of salad forks.

Elizabeth smiled at the fun of an evening out with real people who talked to each other and shared thoughts and ideas, having real fun.

Lily Cup told stories of cases she has solved and of criminals she has gotten off of death row.

While Lily Cup distracted Peck with her tales of the law, Elizabeth would lift the bottle of wine and fill three glasses.

They traded stories, Lily Cup of defending a gambler of shooting a card cheat, Peck of getting bitten by a snapper and Elizabeth of burning a poached salmon. They broke into laughter and thought of more stories and the ice was broken. After their salads they stood, locked arms and followed the Louisiana moon on their walk to the apartment.

Elizabeth switched a lamp on in the living room and then the kitchen lights. She rummaged two cabinets looking for seasonings and her crepe pan. Peck went back into the bedroom.

"This is a nice apartment, right downtown," Lily Cup said.

"It's close to my school, and now my work," Elizabeth said. "I like it."

Lily Cup asked where the bathroom was and managed to find it in the dark hall and bedroom.

"Peck's conked out on the bed with one shoe in his hand," Lily Cup said. "He's out like a light."

"Oh my, he'll blame the wine," Elizabeth said.

"Do you have any cognac?"

"I do."

"What's say we forget the crepes and sit on the floor with some cognac and talk?"

Lily Cup removed her jacket and set it on the arm of the sofa and they kicked off their shoes and squatted on the floor like campfire girls holding snifters of cognac and they talked about Baton Rouge, about what a sous chef does and how hard it was to get into law school.

"Are you in love with Peck?" Lily Cup asked.

"I love him, but I'm not in love with him, if that makes sense."

"It makes perfect sense. How long have you two known each other?"

"Oh my, it's been maybe seven years, maybe more. I met him when I lived in Anse La Butte."

"So, he was a babe in the woods?"

Elizabeth blushed.

"Do you think you were his first?"

"I definitely was. I could tell."

"You popped him? Yum! So how was it? Like how did it play out first time? Was it a quickie and he fell asleep, or was there a big seduction scene?"

"We got in the tub together, I washed his back and he told me stories. I let him watch me shave my legs."

"Your legs and...?"

"Yes."

Lily Cup raised her snifter and clanked the one in Elizabeth's hand.

"Did he go bananas?"

"Banana might be the wrong, how you say, expression—but yes, William showed a great deal of interest."

"Did you do it in the tub?"

"No. He looked big and I wasn't sure if I could take it without some practice."

Lily Cup guffawed. "So you both decided to go to a gym and work out?"

"I toweled him down."

"By down you mean?"

"How you say, blow dry?"

"Oh, a girl after my own heart."

Elizabeth nearly choked on a sip in her mouth. She swallowed, set the glass down and went through a silent giggle with lips pursed.

"Well we have Peck in common just between us girls. I had him the first night I met him too, but I was drunk," Lily Cup said.

"When was that?"

"Last year."

"And he seduced you?"

"Well, it was more like he asked me where the men's room was and I took him to the lady's room and seduced him on the sink."

They poured more cognac and discussed calorie counts of shellfish and seafood. By 2:00 a.m. they had emptied the bottle and were on to finishing the open bottle of wine with two glasses left in it, and they spoke of how Elizabeth was going to go about breaking up with her man on the rig.

By 2:30 a.m. Lily Cup had to pee and she reported that Peck was asleep in his clothes and wouldn't it be polite of them to take his clothes off?

In the dark, with only the hall light on, they had him down to his skivvies when his eyes opened enough to see them both standing there. He rolled over and closed his eyes again.

The ladies looked at each other.

"Rock, paper, scissors?" Lily Cup chided.

"Let's drink cognac," Elizabeth said.

By 3:34 a.m. they were asleep, and from that moment forward, on this particular bend in Huckleberry's Mississippi River, not even the gods of night could predict what legends were seeded from quiet secrets shared in a second-floor apartment in Baton Rouge.

CHAPTER 45

AUDREY, I JUST WANTED YOU TO MEET my good frien' who helps Peck," Peck said.

Peck introduced Lily Cup to Audrey. He described a special good friend who has helped him in the past and how she is worried about him and asked if she could meet Audrey to talk. Lily Cup offered her hand.

"Hi Audrey—Elizabeth has said nice things. I wanted to meet and maybe have a few words before you got started today and I drive to New Orleans," Lily Cup said.

"Nice to meet you. Peck and Elizabeth, why don't you go to the kitchen, take a seat and have some coffee or there's fresh squeezed orange juice while we chat out here," Audrey said. "I'll come get you when we're ready."

Peck followed Elizabeth through the house.

"Peck, maybe orange juice for you. It's in the fridge. Coffee is a stimulant. Best you don't drink any more coffee this morning," Audrey said.

Lily Cup had picked up and was admiring a set of oyster-shell pink plastic rosary beads from the shelf holding a statue of the Virgin Mary.

"You may keep it," Audrey said.

Lily Cup opened her purse, pulled a ten and set it on the table. She held the rosary in her hand, rolling beads between her thumb and finger.

"My best friend and I sit on the roof under full moons and star-gaze and wonder about the supernatural. I'm no expert, but I do believe in it," Lily Cup said.

"It's always been a wonder to me. I find searching for answers fulfilling somehow," Audrey said. "How can I help you?"

"I've been a criminal attorney for some time," Lily Cup said. "I'm conflicted between what I've learned about the darker side of some of the regions in Acadiana over the years and the journey Peck is about to head out on."

"Let's sit over here," Audrey said.

"There was that serial killer who lured his victims with the promise of sex, tied them up—I don't remember how many, twenty or so—and cut their throats or strangled them," Lily Cup said.

"How tragic," Audrey said.

"I hear it all in Angola prison. One, I heard was a wise guy disposing bodies on carnivore feral pig farms. Another, when in the old days they would execute enemies with their feet in cement and drop them overboard—now victims being pushed out of low-flying airplanes deep into swamps after the advance plane signals an alligator congregation below."

"What a morbid world you must witness," Audrey said.

"I picked it, it didn't pick me," Lily Cup said. "If I can help one innocent person break the shackles of so many misunderstood public perceptions of what poverty actually is and that it is not a disease but a symptom of despair, it makes my effort worth it. Being poor does not mean a person is criminally oriented."

"And the criminals?" Audrey asked.

"Being a criminal doesn't preclude you from being defended."

"You're worried about Peck going back into these swamps?" Audrey asked.

"In New Orleans, most violence is drug-related. Peck would avoid that world. But there is a *Gris Gris* in the swamps by their almost prehistoric nature, and it's the bayous where there's a frightening anonymity. I live in a world that is reminded of the silt and darkness of the bayou and swamp. I hear about it in Angola."

"Are you suggesting you don't want me to help Peck explore his past because of the physical dangers in the swamps?" Audrey asked.

"I think what I'm trying to say is it frightens me to see Peck exploring. Exploring can be fraught with danger. If he doesn't know where he's going he'll be exploring," Lily Cup said.

"But if we can give him specific destinations to go to, there would be less danger?" Audrey asked.

"Yes. Exactly," Lily Cup replied.

"I understand," Audrey said.

"Can this be done, or am I deluding myself, hoping for the impossible?"

"With hypnosis, I believe it can be a definite possibility. I've seen it work many times, and I think Peck would be a good candidate for it. There is something eternally spiritual about him. He's of the mind."

"I've heard Peck described quite like that in different words. You express it well. I see him as a man of nature, of God and of the wind and the rain," Lily Cup said. "While we would hide from lightning, Peck would be of a mindset to lean against a tree or fence post and watch thunder and lightning split a sky open and he'd wait through it for the full moon to once again reappear."

"Do you believe in tarot?" Audrey asked.

"I believe in spiritual magnetism and of the windows that tarot opens to little rooms in our brains making us think. So yes, I do."

"The last card Peck selected yesterday was a destiny card. What card do you suppose he selected?" Audrey asked.

"Will I faint?"

"He picked the Moon card."

Rosary in hand, Lily Cup blessed herself.

"In the name of the Father, Son, and Holy Ghost," Lily Cup said.

"He told me the moon is his momma," Audrey said.

"Is that all he told you it was?"

"Yes."

"Let me tell you things for the hypnotist. By the way, will the hypnotist be a medically licensed psychiatrist?"

"If his budget would allow, it could be," Audrey said.

Lily Cup handed Audrey a business card.

"Make that happen and send me the bill. I'll get it paid."

"Very good."

"I don't know any of the circumstances of his birth, but I do know his birth certificate says race unknown. I'm not certain what he will remember from back then. I do know there was an Alayna Prudhomme somewhere near Bayou Sorrell and Choctaw. I believe she was what he called a foster nanna, but there are no records of an adoption or of his being in foster care. I do know from his own account he was chained under a back porch by some fisherman with a padlocked dog collar and he would look up at the full moon and talk to his momma by way of the moon. I also know they would tie his hands and drag him behind boats trolling for alligators when he was a child. They'd tape his mouth to keep him from screaming."

"I find it interesting that you know of this Alayna Prudhomme, and yet he's never mentioned that name to me. He's only mentioned a foster nanna," Audrey said.

"In eight months he's learned to read and write and he gets his GED this month. I could see why he'd block out his childhood," Lily Cup said.

"In eight months he learned to read? Such a passion he must have. We should be so lucky to have such a passion."

"He has an amazing mind," Lily Cup said. "I sometimes wonder if it's wise to encourage him to learn about his past."

"He'll always wonder, and until he knows, it could haunt him if he didn't at least try."

"Has he mentioned Millie?"

"He's mentioned her, yes. Are they close?"

"He's flipped for her—almost a year now. She was the start of this whole thing. She asked him if she could meet his mother."

"I'm certain her asking wasn't meant to be spiteful."

"I'm sure. They're talking about getting married. Most any girl would ask the same thing."

"Yes."

"How about my idea of Millie traveling with him to help with research and the driving?" Lily Cup asked.

"I think it could go a long way to build a strong, lasting bond between them, if the girl is meant for him and it would protect him and allay your fears."

"How would it protect him?"

"By virtue of his nature he'd go out of his way to protect her. That would keep him from being distracted. It would help keep him from putting either of them in harm's way."

"You're very good," Lily Cup said.

"I majored in psyche at LSU. I don't practice, I enjoy tarot insights."

"You are good because you care."

"I've been at this for some time now. I can always tell the differences between the couple who come in on a date like I'm a carnival reader, wanting to hear that they will live happily ever after if one of them would commit. I also know when there is a depth to my work when it comes to persons in situations like Peck or Elizabeth. There is much reward deep in my soul for helping people like them."

"And the rosary beads and the blessed Virgin Mary? Do you tie religion in?"

"Religion isn't an occult here when I read. By displaying my Catholicism, I try to project a message that a guide for happiness is the Ten Commandments—and in any religion – Christian or Jew or Hindu, whatever."

"Elizabeth is a beautiful woman," Lily Cup said.

"Such a beauty, inside and out," Audrey agreed.

"I wonder why they aren't together?" Lily Cup asked.

"Peck means the world to Elizabeth, and he means so much because he's comfortable knowing exactly what he is to her. Two closer friends you will search long and hard to find...but both he and Elizabeth know he is one color on her palette, and he knows that Elizabeth is an artisan of a world that will discover her one day."

"One color," Lily Cup said. "I like that Peck is secure in his own skin. It's so refreshing."

"That one color, his, will always be on her palette. He will always be a part of her life."

"Always goes such a long way, doesn't it?" Lily Cup asked.

"She speaks of him almost with reverence. They are blessed to have found each other. It was in the stars for them," Audrey said.

"In the moon?" Lily Cup asked.

Audrey started and held her hand to her mouth, looking at Lily Cup in awe for the depth of her perception.

"The Moon card," Audrey said.

"I feel good," Lily Cup said. "Elizabeth did well finding you, Audrey. Let me go say goodbye to them and be off."

"Do come by whenever you get to Baton Rouge. You are a most interesting woman. We can do lunch."

Lily Cup made her way back into the kitchen. Peck was sitting with a glass of water; Elizabeth had a cup of coffee. They both stood when she walked in.

"She's fabulous. She's a caring reader with real depth. I may have her read for me some time."

"I like coming to her," Elizabeth said.

"Peck, you be patient. She's getting an appointment with a doctor who might be able to hypnotize you and bring you the information you'll need for going back. I'll see Millie comes to go with you."

"Is she coming here?" Peck asked.

"No, New Orleans, first."

"Does she know? You say last night Baton Rouge."

"I'll tell her about this when we can sit down and talk. I don't want to just throw it at her over the phone."

"Good idea, cher."

"I'll call her when I get to my office and have her come to New Orleans first. She can stay at your place with Gabe. I'll put her to work in my office for colleagues until you have a better grasp on where it is you have to go. Then I'll drive her up and drop her off, or Sasha will."

"Peck drank too much wine last night. Dass for true," Peck said with a sheepish grin.

"Do you remember anything about last night?" Lily Cup asked.

"Nah, nah," Peck said. "I remember eating is all, and you calling Millie."

"Then I'd say you had just enough of the wine—right, Elizabeth?"

Elizabeth smiled.

"*La prochaine fois, c'est moi qui cuisine*," Elizabeth said. ("Next time I cook.")

Lily Cup kissed Peck on both cheeks. He kissed hers in return. She did the same with Elizabeth. They followed her into the reading room and waved goodbye.

"Did you remember to bring maps, Peck?" Audrey asked.

Peck pulled three copies of maps from an envelope and set them side-by-side on the table.

"Let's sit at the table," Audrey said.

"May I ask what we are to do today?" Elizabeth asked.

"Today I'd like to make a list of words that might stir memory in Peck's subconscious. Words the hypnotist may or may not use in helping Peck remember," Audrey said.

"When we do it?" Peck asked.

Audrey brought her cellphone from the side table drawer and turned the volume up. She pressed a button.

"Dr. Price's office, may I help you?"

"Audrey here."

"Oh hi, how are you?"

"Doing well, thank you. I have a man who I need to set an appointment for a hypnotherapy session as soon as possible. Can one be arranged?"

"What's the patient's name?"

"Boudreaux Clemont Finch."

"May I tell Dr. Price what the nature of your concern is, Audrey?"

"He's twenty–four. I think it would be easiest to say childhood abuse."

"One moment please, I'll check his schedule."

"Thank you."

"Audrey, would tomorrow between twelve-thirty and three p.m. work for you? Dr. Price would want to meet with you from twelve-thirty to one p.m. and with Mr. Finch from one to three."

"That will be perfect."

Audrey ended the call. "It's set then for tomorrow."

"Will I need to be there?" Elizabeth asked.

"Not unless you want to. Right now, I want to make the list of words for Dr. Price. Can you help?"

One by one, Elizabeth listed the words and names she had learned from knowing Peck almost ten years and from several hours in the library with him.

"Carencro, nanna Prudhomme, Atchafayalaya River, Lake Maurepas, Frenchman Settlement, Killian..."

Audrey patiently waited as they thought, and she wrote down each word, occasionally looking into Peck's eyes sympathetically. After Elizabeth had exhausted her memories, she paused.

"Bayou Chene," Peck said.

"Oh—and weeps," Elizabeth said.

"Weeps?" Audrey asked.

"Yes—like the song—Willow weeps for me," Elizabeth said.

Audrey made a note of it.

They chatted a while, Audrey jotting things down and describing what Peck might expect in tomorrow's hypnotherapy. Peck paid what he owed, and he and Elizabeth walked home without speaking. She splashed her face and changed into her chef school uniform and headed to school.

"Want to do Bistro tonight, Peck?"

"*Oui*, cher."

"Why don't you get some rest? We were up late last night."

Elizabeth smiled and closed the door behind her.

CHAPTER 46

HELLO?" Peck asked.

"Were you ever going to call me?" Millie asked.

"We just gotted home, Millie. How you are?"

"I'm lonely."

"I'm sorry."

Peck unbuttoned and dropped his jeans to his ankles, preparing to take a shower.

"Seems like I've been waiting for hours."

He sat on the sofa, stretched to reach a side pillow and folded it behind his head as he lay back.

"We talk now. All you want."

"I'm happy Lily Cup called me last night about working for her. Won't it be fun?"

"She happy too, cher."

"If you show me how, I can cook for you and Gabe."

"I can show you. Gabe knows too."

"I can't wait to see you. I'm looking at bus schedules to Baton Rouge after I go to the library."

Peck knew Lily Cup had a change of plans and was going to have Millie go to New Orléans first, but as he wasn't certain, he decided not to confuse Millie by opening it up.

"I'm nervous," Millie said.

"Don't be nervous, cher."

"I want to make a nice impression—do a good job."

"You will, no worries."

"Like what does she wear to the office?"

"Lily Cup dresses good—business clothes, lady suits, ya know."

"So, not jeans, things like that?"

"Nah, nah—dressy."

"Mommy will send things."

"Wait for Lily Cup to call you," Peck said. "She just left Baton Rouge and should be in New Or–lee–anh soon."

"I got a C in French, Peck. Will you just hate me?"

"Nah, nah."

"I'm so embarrassed."

"Peck will larn you French."

"You mean teach me French."

"See? Already my Millie teach me English, so I teach you the French."

She asked about Elizabeth and was he alone to talk, and she learned which jams were best on crepes and how to get a perfect lace in a crepe without burning it by gently rocking the pan above the burner. They spoke of Steinbeck and *Cannery Row* and of soft-shelled crabs and would chickens eat the okra seed if the garden wasn't fenced and how rice came from wet paddies called marshland and not swamps and how crawfish could be farmed with rice.

They mused about baby names and whether Peck would walk or drive to Tulane. Millie's schoolwork was important to her sense of worth, just as Peck's keeping his promises of growing and learning were to him. It would be another year before she could live with him full-time. He told of the x in downtown Baton Rouge, and did she know Baton Rouge meant *red stick*, and she suggested colors for curtains in Peck's room in New Orleans.

The warmth of the call wasn't the small talk or the sounds of voices, and it wasn't the topics. It was being together, like logs on a fire, if only by phone, that made them feel whole. They expressed their love with a softness in tone as if their heads were on the same pillow, and Millie stalled saying goodbye until her clock told her she had to go to the Baylor library to return books and Peck nodded off with his jeans at his ankles.

Peck was in the shower washing his hair after shaving when Elizabeth came into the bathroom bare breasted and lowered the chef pants and white cotton panties to her thighs and sat on the commode.

"It's me, Peck."

She stood, dropped the pants to the floor and removed her panties. She pulled the shower curtain aside just enough to step in behind Peck and put her hands on his shampoo-covered scalp and massage it with her fingers.

"*J'ai pensé a plus de mots*," Elizabeth said. ("I thought of more words.")

"*Mots*?" Peck asked. ("Words?")

"For tomorrow, in case you need more. Want to hear them?"

"Nah, nah, cher, not now."

"Give me the cloth," Elizabeth said.

Peck picked a cloth from the soap dish and handed it over his shoulder to her. She began at his shoulders and created suds and washed his back slowly.

"Are you frightened about tomorrow?"

"I don't know."

"Hypnosis doesn't hurt, Peck. I had it done once. It doesn't hurt. It's like you're asleep."

"Nah, nah—what if I die, cher?"

Elizabeth bolted. She pulled Peck's arm around until he was facing her.

"*Mon dieu*, you are not going to die. Hypnosis does not make you die, Peck."

Peck clenched his jaw, his eyes closed to keep soap away.

"What is it you're afraid of, Peck? Please tell me."

"Audrey say this man will, how you say, put me under like asleep, right?"

"Yes, and he only talks to you. He sits a distance away from you, so he can't hurt you."

"Audrey say I will remember t'ings, like being chained under gator man's porch."

"I'm sure you'll remember some things, yes. That will be good if you want to find your foster nanna."

"So, Peck could die—dass for true."

"*Je ne comprend pas.*" ("I don't understand.")

"English, cher."

"What do you mean you could die?"

"I can see the porch where he chained me again?"

"Maybe."

"I can see gator man again?"

"Maybe, but he can't hurt you."

"Gator man can tape Peck's mouth and tie my hands and pull Peck behind his pirogue looking for gators?"

"I guess, but..."

"Then Peck will die, cher. I maked myself die when he did that."

"I don't know how it works Peck, but I think you're allowed to ask the doctor to wake you so you don't have to be tied up. Ask him before you do anything. Then decide if you want to go through with it."

Peck raised his head back to rinse under the shower.

"Peck needs wine."

Elizabeth laughed. "You don't like wine, remember?"

"Peck need the wine tonight."

"Bistros, wine, and dinner, and maybe..." Elizabeth said.

"Maybe what?"

"Maybe I talk to the owner and he gives me a job as sous chef—or on salads."

"That would be good, *non?*"

"That would be good, *oui.* And we can talk and you tell me about your Millie, and we'll drink the wine and we get in the pool tonight?"

"No gators or snappers?"

Elizabeth reached and took William in hand with firm pulls and strokes.

"Only wild women with much wine."

Peck turned full circle in a final rinse and stepped out of the tub onto the towel on the floor. Elizabeth tied her hair in a knot on top of her head and let the shower splash her face.

"I feel like meat tonight, cher."

"Lamb chops with herbes de Provence. You will like them, Peck. You ever had lamb chops?"

"Nah, nah."

"They're good."

"Bistro?" Peck asked.

"*Oui,* very good."

While dressing, Peck saw that he had two calls from Lily Cup. He pressed the return button.

"Hey Peck," Lily Cup said.

"You in New Or–lee–anh, cher?"

"I've been here an hour or so, stopped over and saw Gabe. We talked about Millie coming and about the party for Sasha's engagement. He gave me a key for Millie."

"You need me?"

"I wanted to let you know Millie will be here late tomorrow night. The bus ride from Waco is about twelve hours. I'm only bringing her here just until you feel you are ready to go to wherever it is you have to go."

"Is that why you called me?"

"Sort of. I also wanted to ask you if you thought it would be a good idea or a bad idea for me and Sasha to have a talk with her. Give her some background about before you ran away when you were a kid."

Lily Cup paused and waited for a reaction.

"We wouldn't do it without your approval, Peck. Do you want to think it over and call me back when you decide yay or nay?"

"You plenty sm'at, dass for true, cher. I t'ink you know'd what to say, so it would be good. I t'ink it be hokay."

"It would be best this way. We don't want to scare her the minute she gets up there," Lily Cup said.

"*Oui.*"

"That's what I called about."

"Cher, do you read the tarot cards?"

"Sasha can—not so much me."

"Maybe she read cards for Millie before she comes here, maybe?"

"Does Millie drink?"

"She likes the frozen daiquiris."

"We'll take her to the roof and have a séance. Don't worry about a thing."

Peck finished the call and he and Elizabeth left the apartment to walk to the Bistro. The night air was dry and warm, the stars were there, hidden by an occasional streetlamp. Elizabeth asked the host to send the owner or manager to the table when they had time. Their table was in a corner and the unlit candle was lighted and placed in the center. Elizabeth opened the menu and started to speak in French.

"Oh, *oui,* English...sorry," she started.

She ordered a bottle of red Bordeaux, escargot for two, and a plate of cheeses and French bread for starters. The server expressed his approval and stepped from the table. Elizabeth watched him walk away, and then she folded her arms on the table, leaning in.

"Peck, it's time."

"It's time?"

"I'm going to tell him."

"Hanh?"

"My man on the rig."

"What about him, cher?"

"It's time I tell him."

"You mean...?"

"It's over between us. I think he knows it. I know it. It has to be said."

Peck reached for her hand.

"You're not doing this for Peck?"

"I'm doing it for me. I want to be free to do things I want to do. I'm going to be a good chef. I want to travel."

"When will you call him?"

"I respect him too much for that. I'll wait for when he comes back."

"Dass good."

"I really think he knows. We hardly talk on the phone anymore. He'll tell me the weather offshore or I'll tell him what I'm cooking at school."

"Where will you live?"

"The apartment is in my name. I paid the deposit and six months in advance when we moved in. He'll move. Probably to New Orleans. He would like that better."

The wine was opened and a sample poured and approved. Peck lifted his glass.

"*À ma meilleur amie courageuse. Ma deuxiéme cousine pour toujours,*" Peck said. ("To my brave best friend. My second cousin always.")

"You mean kissing cousin, don't you?"

"Ahh *oui, oui* – kissing cousin."

They sipped their wine.

"Peck, know what I want to do tonight?"

"What?"

"First I want to enjoy the escargots."

"*Oui.*"

"Then Peck will have the lamb chops herbes de Provence and Elizabeth will have the duck."

"This is your night, cher. Anything tonight for my frien'."

"Will you swim with me later, Peck?"

"*Oui.*"

"*Nue?*" ("Naked?")

"Is there any other way, cher?"

Piping hot garlic butter, for dipping the crusts of baguette to best savor the snails was the perfect start to a beautiful evening. Elizabeth putting the rig out of her mind and Peck putting tomorrow from his. Tonight, they celebrated the death the tarot cards predicted. They knew that with it came a new life, a new vision. It was all good. Tonight, they belonged to the stars.

CHAPTER 47

PECK WAS IN THE WAITING ROOM while Audrey and Dr. Price visited in a small conference room. When they came out, Audrey kissed Peck on both cheeks and said goodbye.

"Have Elizabeth call me," Audrey said.

"Yes'm."

Dr. Price shook hands with Peck. "Audrey tells me you go by Peck, while your given name is Boudreaux Clemont Finch," Dr. Price said.

"Yes, sir," Peck said.

"Do you have one you are more comfortable with, may I ask?" the doctor asked.

"Peck is hokay, Doctor," Peck said.

"Tell me, does Peck date back to your childhood or was it a nickname you took on as you got older?"

"Mrs. Feller, church school I t'ink," Peck said.

"That'll be fine, then. Peck, it is. Let's step into our small conference room and talk."

It was a comfortable room with pictures of honeybees on red roses and birdhouses on the side of a tree—–decorated to not arouse either suspicion or angst. Peck handed the doctor a sheet of paper Elizabeth had printed out from her computer—the words that might be of help to the doctor. Dr. Price studied them without comment. He set the paper on the table face-down.

"Peck, I think a good start would be for me to tell you a little about me, and what I hope to accomplish today...and how we go about it. I would like you to ask me anything. It could be things you're concerned about, or just things or procedures you want to know more about."

"Yes, sir."

"My name is Dr. John A. Price. I'm well aware the word *doctor* might intimidate some, so it's not necessary that you call me 'doctor.' 'Mr. Price' will do. I studied medicine at Tulane Medical University and got my medical degree at LSU, right here in Baton Rouge."

Peck started and sat up straight. "You go to Tulane, doctor? Dass for true?"

"I did."

"Peck is going to Tulane night school, in New Or–lee–anh, start in June," Peck said.

"That can only mean one thing, Peck."

"What?"

"Us Tulane men have to stick together. From now on you call me John. Okay with you?"

"Hokay with me."

"Okay with me, John," the doctor said.

Peck beamed.

"Hokay with me, John."

"This is a good start. Now Peck, hypnotherapy is just a big word for trying to get you to relax."

"Relax?"

"Do you sometimes take a nap in the middle of the day? Other times you just stretch out on the bed or a sofa and take a nap?"

"Yes."

"Well, hypnotherapy is trying to relax you so you can take a nap."

"I can did that," Peck said.

"But the difference between hypnotherapy and the everyday nap is that I'll try to get you to talk in your sleep."

Peck listened with an inquisitive eye.

"You see, when a person talks while they are wide awake, that's their conscious mind helping them remember things and what to say. But when a person talks in their sleep, that is their subconscious mind talking."

"What does sub mean?" Peck asked.

"Sub means lower, or deeper. Subconscious means to go deeper into your memory. Like a submarine goes deep in the water."

Peck stiffened.

"I said submarine and you reacted, Peck. Does that word, submarine, bother you in some way or remind you of something bad?"

"Gator man tied my hands and threw me in the bayou and pulled me with his pirogue for gator bait. Dass for true. Peck died ever' time, dass for true."

"Well this is a different sub than what you're describing, Peck. This sub will only be in your brain, not in any water, bayou, or swamp. You have my word."

"For true?"

"For true, Peck. If your subconscious even so much as puts your toe near the water, I'll simply wake you and we'll start all over another time if we have to."

"So, Peck won't die?"

"Not on my watch, Peck."

"So good. Peck is good. You can do it."

"Shall we get started?"

They stood, shook hands, and went into a room with a leather-upholstered chaise for the patient with a leather chair beside it. Peck asked about the pictures on the walls and if John had to take English at the university. Doctor John talked about trying to learn how to fly-fish and he was pretty good with English and words because he had to take so much Latin, but he couldn't spell.

Peck lay on the chaise with his eyes closed. In thirty to forty-five-second segments each, the doctor asked Peck to tighten his feet and toes and then in about a minute relax them; then tighten his calves for a minute and relax them. Then his thighs, his stomach muscles, his chest, and each hand and arm in turn. The doctor asked him to tighten his lips and hold for a minute, and then his brow for a full minute. When the doctor said to relax his brow, Peck fell into a deep sleep, as though he was floating on a feather cloud. The room stayed silent while the doctor watched.

"Peck, I want you to go back to the earliest you can remember. Travel back through your mind to the first thing you can remember."

"*Je suis la*," Peck said. ("I am there.")

"Where are you, do you know?"

"*Je ne sais pas.*" ("I don't know.")

"Peck, can you tell me what you see?"

"*Maman.*" ("Mamma.")

"You see mamma. Do you see anything else?"

"*Je vois la lune.*" ("I see the moon.")

"Peck, can you look around where you are?"

"*Oui.*"

"Look carefully. Are there any words you can see? Words on books you see, envelopes, on signs or maybe wall calendars."

"*Il fait somber.*" ("It's dark.")

"Do you see any words at all, Peck?"

"*Oui.*"

"What words do you see, Peck?"

"*Ward, je vois ward.*" ("Ward, I see ward.")

"Are you saying *word*, Peck?"

"Ward."

"Can you tell me how to spell *ward*, Peck?"

"W-A-R-D."

"I want you to go to another place now. I want you to go to a place where you see mamma and the moon again."

"*Saule pleureur.* Peck see'd the willer tree."

"Is the willow tree an important tree, Peck?"

"Mamma nanna houseboat tied with rope to tree."

"Peck, are you on the houseboat with your mamma nanna?"

"*Oui.*"

"What are you doing?"

"Highchair."

"You're in a highchair?"

"*Oui.*"

"Are you eating?"

"Nah, nah. Mamma nanna has mail from man come by."

"The mailman?"

"*Oui.*"

"From where you're sitting, can you see any mail? Letters? Envelopes? Can you see any words from where you are? On books, on walls?"

"*Oui.*"

"What can you see? Can you tell me?"

"A paper."

"A paper. Is there anything on the paper?"

"Killian National Bank."

"Killian National Bank. Very good. Does it say anything else?"

"Alayna Prudhomme."

"Alayna Prudhomme. This is good. Does it say anything else?"

"Maurice Pontelban. It say Maurice Pontelban."

"Peck, now this is important. Can you tell me how Pontelban is spelled? Can you see it well enough?"

"p-o-n-t-e-l-b-a-n-m-d."

"Peck, look at that word again and tell me how it is spelled one more time."

"p-o-n-t-e-l-b-a-n-m-d"

"Now Peck, take your time and look about where you are right now. Just look about."

The doctor could see Peck's pupils rolling under his eyelids.

"Peck, when you're ready, you can wake up."

His eyes opened.

"How do you feel, Tulane man?"

"Peck feels good, cher...oops, I mean...?

"Cher will do fine—or John. Whatever suits you. I'm going to my office to jot down a few things. Take your time. When you're ready why don't you go to that small conference room area and have a seat? I'll be in in a minute and we'll talk about what I've learned."

"Can I see if Elizabeth is here, and can she come with me?"

"Is it important to you that Elizabeth be with you?"

"Oh, *oui.* She my good frien'. Elizabeth got me to go to Audrey."

"By all means, bring her in, if she's here. There's coffee somewhere. Ask the girl at the desk. I'll be no longer than fifteen minutes or so."

Peck stood and tightened his buckle. He stepped out into the waiting room where Elizabeth was standing, arms outstretched. She wrapped them around Peck and nuzzled his neck in a complete silence.

She lifted her head back.

"*Comment vas-tu?*" Elizabeth asked. ("Are you okay?")

"I'm good, cher. So good."

"And you didn't...you know?"

"Peck didn't die. Not ever today."

"Do we leave now?"

"No. He wants to talk and he say it good you come too. Hokay with you?"

Peck led Elizabeth into the conference room. He passed on getting coffee, as none would come close to his Cajun chicory home brew. Dr. Price came into the room, shook Elizabeth's hand and sat.

"Peck, I feel good about our session today. How about you?"

"So good."

"I want to start by telling you that from my experience, if one uses an approach to find the seed first, the plant will grow on its own accord. What this means is I think if I can tell you the beginnings of your life as your subconscious remembers it, that alone will give you the tools internally to slowly remember more...and you will discover more each day."

"Peck didn't die?"

"Peck didn't die, and the fact is you didn't see this gator man fellow—not a pirogue and definitely no alligators."

"So good."

Dr. Price handed Elizabeth a small spiral pad and a pen.

"You may want to take some notes for your friend, Elizabeth."

He looked at Peck.

"Are you ready?"

"Peck is so ready."

"It's important you understand that what I tell you are my interpretations of what I think I heard listening to you answer my questions while you were under. Do you understand that?"

"*Oui.*"

"Peck, I have a feeling the woman who raised you is named Alayna Prudhomme."

"Dass for true. Mamma Nanna."

"Peck, I have a feeling this Alayna Prudhomme is your real mother."

Peck started. His fists clenched. He waited for more.

"Peck, I knew of your talking to the moon as if it were your momma."

"*Oui.*"

"And the moon would give you great comfort, especially when you were stressed or felt abandoned?"

"*Oui.*"

"Peck, you weren't saying momma nanna. You were saying *mamma* nanna."

"*Quoi?*" ("What?")

"You said *mamma*, and you could see the moon. Peck, mamma means a mother's breast milk for her baby. You said the room was dark. You were suckling and could see the moon. When you see the moon, you think of your mother."

A tear grew in Peck's eye. His head dropped. The tear rolled down his face as Elizabeth clenched his hand.

"Peck, you mentioned a Maurice Pontelban. You spelled it p-o-n-t-e-l-b-a-n-m-d. The MD at the end meant this Pontelban fellow was a doctor. You also mentioned the Killian National Bank. I called the bank and they said Maurice Pontelban was a doctor at a hospital near Choctaw."

"Choctaw. I know'd Bayou Sorrell and Choctaw."

"The banker told me that Dr. Pontelban passed away four years ago."

Peck wiped his eyes with his wrist.

"Peck, you saw the word *ward* when you spoke of your 'mamma' nanna. Dr. Pontelban worked at a woman's mental health hospital near Choctaw. The hospital was for women with mental issues. They first called it an insane asylum. Peck, you saw a sign that read 'Ward.' It was likely a psychiatric ward and your mother was breastfeeding you at night by a window—the woman who you call mamma nanna. I'm afraid your mamma nanna and Alayna Prudhomme are the same person—a patient in the mental hospital. You could have been born in that hospital."

Peck couldn't have been more stunned if an alligator had taken a leg off. Elizabeth held his arm with a hug.

"Peck, will this help get you started?"

Peck sat with a tear slipping down his cheek. Elizabeth dabbed it with a tissue. She kissed his cheek.

"Are you okay, Peck?" the doctor asked.

"It will help, *oui.* T'ank you."

"If you want to meet with me on a regular basis to work out some issues, I'm here for you, at any time."

Peck stood and shook the doctor's hand.

"Thank you, John."

Doctor Price smiled. Peck and Elizabeth went into the hall and rode the elevator in silence and stepped out onto the sidewalk. They crossed one street at the corner and came to a park with a tall bronze statue of Governor Huey Long, stopped and gazed.

"Can we go to Maison Lacour tonight?" Elizabeth asked. "My treat."

"Where Lily Cup taked us?"

"*Non, non, c'est un bon restaurant français,*" Elizabeth said. ("No, no, this is a fine French restaurant.")

"Will you order for me, cher?"

"Can we swim again? A long time tonight, and perhaps a shower and maybe crepes with jam?"

"And whipped cream?"

"*Mais oui...mais oui.*"

They held hands like school children and Peck walked briskly, running his fingers against the wrought iron fences they passed by like they were playing cards in a bicycle wheel, Elizabeth skipping from time to time. They didn't speak of it but they both knew change was coming for them both—good change. Peck now had a mother that he didn't know he had, and he knew where to go to find out more—and where to find her. Elizabeth was happy for Peck, while sad about some things he learned. But any answers to a lifetime of questions had to be good for the soul.

Tonight, she would celebrate her commitment to a new freedom and she would shower and wear provocative perfumes and her alluring imported black Chantilly lace bra and perhaps garter straps and sheer hosiery.

Tonight, Elizabeth would lasso a sensual encore of flavors for the palate and the whirling tornado that was now in Peck's brain—and she would ride the night wherever the winds pointed their sails.

Chapter 48

STANDING ON THE SMALL BALCONY in Baton Rouge, Peck watched the setting sun rest on the Mississippi River in a quiet moment of glassy calm; the crawling waterway was that one vein Peck imagined physically connecting him to Millie this night. His Millie, whose bus was just now driving through the city traffic into the soul of New Orleans. It was as if mythical candles were being gathered along the shoreline by spirits for a special lighting.

Something was in the air. It was like how we feel on the last day of school, or after a first prom, a first kiss; how it feels when you sit by the window while your plane lands in a brand-new city. This evening was spoken for and with it was a promise of the biggest full moon ever, just to match the mood. Acadiana and Southern Louisiana was about to celebrate Millie's arrival in a big way, a Sasha and Lily Cup way in the heartland of jubilee, the Big Easy, while miles away Elizabeth and Peck, in downtown Baton Rouge, would be savoring herbs of their new life awareness with fine Bordeaux and decadent chocolate souffles with Grand Marnier Cordon Rouge.

In that apartment of so many memories on Baton Rouge's South Fourteenth street, the shower was recently turned off to a drip, but sink and door mirrors were coated with a steam of concealing opaque, while Elizabeth stood in the tub, her hair wrapped in a towel, shaving her legs and her lovely. Peck was now in the living room finishing his hundredth pushup on the floor. He could always think best while doing pushups.

By watching his face, one couldn't discern if he was thinking of the road ahead to finding his mother, or of the mischief he saw in Elizabeth's eyes when she stepped into the bathroom. It was the inviting smile in her eyes that caught his imagination. Add to that the blind embossed, ivory-toned gift box wrapped in ribbon on the coffee table with his name on the card. In its tissue papers lay an imported black Mouline fabric shirt with black onyx buttons. Peck held the shirt and felt the texture of its collar and buttons with a look on his face as if it was likely that this was to be a joyous evening of *adieu, mais pas au revoir.* (farewell, but not goodbye.)

As he lifted the shirt and unbuttoned its collar it dawned on him this special evening could only end one way...at dawn. Peck set the shirt on the sofa and dropped to the floor for fifty more.

On Loyola Avenue in New Orleans Sasha parked her light blue Bentley convertible with top down in front of the bus depot and waited, listening to jazz while Lily Cup went in to find Millie. They came out with Millie pulling her bag. Lily Cup opened the car door and Millie climbed into the back seat.

"It's so good to see you," Millie said.

"One bag for the whole summer?" Sasha asked.

"Mommy is sending my things for work."

"Did you bring your baby Charlie?"

"Charlie's in my bag," Millie said.

"My Teddy still sleeps with me," Lily Cup said. "He's pushing forty."

"I promise I'll look presentable soon," Millie said.

Sasha pulled the Bentley into traffic and toward Canal Street with a wry smile.

"You'll be presentable tonight, darling. You're in good hands," Sasha said.

"You thinking what I'm thinking you're thinking?" Lily Cup asked.

"Saks Fifth Avenue?"

"I thought so."

"I do have some nice things, I promise," Millie said.

"Honey, there's a full moon tonight and we have a séance planned on a rooftop. We three must always look our best in the light of the moon," Sasha said.

"For alone and on a rooftop?" Millie asked.

"For after, love, for when we go to Frenchmen Street and dance," Lily Cup said. "Gabe will be there."

Millie shrugged a relenting grin and sat back with her arm rested on the opened car window ledge.

"This is such a beautiful city," Millie said. "It's filled with so many chapters, like in a picture book."

"Driving through N'Orleans is like crawling through an attic," Lily Cup said. "Every neighborhood is opening another box of something timeless—something that was once a part of someone's life, that got stored and tucked away like memories. Good or bad memories, but regardless, they held memories in a person's life, and memories were always better times."

"That's beautiful," Millie said.

They bantered and laughed and spoke of architecture and of the sounds and how music on street corners reminded passersby that life was good, and they talked of how many different streetcar lines there were in New Orleans.

In Saks Fifth Avenue, Sasha did a beeline to Women's Wear with Millie and Lily Cup in tow like children on a field trip.

"Shoe size?" Sasha asked.

"Seven," Millie said.

"Dress?"

"Three."

"Bra?"

"Thirty-two C."

"Lily Cup, take our Miss Millie to a fitting room and camp there while I look. I'll hand things over the door for her to try for fit."

"But I—" Millie started.

"Save your breath," Lily Cup said. "Sasha is in Saks, and something always comes over her when we're in Saks. It's like she's rabid or something. That's how she is. Just go with the flow. Strip."

"Huh?"

"Strip."

"Everything?"

"Honey, strip to what you would be wearing if you were alone with Peck in the bedroom."

Millie grinned and pulled her T-shirt over her head and was unfastening her bra when two hands came over the top of the fitting room door, one hand holding a large plastic cup with rye on the rocks and the other a large, frosted frozen daiquiri. Lily Cup took them in hand and held them up like prizes.

"The only large every woman prays for in a fitting room," Lily Cup said.

Millie dropped her jeans to the floor and kicked them aside.

Lily Cup handed the daiquiri to Millie and settled on the stool by the door, sipping her rye. There was a hook holding empty hangers above her head.

"Lose the panties," Lily Cup said.

"Huh?"

"Off."

"Why?"

"Trust me, I just saw Sasha head to the lingerie counter. It's a mile long. This ain't Target." She pointed her cup at Millie's midsection.

Millie looked down at her panties.

"Drop 'em."

Millie hesitated, looked in the large cup in her hand and belted back a swig and followed that with another quick swallow that would keep her awhile. She handed the cup to Lily Cup while she took her panties to the floor and stood with her feet pigeon-toed, as if by holding her knees together she could hide her girl power. Lily Cup glanced over the beautiful, freckled body with perky, full young breasts and her eyes rested on Millie's pelvis.

"What's with the lady garden?" Lily Cup asked.

Millie jerked her hand to cover her crotch. "Well, one day I'll be on a farm, and I didn't think..."

"You were going to grow a bird nest for the farm?"

Millie started to giggle uncontrollably. She reached for the daiquiri and took another slug, this time spreading her legs to keep from falling. Three sets of panties and bras flew over the door.

"How're your drinks? Need anything?" Sasha asked from outside.

"We could use a weed-wacker," Lily Cup said.

With that, the New Orleans' night was broken open like a Humpty Dumpty cracked egg, and the ladies were ready for any omelet it might serve up. More drinks were followed by more laughter and more fittings of gorgeous lace undies, Parisian hosiery and Chanel evening wear, with and without straps.

Millie exaggerated poses in the mirror and admitted she had a lovely cleavage, but opted for conservative sexy, the shorter skirt and thigh-high look, and Lily Cup confessed she couldn't help, as her own taste was mostly in her mouth, and Sasha had dressed her since high school and hated the diamond brooch she wore and the white Nike driving shoes.

When Millie finally stepped through the fitting room door, her cinnamon hair combed back neatly with a Jeffersonian flair and tied with a black and red striped ribbon, she looked as an Audrey Hepburn with freckles might look in the same black

Chanel cocktail dress, hand-sewn, black lace stockings and Prada's finest red satin heels with ankle straps.

"You are such a beauty," Sasha said.

"She doesn't dye her hair," Lily Cup said.

Sasha picked from the four handbags in her hand and handed Millie a red satin Chanel bag as the fitting room door closed behind her.

"Didn't you have braces last time?" Lily Cup asked.

"I got them off three weeks ago," Millie said.

"You are a beauty."

"This has been so much fun, but my debit card has a limit, and I don't think—" Millie started.

"The outfit is a wedding present," Sasha said.

"For me? But Peck and I—"

"My wedding," Sasha said. "You'll look smashing walking down the aisle as my bridesmaid."

They first drove to Lily Cup's house.

"See you in an hour?" Sasha asked.

"I'll be there."

Sasha drove home to the Garden District.

While Millie explored the art and bric-a-brac in the living and dining rooms, Sasha dressed and made an entrance, delicately sliding her palm on the wrought-iron handrail of a winding staircase. In strapless Chanel she stepped from the bottom stair with a smile and fabled cleavage, setting a tone that the night was young, the moon was full, and it was meant for a dry martini and how lovely they both looked. She handed Millie a sealed deck of tarot cards to bring to the séance. Millie glanced in every mirror or reflective glass window or picture frame she could. She felt like the million dollars she looked like when they stepped from the house into a waiting limousine.

"Parking in the Quarter is such a pain," Sasha said.

"Is that where the rooftop is?" Millie asked.

"Yes. It has an umbrella table with chairs that won't rip our dresses and a box of candles. It's cozy."

"Do you like know somebody who lets you on their roof?" Millie asked.

"I do."

"That's awfully nice of them."

"Lily Cup," Sasha said.

"Lily Cup?"

"Lily Cup owns the building. My realty office manages the rentals."

Millie pulled a lighted mirror down from the ceiling and checked her makeup.

"I would have drinks for us in here, honey," Sasha said. "But dry-cleaning Chanel costs a mortgage, so I take no chances drinking in moving vehicles."

Millie sat up like royalty and watched through every window, catching lights and motions in a New Orleans night with a determination in her eyes that she would take in every minute, every sight, every sense and sound and enjoy every drip of it.

"When we go to Charlie's later, do you think someone will ask me to dance?" Millie asked.

"Count on it," Sasha said.

In Baton Rouge the maître d' let Elizabeth examine the Bordeaux label and then uncorked it.

"Do you mind decanting it?"

"Not at all, Miss."

Elizabeth explained to Peck that a decanted dry red was smoother because it breathed deeper breaths of air, or so it seemed to her. Once the ceremony was completed and they felt alone in the room filled with chatting, laughing lovers, and other patrons, Elizabeth lifted her glass in toast. Peck followed suit.

"To my new job at Bistro," she said. "You happen to be dining tonight with the brand-new sous chef."

"Oh, cher, this couldn't be better news. Everything is changing for us, dass for true," Peck said.

"*Ce soir, je me sens comme une femme*, Peck," Elizabeth said. ("Tonight, I feel like a woman, Peck.") Tonight, I feel fresh and flavorful and a bit sassy. Isn't it wonderful?"

"It is so wonderful. Such a day."

"And to think, I'm sitting at this table with all the lovely silver and wax candles and fine linens—across from such a sexy thing."

"Aw."

"Oh, not you, Peck. Did you think I was talking about you? *Mais non, mais non!* William. I was talking about William."

They guffawed and snorted and sipped their wine and lifted cheeses to smell the piquant and their cheeks would puff with a bite of baguette as they tried to finish a sentence, sometimes their own. The food moved from plate to palate and they talked of Paris and of how long cooking school was and of Tulane.

"Will you bring Millie to Paris?"

"Nah, nah. You say yourself Peck is, how you say, chopped liver? You only speak of William."

"Well, you're important too."

"I am, for true?"

"But of course, you are, you're William's driver. You're his portage." She giggled.

There was an air about the table that everything was fine in the world. Elizabeth could taste Paris and her corner café or bakeshop with the crepes and jams and French country mushroom soups with the richest of creams. Peck knew now his momma was in sight of the moon not far away, and he and Millie would see her soon, and didn't Elizabeth look like heaven, her green eyes inviting him with lips, glistened with a buttery hollandaise, closing on an asparagus stalk she held delicately in her fingers.

The French Quarter was busy with people in the streets milling about, listening to street performers or looking through the windows of antique shops. The limo stopped a block away as a group sat in a circle in the center of the street playing Dixieland for a growing crowd. Each musician had a can or jar on the ground before them in case anyone wished to show appreciation for their sounds.

Sasha's leg stepped out and with a hand from the driver she stood and adjusted her bodice and waist. To the onlookers' delight, Millie bounced across the back seat to the door almost as if she were in her shorts, and with an awkward step out her leg revealed red panties that matched her shoes and bag, fine hosiery, and a delightfully freckled bare thigh. She was none the wiser for the stir she caused and read the smiles on faces in the crowd as official welcomes into the Quarter. In a certain sense, they were.

Lily Cup's building in the Quarter had two elevators. One was installed with the building in the late 1930s. The other was Lily Cup's private elevator, less than ten years old. This private elevator required a key only three people had—Lily Cup, Sasha, and a neighbor's housekeeper, who cared for the plants on the roof garden. The two walked arm-in-arm and stopped to hear a riff of the Tuba Skinny jazz street band performers. Millie clapped her hands to the beat and rhythm with a delightful grin and bright, excited eyes, and Sasha swayed her hips, while looking through her purse for a fifty.

"Which can is for all of you," Sasha mouthed to the clarinetist.

The player, a young lady, lifted a finger from her clarinet and pointed to the large can in the center of the circle.

"Oh, can I do it?" Millie asked.

Sasha handed Millie the fifty. Millie added a ten from her bag and stepped between the tuba and trombone in grins, bent over with her Chanel doing a proper job of showcasing a delectable hint of bare thigh above exquisite French hose. The elevator door opened and they stepped in and pushed the button with the arrow pointing up.

"Lily Cup is here," Sasha said.

"How can you tell?"

"Smell the perfume?"

"I do."

The door opened to find the candle in its proper holder on the table, but unlit. Lily Cup was standing by the rail looking down into the street with her phone to her ear. She was in black tights with four-inch, black, sequined heels and a shimmering sleeveless top. She turned and held her index finger up to be patient while she finished a call she didn't seem to be talking on.

"Sit where the moon is to your best advantage," Sasha said.

Millie stepped behind one chair, then another and selected the second, pulled it and sat. Sasha lit the candle.

"Do you have the cards?" Sasha asked.

Millie took them from her bag and handed them over. Sasha broke the seal and took them out. While standing, she leaned and shuffled the deck four times on the tabletop and set them there.

"Okay, I'm ready," Lily Cup said.

Sasha pulled a chair and sat down.

"My, but don't you two look absolutely gorgeous," Lily Cup said.

"You look pretty amazing yourself," Millie said.

Lily Cup opened the door of a small refrigerator and pulled out a plastic tray with three drinks on it. She held it for Sasha and Millie to take theirs, and she set hers in front of the empty chair.

"No trial tomorrow, no clients to bail out of jail. Tonight we party and dance," Lily Cup said.

"We're dancing tonight," Sasha said. "Gabe is probably at Charlie's already, so let's get started."

"I'm ready," Millie said.

Sasha raised her martini in toast. Lily Cup and Millie followed suit.

"Millie, it's been a whirlwind year for you. It was just about ten months ago when you came into our lives like the most welcome child a family could ever have," Sasha said.

Millie started to tear up.

They each sipped to the thought and set their drinks on the table.

"Millie, I want you to take your mind back a whole year. If you do, you will see your life before Peck and us, your family here—and you will have it to compare with your life now."

"I can do that."

"As you do, I want you to think of the most important number you can think of—the first number that comes to your mind."

"Easy," Millie said.

One at a time she pointed at each of her friends at the table.

"One, two," Millie said. "Two is the number."

Sasha placed her palm on the tarot deck and fanned them across the table.

"Pick any two cards, Millie. Take your time. We have all night. But pick two and slide them out of the deck. Don't lift them."

Millie used the index finger of both hands and lowered them both to the fan of cards and pushed two cards at the same time to the tabletop. Sasha picked up the remaining cards and handed them to Lily Cup to put back in the case.

"Two cards will tell us a story tonight. A story of our sweet Millie and what lies ahead for her."

Millie reached to her right and took Lily Cup's hand and held it for security. Sasha turned both cards over and left them side-by-side, face-up.

"Oh my," Sasha said.

"Is that good?" Millie asked.

"Well this one is the Lover card. That looks pretty good to me."

"What does it mean?"

"The Lover card tells you that in the coming days and years you will have strengthening of an existing love relationship."

Millie beamed, holding fingers over her mouth to cover braces she had forgotten were no longer there.

"Peck?" Millie squeaked.

"Seems like," Sasha said.

"Watch the moon, everybody," Lily Cup said. "Let's watch for a shooting star."

Millie sat tall, her eyes embracing the thought of a lifetime with Peck and her body lurched when a star raced across the heavens, and she bounced in her chair while pointing up.

"There's one! I see one!"

"A shooting star," Lily Cup said.

"What's that mean?" Millie asked.

"So, because you saw it first, it will all come true for you."

Millie's palms touched her cheeks, tears in both eyes, evaporating in the gentle night's air.

"The second card is Nine of Pentacles," Sasha said. This is a most enlightening card."

Millie leaned in to take a closer look at the card.

"What does it mean?" she asked.

"The Nine of Pentacles means you have reached a point in your life where you are feeling self-confident and self-sufficient."

"Are you feeling more self-confident, Millie?" Lily Cup asked.

Millie reflected, shoved her chair back, stood and pulled her dress up to her hips, displaying a red garter belt, matching thong panties, young bare thighs and hosiery that cost more than three graduate school textbooks.

"Why, I wouldn't know. Whatever would give you the impression I lacked self-confidence? Well, I mean, I just wouldn't have the foggiest idea how you could ever..."

Roaring in laughter, Lily Cup spilled her drink on the table, Sasha snorting three, four, five snorts, slapping a flat hand on the tabletop. Millie stood stoically, lips clenched to keep from laughing. Just as the laughter subsided, Millie went into act two. She reached with both hands and pulled the front of her top and the bra beneath down.

"And my tits are pretty confident too!"

Almost as soon as act two was over, Millie's face turned a beet red in embarrassment, but grinning as she covered her girls. Sasha, still laughing almost to tears, picked the two tarot cards from the table, reached and stuck them under the thigh strap of Millie's garter belt. They sat and enjoyed the moment and the friendships. Such a day it has been and such a celebration the night promised. At what she thought was the right moment, Lily Cup interrupted.

"I heard from Peck," Lily Cup said.

"What'd he say?" Millie asked.

Lily Cup looked at Sasha and nodded a wink.

"Millie, do you remember how I told you I want you to go with Peck to see about finding his mother?"

"Yes, why?"

"What if you find her, and she's not well? Or maybe she has dementia, or it could be anything? What then?" Lily Cup asked.

"His mother is his mother. I would love her just for that. Why? What did he tell you?"

"I didn't talk to him, but he left a voicemail for me this afternoon. I was listening to it when you both came up here tonight. Would you like to hear it?"

"Yes."

"It's a long one."

"Please."

Lily Cup pressed the voicemail button and the speaker button and set her phone on the table.

"Lily Cup, I see'd this doctor John today, and he did good, I t'ink. He say my mamma I see'd in the moon is what I thought was my foster nanna, and she been my mamma all along. He told me where to go to ax a banker where she lives and I see'd it on a map, so I'm ready to go. I want to ax you somet'ing, and I do what you say, but I got to ax, or I can't live with myself. Lily Cup, when I runned away from home and my foster nanna, I was running from my own mamma, and dass for true. Lily Cup, what

kind of man runs away from his own mamma and don't stay to take care of his own mamma? I need you to tell Millie what kind of a man I am and tell her Peck understand should she never want to see me again ever. Would you tell her, please, for me please? I'm going to turn my phone off until tomorrow, then I'll call you back."

The message beeped to a close.

Sasha and Millie were in tears. Millie was sobbing. No one spoke. The moment was for thought, for garnering strength. Millie dabbed her face with a tissue Sasha handed her.

"I love that man more than I dreamed I could ever love someone," Millie said.

Sasha and Lily Cup waited to react.

"You okay?" Sasha asked.

"Lily Cup, will you drive me to Peck tomorrow, please?"

"Damn straight."

"Millie, Millie, you are so fucking perfect for Peck. You go girl!" Sasha said.

"What now?" Lily Cup asked.

Lily Cup and Sasha looked into Millie's eyes. It would be her call. Millie looked at them, and a smile broke into a grin through the tears. She pushed her chair back, stood and pulled her skirt up over her hips for an encore.

"If all this doesn't get me a dance with a drunken sailor tonight, nothing will. Let's go girls!"

Sasha and Lily Cup stood and howled and applauded.

Millie lifted her cell from her bag and held it up as she pressed the off button.

"I'll turn it on when we get to Baton Rouge tomorrow. Tonight I'm Catholic."

"Ha ha, you are such a Baptist. What's with the Catholic trip?" Lily Cup asked.

"Southern Baptists aren't supposed to drink or dance. You Catholics can drink on the dance floor." She blessed herself. "Look out tonight."

Lily Cup called Uber and arranged a pickup spot.

In Baton Rouge the dinner and conversation carried to closing and a walk to the apartment was settling. Peck was feeling his wine and opted not to swim, so he sat on the floor, leaning back on the sofa, as Elizabeth stretched on the sofa, her head near his, and told him in a sensual whisper that it had been a perfect evening. Peck asked about wild mushrooms and if there was a market for them and what Lily Cup was going to tell Millie when he tells her he's ready to go meet the banker so he can find his mamma. His head fell back from time to time. Could have been the drink, could have been all that was on his mind.

He turned and looked into Elizabeth's eyes and told her he would always love her, and maybe if he sold enough crawfish and soft-shell crab, he and Millie will come to see her in Paris, and she could make crepes with jam. Elizabeth leaned over as though to kiss him, but she reached her arm around his waist, sliding her hand in behind his opened belt buckle. She found William, and she held it firmly and could feel the head on her wrist and Peck began to grind his hips and her hand held the skin tightly and William moved up and back, up and back in the sheath of nerves and she kissed his neck, his hips thrusting William again and again. She nibbled his ear and licked it with her warm tongue and his pelvis held and quivered, his butt lifted from the floor and then down. Elizabeth left her hand on William, tenderly feeling the wet warmth of his still firm love and Peck turned his head to her and smiled. She spoke softly into his ear.

"*Nous devons dire au revoir a Peck avant que ton Millie ne vienne,*" Elizabeth said. ("We need to say goodbye, Peck, before your Millie comes.")

"Goodbye, cher?" Peck asked.

"Make love to me Peck."

Peck unzipped his pants and pushed them down first with his hands and then with each foot pushing a pantleg off, his back resting against the sofa. Elizabeth stood in her black, sleeveless French cocktail dress and stood over Peck, straddling him while facing him. She lifted her skirt briefly to show she was without panties and then she reached down and she held the sides of his head for leverage as she lowered herself to just above a still glistening William. Her hand between her thighs guided it in with a slow compression down to its base, every centimeter a lighted fuse of nerve endings about to burst. Their friendship would not wane, but just this once, an electric au revoir.

Was she thinking of her lonely nights without him or of the first time he walked her home stepping backwards in front of her because they couldn't take their eyes from each other? Was he thinking of how being held by her took him from the nightmare of carrying bait buckets and sleeping under saw blades? She kissed and sucked on his lips as her buttocks would rise and lower with a passionate squeeze and flexing a conjuring of so many memories of so many empty nights filled. She came while kissing him and then soon again with still another kiss until his hands reached under her dress and grasped her buttocks, now lifting and lowering her on William to share a final, long-lasting climax they both needed before they went their own separate ways. The kiss lingered patiently, their bodies at rest. Elizabeth lifted her head back. She wasn't quite ready to get up and end the physical connection. She leaned in and whispered in his ear?

"*Un bain chaud*, Peck?" ("A hot tub, Peck?")

"*Oui.*"

They held each other while the tub filled and they stepped into it like it was their private tree house where it all began.

CHAPTER 49

THE DOORBELL RANG. Gabe stood from his easy chair.

"Is she up?" Lily Cup asked.

"I haven't heard a peep. How late did you stay at Charlie's?"

"You and Sasha left, what—at midnight?"

"About then."

"We closed the place. Twinkle-toes in there danced with two different guys. One couldn't keep his hands off her."

"I saw the one with the Saints hat. I didn't see the other."

"He came in after you left. She told Sasha the Saints hat was a sexy guy and made her want Peck."

"The other?"

"He was the all hands, kept feeling her. She even asked Sasha what to do about him besides slap him or not dance with him."

"And?"

"Sasha asked her if he was a good dancer and when Millie said he was the better dancer of the two, Sasha told her to tell the guy to wash his hands. The dress was twenty-eight hundred bucks."

"That's our Sasha," Gabe said.

Gabe brought in a cup and the pot of coffee for Lily Cup. He poured.

"Has anybody told her?"

"Told her?"

"About the jam I was in. She has the right to know she's living with a..."

"Knock it off, Gabe. Get a grip. I'll tell her before I take her to Peck today."

"She has a right to know," Gabe said.

"I'll handle it. Put it out of your head."

"Let me hear the voicemail," Gabe said.

Lily Cup picked up her cellphone and pushed the voicemail button and the speaker button. Gabe listened to Peck's voice talking through his experiences with the psychiatrist.

"This is pretty heady stuff," Gabe said.

"What do you think?" Lily Cup asked.

"I'm not worried about the boy. The life he's lived would have broken most men. He hasn't so much as flinched or yelled uncle one time since he was nine. He's fed himself and kept a roof over his head, and he's done it with honor. I'm not worried for a second for him or for what he's going to find in those swamps."

"Is this one of those black epiphany moment things you were telling me, Gabe?"

Gabe chuckled. "Actually, it could be. There isn't one of my brothers or sisters who couldn't go back in time and not find ghosts and spirits haunting the barns and haylofts and church steeples in alleys of pain."

"What the hell does that mean?"

"My papaw was a slave. You think I wouldn't find more slaves in my bloodline if I went back far enough—maybe a family of slaves? Maybe a great, great uncle whose body was dropped in chains overboard when he died at sea on his way over from scurvy or something. Maybe a grandmother who jumped overboard or ran into a burning barn to kill herself after she was raped by a slave trader or owner."

"Jesus."

"What?"

"Do you sit up at night dreaming this stuff?"

"It's like our chicken pox, little sister."

"Your chicken pox?"

"Something we're born with...sorry. You have your *Goldilocks and the Three Bears*, we have our, 'don't be lookin' the Massah in the eye, les' you want to get a whuppin', boy.'"

"Christ, Gabe, you're depressing me."

"You asked me what I thought."

"Can't you at least tell me you're in a happy place now—that you're a happy man, and all that crap is behind you, and you're going to go out in style with a smile on your kisser with us as your friends and family?"

Gabe looked at Lily Cup. He grimaced a smile and reached his cup over to click on hers.

"To the end, my friend," Gabe said. "To the end."

"Damn," Lily Cup said. "If I didn't have to drive Millie to Baton Rouge I'd go buy a fifth of rye."

"You'll tell her?"

"I'll do it before I take her to Baton Rouge."

"Wasn't that something in the voicemail about Peck's mammas and the moon?" Gabe asked.

"It gave me chills. He told Sasha since he was a kid he would talk to the moon, thinking it was his mamma. It had Sasha and Millie in tears. Now that's the real hoodoo, in real time."

"I'll make a fresh pot, go see if Millie is up. I have Danishes and crumb cake."

"I feel like I need another fucking shower," Lily Cup said.

Lily Cup and Gabe shared a grin.

"Try to get it out of your head, Gabe. Life's too short. He would have killed you. You protected yourself. End of story."

She followed him to the kitchen, took an empty coffee mug from the shelf.

"How does she take it?" Lily Cup asked.

"Two Splenda. It's on that shelf over there, and a bit of milk."

Lily Cup prepared a cup and quietly pushed Peck's bedroom door to find the sleeping Cinderella. She was lying on her side, facing the window, the sheet and blanket over her head, blocking sunbeams coming in. She stepped around and adjusted the blinds to deflect the sun. She sat on the side of the bed and just nestled in the fold of Millie's stomach and thighs. A voice came from under the sheets.

"What time is it?"

"What's it matter? You're out of school."

"Where am I?"

"You're in a hotel room off Canal Street. Some guy wearing a Saints cap just left your room, counting the money in his wallet."

Millie slapped the sheet and blanket from her face; her eyes blinked a grin and focused on Lily Cup's eyes.

"Who are you?" she demanded, just before she giggled and turned on her stomach.

"I'm your worst nightmare. I'm your new boss and this is your first day of work and you're already two hours late, for Pete's sake. I'm thinking of canning your ass."

Millie turned and sat up.

"You never told me when to come to work."

"Here, drink some coffee."

Millie took the mug and had a temperature sip.

"What time is it?"

"We'll have a Danish and I'll show you my office, and we'll do some things before we head on up to Baton Rouge."

"Did Peck call?"

"His phone is still off, but I left a message we'll be there by two."

"Who'd you leave a message with?"

"I texted Elizabeth, and she texted me right back that he was sleeping and she would leave a note for when he wakes up."

"He's still asleep?"

"My accountant says I should intern you. Would that be okay with you?"

"Of course. Do it however you want. Do you think Peck and Elizabeth are having sex?" Millie asked.

"What brought that up?" Lily Cup asked. "You heard the message and how much he loves you."

"I know, but he's been with her a long time this week. Who is she to him anyway?"

"So, tell me—who was the better dancer last night, the Saints hat guy or the grabber stud?"

"Larry..."

"Larry? Oh, really? Larry? Aren't we getting a bit personal?"

"He was sweet. He has a girlfriend in Jackson. He was only in New Orleans on a job interview. He danced like a gentleman. I didn't mind so much that he wasn't a good dancer."

"Now I get it little lady, you're feeling guilty about your Larry last night so you're thinking Peck is hiding the salami in Baton Rouge?"

Millie did a doubletake at the concept and broke into a giggle, which ended with her head down on the pillow and a sigh.

"Well, it's not about Larry," Millie said.

"So how was Curley? Or was it Moe? The grabber?"

"He's a really good dancer. He pinched and grabbed, which was a pain, but he was such a good dancer."

"Aha," Lily Cup said. "He's the guilt trip you're having."

Millie looked up with a sheepish smile.

"Ain't that a bitch? The good ones are always copping a feel."

"That's not true. Gabe doesn't grab Sasha."

"Well did the grabber get his hands on the lady garden?"

Millie turned her head away.

"He did, he copped a feel of your kitty."

"He didn't get under my panties and it was only once...twice. I told him to stop and he stopped. I feel so bad, I've got to tell Peck. I was drinking."

"He was a hunk. Did you get his name?"

Millie reached into her red Chanel purse on the side table and pulled a business card from it.

"Here's his number. Keep it."

Lily Cup looked at the card.

"Well, what do you know about that?" she asked.

"What?"

"His name really is Curley," Lily Cup said.

"Shut up," Millie said with a giggle.

"Curley Moe, that's his name."

"Shut up."

"How's his willie, did you get a grab of his willie?"

"What!?"

"Aha, you did, I can tell."

"He knew all the song names to the music we danced to."

"So, you had to feel his baton."

"Shut up."

"Don't you just hate that? The grabbers are like that. They know all the words."

Millie handed the coffee mug back to Lily Cup, lifted the sheet and crawled to the other side of the bed and stood in her new, red satin panties.

"At least you were sober enough to take your garter belt and stockings off."

"I wasn't that drunk. After the first one on the roof and one at Charlie's I just sipped. I'm a stupid drunk."

"Plus, the two you had at Sak's and it was two, not one, on the roof," Lily Cup said.

Millie donned a T-shirt, and they went into the kitchen, and she told Gabe how embarrassed she was to get a C in French and that she was studying about crawfish farming online, and would her new dress be protected from the elements better in a closet or at a dry cleaner? They spoke of Peck's trip and how Gabe wanted her to use her phone and always find a hotel room if they had to stay over and to not stay with strangers or sleep in the truck. They lifted and bumped fists and he took her hand.

"You could be going into some dark waters, maybe, darlin'. You going to be okay?" Gabe asked.

"I watched him kill the dog," Millie said.

Gabe hesitated, wrinkled his brow and remembered. The other knife man's dog—the thief who stole Gabe's pills under the bridge the year before. Peck killed the dog when that knife man told his dog to 'sic 'em' and it sprung into attack.

"You're a good woman."

Millie grinned, lifted and dropped her shoulders with pride.

"What's on the agenda for you ladies today—besides taking Millie to her Boudreaux Clemont Finch?" Gabe asked.

"I'm going to show her my office and where her desk is. Then we're meeting Sasha at Coquette for an early lunch, and after that she and Millie are hitting the Ritz-Carlton spa for a mani-pedi and a mow."

Millie broke into a red-faced grin at the "mow" and Gabe, ever the gentlemen, held his coffee cup up with a silent approval.

"Will I see you before you leave for Baton Rouge?" Gabe asked.

"Probably not," Lily Cup said. "I have to be back by four. Best you get your hugs in before we leave here."

Gabe lifted the lid on the box of Danish for the ladies to see, turned and went to his easy chair to finish the morning paper.

"Help yourselves."

In Baton Rouge, Elizabeth, in her morning garb of chef school pants and bare top, was in her usual ritual of gathering dishware and utensils for the dishwasher when Peck came from the bedroom in his briefs.

"You up for good? I want to make the bed before I leave for school," Elizabeth said.

Peck didn't say a word. He walked into the kitchen rubbing his face and leaned against the counter to her left. Elizabeth started the dishwasher, and sidled over to Peck and leaned against him, skin on skin, folding her arms around him. They let their body language say good morning.

"That was beautiful, Peck. Thank you," Elizabeth said.

"I can make the bed, cher. Gabe teach'd me how he did it in the army. I'll make it," Peck said.

"I want to change the sheets," Elizabeth said.

"They look clean."

Elizabeth raised her head and looked Peck in the eyes.

"*Ta Millie arrive aujourd'hui, et tu voudras lui faire l'amour passionnément, non?*" Elizabeth asked. ("Your Millie is coming today, and you'll want to make passionate love to her, no?")

"*Oui.*"

"*Des draps propres, alors. Une femme sait ce qu'il faut faire dans ce cas,*" Elizabeth said. ("Fresh sheets, then. A woman knows these things.")

Peck ran his flat hands down under her chef pants waistband and grasped a buttock cheek in each hand and gently squeezed.

"If we don't speak English, Peck will be forty when I graduate Tulane."

Elizabeth lifted her head and smiled.

"When will you and Millie be leaving to find your mamma?"

"Tomorrow."

"Tonight, you take her to Bistro, and I see you get free wine and a beautiful dinner, and you bring her here after your chocolate souffle and make love. I'll sleep on the sofa."

"You're good to Peck, cher. T'ank you."

Elizabeth stood.

"You go shower. I'll make the bed and pick things up. I can't be late for school. Come to Bistro at six. There will be a table for you."

As Peck was stepping into a morning shower in Baton Rouge, on Carrolton Avenue in New Orleans, Lily Cup was touring Millie through her law offices and to her private office.

"We all get our own coffee here."

"This is beautiful," Millie said.

"Before the summer's out, you'll learn your way around all these files and cabinets, and you'll know who's who around here."

"Why are those files against that wall red and the ones on that wall green?" Millie asked.

"Very observant, young lady. You must have some Peck in you…"

Lily Cup started a second as they both realized what she had said. They did double-takes at the double entendre and guffawed.

"Simple. The red filing cabinets are for violent crime case files. The green ones are for nonviolent felony case files. We have everything on computer, but it's easier to take files into meetings or to court."

"Have you had any murderers for clients?" Millie asked.

Lily Cup turned and hesitated. She reached and took Millie by the arm.

"Come with me. We have to talk."

They went into her office, and Lily Cup pointed to a chair for Millie as she stepped around and plopped into her leather wingback.

"Push the door," Lily Cup said.

Millie obliged and sat down. Lily Cup leaned in, elbows folded on her desk.

"Millie, ever pinky-swear a secret?"

"Duh?" Millie asked.

"And duh is?"

"I'm a southern Baptist girl. My Daddy is a southern Baptist minister and my mother is a Baptist Evangelical missionary to the poor."

"And this means exactly? Help me out here."

"They didn't know until I was a junior that I started on birth control pills my freshman year at Baylor, and I could make frozen daiquiris for my thermos by the time I was nineteen. I can keep a secret."

"Good, because there's something I have to tell you, and I need you to keep it a secret always."

"I can do that, I promise."

"Peck, Sasha, Gabe and I have been trying to come up with a way to tell you, and they asked me to spill it as I knew all the facts."

"Should I be worried?"

"It's nothing like that, It's just something that happened, and we want to make sure you heard the whole story so you can decide for yourself."

"Now I am worried."

"Millie, do you know what self-defense is?"

"I do. I took two law courses."

"Well about a week or so ago, somebody down at Lee Circle tried to rob Gabe with a knife."

"Was Gabe hurt?"

"Gabe had to fight the man with his cane."

"I remember something about self-defense—"

"And Gabe hit the man when he tried to stab him with the knife."

"Did he stab Gabe?"

"No, but Gabe hurt him really bad when he hit him."

"What is it with Louisiana and men with knives? Peck was attacked with a knife too. Remember, we caught the guy?"

"I do remember, and it was in Mississippi."

"Oh, that's right, sorry. Well, if the crook with the knife got hurt by Gabe's cane, it's just too bad for him. He deserved it."

"He died."

"Oh."

Lily Cup kept silent to let it all play out in Millie's mind. She knew if she dealt with it in her own way, it would be more lasting than if she were "sold" the rationale.

"Is Gabe okay?"

"He was sad about it—almost in a stupor for a while. It was like a depression when the man died, knowing he did it, but he was frightened for his life. He had to defend himself."

"Yes."

"Like he would defend you or me or anyone."

"Yes."

"It's just that we try not to talk about it. It still upsets him, and he's an old man, and we try not to bring it up. That's why I'm telling you so you don't learn it from some stranger, or by looking in our files."

Millie placed both hands on the edge of Lily Cup's desk. She lowered her head and rested her forehead on the back of her hands and meditated, motionless. When she lifted her head she sat tall.

"If the thief is found breaking in and is struck so that he dies, there shall be no bloodguilt for him..." Millie was quoting scripture.

Lily Cup sat in awe, with gaping mouth. She started, shook her head awake and came to life again.

"You're one amazing kid," Lily Cup said.

Millie lifted her hand, pointing a curved pinky finger.

"Pinky-swear, I won't tell," she said.

Lily Cup lifted both hands, with both pinky fingers out and curled.

"Two pinky-swears—one for the secret about Gabe, and one for you're one amazing kid."

They clasped pinkies on the swears, and Millie sat back. She lifted a comical twisting of her index finger to her cheek to the "kid" remark.

"I'm not a kid, ya know. Why I'm near fully growed," Millie replied.

"I'll say your fully growed. I've been in your dressing room."

Millie grinned.

"And you're beginning to sound like Peck."

Lunch was more laughs than it was lunch. Sasha was seated and had ordered off-menu cucumber sandwiches and a large fruit and cheese plate they would share.

"I'm impressed, Millie," Sasha said.

"Huh?"

"You are quite the dancer. Do you and Peck dance?"

"We will this summer. It wasn't easy going out when I'd come for a weekend."

They spoke of Charlie's Blue Note and of slow jazz and Dixieland, and whether Prada or Dior or a Christian Louboutin made a better shoe and how a thong needed some getting used to. Lily Cup told Sasha they had a talk about the Gabe episode and how Millie was good with it and would keep it under wraps. Millie asked if it was necessary that she get a waxed *coochie,* as she didn't want an itch like she was told it caused.

"Coochie?" Sasha asked. "I love it."

"You know what I mean. I heard it like itches after waxing."

"Ask them for a trim. They'll do a trim," Lily Cup said.

In the midst of the lunch Millie was impressed when Sasha asked them all to hold hands and they each said a prayer for Millie and Peck to find his mother and that their journey be rewarding, and they would return to New Orleans safe and soon. They said one for Gabe, as well.

The friendship the three of them had bonded in the past eighteen hours brought a tear to Millie's eye, and she suggested they treat themselves to sherbet and cookies if Coquette had them. Pecan or key lime pie if they didn't. Sasha and Lily Cup took turns expressing their views on why there were no spoons or dessert forks on the table and the nuances of differences between diets for women pushing forty and young college bitches who could eat anything and still not know what a tummy is.

The drive to Baton Rouge was uninterrupted by conversation or radio noise. It was a blending of silences between two new friends perhaps playing the evening together in their minds, the rooftop séance, the dancing. Talk of the week that lay before Peck and Millie would be a spoiler. Conjecture was not a good way to start anything of this nature. Millie couldn't take her eyes off the bridge to Baton Rouge as it carried them over the longest stretch of Acadian bayous and moss-dripping cypress trees Millie had ever seen. It looked as if she was imagining the gators and snappers Peck had talked of so many times before, with his arms around her as they lay on the bed, looking up through the window at a full moon.

Lily Cup pulled into a parking space on South Fourteenth Street just behind Peck's pickup. She lifted her cell and pressed a key and put the phone to her ear.

"We're here; come get your lady. I have to get back."

Lily Cup leaned over and kissed Millie on both cheeks. They squeezed hands.

"It's been fun, sweetie. We'll see you soon. You're on the payroll. Keep me posted by text once a day. Call me if you need help with something."

Millie stepped out of the car with her bag as Peck came through the front doors and with a wave Lily Cup made a wide U-turn and drove off.

CHAPTER 50

AS THOUGH SHE WERE SLEEPWALKING, Millie closed the medicine cabinet and switched off the bathroom light before pulling its door open. She could see Peck's leg sticking out from under the sheet. She stepped quietly into the hall and followed a glowing kitchen nightlight until she could see Elizabeth asleep on the sofa, a summer quilt blanketing her. Millie knelt beside her.

"Elizabeth?"

"*Oui?*" Elizabeth asked, raising her head.

"I'm so sorry to wake you."

"Is there a problem?"

"Do you have any Tampax?"

"Look in the cabinet under the sink."

"In the bathroom?"

"*Oui.*"

"Thank you."

"No worries. Help yourself."

"The dinner was totally awesome. Did you cook all that?"

"Some, but no, I'm not the head chef."

Millie stood.

"G'night. Sorry to wake you."

Millie made her way back to the bathroom, did her business and crawled in behind Peck, putting her arm over his chest and kissing him on the back.

"You hokay, cher?"

"I had a visitor."

Peck raised his head. "Hanh?"

"Mother Nature."

Peck turned inquisitively.

"A girl thing. Go to sleep."

Peck rested his head as if he understood. They lay silently, Millie gathering her thoughts.

"Peck?"

"*Oui?*"

"Lily Cup told me about Gabe and that man. It's so sad for Gabe."

"*Oui.*"

"He had every right to hit a man who was like attacking him with a knife."

"*Oui.*"

"He hit him like the dog. Remember that dog, Peck?"

"*Oui.*"

"It'll be better coming from you. Will you tell him I still love him and nothing will ever change that?"

"I will."

"When are we leaving?"

"When we get up."

"Where're we going?"

"Millie, I t'ink I should tell you about some t'ings like when I growed."

"I know some of it, like you ran away because your stepfather was mean."

"Do you know what he did to me?"

"How would I know?"

"I was t'inking maybe Lily Cup or Sasha tole you."

"Nobody told me anything."

Peck was silent.

"Well, that's not all true," Millie said.

Peck waited.

"Lily Cup let me hear the voicemail."

Peck bounced on his elbow and turned over, facing Millie's silhouette shaded from a streetlamp leaking through the center of nearly closed bedroom drapes.

"You heard it?"

"I listened to it. It only made me love you more."

"I love you, cher—so much."

"I know you ran away from home when you were young. There must have been a good reason, and you didn't know she was your momma."

"I love you, Millie."

"We have all our lives for you to tell me about those things. Let's go try to find your momma in the morning. Do you know where to start?"

"Killian, to the bank there. A man at the bank knows maybe where mamma is."

The room was still. They heard a car driving by on the street below. Peck was nodding off.

"Elizabeth is nice," Millie said.

"Nice."

"Do you love her?"

Peck lifted a hand sleepily, touching Millie's cheek and he thought.

"Charlie?" Peck asked.

"My baby doll, Charlie, or the Blue Note Charlie?" Millie asked.

"Your baby doll Charlie."

"What about baby Charlie?"

"Peck loves Elizabeth like Millie loves her Charlie."

"That's so sweet. Would you say you and Elizabeth are like brother and sister?"

"Why you ask me, cher?"

"Because I drank too much last night and let a man get fresh with me dancing at Charlie's. I could have stopped it but he was holding me and I was thinking of you up here with Elizabeth."

"Cousins. Elizabeth and Peck like cousins."

"Did you make love?"

"Peck drank too much wine and, yes, I made goodbye love with Elizabeth, dass for true. I know'd her like ten years. She'll be our good friend always. I love you, Millie, and only you. Elizabeth knows this and she likes you very much."

Millie pouted.

"Will Millie forgive me?"

"Will Peck forgive me?"

"*Oui.*"

"*Oui oui,*" Millie said.

Peck lifted and kissed Millie's hand.

"We need to do something nice for her. You know, for her letting us stay here," Millie said.

"Okay. Millie tell me what we do and we can do that."

"When we go home, you know back to New Orleans after we find your momma will we be coming through Baton Rouge?"

"Yes, I'm t'inking."

"So, we tell Elizabeth we're taking her out to a nice dinner when we come through."

"Good, cher. You tell her that."

Millie kissed Peck on the back as he turned and began dozing off.

"Peck, have you and Lily Cup ever…?"

"Hanh?"

"Go to sleep."

Millie awakened with the brushing sounds of the early morning street washer. She rolled to the edge of the bed, got up and went into the bathroom. The aroma of percolating coffee was in the air, and she followed the scent to the kitchen only to find Elizabeth standing in her chef school pants and no top, scratching marmalade onto both halves of a toasted English muffin.

"Oh?" Millie asked.

"Would you like an English muffin?" Elisabeth asked.

"Sure."

Elizabeth took one from the package, split it in half with two forks and dropped it in the toaster.

"My uniform top is in the bedroom closet. It's on the left. White, heavy starch. Do you mind getting it for me?"

Millie walked down the small hall into the bedroom and brought the chef school coat back on the hanger.

They stood drinking coffee and munching on crisped English muffins and Millie inviting Elizabeth to be their guest for dinner when they came back through and Elizabeth admiring Millie's cinnamon hair and did they enjoy their meal last night? They spoke of how charming downtown Baton Rouge was and of Elizabeth's wish to live in Paris when she graduated and for Millie to take several tampons until she could get to a drugstore. In the bedroom they heard Peck moving about. He came into the kitchen dressed, packed, and ready to go.

"What time are you leaving for school, Elizabeth?" Peck asked.

"I'll go at nine."

"Hokay, we can leave when you do, so you can lock the door. We drive an hour and the bank will be open at ten, so all is good."

"You want coddled eggs, Peck?" Elizabeth asked.

Peck looked at Millie. "Oh, cher, you have to taste Elizabeth's coddled eggs. They are so good, dass for true."

"Sure," Millie said.

"I'll make four," Elizabeth said.

"I better get ready. I'll be right back," Millie said.

Millie went and closed the bathroom door behind her.

"She's nice. You're a lucky man," Elizabeth said.

"The first time I saw her I knew I wanted to be with her. I never thought Peck would ever have a chance, dass for true, but here we are. She loves me."

"She adores you, Peck."

Elizabeth leaned and kissed Peck on the cheek.

"*Tu es un homme tres chanceux*," Elizabeth said. ("You are a very lucky man.")

After small talk over breakfast snacks, Peck and Millie bid adieu and tucked bags behind the seat of the truck. Peck drove first to a service center station and filled the tank. He went inside with Millie where she picked up a few things, and he bought water bottles and Fritos. When they got back to the truck he asked if they should maybe get the truck washed before they left. It was an hour drive to Killian where the bank was. Just as he was about to start the engine Millie took his wrist in her hand and pulled it to get his attention.

"Peck, do you remember when I first met Gabe, that time you came up for Thanksgiving..."

"I remember."

"Gabe would come down and sit with me on Daddy's fishing dock while I fed the ducks and he told me stories of the times he was at the hospice and how he couldn't wait for Thursdays to come because that was the day you came to mow the lawn and how excited he was that you were coming. He told me everything you did and how you would wave hello and walk right to the bayou without stopping and you would put your gear on the ground and you would stretch out your trotline and you'd put bait on those things..."

"Snoods."

"That's it, the snoods—and right after you had the bait on he told me how you would twirl it around and throw it out as far as you could into the bayou, and then how you would tie it on a tree root, and you'd stand and watch it for a minute and then go mow the lawns."

"Dass for true, cher."

"Peck, you got all that done quickly every Thursday morning before you mowed?"

"Yeah?"

"So why are you stalling about going to find your momma? Why are you coming up with excuses—these things you have to do?"

Peck smiled with clenched lips of defeat. He looked over at Millie. "I love you," he said.

He started the pickup.

"I have to find Interstate 12," Peck said.

Millie lifted her phone, tapped into her Maps app and typed Interstate 12 and pressed.

"See the second light up there?" Millie asked.

"*Oui*."

"Go to that light and turn right."

Off they went.

"What's the name of the place we're going?"

"Killian National Bank."

Millie pressed some buttons.

"It's fifty-five minutes. Turn up here on Interstate 12 and stay on it until I tell you to get off."

Peck reached in the paper sack sitting between them. He pulled a small bag of Fritos corn chips and began to tear them open. Millie took them from his hand, reminding him they had just eaten and they would need them for a snack later, and he didn't want to make a mess in his new truck and what a pretty truck it was, if trucks were pretty.

The last two days had been such a fun whirlwind for Millie, it hadn't dawned on her to charge her cellphone. Peck examined every home and farm and swamp they passed. Nothing from his childhood seemed to come to his memory. It was when Millie saw the painted wooden sign for a bait shop on the Livingston exit she figured they had gone too far.

"My phone is dead. Where's yours?"

"In my bag."

"Better get off here. We need to ask directions."

Peck slowed and exited while glancing about for a service station—anyplace where there would be someone they could ask.

"The arrow on that bait shop sign over there points this way. Let's go see if it's open," Millie said.

The exit was a paved road and the arrows pointed to the right. The road turned into a narrow dirt path. Not far into it, nestled back under low, hanging pine tree branches was a medium size, egg-shaped travel trailer from the 1960s. There were six Styrofoam ice chests on a long wooden harvest table in front. The visible tire was flat and the front trailer hitch was resting on two cinder blocks. It had an awning over a two-by-twelve counter on the ledge of an opening that appeared to have been hacksawed out of its side, framed with cedar.

A flat, painted board sign read, BAIT. Crushed shells lined the drive up to and around the bait shop trailer. Peck pulled in and turned the engine off. He got out while Millie moved the seat and pulled his bag from the floor behind and looked for Peck's phone and charge cord. There was no sign of life in the trailer until a voice from inside sounded.

"You fishing for catfish or bass, friend?" the voice asked.

"Nah, nah, not fishin' today, frien', just driving," Peck said.

"I got fresh bait case you do."

Peck felt French was a door opener in Acadiana, a signal he was friendly.

"*Je lance pas fois des trotlines dans Carencro bayou, mon ami*," Peck said. ("I throw trotlines in Carencro bayou at times, friend.")

"I don't speak z'ee French, friend. My wife speaks it. She's Creole. Oh, I know zee *oui* and zee *merci* if I have to and enough to let her z'ink I'm learning zee French, so I can be a good American."

"You're not American?"

"I'm from Russia. Been a citizen three years now. I come here to read my books and sell my bait to buy more books. What you fishing—catfish or bass?"

"Nah, nah..." Peck started.

"Catfish go for smells. I've got good frozen chicken livers. Z'ay love chicken livers. Have lots of cut-up shad too. Z'at smells too. Catfish go for smells."

The curiosity of the fisher in Peck peaked.

"Shicken livers?"

"Z'ay smell so good to catfish. Why, what you use?"

"Purdy much cut snake and maybe snapper innards," Peck said.

"Chicken livers work good for catfish around here. Just keep checking your hook, z'ay crumble off easy. You want to try my chicken livers? Frozen quick, z'ay'll keep 'til you get to where you're going."

"Nah, nah, not today, but t'anks," Peck said.

"Ahhh, I understood you said Carencro. I never been z'are—Carencro. Been to Lafayette, z'o," the voice said.

"Mister, I t'ink we lost, t'inking maybe you can help."

"What, you both driving z'at new truck to get lost?"

"No, I'm drivin' it. The name's Peck."

"Well z'en, seems Peck is the one z'at's lost, seems to me," the voice said.

The voice snorted chuckles as the trailer began to rock with motion inside. A large hand set a hardcover book on the counter and the end door pushed open.

He was a tall man, looking to be 275 pounds or more, like Sydney Greenstreet from a vintage Humphrey Bogart movie. He stepped down, causing the trailer to rock, squeaking on broken springs. Bright red suspenders held up his khaki pants. He had an apron tied around his waist with gloves in the pocket. His posture was proud, his head up with full, black, curly hair. It looked as though he was looking under his glasses to see Peck. Broad shoulders with chest out. As imposing as his body was on first impression, he had a gentle, warm smile with his large hand outstretched to officially welcome this lost traveler. It was as if Peck were a break in his morning. Someone to talk to.

"I'm Alex," he said.

"Good to meet you, Alex. How you are?"

"What you need, friend?" Alex asked.

"Where'd you get this oyster shell in your drive, frien'? No oysters hereabouts – maybe in New Or–lee–anh, though," Peck said.

"Z'ay aren't oysters."

"Hanh?"

"Z'ay're mussel shells."

"Mussel shells? Where from?"

"My wife's broodher, in Alabama. He fishes the Tennessee River. He gets z'em just for haulin z'em off."

This was when an exasperated Millie walked up.

"In Carencro, where did you get your snake, was it good bait?" Alex asked.

"I catched 'em mostly by hand. On a snood sometimes. Snakes are good for snappers. Turtle innards good for catfish."

"What did you find out, Peck?" Millie asked.

"Oh, we talkin' bait. Millie, meet Alex, here. He's from Russia."

Alex extended his hand, and measuring the look on her face, he'd felt he best leave oral cordialities to her.

"Ma'am?" Alex asked.

"We're looking for Killian," Peck said.

"Which way you been driving?" Alex asked.

"From Baton Rouge."

"Well, you missed it, I'll say."

Alex pointed. "Go get on 12 and head z'at way. Go one exit. Get off and go south on Satsuma Road. You can't miss it," Alex said.

"You know anything about Killian?" Peck asked.

"I know Killian. What you need to know, friend?"

"Killian National Bank," Millie said.

"Z'ay'res old man Aucoin and old man Hebert. Z'ay own z'ee bank," Alex said.

"You know them?" Peck asked.

"Z'ay don't loan money on bait, but z'ay love to fish—least'n Aucoin does. Gets his bait here," Alex said. "He brings me books in trade for chicken livers."

"I have to go meet them," Peck said.

"If you want to come back by, come try my chicken livers. We'll go fishing, Millie too," Alex said.

Peck and Millie walked to the truck. Millie crawled up and in. Peck turned to wave, then hesitated with second thoughts. He left his door open and walked back to Alex.

"Alex, you ever heared of gator man? You ever heared of him?"

"Important to you, friend?" Alex asked.

"Very important," Peck said.

"Lots of men call z'emselves gator man, but I don't know a, like you say, 'gator man,' but I can ask cousins." Alex said.

"You got a lot of cousins?" Peck asked.

"My wife does."

The tracker in Peck's eyes lighted up. "This is good."

"You got a phone, Peck?"

"I do."

"What's your number?"

Peck gave him his number. Alex pulled his phone from his apron and punched it into his phone and pressed send.

"I'll send you a text. If her cousins know of z'ees 'gator man,' Alex will text you, friend."

"T'anks, frien," Peck said.

Peck turned to walk to the truck. He paused, considering if he had more questions.

Millie sang out.

"Oh, Boudreaux Clemont Finch?"

Peck looked at her.

"You're stalling again. There's nothing to be afraid of in Killian. So climb in the truck and let's go."

Peck paced their ride to best give him advantage looking at every yard, house and barn. He recognized nothing on Satsuma Road, and nothing on his drive into Killian. He pulled up to the bank and parked.

"You goin' in with me, cher?" Peck asked.

"I think you need to go in alone," Millie said. "I'll wait here. I saw a drugstore down that street. I may walk over and see if they have a charger cord for me."

CHAPTER 51

MAY I HELP YOU, YOUNG MAN?" the bank teller woman asked.

"Dr. John Price called a man here to talk about Alayna Prudhomme. Can I see the man, please ma'am?" Peck asked.

"Do you know who your doctor spoke with?"

"Nah, nah. I forgot to ax, sorry."

"Let me check," the teller woman said. "What's your name?"

"Boudreaux Clemont Finch, ma'am."

She went to the end of the booth and pulled a door open, stepped through and closed it. Peck looked about the bank, at the pictures on the wall, the flags. He looked through the front window at his truck. Millie was not in it. Two boys rode by on bicycles, the taller one holding two fishing poles, the shorter one with a back bag.

The teller woman came through the door and held it for an elderly gentleman, using a cane. He had thin, neatly combed hair, wire-rimmed glasses. He peered out at Peck.

"Why don't you come in, son? Come in," the old man said.

Peck obliged and stepped into the office.

The old man extended his hand. "Walter Aucoin," he said.

Peck shook his hand. "Boudreaux Clemont Finch," Peck said. "Proud to meet you, sir."

They both sat.

"Mr. Finch, do you have any form of identification?" Mr. Aucoin asked.

"Oh, *oui*," Peck said.

Peck lifted his wallet from his back pocket. From it he pulled his driver's license, his social security card, and a copy of his birth certificate. He handed them to Mr. Aucoin, who in turn looked at each and set them on his desk before him.

"I'm not familiar with a Dr. Price, young man. Let me phone my partner and ask if he knows the man."

Mr. Aucoin dialed and waited.

"Hello?" a voice in the phone asked.

"Harold, there's a young man here, a Boudreaux Clemont Finch."

"Finch?" Harold repeated.

"That's right, a Mr. Finch," Mr. Aucoin said.

"Can't say I know a Mr. Finch," Harold said.

"No, Harold, I don't think you have ever met Mr. Finch, but he mentions a Dr. John Price. Are you familiar with a Dr. Price?"

"Oh yes, Dr. Price. I recall the name. I spoke with him not long ago," Harold said.

"Well, the young man, Mr. Finch, is here to speak with you. Should I put him on the phone?"

"No, don't put him on. I'm leaving the house in ten minutes. Have to stop by the hardware store. Walter, tell the young man to get himself a cup of coffee at the café and when I get in I'll fetch him. Ask the young man if that will work."

Mr. Aucoin looked over at Peck.

"He knows Dr. Price, but it'll take him an hour or so to get here. Will that be okay with you, son?"

"Oh, *oui*, sir. That'd be good. I wait."

Mr. Aucoin spoke into the phone. "Harold, the young man will wait. Tell Constance hello."

"Who's there with you?" Harold asked.

"Flo and Norman. Why?"

"There are three boxes in the old vault. I'll need them in my office, and they'd be too heavy for Flo."

"I'll have Norman get them out."

"Good. Tell Norman there're three boxes marked 'Pontelban' on them. I need them in my office."

"Oh my," Mr. Aucoin said. "How long has it been since the doctor passed?"

"It'll be five years this October," Harold said.

"I'll have Norman move the boxes. See you when you get in, Harold."

Mr. Aucoin set the phone on its cradle.

"Mr. Finch, there's a café and grill just up the street. If you go have a coffee, Mr. Hebert will come get you after he runs a couple of errands. Will that be all right with you?"

"Yes, sir, Mr. Aucoin, sir. Alex tells me you're a fisher. What you fish for?"

"You know Alex?"

"He give'd me directions to come here," Peck said.

"I fish mostly bass. Did Alex tell you I wasn't much good at it?"

"Nah, nah." Peck smiled.

"He's a good man, Alex. He's a big reader. Russians love to read. I trade him old books for his bait, so neither of us lose out," Mr. Aucoin said.

"Nice man, Alex," Peck said.

Peck stood and started toward the door.

"The café is to the right, from the front door, son," Mr. Aucoin said.

Peck waved and walked out to find Millie sitting on a park bench near the street corner.

"I found a charger," Millie said. "How'd it go with you?"

Peck spoke of the Mr. Hebert who was coming in to see him and how they should go have a cup of coffee and wasn't it a nice town?

Millie observed that people in Louisiana were friendly, and it wasn't as dark and frightening a place as Gabe thought it might have been. They ordered coffee and one grilled bacon and cheese sandwich they would share. They spoke of where their farm might be and was Peck thinking more softshell crab or crawfish and had he ever eaten a snake? Peck told Millie her nail polish was pretty and did she have fun with Sasha and Lily Cup in N'Orleans?

An elderly gentleman edged up to their booth.

"Young man, are you Mr. Finch?"

"Yes sir."

"I'm Harold Hebert. Would you like to step over to my office?"

"I'll just wait here," Millie said. "You all have things to talk about."

"You can come too, cher," Peck said.

"You go on. You can tell me about it later."

Millie loved Peck too much to not let him paint his past from his own pallet, using his brushes. She would respect any story he told her, and she would respect the privacy he held to his chest.

Peck and Mr. Hebert walked over to the bank.

"Flo?" Mr. Hebert asked.

"Yes, sir, Mr. Hebert?"

"Can you see Mr. Finch and I don't get disturbed? We may be some time. We have things to go through."

"I'll see you aren't bothered, Mr. Hebert. How's Mrs. Hebert, sir?"

"It was a late bronchitis. Gave her a devil of a time. It's passed now. Thank you, Flo. She'll appreciate hearing you asked about her."

Mr. Hebert led Peck into his office and closed the door. He pointed to a chair for Peck. On top of his desk were three large cartons labeled with black marker, "Dr. Pontelbon." He walked around his desk and rolled his chair to a spot to best have Peck in sight and sat down. He picked up some papers clipped together.

"You left your papers, son."

He handed Peck his driver's license, social security card, and birth certificate. As Peck organized them in his wallet, Mr. Hebert studied Peck's face, just as if he were in a garden studying the new bloom on a wild flower.

"What do you go by, son?" Mr. Hebert asked.

"People mostly call me Peck, sir."

"Peck it is, then. Call me Harold, son. I'll be helping you today, best I'm able."

Mr. Hebert took a pocketknife from his desk drawer and cut the packing tape.

"Let's have a look," Mr. Hebert said.

He cut the tape on all three boxes and folded the flaps down.

"Mr. Hebert, sir – can I go get my Millie?"

Mr. Hebert looked at Peck as he folded his knife and returned it to his desk drawer.

"Go get your Millie, son."

Peck grinned and made his way through the lobby down the street and into the café and grill."

"Millie, I want you with me."

"Peck, it's personal. Won't you be more comfortable finding out what the man has to say first?"

Peck knelt on one knee, took her hand and looked Millie square in the eyes.

"Do you remember the day we met, Millie? In North Carolina?"

"On the bus. I remember. Why?"

"You remember first thing you told Peck, cher?"

Millie wrinkled her brow with a broken guess.

"That I needed to use the bathroom?"

Peck guffawed. "After that, the first was you told me you had water and then you told me about Charlie. Remember, cher?"

"I remember, and you held my Charlie and didn't laugh at me."

"*Oui.*"

"Today is different, Peck. Mr. Hebert is going to maybe tell you some very personal things."

"When I holded your Charlie I know'd I wanted to be with you for the rest of our whole lives, and dass for true."

"You're the sweetest man."

"Come with me, cher. We together forever. Please."

Millie dabbed a tear from her eye. She paid the check and hand-in-hand they walked the street in downtown Killian to the brass door of the vintage bank. Mr. Hebert stood and welcomed them in and reached for a picture of his wife, Constance, and handed it to Millie.

"I do understand these things, Miss Millie. When love is true, there are no walls."

Millie handed the picture frame back with a gentle smile.

"Romans 12:9 and 10 tell it, Mr. Hebert. I learned it in bible study. *Love must be sincere. Hate what is evil; cling to what is good. Be devoted to one another in love. Honor one another above yourselves.*"

"Such a lovely thought, young lady. I'd say whatever we unfold in these boxes that might pertain to your young man here, will be no match for the love you share."

"Thank you, sir," Millie said.

Mr. Hebert set the picture of his Constance on the side table and sat. He lifted a yellow legal pad and pen and handed it to Peck for notes. Peck handed it to Millie.

Mr. Hebert rummaged through the boxes that appeared to be filled with heavy manila envelopes with large rubber bands holding them secure. Dates were scrawled on each from a marker pen. Mr. Hebert lifted each envelope with the tips of his fingers, scratching at them from the side, like a squirrel digging for a buried nut. He came upon two white envelopes, one with "Finch" penned on it, one with "Dr. Pontelban" on its flap.

"Here we are," he said.

He set the two envelopes before him on the desk.

"You're on a great search for truths, son. I know a little about you. Not much, but least what I've been told. I do know about Dr. Pontelban though, son. I've known him since the early days when he moved nearby. We would fish together. Are either of you fishers?"

"I'm a fisher, sir. Trotlines mostly, though. Five snoods, what I can throw," Peck said.

"I didn't have the arm for a net cast or a trotline throw," Mr. Hebert said.

"Big sinker helped me, sir," Peck said.

"You being a fisher, son, I don't have to tell you that two bodies can spend years together in a boat waiting for that strike, and not talk too much more than the pleasantries. Fishing time is a restful meditation between you and nature…or God, as my Constance would say."

"Dass for true," Peck said.

"Best I start by telling you about Dr. Pontelban. Why don't I read his obituary? I think that would be best."

"Nah, nah," Peck said. "Did you fish wi'd this Dr. Pontelban a lot of times, Mr. Hebert?"

"I'd say twice a week for twenty-five years or so, son. We'd meet here at the bank or at the lake. He had a skiff we'd take off shore and anchor maybe a hundred yards or so out."

"What lake?"

"Lake Mourepas. We'd catch mainly bass or catfish. We'd throw the sunfish back. More luck with bass, I'd say."

"Peck think you can tell me more about this doctor man than a newspaper thing."

"You would have liked the man, Peck. He had a gentle kindness about him. I know he was dedicated to his work, and I know he was a generous man. Lived simply. Always helping others. He worked at the women's insane asylum since the sixties. They call it *mental health* now. He passed in his sleep."

"Did he leave anyone behind, Mr. Hebert? Any family?" Millie asked.

"Not that I was aware of. He never married. Oh, the funeral was a large one. More than a hundred at the gravesite, but no family."

"Happy and sad at the same time," Millie said.

Mr. Hebert opened his desk drawer and pulled an opened envelope from it.

"I received this letter a few weeks before he passed. It was from him, and it was postmarked Killian. He could have just dropped it by. He had to walk by the bank to get to the post office. It says on the outside, 'Open after I'm gone.' I waited."

"The doctor know'd he was goin'," Peck said.

"Was he sad?" Millie asked.

"Sad?"

"If you fished with him two times every week you could tell, did he look sad?" Millie asked.

"He looked tired," Mr. Hebert replied "Let me read the letter to you."

He pulled a single page from the envelope and unfolded it.

"'Hal'—he always called me Hal – my nickname for Harold.

'Hal, I've been on the mend, but I need you to do something for me, dear friend. Keep the Prudhomme checks going until she passes and then give any balance to your church and close the account. My safety deposit box key is in the envelope. When I go, can you empty it and put the contents—there's two envelopes and my granddaddy's pocket watch. Put them with my bank records and store them, if you will. If you ever hear from a gentleman by the name of Boudreaux Clemont Finch, there's an envelope marked with his name that you may read to him. Hold the other. You may give him the watch. Hal, we most never said goodbye when we fished, we waved. You've been a good friend, good company. Here's a wave, my friend. My best to Constance.'"

Mr. Hebert held up the watch and chain as if it were his old friend, and he dabbed his eye with a handkerchief. He started to talk, choked a sob and waited.

"He signed it 'Doc,'" Mr. Hebert said.

"What a beautiful friendship," Millie said. "You were both so lucky to have your lives cross."

Mr. Hebert nodded, lips clenched.

"I need some air," Mr. Hebert said. "Would either of you like to join me for a stroll around the block?"

Peck and Millie stood.

"We'll read the envelope when we get back," Mr. Hebert said.

On the first street they walked without talking. On the second street Mr. Hebert pointed to the old church that was built by a Cajun French community in 1831. On the third street Peck asked Mr. Hebert what he used for bait and had he ever tried shicken livers. On the street back to the bank, they set a promise to get Alex the bait man one day and go fishing. Before entering the bank, Mr. Hebert stood looking up at the town clock on the corner. He lifted the watch and chain from his pocket and set the time to the clock and wound it. He lifted it to see under his bifocals before handing it to Peck.

"Wind it once a day, son, in one direction, forward, not too tight."

CHAPTER52

MR. HEBERT ASKED PECK to lift the three cartons to the floor so he could best see over his desk as he read the contents in the envelope. Peck obliged and was about to sit when his phone rang. It was Lily Cup's phone calling.

"Hello?"

"My brother, I just had to call to see if you were okay," Gabe said.

Peck excused himself and stepped from the office, through the lobby and onto the sidewalk.

"Hey Gabe, how you are?"

"Lily Cup and I've been sitting here trying to get organized so you and I can throw an engagement party for Sasha and James. I'm just scribbling notes. She came by for coffee. How are you son? Are things going well up there?"

"It's all good, Captain. Nice people are helping Peck. This old man in Killian give'd me a, how you say, pocket watch that belonged to a doctor's granddaddy. The doctor know'd my mamma, he say."

"Sounds like it's an eventful trip. If you need anything, you know who to call."

"I know, Gabe. Millie and me, we doing so good. People are nice."

"I'll share that with Sasha and Lily Cup. They'll be happy to hear it's going well."

"Yes, sir. It's good."

Peck made his way back into the office where Mr. Hebert was lifting a stack of typed pages an inch or so deep. He read the title page: A Story for My Best Friend. He pondered it as if he were looking the doc in the eye. He clutched it to his chest with his left arm and with his right hand he cleared the top of his desk, setting things on the console table behind. He placed the stack of papers on the desk and sat down. He looked over at Peck.

"You ready, son?"

Peck nodded.

Mr. Hebert turned the title page and set it to the right of the pile. He picked up the first page and began reading.

"Dear Hal,

"I don't mind telling you that God and I have not always seen eye to eye, but in all the years I shared my skiff with you, Harold Hebert, my dear friend, for longer than I can remember at this writing, I could always trust the man in you to do the right and good thing.

"I have no way of knowing what time has passed since my own passing. Has it been weeks, months, or years? I was raised to believe in miracles, and I did pray that it would be you reading this letter, Hal, and if you are reading it, *it would be a miracle at this time in your life because I'll assume there's a gentleman, alive and sitting across from your desk with the name Boudreaux Clemont Finch. I also prayed that the young man's mother, Alayna Prudhomme, would be alive if and when this time came. There is so much to say, it would only be fitting if Mr. Finch knew the story and then shared it with her, if that was his choice."*

"Mr. Hebert, do you have any tissues?" Millie asked.

Mr. Hebert opened a console door and pulled three Puffs boxes, handing one to Peck, one to Millie, who was weeping, and he opened one for himself. He picked up another page and read aloud.

"Louisiana in 1963 and 1964 was not like the Louisiana you and I fished in all those years, Hal. They were darker times in a state fraught with levee breaks and lost lives, a time when New Orleans was a boiling caldron both with equal measure of celebration and sorrow over the shooting death of President John F. Kennedy. His killer, New Orleans own Lee Harvey Oswald from Magazine Street, was considered a hero in some non-Catholic circles. I was ashamed to hear there was cheering in some schools. It was following that time, in January of 1964, that I was assigned to do my residency program riding with the Louisiana State Police, observing and serving what was to later become paramedics at scenes of accidents, fire, spousal abuse, suicide, and murders.

"My story begins at seven in the morning on February 25th,1964. There was a blackened, moonless sky with a pouring of rain, and I was answering an emergency call about a pregnant woman disturbing the search and rescue craft on the north shore of Lake Pontchartrain in Mandeville. When we arrived, we found the woman standing among the floodlights at the water's edge, with no coat and her sweater soaked with rain. At the risk of losing her unborn baby she stood there like a cold marble statue, her hands to her face. She was staring out at a child's baby doll that was floating on its back about thirty feet out, bobbing up and down in the wakes of the search boats."

Mr. Hebert set the page down and picked another and studied it.
"Here he's addressing you, son."

"Mr. Finch, in all my life, I've never forgotten this day. It was the day I first met your grandmother. That desperately dark, cold, raining, predawn morning was the day. The woman standing there at water's edge was your grandmother. Another two feet and she would have been lost in the abyss. It happened she was standing in that very same spot the day before when an enormous DC8 jetliner, an Eastern Airlines Flight 304, taking off from New Orleans airport, lost altitude and exploded above her head and crashed into Lake Pontchartrain in front of her. Mr. Finch, fifty-eight men, women, children, babies, and dreams sank to hundred-foot depths under the nightmare of silt that hides sin and so many souls. That was the morning, Mr. Finch, and that was how I met your grandmother. She was pregnant with your mother. That was how I met the woman. She was standing in a long skirt

and sweater, as though she had lost her belongings in a fire. She had no purse, no wallet or identification of any kind. She clenched a bible in her hand. She appeared to be in her late twenties, perhaps thirty. I remember the icy rain on my back when I removed my trench coat and wrapped it around her. She was reluctant to move from the shore. She kept pointing at the floating doll and whimpering, 'Mommy? Mommy? Mommy?' The floating doll wasn't hers, but it had fallen from the plane in front of her and I could only imagine her picturing in her mind a face of a little girl who seconds before had her arms around the doll. Signs and superstitions were a norm in the day. They were compounded by Kennedy's death and now this, just a few months later.

"The crash was as though New Orleans was being cursed for the death of a president–a Catholic president. Mr. Finch, your grandmother would cry in haunting voice that disturbed the crews volunteering to search for bodies. No one offered to retrieve the doll. They claimed there wasn't enough fuel to go out of their way. From that morning on your grandmother convinced her mind that her mother or her father, even perhaps her baby's father—we were never certain which—was aboard when that enormous plane she watched exploded into flames and was swallowed alive by Lake Pontchartrain.

"From that day forth your grandmother was in a continual shock, Mr. Finch. We took her to a Mandeville hospital emergency for sedatives and warmth, but as it turned out, she never came out of the shock and the nameless woman was taken to the women's insane asylum in Acadiana, built in the 1940s. I was so moved by the incident, the look on her face, I joined the asylum's staff and continued my education in psychiatry. It was as though she were in a constant state of an awakened coma. I was young and in the innocence of the times, and I would spend late evenings searching through newspapers and local police blotters looking for missing persons reports. No one ever came forward inquiring about your grandmother, Mr. Finch. For days on end, although it gradually turned into whispers, your grandmother would look at a spot on a wall and repeat, 'Mommy? Mommy? Mommy?'

"Mr. Finch, your mother was born in that mental hospital and in the day, we were required to register a name on birthing certificates. The delivering midwife lovingly gave the new baby girl that would grow up to be your mother the name, Alayna Prudhomme. It was the midwife's own grandmother's name. Those were times when medicine was experimenting with mental health issues, and when we witnessed a noticeable change in your grandmother's demeanor after your mother's birth, we observed her carefully around the clock for several days. There was a calm that came over her whenever she held her new baby. With the baby in her arms, her heart rate would drop to levels of a calm. We felt leaving the baby in her care under close supervision could bring her around. That was our choice.

"Whenever your mother was swaddled and in your grandmother's arms, she would hold her and rock and sing quietly. As your mother grew we arranged homeschool for her close to the hospital and she would come and go with the blessing of the staff. Throughout her high school years, I saw to it she was cared for at a girl's boarding school where she could receive a proper education and perhaps a perspective of who she was. Alayna, your mother, Mr.

Finch, would visit your grandmother every weekend, sacrificing a high school private and social life of her own to be with her mother."

Mr. Hebert set that page down and looked over at Peck. Peck appeared to be squirming in his seat. Millie was in tears, her elbows on her knees, her head lowered, tissues in both eyes.

"Is this making you uncomfortable, son?" Mr. Hebert asked.

"Nah, nah."

Peck turned his head, staring at a wall.

"Perhaps this isn't a good time," Mr. Hebert said.

"It's just—well, I don't remember all dat, sir."

"You can't remember it, son. You weren't born while this was going on."

"Nah, nah. It's I don't remember my mamma nanna so nice like she is in dat letter, sir," Peck said.

Mr. Hebert pursed his lips with a knowing, gentle smile. He nodded his head as if he could see what was happening. He reached for his phone.

"I think we need a small break. Let's have some coffee."

"Coffee would be good," Peck said.

"Yes, Mr. Hebert?" Flo asked.

"Flo, can you be a dear and run over to the café and get three large coffees to go? With cinnamon and bring some sugar packets if you would be so kind."

"Yes, sir."

Mr. Hebert cradled the phone and leaned on his desk, facing Peck. "Let me tell you a story, young man."

Peck appreciated the break. His face looked tormented. He leaned in to listen.

"Peck, I'm an old man. Back when it was time for me to go to college, I wanted to go out of state, so I went away to Ole Miss. Jackson was only about a hundred–fifty miles, but it was out of state. It was a grand time, son. I sang in the men's choir, I was on the debate team. I was away from home for the first time in my life...and son, it seemed every year I was there at Ole Miss my childhood memories became suspect to my bad memory and good imagination. Why it could have gone on for all the years I was there until that one Christmas break when it came to an end."

"End?" Peck asked.

"It was the time I brought two of my best college–campus friends home. They couldn't afford plane fare to go home for the holidays—one lived in Seattle and one lived in Toronto."

Peck put his two stacked fists on the edge of Mr. Hebert's desk and rested his chin on them.

"We were at dinner on Christmas day. My dad had just carried in the silver platter with the large, crispy golden-brown turkey on it. I remember it was surrounded by baked apples and sweet-potato halves. It was just as my dad was slithering the carving knife to the sharpener rod when one of my friends opened his mouth and a door of conversation that changed my life."

"Hanh?" Peck asked.

"His name was Riley. He was a junior at Ole Miss. The lad, this Riley fellow, was mesmerized by the sounds of the long carving knife with deer-horn handle slithering against the steel sharpener rod. He looked at my dad and said, 'Mr. Hebert, you sure don't look all that mean.'"

"With that I dropped my fork and my dad said, 'Excuse me, son, I don't think I caught that.' And of course, as the young tend to do, my friend Riley kept on digging the hole deeper. That's the time he said, 'Harold told us how you'd whipped him with a bullwhip until he learned to make his bed. That sure must have worked, Mr. Hebert. He makes a good and tidy bed.' Of course, it was about that time, I felt like I blacked out and came to, chagrinned to know I was still sitting at the same table that my dad was hearing all this. And that is when my daddy said, 'Bullwhip?' and Riley just went on and on like a Gomer Pyle and said, 'My father would threaten a belt, but a rolled-up newspaper was all we ever needed. Good thing he didn't have a bullwhip like you do, Mr. Hebert.' Peck, that was the exact moment, I remember it like it was yesterday when my daddy set the carving knife and sharpener rod on the table and he said something that changed my life."

"What'd your daddy say?" Peck asked.

"He said, 'Riley, I don't own a bullwhip. I have never owned a bullwhip, and I wouldn't even know what a bullwhip looked like.' I remember him finishing that sentence with a fire in his eyes looking at me, his college junior son who had gone off and made some mountains from memories and the more I told them the bigger the tales grew. Boys of the same ages would try to outdo each other about the stories from home and their tragic lives. We learned in English comp that novels without tragedy weren't near as good."

"It wasn't true about your daddy?" Peck asked.

"It was my imagination taking liberties with exaggeration, son. Like most young boys I took a proper scolding about keeping my room clean, but then I took it to the extreme. Those were days without television and we were fond of our books and comic novels—and exaggeration was a part of giving our young lives and the hot summers some spark."

"Mr. Hebert, gator man tied me and pulled me back of his boat for gators, dass for true. He belt-strapped me for dropping bait buckets, dass for true. He dog-collared me and chain me under the porch, dass for true. S'why I hided in the cypress tree holler for three days standing on buzzard eggs and ants and runned away to Carencro."

Mr. Hebert let the moment rest. He watched Peck's eyes.

"Young man, I have known you for less than a morning and I already have a sense I can trust you at your word. An old man knows these things. I believe all of this, as you describe it, happened to you—just as you say it happened."

Peck sat up, settled in his face that someone was listening.

"But I ask a small consideration, young man," Mr. Hebert said.

"Hokay, what is it, sir?"

"Peck, did this gator man do these things to you at your house or at his house?"

"His house," Peck said.

"Was your momma ever there when he did these things to you?"

"Nah, nah. Mamma nanna not there."

"Peck, these papers are about your momma. They're not about that gator man. Why don't we give it some time and see where the story goes?"

"So maybe gator man is Peck's bullwhip, not my mamma nanna?"

"Maybe, son."

It made sense to Peck. He was learning about his mamma from the doctor's story and he was eager to learn new things. Mr. Hebert smiled as though his offering made a difference. He sat back and picked up the next page and read aloud.

"Mr. Finch, your grandmother had only one possession when we found her at Lake Pontchartrain—a bible. The pages were stuck together and when we were able to pull the covers back there was no name in it, so it was left by her bedside. It was when your mother, Alayna, was of high school age, she wanted to take the bible as a keepsake and was trying to unstick the pages when she found a page with a name penned on it. It was written on a page under Proverbs 22:1 about names. That was the day we learned your grandmother's name was Abella Blanchard. There were no Blanchards on the plane that crashed. We were able to trace her family name to Bayou Chene, eighty-nine miles away. We could only assume she had walked that far."

"I know'd what happened," Peck said. "I know'd what happened, Mr. Hebert."
Mr. Hebert paused and looked up.
"Go on, son," Mr. Hebert said.
"Bayou Chene drowned, dass for true. Church and all the houses and lots of people drowned when the levee broke. It was same time like that. Flora told'd me."
"That's right, Peck, it was in the early sixties," Mr. Hebert said.
Mr. Hebert continued reading.

"The town sank under silt and many died. It's very probable that your grandmother's husband and parents died in that flood and she walked in shock to Lake Pontchartrain."

"You ran from your demons, Peck. Gabe told me you ran ninety miles," Millie said. "Your gramma ran from hers and she got stopped at the edge of Lake Pontchartrain. She could have fallen in and drowned. Dr. Pontelbon may have saved her life."
Mr. Hebert continued reading.

"Mr. Finch, when your mother graduated from high school, I let her live on a houseboat I owned but seldom used. I eventually gave her title to it. It was on a short inlet by the Diversion Canal and Amite River."

"The willer," Peck said. "Tied to a willer."

"Your mother had a fondness for the flora and she'd read many seed catalogues and books on the subject and she took jobs and made a proper living minding gardens for some and plants for homes and buildings for others within distance of a bicycle ride. I offered to get her a used car or a Toyota pickup, but she insisted on her bicycle and its oversized basket on the front and wire saddle baskets on the back fender. Every Saturday morning and every Wednesday morning, like clockwork, your mother would catch a ride to the clinic to visit and spend the day with her momma, and she would read to her

and they would speak a Cajun French and she would bring flowers and arrange them in a green vase on her momma's bedside.

"Mr. Finch, I'm about to tell something I've always kept from everyone. I'm sorry, Hal—even you, my friend. I'm not proud of it. Only one man has ever known about it. It's important that you know it from me, Mr. Finch. I would have told you in person had I known your whereabouts. In late 1990, the mental health hospital hired a handyman in their maintenance department. His name was Guillaume Devine, a Creole who worked shrimp boats in the gulf most of his life. He was maybe thirty when he started working at the hospital. Hal, three women were raped at the hospital, one staff, one patient. The third was Alayna. He attacked her in the lady's restroom. This Devine fellow threatened the women's lives if they ever talked to anyone. A patient by the name of Ellen McDowell and your mother, Alayna, were impregnated. Ellen McDowell and her child died that same year in childbirth. Alayna, with the help of a midwife and myself, gave birth to a healthy baby boy. That was in a day a single woman could explain an adoption, so I took the birthing papers and named the new baby boy Boudreaux Clemont Finch. Mr. Finch, if you're still in the room, please take a look at your new pocket watch."

Peck pulled the watch and chain from his pocket.

"You'll see, Mr. Finch, the engraving on the watch is BCF—for my granddaddy—and it's now etched there for you, friend. My granddaddy was a good man and he would have been proud for you to have the watch, Mr. Finch.'"

Millie stood and stepped over to Peck and knelt on the floor, her arms around him.

"Mr. Hebert, I love this man so much. We are so blessed and fortunate to have this strong name from such a wonderful man."

Millie looked in Peck's teary eyes.

"Peck, I will be proud to be your Mrs. Finch. So proud and I will be so proud to know your mamma and to call her Mamma."

Millie kissed his cheek.

"Peck," Mr. Hebert said. "I know when the doc set up the account to have checks sent to your mother every month, the word was you were dead."

Millie and Peck started, heads up.

"Hanh?" Peck asked.

"Everyone assumed an alligator had taken you under, son," Mr. Hebert said. "Things would have been different had the doc known you were alive, Peck. I know the man. He would have put out searches."

Peck was stunned to learn they thought he was dead. As an experienced fisher and tracker, it was beginning to make sense to him.

"They find d'is man?" Peck asked.

"Which man, son?"

"The man what raped..."

"Keep reading, Mr. Hebert," Millie said.

Peck sat back and Millie returned to her seat and her tissues.

"Peck, may I continue?" Mr. Hebert asked.

"*Oui*," Peck said.

Mr. Hebert lifted another page.

"Since the rapes weren't reported, no suspicions were hovering. I knew the two pregnancies were illegitimate, and I chose not to make uncomfortable inquiries, but to help as I could. Alayna would always bring you, her young Boudreaux, to the hospital for her regular visits and you would spend the day with your grandmother. The grandmother would rock you and bottle feed you in daylight feedings and Alayna would stand by the window and breastfeed you under the moonlight."

Peck leaned his face down into his hands. He was in tears.

"Two things you need to know, Mr. Finch. The first, my friend, Hal, is about to read to you. The other is something special for you in the second envelope.

"The first happened two years after you were born, Mr. Finch. Mr. Devine and I planned a day of fishing. Before he got to the lake, I packed my end of the boat with a thermos of lemonade, my small iced cooler with sandwiches, and a paper sack with two bags of potato chips. I rolled my yellow slicker around my shotgun in case I saw a low-flying duck. It wasn't legal, but the thought of duck for dinner crossed most fishers' minds and most law would turn a blind eye on a single duck. Devine eventually showed. He packed his end of the boat with a small cooler, some beer, and a hoagie sandwich. I backed the boat into the lake and then parked my car and trailer before we headed out on the Mourepas. We went to the middle of the lake for the bigger bass.

"Mr. Finch, it was after his fourth beer when the man asked me whatever happened to that gal that used to come by. When I asked him who he was referring to, he described your mother. When I told him she still came by to visit her mother he made a comment...he said he sure would like to get with her. Mr. Finch, I'm not the sort of a man who blurts out without thinking, but for some reason all that came to my mind was to say, 'You're the one, aren't you?' I remember him looking at me, first in surprise, then with a low sneer. 'So, what if I am?' All I remember, Mr. Finch is that I wasn't afraid. I even repeated 'You did it.' Two women—or was it more? He tossed his sandwich in the lake and began unsnapping his hunting knife. 'You'll never know, old man—and you'll never tell, neither. You're about to get out and swim with the gators.' I remember every word he said. I reached in my slicker and took my shotgun and just that fast I shot him in the face, pumped quickly and shot him again in the chest. He fell overboard and floated face down. I motored back to shore where, off in the distance, I could see him floating. I went directly to the Sherriff's office and told him the story. He sent me home and that was more than twenty years ago and he hasn't said a word about it.

"I'm sorry, Mr. Finch. I don't know what came over me that day. I hope you have a good life. Please say hello to your mother. She's a very nice lady."

Mr. Hebert turned the last page and set it on the stack.

"That's his story, Peck. I don't know what more there is to say."

"He's a good man, that doc, dass for true. A good man."

"So you're all right with the…?"

"Him shootin' that man? I'm good wit' that. I see it haunted the doc, though. The man would have killed him sure."

"I believe he would have," Mr. Hebert said. "Here's the other letter, Peck. Do you want some privacy so you can read it?"

"Nah, nah," Peck said while taking the envelope and removing a blue envelope and letter inside. The envelope inside was addressed to the doc. The letter was handwritten and it was from Peck's mamma. It was in script and Peck couldn't read script. He looked at Millie to help. He handed the letter to her. She read it to herself, her tears turning to sobs.

"Read aloud, cher," Peck said.

Millie read it aloud the second time. In it Peck's mother was telling the doc that on a few occasions a man she knew from church, a man known as gator man, would offer to watch Peck for her while she had to go garden hoe or reseed a place or pull weeds somewhere. The letter went on that she heard Peck talking in his sleep about dying and of alligators and of his tossing and turning while having nightmares, and she was scared for what it meant, and could the doc talk to the boy to see if the gator man was maybe causing the nightmares and tell her what she should do about the boy's dreams. Millie held the letter in her hand and Peck was in a daze, looking off into nowhere.

"I didn't know your momma had written this letter, son. I remember we all thought you were dead. I remember the talk. A gator grabbed you, was the thinking. We had no evidence of foul play," Mr. Hebert said. "I know your momma stopped seeing that man at the church."

Peck reached and took Millie's hand. He took the letter and envelope and held it.

"Are you all right, young man?" Mr. Hebert asked.

"Nah, nah, I'm good, Mr. Hebert. Peck is good."

"Is there anything I can do?"

"Can you tell me how I find my mamma, sir?"

CHAPTER 53

MILLIE EXCUSED HERSELF to go to the ladies' room; Peck stood and paced, stirring around Mr. Hebert's office pensively looking on tabletops cluttered with civic awards and photographs framed and hanging on the walls. He studied one that caught his attention. It was a dated eight-by-ten black and white photograph of a younger Mr. Hebert standing with someone in front of a trailered skiff with a string of bass and with smiles on their faces.

"That's the doc and me," Mr. Hebert said as he lifted his phone and pressed a button.

"Flo, can you make copies of something please?"

"How many copies, Mr. Hebert?"

"One copy, but it's many pages."

"Yes, sir, I'll be right in."

"Peck if you don't mind, I'd like to make a copy of my old friend's words here as a keepsake and I'll give the original to you," Mr. Hebert said.

"That'd be good, Mr. Hebert."

"How are you feeling about today, son? I know it's been a long day for you and your lady."

"I feel so good, Mr. Hebert—sorry though, I didn't know all d'is and just runned off like I did. I was plenty scared bag then, I'll say. Plenty scared. Gator man tape my mouth and pulled me back of his pirogue for gator bait."

"You did what you felt was right. You protected yourself, son. I would have run off too."

"Dass for true, Mr. Hebert?"

"That's the truth, son. In the same situation I would have probably run off."

Peck stared out the window.

"Peck, I know you want directions to see your momma. I have good maps at home. Let me suggest you and your Millie join my Constance and me for a home-cooked meal. You need a break. We're having grilled chicken and bratwurst and cob corn. You both have to eat. You can rest up at our place and we'll look at maps."

"That'd be hokay with us," Peck said. "T'ank you, Mr. Hebert."

"It's settled, then. May I ask you to step out of my office for a bit? Perhaps you and Millie can take a walk? I have one call I have to make."

"Yes, sir," Peck said.

"I promised I would call your Dr. Price and tell him about our day. Will that be all right with you, son?"

"Nah, nah, it's all good. Tell John—dass his name—tell him Peck is doing so good."

Mr. Hebert smiled.

"We'll leave for home after I'm finished the call. I'll find you. The old church has some historic photos hanging in the vestibule, if you're interested in that sort of thing."

Peck left the room, and he and Millie walked a city block and then another, with Millie letting the love of her life ramble on as if he had seen Santa Claus under the tree. Peck talked about the frightening airliner crash in Lake Pontchartrain and what it must have been like for his grandmother. He talked of what his mamma must have thought when she thought he was gator-grabbed and dead. He talked about whether she would forgive him for running off as he had or not speak to him.

"A momma will always forgive," Millie said. Millie was measured with her words. This was Peck's time...his reawakening.

Mr. Hebert was able to get through to Dr. Price and the feedback was positive, and Dr. Price offered his best to Peck and his word that his door was always open to him if he ever wanted to talk. Dr. Price added that he had talked to the mental health hospital and the grandmother was still alive, passed eighty, but not in good health. The fear was she could develop pneumonia, or lung blockage of some kind. Flo rested his copy and the original manuscript on the desk in front of Mr. Hebert. While talking, he rustled through his stack and found the page he was hoping to find.

"Dr. Price, tomorrow is Wednesday. Alayna always visits her momma, the young man's grandmother on Wednesday and Saturday. Do you think it might be wise that Peck reconnect with them both at the same time?" Mr. Hebert asked.

There was a pause.

"Mr. Hebert, I think that could be a blessing, both for the grandmother who rocked that young man in her arms and for the momma who nursed him and unwittingly trusted a churchgoing man from the devil's own. I think it would be a wonderful idea. I would even have Millie join him. Let them both, grandmother and mother, witness a sense that they had a hand in raising such a good and caring young man."

"Any suggestions I can share with the young man?" Mr. Hebert asked.

"Just tell Peck to be himself. Tell him it would be a blessing if he could forget the past—to put it behind him. Suggest to him that that past has been a nightmare for the mother and sleepless nights for her all these years thinking an alligator ate her only son. Tell him I suggested that closing that book and opening a new book with Millie at his side would be the greatest gift he could bestow on his mother and grandmother."

"Anything else, Doctor Price?"

"You say his mother likes flora?"

"She earns a living at it."

"Suggest he and Millie take them each a bouquet of flowers. That would be nice."

Dr. Price and Mr. Hebert spoke of other pleasantries and what a marvelous day it had been for the lad, his lady and for Mr. Hebert himself. He didn't share Dr. Pontelbon's darker secrets, but he did say how comforting it was to hear from his dear old friend nearly five years after his death. Mr. Hebert put Peck's original copy of the manuscript into a manila envelope, left the office and found Peck and Millie holding hands and walking with strawberry ice-cream cones. They followed behind Mr. Hebert's car to his home and parked in front.

"This place has been in my family since 1888," Mr. Hebert said.

"It's beautiful," Millie said.

"How many acres do you farm?" Peck asked.

"It once was a section, so that's 640 acres. Sold much of it off, a little at a time over the years. It got to be too much for me. We have the three acres fenced here. No farming now, but in the day, we planted soybeans or sugar cane, depending on prices. We mostly enjoy counting our sunsets now. I have a woodshop in the barn for making birdhouses for friends. It keeps me out of trouble with Constance."

Constance was a pleasant, grandmotherly looking woman, a gracious hostess, and she suggested they consider staying over so they could be properly rested for the day ahead. Peck asked Millie if they should, or should they go to Baton Rouge and stay with Elizabeth and come back in the morning to find his mamma? It was just as Constance was finishing mixing her homemade potato salad that Millie's phone rang. It was Lily Cup calling. Millie excused herself and stepped into another room.

"Hello?"

"Millie, are you two okay?"

"We're good. We're with Mr. and Mrs. Hebert and about to have dinner. They're so nice."

"You'd tell me if anything was wrong, right?"

"Of course, I would. Peck would too. Mr. Hebert is the man from the bank. Everything is just fine. Today was a beautiful day, but I think Peck should be the one to tell you about it. We learned a lot. All I can say is everyone here has been so nice," Millie said.

"Where are you?"

"Just outside of Killian. We're at their house. It used to be a farm."

"I'll tell Gabe and Sasha you're okay. Where are you staying tonight?"

"We don't know yet. Peck suggested maybe we drive to Baton Rouge and come back tomorrow. I'm not sure. Mrs. Hebert invited us to stay here. I'll know more after dinner."

"Text me when you know, so I can tell Gabe."

"I will. Love you."

"Love you back."

Millie offered the blessing before Mr. Hebert began passing platters of chicken, bratwurst, and boiled cob corn. Peck particularly liked the barbeque sauce. He held the bottle and wrote the name of it on a paper napkin for later reference. Constance asked Millie if, while at Baylor in Waco, she got to enjoy the wonderful Texas grapefruit as much as she did and how with his heart medicine poor Harold couldn't eat grapefruit. Peck recounted his recipe for turtle soup and Millie spoke of the farm they wished to have one day and was it safe to free range chickens in Acadiana with the predators about?

Mr. Hebert kept his eyes on Peck's expressions as a father might watch a maturing son at one of life's crossings. It was as if he could sense what depth the boy went through that day emotionally and what must be going through his mind now—or later, as it replayed in his memory. Mr. Hebert would glance over at the coffee table with the envelope holding his copy of the doc's letter to him and Peck, and there would be a small bubble of glassy tear in his eye. It was as if his old friend, the doc, was sitting there on the sofa, waiting for an after-dinner coffee and chat.

"Peck, I had a nice talk with your friend, Dr. Price." Mr. Hebert said.

"John?" Peck asked.

"John," Mr. Hebert said. "Care to talk about it now, son?"

"It'd be good. Sure," Peck said.

"Peck, if you can remember in that letter we read today…"

"I remember."

"It spoke of your mother visiting your grandmother at the clinic every Wednesday and every Saturday. Do you remember that?"

Peck set his fork down and looked over at Mr. Hebert.

"I remember."

"Tomorrow is Wednesday, son. I was thinking tomorrow would be good. Dr. Price thought it could be a blessed time if you and Millie would meet them both at the clinic."

Mr. Hebert set his fork down and waited. He kept his eyes on Peck's eyes, giving him the courtesy of silence as he waited for a reaction. Peck took his eyes from Mr. Hebert, turned them to Millie's eyes, her brow raised in anticipation, and then he too glanced over at the envelope sitting on the coffee table.

"I t'ink dat'd be good, Mr. Hebert. Peck and Millie will go and see my mamma and gramma tomorrow. John know'd these t'ings best, I say," Peck said.

Millie grasped her hands in joy. The nightmares that had been predicted of the giant evil cypress, the desperate swamps and forbidden bayous, were leveling themselves over a linen tablecloth on a dinner table and being replaced with an excitement of angst and anticipation born adventurers loved to feel. Peck and Millie were as one soul in this world of wonder. They were ready.

"Miss Hebert," Peck said. "Maybe can my Millie and me stay here tonight, please?"

CHAPTER 54

UNBEKNOWN TO PECK AND MILLIE and even Mr. Hebert, Dr. Price had called ahead to the clinic, telling them the visit was happening on Wednesday. The call virtually eliminated red tape. A caring ward attendant went out of her way to brush his grandmother's hair and put her in a flowered dressing robe before visits started that day. Although she was able to walk, the grandmother was in a wheelchair next to the bed at the time Alayna, Peck's mamma, came in and soon after, the wheelchair was over by the window.

Alayna was sitting in a rocker next to the wheel chair, reading aloud in French when the door first pushed open. Peck held the door with his right hand and Millie's hand with the other. His eyes were wide, inquisitive, wary.

Alayna glanced up and then back at the book she was reading, as if Peck was a service attendant of some kind. The door closed behind them both, and Peck let go of Millie's hand. He stood and watched his mamma's eyes as she read. Her eyes looked up at him and away...and then up again. Peck froze in fright.

Millie stood with her hands clasped as if in prayer, a tear rolling down her cheek. Alayna set the book in grandmother's lap and stood slowly. She moved tentatively toward Peck, her eyes riveted to his. Two fingers buttoned her collar and she ran both hands and fingers back through the sides of her graying hair, as if to look as presentable as a moment's notice might allow for this haunting stranger.

Standing before him, she studied his eyes, his mouth, his chin, his ears. She leaned to the left to see a profile. She looked over at Millie, standing behind him with a wrenched smile on her face, in tears.

With a mother's instinct, she stepped closer to Peck and put her hands on both sides of his temple and gently lowered his head, running her thumbs through his scalp.

"*C'est toujours là, Mamma,*" Peck said. ("It's still there, Mamma.")

Peck let his mamma know he still had the birthmark on his scalp.

Alayna's eyes squinted nearly to tears as she raised her son's head and studied his eyes as if they were the last thing she would remember every night as she had knelt in prayer from that day he went missing.

She pulled him to her, her head on his cheek, and she hugged her baby boy as closely as she promised God she would if He ever graced her with her son just one more time before she died.

Peck wept with his eyes closed, his arms around his mamma. They didn't have to say a word. Not a single word.

His mamma was a seasoned gardener with strong legs and heart from bicycling. She knew what God could do. She witnessed it every day in gardens.

Peck was a seasoned tracker and fisher. He knew patience. He knew that everything good could come true with time. His life was rich now, rich with his Millie, rich with his being able to read. He was even richer today. Having his mamma in his arms, it was as though he knew it was time to put the nightmares that hung over his life like sawblades in a sharpening shanty into a drawer and to push it closed and locked.

He took his mamma by one hand, his Millie's hand with the other and stepped over to his grandmother, who looked off at the rocker her baby girl would sit in every Wednesday and Saturday and read to her.

Peck turned to his mamma.

"*En Anglais, Mamma*? ("English, Mamma?")

"Yes," his mamma said.

"Mamma, this is my Millie. We getting married after Peck finishes school. I'm going to university, Mamma."

Peck smiled, letting his mamma take it all in. She looked over at Millie, placed a gentle hand under Millie's chin and smiled approval with her eyes.

"Millie," his mamma said.

"She loves me, Mamma. She loves your Peck and I love her so much."

Mamma turned her eyes to Peck, reached her hand to his face and grasped his chin in a smiling scold.

"Boudreaux!" Mamma said. "No Peck."

"But Mamma…"

"No Peck…*non, non, non.*"

"I love Boudreaux too, Mamma," Millie said.

Mamma looked at Millie, who had just called her Mamma. A tear appeared.

"Watch this, Mamma," her Boudreaux said.

He sat on the rocker, took the book from his grandmother's lap and held it up to read. He glanced at the book in puzzlement and looked up at his mamma.

"*Anglais, Mamma?*"

Mamma took the book from him and got another from the bed table and handed it to her Boudreaux. His eyes gleamed as he proudly opened it, read the title page and turned to chapter one. His grandmother gazed at his hands as he read slowly, his mamma standing at his side, running her fingers through his hair, as though she was braiding closed the void that had consumed nearly two empty decades of her life. His words were measured, careful; his annunciation was with an effort, but warm.

"Wait, I have an idea," Millie said.

Peck started, looked up at the interruption, but there was a look in Millie's eyes that only he could know would be a good interruption.

"Hanh?" he asked.

"Peck—I mean Boudreaux—let me have the keys," Millie said.

"Keys?"

"The truck keys. I have an idea."

Boudreaux handed Millie the keys and picked up the book again.

"I'll be right back," Millie said.

She scooted from the room. It was just as the door closed behind her when Mamma knelt beside Boudreaux.

"I like your Millie, Boudreaux. You must marry the girl."

"I will, Mamma. I promise I will."

It was on the eighth page of chapter one when the room door opened with Millie pushing it with her back. Her smile was a Christmas morning smile, and her arms cradled her baby doll, Charlie, swaddled in his baby blanket. Without speaking a word, she walked over to the wheelchair and leaned down.

"Gramma, this is your grandbaby. Isn't he such a sweet baby boy, Gramma?"

Millie handed the baby doll to the grandmother, who turned her eyes from beyond to the baby's face and blue eyes looking up at her. She smiled a tear and took the baby in her arms and cradled him, rocking her shoulders back and forth. It was her baby girl's Boudreaux Clemont Finch. Baby came home to grandmamma.

"He's such a pretty baby," Mamma said.

"He's her Charlie, Mamma," Boudreaux said.

"No, he isn't, P—I mean, Boudreaux. That's little Boudreaux Clemont Finch now, and he's Gramma's little baby to take care of, always.

Boudreaux looked into Millie's eyes with a love only true love knows. He looked at his gramma, rocking with the baby doll in her arms. She was humming as if she was trying to remember the words. As he opened the book to page nine of the first chapter he looked over at his mamma.

"I'm going to marry her, Mamma, dass for true."

CHAPTER 55

MAMMA WASN'T COMFORTABLE letting her son and his Millie see the houseboat until after she straightened it up, maybe had it painted for company, but she did accept an invitation for dinner with them at the Hebert's. This was a blessed time for her, she wanted to spruce it up for her son's first visit home.

Alex, the Russian bait man was also invited for the cookout of fresh chicken livers and dove breasts stuffed with jalapeno, wrapped with bacon. Mamma said Labor Day weekend would be a good time for them to come visit her on the houseboat.

Peck pulled his wallet from his back pocket, assuring his mamma with his debit card and driver's license he was a real Boudreaux Clemont Finch, and Peck was only a friendly nickname. He and Mamma were smiling and chatting almost as if he had been off to war and had finally come home. Mamma relented to his using Peck, but only with Millie's vow that her babies aren't named Peck. Peck said Labor Day was a perfect time, as university would be out and could they bring their friends and he explained about Gabe and Sasha and Lily Cup and was there a place to dance nearby?

Mamma was good with all that and Mrs. Hebert said Gabe and Sasha and Lily Cup could stay at their house and Millie and Peck on the houseboat and Alex spoke of taking everyone fishing and the bait and the use of his wife's cousin's boat would be his gift.

When back in New Orleans, Millie was immersed in research projects for the summer at Lily Cup's office, while learning to cook at home when she and Peck were not making love.

Peck got his GED and Gabe had it framed to make it two pictures on the mantle, and everyone celebrated at Dooky Chase's, filling a table with laughter and love. Sasha and James decided they liked the arrangement as it was, and why spoil it with marriage, as that would require he go to Charlie's Blue Note on occasion, but Gabe and Peck threw them a party anyway, an un-engagement party.

On the Thursday before Labor Day the plan was for everyone to make an early morning drive to Killian in Sasha's Caddy SUV. Lily Cup asked if she and Peck could ride alone together in his pickup. Having the pickup there he and Millie could stay on a day or so if Mamma was good with that. She wanted to ride alone with Peck just so she could take him to Angola for an early morning visit. Gabe and Sasha knew what she had in mind, and they suggested it would be a good learning experience for him, and they'd meet at the Heberts' for a late breakfast. Lily Cup said they wouldn't be more than two hours behind them.

Early morning visitation at Angola was celebrated on holidays. Lily Cup's client, André, was permitted to meet visitors in the sitting room as his was a nonviolent crime—illegal gun sales. The guards couldn't let her take a thermos of coffee in and apologized to her. He was due to be released by Thanksgiving.

Peck and Lily Cup sat in adjoining chairs.

"Peck, you can't shake hands with him and you have to keep your voice down, but say hello to André," Lily Cup said.

"How you are?" Peck asked.

"This is that boy, Lily Cup, the one you maybe told André about?"

"Yes."

"The tracker?"

"This is him, André. Ain't he a looker?"

André laughed, his head back. "I'll say. Cher, what you doing with someone so young and so handsome?"

"It's not like that, André. Peck here is engaged to a wonderful girl," Lily Cup said.

"Engaged? So when you getting married, young man? André wants to get you a wedding present. Any friend of Lily Cup here."

"They're waiting until they're out of school, André."

"So why does André have this honor? What's on your mind?" André asked. "Something always on that pretty mind of yours."

"André, I'm really proud of you. You've been a good boy and they're cutting you loose in November. That's a whole year early."

"You're the best. I'll see you get paid proper."

"You've already paid me, André. Just promise me no more guns."

André held up his hand as a promise.

"So why you bring this boy all the way out here, Lily Cup—just to congratulate me?"

Lily Cup leaned in, motioned her head, asking Peck to lean in as well.

"It's time you know," Lily Cup whispered.

"Me, cher?"

"Keep your voice down, just listen, Peck."

"Know what, cher?" Peck asked.

"Last year I was telling André about how a gator man had treated you when you were a helpless little kid. You don't mind I told him that, do you? André is my friend."

"Nah, nah, cher. Gator man was a bad man, dass for true."

"André, tell Peck what you 'heard' about that gator man—you know, the Christmas Story you told me."

André caught Lily Cup's wink. He looked at Peck, thought for a moment, as if he were reflecting a best approach.

"It was just something I heard about this rich man from England or France or somewhere—André doesn't remember. You know those rich men who travel all over trying to spend money? Well this one rich man, see, he hired a gator man to find him a big ole gator. He wanted a prize gator, maybe twenty feet, and story is I guess the rich man's money was good, so that gator man sure enough found him a twenty-foot alligator and, *oops*, wouldn't you know—the pirogue tipped and don't you know that gator man standing in that pirogue fell in that bayou and *chomp*, that was all it wrote for gator man?"

"Dey both fall in?" Peck asked.

"Oh, no—that's just it—you see that rich man, he was in his own, what you'd call a party boat. He was following behind gator man's pirogue and watching, like a tourist. Lucky for him too, my friend. Gator man's boat up and jerked and over the side he went and *chomp*. Yum yum, for that big ole gator, I'll say."

André stopped talking and looked Peck in the eye.

"Least that's what I heard," Andre said.

Lily Cup watched Peck. Peck was in a blank stare.

"Are you okay, Peck?"

"Nah, nah, I'm good, cher," Peck said.

In the parking lot Peck pulled his door and sat holding the steering wheel, looking through the windshield in thought.

"You sure you're okay, Peck?" Lily Cup asked.

She waited a time for him to gather his thoughts.

"How'd they do it, cher?" Peck asked.

"Do what?"

"How'd they do it?"

"I don't know what you're talking about, Peck."

Peck turned his head and looked into Lily Cup's eyes and stared. It was just less than a full minute when Lily Cup broke the stare, reached in her bag and pulled the empty spool of 200-pound test fishing line out and handed it to Peck.

"Is that mine?" Peck asked.

"No."

"I got one like that in Memphis and lost it, cher," Peck said. "Where'd you find this one?"

"This isn't the same one."

"Hanh?"

"This isn't your spool, Peck. I took your spool from your bag one night when you were cleaning our offices. I emptied it and showed it to André. I told him how gator man would tie gator's snouts with it. The guards wouldn't let me bring one in with fishing line on it. Your empty spool is back at my office in my drawer."

"Whose is this one—this spool, cher?"

"Andre wrapped this one with a bow on it and gave it to me as a present last Christmas."

"Last Christmas?"

"It was empty when he gave it to me. That's when he first told me the story he just told you."

Peck started the truck, backed around and pulled onto the highway. He drove without talking for twenty minutes. It was another twenty miles when he raised his fist slowly with a smile for an approving fist pump.

"You know somet'ing, cher?"

"What?"

"They ain't no such t'ing as a twenty-foot gator."

"And now there's no such thing as gator man," Lily Cup said.

Lily Cup obliged his fist pump with a smile of satisfaction, knowing this Angola visit wouldn't be spoken of again.

Peck's nightmares were over.

"Look at the morning moon, Peck. It's huge."

"Ah *oui* – it's a crepe, cher."
Peck had found his mamma.

Lest I forget...

Thank you, New Orleans.

Thanks to Orleans Criminal District Court especially to Counselor Lindsay Jay Jeffrey for patience in putting order in my court.

Thank you Donald W. Gaffney, my dear friend and early writing coach for inspiring this book by waking up from your hospice death bed at the sound of my voice on the phone, going home and living another year and a half so you could finish your book on WWII in the South Pacific.

A heartfelt thank you to the esteemed Leah Chase, matriarch of the historic Dooky Chase Restaurant and the iconic leading lady of New Orleans for the best part of a century. I'm humbled and flattered by the hours given myself and my researcher by Leah Chase. What you taught me about life, the hope you always saw for America, the roads you have traveled inspired my painting an accurate mural of my Acadian heritage and of New Orleans in my story.

Thanks Marty and Corneilius, my research assistants; Eddie (Ned) Reid for my Gabe—thank you for the jazz lessons. I could write 30 books on being black and not even come close...but I can write Ned – my Gabe. Thank you Big Easy and your legendary Pontchartrain Hotel and The Columns Hotel. Thank you for your input bestselling Tom Hyman – you're still a legend.

Special thanks to the one who made it possible - Judge Laurie A. White for encouraging members of the courts of New Orleans to help the arts, and this storyteller in attempting to present an accurate picture of events in the city of flavors she loves so much...and thank you Judge Laurie A. White for turning a blind eye on a bit of my 'misspelling' the letter of the law here and there for my spin of a tale.

JMA